DEFINING A PHENOMENON

What *Star Trek* is or is not, it is unmistakably an astonishing cultural phenomenon so profound that it must now be treated as a defining process of American popular culture. . . .

Some analysts might say that this is because *Star Trek* represents a vision that inspires the viewer. I think that this is a misstatement. It puts the warp drive before the dilithium crystals.

The truth is that the dream of a better tomorrow already exists in the viewer. *Star Trek* merely gives it a focus. . . . For many people, before there was *Star Trek* that vision was unformed, unspoken, and rarely consciously realized; but it was there—expressing itself in every dream of the future since human beings first climbed down out of the trees and began staring at the moon and wondering. That essential human ability to dream of something better is the spark of transformation that exists as the core of every human soul.

Star Trek's real success is not simply that it is an extraordinary television show, but that is connects itself to that extraordinary vision that already exists. . . .

—From the introduction
by David Gerrold

Please be sure to ask your bookseller for the Bantam Spectra Books you have missed:

STAR TREK®

THE CLASSIC EPISODES 2

adapted by James Blish

Introduction by David Gerrold

SPECTRA™

BANTAM BOOKS
NEW YORK • TORONTO • LONDON • SYDNEY • AUCKLAND

STAR TREK: THE CLASSIC EPISODES 2
A Bantam Spectra Book

PRINTING HISTORY
*Stories appearing in this volume were published
in a slightly different form by Bantam Books.*
Special Bantam edition / September 1991

*SPECTRA and the portrayal of a boxed "s" are trademarks of
Bantam Books, a division of Bantam Doubleday Dell Publishing
Group, Inc.*

ISBN 0-553-29139-4

Published simultaneously in the United States and Canada

Bantam Books are published by Bantam Books, a division of Bantam
Doubleday Dell Publishing Group, Inc. Its trademark, consisting of
the words "Bantam Books" and the portrayal of a rooster, is Reg-
istered in U.S. Patent and Trademark Office and in other countries.
Marca Registrada. Bantam Books, 666 Fifth Avenue, New York, New
York 10103.

PRINTED IN THE UNITED STATES OF AMERICA

OPM 0 9 8 7 6 5 4 3 2 1

CONTENTS

≡

THE TRANSCENDENTAL VISION

by DAVID GERROLD

As I write this, it is almost twenty-five years since the first episode of *Star Trek* was aired on the NBC television network on September 8, 1966. It has been an amazing quarter century.

A little history:

That first season, *Star Trek* aired on Thursday nights at 8:30. During the second season, the time slot was Friday nights at 8:30; and for the third and final season, the show was aired on Friday nights at 10:00. Surprisingly, even though the 10:00 time slot was considered a "death slot" for any program, *Star Trek*'s ratings held up all season long. Despite this, NBC executives decided not to renew the series for a fourth season. A total of seventy-nine hours were produced, at an average cost of $186,000 per hour.[1]

After *Star Trek* was canceled by the network, it went into immediate syndication. Local stations were able to "strip" the show, putting it on five nights a week, usually at 5:00 or 6:00 in the evening. In almost every single market,

---

[1] The single most expensive episode of *Star Trek* was the "City on the Edge of Forever" episode that ended up costing $262,000. That episode, written by Harlan Ellison (with an uncredited rewrite by Gene Roddenberry), also won the coveted Hugo Award for Best Dramatic Presentation of 1967.

Star Trek captured its time slot. Very quickly, Paramount's accounting department dubbed the original seventy-nine episodes "the seventy-nine jewels," and for the next two decades, those episodes would be an important cash cow for the studio. *Star Trek* would become one of the most successful syndicated series in television history, second only to *I Love Lucy*.

Most of us who were connected with the original show always knew it was something special. That it had become a ratings success in syndication was a validation of that conviction; nevertheless, most of us who were connected with the original show also believed (at that time) that it was over and that after a while the syndicated shows would also run their course and eventually disappear and be forgotten like so many other TV series.

Okay. So we were wrong.

Let's talk about the *Star Trek* phenomenon. Conventions first:

In February of 1972, a group of fans in New York staged the very first *Star Trek* convention. They expected 600 people; 3000 showed up. That was the first clue. . . .

In February of 1973, the same group of fans held another *Star Trek* convention. They expected 3000 people; 6000 showed up. In April of 1973, a group of fans in Los Angeles held their first *Star Trek* convention. They expected 3000 attendees; 6000 showed up.

Within a year, *Star Trek* conventions began popping up all over the country. In 1975 and '76, there were conventions in Boston, Detroit, Philadelphia, Los Angeles, New York, San Francisco, Chicago, and New Orleans. Almost every single one of these conventions was a grass-roots operation, put on spontaneously by local fans of the show; profit was not the motive; love of *Star Trek* was. It was an astonishing phenomenon—and unfortunately one that didn't last. *Star Trek* conventions still exist, but many of them are now put on by professional convention promoters who operate on a regular circuit; the spontaneity and family sense of the original conventions is no longer part of the experience.

Let's talk about fanzines:

A fanzine is an amateur magazine, usually with a print run of less than 200 copies. A quarter of a century ago, fanzines were usually typewritten and mimeographed—today, many of them come rolling smoothly out of laser printers, with perfect columns of justified text, looking like they've been professionally published.

Many of the early fanzines had titles like *Spockanalia* or *Grup*, titles derived directly from the show. They had articles about the series, sometimes interviews with people who had worked on the show, sometimes analyses of episodes or characters, sometimes speculations or extrapolations about the *Star Trek* universe, and, most often, amateur stories about the *Star Trek* characters.

Some of the fanzines were very handsomely produced, and at least one, *Starlog*, almost immediately evolved into a professional-level media magazine focusing on all science fiction movies and television shows, but *Star Trek* in particular.

Let's talk about the books:

The first *Star Trek* books were the James Blish adaptations of the episodes of the original series. These sold so well that other *Star Trek* books quickly followed. In the quarter century since *Star Trek* premiered, there have been several hundred *Star Trek* and *Star Trek*-related books published. There have been adaptations of all of the original episodes, photo-novels, adaptations of the *Star Trek Animated* episodes, novelizations of all of the movies, original novels using the *Star Trek* characters, original novels using the characters from *Star Trek: The Next Generation*, StarFleet manuals of all kinds, books that detail the history of the *Star Trek* phenomenon, books that focus on individual characters, books of articles culled from fanzines, books that analyze the phenomenon through a religious lens, even a Klingon language guide, a history of the first *Star Trek* conventions, and a book of *Star Trek* quotes. This does not include the comic book adaptations of *Star Trek*, which seem to have been going strong for several hundred years.

Let's talk about *Star Trek*:

After seventy-nine episodes of the original TV series, *Star Trek*'s next incarnation was as a Saturday morning animated series. Twenty-two episodes of this show were produced in 1973 and 1974. In 1979, the first *Star Trek* movie premiered. Despite a lukewarm critical reception, the film was profitable enough to justify a second *Star Trek* movie

. . . and a third, and a fourth, and a fifth, and (at the time of this writing) even a sixth.

In 1986, the success of *Star Trek* as a twenty-year phenomenon encouraged Paramount to take a bold gamble, a *new* television series called *Star Trek: The Next Generation*, which introduced a new *Enterprise*, seventy-eight years after the original, and a new crew. At the time of this writing, four full seasons of *Star Trek: The Next Generation* have been produced. The original plan for the series was that it would go for a full five seasons, totaling 150 episodes. This time around, it seems that the *Enterprise* will complete her five-year mission. (Some fans of the show have christened the original *Star Trek* series "Trek Classic" and *Star Trek: The Next Generation* as "New Trek." Obviously, then, *Star Trek Animated* is "Diet Trek.")

Which brings me back to the original series, which was canceled by NBC in 1969.

In speaking of that cancellation, Gene Roddenberry, the creator of *Star Trek*, has said that NBC didn't understand what they had. They didn't understand what *Star Trek* really was.

At the risk of ruffling a few feathers, let me say that it's my own conviction that no one at Paramount—not even Gene Roddenberry—*fully* understands what *Star Trek* has become or what it represents to its audience.

If you were to ask almost anyone at Paramount why *Star Trek* has been such a success over the years, you would hear (a variation of): "*Star Trek* offers an optimistic vision of the future. It says that there will be a future and it will be a good one; it says that we will solve today's problems to become the kind of people who can solve even the biggest problems the universe can throw at us."

That statement, or some form of it, has been repeated so many times, by so many people, it has almost become the "official" explanation. But it's only partly true; because it barely scratches the surface.

During the past quarter century, I've had the opportunity to meet *Star Trek* fans from all over the world—just about every kind of *Star Trek* fan there is. I've met those who put on conventions, those who attend conventions, those who make their own costumes and put on masquerades, those who write computer games, those who build their own working bridge mock-ups (yes!), those who collect the videotapes and laser disks and books and records and CDs and action figures and games and toys and comic books, those who write their own amateur stories, those who publish fanzines, those who write pornographic fanzines about the characters in the show, and even those who just like to sit and watch the show on television.

I've also had the opportunity to meet many of the people who've worked on the various incarnations of *Star Trek*, both in front of and behind the camera: actors, writers, art directors, costumers, prop men, set dressers, directors, makeup artists, special-effects wizards, animators, model builders, matte painters, and visionaries of all kinds.

If I were to try to *explain* the phenomenon, I would tell you three things about it.

First, it's a mirror.

Second, it's a Rorschach test.

And third, whatever is magic about *Star Trek* isn't really in *Star Trek*. It's in the audience.

Allow me to elucidate:

Star Trek is a mirror because people see themselves in it; they identify profoundly with the crew of the *Enterprise*, imagining themselves as part of the continuing team. But *Star Trek* is also a two-way mirror. Just as the show reflects the desires and fears of the audience, so does the audience reflect the behaviors depicted. Many of the viewers model themselves after the main characters and their behaviors, adopting the same body postures, mannerisms, and patterns of speech; often even parroting lines from the show in equivalent situations: "I'm a doctor, not a drama critic." "Shut up, Wesley." Or creating new dialogue of their own: "He's dead, Jim. You take his wallet, I'll get his tricorder." "I'm not stupid, I'm not expendable, and I'm not going."

But *Star Trek* is also a Rorschach test because each person perceives it as a different phenomenon:

To some people, *Star Trek* is a sexual fantasy—the universe is filled with beautiful men and beautiful women, all of whom want to jump into bed with each other, in a variety of combinations: there is a whole subgenre of fans dedicated to this particular interpretation.

To some people, *Star Trek* is a cash cow; it's another way to generate large amounts of money quickly. Once, at a *Star Trek* convention, a man in the lobby started hawking "official program books'' that he had printed up in his own print shop—without permission from either Paramount or the convention; when accosted, he said, ''Why not? Everybody else is making a profit off *Star Trek*. Why shouldn't I?'' Others may not be quite so blatant, but the dealers' room of almost any *Star Trek* convention is sure to have a fair sampling of unlicensed or even bootlegged or stolen material.

To some people, *Star Trek* is their personal property, and heaven help the person who doesn't agree with that vision. The arguments about what *Star Trek* is or should be have generated some of the heaviest message traffic on computer bulletin boards for at least two decades, and probably since the day the show began. These arguments have explored every nuance of the show: Is the *Enterprise* a military vessel or not? Should children be allowed on a starship? What do Klingons eat for breakfast?

And so on.

But to some people, *Star Trek* is something so special that it is not a single event, but rather an enveloping context for everything else in life. To those viewers, *Star Trek* is a future in the process of becoming. It is a different vision of the possibilities available to human beings.

Let me talk about that vision.

I have often thought that *Star Trek* is not very good science; the science portrayed in the TV series and the movies bears little relationship to science as it is practiced in the real world, often giving viewers a distorted and unreal sense of how scientists and engineers actually solve problems. I've also thought, from time to time, that *Star Trek* in some of its incarnations has not even been very good fiction. And, if I may be so bold as to risk offending some of the fundamentalists who might be reading this, I might even go so far as to state that by the purest of definitions, *Star Trek* is not even very good science fiction. (Too much fantasy, too much double-talk, too much make-believe; not enough real science, not enough real storytelling.)

But—whatever else *Star Trek* may or may not be—it is, first and foremost, *extraordinary* television; which is not only a whole other kind of storytelling, it is a whole different medium of communication, one that is exceedingly difficult (if not impossible) to master. The technical problems of television production are multiplied a thousandfold when every prop, every costume, every set, every hairdo, and every line of dialogue must be deliberately calculated to create the appearance of a whole other culture. In addition to this, *Star Trek* requires more special visual effects and sound effects per episode than any other television show ever produced. The pressures and complications of coordinating all of these separate elements, week after week, make *Star Trek* the single most daunting dramatic production challenge in television history.

Whatever else *Star Trek* is or is not, it is unmistakably an astonishing cultural phenomenon so profound that it must now be treated as a defining process of American popular culture. It has become more than an icon; it has become, like Mickey Mouse and Coca-Cola, a symbol as well as a role model for the American people.

Some analysts might say that this is because *Star Trek* represents a vision that inspires the viewer. I think that this is a misstatement. It puts the warp drive before the dilithium crystals.

The truth is that the dream of a better tomorrow already exists in the viewer. *Star Trek* merely gives it a focus, it is only one of many possibilities in the universe. For many people, before there was *Star Trek*, that vision was unformed, unspoken, and rarely consciously realized; but it was there—expressing itself in every dream of the future since human beings first climbed down out of the trees and began staring at the moon and wondering. That essential human ability to dream of something better is the spark of transformation that exists at the core of every human soul.

Star Trek's real success is not simply that it is an extraordinary television show, but that it connects itself to that extraordinary vision that already exists inside every human being, amplifies it, focuses it, expresses it, and reflects it back to the viewer in a way that he or she recognizes it as part of his or her own yearning for a better, brighter tomorrow. Call it a transcendental vision; it is the ability to dream of other possibilities. It is the ability to think that, "the universe that exists today does not have to be the universe that exists tomorrow. The way things are is not necessarily the way things have to be."

Which brings me, of course, to the writers.

I admit to some bias here, but I've always felt that the real success of *Star Trek* has always belonged to the writers. Without the story, without the script, without the words on the page, all you have are a bunch of good-looking people standing around in silly costumes in front of some cardboard walls waiting to be told what to do. Before any of it can come to life, you have to have someone who believes in it enough to sit down at a keyboard and deliberately, carefully, construct a whole world and an adventure to happen inside it.

The writers are the real creators of *Star Trek*. Everybody else is only interpreting the writer's vision.

Proof? The work stands by itself. The very best episodes of *Star Trek* are those that were written by individuals who are already in touch with aspects of the transcendental vision within themselves.

To give fair credit to every other person involved in the creation of *Star Trek*, the same transcendental vision has clearly been expressed in the other aspects of the production as well; most noticeably in the music, the special effects, the makeup, the art direction, the props, the costuming, and, of course, the acting.

Nevertheless, if you were to ask the fans of the show to list the very best episodes, and then if you were to look at the names of the writers of those episodes, you would see these names: Harlan Ellison, Norman Spinrad, Theodore Sturgeon, Fredric Brown, Jerome Bixby, Jerry Sohl, Robert Bloch, Richard Matheson, Max Erhlich, George Clayton Johnson, Gene L. Coon, and Dorothy C. Fontana. Most of these writers are better known for their short stories and novels in the science fiction and fantasy genres. All of them share one thing in common: an ability to dream believably. In fact, if you were to spend some time browsing through the science fiction and fantasy shelves of your local library or favorite bookstore, you would probably find works written by most of these writers.

The same holds true for the various *Star Trek* novels that have been published. The most popular of these books have been written by authors who have also demonstrated their skills as science fiction or fantasy writers: Vonda McIntyre, Diane Duane, Peter Morwood, Joe Haldeman, Jack Haldeman, Joan Vinge, Gordon Eklund, Melinda Snodgrass,

Greg Bear, Janet Kagan, Lee Correy (G. Harry Stine), Barbara Hambly, John M. Ford, Gar and Judy Reeves-Stevens, and others. Again, if you were to spend some time browsing through the non-*Star Trek* sections of your favorite bookstore, you will find many other books written by these authors.

In fact, let me encourage you to do precisely that. There are wonderful discoveries to be made in every bookstore in the world. *Star Trek* is only one place to visit in a whole landscape of science fiction and fantasy. Indeed, *Star Trek* is only a very small part of what's possible in the literature of the impossible. In that sense, *Star Trek* is science fiction with training wheels. It's the first tentative step toward some places that will *really* explode the event horizon of your imagination.

Science fiction—the hard-core stuff—has been described as a literature of ideas. But that definition is incomplete. Science fiction is a literature of change; it is a literature of transformation. It is the reader who is transformed, when his perception of what is possible is expanded to include a new vision.

There is a great debt that *Star Trek* owes to the science fiction field. If the writers of the show sometimes seem to have a million-light-year vision, it is because they are standing on the shoulders of those who went before, charting the unknown territory and leaving as their legacy a fantastic body of work.

Star Trek has mined the field of science fiction not only for writers, but for ideas since the first day it began. One of the first things that Gene Roddenberry did when he began producing the series was to assign Dorothy C. Fontana (at that time his secretary, later his story editor) to write summaries of the stories in every available science fiction anthology, so that the synopses could be used as reference material, to show what had already been established in science fiction, and even to suggest what stories might be available for adaptation. This was one of the best ideas he ever had, because it sensitized the entire staff to the realm of imaginative possibilities already explored in the genre.

That debt is repaid every time a *Star Trek* fan gets curious about what lies just beyond the realm of *Star Trek* and goes prowling through the rest of the science fiction shelves in the bookstore to see what else is possible. In the twenty-

five years since the first episode of *Star Trek* was aired, the
sales of science fiction books have expanded from 3 percent
of the market to 12 percent of the market. The science fiction
shelves are usually one of the biggest sections in any bookstore; they are one of the most lucrative sources of revenue
for a bookstore owner. *Star Trek* has been a large part of that
success, drawing more and more new readers into the world
of science fiction every year. The number of science fiction
novels published per year has expanded considerably, and
most of those books are now selling many more copies than
they would have ten or fifteen or twenty-five years ago.

   Star Trek books, of course, regularly hit *The New York
Times* Best Sellers list.

   Let me tell you about the stories you are about to read:

   Betty Ballantine, who almost single-handedly invented the
genre of science fiction paperback originals, gambled that there
was a large audience for *Star Trek* books. The first book she
published was *The Making of Star Trek*, which author Stephen
Whitfield assembled from Gene Roddenberry's notes, the bible
of the series, Paramount's official publicity, and many extensive
interviews with the cast and crew. That book sold so well that
she licensed the right to publish adaptations of all seventy-eight
episodes* of the original TV series, and because she wanted the
adaptations to be well written instead of mere exploitation pieces,
she hired science fiction writer/critic James Blish to do the work
of translating the scripts for the television episodes into publish-
able stories. To say that the Blish adaptations sold well would
be an understatement. They sold better than almost any other
science fiction book published up to that time. The success of
those early efforts was so remarkable that it opened the flood-
gates for the publication of hundreds more *Star Trek* books of
all kinds in the decades to follow.

   This book that you're holding in your hands now is the
second of three, published by Bantam-Spectra, offering all of
James Blish's original episode adaptations in one set. All of
the episodes included here were produced during the second
season of *Star Trek*'s three-year production schedule. Most of
these episodes were produced under the direct guidance of
Gene L. Coon, a man who probably understood *Star Trek*

---

*79 hours. ''The Cage'' was a two-part episode.

better than anyone else ever entrusted with that responsibility. It's my own personal conviction that Gene L. Coon has not received anywhere near as much credit as he deserves for the success of this accomplishment. Gene L. Coon loved *Star Trek;* he put his heart and soul into every episode he produced, he cared about stories, and best of all he cared about writers; in many respects, Gene L. Coon embodied what I think is the true spirit of *Star Trek:* it is not enough to portray a better world, you have to live your life as if you are a representative of that world. That is a lesson that I have carried with me for twenty-five years and I remain profoundly grateful to the man who taught it to me.

Now, let me talk about James Blish:

I had the unique pleasure of meeting James Blish in 1971.

How I got to Ireland, and from there to England, and eventually to a British science fiction convention is another story altogether. The most important thing that I remember about that convention was the opportunity to meet and chat with James and Judy Blish.

Now, James Blish was a gentleman in the truest sense of the word. He treated the people around him with genuine respect and interest. He had an unfettered curiosity about the way the universe worked, why things had happened, and what possibilities might be extrapolated from what was already known. This was amply demonstrated in his conversation as well as in his writing.

Blish was the consummate novelist. His command of the language was (and remains today) a model of carefully crafted writing. He used words like flavors; his phrasing was both lucid and delicious; his narrative was fluent without ever sacrificing clarity of thought or purpose; and his attention to detail was exquisite.

James Blish brought an understanding to his work that transcended mere storytelling; it was clear that he gave much thought not only to the purpose of the work, but to the underlying processes as well. His approach to characters and ideas demonstrated a maturity and depth that was lacking even in many mainstream novels of the time. The stories he wrote were landmarks in the field, affecting the perceptions of nearly every other writer in the field; time and time again, he broke new ground in science fiction, inventing new realms of thought for others to explore in his wake.

For example, Blish's classic story *Surface Tension* was the first science fiction exploration of genetic reconstruction of human beings; in that story, the descendants of the crew of a crashed seeding starship live a microscopic existence among the protozoan life forms of the planet Hydrot; eventually a team of bold explorers build a wooden "spaceship" that runs on wheels, to explore the dry land that surrounds their puddle.

Blish's Hugo-winning novel *A Case of Conscience* was the first science fiction novel to explore the relationship of man and God. In that landmark work, a Jesuit priest must help write the recommendation of how the human race should deal with the people of a newly discovered planet. As he discovers the life cycle of the people of Lithia, his own faith is sorely tested; the planet seems to have been deliberately designed to refute every precept of what his religion postulates about the purposes of God.

In *Earthman, Come Home* Blish wrote of a time when the great cities of the world have all gone into space, encapsulated in force-field bubbles and driven by gigantic spindizzy engines. He wrote of the social effects that such macroengineering was certain to produce upon the populations who went into space, the worlds they visited, and those who stayed behind.

Even when Blish went beyond the bounds of science fiction, he still took with him the same methodical approach to asking questions and seeking answers. In *Black Easter* he considered the religious fantasy as a kind of scientific inquiry into the theological realm; a group of monks confront the forces of Hell as an investigation of the existence of supernatural powers, thereby proving the existence of God.

The evidence of his work proves that James Blish was not just a good storyteller, he was also a profound thinker. He asked questions. He considered possibilities. And then he asked more questions. He explored the realms of the imagination with the rigors of an engineer and the curiosity of a philosopher.

As a result, he understood storytelling on a much deeper level than the average practitioner of the craft. It was no accident that he was also one of the very best critics that the science fiction field has ever had. He had no patience for sloppy writing. He skewered it. The English language was like a violin, an instrument that, in the hands of one who has dedicated years of training and practice, can be played to produce exquisite and compelling images. Blish had little tolerance for those who merely pulled horsehair over catgut to make a squealing noise.

As a critic, James Blish demanded that the field of science fiction be more than just a subgenre of pulp writing; he envisioned the literature of imagination as a research and development lab for humanity and its perceptions about itself and the universe. In his regular columns for *Galaxy Science Fiction*, he functioned as a preacher, a cheerleader, a taskmaster, and a weatherman. His analyses of the landmark novels of the time were insightful and thought-provoking; something to be anticipated with a mixture of eagerness and dread if you were an author, but to be anticipated with relish if you were a reader.

Let me share one of his insights:

At that aforementioned meeting with James Blish in 1971, the conversation eventually wound its way around to a consideration of the craft of storytelling. At one point, Blish looked at me and said, "Who does it hurt? That's who the story is about."

At the moment he said it, my reaction was: "Well, that's obvious—" But in the moments that followed, as the meaning of what he had really said began to sink in, as I continued to think about it, I began to *experience* the profound truth of it. James Blish had reduced the core of storytelling to a single question. Everything that there is to learn about characterization and plotting can be derived from that single insight. *Who does it hurt? That's who the story is about.*

(As an aside, let me mention that I teach screenwriting at Pepperdine University in Malibu, California. The class is a sixteen-week course. We spend at least eight of those weeks on story structure; and at least half of those eight lectures are derived from Blish's original question: *Who does it hurt?* If you have ever entertained any thoughts of writing your own stories, write this on a note card and paste it to your keyboard.)

Which brings me finally back to this book and these stories:

It is a profound irony that while James Blish's *Star Trek* adaptations were the least important works in his career, they were also the most financially rewarding. He also acknowledged, with some wry amusement, that he had received more fan mail for his *Star Trek* books than he had received during the whole previous part of his career. He did not feel at all slighted by this, only somewhat bemused at the whole *Star Trek* phenomenon; but he was also quite pleased at the interest that *Star Trek* fans were beginning to demonstrate in the rest of his work.

Okay, ready? Here's the best part of the joke:

James Blish wrote his *Star Trek* adaptations before he was able to see most of the episodes he was writing about.

James and Judy Blish lived in England; the British Broadcasting Corporation did not purchase the rights to show *Star Trek* until the early seventies. Blish had to write all of his adaptations based *only* on the scripts that were sent to him from Paramount Pictures. In some cases, he was not even working from final draft shooting scripts, but from earlier drafts of the same episode; this is why you'll find occasional small discrepancies between the Blish adaptations and the episodes as telecast. (For example, Sulu is present in the Blish adaptation of "The Trouble With Tribbles," but the character was not present in the episode because George Takei was off shooting a movie at the time. Sulu was only present in the first draft of the script, which was all that James Blish had to work from.)

I know that James Blish enjoyed writing these stories that you're about to read; I know that he enjoyed hearing from *Star Trek*'s fans; and I know that you will enjoy reading these stories and revisiting the early days of one of America's most popular television series.

And when you finish, go to the library or to your favorite bookstore and see what else is available by James Blish.[2] I promise that you will not be disappointed.

---

[2] And all the other authors mentioned above, too.

CATSPAW

Writer: Robert Bloch
Director: Joseph Pevney
Guest stars: Antoinette Bower, Theo Marcuse

≡

The persistent static crackling from Lieutenant Uhura's communications panel was just the minor worry presented by the planet Pyris VII. A dark and forbidding star it had shown itself to be ever since the *Enterprise* had entered its orbit—a chunk of black granite hurled into space to no ostensible purpose, lightless, lifeless except for members of the Starship's landing party beamed down to it for routine investigation and check-in reports. That was the big worry—the absence of any check-in reports. Yet Scott, Sulu and crewman Jackson were all aware of standard landing-group procedure. They knew it required an hourly check-in from any team assigned to explore an unknown planet.

Uhura looked up at Kirk. "Still no response, sir."

"Keep it open."

He frowned at another burst of static from the communications panel. "I don't like this. Nothing since the first check-in. Scott and Sulu should have contacted us half an hour ago."

Spock said, "Perhaps they have nothing to report. Though Pyris VII is a Class M planet capable of sustaining humanoid life, our own people are the only evidence of it our sensors have been able to pick up."

"Nevertheless, Scott and Sulu are obliged to check in, regardless of whether they have anything official to report. Why don't they answer?"

Uhura adjusted a control. A look of relief came into her face. "Contact established, Captain."

Kirk seized the audio. Jackson's voice said, "Jackson to *Enterprise*."

"Kirk here."

"One to beam up, sir."

"One? Jackson, where are Scott and Sulu?"

"I'm ready to beam up, sir."

"Jackson! Where are—" A roar of static overwhelmed his words. Uhura tried to control it; and failed. "I'm sorry, sir. I can't clear it."

"All right," said Kirk. "Notify Transporter Room to prepare to beam up one member of the landing party. Have Dr. McCoy report to me in Transporter Room on the double."

"Yes, sir."

It was the measure of their anxiety that Kirk and Spock both ran for the elevator. They opened the door of the Transporter Room to the steady, throbbing hum of thrown switches.

"Ready, sir," the technician said.

"Energize!" The humming rose to a keening pitch and McCoy hurried in with his medikit.

"What's on, Jim?"

"Trouble."

The Transporter platform glowed into dazzle. Then its sparkle gathered into the full figure of crewman Jackson. He stood, stiff and unmoving, his face wiped clean of all expression, his eyes unseeing, fixed in a glassy stare. The hum of materialization faded. Kirk strode to the platform. "Jackson! What happened? Where are the others?"

The mouth moved as though preparing to speak. But Jackson didn't speak. The mouth twisted into a grimace— and Jackson, pitching forward, toppled to the floor.

Kneeling beside him, McCoy looked up at Kirk. He shook his head. "The man's dead, Jim."

Kirk stared down at the body. Its glassy eyes were still fixed on nothing. Then, horribly, the jaw dropped and the mouth opened. Out of it spoke a voice, deep, harsh, guttural. "Captain Kirk, you hear me. There is a curse on your ship. Leave this star. It is death that waits for you here . . ."

There was a moment of appalled stillness. Jackson's dead mouth still yawned open. But his lips had not moved.

At his desk in Sickbay, McCoy leaned his head on his hand. He didn't look up as Kirk opened the door. Shoulders sagged, he pushed wearily at a heap of tape cartridges in front of him.

"Well?" Kirk said.

McCoy lifted a handful of the cartridges. Then he dropped them. "These are the reports of every test I've run. There's no sign of any injury, none. No organic damage, internal or external."

Kirk was silent for a stretched moment. Scott and Sulu—they were still down there on the planet that had returned a dead man to the *Enterprise;* a dead man whose mouth had been used by that awful voice. *"Then why is Jackson dead, Bones?"*

"He froze to death," McCoy said.

Spock had quietly joined them. "That doesn't seem reasonable, Doctor," he said. "The climate of Pyris VII approximates that of Earth's central Western hemisphere during the summer solstice."

McCoy said irritably, "I know that, Spock. But reasonable or unreasonable, Jackson froze to death. He was literally dead on his feet when he materialized in the Transporter Room."

"He was about to speak," Kirk said.

"He was dead, I tell you!" McCoy shouted.

"Someone spoke." Kirk slowly shook his head. "There seems to be a good deal more to that planet than our sensors have been able to detect! With Scott and Sulu virtually marooned down there . . ."

He was interrupted by the buzzing intercom on McCoy's desk. He hit the switch. "Kirk here."

Uhura, her voice urgent, said, "Sir, we've lost all traces of Mr. Scott and Mr. Sulu. The sensors no longer register any indication of life on the planet's surface. That's Mr. Farrell's last report."

"Well," said Kirk, "that tears it." He paused. "Thank you, Lieutenant. Have Mr. Farrell maintain sensor scan." He snapped off the intercom. "Spock, Bones, get your gear together for a landing party. We're beaming down to find them.''

Fog was what they found. Clammy swirls of it drifted around them as they materialized on a twilight world of rock, barren, desolate. From the craggy knoll they stood on, no green was visible—just a gray vista of mist that moved sluggishly, only to reveal more mist, more rock, black fields, black hills of rock.

"Odd," Kirk said. "Our probe data didn't indicate fog."

"Odd, indeed," Spock agreed. "No bodies of water. No cloud formations. No variations in surface temperature. Under such conditions, fog is impossible." He had unslung his tricorder and was taking readings.

"It was impossible for Jackson to freeze to death in this climate," McCoy said. "Yet that's what happened. By the way, just where are we?"

"According to Transporter Room coordinates, this is the exact spot from which Jackson was beamed up to the ship," Spock said.

"Readings, Mr. Spock?"

"No indication of—wait! I'm picking up a life forms reading at 14 degrees mark 7—distance 137.16 meters." He looked up from the tricorder. "Multiple readings, Captain!"

Astonished, Kirk snapped on his communicator. "Kirk to *Enterprise*."

Static distorted Uhura's voice. "*Enterprise*, Captain."

"How do the ship's sensors read now, Lieutenant?"

"All we're getting are physical impulses from you, Mr. Spock and Dr. McCoy, sir. There's nothing else alive down there."

The static almost obliterated her last words. "I can hardly hear you, Lieutenant," Kirk said. "Can you hear me?"

His communicator cracked with a crash of static. Disgusted, Kirk snapped it off and was returning it to his belt when McCoy said, "The fog's getting thicker. Maybe it accounts for the interference."

It *was* getting thicker. Fog rolled around them so dense now that they could scarcely see each other. "There has to be some explanation for the disparity in the readings," Kirk said. "Ours are the only life forms picked up by the ship's sensors but Spock's tricorder registers multiple forms. Do your readings still hold, Mr. Spock?''

''No change, sir.''

''Phasers on the ready,'' Kirk said.

Then they all heard it—a high-pitched wailing. Faint at first, it grew in volume to a mournful shrieking. ''They must have heard us,'' McCoy whispered.

''Quiet, Bones!''

McCoy gripped Kirk's arm as he pointed with the other hand. Ahead of them the coiling fog had begun to glow with a greenish, sickly luminescence. Then it gathered, shaping itself into three cloudy faces, vaguely featured, indistinct, wrinkled by a hundred years. Elf locks of wispy white hair hung about them, their sex as blurred as their features. One of the faces spoke.

''Captain Kirk . . .''

Its long-drawn-out whine had the same creepy cadence as the wailing.

Kirk stepped forward. ''Who are you?''

''Go baaack—'' wailed the toothless mouth.

The mist was sending the bodiless faces in and out of focus.

''Winds shall rise,'' one of them whimpered

''And fogs descend . . .''

''Death is here . . .''

On a cackle of rheumy laughter, the faces suddenly came apart. Then they dissolved into mist.

Quiet, unmoved, Spock said, ''Illusion, Captain.'' He lowered his tricorder. ''They contained neither physical substance nor energy. It may have been a projection of some sort.''

''Shakespeare wrote of a blasted heath,'' Kirk said. ''And of warning witches. But why should these have appeared to us? None of us care to become the King of Scotland. Spock, did the life form readings change during that little encounter?''

''They remained the same, Captain.''

Kirk nodded. ''That may be part of our answer.''

They moved on—and an abrupt gust of wind whistled past them. It grew stronger. It should have tattered the fog into shreds. It didn't. The stuff became clammier, more blinding. The wind now rose to a gale force that compelled them to turn their backs to it, clinging to each other for support. "Hang on!" Kirk shouted. As though the words were some form of exorcism, the wind was gone as suddenly as it had come.

Panting, McCoy said, "That was one very realistic illusion." He drew a deep lungful of breath. Then, incredulously, he whispered, "Jim—ahead of us—there . . ."

It looked like the keep of a medieval castle. It reared itself up before them, huge, battlemented, its masonry of massive stones hoary with age. Its great oaken door, beamed and iron-bound, was slightly ajar. On one of the worn steps that led up to it crouched a sleek black cat. A glittering gold chain was hung around its neck. As they approached it, they saw that a translucent crystal pendant was attached to the chain. The pose of the cat suggested it was waiting for something. Mice, perhaps.

Spock said, "This is the source of the life forms reading, Captain. They are inside somewhere."

Kirk tried to use his communicator again, only to be defeated by an explosion of static. Once more he hung it back on his belt.

"Is this how we lost contact with the first landing party?" McCoy wondered.

"What about that, Spock?" Kirk put it to him. "Does this apparent castle have anything to do with the static?"

The Vulcan consulted his tricorder. "I would say not, sir. There's no evidence of anything that would directly cause the interference. Both the castle and the cat are equally real."

"Or unreal," Kirk said. "Some illusions can manifest themselves in solid substance. Why didn't our sensors pick up this castle? And why didn't they register the life forms inside it?" He looked up, frowning, at a turreted wall. "It could be exerting a force field that has cut off our sensor scan."

"Then it would also affect Spock's tricorder, wouldn't it?" McCoy asked.

"Would it? I'm beginning to wonder—" It was as Kirk spoke the last words that the cat mewed, rose gracefully and disappeared through the partly open door. Lost, it seemed, in some private speculation, he watched it go. Then pulling himself out of it briskly, "Well," he said, "if Scott and Sulu are anywhere around, this is the most likely place. Come on."

Phasers in hand, they pushed the door open. A squeaking shrilled over their heads—and a cloud of bats swooped through the door, chittering, their leathery wings almost brushing their faces.

Ducking, McCoy cried, "What the devil was that?"

"Desmodus rufus," Spock said. "Vampire bats."

"That's an Earth species," Kirk said. The cat, moving restlessly before them, mewed again as it turned into the darkness beyond the doorway. He looked after it, the look of private thoughtfulness back on his face. "And so is the cat an Earth species. The plot thickens. Castles, black cats, vampire bats and witches. If we weren't missing two live officers and a dead crewman, I'd say someone was putting on an elaborate Halloween trick or treat."

"Trick or treat, Captain?"

"An old Earth custom, Mr. Spock. Explanation later."

The castle walls appeared to be hewn from solid rock. The cat padded silently ahead of Kirk as he and the others groped along the chilly corridor. It was dim, its uncertain light provided by occasional torches whose flames flared and ebbed above their iron sconces, cobwebbed and rusty.

"Dust. Cobwebs. Halloween is right," McCoy said.

The cat slipped around a corner into a darker corner. As they followed, the floor gave way beneath them, and they were plunged into blackness.

Kirk was the first to recover his senses. Someone with a bizarre sense of humor had arranged to place a spiked Iron Maiden right before him. The skull of the human skeleton inside it grinned at him. He refused to be horrified. What concerned him was the discovery that he was shackled to the dungeon's wall. So were Spock and McCoy. Then he realized that all their equipment—phasers, communicators, tricorders—had been removed.

"Mr. Spock . . ."

The Vulcan stirred in his fetters. "I am undamaged, Captain."

"Is Bones all right?"

McCoy spoke for himself. "Nothing broken—just a lot of bruises. What was that you said about trick or treat, Jim?"

"Curses, dungeons, Iron Maidens, skeletons. The point is, these are all Earth manifestations. *Why?*"

"The tricorder registered this castle as real, Jim." McCoy rattled his chains. "And *these* are no illusion. This place could be an Earth parallel."

"But it would be a parallel only of Earth superstition, Doctor," Spock said. "Something that exists only in the minds of men."

"Exactly," Kirk said. "It's as though—" He broke off. Muffled footsteps had sounded from the corridor outside. A key scraped in the dungeon's lock; to Kirk's astounded relief, its heavy door was swung open by Scott and Sulu.

"Scotty! Sulu! You're safe!"

There was no sign of responsive joy on either of their faces. Silent, stone-faced, Scott pulled a phaser from his belt—and leveled it at them.

"Scotty," Kirk said, "put that phaser down!"

Unmoving, unblinking, Scott maintained the phaser at aim.

"Scott!" Kirk shouted.

"Jim, I think they've been drugged. Look at their eyes—no nictation. They don't blink at all."

"Neither did Jackson," Spock said.

"These two are alive! Scotty, Sulu—do you know who I am?"

Sulu nodded.

"What's happened to you?" Kirk demanded.

For answer, Sulu shuffled past him to lean over McCoy. While Scott covered the *Enterprise* physician with the phaser, Sulu selected a key from a bunch he was carrying on a ring, and inserted it in the bolt's lock that bound the chains to McCoy's arms. Watching, Kirk said, "They're just taking off the chains, Bones. They're not going to let us go. Are you?"

Silence. In absolute silence, their manacles were unlocked. At the dungeon door, Sulu motioned them into the corridor. Gauging Scott's distance behind him, Kirk whirled around to throw a punch at his jaw. The butt of the phaser caught him in the temple. As he stumbled to his knees, Spock jumped Scott and McCoy made a leap for the unarmed Sulu.

But even as they touched them, their faces were lit by the sickly greenish light—and they dissolved into it.

"*Stop!*"

It was the voice that had spoken through the dead mouth of Jackson.

They stopped. The green glow seemed to have dissolved the corridor and the dungeon, too. All that was familiar was the strangeness of Scott and Sulu. They had reappeared, as unblinking, as blank-faced as before. Everything else was new.

And old. The large chamber to which they'd somehow been transported was heavy with medieval magnificence. Dark tapestries covered its walls. The flare of its sconced torches shone on the bare surface of a huge table, flanked by high-backed chairs. But Kirk's eyes had fixed on a man. He sat on an ornately carved chair, set on a dais that was canopied by a domelike structure. He was bearded, and the long robe he wore glittered with the gold-embroidered symbols of the Zodiac. The black wand he held was topped by a dazzling crystal ball. The cat was stretched out at his feet.

Kirk strode up to the chair. "Whoever you are, you've proved your skill at creating illusions. Now what I want to know is what you have done to my men."

The man leaned forward. "Your race owns a ridiculous predilection for resistance. You question everything. Is it not sufficient for you to *accept* what is?"

"Not when one of my men is dead and two others have been turned into mindless . . ."

"Not mindless, Captain Kirk. The live ones are merely—controlled."

Spock and McCoy had made startled movements at the man's use of Kirk's name. They were noted. "Yes, we know you, all of you. Don't we, my precious?" He lowered a hand to stroke the cat.

"Who are you?" Kirk demanded. "Why did you bring us here?"

The bearded mouth smiled. "My name is Korob. As for bringing you here, you insisted upon coming. You were warned away from here."

"For what reason?" Kirk waved a hand that embraced all

the mystic trappings of the room and the man. "What is all this—farce about?"

"Farce? I assure you, it is not that, Captain."

Spock spoke. "Clearly, you are unfamiliar with your planet, Korob."

The piercing eyes searched the Vulcan's face. "What did you say?"

"No life exists on your planet," Spock said. "Mapping expeditions have charted this solar system. Their scientific surveys prove that no life forms have ever lived where you appear to live."

The cat stirred, mewing. Lids lowered over the piercing eyes. "That we are not native to this planet is of no importance," Korob said softly.

"It's important to the Federation," Kirk said. "What are you doing here?"

"All in good time, Captain." The cat mewed again, and Korob bent his head as though listening to a secret message. When he raised it, he said, "You must forgive me. I have been an inattentive host. You will join me in something with which to refresh yourselves." Followed by the cat, he rose to lead the way toward the empty table.

"That cat—" McCoy said quietly.

"Yes," Spock said. "It reminds me of certain ancient Earth legends concerning wizards and their 'familiars'— demons in animal form sent by Satan to serve the wizards."

"Superstition," Kirk said.

"I did not create the legends, Captain. I merely repeat them."

Korob turned. "You are the different one, Mr. Spock. There are no colors in your patterns of logic. You think only in terms of black and white. You see all this around you. Yet you do not believe in it."

"He doesn't know about trick or treat," McCoy said.

Korob smiled faintly. "I see." He waved toward the empty table. "But, gentlemen, please join me at dinner."

Nobody moved. Scott and Sulu made a menacing move, Scott lifting the phaser. Korob held up his hand. They both backed up to stand stock-still again. "I had hoped you would be more flexible," Korob said, "but—" He raised his wand.

The green glow grew into a dazzle, dazzling as the

crystal ball on the wand's end. The room and all its objects spun in it like dust motes. It blinded Kirk. When he could see again, he, Spock and McCoy were seated at the table. A boar's head gaped in front of him. There was a platter of stuffed peacock. In the table's center a giant beef roast, browned to succulence, was surrounded by silver bowls of fruit, great plates of creamy cheeses. Massive candelabra refracted light on crystal wine decanters and golden goblets. As a display of medieval food and sumptuous service, it was a feast to be seen only by tourists who had booked passage in a Time Machine.

"How in the name of—" McCoy began.

"Not a trick, Doctor," Korob said. "A treat this time. Believe that."

"What do you want from us, Korob?" Kirk asked.

"For the moment, merely that you eat and enjoy yourselves. Please try the wine, Doctor. You will find it excellent."

"No, thank you," McCoy said.

Mewing, the cat suddenly leaped to an empty seat at the table, light glinting from the crystal pendant hung around its neck. Despite his refusal of wine, McCoy's hand reached for the decanter in front of him. He made a visible effort to pull it back—and failed. Kirk made a move toward him only to be slammed back in his chair by Scott.

"Bones . . ."

"He can't obey you, Captain," Korob said. "He will not be harmed."

Will paralyzed, McCoy poured wine from the decanter into his goblet. The cat, its crystal pendant shining against its black fur, watched steadily as he raised the goblet to his lips. He touched it with them—and the wine burst into vivid red flames.

Clearly alarmed, Korob raised his wand. The flames subsided, and McCoy dashed the goblet to the floor. It vanished, leaving a smell of smoke in the air.

The cat hissed.

Furious, Kirk said, "If you've amused yourself sufficiently, Korob . . ."

But Korob's eyes were on the cat. "That was not my wish," he said. "I—perhaps I can make proper amends."

The black wand pointed to the table's empty plates. They filled with gems, pricelessly exotic jewels come together in their multicolored glitter from the multiworlds of the galaxy—the ruby reds of what were not rubies, the sapphire blues of what were not sapphires but the alien treasures of an unearthly star system.

"They look genuine," McCoy said.

"They are, I assure you," Korob said. "That is a masgar, Doctor—a lorinium—a pavonite. There is a fortune for each of you in the richest gems of the galaxy if you will leave here without further query."

"We are not ready to leave here," Kirk said quietly.

"Captain, you are a stubborn and unreasonable man. However, you have passed the tests."

"Tests?" McCoy queried.

Korob nodded. "You proved your loyalty by coming here to rescue your comrades in spite of warnings to stay away. Your courage was also tested. I learned you couldn't be frightened. Now I've learned that you can't be bribed. I congratulate you."

The cat mewed. Korob patted it. "Quite right," he said. "Go at once." The animal jumped from the chair and was gone through the tapestried archway at the other end of the chamber.

Kirk got up. "All right. Now that you've tested our integrity, suppose you demonstrate yours."

"Gladly, Captain."

"Begin by explaining what you've done to Scott and Sulu. How are you 'controlling' them?"

"I cannot answer that question?" Korob said. "But I have sent for someone who can."

That someone entered, a tall, slim woman. Her black hair, parted in the center above her acquiline features, fell below her waist. Perhaps it was her high cheekbones that gave her green eyes an oblique look. On the breast of her red gown she wore a crystal pendant like the one they had seen on the cat.

Korob said, "This is my colleague, Sylvia."

As she approached Kirk, he became conscious of her remarkable grace. Bowing slightly, she said, "Captain Kirk, I understand you want to know what we did to your men. We probed their minds. For us it is a simple matter to probe the minds of creatures like yourself.''

"Hypnosis?" Spock asked.

She ignored him to move to McCoy. As she did so, she said, "Our methods go a little deeper than hypnosis." McCoy made no comment. Eyes held by the glowing pendant, he had gone suddenly rigid, unblinking. She smiled at him. "Let me tell you what you said of the man Jackson who was returned to your ship. You said, 'There's no sign of any injury . . . no organic damage, internal or external. The man simply froze to death.' ''

"How do you know that?" Kirk was watching her closely.

The green eyes turned to him. "You like to think of yourselves as complex creatures, Captain, but you are flawed. Your minds have many doors. Most of them are left unguarded. We enter your minds through those unguarded doors.''

"Telepathy?" Spock suggested.

This time she answered him. "Not entirely. Telepathy does not include control. And I assure you, I am in full control of your friends.''

Abruptly, Kirk lost patience with the charming lady and her conversation. Moving swiftly, he shoved his heavy chair back into Scott. Scott stumbled, losing his guard stance behind the chair. He lost his phaser, too; Kirk grabbed it from him all in that same swift, unexpected movement. Scott, recovering his balance, lunged. Kirk leveled the phaser at him. He backed up, and the phaser swung around to cover all of them—Sylvia, Korob, Sulu, Scott.

"Don't move—any of you!" Kirk said.

McCoy relaxed. His eyes blinked. Kirk motioned Scott and Sulu over to Korob, the phaser steady in his hand. "No more hocus-pocus!" he said. "Korob, I want our other weapons and our equipment. I want them now. I also want some answers—real ones.''

Sylvia said, "Put that weapon down, Captain."

Kirk laughed. The green eyes didn't flash with anger. They merely regarded him appraisingly. Then, reaching a hand into a pocket slit in her gown, Sylvia withdrew from it what appeared to be a small silver toy. She left Kirk to go to Spock and McCoy.

"Do you recognize this?" she asked them.

"It looks like a miniature model of the *Enterprise*," McCoy said.

"No. In a sense it *is* the *Enterprise*."

Frowning, Spock said, "Where did you get it?"

"From the minds of your two crew members. I absorbed their knowledge of the ship."

"With what purpose in *your* mind?" Spock asked.

She moved to the table where the huge candelabra held its tall, lit candles. "In the mythology of your race," she said, "this is called 'sympathetic magic,' Captain. One may call it what one chooses. It is an interesting tool."

Kirk, still holding the phaser on Korob, spoke over his shoulder. "Lady," he said, "that won't do as an explanation."

Spock's face had grown grave. He watched her intently as she stood at the table, the candlelight throwing come-and-go shadows across her face. "Jackson," she said, "you all wondered why he froze to death in a moderate climate. How is *this* explanation, Captain? I made an exact image of him. Then I froze the image. When I knew it was frozen, he died."

"Rubbish!" Kirk said. "You can't *think* a man to death!"

"Your communicator is in the pocket of Korob's robe, Captain. Please take it."

He hesitated a moment before he obeyed. As he turned, he saw that she was holding the toy model of *Enterprise* about six inches above a candle flame. "Signal your ship," she said.

He clicked the communicator open. Uneasy in spite of himself, he realized that she had lowered the silver model closer to the candle flame.

Korob said, "Sylvia—don't . . ."

The model sank closer to the candle flame; and Kirk spoke hastily into the communicator, "Kirk to *Enterprise*! *Enterprise*, come in, please. Kirk here. Come in . . ."

"Captain, it's you!" It was Uhura's voice but there was desperation in it. "Where are you? We can't . . ."

"Never mind us. What's happening up there?"

"Something's—gone wrong with the temperature control. We—can't locate it. The heat has risen—sixty degrees in the past thirty seconds. The *Enterprise* is burning up, sir . . .''

"Beef up the refrigerator units, Lieutenant!"

The voice came more weakly now. "We did, sir—but they're—breaking down . . ."

Kirk, visualizing his Starship, saw it streaking through space like a comet on fire. He imagined Uhura and Farrell, hanging onto their posts, gasping for air, their uniforms sweat-drenched. "The heat will go," he said. "I'll take care of it, Lieutenant."

He snapped off the communicator, walked over to Korob and returned it to him. "All right," he told Sylvia. "You can stop it now." He handed the phaser, too, to Korob.

She removed the little ship from the flame.

"Now that you've seen our science," Korob said, "perhaps you'd better tell us something of yours."

"I'd rather know more about yours," Kirk said. "First you call it magic. Now it's science. Which is it?"

"What would you call it, Captain?"

"Transmutation—telekinesis. You seem to have a strange ability, not just to change the molecular structure of objects, but to move them from point to point by merely willing it. What could you want with our comparatively clumsy science?"

"Ours requires machines, matter, energy, chemicals," Spock added. "Compared with your techniques, it is imperfect and cumbersome. Then why is it important to you?"

"There are things you know that we do not. We can alter the molecular structure of matter. But you can release the energy within it."

"Korob! You talk too much!" Sylvia snapped. Recovering herself, she went on, "Besides, you three are not so specialized as those two." She indicated the motionless figures of Scott and Sulu. "That one thinks only of machines. The other's mind is full of trivia, thoughts about his collections, the physical exertions he calls exercises. But in your minds is an accumulated knowledge of worlds, of this galaxy."

"If so, in our minds is where the knowledge stays," Kirk said.

"You have used Scott and Sulu as catspaws," McCoy said. "You used them to lure us down here. How did you know we'd come?"

"*They* knew you'd come," Korob smiled.

"Enough of this," Sylvia said impatiently. "You will tell us what we want to know, one way or another!"

"It's a little late for threats," Kirk said. "I contacted my ship, remember? How long do you think it'll be before there's another landing party here?"

"Quite some time," Korob said. He touched the tiny ship on the table with the crystal ball of his wand. The now familiar greenish light glowed over it. When it faded, the model was encased in a solid block of crystal. "An impenetrable force field now surrounds your ship, Captain. It will not hinder orbit. It does, however, make prisoners of everybody inside your ship."

"I advise you to cooperate, Captain." Sylvia said. "Though it is simple to extract the information we want by forcible means, they are extremely painful. And they have a certain—draining effect." She waved a hand toward Scott and Sulu.

"We have nothing to discuss," Kirk said.

Korob turned to Scott and Sulu. "Take them back to their cell."

"Wait." Sylvia's green eyes moved over them, cold, icily analytical. "The Doctor will stay."

"Bones—" Kirk began.

"Don't waste your sympathy, Captain. You will be next. It really makes little difference." She turned, speaking sharply to Scott and Sulu. "Take the others away."

Korob handed Sulu the phaser. It thrust hard into Kirk's back as he and Spock were herded from the chamber.

This time his shackles seemed tighter to Kirk. His eyes fixed anxiously on the dungeon door, he moved restlessly in the chains, feeling them grind into his flesh.

"How long has it been?" he fretted.

"Twenty-two minutes, seventeen seconds," Spock said.

The question gnawing at Kirk burst out of him. "What are they doing to him?"

"Perhaps," Spock said, "the real question is '*what* are they?' They've admitted they are alien to this planet. And I find their total ignorance of our instrumentality and science most curious."

Kirk gave him an interested glance. "They also refer to us as 'creatures,' as though our species were unfamiliar to them."

Spock nodded. "The fact that everything around us seems solid and real may not be the fact. Sylvia and Korob look humanoid. But they fabricated that food and the gems. They may also have fabricated the way they appear to us. Suppose they are not biped humanoids? Suppose they've just drawn all this from the subconscious minds of Scott and Sulu?"

Kirk frowned. "Scotty and Sulu are responsible men. They are not prone to superstition." He paused to digest Spock's speculations. "But Scott, it's true, does *have* a heritage that includes castles, dungeons and witches in its lore. And Sulu—Oriental folk tales also admit the influence of ghosts and spirits."

"Children are still fond of ghost stories, Captain. Even I grew up with a knowledge of them, much to my father's dismay. Perhaps we are all subconsciously afraid of dark rooms, of spectral visions—and this is what these aliens are using to try and gain the information they want."

"But they don't want just our science," Kirk reminded him. "What they're after is knowledge about our worlds—the galaxy itself." He was about to add *"Why?"* when the key scraped in the lock of the dungeon's door.

It opened. Sulu, phaser in hand, pushed McCoy through it. He didn't resist the shove. He just stood there, unblinking, his face emptied of all human expression.

"Ah, Bones, Bones—" Kirk groaned.

But Sulu had bent over him and was unlocking his chains. Then McCoy shambled over to him. He jerked Kirk to his feet, and placing him carefully in line with Sulu's pointed phaser, kicked him toward the open dungeon door.

Sylvia's method for making an obedient imbecile out of McCoy had disturbed Korob. As they awaited Kirk's arrival in the castle's great hall, he put his agitation into words.

"There's no need to torture them!"

"They resist," she said.

"You tease them! You promise them toys and then watch them scream in pain when they reach out to touch them. It amuses you!"

She shrugged. "And if it does, that does not concern you. I get the information I want for the Old Ones; and to get it is why we were sent here."

"You must *stop*!" Korob cried. "At least, let the pain be brief!"

"You cannot command me, Korob. We are equals."

"But not the same," he said.

"No. You are weak. I am strong. That is the reason I was chosen by the Old Ones to come with you. They suspect you of weakness. I am the one they—" She stopped at the appearance of Kirk between McCoy and Sulu.

Her lips moved into a charming smile. In the voice of a hostess greeting a distinguished guest, she said, "Captain, how nice to see you. I'm so glad you have come." The welcoming smile still on her mouth, she turned to Korob. "Leave us—and take those two with you."

Korob hesitated. Then, making Sylvia a formal bow, he picked up the *Enterprise* in its transparent casing—and left the chamber, followed by the listless Sulu and McCoy.

Kirk and Sylvia eyed each other. For the first time he sensed tension in her, a certain wariness as though she knew she'd met her match in strength. The smile he gave her was just as charming as the one that still lingered on her face. "What now?" he said pleasantly. "Do you wave your magic wand and destroy my mind, too?"

He didn't miss the involuntary start she gave at mention of the wand. He also noted how her hand had lifted to touch the crystal pendant on her breast. "There's no real damage done to the mind, Captain—just a drain of knowledge and will."

"You don't call that damage?"

"Why should I when it isn't?" she responded easily.

His eyes swept over her in the immemorial look of the sexually appraising male. "You must forgive me," he said. "I forget that you are not a woman. Perhaps not even human."

"I don't know what you mean," she said.

"All this—" he waved his hand around the room, "all this apparently drawn from our racial superstitions and fantasies. Illusion—the whole thing."

She pointed to one of the wall torches. "Put your hand in that flame and you will be burned, Captain. However created, these things are quite real. I am real, too."

"Why do you need us?" he said.

She walked over to the table. When she turned to face him again, she said, "What does your science teach you about the nature of the universe?"

He laughed. "There's nothing I enjoy so much as discussions on the nature of the universe. Particularly with charming ladies." He gave her a mocking little bow. "You didn't answer my question, you know. Why do you need us?"

"I don't need the others. Nor do you."

She spoke softly. Now she left the table to move closer to him. Human or not, she *was* graceful. "If we combined what you know and I know," she said, "there's no limit to the power we would possess."

"And Korob?" he said.

One thing she *did* know, he was thinking—how to exert sexual witchcraft. She'd laid her hand lightly, very lightly on his forearm. "Korob is a weak and foolish man," she said. "He can be disposed of. But I would find it difficult to dispose of—you."

He smiled down into the green eyes. "Or to probe my mind?"

"That would not be necessary if we mingled our knowledge," she said. "From me you could learn secrets you've never dreamed of. Anything you imagined could be yours . . ."

The hand was slowly moving up his arm. "Your—arguments are quite persuasive," he said. "Suppose I decided to go along with you?"

Her low murmur was a caress. "You would not regret your decision. Power, wealth, all the luxuries of your galaxy would be yours."

"You're a very beautiful woman," he said—and meant it.

"I can be many beautiful women," she said. The green

eyes upturned to his were suddenly sapphire blue. The long black hair disappeared and became a shining tumble of blond curls. Even her red robe drained of its color to change into a creamy white that matched the flawless cream of her skin. Then the blond beauty was gone. Copper braids wreathed her head. The robe deepened to a rich bronze. She was an autumn beauty now, her cheeks flushed with the tone of autumn leaves.

"Do you like me thus?" she asked. "Or do you prefer this?"

She recovered her original appearance.

"I prefer this," Kirk said—and took her in his arms. When she lifted her head from his kiss, she was staring at him with surprised delight. "That was very—enjoyable. What is it called? May I have another?"

He kissed her again. Then he released her. "Your people will guarantee me that I won't be harmed?"

"Yes, when they come. I have only to report to the Old Ones that you will cooperate with us."

"And my friends will be restored to their former condition?"

"Of course—if you wish it."

She reached up her arms to his neck but he removed them.

"What's wrong? What wrong have I done?"

He stepped away from her. "When you took the form of a woman," he said, "you also assumed the female compulsion to talk too much. You've revealed too many secrets, Sylvia. What if your Old Ones find out you've been tricked by one of the creatures you plan to conquer?"

"You tricked me? You do not like me?"

"No," he said.

"Then you just used me?"

"Didn't you plan to use me?"

Her green eyes blazed. She clapped her hands sharply. Scott and McCoy, both armed with phasers, came through the tapestried archway.

She pointed a shaking, sharp-nailed finger at Kirk. "Get him out of here! Take him back to his cell!"

* * *

It was Korob who came to release him from his shackles.

But in spite of the phaser in his hand, he seemed hurried, anxious. Kirk and Spock watched him in tense silence as he unlocked their chains. To their astonishment, they were no sooner freed than he handed Kirk the phaser and pulled the communicator from his robe's pocket.

He spoke in a whisper. "I have broken the crystal that imprisoned the model of your ship, Captain. It was time. Your people had found a way to break out of the force field. It is difficult to control so many things. You must go now before she discovers the weapon is missing."

"We can't leave without our men," Kirk said.

Korob made an impatient gesture. "They are not your men any longer. They belong to Sylvia. I can no longer control them—or her."

He glanced fearfully at the dungeon door. "There was no need for any of this. We could have entered your galaxy in peace. But Sylvia is not content with conquest. She is close to the Old Ones and she wants to destroy."

"You came in a ship?" Spock asked.

Korob shook his head. "We used a power pack." He motioned to the door. "There's no time to explain now. We must go. She plans to kill us all."

Kirk and Spock had started to follow him to the door when Korob suddenly turned, stopping them with a warning gesture. They both heard it at the same time—the sound of a deep, resonant purr. Then through the open door of the cell they saw the shadow; the creeping shadow of a great cat silhouetted against the farther wall of the corridor.

"Keep back," Korob muttered.

He drew his wand from his robe. Holding it poised, he slid into the corridor toward the cat's shadow. But already it had begun to grow in size and was looming black, gigantic against the corridor wall. And the purr had changed. Ferocity had entered into its deep growl. Snarling, the cat now towered over a Korob whose face had convulsed with terror. He lifted his wand, shouting, "No, no—get back! *No!*"

The shadow lifted a monstrous paw. Korob screamed, crumpled, the wand falling from his hand. Kirk and Spock ran to reach him. There was an animal roar of rage as the huge paw lifted again. Kirk had barely time to seize the wand before Spock grabbed him—and slammed the dungeon door closed behind them.

A latch on its outside clanked into its slot. They were locked into the cell again.

Its door shook as some immense body pushed against it. Maddened roars rebounded in echoes from the corridor as the unseen monster-cat hurled itself against the door again. Spock shouted, "It won't hold long against such pressure, sir!"

"Move back," Kirk said. He aimed the phaser at the door and fired. There was no effect. "It's out of energy," he said, examining the weapon. "She must have drained it. We could have jumped Scott or Sulu any time—and we never knew it." He glanced around the cell. "There's no way out of here."

"Only one," Spock said. "The way we got in."

Another thud shook the door. Kirk said, "This wall's too smooth to climb."

Spock had his eyes on the trapdoor above his head. "If you were to boost me up, sir, I could pull you up from there."

"It's a good eight feet. Think you can make it?"

"Ready when you are, Captain."

Kirk nodded, laid the wand on the floor, and bending his back, braced himself on spread legs as Spock climbed up on his shoulders. The Vulcan got his grip on the trapdoor opening. He hauled himself up through it, and Kirk, retrieving the wand, reached for the hand Spock extended down to him. As he found his own grip on the opening, the cell door crashed down. The cat's head, lips drawn back over its teeth, filled the empty space. It opened its jaws in a scream of rage.

Breathless, Kirk said, "That's what I call a close thing. Where are McCoy and the others?"

"Maybe we should return with weapons and another landing party, Captain."

"I'm not leaving them here," Kirk said. He moved on, and was leading the way along the dimly lit passage when Spock paused. "I don't think this is the way we came, Captain."

"Maybe, maybe not," Kirk said. "It's like a maze in

here. Look, there's a turn ahead there. And we *did* come around a turn . . .''

Perhaps it was a sound, not a sixth sense that warned him. He whirled just in time to avoid a blow by the mace McCoy held in both hands. As it struck the wall with a shattering clang, Scott darted from the shadowy angle of the corridor to lift a mace above Spock's head. Spock ducked its swoop and closed with Scott, applying his Vulcan neck-pinch. It felled Scott who dropped his weapon. Spock simultaneously shouted, ''Behind you, sir!''

Kirk had just toppled McCoy with a punch to the jaw. Now he wheeled, to be smashed against the wall by Sulu's booted foot. He grabbed it and brought Sulu crashing down on top of him, knocked out.

He looked up at Spock. ''You were right. We *did* take the wrong turn—but at least we found them.''

''I'd hardly call it that, Captain. But now that we do have them all together . . .''

The snarling roar sounded very close. The shadow of the immense cat grew blacker and blacker on the corridor wall. Its claws were extending from one enormous paw.

Kirk lifted the wand. ''This,'' he said, ''is your 'power pack,' isn't it, Sylvia?''

The cat's shadow vanished. Sylvia, dark-haired, red-robed, stood against the wall.

Kirk fingered the wand. ''This crystal—and the one you wear—both serve as the source of your power, don't they?''

''The source? No, Captain, the mind is the wellspring of our power. My crystal is merely an amplifier. The wand controls much more.''

''With such power at your command, what did you want of us?'' Spock asked her.

''I have wanted nothing of you, Mr. Spock. Your mind is a deep well of facts. It is the people of Earth I wanted. Their minds are the deep wells of dreams—the material we need to create our realities.''

''You consume the minds of others,'' Kirk said. ''What happens to them when you've used their minds to increase your power?''

''Why do you care?'' she countered. ''With that wand you hold in your hand, you could reach out and shatter the stars if you knew how to use it." Her voice softened. "I offered once to share power with you. I offer again."

"No," Kirk said. "I don't know what you are. All I know is that you are not a woman. You are a destroyer."

"That's enough," she said. A phaser appeared in her hand. She aimed it at Kirk. "Give me the wand."

She extended her free hand, palm upward. "The wand—give it to me."

Kirk shrugged in surrender and held out the wand. She reached for it—and he dashed it to the stone floor. Sylvia screamed. Its crystal shattered. A blinding red light lit the corridor with the crimson of blood. It changed into the yellow dazzle of the sun. Then it was white like the light of a dead moon. When it faded, Kirk was standing on a rocky knoll. All around him was the bleak and barren surface of Pyris VII just as he'd first seen it. Only the fog was missing.

Dazed, McCoy said, "What happened, Jim?"

"That will take some explaining, Bones," Kirk told him.

Scott, recovered, said to Sulu, "Everything's vanished."

"Not quite everything," volunteered Spock.

On a rock ledge before them lay two tiny creatures, boneless, mere blobs of jelly, their bodies veined like those of jellyfish. One moved feebly. The other wavered up into the air, squeaking in a thin wail.

"Meet Korob and Sylvia in their true shape," Kirk said. "Their human shapes, like the castle and everything else, were illusion. Only the wand's crystal ball gave them an appearance of reality."

Spock's impassive face had a rare look of fascinated curiosity.

"A life form totally alien to our galaxy. If only we could study and preserve them."

The squeaking little creature was waving its transparent filaments over the now unmoving body of its companion. Soon, collapsing in on itself, it sank down beside it, its pitiful wail growing fainter.

"It's too late," McCoy said. "They're gone."

He sighed. "Illusion and reality. Sometimes I wonder if we humans will ever learn the difference."

METAMORPHOSIS

Writer: Gene L. Coon
Director: Ralph Senensky
Guest stars: Glenn Corbett, Elinor Donahue

It was not often that the *Enterprise* needed the services of her shuttlecraft *Galileo*, for usually the Transporter served her purposes better; but this was one of those times. The *Enterprise* had been on other duty when the distress call had come from Epsilon Canaris III, well out of Transporter range, and not even the *Enterprise* could be in two places at once.

Now, however, the *Galileo* was heading back for rendezvous with the mother ship, Kirk at the controls, Spock navigating. The shuttlecraft's passengers were Dr. McCoy and his patient, Assistant Federation Commissioner Nancy Hedford, a very beautiful woman in her early thirties, whose beauty was marred by an almost constant expression of sullenness. The expression did not belie her; she was not a particularly pleasant person to be around.

"We have reached projected point three, Captain," Spock said. "Adjust to new course 201 mark 15."

"Thank you, Mr. Spock . . . Doctor, how is she?"

"No change."

"Small thanks to the Starfleet," Nancy Hedford said.

"Really, Commissioner," McCoy said, "you can't blame the Starfleet—"

"I should have received the proper inoculation ahead of time."

"Sukaro's disease is extremely rare, Commissioner. The chances of anyone contracting it are literally billions to one. How could we predict—"

"I was sent to that planet to prevent a war, Doctor.

42

Thanks to the inefficiency of the medical branch of the Star-fleet I have been forced to leave before my job was done. How many millions of innocent people will die because of this so-called rare disease of mine?''

Privately, Kirk was of the opinion that she was over-estimating her own importance; her senior officer could prob-ably handle the situation alone—or maybe even better. But it wouldn't do to say so. "Commissioner, I assure you, once we reach the *Enterprise*, with its medical facilities, we'll have you back on your feet in no time. You'll get back to your job.''

"And just how soon will we rendezvous with this ship of yours, Captain?''

"Four hours and twenty-one minutes.''

"Captain," Spock said. "The scanners are picking up some kind of small nebulosity ahead. It seems to be—yes, it is on a collision course.''

"It can hardly matter," Kirk said, "but we'll swerve for it anyhow.''

This, however, proved impossible to do. Every time Kirk changed the *Galileo's* course, the cloud did also. Soon it was within visual distance, a phosphorescent, twisting blob against the immensities of space.

Spock checked the sensors. "It appears to be mostly ionized hydrogen, Captain. But I would say nevertheless that it is not a natural object. It is too dense, changes shape too rapidly, and there is a high degree of electrical activity.''

"Whatever it is, we're about to be right in the middle of it.''

He had scarcely spoken when the view ahead was com-pletely masked by the glowing, shifting cloud. A moment later, the controls went dead. A quick check showed that communications were out, too.

"Readings, Mr. Spock?''

"Extremely complex patterns of electrical impulses, and an intense magnetic field—or rather, a number of them. It seems to have locked onto us.''

The craft lurched, slightly but definitely. Kirk looked down at his console. "Yes, and it's taking us with it.''

"Captain!'' the woman's voice called. "What's hap-pening? I demand to know!''

"You already know about as much as we do, Commissioner. Whatever that thing is outside, it's pulling us off our course for the *Enterprise*."

"Now on course 98 mark 12," Spock said. "Heading straight into the Gamma Canaris region."

"Jim!" McCoy said. "We've got to get Miss Hedford to the *Enterprise*—her condition—"

"I'm sorry, Bones. There's nothing we can do."

"I am not at all surprised," Miss Hedford said coldly. "This is exactly the sort of thing I expect from the Starfleet. If I am as sick as this dubious authority claims I am—"

"Believe me, you are," McCoy said. "You may feel fine now, but nevertheless you're very ill."

"Then why are you all just sitting there? I insist—"

"I'm sorry, Commissioner," Kirk said. "We'll do what we can when we can—but right now we're helpless. You might as well sit back and enjoy the ride."

The *Galileo* was put down—there seemed to be no other word for it—on a small planet, of which very few details could be seen through the enveloping nebulosity. But the moment they had grounded, the cloud vanished, leaving them staring out at a broad, deserted sweep of heathlike countryside.

"Bones, Mr. Spock, get some readings on this place." Kirk snapped a switch. "*Enterprise*, this is the *Galileo*. Kirk here. Come in, please. Come in . . . no good, we're not sending. That cloud must still be around someplace. Any data, anybody?"

"The atmosphere is almost identical with that of the Earth," Spock reported, "and so is the gravity. Almost impossible for a planet this small, unless the core is something other than the usual nickel-iron. But suitable for human life."

"Well, I guess we get out and get under," Kirk said. "Bones, phaser out and maintain full alert. Commissioner, best you stay inside for the time being."

"And just how long a time is that?"

"That's a very good question. I wish I could answer it. Mr. Spock, let's go."

Outside, they went to the rear of the shuttlecraft and

unbolted the access panels to the machinery, while McCoy stayed up forward. Checking the works did not take long.

"Very strange," Spock said. "In fact, quite impossible."

"Nothing works."

"Nothing. And for no reason."

"Of course there's a reason. We just haven't found it yet. Let's go over it again."

While they were at it, Nancy Hedford came out and headed for them, looking, as usual, both annoyed and officious. Patience was evidently not her strong point, either. Kirk sighed and straightened.

"Well, Captain?"

"Well, Commissioner?"

"Where is this strange powerful force of yours, which brought us here? Or could it be that you simply made a navigational error?"

"There was no error, Miss Hedford," Kirk said patiently. "For your information, our power units are dead—so I judge that the force you refer to is still in the vicinity."

"I am not interested in alibis, Captain. I insist that you get us off this dismal rock immediately."

"Commissioner, I realize that you're ill, and you're anxious to receive treatment."

"I am anxious, as you put it, to get this medical nonsense out of the way so I can get back to my assignment!"

McCoy, looking rather anxious himself, had joined them. He said, "How do you feel, Commissioner?"

"I wish you would stop asking that stupid question." She strode angrily away.

Kirk managed a rueful grin. "As long as she answers you like that, Bones, I guess she feels all right."

"But she won't for long. The fever's due to hit any time."

As Kirk started to reply, there was a long, hailing call from no very great distance. "Halllooooo!"

They turned, startled. A human figure had emerged from over the horizon, which on this small world was no more than a mile away. It waved its arms, and came toward them at a run.

"Bones, I want a physiological reading on—whoever that is."

The figure disappeared behind a rise, and then appeared at the top of it, looking down on the party. It was a young, sturdy, tall, handsome man in his mid-thirties, dressed in a one-piece suit of coveralls. His expression was joyful.

"Hello!" he said again, plunging down the rise to them. "Are you real? I mean—I'm not imagining you, am I?"

"We're real enough," Kirk said.

"And you speak English. Earth people?"

Kirk nodded. "From the Federation."

"The Federation? Well, it doesn't matter." He grabbed Kirk's hand enthusiastically. "I'm Cochrane. Been marooned here who knows how long. If you knew how good it was to see you . . . and a woman! A beautiful one at that. Well!"

Kirk made the introductions. Cochrane, still staring at the Commissioner, said, "You're food to a starving man. All of you." He looked over to Spock. "A Vulcan, aren't you. When I was there—hey, there's a nice ship. Simple, clean. Been trying to get her going again? Forget it. It won't work."

He began to circle the shuttlecraft, admiringly. Kirk said in a low voice to McCoy, "Our friend seems to have a grasshopper mind."

"Too many things to take in all at once. Normal reaction. In fact, everything checks out perfectly normal. He's human."

"Mr. Cochrane!" The newcomer rejoined them, still beaming. "We were forced off our course and brought here by some power we couldn't identify—which seems to be here on the surface of the planet at the moment."

"Could be. Strange things happen in space."

"You said we wouldn't be able to get the ship functioning again?" Spock asked.

"Not a chance. Damping field of some sort down here. Power systems don't work. Take my word for it."

"You won't mind if we keep trying?" Spock persisted.

"Go right ahead. You'll have plenty of time."

"How about you, Cochrane?" Kirk said. "What are you doing here?"

"Marooned. I told you. Look, we've got lots of time to learn about each other. I've got a little place not far away.

All the comforts of home." He turned to the woman. "I can even offer you a hot bath."

"How acute of you to notice that I needed it," she said icily.

"If you don't mind, Mr. Cochrane," Kirk said, "I'd like a little more than just the statement that you were marooned here. This is a long way off the beaten path."

"That's right. That's why I'm so glad to see you. Look, I'll tell you everything you want to know. But not here." He eyed the shuttlecraft again. "A beauty."

"You've been out of circulation a while. Maybe the principles are new to you. Mr. Spock, would you like to explain our propulsion methods to Mr. Cochrane?"

"Of course, Captain. Mr. Cochrane?"

As the two moved off, McCoy said, "He talks a lot but he doesn't say much."

"I noticed," Kirk said. "And I noticed something else. There's something familiar about him, Bones."

"Familiar? . . . well, now that you mention it, I think so too."

"I can't place him, but . . . how about Miss Hedford?"

"No temperature yet. But we've got to get under way soon. I guarantee you it'll develop."

"You're sure there's no mistake? It is Sakuro's disease?"

"Positive. And something else I'm not mistaken about. Untreated, it's fatal. Always . . . well, what do we do now?"

"I think we'll take Mr. Cochrane up on his offer. At least we can make her comfortable."

Cochrane's house was a simple functional cube, with a door, but no windows. The surrounding area was cultivated.

"You built this, Mr. Cochrane?" Spock said.

"Yes. I had some tools and supplies left over from my crash. It's not Earth, of course, but it's livable. I grow vegetables, as you see. Come on in."

He led the way. The house contained a heating unit which apparently served as a stove, a climate control device, and some reasonably comfortable furniture, all decidedly old. Miss Hedford looked around with distaste.

"What a dreadful, dingy place," she said.

Cochrane only smiled. "But I call it home, Miss Hedford."

"Where did you get the antiques?" Kirk said.

"The antiques? Oh, you mean my gadgets. I imagine things have changed a lot since I wrecked."

"Not that much."

"Must you keep it so terribly hot?" the woman asked.

"The temperature is a constant seventy-two degrees."

"Do you feel hot?" McCoy asked Miss Hedford.

She flopped angrily down in a chair. "I feel infuriated, deeply put upon, absolutely outraged."

"It was quite a hike here," McCoy said. "You're tired. Just take it easy for a while."

"I'll rest later, Doctor. Right now I am planning the report I will make to the Board of Commissioners on the efficiency of the Starfleet. I assure all of you it will be very, very complete."

"Captain! Doctor!" Spock called from the door. "Look at this, please!"

Alarmed at the urgency in his voice, Kirk crossed to the door in one bound. Outside, perhaps half a mile away, was a columnar area of blurry, misty interference, like a tame whirlwind, except that there was no wind. Faint pastel lights and shades appeared and disappeared inside it. With it there was a half sound, half feeling of soft chiming music. For a moment it moved from side to side, gently; then it disappeared.

Kirk turned quickly to Cochrane. "What was that?"

"Sometimes the light plays tricks on you," Cochrane said. "You'd be surprised what I've imagined I've seen around here."

"We imagined nothing, Mr. Cochrane. There was an entity out there, and I suspect it was the same entity that brought us here. Please explain."

"There's nothing to explain."

"Mr. Cochrane, you'll find I have a low tolerance level where the safety of my people are concerned. We find you out here where no human has any business being. We were virtually hijacked in space and brought here—apparently by that thing we just saw out there. I am not just requesting an explanation, Mister. I am demanding it!''

Cochrane shrugged. "All right. Out there—that was the Companion.''

"The what?''

"That's what I call it. The fact is, Captain, I did not crash here. I was brought here in my disabled ship. I was almost dead. The Companion saved my life.''

"You seem perfectly healthy now," Kirk said. "What was wrong?''

"Old age, Captain. I was eighty-seven years old at the time. I don't know how it did it, but the Companion rejuvenated me. Made me—well—young again, like I am now.''

Kirk and Spock exchanged glances. Spock's eyebrows were about to crawl right off the top of his forehead. He said, "I would like to reserve judgment on that part of your story, sir. Would you mind telling us exactly what this Companion of yours is?''

"I told you, I don't know what it is. It exists. It lives. I can communicate with it to a limited extent.''

"That's a pretty far-out story," McCoy said.

"You saw the creature. Have you a better story?''

"Mr. Cochrane," Kirk said. "Do you have a first name?''

Cochrane nodded. "Zefram.''

McCoy's jaw dropped, but Spock had apparently been expecting the answer. Kirk said, "Cochrane of Alpha Centauri? The discoverer of the space warp?''

"That's right, Captain.''

"Zefram Cochrane," McCoy said, "has been dead a hundred and fifty years.''

"His body was never found," Spock said.

"You're looking at it, Mr. Spock," Cochrane said.

"You say this Companion of yours found you and rejuvenated you. What were you doing in space at the age of eighty-seven?''

"I was tired, Captain. I was going to die. And I wanted to die in space. That's all.''

McCoy turned to Miss Hedford, whose eyes were now closed. He felt her forehead, then took readings. He was obviously concerned by the results.

"These devices," Spock said. "They all date from the time indicated. From your ship, Mr. Cochrane?"

"I cannibalized it. The rest—the food, water, gardens, everything I need—the Companion gives me. Creates it, apparently, out of the native elements."

"If you can communicate with it," Kirk said, "maybe you can find out what *we* are doing here."

"I already know."

"You wouldn't mind telling us?"

"You won't like it."

"We already don't like it."

"You're here to keep me company," Cochrane said. "I was always pretty much of a loner. Spent years in space by myself. At first being alone here didn't bother me. But a hundred and fifty years is a long time, Kirk. Too long. I finally told the Companion I'd die without the company of other humans. I thought it would release me—send me back somehow. Instead, it went out and obviously brought back the first human beings it could find."

"No!" Miss Hedford cried weakly. "No! It's disgusting! We're not animals!"

She began to sob. McCoy, with Kirk's help, lifted her and put her on a cot, where McCoy gave her a shot. Gradually, her sobbing subsided.

"Bad," said McCoy. "Very bad."

"You can't do anything?"

"Keep her quiet. Keep secondary infections from developing. But the attrition rate of her red corpuscles is increasing. I can't stop it."

Kirk turned to Spock. "Mr. Spock, the next time that thing appears, don't fail to get tricorder readings. Find us a weapon to use against that thing."

"Captain, I have already drawn certain tentative conclusions. Considering the anomalously small size of this planet, and the presence of the damping field Mr. Cochrane mentioned, plus the Companion, leads me to believe that it was the moon of some larger body now destroyed, and was colonized by a highly advanced civilization."

"I agree," Cochrane said. "I've found some artifacts which suggest the same thing."

"The point, Spock?"

"One can deduce further that the Companion may be the last survivor of this long-dead culture. You ask me to find a weapon. Do you intend to destroy it?"

"I intend to do whatever is necessary to get us away from here and Commissioner Hedford to a hospital," Kirk said grimly. "If the Companion stands in the way, then we push it out of the way. Clear, Mr. Spock?"

"Quite clear, Captain." Spock picked up his tricorder and left, heading for the shuttlecraft.

"Cochrane, if you left here, what would happen to you?"

"I'd start to age again, normally."

"You want to get away from here?"

"Believe me, Captain, immortality consists largely of boredom. Of course I do . . . what's it like out there? In the galaxy?"

"We're on a thousand planets, and spreading out. We're crossing fantastic distances . . . and finding life everywhere. We estimate there are millions of planets with intelligent life. We haven't begun to map them." Cochrane's eyes were shining. "Interesting?"

"How would you like to go to sleep for a hundred and fifty years and wake up in a new world?"

"Good," Kirk said. "It's all out there, waiting for you. And you'll find your name honored there. But we'll probably need your help to get away."

"You've got it."

"All right. You seem to think this Companion can do almost anything."

"I don't know its limitations."

"Could it cure Commissioner Hedford?"

"I don't know."

"It's worth a try. We're helpless. You say you can communicate with it?"

"To a degree. It's on a non-verbal level, but I usually get my messages across."

"Try it now. See if it can do anything."

Cochrane nodded and stepped outside, followed by Kirk and McCoy. "How do you do it?" Kirk said.

"I just sort of . . . clear my mind. Then it comes. Better stay back."

Cochrane closed his eyes. A long moment passed, and then Kirk heard the melodic humming of the Companion. It appeared near Cochrane, shimmering, resplendent with a dozen beautiful colors, to the sound of faint bells. It moved to Cochrane, enveloped him, gathered around him, hovering. The lights played on Cochrane's face.

"What do you make of that, Bones?" Kirk said softly.

"Almost a symbiosis of some kind. A sort of joining."

"Just what I was thinking. Not exactly like a pet owner speaking to an affectionate animal, would you say?"

"No. More than that."

"I agree. Much more. Possibly . . . love."

Now the Companion was moving away from Cochrane, who was slowly returning to normal. The Companion faded away, and Cochrane shook his head and looked about as if to get his bearings. His eyes settled on Kirk.

"You all right?" Kirk said.

"Oh. Yes. I . . . it always kind of . . . drains me. But I'm all right."

"Well?"

Cochrane shook his head again. "The Companion can't do anything to help Miss Hedford. There seems to be some question of identity involved . . . I didn't understand it. But the answer is no, I'm sure of that."

"Then she'll die."

"Look, I'm sorry. If I could help you, I would. But the Companion won't."

It was several hours before Spock came back from the shuttlecraft. When he returned, he was carrying with him a small but complex black device, obviously in very rough form, as though it had been hastily put together by a gifted child. He took it into the house. "Your weapon, Captain."

"Oho. How does it work?"

"The Companion, as we already know, is mostly plasma—a state of matter characterized by a high degree of ionization. To put the matter simply, it is mostly electricity. I propose to, in effect, short it out. Put this in proximity to the Companion, throw this switch, and we will scramble every electrical impulse the creature can produce. It cannot fail."

Cochrane was staring unhappily at the device. Kirk said, "It troubles you, Cochrane?"

"The Companion saved my life. Took care of me for a hundred and fifty years. We've been . . . very close . . . in a way that's hard to explain. I suppose I even have a sort of affection for it."

"It's also keeping you a prisoner here."

"I don't want it killed."

Spock said, "We may simply render it powerless—"

"But you don't know!" Cochrane said intensely. "You could kill it! I won't stand for that, Kirk."

"We're getting away from here, Cochrane. Make up your mind to that."

"What kind of people are you nowadays?" Cochrane demanded. "Doesn't gratitude mean anything to you?"

"I've got a woman dying in here, Cochrane. I'll do anything I have to to save her life."

Cochrane stared at Kirk, and slowly the fight went out of him. "I suppose, from your point of view, you're right. I only . . ."

"We understand how you feel, Mr. Cochrane," McCoy said. "But it has to be done."

"All right. You want me to call it, I suppose?"

"Please," Kirk said. "Outside."

McCoy remained with his patient. Spock hefted his device, and he and Kirk left the house. Already, Cochrane and the Companion were approaching each other. Soft lights and soft music came from the creature. It almost seemed to be purring.

"Is this close enough?" Kirk whispered.

"I think so," Spock whispered back. "But there is a certain risk. We do not know the extent of the creature's powers."

"Nor it ours. Now, Spock!"

Spock closed the switch. The blurring of the Companion abruptly increased, and a sharp high-pitched humming sound came from it, alarmed, strong. The pastel colors changed to somber blues and greens, and the hint of bells changed to a discordant clanging. Cochrane, only a few feet away from it, grasped his head and staggered, then fell. The

evanescent, ever-changing column of plasma swept down
upon the house.

Kirk and Spock ducked inside, but there was no safety
there. The room was filled with the whirling and clanging.
With it, Kirk felt a terrible sense of pressure, all over his
body. The breath was crushed out of him. He struck out, but
there was nothing to strike at. Beside him, he was aware that
Spock had dropped the device and was also gasping futilely
for air.

"Stop it! Stop it!" McCoy's voice shouted, as if from
a great distance. "It's killing them!"

Cochrane came in, and, immediately divining what was
happening, went into the position of communion. The Companion's colors returned to the pastel, and the creature faded
away. Kirk and Spock both fell to their knees, gulping in
great gasps of air. McCoy knelt beside them; Cochrane went
out again.

"Are you all right?" McCoy said. "Can you breathe?"

Kirk nodded. "All . . . right, Bones." He got shakily
to his feet, followed by Spock, who also seemed to be regaining his strength rapidly. "Cochrane's got it off us. I don't
know whether he did us a favor or not."

"What kind of talk is that?" McCoy said sharply.

"How do you fight a thing like that? I've got a ship
somewhere out there . . . the responsibility for four lives here
. . . and one of them dying."

"That's not your fault."

"I'm in command, Bones. That makes it my fault. Now
I've had it. I can't destroy it. I can't force it to let us go."

After a moment McCoy said, "You're a soldier so often
that maybe you forget you were also trained to be a diplomat.
Why not try using a carrot instead of a stick?"

"But what could I offer . . . Hmmm. Maybe we can.
Spock!"

"Yes, Captain."

"The universal translator on the shuttlecraft. We can
try that. Talk to the thing."

"The translator is for use with more congruent life-
forms."

"Adjust it. Change it. The trouble with immortality

is that it's boring. Adjusting the translator would give you something to do.''

"It's possible. If I could widen its pattern of reception—"

"Right down your alley, Mr. Spock. Get it here and get to work.''

The translator was small but intricate. Cochrane eyed it interestedly, while McCoy tended his patient. "How does that gadget work?'' he said.

"There are certain universal ideas and concepts, common to all intelligent life," Kirk explained. "This device instantaneously compares the frequency of brain wave patterns, selects those it recognizes, and provides the necessary grammar and vocabulary.''

"You mean the box speaks?''

"With the voice, or its approximation, of whatever creature is on the sending end. It's not perfect, of course, but it usually works well enough. Are you ready, Mr. Spock?''

"Quite ready, Captain.''

"Mr. Cochrane, call the Companion, please.''

Cochrane left the house, Kirk and Spock once more following, with the translator. And again the sound of the Companion preceded its appearance; then it was there, misty, enigmatic. Spock touched the translator and nodded to Kirk.

"Companion . . . we wish to talk to you.''

There was a change in the sound. The Companion drew away from Cochrane. Then a voice came from the translator. It was soft, gentle—and unmistakably feminine.

"How can we communicate? My thoughts . . . you are hearing them. This is interesting.''

"Feminine, Spock," Kirk said. "No doubt about it.''

"Odd. The matter of gender could change the entire situation.''

"Dr. McCoy and I are way ahead of you, Mr. Spock.''

"Then it is not a zoo-keeper.''

"No, Mr. Spock. A lover . . . Companion! It is wrong to hold us here against our will.''

"The man needs the company of his own kind, or he will cease to exist," the gentle voice said. "He felt it to me.''

"One of us is about to cease to exist. She must be taken to a place where we can care for her."

"The man needs others of his species. That is why you are here. The man must continue."

"Captain, there is a peculiar, dispassionate logic here," Spock said. "Pragmatism unalloyed. From its words, I would say it will never understand our point of view."

"Maybe. Companion, try to understand. It is the nature of our species to be free, just as it is your nature to stay here. We will cease to exist in captivity."

"Your bodies have stopped their peculiar degeneration. You will continue without end. There will be sustenance. There will be nothing to harm you. You will continue and the man will continue. This is necessary."

"Captain!" Spock said. "This is a marvelous opportunity for us to add to our knowledge. Ask it about its nature, its history—"

"Mr. Spock, this is no classroom. I'm trying to get us away from here."

"A chance like this may never come again. It could tell us so much—"

"Mr. Spock, get lost. Companion, it is plain you do not understand us. This is because you are not of our species. Believe me, we do not lie. What you offer us is not continuation. It is non-existence. We will cease to exist. Even the man will cease to exist."

"Your impulses are illogical. This communication is useless. The Man must continue. Therefore, you will continue. It is necessary."

The voice fell silent. The Companion moved away. Slowly it started to grow fainter, and finally was not there at all.

Kirk's shoulders sagged, and he went back into the house, followed by Spock. Cochrane came in after them.

"Captain," he said, "why did you build that translator of yours with a feminine voice box?"

"We didn't," Kirk said.

"But I heard—"

"The ideas of male and female are universal constants, Cochrane. The Companion is definitely female."

"I don't understand."

"You don't?" said McCoy. "A blind man could see it with his cane. You're not a pet, Cochrane. Nor a specimen kept in a cage. You're a lover."

"I'm—what?"

"Isn't it evident?" Kirk said. "Everything she does is for you. Provides for you. Feeds you. Shelters you. Clothes you. Brings you companions when you're lonely."

"Her attitude, when she approaches you, is profoundly different from when she contacts us," Spock added. "In appearance, in sound, in method. Though I do not completely understand the emotion, it obviously exists. The Companion loves you."

Cochrane stared at them. "That's—that's ridiculous!"

"Not at all," Kirk said. "We've seen similar situations."

"But after a hundred and fifty years—"

"What happens when you communicate with it?" Spock said.

"Why, we sort of . . . it—it merges with my mind."

"Of course. It is nothing to be shocked by. A simple symbolic union of two minds."

"That's outrageous! Do you know what you're saying? No, you couldn't! But . . . all the years . . . letting something . . . as alien as that . . . into my mind, my feelings—" Suddenly Cochrane was furious as well as astonished. "It tricked me! It's some kind of an . . . emotional vampire! Crawling around inside me!"

"It didn't hurt you, did it?" Kirk said.

"Hurt me? What has that to do with it? You can be married to a woman you love for fifty years and still keep your private places in your mind. But this—this thing—fed on me!"

"An interesting attitude," Spock said. "Typical of your time, I should say, when humanity had much less contact with alien life-forms than at present."

"Don't sit there and calmly analyze a disgusting thing like this!" Cochrane exploded. "What kind of men are you, anyway?"

"There's nothing disgusting about it, Cochrane," McCoy said. "It's just one more life-form. You get used to these things."

"You turn my stomach! You're as bad as it is!"

"I fail to understand your highly emotional reaction," Spock said. "Your relationship with the Companion was, for a hundred and fifty years, emotionally satisfying, eminently practical, and totally harmless. It may, indeed, have been quite beneficial."

Cochrane glared at them. "So this is what the future looks like—men who don't have the slightest notion of decency or morality. Well, maybe I'm a hundred and fifty years out of style, but I'm not going to be fodder for some inhuman—monstrous—" Choking up, he swung on his heel and walked out.

"A most parochial attitude," Spock said.

"Doctor," Nancy Hedford's voice called weakly. "Doctor."

McCoy hurried to her, Kirk following. "Right here, Miss Hedford."

She managed a very faint, almost bitter laugh. "I . . . heard him. He was loved . . . and he resents it."

"You rest," McCoy said.

"No. I don't want . . . want to die . . . I've been . . . good at my job, Doctor. But I've . . . never been loved. What kind . . . of a life is that? Not to be loved . . . never . . . and now I'm dying. And he . . . runs away from love . . ."

She fell silent, gasping for breath. McCoy's eyes were grim.

"Captain," Spock called from the door. "Look out here."

Outside, the Companion was back, looking much the same as usual, but Cochrane was standing away from it, barely controlling himself, icily furious.

"Do you understand?" he was saying. "I don't want anything to do with you."

The Companion moved a little closer, chiming questioningly, insistently. Cochrane backed away.

"I said keep away! You'll never get close enough to trick me again! Stay away from me! I know you understand me! Stay away! Leave me alone, from now on!"

Shaken, white-faced and sweating, Cochrane came back to his house. Kirk turned back to McCoy. Nancy was lying quite still.

"Bones? Is it over?"

"No. But she's moribund. Respiration highly erratic. Blood pressure dropping. She'll be dead in ten minutes. And I—"

"You did everything you could, Bones."

"Are you sorry for her, Kirk?" Cochrane said, still in an icy rage. "Are you really feeling something? Don't bother. Because that's the only way any of us are going to get away from here. By dying!"

An idea, a forlorn hope, came to Kirk. He picked up the translator and went outside. The Companion was still there.

"Companion. Do you love the man?"

"I do not understand," said the feminine voice from the translator.

"Is he important to you—more important than anything? Is it as though he were a part of you?"

"He is part of me. He must continue."

"But he will not continue. He will cease to exist. By your feeling for him you are condemning him to an existence he will find unbearable."

"He does not age. He remains forever."

"You refer to his body," said Kirk. "I speak of his spirit. Companion, inside the shelter a female of our species lies dying. She will not continue. That is what will happen to the man unless you release all of us."

"I do not understand."

"Our species can only survive when there are obstacles to overcome. You take away all obstacles. Without them to strengthen us, we weaken and die. You regard the man only as a toy. You only amuse yourself with him."

"You are wrong," said the translator. Was there urgency as well as protest in that voice? "The man is the center of all things. I care for him."

"But you can't really love him. You don't have the slightest knowledge of love—of the total union of two people. You are the Companion; he is the man; you are two different things, and can never join. You can never know love. You may keep him here forever, but you will always be separate, apart from him."

There was a long pause. Then the Companion said, "If I were human . . . there can be love . . ."

Then the creature faded from sight. Kirk went back into the shelter, almost bumping into McCoy, who had been standing behind him. "What did you hope to gain by that?" the surgeon said.

"Convince her of the hopelessness of it. The emotion of love frequently expresses itself in sacrifice. If love is what she feels, she might let him go."

"But she—or it—is inhuman, Captain," Spock said. "You cannot expect her to react like a human."

"I can try."

"It won't do any good," Cochrane said. "I know."

From the direction of the cot, a voice said, "Zefram Cochrane." It was Nancy's voice, clear and strong, but somehow as if the use of human lips, tongue and vocal cords had become unfamiliar. They all spun around.

There stood Nancy Hedford—but transformed, radiant, soft, gentle, staring at Cochrane. The rosy glow of health was evident in her cheek. McCoy raised his medical tricorder and stared at it, thunderstruck, but Kirk had no need to ask what he saw. The Nancy Hedford who had been about to die was not sick at all now.

"Zefram Cochrane," she said. "We are understanding."

"It's—it's her!" Cochrane said. "Don't you understand? It's the Companion!"

"Yes," said Nancy. "We are here—those you knew as the Commissioner and the Companion. We are both here."

Spock said, "Companion, you do not have the power to create life."

"No. That is for the maker of all things."

"But Commissioner Hedford was dying."

"That part of us was too weak to hold on. In a moment there would have been no continuing. Now we are together. Now we understand that which you called love—both of us. It fills a great need. That we did not have, we now have."

"You mean—you're both there in one body?" Kirk said.

"We are one. There is so much hunger, so much wanting." She moved toward Cochrane, who retreated a step. "Poor Zefram Cochrane. We frighten you. We never frightened you before." Tears formed in her eyes. "Loneliness.

This is loneliness. We know loneliness. What a bitter thing. Zefram Cochrane, how do you bear it?''

"How do you know what loneliness is?" Cochrane said.

"To wear this form is to discover pain." She extended a hand. "Let us touch you, Zefram Cochrane."

His hand slowly went out, and they touched.

Kirk turned his head and said in a low voice: "Spock. Check out the shuttlecraft. The engines, communication, everything."

"We hear you, Captain," Nancy said. "It is not necessary. Your vehicle will operate as before. So will your communications device."

"You're letting us go?" Cochrane said.

"We would do nothing to stop you. Captain, you said that we would not know love because we were not human. Now we are human, all human, and nothing more. We will know the change of the days. We will know death. But to touch the hand of the man—nothing is as important. Is this happiness, Zefram Cochrane? When the sun is warmer? The air sweeter? The sounds of this place like gentle currents in the air?''

"You are very beautiful," Cochrane said in a low voice.

"Part of me understands. Part does not. But it pleases me."

"I could explain. Many things. It'll be an eye-opener to you." He was alive with excitement. "A thousand worlds, a thousand races. I'll show you everything—just as soon as I learn my way around again. Maybe I can make up for everything you did for me."

Sadness appeared in Nancy's eyes. "I cannot go with you, Zefram Cochrane."

Cochrane was stunned. "Of course you can. You have to."

"My life emanates from this place. If I leave it, for more than a tiny march of days, I will cease to exist. I must return, even as you must consume matter to maintain your life."

"But—you have powers—you can—"

"I have become almost as you. The march of days will

affect me. But to leave here would mean a cessation of my existence.''

"You mean you gave up everything to become human?''

"It is nothing . . . compared to the touch of you.''

"But you'll age, like any other human. Eventually you'll die.''

"The joy of this hour is enough. I am pleased.''

"I can't fly off and leave you here,'' Cochrane said. "You saved my life. You took care of me and you loved me. I never understood, but I do now.''

"You must be free, Zefram Cochrane.''

Kirk said gently: "The *Galileo* is waiting, Mr. Cochrane.''

"But . . . If I take her away from here, she'll die. If I leave her . . . she's human. She'll die of loneliness. And that's not all. I love her. Is that surprising?''

"Not coming from a human being,'' Spock said. "You are, after all, essentially irrational.''

Cochrane put his arms around her. "I can't leave her. And this isn't such a bad place. I'm used to it.''

"Think it over, Mr. Cochrane,'' Kirk said. "There's a galaxy out there, waiting to honor you.''

"I have honors enough. She loves me.''

"But you will age, both of you,'' Spock said. "There will be no more immortality. You will grow old here, and finally die.''

"That's been happening to men and women for a long time . . . and I've got the feeling that it's one of the pleasanter things about being human—as long as you do it together.''

"You're sure?'' Kirk said.

"There's plenty of water. The climate is good for growing things. I might even try to plant a fig tree. Every man's entitled to that, isn't he?'' He paused, then added soberly, "It isn't gratitude, Captain. Now that I see her, touch her, I know. I love her. We'll have a lot of years, and they'll be happy ones.''

"Mr.Cochrane, you may or may not be doing the right thing. But I wish you the best. Mr. Spock, Bones, let's go.''

As they turned, Cochrane said, "Captain.''

"Yes?''

"Don't tell them about Cochrane. Let it go."

Kirk smiled. "Not a word, Mr. Cochrane."

As they settled into the *Galileo*, Spock said, "I pose you an interesting question, Captain. Have we not aided in the commission of bigamy? After all, the Companion and Commissioner Hedford are now sharing the same body."

"Now you're being parochial, Mr. Spock," McCoy said. "Bigamy is not everywhere illegal. Besides, Nancy Hedford was all but dead. Only the Companion is keeping her alive. If it withdrew, Nancy wouldn't last ten minutes. In fact, I'm going to report her dead as soon as we hit the *Enterprise*."

"Besides, what difference does it make?" Kirk said. "Love was the one thing Nancy and the Companion wanted most. Now they have it."

"But not for eternity," McCoy said. "Only a lifetime."

"Yes. But that's enough, Bones. For humans."

"That's a very illogical remark, Jim." As Spock's eyebrows climbed, McCoy added, "However, it happens to be true."

Kirk grinned and raised his communicator. "Kirk to *Enterprise*."

The communicator fairly shouted back. "Captain! This is Scotty. Are you all right?"

"We're perfectly all right. Can you get a fix on us?"

"Computing now . . . yes, locked on."

"Very good. I'll continue transmission. Assume standard orbit on arrival. We'll transfer up on the shuttlecraft."

"But what happened, Captain?"

"Not very much, in the end," Kirk said. "Only the oldest story in the world."

FRIDAY'S CHILD

Writer: D.C. Fontana
Director: Joseph Pevney
Guest stars: Julie Newmar, Tige Andrews

═══

Monday's child is fair of face.
Tuesday's child is full of grace.
Wednesday's child is loving and giving.
Thursday's child works hard for a living.
Friday's child is full of woe.
But the child that is born on the Sabbath Day
Is brave and bonny and good and gay.
                    (*Harper's Weekly*, 1887)

Even had Kirk not already known that Teer Akaar was High Chief of the ten tribes of Ceres, it would have been plain from the moment that he, Spock and McCoy materialized before the encampment that the Akaars were persons of consequence. Before each of the tents—which were on the edge of a brushy area—stood a pole bearing a family banner, and each of these was surmounted by another flag emblazoned with Akaar's tribal emblem, a flight of abstract birds.

A few tribesmen and women, wearing vividly colored robes cut in simple tunic style, stared in astonishment as the three from the *Enterprise* shimmered into existence out of nothing, and then silently ducked away into their own tents as another man stepped into view from the largest pavilion. This man's tunic was plain black, with the distinctive bird design embroidered on the shoulder. He seemed to be about forty-five, reed slim, tough as a leather quirt. Looking straight at Kirk, he put his right fist over his heart and then extended the hand out before him, palm up. The gesture was easy to read: *My heart and all that I own are open to you.*

"I am Maab, of the House of Akaar," he said. "Our tents are honored."

"You honor us," Kirk said. Thinking fast, he made a half-bow with both hands out before him, palms up, and then drew the hands to his chest. *Your hospitality is accepted with open heart.* It might not have been the right answer, but it seemed to do.

"The High Chief awaits your coming," Maab said, gesturing toward the tent and then leading the way. The people of Ceres were friendly toward the Federation, but Klingon ships had been reported in this sector, and though technically the Federation and the Empire were at peace, there had been an increase in the number of 'incidents' in the past month. It was vital that the mission to Ceres not become an incident.

There were two men, as well as a woman, inside the tent, but Maab's full, deep bow of total subservience instantly made evident which man was Teer Akaar, a tall, broad-shouldered man in his late fifties, in a white robe with black birds. The ritual gestures were exchanged, and introductions made all around. Maab, it developed, was Teer Akaar's brother. The tall man in his late teens was Raal, the chief's son; and the kneeling young woman, who was quite lovely, was the chief's wife Eleen ("My second wife, and an honor to my house"). As Raal helped her to rise, it became clear that she was pregnant.

"Come," Akaar said, gesturing toward a table so low that it almost scraped the carpets. "I wish to hear your words about the rocks of the mountains."

Kirk motioned to Spock, who set upon the table several pieces of raw stone and the many-paged, pre-prepared formal agreement. They all sat down on cushions, except the woman, who retired to a curtained-off area, and Raal, who quietly left through the front entrance. It was getting dark outside.

"A geological survey," Kirk said, "has revealed that your world has valuable deposits of a mineral called topaline. I have been authorized to negotiate for Federation mining rights for this mineral."

"My people are herders and tradesmen, Captain,"

Akaar said. "We do not understand how a rock may be of value."

"You make your weapons of iron. You often trade in gold and silver."

"Iron has long been known to our weapons makers. Gold and silver came with Federation trade ships—they have little meaning to us. But they are metal, not rock such as this." He nudged the chunk of topaline ore.

"Chief Akaar, I trust you will bear with me for a long explanation. The Federation has hundreds of colonies which are mining operations, and research projects, on planets and asteroids that normally could not maintain our life forms. As your own legends hint, you yourselves are descendants of an Earth colony. Those colonists named your planet after an asteroid in Earth's own solar system, a five-hundred-mile ball of rock that was the first asteroid to be colonized—though it hasn't even an atmosphere."

"Then how is this done?" Akaar said.

"We create artificial domes under which we maintain air we can breathe," Spock said. "Topaline contains minute quantities of a metal which is essential to such life-support systems. Not only is it rare, but it must be constantly replaced."

"Why?" Maab said. "Does it rust, or wear out?"

Spock was obviously starting to explain, but Kirk held up his hand. These people had utterly forgotten the technology which had brought them to this planet, centuries ago. Nothing short of a cram course in physics would make clear to them the concept of radioactive half-life.

"Something like that," Kirk said. "And the fact that there is so little of it even in topaline means that the ore has to be transported in bulk to special refining plants."

"Then clearly it is of enormous value," Maab said. "What then do you offer for it?"

"An honest price," Kirk said, "in whatever medium of exchange you favor."

Maab leaned forward. Suddenly, he looked angry. "You Earthmen," he said harshly, "come hiding your lies behind papers of promise. Then you steal . . ."

Akaar slammed a hand flat on the table top. "Maab!"

"They have cheated others," Maab said, staring hard at his brother. "We have heard. They have no honor . . ."

"You will be silent!"

"Nay, I will not. We are not of one mind on this. There are many who do not wish this treaty."

"Leave us. You cannot speak for the tribes."

Maab arose. "I will leave. But many are not as gullible as our High Chief. We will be heard."

He turned and strode out furiously, leaving behind a thick, heavy silence. Finally, Akaar stirred uncomfortably and said, "My brother dishonors me. Yet it may be said that your history gives him some reason to distrust you."

"Our ancient history, perhaps," Kirk said. "And perhaps dimly and inaccurately recalled."

"Certainly you have done us no wrong. But Maab has heard of other places and other peoples. He uses these to speak against you."

"How has he heard such stories?"

"By truth, I do not know," Akaar said. "Earth traders, perhaps. A few come for the wool of our *zakdirs*."

"Then these are mere rumors, at best," Kirk said. "Our treaties are faithfully upheld."

"I take your word, Captain. I understand the things in this paper, and I will give it to the council of tribes this night. In the meantime, I bid you hang your weapons in my tent while you eat, and then rejoin us."

Kirk had known this was coming, for Spock had earlier made a most thorough study of the culture. But there was nothing that could be done about it. At a clap of Akaar's hands, a tribesman appeared, and the three men from the *Enterprise* handed over their phasers to him, and also their communicators, for to these herdsmen any machine seemed likely to be a weapon—especially if its custody was refused.

"I accept the guardianship of these weapons," Akaar said with singsong formality, "as an earnest of long peace between us. Keel, you will show these visitors to their tent, and have food brought them."

The meal was strange, but sumptuous, and served by a most scantily-clad Cerean girl of whom it was impossible not to be aware. Trying not to look pointedly the other way,

McCoy said, "But I thought topaline deposits on Altimara would be sufficient for another two years."

"Altimara was a disappointment," Kirk said. "The two most promising veins petered out. They'll be able to maintain full supply for all colonies for six months. By then, the mining project here has to be in full operation."

"No reserves?"

Spock said, "There is a convoy of freighters on its way now from refineries on Lorigan to the colonies in this quadrant. But it will be the last; Lorigan has been shut down. Exhausted."

"Umph," McCoy said. "These endless mineralogical assignments are dull work. And Jim, this argument between Akaar and Maab—I don't like the feel of it."

"Nor I. But it's not our quarrel. We have to abide by the Council's ruling. Clearly Maab will have a strong voice in it. If he wins, well, maybe he has a price of his own."

"You'd deal with him?" McCoy said.

"I'm authorized to deal with whoever can give this planet's mining rights to the Federation," Kirk said quietly. "I am *not* authorized to take sides in any local struggle for power, Bones."

"In that connection," Spock said, picking up a slice of some pink fruit and eyeing it as if it were an unusually uninteresting insect, "I found it odd to see that two guards were placed in front of the High Chief's tent as soon as Keel led us away from it. In addition to the usual swords and knives, these carried the boomerang-like instrument these people call the *klugat*. Such an arsenal makes me wonder whether the guards were posted to defend Teer Akaar from attack—or from escaping."

Outside the tent there was a sudden shout, then another, and then the unmistakable clash of metal on metal.

"I think we're about to find out," Kirk said, springing up. All three dashed for the entrance.

They were met outside by three tribesmen, whose swords were instantly at their throats. The encampment was a bedlam. Akaar was in the center of a swirl of combat, defending himself like a hawk at bay. He was not alone, but his party was clearly outnumbered. His son was already dead. In the light of the campfire, Kirk could see that Maab was directing the attackers, and also prominent among them was Keel.

A *klugat* struck Akaar. He staggered, wounded in the side, blood flooding the side of his tunic. He had only two defenders left.

"Jim! We can't just . . . ."

"Stand fast, Bones," Kirk said in an iron voice.

Akaar tried for his brother with one last thrust of his sword. Maab sidestepped it easily, and Akaar fell. His two last defenders, though apparently not seriously hurt, fell with him, kneeling before Maab in servile supplication.

The guards around Kirk's party prodded them forward. Maab waved Keel and another tribesman into what had been Akaar's pavilion. Then he smiled slightly at Kirk.

"You were wise not to try to interfere, Captain. This is none of your concern."

"We would have interfered if we could. We don't approve of murder."

"There has been no murder," Maab said stiffly. "We gave my brother an honorable death. This is revolution."

"I'm not interested in what you call it. However, you are not the man into whose custody we gave our equipment. I want it returned."

Maab's answer was predictable, but he did not have to give it, for at this moment Eleen stumbled out of the tent, herded at sword point by Keel and his fellow assassin. She was already frightened, but her fright became terror as she saw Akaar's body. Maab tripped her and simultaneously shoved her with the flat of his sword, so that she fell partly into the still red ashes of the campfire.

She screamed, half with pain and half with the doom of Maab's sword raised above her. Moving like lightning, Kirk slammed Maab aside, at the same time twisting his wrist in one of the very few directions the human wrist is not built to go; the sword fell. McCoy, only half a step behind, knelt beside Eleen; and with a smooth gesture, Spock scooped up the fallen sword.

Vulcans are tightly rational creatures, but in background they are a warrior race. Spock with a sword in his hand was a sight to give even a Cerean pause. They closed in with exaggerated caution.

And then, as McCoy lifted Eleen gently to examine her burned arm, all the Cereans gasped—and the woman herself, with an expression of loathing impossible to misinterpret, jerked herself free of the doctor's support.

"What's the matter with you, woman?" McCoy said sharply. "None of that, now. I'm only trying to help."

"And you have brought death upon yourself," Maab said slowly. "I would have let you go. But now . . ."

"You talk nonsense," Kirk said. "Killing an armed man who has a chance to defend himself is one thing. Murdering a defenseless woman is something else. She can't hurt you. You have the Chieftanship—you don't need her life."

"It is you who talk nonsense. Raal is dead, but this child that is to come is also of Akaar and still lives. It too must die before I may become chief—cleanly, by the sword. Moreover, Captain, by our law, only a husband may lay hands on his wife; for any other man, the penalty is death. I have not touched Eleen, nor would I have; but this your officer . . ."

"We're not governed by your law. Any charges against us will have to be brought before Starfleet Command, which will weigh them on their merits, one set of laws against the other."

"We know who would lose that judgment," Maab said. "On our world, our laws, and only our laws, prevail."

"Our ship will send a landing party to investigate our silence," Spock said, leveling the captured sword at the bridge of Maab's nose.

Maab did not flinch. "I think not," he said, with an odd, lopsided smile. "I think they will be too busy."

Kirk and Spock shot a swift glance at each other. Each knew precisely what the other was thinking. With that single, irresistible, and absolutely unnecessary brag, Maab had let slip the fact that there was more to this situation than simple tribal politics—a *lot* more.

Now had to come the hardest game of all: waiting in patience, even to the verge of death, to find out what it was.

In the guest tent, which was now their jail, Kirk, Spock and McCoy sat around the table where once they had been fed so sumptuously. Now two assassins were on guard inside the tent entrance. Eleen sat as far away from them all as she could, a light cloak over her tunic, but even more markedly huddled behind a wall of self-imposed isolation. Her arm had still not been tended; she had refused, and now she was refusing also to show any pain.

McCoy leaned his elbows on the table and looked unhappily at his colleagues. In a deliberate hash of English, Vulcan, Old High Martian, medical Latin and Greek, and Fortran—the language used to program very simple-minded computers—he said, "Maab still claims he would have let us go if it hadn't been for my laying hands on that poor girl. But now, apparently, we're sunk. Why do you suppose Scotty hasn't sent down a landing party?"

"By my calculation," Spock said, "it is an hour past the longest time Mr. Scott would wait before taking action. No other conclusion is possible but that he has become engaged in some other duty which he considers more important, as Maab hinted."

Since the First Officer, picking up McCoy's clue, put out several words of this speech in the operative terms of the calculus of statement, he had to repeat it with these parts translated into Vegan before Kirk or McCoy could be sure of it; but once understood, there was no arguing it.

Kirk eyed everyone in the room with slow calculation. Then he said, slowly and in Cerean, "Bones—I think you ought to do what you started out to do before. That girl's burned arm is still untended."

The guards stiffened.

"Might as well," McCoy said, also in Cerean. "They can only kill me once for touching her, after all."

"Mr. Spock, what is your advice?"

"I believe, Captain, that the risk is defensible."

Good; they understood each other. McCoy stood up. As his shadow fell across the girl, she looked up, and then pulled herself together. McCoy kneeled beside her.

"Your arm," he said, very gently.

"You will not touch me!"

The guards took a step forward. McCoy reached out. Eleen promptly turned into a scratching, biting wildcat. Somehow or other, it had occurred to none of them, in their swift and necessarily cryptic plotting, that she would also squeal. McCoy clamped a hand down hard over her mouth.

It was this, evidently, that made up the guards' minds. They lunged away from the entrance toward the struggle. Their backs were toward Kirk and Spock for perhaps three seconds. No more than three seconds later, they were decked.

While Spock disarmed the unconscious men, Kirk leaned over the girl, whom McCoy was still holding silent with grim difficulty.

"Listen, Eleen," Kirk said. "We're leaving. We can leave you behind, if that's what you want. Or you can cooperate and come with us. Maybe, just maybe, we can get you safely to our ship. We offer you the choice. Will you come with us?"

Cautiously, McCoy removed his hand from her mouth, ready to clamp it back down at the slightest intake of breath for a scream. But the girl only glared. At last she said, "I am dishonored. But I wish to live. I will come."

McCoy helped her up by the uninjured arm. She pulled away from him and stood immobile, not deigning to speak further, and waited while Spock distributed the guards' weapons to Kirk and McCoy, retaining a *klugat* for himself.

"Now," Kirk said, "let's get those phasers and communicators back."

This was not as easy in the doing as in the saying. Outside, the tribesmen were seated around the rebuilt campfire in an open square, the open end of which was occupied solely by Maab, with Keel standing in the background. Kirk and Spock approached the back of Akaar's tent stealthily, slit the fabric, and slipped inside.

While they searched, they heard Maab's voice: ". . . Only the woman lives now. All know her. And it is not only the child that dooms her."

A general rumble of agreement.

Kirk threw back a carpet over a chest. There were the belts with the communicators still on them, but the phasers were gone. Somebody in this crowd, then, knew which was which—another oddity. He and Spock had just begun to look further when there was a mutter of movement and conversation outside, and a second later McCoy's head popped through the slit in the tent fabric.

"Jim," he whispered urgently. "The Council meeting's over. They're going to find out we're gone . . ."

As if in confirmation, there was a shout of alarm in the near distance.

The three men and Eleen stumbled through the scrub until the light from the fire and the torches was the dimmest possible glow in the distance before Kirk chanced calling a halt. Kneeling and motioning the others to cover—what there was of it in this brush—he snapped open his communicator. "Kirk to *Enterprise* . . . Kirk to *Enterprise* . . . Come in, Scotty . . . Kirk to *Enterprise* . . ."

There was no answer. Had the device been sabotaged? Kirk held out his hand for Spock's communicator, but that produced no better results.

"They are operative," said the First Officer. "It would appear that the *Enterprise* is simply out of range."

"Out of range?" McCoy said. "Where would they go?"

"The answer to that would involve a great deal of useless speculation on our part, Doctor, since we have no facts at hand. A better question is, what do we do until the ship returns?"

"No place can hide you from the *makeen*," the woman said abruptly.

"What are they?" Kirk said. "Or it?"

"There are legends," Spock said, "of a guild of assassins among the Cerean tribes—a secret society, outside the law."

"They are not outside the law," Eleen said. "They are a part of our society. Certain deaths are always—necessary."

"Criminals like us?" Kirk said. "And 'traitors' like your husband? And you?"

"*Not* me," Eleen said. Her voice was angry, harsh, bitter. "It is because I bear Akaar's child. I did not want it. I would kill it myself, if that would save me."

McCoy took her by the wrist, and his own voice was just as angry. "You listen to me, Missy. You're not killing anything while I'm here to prevent it. We intend to keep both you *and* your baby alive, whether you want it or not. Hear me?"

She twisted herself free, her face contorted with anger and loathing. "You are heard. And I come with you because you will give me a few more hours to live. But in the end you will not escape the *makeen*."

"Maybe not," Kirk said. "But we sure in blazes are going to try."

By the first wash of daybreak there were ample signs that they were being followed. Kirk was almost sorry to see the intimations of dawn, for at night he had at least been able to guess how far ahead they were of their pursuers by the distant sparks of torches.

The light found them in rocky country, the foothills of a mountain range. It was chill and desolate, even in the pale gold of early sunlight. The trail they were following seemed to wander aimlessly; Kirk could only hope that this was because it was following the contours of the land, rather than being simply an animal trail.

He and Spock led the way, with Eleen close behind. As bulky as her physical condition made her, she was surprisingly fresh and strong; McCoy, puffing along behind her, looked more the worse for wear than she did.

But the day grew hotter, the slopes steeper, the footing strewn with slippery shale and broken rock. At last Eleen stumbled and would have fallen had McCoy not caught her. She still had the energy to break free of him, however.

"Stay here with her and let her rest, Bones," Kirk said. "We're going to look around. While you're waiting, treat that arm—by force, if necessary."

He moved off with Spock. Shortly, they found the trail entering the narrow mouth of a steep defile. The slopes were shale-strewn and very high.

"Nice place to get trapped in," Kirk said.

"It has advantages as well, Captain. A defensible entrance, and walls that provide difficult access for attackers."

"That may be. At least there also seems to be a way out. If we could block this entrance, that would hold them up; they'd have to go around, over the hills."

Spock's eyebrows went up. He looked about speculatively. "The entrance is narrow enough, and there seems to be enough loose rock."

"What do you have in mind?"

"Do you remember our discussion of the kinds of

weapons that might be made with a communicator in an emergency? In this instance, I think the device I called a 'sound bomb' might be in order.'' Kirk promptly handed Spock his communicator, but the First Officer shook his head. ''Captain, it's only a chance. I would have to phase *two* communicator signals into exact synchronization. We only have three. The odds . . .''

''I'm not interested in the exact odds—only in lowering them. I'll go get McCoy's communicator.''

He went back. He found Eleen's arm bandaged. He shook hands with himself at McCoy with approval, but McCoy was frowning.

''Jim, she says the baby isn't due until next week, but as far as I can tell with the few instruments I have, it's due *now*.''

''Oh, brrrotherrr. Well, you've doubtless delivered plenty of babies.''

''Sure. But the Cereans have been away from Earth a long time, and they've developed some differences from the basic humanoid stock—a process called 'genetic drift' that's common in small, inbred populations. And if surgical intervention's necessary . . .''

''We may not live long enough to worry about it. Give me your communicator, Bones, and come along. We're planning a surprise.''

Spock worked quickly, explaining to McCoy as he went along. ''I have placed these so the sound beams they put out will meet and focus on a weak point, a potential slide area. The phased beams should set up a vibration in the rocks, *beneath* the loose material. There the rock is cohesive enough so that the vibration should build to the equivalent of explosive force.''

''And the whole thing,'' Kirk said, ''will end up in Maab's lap. We hope.''

''Theoretically, if the loose rock does not slide away too soon and allow the sound energy to escape as heat. In either event it will destroy the communicators.''

Kirk glanced back. Tiny figures were on the horizon. Their pace obviously had picked up. These tribesmen were like bloodhounds, and the track was fresh.

''Let's go.'' Kirk and Spock twisted the dials of the

two communicators. The dull black little instruments each began to emit a hum which rose quickly in pitch to an ear-splitting screech. Hastily, the party ran up the trail into the defile.

A glance back showed that their harriers were also running. The sound had located their quarry for them.

The rising sounds merged into one intolerable note. Eleen clutched at her head, then at her belly. McCoy grabbed her around the waist, kept her moving.

The screaming note was joined by a groaning rumble of rock shaking free of its moorings. Suddenly, the screaming wail was gone, leaving a silence which only seemed underlined by the moan of protesting rock.

Then came the explosion, the confined energy bursting out of the cliffside as though an actual charge had been planted there. The rocks crumbled and fell apart, their grumbling rising to a thunder as the shale and dirt smashed down the slope.

Maab, Keel and their party were almost in the defile. They looked up as the rock slide bore down on them. After a split second of frozen terror, they wheeled and scattered like a flight of pigeons. But some of them were caught, all the same.

And in the end, the entrance to the defile was gone. Instead, there was only a massive heap of shale, boulders and dirt.

"Very nice, Mr. Spock," Kirk said, when he could hear again. "Now, we'd better push on. There's still the problem of food and water . . ."

"Not a chance, Jim," McCoy said. "We might carry Eleen—but not very far. She's started labor."

Since they had no choice, they did carry her out the other end of the defile; they did not want the *makeens* to return the favor by dropping rocks on them from above. At the exit, the country opened out a little, and off to the right some green shrub growth and contorted young trees indicated the possible presence of water.

Kirk looked up the slopes. A peculiar formation caught his eye: several huge boulders tumbled together, with a narrow, dark opening just visible between them. Kirk pointed.

"We might take shelter under those rocks. It's probably the best we can do on such short notice. Spock, stay here while we take her up and stand guard."

The First Officer nodded, and unhooking the *klugat* he had taken from the guard, twirled it experimentally.

The hole proved to be a genuine cave. The entrance was low, but inside the roof was high enough to permit them to stand erect. It was far from spacious, however. The walls were rough and pitted, and the floor sloped. Eleen lowered her bulky body and sat huddled in pain.

"Even eighteenth-century surgeons had more to work with than this," McCoy said, "but I guess beggars can't be choosers."

"We'll be outside if you need help."

"Don't make any rash offers."

Kirk went outside to find Spock experimenting with the *klugat*. "A most unusual weapon," the First Officer said. "Observe that the cutting edge is along the *inside*. If you throw it with a snap of the wrist, thus . . ."

The whirling knife spun in flight, its silver blades flashing. It sliced into a low bush and nearly cut it free of the ground before becoming entangled.

"And if you miss, it comes back to the owner," Spock said, retrieving the weapon. "A nice instance of economy."

"We'll need the economy. We've only got two. I'm more interested in those saplings. They look resilient. We might make bows and arrows—if we only had something to use for bowstrings."

"Hmm," Spock said. "A very pretty problem. I see nothing that would serve. But Captain, I suggest that an even more primitive weapon might serve our purposes: a throwing-stick."

"What in blazes is that?"

"It consists of a grooved handle with a cupped end. The arrow is fitted into the groove with the arrowhead toward the hand and the feathered end in the cup. You swing the throwing-stick overhand, and the arrow leaves it with considerable force, on the lever principle."

"There's plenty of flint here for arrowheads," Kirk said thoughtfully. "But we have nothing to use for feathers."

"True. However, if we notch the end of the arrow and tie

on a length of rag, that may afford some stabilization, on the principle of a kite's tail. And may I point out, Captain, that the only missile weapon possessed by the Cereans is this *klugat*, which has a range limit built into it by the very fact that it is designed to return to the thrower. Our arrows will fly somewhat farther—and will, of course, be quite unfamiliar to the Cereans. These advantages are small, but they may be all we have.''

"You're right, Mr. Spock. Let's get to work.''

As they climbed toward the cave, a cry of pain came from it.

They were practicing with the throwing-sticks when McCoy at last appeared at the cave entrance, mopping his hands. "Come on in,'' he said.

Eleen lay in a shadowed corner. Her light cloak was her only bed; the lower half of her long tunic had been torn off to provide a blanket for the small bundle lying beside her. She propped herself up as the men entered, but made no protest as Kirk and Spock peered down at the bundle.

Tiny fists that resembled minute starfish wriggled aimlessly. The baby yawned into Kirk's face, seeming to suggest that the whole thing had been a snap, and all McCoy's worries had been needless.

"It seems a rather average specimen on the whole,'' Spock said.

"You think so, Spock?'' McCoy said tiredly. "Well, look again. That is the High Chief of the ten tribes of Ceres.''

He picked up the baby and put it in its mother's arms. The woman took it, passively, but she said, "I do not want it.''

"He's your son,'' Kirk said.

"I did not wish it. It was good to become wife to Akaar. He was High Chief and had wealth. I thought because he was old and already had a son . . .''

"I don't care why you married Teer Akaar,'' Kirk interrupted harshly. "You did, and you bore his son, who is now the High Chief. You're bound by honor and position to care for him as long as you live. That's your tradition as well as ours, and I'll enforce it if I have to. Bones, how soon can she travel?''

"All these Cereans seem to have remarkable stamina,

and I'd say this one is strong as an ox, even now. We might be able to move as soon as tomorrow.''

"If so," Spock said, "I suggest that we climb the ridge behind us when we leave, and move cross-country. It will be difficult, but I believe safer.''

Kirk thought about this. Maab might well have figured that they would follow the defile all the way, because of the woman. Or he might even already be moving in on them from the other end.

"Even odds," he said "We'll try it. But first, let's get some sleep. McCoy, you need the rest most; you'll stand last guard. I'll take the first.''

He awoke to hear McCoy's voice calling his name and feeling his shoulder being shaken. As he sat up, McCoy was already leaving his side to rouse the sleeping Spock.

"Wake up, Spock. Jim, we're in more trouble. My, uh, patient has taken the child and gone.''

"She got past *you*?" Kirk said.

"She struck me from behind with a rock. We've got to have more respect for the medical profession around here.''

"How long has she been gone?''

"By the sun, I was out no more than half an hour. Her trail leads toward the defile exit. If Maab's men catch her . . .''

"I suggest," Spock said, "that henceforth we leave the matter to tribal justice, and devote ourselves to our own survival.''

"Why, you ice-hearted, unfeeling . . .''

"The lady is *not* honorable, or charitable, or cooperative, or of much total worth," Spock said. "Even you can see that, Doctor.''

"Yes? And what about the baby?''

"You both have a point," Kirk said. "Granted that the lady has few shining virtues. But the baby has done nothing but come into this world. I'd like to see him get a chance to grow up in it. Let's get going.''

They moved cautiously along the defile, keeping as high up on the slopes as the footing would allow. At the exit, they came upon an astonishing scene.

The assassins, or all that had survived the rock slide,

were all there, and so was Eleen. Most of the men were staring at her in amazement, and small wonder, for she was holding out the child to Maab.

"I have the child, Maab," she said, her voice distant but clear. "He is yours. Do as you will."

Keel and Maab looked at each other. At last Maab said, "Why?"

"I claim nothing but my life. Take the child, Maab— but let me go free. I care not for *him*."

Finally Maab nodded. When he spoke, his voice was sarcastic. "It is much like you, Eleen. Come with us."

At this point, Kirk rose from cover and swung the throwing-stick, then fell flat again in the brush. No one saw him. The arrow cut through the air straight at Maab, its rag tail fluttering, and at the last minute veering and hitting another man in the leg. Evidently feathers were much better for arrows than tails were. The struck man fell, with a cry as much of surprise as of pain.

Everyone turned toward him. Spock popped up from behind a rock and threw, then also vanished. The arrow winged Keel; a red stain began to spread on his sleeve.

McCoy now appeared suddenly on the trail, just behind Eleen. Grabbing her from behind, he dragged her screaming to cover. The assassins were now beginning to realize what had happened, and made an abortive move after McCoy, but a scatter of arrows from Kirk and Spock threw them into confusion. The volume of fire was, tactically, not nearly great enough to produce such an effect; evidently Spock's guess about the effect on morale of the unfamiliarity of the weapons had been correct.

"Bones, get out of there!" Kirk shouted. "General retreat!"

He ducked as Keel threw a *klugat* at him. The vicious scything blades slashed the air whisperingly over his head. Below, McCoy, dragging Eleen, made his way up the slope from cover to cover. Kirk slipped to another rock, rose, and threw again, and this time was rewarded with a full-throated scream. He was getting the hang of the thing.

They moved backward slowly, covering for Eleen, hampered by the baby. As they went, Spock picked up the *klugat* Keel had thrown, which had been blocked from boomeranging by a boulder. Oddly, the *makeen* were no longer following.

Back inside the more defensible defile walls, the *Enterprise* men paused to assess the situation. They were nicely trapped—and the arrows were running out.

"What did you think you were going to do?" McCoy said, glaring at Eleen.

"You heard," she said coldly. "I would trade my life. Maab will let me go—to get the child."

"Oh? Aren't you overlooking something? We were close enough behind you to surprise Maab. It might even have looked to him like you were bait for a trap. He won't trust you again, Missy—if he ever did. He'll kill you both, just to be sure."

"And of what use was this grand surprise?" the woman said with contempt. "Here he can simply starve us out."

As Kirk digested the truth of that, Maab's voice rang out.

"Captain!"

"What is it?"

Maab came forward, slowly, accompanied by two henchmen. The other assassins followed, stopping just out of arrow range. They learn fast, Kirk thought ruefully.

"A fine fight, Captain. And fought with much ingenuity. But useless, as you can see. I suggest that you put down your weapons now."

Clearly, there was no choice. "Do as he says, Doctor, Mr. Spock," Kirk said quietly. "It appears that the cavalry doesn't come over the hill any more."

Eleen pushed forward, the child held out in her arms. "Take him, Maab. He is all that prevents your true Chieftanship."

Maab signaled to a henchman, who came forward and took the child.

"I will go now," Eleen said, hopefully.

"No," Maab said. "You stand condemned for other treasons. You know the penalty for unfaithfulness."

The woman backed away in terror. "No, no! I was not unfaithful—there was no one . . ."

"There is proof," Maab said heavily. "Keel saw it done, though he did not name the man before he was slain by this alien Captain's arrow. My brother may be dead, but his honor is my honor. Let justice be done!''

"No! No!"

Eleen began to run. The *makeen* silently cleared for her what seemed to be an avenue of escape. Then a *klugat* whirled through the air. She fell, and was still.

Maab looked sharply at Kirk. "You do not protest as before."

"Your justice is served," Kirk said, fighting down his nausea. "Perhaps it was merited. But the child is a different matter. He has harmed no one."

"He lives. The High Chieftanship must be mine."

"Why? Clearly you have only sown the seeds of still more factionalism, still more assassination. What do you really gain in the end, Maab? And who else gains with you?"

"You are a clever man, Captain," Maab said reflectively. "You see beneath surfaces. Well, you are not the only ones who wish this rock in our hills. The Klingon Empire offered my brother much for mining rights. Wealth, power, a seat in their Empire. The fool chose to honor a promise made to your Federation. He did not trust the Klingons."

"But you did."

"I had to be Chief to give them what they wanted. A Klingon ship drew yours away so your men could not stop Akaar's death. You could have returned without harm if you had not broken taboo to save Eleen. She was not worth your deaths."

"She was," McCoy said, "then."

"Because of the child within her? But both die in the end. All this that followed was fruitless."

"One thing, then," McCoy said. "Let me have the boy I brought into the world. If you're going to take us out of it, I'd rather have him with me."

Maab shrugged and signaled to his henchman, who paused and then passed the child to McCoy. The remaining assassins raised their *klugats*. The resemblance to a firing squad was inarguable . . .

"Drop those weapons!"

The voice—Scott's voice—came from the lip of the cliff. With him was Sulu and a crewman. At the edge of the other side of the defile were Frost and two more crewmen—all with phasers at the ready.

"What the devil?" McCoy said.

"I would say, Doctor," Spock said, "that the cavalry has just come over the hill."

The crewmen came down, herding the assassins together. "But *how*?" Maab said. "How did you escape the Klingon ship? They were not to let you through until I signaled . . ."

"They backed off and ran when we came straight at them," Sulu said with a grin. "At first they decoyed us away with false distress calls, but when we saw through that and went right down their throats—well, their ships have speed, I'll grant them that."

Scott added, "I didn't think the Klingons were ready for a war, even to please this gentleman. Not even for topaline mining rights."

"Mr. Scott," Kirk said, "I know you for a resourceful man, but how did you find us out here?"

"When we beamed down to the main camp, we found what had happened. A lot of Akaar's followers are left; only the assassins of Maab's group went hunting you. They told us you'd escaped to the hills, we used our sensors to pinpoint you, and beamed down again.'Twas a near squeak."

Abruptly, there was movement behind Maab and a knife flashed. Maab gasped and fell. His killer stolidly wiped the knife on the sleeve of his tunic and held it out to a stunned Kirk.

"For treason to Akaar," the man said, "and for treason with the Klingons. I now stand ready for justice."

"And who in blazes may you be?" Kirk demanded.

"I," the man said, "am the father of the High Chief born of Eleen."

The treaty was signed, by the father, who after a long tribal party had been named the High Chief's guardian-regent. What complicated tribal politics and concepts of justice produced this result, Kirk could not fathom, nor did he care any longer. It was enough for him that the man had bound himself to serve the child until it came of age.

The last surprise was the naming of the High Chief. The father dubbed him, Leonard James Akaar.

It was Spock's opinion that McCoy and the Captain were going to be insufferably pleased with themselves about that for at least a month.

WHO MOURNS FOR ADONIS?

Writer: Gilbert A. Ralston and Gene L. Coon
Director: Marc Daniels
Guest stars: Michael Forest, Leslie Parrish

All heads in the *Enterprise* bridge turned as the elevator door opened.

Kirk made a bet with himself: it was Lieutenant Carolyn Palamas with her report on those marblelike fragments they'd beamed up from the dead planet in the Cecrops cluster. He won the bet. She handed him some stapled sheets and he said, "Thank you," his eyes carefully averted the girl's lustrous slate-gray ones.

Supreme beauty, he'd decided, could be a cruel liability to a woman. The stares it attracted set her apart. And he didn't want Carolyn Palamas to feel set apart. If she was the owner of copper-glorious hair and those slate-gray eyes, she was also a new member of his crew and a highly competent archeologist. She'd been stopping traffic since the day she was born. Well, he wasn't adding his gapes to the quota. He said, "Continue with standard procedures for Pollux Four, Lieutenant."

Dr. McCoy appeared to share his defensiveness toward the traffic-stopper. "You look tired, Carolyn," he said.

"I worked all night on my report," she said.

"There's nothing like a cup of coffee to buck you up," Scott said. "Want to join me in one, Carolyn?"

She smiled at him. "Just let me get my chemicals back into the lab cabinet first." She left the bridge and Kirk said, "Could you get that excited over a cup of coffee, Bones?"

"I'm in love with her," Scott said briefly. As he hastened after her, a slight frown pulled at McCoy's brows. "I'm wondering about that, Jim."

"Scotty's a good man," Kirk said.

"He thinks he's the right man for her, but *she*—" McCoy shrugged. "Emotional analysis of this love goddess of ours shows up strong drives for wifehood and motherhood. She's all woman, Jim. One of these days the bug will find her and off she'll go—out of the Service."

"I'd hate to lose a good officer, but I never fight nature, Bones."

Chekov spoke from his station near Kirk's command chair. "Entering standard orbit around Pollux Four, sir."

On the screen Pollux Four had already appeared, not unearthlike. Continents, seas, clouds.

"Preliminary reports, Mr. Spock?"

"Class M, Captain." Spock didn't turn from his mounded computer. Kirk, his eyes on the screen, saw the planet, rotating slowly, come into closer focus. He heard Spock say, "Nitrogen-oxygen atmosphere, sir. Sensor readings indicate no life-forms. Approximate age four billion years. I judge no reason for contact. In all respects quite ordinary."

Kirk pushed a button. "Cartographic section, implement standard orders. All scanners automatic. All—"

"Captain!" shouted Sulu. "On scanner twelve!"

Something had suddenly come between them and the planet—something formless and so transparent Kirk could see the stars through it. It was rapidly growing in size.

"What in the name of . . ." McCoy fell silent.

"Mr. Sulu," Chekov said, "am I seeing things?"

"Not unless I am, too," Sulu said. "Captain, that thing is a giant hand!"

Kirk didn't speak. On the screen the amorphous mass had begun to differentiate itself into five gigantic fingers, into a palm, the hint of a massive wrist extending down and out of the viewer's area. "Readings, Mr. Spock." His voice was toneless. "Is it a hand?"

"No, Captain. Not living tissue."

"A trick then? A magnified projection?"

"Not a projection, sir. A field of energy."

"Hard about!" Kirk ordered briskly. "Course 230 mark 41."

The palm now dominated the screen, its lines deeply shadowed valleys, the huge, contrasting mounds of its construction simulating the human-size mounds of a human palm. The valleyed lines deepened, moving—and Chekov cried, "It means to grab us!"

For the first time Spock turned from his computer to look at the viewer. "Captain, if it's a force field—"

"All engines reverse!" Kirk shouted.

Lights flickered. Shudders shook the starship. Strained metal screamed. Bridge seats tumbled their occupants to the floor. Scrambling up to wrestle with his console, Sulu grasped it with both hands as he fought to pull it backward. "The helm won't answer, Captain! We can't move!"

Scott had rushed in from the elevator; and Kirk, regaining his chair, addressed Uhura. "Lieutenant, relay our position and circumstances to Star Base Twelve immediately. Report that the *Enterprise* has been stopped in space by an unknown force of some kind." He swung his chair around to Sulu. "Mr. Sulu, try rocking the ship. Full impulse forward, *then* back."

"Damage report coming in, Captain," said Uhura. "Situation under control. Minor damage stations three, seven and nineteen."

"Mr. Sulu?"

"Applying thrust, sir."

The ship vibrated. "No results, Captain. We're stuck tight."

Kirk glanced at the screen. The palm still owned it; and stars still shone through it. He looked away from it. "Status, Mr. Spock?"

"The ship is almost totally encircled by a force field, sir. It resembles a conventional force field but of unusual wavelengths. Despite its likeness to human appendage, it is not living tissue. It is energy."

"Thank you, Mr. Spock. Forward tractor beams, Mr. Sulu—and adjust to repel."

"Aye, aye, sir."

"Activate now!"

The ship quivered, groaning. "Ineffective, sir," Sulu said. "There doesn't seem to be anything to push against."

Spock spoke. "I suggest we throw scanner twelve on the main viewing screen, Captain."

"Do so, Mr. Spock."

The palm slid away. In its place, nebulous, still transparent, the features of a great face were shaping themselves into form on the screen. Silence was absolute in the bridge of the *Enterprise*. The immense face could be seen now, whole. But its immensity struck Kirk as irrelevant. It was an intensely masculine face; and whomever it belonged to was the handsomest male Kirk had ever seen in his life. The dark eyes were fixed on the ship. Diademed with stars, the brow, the nose and mouth conformed to convey an impression of classic beauty, ageless as the stars.

The voice that came from the screen suited the face.

"The aeons have passed, and what has been written has come about. You are welcome here, my beloved children. Your home awaits you."

Kirk shook his head as though to clear his ears of the deep organ tones reverberating through the bridge. He tore his gaze from the screen to address Uhura. "Response frequencies, Lieutenant."

"Calculated, sir. Channel open."

He pulled the mike to him. "This is Captain James T. Kirk of the *USS Enterprise*. Please identify yourself."

The request was ignored. "You have left your plains and valleys to make this bold venture," said the voice. "So it was from the beginning. We shall remember together. We shall drink the sacramental wine. The pipes shall call again from the woodlands. The long wait is ended."

The words had the sound of an incantation. Kirk said, "Whatever you are, whoever you are, are you responsible for stopping my ship?"

"I have caused the wind to withdraw from your sails."

"Return it," Kirk said. "Then we'll talk. You seem unwilling to identify yourself, but I warn you we have the power to defend ourselves. If you value your safety, release this ship!"

The lips moved in an approving smile. "You have the

old fire. How like your fathers you are. Agamemnon . . .
Achilles . . . Trojan Hector . . .''

"Never mind the history lesson. Release this ship or
I'll—''

The smile faded. ''You will obey—lest I close my
hand—thus—''

The ship rocked like a toy shaken by a petulant child.

"External pressure building up, Captain,'' Scott called
from his station. ''Eight hundred GSC and mounting.''

"Compensate, Mr. Scott.''

"Pressure becoming critical, sir. One thousand GSC.
We can't take it.''

Savagely Kirk swung around to the screen. ''All right,
whatever you're doing, you win. Turn it off.''

"That was your first lesson. Remember it,'' the voice
said. The sternness on its face was replaced by a smile radiant
as sunlight. ''I invite you and all your officers to join me,
Captain. Don't bring the one with the pointed ears. Pan is a
bore. He always was.''

Kirk said hastily, ''Take it easy, Mr. Spock. We don't
know what we're up against.''

"Hasten, children,'' urged the voice. ''Let your hearts
prepare to sing.''

"Well, Bones, ready for the concert?''

"Is that wise, Jim?''

"It is if we want a ship instead of a crushed eggshell.''

Kirk got up to join his First Officer at the computer
station. ''You're in command, Mr. Spock. Get all labs working on the nature of the force holding us here. Find a way to
break clear.''

"Acknowledged, sir. Beam-down?''

"Yes, Mr. Spock.''

The party materialized among olive trees. Ahead of
them on a grassy knoll stood a small edifice of veinless marble. It was fronted by six fluted columns of the stone, lifting
to capitals that flowered into graceful curves. Above them
rose the white temple's architrave, embossed with sculptured
figures. They looked ancient but somehow familiar. A semi-
circled flight of steps led upward and into the structure.

As Chekov and Scott moved into position beside him,

Kirk said, "Maintain readings on tricorders. That goes for everybody."

Behind him, unusually pale, Carolyn Palamas edged nearer to McCoy. "What am *I* doing here, Doctor?"

Unslinging his tricorder, McCoy said, "You're the student of ancient civilizations. This seems to be one. We'll need all the information you've got about it." He moved on to follow Kirk, adding, "The Captain will want us with him when he enters that door."

There was no door. They found themselves at once in a peristylelike open space. At its far end a dais made a pediment for a carved throne of the same spotless marble. There were benches of marble, a table that held a simple repast of fruit and wine. From somewhere came the sound of pipes, sweet, wild, pagan. On a bench beside the table sat a man-size being. Kirk had seen some good-looking men in his life, but this male, human or non-human, was in a class of his own. His face held the same agelessly classic beauty as the huge image of the *Enterprise* screen. A thigh-length garment was clasped to his sun-browned, smoothly muscular shoulders. Beside him lay a lyre. He rose to his tall six-foot two-inch height and walked to meet them.

"My children, greetings. Long, long have I waited for this moment."

His youth should have made the term "children" absurd. It didn't. He could get away with it, Kirk thought, because of the dignity. The whole bearing of the creature exuded it.

Low-voiced, he said, "Bones, aim your tricorder at him."

"Ah, the memories you bring of our lush and beautiful Earth!" The being flung up his arms as though invoking the memories. "Its green meadows . . . its blue skies . . . the simple shepherds and their flocks on the hills . . ."

"You know Earth?" Kirk asked. "You've been there?"

The white teeth flashed in the radiant smile. "Once I stretched out my hand—and the Earth trembled. I breathed upon it—and spring returned."

"You mentioned Achilles," Kirk said. "How do you know about him?"

"Search back into your most distant memories, those

of the thousands of years that have passed . . . and I am there. Your fathers knew me and your fathers' fathers. I am Apollo."

It was insanely credible. The temple . . . the lyre. Apollo had been the patron god of music. And the speech of this being was marked by an antique cadence, an almost superhuman assurance. There was also his incomparable symmetry of body and gesture.

Chekov broke the spell. "Yes," he said, "and I am the Czar of all the Russias!"

"Mr. Chekov!"

"Sorry, Captain. I never met a god before."

"And you haven't now," Kirk said. "Your readings, Bones?"

"A simple humanoid. Nothing special."

"You have the manners of a satyr. You will learn." The remark was made abstractedly. The dark eyes had fixed on Carolyn Palamas. The creature stepped forward to lift her chin with his hand. Scott bristled and Kirk said, "Hold it, Scotty."

"Earth—she always was the mother of beautiful women. That at least is unchanged. I am pleased. Yes, we gods knew your Earth well . . . Zeus, my sister Artemis, Athene. Five thousand years ago we knew it well."

"All right," Kirk said. "We're here. Now let's talk. Apparently, you're all alone. Maybe we can do something to help you."

"Help me? *You?* You will not help me. You will not leave this place." The tone was final. "Your transportation device no longer functions."

Kirk, flipped open his communicator. There was no responding crackle. The being said casually, "Nor will that device work either, Captain." He paused. Just as casually, he added, "You are here to worship me as your fathers worshipped me before you."

"If you wish to play god by calling yourself Apollo, that is your business," Kirk said. "But you are not a god to us."

"I said," repeated the humanoid, "you shall worship me."

"*You've* got a lot to learn, my friend," Kirk retorted.

"And so have you! Let the lesson begin!"

Before Kirk's unbelieving eyes, the body of the man-size being began to rise, taller, taller, taller. He towered twelve feet above them—and still grew higher. He was now a good eighteen feet in stature, a colossus of mingled beauty and rage. As the black brows drew together in fury, there came a deafening crash of thunder. The translucent light in the temple went dim, streaks of lightning piercing its darkness. Thunder rolled again. Around the temple's columned walls far above him, Kirk could see that lightning spears were gathering about the great head in a dazzling nimbus of flame.

Crowned with fire, Apollo said, "Welcome to Olympus, Captain Kirk!"

Dazed, the *Enterprise* commander fought against the evidence of his senses. His reason denied the divinity of the being; but his eyes, his ears, insisted on its truth. Then he saw that a look of weariness, of pain, had appeared on Apollo's face. The massive shoulders sagged. He vanished.

It was McCoy who spoke first. "To coin a phrase—fascinating."

Kirk turned to the girl. "Lieutenant Palamas, what do you know about Apollo?"

She stared at him unseeingly. "What? . . . oh, Apollo. He—he was the son of Zeus and Latona . . . a mortal woman. He was the god of light, of music, of archery. He—he controlled prophecy."

"And this creature?"

She had collected herself. "Clearly he has some knowledge of Earth, sir. His classic references, the way he speaks, his—his looks. They resemble certain museum sculptures of the god."

"Bones?"

"I can't say much till I've checked out these readings. He looks human, but of course that doesn't mean a thing."

"Whatever he is, he seems to control a remarkable technology," Chekov said.

"Power is what the thing controls," Scott said. "You can't pull off these tricks without power."

"Fine. But what power? Where does it come from?" Kirk's voice was impatient. "Scout around with your tricorders and see if you can locate his power source."

Scott and Chekov moved off and Kirk, his face grown thoughtful, turned to McCoy. "I wonder if five thousand years ago a race of—"

"You have a theory, Jim?"

"I'm considering one. What if—"

"Jim, look!"

Man-size again, Apollo was sitting on his marble throne.

"Come to me," he said.

They obeyed. Kirk spoke. "Mister—" he began. He hesitated, then plunged. "Apollo, would you kindly tell us what you want from us? Omitting, if you please, all Olympian comments?"

"I want from you what is rightfully mine. Your loyalty, your tribute and your worship."

"What do you offer in exchange?"

The dark eyes brooded on Kirk's. "I offer you human life as simple and pleasureful as it was those thousands of years ago on our beautiful Earth so far away."

"We're not in the habit of bending our knees to everyone we meet with a bag of tricks."

"Agamemnon was one such as you. And Hercules. Pride, hubris." The deep voice was somber with memory. "They defied me, too—until they felt my wrath."

Scott had rejoined Kirk in time to hear this last exchange. "We are capable of some wrath ourselves," he said hotly.

"I have four hundred and thirty people on my ship up there," Kirk said, "and they—"

"They are mine," said Apollo. "To cherish or destroy. At my will."

Carolyn suddenly broke in. "But why? What you've said makes no sense."

The dark eyes veered from Kirk's to linger on the cloud of copper-glorious hair. "What is your name?"

"Lieutenant Palamas."

"I mean your *name*."

She glanced at Kirk as though for help. "Carolyn."

"Yes." Apollo leaned forward on the throne. "When she gave you beauty, Aphrodite was feeling unusually generous. I have a thousand tales to tell you. We shall speak together, you and I, of valor and of love."

"Let her alone!" Scott cried.

"You protest?" Apollo was amused. "You risk much, mortal."

Scott whipped out his phaser. "And so do you!"

With a lithe movement, Apollo was on his feet. He extended a finger at the phaser. A blue-hot flame leaped from it—and Scott yelled in pain. He dropped the weapon, recoiling.

Kirk bent to pick it up, but Chekov had already retrieved it. The phaser was a lump of melted metal. Chekov handed it to Kirk. It was still hot to the touch.

"Quite impressive." The respect in Kirk's voice was genuine. "Did you generate that force internally?"

"Captain!" shouted Chekov. "The phasers—all of them!"

Kirk withdrew his from his belt. It had been fused into the same mass of useless metal.

"None of your toys will function."

Apollo dismissed the subject of the ruined phasers by stepping from his white throne. He strode over to Carolyn to search the slate-gray eyes with his. "Yes," he said, "the Cyprian was unusually generous to you. But the bow arm should be bare . . ."

He touched her uniform. Its stuff thinned into soft golden folds. They lengthened to her feet. She was gowned in a robe of flowing archaic Greek design that left one white shoulder naked. Golden sandals had replaced her shoes. Wonderingly, she whispered, "It—it is beautiful."

"You are beautiful," he said. "Come."

"She's not going with you!" Scott shouted. He took an angry step toward them—and was slammed against a marble bench. McCoy ran to him.

"That mortal must learn the discipline of my temple," Apollo said. "So must you all." He had Carolyn's hand in his. "But you—you come with me."

Kirk made a move and the girl shook her head. "It's all right, Captain."

The sunlight smile was for her. "Good," Apollo said.

"Without fear. You are fit." A radiance suddenly enveloped them. Their figures were absorbed by it. They disappeared.

McCoy called to Kirk. "Scotty's stunned. He'll come around. But the girl, Jim—I'm not sure at all it was wise to let her go off like that. Whatever this Apollo is, we'd better be careful in dealing with him."

"He'd have been hard to stop," Kirk said. "Scotty tried."

"It's his moods that worry me. You've seen how capricious he is. Benevolent one moment, angry the next. If she says one displeasing thing to him, he could kill her."

"Yes, he could." Kirk turned to Chekov. "Mr. Chekov, continue your investigations. You all right, Scotty?"

Leaning against McCoy's shoulder, the engineer shook his head dazedly. "I don't know. I'm tingling all over . . . a kind of inside burning. Did he take her with him?"

"So it would seem, Scotty."

"Captain, we've got to stop him! He wants her! The way he looks at her—"

"Mr. Scott, the Lieutenant volunteered to go with him, hopefully to find out more about him. I understand your concern—but she's doing her job. It's time you started doing yours. We've got to locate the source of his power. You have a tricorder. Use it. One thing more. I want no more unauthorized action taken against him. I don't want you killed. That's an order."

Sullenly Scott stumbled away after Chekov and McCoy said, "Scotty doesn't believe in gods, Jim."

"Apollo could have been one though—once."

"Is *that* your theory?"

"Bones, suppose a highly sophisticated group of humans achieved space travel five thousand years ago. Suppose they landed on Earth near the area around the Aegean Sea. To the simple shepherds and tribesmen of primitive Greece wouldn't they have seemed to be gods? Especially if they were able to alter their shapes at will and command great energy?"

McCoy stared. Then he nodded soberly. "Like humans, occasionally benevolent, occasionally vindictive. Maybe you've got something. But I certainly wish that love-goddess girl were safely back on the *Enterprise*."

* * *

Under the golden sandals of the love-goddess girl, the grass of the olive-groved glade was soft. "A simple humanoid" was how Dr. McCoy had defined the man who strolled beside her. Birds threaded the air she breathed with melody. Her hand felt very small in his. He lifted it to his lips—and they were as warm as human lips. Above the bird song, she could hear the splashing of a waterfall. Vaguely Carolyn Palamas thought, "I am both afraid and not afraid. How is it possible to feel two such different feelings at once?"

"I have known other women," he said. "Mortals . . . Daphne, Cassandra. None were so lovely as you. You fear me?"

"I—don't know. It isn't every day a girl is flattered by—"

"A god? I do not flatter."

She reached for another subject. "How do you know so much of Earth?"

"How do you remember *your* home? Earth was so dear to us, it remains forever a shrine. There were laughter, brave and goodly company—love."

"You are alone, so alone," she said. "The others— where are they? Hera, Hermes, your sister Artemis?"

"They returned to the stars on the wings of the wind," he said.

"You mean they died?"

"No. We gods are immortal. It was the Earth that died. Your fathers turned away from us until we were only memories. A god cannot survive as a memory. We need awe, worship. We need love."

"You really consider yourself to be a god?"

He laughed. "It's a habit one gets into. But in a real sense we were gods. The power of life and death was ours. When men turned from us, we could have struck down from Olympus and destroyed them. But we had no wish to destroy. So we came back to the stars again."

A note of infinite sadness entered his voice. "But those we had to leave behind, those who had loved us were gone. Here was an empty place without worship, without love. We waited, all of us, through the endless centuries."

"But you said the others didn't die."

"Hera went first. She stood before the temple and spread herself upon the wind in a way we have . . . thinner and thinner until only the wind remained. Even for gods there is a point of no return." He paused. Then he turned her around to face him.

"Now you have come," he said.

A breeze stirred the grass at her feet. The urgency in his eyes was familiar to the traffic-stopper. But in his it seemed uniquely moving. Abruptly she had a sense of imminent glory or catastrophe.

"I knew you would come to the stars one day. Of all the gods, I knew. I am the one who waited. I have waited for you to come and sit by my side in the temple. Why have you been so long? It has been . . . so lonely."

She didn't speak. "Zeus," he said, "took Latona, my mother. She was a mortal like you. He took her to care for, to guard, to love—thus . . ."

His arms were around her. She whispered, "No—no, please, not now. I—I feel you are most kind and your—your loneliness is a pain in my heart. But I don't know. I—"

"I have waited five thousand years."

He kissed her. She pulled back; and he released her at once. "I will leave you for a little to compose yourself. The temple is not far." He stopped to brush the burnished hair with his lips before turning to stride up the swell of the glade. She watched him go. A sob broke from her; and she covered her face with her hands. Glory—or catastrophe. Who could know which lay in wait? The bird song had sunk into silence and shadows were lengthening through the leaves of the olive trees. She waited another moment before she climbed the gladed upswell that led back to the temple.

The *Enterprise* party was quartering the area before it with tricorders. As she emerged from the trees, Chekov was calling to Kirk. "There's a repeated occurrence of registrations, Captain. A regularly pulsating pattern of radiated energy."

She was glad Scott's attention was fixed on the ground. "I can detect the energy pattern, too, Captain. But I can't focus on it."

"Apollo seems able to focus on it, Mr. Scott. He taps that power. How?"

"The electric eel can generate and control energy without harm to itself," Chekov said. "And the dry-worm of Antos—"

"Not the whole encyclopedia, please," McCoy begged.

"The Captain asked for complete information," Chekov said stiffly.

"Jim, Spock is contaminating this boy."

"Mr. Chekov, what you're suggesting is that Apollo taps a flow of energy he discharges through his own body," Kirk said.

"That would seem to be most likely, sir."

"But we don't *know* where the energy comes from! That's what we've got to find out if we're to cut off its source!"

"Number one on our 'things to do,' " murmured McCoy.

"Is that all you can offer, Bones?"

"Yes, except for this finding. Your Apollo's got an extra organ in his gorgeous chest. I can't even make a guess at its function."

"An extra organ. Bones, is there any chance—"

"Captain!" Scott shouted.

Apollo had assumed shape and substance on the temple steps. Kirk walked up to him. "Where is Lieutenant Palamas?"

"She is well."

"That's not good enough—"

"She is no longer your concern, Captain Kirk."

"You blood-thirsty heathen, what have you done with her?" Scott cried.

Kirk's stern "No!" came too late. Scott, snatching up a stone, charged Apollo, headlong. The finger extended—and the blue-hot streak lashed from it. Heels over head, Scott was whirled through the air. He fell with a crash; and the rock in his hand rolled down the knoll.

"Well?" Kirk said.

McCoy was kneeling beside Scott's crumpled body. "Not so well, Jim. He's in deep shock."

Kirk glanced at Scott's white face. Blood was seeping from a gash near his mouth. He stood immobile for a long moment, half-seeing the injection McCoy was preparing. Then he whirled to stride up to the temple steps. "All right,

Mr. Last of the Gods. You wanted worshippers? You've got enemies. From now on—''

The finger pointed directly at him. The blue-hot flash struck him directly in the chest. It didn't fade. It didn't waver. Kirk choked, hands groping at his heart. He spun around—and fell flat on his face into unconsciousness.

McCoy, instantly beside him, lifted an eyelid. ''Two patients,'' he muttered to nobody. ''Two damn fools.''

From behind the tree whose trunk had sheltered her from Scott's notice, Carolyn burst out of the dismay that had benumbed her. She flew to the temple steps, crying wildly, ''What have you done to them? What have you done?''

''They—needed discipline.'' Apollo spoke wearily.

She turned her back on him to run to the two stricken crew members. Kirk was climbing slowly to his feet, McCoy's arm about his shoulders. She knelt beside Scott to wipe the blood from his chin with her robe. He opened his eyes at her touch and smiled faintly at her. ''What happened?'' he said.

''You let your enthusiasm get the better of your pragmatism,'' McCoy told him dryly.

''I—I was going to separate his head from his ruddy neck,'' Scott said.

''And you disobeyed an order not to do it! When we get back to the ship, you'll report for a hearing, Mr. Scott!''

''She's—worth it, Captain.''

''You're an officer of the Starfleet! Start acting like one! Besides, you stiff-necked thistlehead, you could have got yourself killed!''

Carolyn leaped to her feet, eyes blazing. ''Apollo would not kill!''

Kirk stared at her. ''*Women!*'' he thought. ''They'll believe anything's true if they want to believe it is true.'' He said icily, ''Lieutenant, he very nearly has killed—and several times.''

''He could—but he *didn't*! Captain, you've got to see! He doesn't want to hurt anyone. He's just—terribly lonely. Please try to understand. He's the god of light, of music. He wouldn't hurt us!''

Kirk gripped her shoulders. ''What happened when he took you away?''

"We—just talked."

"What about?"

"Captain, I—"

Kirk's voice was hard as the temple's stone. "Answer me, Lieutenant. What he said may help us."

Her eyes sought the ground. "He—said there was a point of no return . . . even for gods. Of course he's not a god—but he is *not* inhuman!"

"He's not human, either," Scott said grimly.

"No!" she cried. "He is something greater than human, nobler!"

"Lieutenant, there are four hundred and thirty people on our ship and we're all in trouble."

"Oh, I know it, Captain! Don't you think I know it? I just don't know what—" She burst into tears.

"Go easy on her, Jim."

"Why? So she can play around with an exciting new romance?"

"A god is making love to her. That's strong stuff, Jim."

Kirk shook his head in irritation. "How do you feel, Scotty?"

"I can't move my left arm."

"You won't for a while. There's some neural damage to the arm, Jim. I could repair it if I had the facilities."

"One more reason why we have to get out of here." Kirk walked over to a log, kicked it aside and turned to beckon to McCoy. "Bones, listen. I've been trying to remember my Greek mythology. After expending energy its gods needed rest just as humans do. At any rate, I intend to assume they did."

"You think this Apollo is off somewhere recharging his batteries?"

"That's not so far-fetched. He's disappeared again, hasn't he? Why shouldn't he be resting after the show he put on? Remember he's maintaining a force field on the ship while he drains off energy down here. Point? If we can overwork him, wear him out, that just might do it."

"The trouble with overworking him is that it could get us all killed."

"Not if we can provoke him into striking one of us

again. The energy drainage could make him vulnerable to being jumped by the rest of us.''

"I still think we might all get killed.''

"Bones, you're a pessimist. It's our only out. When he comes back, we'll try it. Cue Chekov in on the plan. Scotty's useless arm counts him out of any scramble. By the way, let's get him into the shade of the temple. It's hot in the sun.''

But Carolyn Palamas had already assisted Scott into the temple's coolness. She was easing him down on a bench. Kirk, following them, heard her say, "I am so sorry, Scotty.''

"I'm not blaming you,'' Scott said heavily, his eyes on her face. He shoved himself up with his right arm. "Carolyn, you must not let yourself fall in love with him!''

"Do you think I *want* to?''

Kirk had had enough. He interrupted them. "You are the one to answer that question, Lieutenant. What is it exactly you *do* want? If you've pulled yourself together, I'd be glad to hear.''

"Jim, he's recharged his batteries.''

McCoy's warning was very quiet. Kirk spun around.

Strong, glowing, glorious with health, Apollo was reclining against the side of his marble throne, chin on fist, the dark eyes on all of them, watchful.

"Come here,'' he said.

Kirk, McCoy and Chekov obeyed. "You are trying to escape me. It is useless. I know everything you mortals do.''

"You know nothing about us mortals,'' Kirk said. "The mortals you know were our remote ancestors. It was they who trembled before your tricks. They do not frighten us and neither do you.'' He spoke with deliberate insolence. "We've come a long way in five thousand years.''

"I could sweep you out of existence with a wave of my hand.'' The radiant smile flashed. "Then I could bring you back. I can give life and I can take it away. What else does mankind demand of its gods?''

"We find one sufficient,'' Kirk said.

Apollo sighed, bored. "No more debate, mortal. I offer you eternal joy according to the ancient way. I ask little in return. But what I ask for I shall have.''

He leaned forward. "Approach me.''

They didn't move. Instead, they turned their backs on him and strolled toward the temple entrance.

"I said *approach* me!"

"No." Kirk flung the word over his shoulder.

"You will gather laurel leaves! You will light the ancient fires! You will slay a deer—and make your sacrifice to me!"

Kirk roared with laughter. "Gather laurel leaves? Listen to him!"

"It's warm enough without lighting fires!" shouted McCoy.

Chekov chuckled. "Maybe we should dance around a Maypole."

Apollo rose. "You shall reap the reward of this arrogance."

"Spread out. Get ready," Kirk said quietly. Then he turned, shouting, "We are tired of you and your phony fireworks!"

"You have earned this—"

Apollo had lifted an arm when Carolyn's *"No!"* came in a scream. "No, please, *no*! A father does not destroy his children! You are gentle! You love them! How can they worship you if you hurt them? Mortals make mistakes. You know us!"

"Shsssh," Kirk hissed. She didn't so much as glance at him. She was on her knees now before the throne. "Please—you know so much of love. Don't hurt them!"

The raised arm lowered. Apollo stepped from the dais and bent to lift her in his arms. Then he placed her on his throne. His hand on her neck, he turned to face them.

"She is my love of ten thousand years," he said. "In her name I shall be lenient with you. Bring the rest of your people down to me. They will need homes. Tell your artisans to bring axes."

Kirk's voice was acid with disappointment. "And you'll supply the sheep we herd and the pipes we'll play."

Apollo took Carolyn in his arms. The sunny radiance gathered around them. They dissolved into it—and were gone.

"Captain, we must *do* something!"

Kirk strode over to Scott's bench. "We *were* doing something until that girl of yours interfered with it! All right, she stopped him this time! How long do you think her influence will last?" It was a question Carolyn was asking herself.

Gods were notoriously unfaithful lovers. Now the summer grass in the olive-groved glade was still green beneath her sandals. But autumn and winter? They would come in their seasons. Summer would pass . . . and when it went, she would know. Catastrophe—or glory. Now there was no knowing, no knowing of anything but the warmth of his arm around her shoulder.

"They are fools," he was saying. "They think they have progressed. They are wrong. They have forgotten all that gives life meaning—meaning to the life of gods or of mortals."

"They are my friends," she said.

"They will be with you," he said. "I will cause them to stay with you—with us. It is for you that I shall care for them. I shall cherish them and provide for them all the days that they live."

She was trembling uncontrollably. She wrung her hands to still their shaking. He took them in his.

"No dream of love you have ever dreamed is I," he said. "You have completed me. You and I—we are both immortal now."

His mouth was on hers. She swayed and his kiss grew deeper. Then her arms reached for his neck. "Yes, it is true," she whispered. "Yes, yes, yes . . ."

Kirk glanced at her sharply as she re-entered the temple.

"Lieutenant, where is he?"

She didn't answer; and Scott, raising his head painfully from his bench, saw her face. "What's happened to her? If he—"

She passed him to move on toward the throne. Her look was the absent look of a woman who has just discovered she is one. It was clear that the men of the *Enterprise* had ceased to exist for her.

"She can't talk," Scott said bewilderedly. "He's struck her dumb."

"Easy does it, Scotty," Kirk said. "She won't talk to you. You're too involved. But she'll talk to me."

"Want some assistance, Captain?" Chekov asked.

"How old are you, Ensign Chekov?"

"Twenty-two, sir."

"Then stay where you are," Kirk said. He walked over to the girl. "Are you all right, Lieutenant Palamas?"

She stepped down from the dais. "What?"

"I asked if you are all right."

"All right? Oh yes. I—am all right. I have a message for you."

"Sit down," Kirk said. "Here on this bench. Beside me—here."

She swallowed. "He—he wants us to live in eternal joy. He wants to guard . . . and provide for us for the rest of our lives. He can do it."

Kirk got up. "All right, Lieutenant, come back from where you are. You've got work to do."

"Work?"

"He thrives on love, on worship. They're his meat."

"He gives so much," she said. "He gives—"

"We can't give him worship. None of us, especially you."

"What?"

"Reject him. You must!"

"I love him," she said.

Kirk rubbed a hand up his cheek. "All our lives, here and on the ship, depend on you."

"No! Not on me. Please, not on me!"

"On you, Lieutenant. Accept him—and you condemn the crew of the *Enterprise* to slavery. Do you hear me? *Slavery!*"

The slate-gray eyes were uncomprehending. "He wants the best for us. And he is so alone, so . . . so gentle." Her voice broke. "What you want me to do would break his heart. How can I? How can I?" She burst into passionate weeping.

"Give me your hand, Lieutenant."

"What?"

He seized her hand. "Feel mine? Human flesh against human flesh. It is flesh born of the same time. The same century begot us, you and I. We are contemporaries, Lieutenant!"

All sympathy had left his voice. "You are to remember what you are! A bit of flesh and blood afloat in illimitable space.

The only thing that is truly yours is this small moment of time you share with a humanity that belongs to the present. That's where your duty lies. He is the past. His moment in time is not our moment. Do you understand me?''

The slate-gray eyes were anguished. But he sustained the iron in his face until she whispered, "Yes—I understand." She rose, left him, bent distractedly to pick up a tricorder; and half-turning, looked up at the temple's ceiling as though she was listening.

"He's—calling me," she faltered.

"I hear nothing," he said.

She didn't reply. The iron in his face was steel now. Desperate, he grabbed her shoulders. As he touched them, their bone, their flesh seemed to be losing solidity. She grew misty, fading. Kirk was alone with the echo of his own word "nothing".

Sinking down on the bench, he put his head in his hands. *Slavery.* It would claim all of them, McCoy, Scotty, Chekov. And up on the ship, they, too, would be enslaved to the whims of this god of the past. Sulu, Uhura, Spock . . .

"Spock here, Captain! *Enterprise* to Captain Kirk! *Enterprise* calling Captain Kirk! Come in, Captain!"

"I've gone mad, " Kirk said to his hands. His useless communicator beeped again. "Communication restored, Captain! Come in, Captain. First Officer Spock calling Captain Kirk . . ."

"Kirk here, Mr. Spock."

"Are you all right, sir?"

"All right, Mr. Spock."

"We have pinpointed a power source on the planet that may have some connection with the force field. Is there a structure of some sort near you?"

Kirk had a crazy impulse to laugh. "Indeed there is, Mr. Spock. I'm in it."

"The power definitely emanates from there."

"Good. How are you coming with the force field?"

"Nuclear electronics believes we can drive holes through it by synchronization with all phaser banks. We aim the phasers—and there'll be gaps in the field ahead of them."

Kirk drew a deep lungful of air. "That ought to do it, Mr. Spock. Have Sulu lock in every phaser bank we've got on this structure. Fire on my signal—but cut it fine. We'll need time to get out of here."

"I would recommend a discreet distance for all of you, Captain."

"Believe me, Mr. Spock, we'd like to oblige but we're not all together. One of us is hostage to the Greek god Apollo. This marble temple is his power source. I want to know where he is when we attack it. Kirk out."

"I seem to have lost touch with reality." McCoy was looking curiously at Kirk. "Or maybe you have. Was that Spock you were talking to on that broken communicator—or the spirit world?"

"Function has been restored to it. Don't ask me how. Ask Spock when you see him again. Now we have to get out of here. All phaser banks on the *Enterprise* are about to attack this place. I'll give you a hand with Scotty."

Scott said, "I won't leave, sir." Then his anxiety burst out of him. "Captain, we've got to wait till Carolyn comes back before you fire on the temple. We don't know what he'll do to her if he's suddenly attacked."

"I know," Kirk said. "We'll wait, Scotty."

As he arranged the paralyzed arm around his shoulder, he said, "That mysterious organ in the gorgeous chest, Bones—could it have anything to do with his energy transmissions?"

"I can't think of any other meaning it could have, Jim."

The gorgeous chest, its extra organ notwithstanding, had another meaning for Carolyn Palamas. Its existence had plunged her into the battle of her life. Walking beside her god in the olive-groved glade, her eyes were blank with the battle's torture. It centered itself on one thought alone. She must not let him touch her. If he touched her . . .

"You gave them my message," he said. "Were they persuaded?"

They'd said he was the source of the mysterious power. He was not. He was the source of mysterious rapture. People, millions of them, shared her moment of time. They crowded it with her. But not one of them could evoke the ecstasy this being of a different time could bring to birth in her just by the sound of his voice.

"*You* persuaded them," he said. "Who could deny you anything?"

His eyes were the night sky, starred. He caught her in his arms; and not for her soul's sake or humanity's either, could she deny him her mouth. She flung her arms around his neck, returned his kiss—and pushed him away.

"I must say that the way you ape human behavior is quite remarkable," she said. "Your evolutionary pattern must be—"

"My what?"

"I'm sure it's unique. I've never encountered any specimen like you before."

"Haven't you?" he said. Running laughter sparkled in the dark eyes as he reached for her again. She held herself rigid, tight, withdrawn. The sparkle flamed into anger. "I am Apollo! I have chosen you!"

"I have work to do."

"Work? *You?*"

"I am a scientist. My specialty is relics—outworn objects of the past." She managed a shaken laugh. "Now you know why I have been studying you." She unslung her tricorder, aiming it at him. "I'd appreciate your telling me how you stole that temple artifact from Greece."

He knocked the tricorder out of her hand. "You cannot talk like this! You love me! You think I do not know when love is returned to me?"

"You confuse me with a shepherd girl. I could no more love you than I could love a new species of bacteria." Lifting the hem of her golden robe, she left him to climb back up the gladed hill. Then he was beside her. Anguish struggled with fury in his face.

"Carolyn, what have you said to me? I forbid you to go! I command you to return to me!"

"I am dying," was what she thought. What she said was: "Is this rage the thunderbolt that dropped your frightened nymphs to their knees?"

An eternity passed. His hand fell from her shoulder. Then a wild cry broke from him. He raised an arm and shook a fist at the sky. The air in the glade went suddenly sultry, oppressive. The sun disappeared. A chill breeze fluttered her robe as she began to run up the glade's incline.

* * *

It did more than flutter Kirk's jacket. A fierce gust of wind blew it half off his shoulders. Under its increasing howl his communicator beeped feebly. "Spock, Captain. Sensors are reporting intense atmospheric disturbance in your area."

The sensors hadn't exaggerated. The clouds over Kirk's head darkened to a sickly, yellowish blackness that hid the glimmer of the temple's marble. It was cleaved by a three-pronged snake of lightning before it flooded in again. There followed a crack of thunder; and another lightning flash struck from the sky. Kirk heard the sound of splitting wood—and an olive tree not five feet away burst into flame. Grabbing his communicator, he shouted into it. "Stand by, phaser banks! Mr. Spock, prepare to fire at my signal!"

Scott rushed to him. "Captain, we've got to go and find her!"

"Here is where we stay, Mr. Scott. When he comes back—" The wind took the words from his mouth.

"What if he doesn't, sir?"

"We'll bring him back. When that temple is—"

There was no need to bring him back.

He was back. The God of Storms himself. He topped the olive trees. A Goliath of power, Apollo of Olympus had returned in his gigantic avatar. The great head was flung back in agony, the vast mouth open, both giant fists lifted, clenched against the sky. It obeyed him. It gave him livid lightning forks to hurl earthward and filled his mouth with rolling thunder. Leaves shriveled. The tree trunk beside Kirk began to smoke. Then it flared into fire—and the black sky gave its God of Storms the lash of rain.

Stumbling toward the temple, Carolyn Palamas screamed. The gale's winds tore at her drenched robe. She screamed again as the bush she clung to was whipped from the ground, its branches clawing at her face. Apollo had found her. He was all around her, the blaze of his eyes in the lightning's blaze, in the rain that streamed down her body, the wild cry of the wind in the ears he had kissed. The she saw him. The God of Storms stooped from his height above the trees to show her his maddened face. He brought it closer to her, closer until she shrieked, "Forgive me! Forgive me!—" and lay still.

"Captain, you heard her! She screamed!"

"*Now*, Mr. Spock," Kirk said into his communicator.

The incandescing phaser beams struck the temple squarely in its central roof.

"*No! No! No!*"

The god who had appeared before the temple dwarfed it. He had unclenched his fists to spread his hands wide on his up-flung arms. Bolts of blue-hot fire streamed from his fingers.

"Oh, stop it, stop it, *please*!"

Carolyn, running to Apollo, halted. Behind him the temple was wavering, going indistinct. It winked out—and was gone.

She fell to her knees before the man-size being who stood in its place.

He spoke brokenly. "I would have loved you as a father his children. Did I ask so much of you?"

The grief-ravaged face moved Kirk to a strange pity. "We have outgrown you," he said gently. "You asked for what we can no longer give."

Apollo looked down at the girl at his feet. "I showed you my heart. See what you've done to me."

She saw a slight wind stir his hair. She kissed his feet— but she knew. The flesh under her lips, his body was losing substance. Kirk made no move; but he had noted that the arms were spreading wide.

"Zeus, my father, you were right. Hera, you were wise. Our time is gone. Take me home to the stars on the wind . . ." The words seemed to come from a great distance.

It was very still in the empty space before the ruined temple.

"I—I wish we hadn't had to do that," McCoy said.

"So do I, Bones." Kirk's voice was somber. "Everything grew from the worship of those gods of Greece— philosophy, culture. Would it hurt us, I wonder, to gather a few laurel leaves?"

He shook his head, looking skyward.

There were only the sounds of a woman's sobbing and the drip of raindrops from olive trees.

McCoy, sauntering into the *Enterprise* bridge, strolled over to Kirk and Spock at the computer station.

"Yes, Bones? Somebody ill?"

"Carolyn Palamas rejected her breakfast this mornin."

"Some bug going around?"

"She's pregnant, Jim. I've just examined her."

"What?"

"You heard me."

"Apollo?"

"Yes."

"Bones, it's impossible!"

McCoy leaned an arm on the hood of the computer.

"Spock," he said, "may I put a question to this gadget of yours? I'd like to ask it if I'm to turn my Sickbay into a delivery room for a human child—or a god. My medical courses did not include obstetrics for infant gods."

AMOK TIME*

Writer: Theodore Sturgeon
Director: Joseph Pevney
Guest stars: Arlene Martel, Celia Lovsky

*Hugo Award nominee

It was actually Nurse Christine Chapel who first noticed that there seemed to be something wrong with Spock. Nothing serious—only that he wasn't eating. McCoy, observing him more closely, saw no further sign but what seemed to be a gradual increase in tension, something that might almost have been called "nervousness" if Spock hadn't been half Vulcan. This, McCoy thought, might have been purely a subjective impression on his own part.

It wasn't. On the third day of the apparent fast, Nurse Chapel tried to tempt the First Officer with a vile green concoction called plomik soup, regarded as a delicacy on Vulcan. Spock threw the bowl at her, soup and all.

This was enough to move McCoy to suggest to Spock, a day after the soup incident and apparently without any connection to it, that it was time for his routine checkup.

The logical, unemotional First Officer's verbatim reply to this was, "You will cease to pry into my personal affairs, Doctor, or I shall certainly break your neck."

Regardless of his state of mind—whatever it was—Spock certainly knew that this would not go unreported. He forestalled inquiry by requesting a leave of absence on his home planet. On the present course of the *Enterprise*, he pointed out, a diversion to Vulcan would cost a loss of only 2.8 light-days.

Unfortunately, Kirk had to refuse him. In all the years that Kirk had known him, Spock had never asked for a leave of any sort, and in fact had refused offers; he had leave enough accumulated for six men. But the *Enterprise* was bound for the inauguration ceremonies of the new president of Altair Six—not, apparently, a vital assignment, but the orders left no leeway for side trips, all the same. Kirk suggested that shore leave facilities on Altair Six were excellent; Spock declined the offer stiffly, and that was that.

At least, that should have been that. Not six hours later, while the First Officer was off duty, Kirk discovered that the ship's course had been altered for Vulcan anyhow, on Spock's orders. Leaving the bridge in Scott's charge, Kirk went directly down to Spock's quarters.

He had seldom visited them before, but he resisted the impulse to look around. He got only the vague impression of a room simple, sparse and vaguely Oriental in decoration and mood, the quarters of a warrior in the field. Spock was seated at a desk studying a small reading screen. Kirk had the briefest of impressions that the screen showed the head of a very young girl, no more than a child, but Spock snapped it off too quickly for him to be sure.

"Well, Mr. Spock?"

"Well, Captain?"

"I want an explanation. Why did you change our course?"

"Sir?"

"You changed our course for Vulcan. I want to know why."

Spock frowned slightly. "I changed our course?"

"You deny it?"

"No," Spock said. "By no means, Captain. It is—quite possible."

"Then why did you do it?"

"Captain," Spock said, "I accept, on your word, that I did it. But I do not know why. Nor do I remember doing it." He looked straight at Kirk, his spine stiffening. "And therefore I request that you put me in confinement—securely—where I can neither see nor be seen by anyone."

"But why?"

"Captain, lock me away. I do not wish to be seen. I cannot . . . No Vulcan could explain further."

"Spock, I'm trying to help you . . ."

"Ask me no further questions!" Spock almost shouted.
"I will not answer!"

"All right," Kirk said evenly. "I'll accede to your request. But first, I order you to report to Sickbay, Mr. Spock.
McCoy's waiting."

"I don't know how Spock exists with his kind of internal setup," McCoy said. "His normal pulse is in the 240
beats-per-minute range, his blood pressure almost nonexistent by our standards—not that I consider that green stuff of
his to be entirely comparable to blood. But that's only Spock
under normal conditions, Jim. As matters stand now, if we
don't get him to Vulcan within eight days—or maybe only
seven—he'll die."

"*Die?* But why? What's the matter with him?"

"I don't know," McCoy said. "All I can tell you is
that there's a growing imbalance of bodily functions. As if in
your or my bodies, huge amounts of adrenalin were constantly being secreted into our bloodstreams. Spock won't say
why. But unless it's stopped somehow, the physical and emotional pressures will kill him."

"You're convinced he knows what it is?"

"Yes. But he won't tell me."

"He's in the solitary confinement he asked for now?"

"Yes, Jim. And—I wouldn't approach him, if I were
you. It's a shocking thing to have to say, but—well, I consider
him irrational."

"I'll see him anyhow. What else can I do? There's *got*
to be an answer."

"I suppose so," McCoy said. "But Jim—watch out."

"Mr. Spock," Kirk said, as gently as possible. "Mc-
Coy gave me his evaluation of your condition."

Spock remained silent, his face averted.

"Spock, he says you'll die unless something is done.
What? Is it something only your planet can do for you?"

No answer.

"Mr. Spock. You have been called the best First Officer in the Fleet. That is an enormous asset to me. If I have
to lose that First Officer, I want to know why."

Spock stirred, and then began to speak in an almost

inaudible voice. "It is a thing that no . . . outworlder may know—except for the very few that have been involved. A Vulcan understands—but even we do not speak of it among ourselves. It is a deeply personal thing. Captain, cannot you let it rest at that?"

"I cannot," Kirk said. "My ship, my command, my duty are all at stake. I require you to explain. If I must, I'll order you to explain."

"Captain—some things transcend even the discipline of the service."

"That may sometimes be true. But nothing transcends the health, safety and well-being of the members of my crew. Would it help to promise you that I'd consider anything you say to me to be totally confidential?"

Spock hesitated a long moment. At last he said, "It has to do with—with . . ."

The last word was quite inaudible. Kirk said, "With what?"

"Biology."

"What kind of biology?"

"Vulcan biology."

"You mean, the biology *of* Vulcans? Biology, as in reproduction? Oh, blazes! That's nothing to be embarrassed about. It even happens to birds and bees."

Spock stared at the floor. "The birds and bees are not Vulcans. If they were—if any creature were as proudly logical as we—and had their logic ripped from them—as this time does to us . . ."

Kirk waited.

"How do Vulcans find their mates?" Spock said. "Haven't you wondered, Captain? How are we selected, one for the other? I'm sure you've heard many jokes on the subject. We are so aloof, so proud, so without feeling, that we invite such jokes."

"Yes, I've heard them," Kirk said. "But jokes aside, I guess the rest of us assume, well, that it's done, uh, quite logically. Eugenically, perhaps."

"It—is not. We shield it with ritual and custom, as shrouded in antiquity as our seven moons. You humans have no conception—it strips our minds from us. It brings a—a madness which rips away our veneer of civilization." Spock slumped, his face pinched with agony. "It is the *pon farr*—the time of mating."

"But you're not a salmon or an eel, man! You're . . ."

"Half human," Spock finished, painfully. "I had hoped that that would spare me this. But my Vulcan blood is too strong. It drives me home, to take a wife in Vulcan fashion. Or else, as Dr. McCoy says, to die."

"Dear God," Kirk said. The lumps in his own belly and throat were now almost too great for him to bear. He could only vaguely imagine what it had cost Spock to tell him this much.

Was there any way out? There were three starships expected to attend the inauguration ceremony: the *Enterprise*, the *Excalibur* and the *Endeavour*. Neither of the others was within range to get Spock to Vulcan in time.

It was not that vital to have three starships at the ceremony, but the orders specified it. If Kirk disobeyed, Starship Command would . . .

Never mind. Kirk owed his life to Spock, not just once, but half a dozen times. That was worth a career. Kirk stepped to the intercom.

"Mr. Chekov, Kirk here. Maintain course for Vulcan. Warp Eight."

"Uh—yes, sir," Chekov's startled voice said.

"Kirk out."

"Captain," Spock said in a low voice.

"Yes, Mr. Spock."

"Something happens to us at this time, almost—an insanity—an insanity you—no doubt would find distasteful."

"Should I? You've been patient with my kinds of madness."

"Then—will you beam down with me to the surface of Vulcan, and stand with me? There is a brief ceremony. By tradition, the male is attended by his closest friends."

"Thank you, Mr. Spock."

"Also—I believe Doctor McCoy has also guessed the reason behind all this, and has kept his own counsel, and my secret. I would like him to accompany us."

"I believe," Kirk said slowly, "that he will be honored."

* * *

The three beamed down to a fairly level arena area. Rocks around its edges gave it a half-natural, half-artificial aspect, as if the wind and rain had carved something like a Stonehenge, or reduced a Stonehenge to something like this. Inside it, there was an open temple—two high arches of stone, an open fire pit, several huge, jade-like wind chimes stirring and chiming in the hot breeze. The rest of the landscape was drifting sand, stretching away to a distant saw-toothed line of mountains jutting up at the edge of the far horizon.

"The land of my family," Spock said. "Our place for mating. It has been held by us for more than two thousand Earth years!" He choked, and gestured toward the temple. "This—is *Koon-ut-Kal-if-fee*. It means, 'The place of marriage and challenge.' In the distant past, we—killed to win our mates. It is still a time of dread for us. Perhaps, the price we pay—for no emotion the rest of the time."

"If it's any of my business—" McCoy began.

"You were invited, Doctor."

"Then—you said this T'Pring you are to meet was already your wife."

"By our parents' arrangement. A ceremony, while we were but seven years of age. One touches the other—thus— as you have seen me do to feel another's thoughts. In this way, our minds were locked together—so that at the proper time we would both be drawn to *Koon-ut-Kal-if-fee*."

There sounded a distant bell, harmonizing well with the heavier notes of the wind chimes, and then figures began to appear among the rocks. There seemed to be eight or ten of them. Heading the procession, four Vulcan men were carrying someone in an ornate litter or sedan chair. Two other members of the party carried bright-colored, ceremonial objects which consisted of dozens of tiny bells attached to an ornate frame on a pole.

As they drew closer, Kirk saw that the person inside the litter was an old woman of immensely authoritative bearing; as the litter was set down and she emerged from it, he recognized her with a shock as one of the high Vulcan elders, T'Pau, the only person who had ever turned down a seat on the Federation Council. Characteristically, Spock had never mentioned that his family was this important.

The bride walked beside her, no child now, but a lithe,

graceful, beautiful woman, even by Earth standards. Behind
her strode a tall, muscular and rather handsome Vulcan male;
and behind him, a slightly shorter but even stronger-looking
man who carried a Vulcan war ax. The rest of the procession
moved in stately grace behind these principals.

Spock turned and walked to one of the huge wind
chimes. Picking up a stone mallet, he struck the chimes,
producing a somber male sound which was answered by the
shaking of the bell banners. T'Pring seated herself on a carved
rock at the temple archway. T'Pau stood in the open in front
of the temple, with her back to it and the girl. The muscular
young Vulcan stood next to the arch, like a big brick gate-
post, while the rest of the entourage lined up in a curve behind them.

With a sudden swift movement, T'Pau raised both her
arms. Spock stepped forward and bowed before her. She laid
both her hands on his shoulders, as if in a blessing, and then
looked beyond him to Kirk and McCoy.

"Spock. Are our ceremonies for outworlders?"

"They are not outworlders," Spock said. "They are
my friends. I am permitted this. Their names are Kirk and
McCoy. I pledge their behavior with my life."

"Very well." T'Pau turned to the bearers of the bell
banners. *"Kah-if-fee!"*

The bell banners were shaken. Spock turned to strike
the wind chimes again with his stone mallet—but at the same
instant the girl T'Pring sprang to her feet and cried out:

"Kah-if-FARR!"

There was a gasp from the Vulcan onlookers; even
T'Pau's eyes flickered in startled surprise. Spock mouthed the
word without speaking it, his breathing quickening, his eyes
narrowed to slits. T'Pring crossed to him, took the mallet
from his hand, and tossed it aside. Her expression was
strangely contemptuous.

The Vulcan with the ax stepped forward. He looked
both amused and dangerous, like an experienced executioner.

"Hey, what's this?" McCoy said. "If there's going to
be hanky-panky . . ."

"All is in order," the old woman said. "She chooses
the challenge."

"What?" McCoy pointed at the executioner. "With *him*?"

"No. He acts only if cowardice is seen. T'Pring will now choose her champion. T'Pring: you have chosen. Are you prepared to become the property of the victor? Not merely his wife, but his chattel, with no other rights or status?"

"I am prepared," T'Pring said.

"Then choose."

T'Pring moved regally out into the arena. She stopped by the huge young Vulcan, who straightened proudly, expectantly, but she moved away from him. Then she turned to T'Pau.

"As it was in the dawn of our days," she said, "as it is today, as it will be through all tomorrows, I make my choice." She turned again. "I choose this man."

And she pointed straight at Kirk.

"Now wait a minute—" Kirk said.

At the same moment, the big young Vulcan stepped forward, obviously outraged. "No!" he cried. "I am to be the one! It was agreed! The honor is mine!"

All at once, everyone in the marriage party seemed to be arguing, all in Vulcan. Under cover of the noise, Kirk said swiftly to McCoy, "What happens if I decline?"

"I don't know, Jim. He'd probably have to fight the young man. And in his present condition, he couldn't win. But Jim, this looks like a situation of total combat—and the heat and the air here are pretty fierce. I'm not sure you could win either—even if you'd want to."

"I'm not about to take a dead First Officer back with me. On the other hand, there's T'Pau over there—all of Vulcan wrapped up in one package. How will it look if a Starship Captain backs off from this, afraid?"

"But . . ."

"And if I can't beat him, if I'm in any danger, I'll give up. Spock wins, honor is satisfied. Or maybe just knock him out . . ."

"*Kroykah!*" T'Pau said explosively. The hubbub stopped as if turned off by a switch.

The big young Vulcan said, "I ask forgiveness." He went back to his post by the arch, sulky, unrepentant, but no longer defiant.

Kirk said, "I accept." He threw a look toward his First Officer, but Spock seemed oblivious of everything but the ceremony.

"According to our laws," T'Pau said, "combat begins with the *lirpa*."

Two Vulcan males stepped forward, each carrying a vicious-looking weapon. At one end of a heavy handle was a circular, razor-edged knife; at the other end, a metal cudgel.

"If both survive the *lirpa*," T'Pau continued, "then combat continues with *ahn woon*, until death. *Klee-et!*"

At this command, Spock wheeled to face Kirk. His eyes blazed with blind savagery as he lifted the weapon. McCoy stepped forward.

"Nothing doing!" McCoy said. "No one mentioned a fight to the death—" his words trailed off as the executioner-like Vulcan stepped in, lifting his ax. Then he swallowed and charged on. "T'Pau, these men are friends. To force them to fight until one is killed . . ."

"Challenge was lawfully given and accepted. Neither party was forced. However, Spock may release the challenger. Spock! How do you choose?"

Spock continued to eye Kirk, scowling. There was still no sign of recognition. Then, suddenly, he shouted his answer, hoarsely, scornfully: *"Klee-fah!"*

"That's it, Bones," Kirk, said. "Get out of the combat area. There's nothing you can do."

McCoy stood fast. "I claim one right for him then. Your temperature is hot for our kind, your air is thin . . ."

He was interrupted by a feint from Spock. Kirk dodged, but Spock, slashing again with the blade, abruptly reversed the weapon and caught Kirk a glancing blow with the cudgel end. Kirk went down, rolling barely in time as Spock reversed again and slashed down hard. The weapon bit into the earth.

Kirk kicked hard at Spock's legs. Now the Vulcan was down, and Kirk was rolling to his feet. He was already sweating, and his breath was whistling in his throat. Out of the corner of his eye, he saw the burly axman advancing on McCoy.

"I can't watch you both, Bones!" he shouted. "Get out before you kill me!"

McCoy held his ground. Turning back toward T'Pau, he produced a hypo from his medical kit. "Are Vulcans afraid of fair combat?" he demanded.

"What is this?"

"A high-G vitalizer shot. To compensate for temperature and atmosphere."

"*Kroykah!*" T'Pau said. Everyone froze. "Very well. Your request is reasonable."

McCoy pressed the hypo against Kirk's arm. It hissed, and the physician turned away.

Spock moved in at once. This time it was Kirk who feinted. Spock countered as if they were marionettes tied to the same string. Kirk tried again, with the same result.

With a wordless rumble, Spock launched a lightning kick at Kirk's left hand. Kirk bent aside, and catching the heel of Spock's boot, dumped him. He dived after him, but Spock rolled with unbelievable quickness, so that Kirk hit only the bare ground.

Then both were up, crouching. Spock raised his weapon as if to throw it, and Kirk tensed, ready to jump aside. Spock, however, suddenly reversed the weapon and rushed.

They came together like the impact of two machines, belly to belly, free hand holding weapon wrist, glaring into each other's eyes. Then, with a bone-cracking wrench, Spock whipped Kirk's weapon to the ground.

With two quick, stamping steps, like a flamenco dancer, Spock snapped the knife blade with a loud crack, and then kicked the cudgel end away. He raised his own blade to striking position.

"Spock!" McCoy cried out. "No!"

They were still at close quarters. Kirk hit Spock's wrist with a karate chop. Now it was Spock's *lirpa* that went flying out of reach.

"*Kroykah!*" T'Pau cried.

Again, Spock froze. The Vulcan weapons attendant came hurrying out, carrying what seemed to be no more than two leather bands about three feet long and four inches wide. One was handed to Spock, who backed up, waiting; Kirk got the other.

"A strip of leather?" Kirk said. "Is that all?"

"The *ahn woon*," T'Pau said. "Oldest and deadliest of Vulcan weapons."

Kirk inspected it with puzzlement. How on earth was one supposed to use this thing? It wasn't long enough to be an effective whip, and . . .

Spock did not hesitate. Scooping up a jagged rock, in the same movement he converted the leather strap into a sling. Kirk understood too late. The rock caught him hard in the ribs, and he fell.

As he staggered to his feet, Spock charged him, now holding one end of the strap in each hand. Whipping it around Kirk's legs, he yanked, and down Kirk went again.

Instantly, Spock was at his back, garroting him with the strap. Kirk shifted to try to throw the First Officer over his shoulder, but something odd seemed to be happening to his muscles; they responded very slowly, and didn't move in the way his brain told them to go.

The pressure around his neck tightened. He made one last grab for Spock's hands, but never even came close. The universe darkened. Blood roared in his ears. He felt himself fall flat, blind and paralyzed.

"*Kroykah!*" came T'Pau's voice, as if from a great distance.

There was a sound of running footsteps, coming closer. Then came McCoy's voice, charged with bitterness:

"Get your hands off him, Spock. It's finished—he's dead."

It was all most peculiar. Kirk could see nothing, feel nothing, was not even sure he was breathing. He was aware of nothing but the voices, as though he were listening to an exchange over the intercom—or attending a play with his back turned to the stage.

T'PAU: I grieve with you, Doctor.

SPOCK: No! I—no, no . . .

McCOY: McCoy to *Enterprise*.

UHURA: *Enterprise*. Lieutenant Uhura here.

McCOY: Have Transporter Room stand by for landing party to beam up. Strange as it may seem, Mr. Spock, you're in command now. Any orders?

SPOCK: I'll—I'll follow you in a few minutes. Instruct

Mr. Chekov to plot a course for the nearest base where I must—surrender myself to the authorities . . . T'Pring.

T'PRING: Yes.

SPOCK: Explain.

T'PRING: Specify.

SPOCK: Why the challenge; why you chose my Captain as your champion.

T'PRING: Stonn wanted me. I wanted him.

SPOCK: I see no logic in preferring Stonn over me.

T'PRING: He is simple and easily controlled. I calculated the possibilities were these: if your Captain were victor, he would not want me, and so I would have Stonn. If you were victor, you would free me because I dared to challenge, and again I would have Stonn. But if you did not free me it would be the same, for you would be gone again, and I would have your name and your property, and Stonn would still be there.

SPOCK: Flawlessly logical.

T'PRING: I am honored.

SPOCK: Stonn! She is yours. After a time, you may find that *having* is not, after all, so satisfying a thing as *wanting*. It is not logical, but it is often true . . . Spock here. Ready to beam up . . . Live long and prosper, T'Pau.

T'PAU: Live long and prosper, Spock.

SPOCK: I shall do neither. I have killed my Captain—and my friend.

Then Kirk's hearing went away too, and for a long time thereafter he knew nothing.

He came gradually back to consciousness in the Sickbay. McCoy was bending over him. Nearby was Spock, his hands over his face. His shoulders were shaking.

Nurse Christine came into his field of view, and turning Spock toward the Captain, gently pulled his hands away from his face. Kirk smiled weakly, and spoke in a faint but cheerful voice.

"Mr. Spock—I never thought I'd see the day . . ."

"Captain!" Spock stared down at him, absolutely dazed with astonishment. Then, obviously realizing what his face and voice were revealing, he looked away.

"Christine," McCoy said, "it might be a good idea for Mr. Spock to get some hot food in him. Why don't you

feed him some of that awful plomik soup. Then bring him
back here for me to run a physical on him. Go on, Spock.
She'll explain it to you.''

Christine led the First Officer toward the door. But just
before he left, Spock said, ''It is not awful plomik soup. It
is very good plomik soup.''

The he was gone. Kirk and McCoy smiled after him.
Then Kirk rolled his head back and wiped the smile off his
face.

''You, Mister,'' he said, ''are a quack.''

McCoy shrugged. ''I made a mistake. Shot you with
ronoxiline D by mistake. Nobody lied. You were dead—by
all normal standards. I had to get you back up here fast, or
you would have been dead by *any* standards.''

''Will Spock be all right?''

''I think so. I'll run a full physical on him to make
sure.''

Kirk started to sit up. ''Where are we now?''

''Stay right there,'' McCoy said, shoving him back.
''We're still orbiting Vulcan.''

Kirk reached out and snapped on the bedside intercom.
''Kirk to Bridge.''

''Bridge, sir. Sulu here.''

''Take us out of orbit, Mr. Sulu. Have the navigator
lay in a course for Altair Six at top warp speed. Tell Scotty
to pour it on—we've got an inauguration to make!''

''Yes *sir*. Bridge out.''

As Kirk dropped back onto the bed, McCoy said sourly,
''You know, Jim, some one of these days these ceremonies
will be the death of you.''

''In which case, Bones, remember: you have standing
orders to bring me back to life.''

THE DOOMSDAY MACHINE*

Writer: Norman Spinrad
Director: Marc Daniels
Guest star: William Windom

*Hugo Award nominee

Shock after shock. First, the distress call from the *Constellation*, a starship of the same class as the *Enterprise*, and commanded by Brand Decker, one of Kirk's oldest classmates; a call badly garbled, and cut off in the middle.

The call seemed to have come from the vicinity of M-370, a modest young star with a system of seven planets. But when the *Enterprise* arrived in the system, the *Constellation* was not there—and neither was the system.

The star had not gone nova; it was as placid as it had always been. But of the planets there was nothing left but asteroids, rubble and dust.

Lt. Uhura tried to project the line of the distress call. The line led through four more former solar systems—*all* now nothing but asteroids, rubble and dust . . . No, not quite: The two inner planets of the fifth system appeared to be still intact—and from somewhere near where the third planet should have been, they heard once more the weak beacon of the *Constellation*, no longer signaling distress, but black disaster.

The beacon was automatic; no voice came from her despite repeated calls. And when they found her, the viewscreen showed that two large, neat holes, neat as phaser cuts, had been drilled through her warp-drive pods.

Kirk called a yellow alert at once, though there was no sign of a third ship in the area, except for some radio interference which might easily be sunspots. Scott reported that all main and auxiliary power plants aboard the *Constellation* were dead, but that the batteries were operative at a low level. Her life support systems were operative, too, also at a very low level, except for the bridge area, which—as the viewscreen showed—was badly damaged and uninhabitable.

"We'll board," Kirk said. "The *Constellation* packed as much firepower as we do; I want to know what could cut a starship up like that. And there may be a few survivors. Bones, grab your kit. Scotty, select a damage control party and come with us. Mr. Spock, you'll stay here and maintain Yellow Alert."

"Acknowledge," Spock said.

Aboard the *Constellation*, the lights were weak and flickering, and wreckage littered the deck. The three crewmen of the damage control party found the radiation level normal, the air pressure eleven pounds per square inch, the communications system shorted out, the filtration system dead. The warp drive was a hopeless pile of junk. Surprisingly, the reactor was intact—it had simply been shut down—and the impulse drive was in fair shape.

But there were no survivors—and no bodies.

Kirk thought this over a moment, then called the *Enterprise*. "Mr. Spock, this ship appears abandoned. Could the crew have beamed down to one of those two planets?"

"Improbable, Captain," Spock's voice replied. "The surface temperature on the inner planet is roughly that of molten lead, and the other has a poisonous, dense atmosphere resembling that of Venus."

"All right, we'll keep looking. Kirk out."

"The phaser banks are almost exhausted," Scott reported. "They didn't give her up without a battle."

"But *where are they?* I can't understand a man like Brand Decker abandoning his ship as long as his life support systems were operative."

"The computer system is still intact. If the screen on the engineers' bridge is still alive, we might get a playback of the Captain's log."

"Good idea. Let's go."

The screen on the engineers' bridge was in fact dead, but they forgot this almost the moment they noticed it; for seated before the console, staring at the useless instruments, was Commodore Brand Decker. His uniform was tattered, his hair mussed.

"Commodore Decker!"

Decker looked up blankly. He seemed to have trouble focusing on Kirk. McCoy was quickly beside him.

"Commodore—what happened to your ship?"

"Ship?" Decker said. "Attacked . . . that thing . . . fourth planet breaking up . . ."

"Jim, he's in a state of shock," McCoy said. "No pressure on him now, please."

"Very well. Do what you can for him here. We've got to question him."

"He mentioned the fourth planet," Scott said. "There are only two left now."

"Yes. Pull the last microtapes from the sensor memory bank and beam them across to Spock. I want a full analysis of all reports of what happened when they went in on that planet."

"I've given this man a tranquilizer," McCoy said. "You can try a few questions now. But take it easy."

Kirk nodded. "Commodore, I'm Jim Kirk, in command of the *Enterprise*. Do you understand?"

"Enterprise?" Decker said. "We couldn't contact—couldn't run—had to do it—no choice at all . . ."

"No choice about what?"

"I had to beam them down. The only chance they had . . ."

"Do you mean your crew?"

Decker nodded. "I was—last aboard. It attacked again—knocked out the transporter. I was stranded aboard."

"But *where* was the crew?"

"The third planet."

"There is no third planet now."

"There *was*," Decker said. "There *was*. That thing . . . destroyed it . . . I heard them . . . four hundred of my men . . . calling for help . . . begging for help . . . and I couldn't . . ." The Commodore's voice went slower and slower, as though he were an ancient clockwork mechanism running down, and faded out entirely.

"Fantastic," Scott said, almost to himself. "What kind of a weapon could do that?"

"If you had seen it—you'd know," Decker said, rousing himself with obvious effort. "The whole thing is a weapon. It must be."

Kirk said, "What does it look like, Commodore?"

"A hundred times the size of a starship—a mile long, with a maw big enough to swallow a dozen ships. It destroys planets—cuts them to rubble."

"Why? Is it an alien ship—or is it alive?"

"Both—neither—I don't know."

"Where is this thing now?"

"I—don't know that either."

Kirk lifted his communicator. "Mr. Spock, still no sign of any other vessel in the vicinity?"

"Well, yes and no, Captain," the First Officer replied. "The subspace radio interference is now so heavy as to cut us off from Starfleet Command; obviously it cannot be sunspots. But our sensors still show only the *Constellation*."

"How is the tape analysis going?"

"We're ready now, Captain. We find that the *Constellation* was attacked by what seems to be essentially a robot— an automated weapon of great size and power. Its apparent function is to smash planets to rubble, and then 'digest' the debris for fuel. It is, therefore, self-maintaining as long as there are planetary bodies to feed it."

"Origin?"

"Mr. Sulu has computed the path of the machine, using the destroyed solar systems detected by ourselves and the *Constellation* as a base course. We find the path leads out of the galaxy at a sharp angle. Projected in the opposite direction, and assuming that the machine does not alter its course, it will go through the most densely populated section of our galaxy."

"Thank you, Mr. Spock. Maintain Yellow Alert and stand by. Commodore Decker, you've had a rough time. I think it would be best if you and Dr. McCoy beam back to my ship for a physical examination."

"Very well," Decker said. "But you heard your First Officer, Captain. That thing is heading for the heart of our galaxy—thousands of populated planets! *What are you going to do?*"

"I'm going to think," Kirk said. "Mr. Spock, have the

Transporter Room beam Dr. McCoy and Commodore Decker aboard immediately.''

A moment later, the two men shimmered out of existence, leaving no one but Kirk and Scott on the dead engineers' bridge.

"They're aboard, Captain," Spock's voice said from the communicator. And then, without any transition at all, "Red alert! Red Alert! Mr. Sulu, out of the plane of the ecliptic at sixty degrees north! Warp One!"

"Mr. Spock!" Kirk shouted, although of course Spock could have heard him equally well if he had whispered. "Why the alert? Why are you running? I'm blind here."

"Commodore Decker's planet-killer, Captain. It just popped out of subspace. Metallic body, a large funnelmouth, at least a mile long. It is pursuing us, but we seem to be able to maintain our distance at Warp One. No, it's gaining on us. Sensors indicate some kind of total conversion drive. No evidence of life aboard. Which is not surprising, since isotope dating indicates that it is at least three billion years old."

"Three *billion*!" Kirk said. "Mr. Spock, since it's a robot, what are our chances of deactivating it?"

"I would say none, Captain. I doubt that we would be able to maneuver close enough without drawing a direct attack upon ourselves. We could of course beam men aboard in spacesuits, but since the thing is obviously designed to be a doomsday machine, its control mechanisms would be inaccessible on principle.''

"A doomsday machine, sir?" Scott said.

"A calculated bluff, Scotty. A weapon so powerful that it will destroy both sides in a war if it's used. Evidently some race in another galaxy built one—this one—and its bluff was called. The machine is now all that's left of the race—and it's evidently programmed to keep on destroying planets as long as it's functioning.''

"Well, whatever happens, we can't let it go beyond us to the next solar system. We have to stop it here. You'd better . . .''

He was interrupted by the filtered sound of a concussion.

"Mr. Spock!" a distant voice called. It sounded like Uhura. "We've taken a hit! The transporter's out!"

"Emergency power on screens. Maximum evasive action! Phaser banks . . ."

And then the communicator went dead.

"Spock! Come in! Spock!" It was useless. "Scotty—we're stuck here. Deaf and blind."

"Worse than that, Captain. We're paralyzed, too. The warp drive is just so much wreckage."

"We can't just sit here while that thing attacks our ship. Forget the warp drive and get me some impulse power—half-power, quarter-power, anything I can maneuver with, even if you have to get out and push."

"But we'd never be able to outrun . . ."

"We're going to fight the thing, not outrun it," Kirk said grimly. "If we can get this hulk going, we may be able to distract the robot, and give the *Enterprise* a better chance to strike at it. Get cracking, Scotty. I'm going to see what I can do with this viewscreen. We can't move until I can see where we're going."

Seated in the Captain's chair, Spock evaluated the damage. Warp and impulse drives were still operative. As he checked, Commodore Decker and McCoy watched him tensely.

"Communications?"

"Under repair, Mr. Spock," Uhura said.

"Transporter?"

Sulu said, "Also under repair."

"Hmm," Spock said. "Random factors seem to have operated in our favor."

"In plain, non-Vulcan English," McCoy said, "we've been lucky."

"Isn't that what I said, Doctor?" Spock said blandly.

"The machine's veering off," Sulu reported. "It's back on its old course. Next in line is the Rigel system."

"No doubt programmed to ignore anything as small as a ship beyond a certain radius," Spock said. "Mr. Sulu, circle back so we can pick up the Captain while we effect repairs. We may have to take the *Constellation* in tow . . ."

"You can't let that thing reach Rigel!" Decker broke in. "Millions of innocent people . . ."

"I am aware of the population of the Rigel colonies,

Commodore, but we are only one ship. Our deflector generators are strained. Our radio is useless as long as we are in the vicinity of the robot. Logic dictates that our primary duty is to survive to warn Starfleet Command.''

"Our primary duty is to maintain the life and safety of Federation planets! Helmsman, belay that last order! Track and close on that machine!"

Sulu looked questioningly at Spock. It was a difficult problem. Kirk had left Spock in command, but Decker was the senior officer aboard. Spock said evenly, "Carry out my last order, Mr. Sulu."

"Mr. Spock," Decker said, "I'm formally notifying you that I am exercising my option under regulations as senior officer to assume command of the *Enterprise*. That thing has got to be destroyed."

"You attempted to destroy it before, sir," Spock said, "and it resulted in a wrecked ship and a dead crew. Clearly a single ship cannot combat that machine."

Decker winced, then stabbed a finger at Spock. "That will be all, Mr. Spock. You're relieved of command. Don't force me to relieve you of duty as well."

Spock got up. McCoy grabbed his arm. "Spock, you can't let him do this!"

"Unfortunately," Spock said, "Starfleet Order one-zero-four, Section B, reads, Paragraph A, 'In the absence of the . . .' ''

"To blazes with regulations! How can you let him take command when you *know* he's wrong?"

"If you can officially certify Commodore Decker medically or psychologically unfit to command, I may relieve him under Section C."

"I can't do that," McCoy said. "He's as sound as any of us. I can say his present plan is crazy, but medically I'd have to classify that as a difference of opinion, not a diagnosis."

"Mr. Spock knows his duties under the regulation," Decker said. "Do you, Doctor?"

"Yes, sir," McCoy said disgustedly. "To go to Sickbay and wait for the casualties you're about to send me." He stalked out.

"Hard about and close," Decker said. "Full emergency power on deflectors. Stand by on main phaser banks."

On the viewscreen, the planet-killer began to grow in size. Decker stared at it with grim intensity, as though the combat to come was to be a personal one, hand-to-hand.

"In range, sir," Sulu reported.

"Fire phasers!"

The beams lanced out. It was a direct hit—but there seemed to be no effect at all. The beams simply bounced off.

In answer, a pencil of solid blue light leapt out of the maw of the planet-killer. The *Enterprise* seemed to stagger, and for a moment all the lights went down.

"Whew!" Sulu said. "What *is* that thing?"

"It's an anti-proton beam," Decker said in an abstracted voice. "It's what the machine cut the fourth planet up with."

"The deflectors weren't built to take it, sir," Spock said. "The next time, the generators may blow."

Decker paid no attention. "Keep closing and maintain phaser fire."

Spock studied his instruments. "Sir," he said, "sensors indicate that the robot's hull is neutronium—collapsed matter so dense that a cubic inch of it would weigh a ton. We could no more get a phaser beam through it than we could a matchstick. If we could somehow get a clear shot at the internal mechanism . . ."

"Now that's more like it, Mr. Spock. We'll cut right across the thing's funnel and ram a phaser beam down its throat. Helmsman, change course to intercept."

Sulu shifted the controls cautiously, obviously expecting another blow from the anti-proton beam; but evidently the monstrous mechanism had no objection to having this morsel sailing directly into its maw.

"Fire!"

The phasers cut loose. Sulu studied the screen intently.

"Those beams are just bouncing around inside," he reported. "We can't get a shot straight through."

"Close in."

"Sir," Spock said, "any closer and that anti-proton beam will go through our deflectors like tissue paper."

"We'll take the chance. Thousands of planets are at stake."

"Sir, there is no chance at all. It is pure suicide. And attempted suicide would be proof that you are psychologically unfit to command. Unless you give the order to veer off, I will relieve you on that basis."

"Vulcan logic!" Decker said in disgust. "Blackmail would be a more honest word. All right, helmsman, veer off—emergency impulse power."

"Commodore," Sulu said in a strained voice, "I can't veer off. That thing's got some kind of a tractor beam on us."

"Can it pull us in?"

"No, sir, we can manage a stand-off, for perhaps seven hours. In the meantime it can take pot shots at us whenever it likes."

On the engineers' bridge of the *Constellation*, the viewscreen finally lit. Kirk stared at what it showed with shock and disbelief. A gasp from behind him told him that Scott had just entered the bridge.

"Is Spock out of his mind?"

"I don't understand it either—I ordered evasive action. What's the situation below?"

"We've got the screens up, but they won't last more than a few hours, and they can't take a beating. As for the impulse drive, the best I can give you is one-third power. And at that I'll have to nurse it."

"Go ahead then. We've got to break up that death-dance out there somehow." As Scott left, Kirk once more tried his communicator. To his gratification, he got Lt. Uhura at once; evidently the *Enterprise*, too, had been making repairs. "Lieutenant, give me Mr. Spock, fast."

But the next voice said: "*Enterprise* to Kirk. Commodore Decker here."

"Decker? What's going on? Give me Mr. Spock!"

"I'm in command here, Captain. According to regulations, I assumed command on finding Mr. Spock reluctant to take proper action . . ."

"You mean you're the lunatic responsible for almost destroying my ship? Mr. Spock, if you can hear me, I give you a direct order to answer me."

"Spock here, Captain."

"Good. On my personal authority as Captain of the *Enterprise*, I order you to relieve Commodore Decker. Commodore, you may file a formal protest of the violation of regulations involved with Starfleet Command—if any of us live to reach a star base. In the meantime, Mr. Spock, if the Commodore resists being relieved, place him under arrest. Is that clear?"

"Not only is it clear," Spock's voice said, "but I have just done so. Your further orders, sir?"

"Get away from that machine!"

"Sir, we can't; we have been pegged by a tractor. The best we can do is prevent ourselves from being pulled inside it, for about the next six point five hours—or until it decides to shoot at us again."

"I was afraid of that. All right, I'm going to move the *Constellation* into your vicinity and see if I can distract the machine. With the power I've got available, it will take at least three hours. Is your transporter working again, too?"

"Yes, sir, but I assure you that you'd be no safer here than there."

"I'm aware of that, Mr. Spock. I just want to be sure you can beam me aboard once we're in range, so I can take command personally from the Commodore if he gives you any trouble. That's all for now. Kirk out."

Kirk set the *Constellation* in creaking motion and then thought a while. Finally he called Scott.

"How's the drive holding up, Scotty?"

"Under protest, I would say, sir," Scott responded. "But if you don't demand any violent maneuvers I think it'll stay in one piece."

"Very well. Now I need an engineering assessment. What would happen if the reactor were to go critical?"

"Why, Captain, you know as well as I do—a fusion explosion, of course."

"Yes, Scotty, but if *this* reactor were to do so, how big would the explosion be?"

"Oh," Scott's voice said. "That's easily answered, the potential is always on the faceplate of a ship's reactor; I'll just check it . . . The figure is 97.8 megatons."

"Would the resulting fireball be sufficient to disrupt a neutronium hull?"

"Neutronium, sir? You mean the planet-killer? What makes you think the hull is neutronium?"

"Because from this distance the *Enterprise* could have cut it into scrap metal by now if it weren't."

"Hmm—aye, that follows. Well, Captain, neutronium is formed in the cores of white dwarf stars, with fusion going on all around it. So I'd say the fireball would just push the machine away, rather than collapsing the hull. And sir, in a vacuum the fireball would be something like a hundred and fifty miles in diameter. That means it would envelop the *Enterprise* too—and *we* don't have a neutronium hull."

"That's true, but it isn't what I have in mind. Scotty, I want you to rig a thirty-second delayed detonation switch, so the reactor can be blown from up here on the engineers' bridge. Can do?"

"Aye, sir," Scott said. "But why . . ."

"Just rig it, fast. Then get yourself and the damage control party up here. Kirk to *Enterprise*."

"Spock here."

"Mr. Spock, I don't have any sensors over here worth mentioning, so I won't know when I'm in transporter range. The instant I am, let me know."

"Acknowledge. May I ask your intent, Captain?"

"Scotty is rigging a thirty-second delayed detonation switch on the impulse power reactor of the *Constellation*. I am going to pilot the vessel right down the planet-killer's throat—and you'll have thirty seconds to beam the five of us aboard the *Enterprise* before the reactor blows."

There was a brief pause. When Spock's voice returned, there actually seemed to be a faint trace of human concern in it. "Jim, thirty seconds is very fine timing. The transporter is not working at a hundred per cent efficiency; our repairs were necessarily rather hasty."

"That's a chance I'll have to take. However, it does change things a little. I'll want you to beam Mr. Scott and the damage control party over as soon as we are in range. I'll be the only one to stay aboard until the last minute."

"Acknowledge. Sir, may I point out two possible other flaws?"

While Spock was talking, Scott came into the room carrying a small black box. Mounted on it was a single three-position knife switch—that is, one with two slots for the blade, the third position being disengaged from either. He set it down on the panel in front of Kirk.

"Go ahead, Mr. Spock, your advice is half your value. Where are the flaws?"

"First, we cannot know the composition of the interior workings of the planet-killer. If they too are neutronium, nothing will happen except that it will get very hot inside there."

" 'Very hot' is certainly a mild way of putting it," Kirk said drily. "All right, Mr. Spock, to use logic right back at you, Proposition A: The planet-killer operates in a vacuum, which means most of its circuits are cryogenic. Heating them a few million degrees may be quite enough to knock it out. Proposition B: Pure neutronium cannot carry an electrical current, because its electron shells are collapsed. Hence, many important parts of the planet-killer's interior cannot be neutronium. Conclusion: an interior fusion explosion will kill it. How is that for a syllogism?"

"It is not a syllogism at all, Captain, but a sorites; however, I agree that it is a sound one. My second objection is more serious. The planet-killer is open to space at one end, and that is the end facing us. The neutronium hull will confine the fireball and shoot it directly out of the funnel at the *Enterprise* in a tongue of flame hundreds of miles long. This is an undesirable outcome."

Kirk almost laughed, although there was nothing in the least funny about the objection itself. "Mr. Spock, if that happens, we will all die. But the planet-killer will have been destroyed. Our mandate is to protect Federation lives, property and interests. Hence this outcome, as you call it, is in fact more desirable than undesirable."

"Now that," Spock said, "*is* a syllogism, and a sound one. Very well, Captain, I withdraw my objections."

When Kirk put down the communicator, he found Scott staring at him ruefully. "Your sense of humor," the engineer said ruefully, "comes out at the oddest times. Well, there is your detonator, Captain. When you pull the switch into the *up* position, it's armed. When you push it down into the other slot, you have thirty seconds until *blooey*!''

"Simple enough.''

"Captain," Spock's voice came again. "The *Constellation* has just come within transporter range. However, when you are ready to have your party beam over, I suggest that you leave the bridge. We do not have fine enough control to pick four men out of five, and even if we did, we would not know which four of the five until it was too late.''

"Very well, Mr. Spock. I will leave the bridge; make your pickup in sixty seconds.''

He got up. As he was at the door, Scott said, "Take care, Jim.''

"Scotty, I don't *want* to die, I assure you.''

When he returned, the engineers' bridge was empty; but Scott's voice was still there. It was coming from the communicator, and it was using some rather ungentlemanly language.

"Scotty, what's the matter? Are you all right?''

"Aye, I'm all right, skipper,and so are we all—but the transporter blew under the load. I dinna ken hae lang it'll take to fix it.''

The return of Scott's brogue told Kirk how serious the situation actually was. Kirk did not even say, "Well, do your best.'' It was unnecessary.

The next few hours were an almost intolerable mixture of loneliness and tension, while the monstrous shape of the planet-killer and its mothlike captive grew slowly on the screen.

Yet not once in all this time did the robot again fire its anti-proton beam, which probably would have gone through the *Enterprise* like a knife through cheese; the ship was using almost all her power in fighting against the tractor ray. That, Kirk supposed, was a present given them by the nature of machine intelligence; the robot, having settled on the course of drawing the *Enterprise* into itself—and, probably, having estimated that in such a struggle it could not lose, eventually—saw no reason to take any other action.

"Mr. Spock?''

"Yes, Captain.''

"Don't fire on that thing again. Don't do *anything* to alter present circumstances—not even sneeze."

"I follow you, Captain. If we do not change the parameters, the machine mindlessly maintains the equation."

"Well, that's what I hope. How is the transporter coming?"

"Slowly. Mr. Scott says half its resistors are burned out. They are easy to replace individually, but so many is a time-consuming task."

"Computation?"

"We may have a most unreliable repair done when the *Constellation* is within a hundred miles of the robot. Sir, we also compute that one hundred miles is the limit of the robot's defensive envelope, inside which it takes offensive action against moving objects under power."

"Well, I can't very well shut off power. Let's just hope it's hungry."

The funnel swelled, much faster now. Kirk checked his watch, then poised his hand over the switch.

"Mr. Spock, I'm running out of time myself. Any luck now on the transporter?"

"It may work, Captain. I can predict no more."

"All right. Stand by."

The funnel now covered the entire star field; nothing else was to be seen but that metal throat. Still the robot had not fired.

"All right, Spock! Beam me aboard!"

He threw the switch. An instant later, the engineers' bridge of the doomed *Constellation* faded around him, and he found himself in the Transporter Room of the *Enterprise*. He raced to the nearest auxiliary viewscreen. Over the intercom, Spock's voice was counting: "Twenty-five seconds to detonation. Computer, mark at ten seconds and give us a fiftieth of a second warp drive at Warp One at second zero point five."

This order baffled Kirk for an instant; then he realized that he was *still* looking down the throat of the doomsday machine, and that Spock was hoping to make a short subspace jump away the instant the robot's tractor apparatus was consumed—if it was.

"Fifteen seconds. *Mark*. Five seconds. Four. Three. Two. One."

Flick!

Suddenly, on the auxiliary screen, the doomsday machine was thousands of miles away. The screen zoomed up the magnification to restore the image.

As it did so, a spear of intolerable light grew out of the mouth of the funnel. Promptly, Kirk ran for the elevators and the control room.

A silent group was watching the main viewscreen, including Commodore Decker. The tongue of flame was still growing. It now looked to be at least two hundred miles long. It would have consumed the *Enterprise* like a midge.

Then, gradually, it faded. Spock checked his board.

"Did it work?" Kirk demanded.

"I cannot tell yet, Captain. The radiation from the blast itself is too intense. But the very fact that we broke away indicates at least some damage . . . Ah, the radiation is decaying. Now we shall see."

Kirk held his breath.

"Decay curve inflecting," Spock said. "The shape—yes, the curve is now exponential. All energy sources are deactivated. Captain, it is dead."

There was a pandemonium of cheering. Under cover of the noise, Decker moved over to Kirk.

"My last command," he said in a low voice. "But you were right, Captain Kirk. My apologies for usurping your command."

"You acted to save Federation lives and property, as I did. If you in turn are willing to drop your complaint against my overriding regulations—which you have every right to make—we'll say no more about it."

"Of course I'll drop it. But the *Constellation* is nevertheless my last command. I cannot forget that my first attempt to attack that thing cost four hundred lives—men who trusted me—and that I had the bad judgment to try it again with *your* men's lives. When a man stops learning, he's no longer fit to command."

"That," Kirk said, "is a judgment upon yourself that only you can make. My opinion is that it is a wise and responsible judgment. But it is only an opinion. Mr. Sulu?"

"Sir?"

"Let's get the dancing in the streets over with, and lay a course for Star Base Seventeen."

"Yes, sir." But the helmsman could not quite stop grinning. Spock, of course, never grinned, but he was looking, if possible, even more serious than usual.

"Mr. Spock, you strike me as a man who still has some reservations."

"Only one, Captain; and it is pure speculation."

"Nevertheless, let's hear it."

"Well, Captain, when two powers prepare forces of such magnitude against each other, it almost always means that they are at a state of technological parity; otherwise they would not take such risks of self-destruction."

"Meaning?"

"Meaning, sir, that the existence of one such doomsday machine implies the existence of another."

"I suppose that's possible," Kirk said slowly, repressing a shudder. "Though the second one may not have been launched in time. Well, Mr. Spock, supposing we were to hear of another? What would you do?"

Spock's eyebrows went up. "That is no problem, sir. I would feed it a fusion bomb disguised as a ship, or better still, an asteroid; that is not what concerned me. The danger, as such, can now be regarded as minimal, even if there *is* another such machine."

"Then if you weren't thinking of the danger, what *were* you thinking of?"

"Of the nuisance," Spock said. "Having to deal with the same problem twice is untidy; it wastes time."

Kirk thought back to those hours aboard the haunted hulk of the *Constellation*—and of the four hundred dead men on the devoured planet.

"I," he said, "prefer my problems tidy. It saves lives."

≡

WOLF IN THE FOLD

Writer: Robert Bloch
Director: Joseph Pevney
Guest stars: John Fiedler, Pilar Seurat

The planet Argelius boasted the most popular Venus-bergs in the galaxy. And spacemen's favorite was a café that featured the belly-dancing of the lushly exotic Kara. The other lovely women who companioned its male guests at their tables were an old, if still pleasing story to Kirk and McCoy. But they were a blissfully new one to Scott. He sat with them, glancing around him, enraptured. Then his eyes returned to Kara's sinuous grace as she twisted it on the dance floor, her transparent gold skirt swirling around her.

Beaming, Scott said unnecessarily, "I like Argelius."

"Very little about it not to like," Kirk said.

"You mean to tell me these women, these beauties—I mean, all this is . . ."

"The Argelians think very highly of pleasure," Kirk told him.

McCoy laughed. "There's an understatement if ever I heard one! This is a completely hedonistic society."

"Like Kara, Scotty?" Kirk asked.

There was a fervent "Aye!" from Scott, at which Kirk said, "Good. I've invited her to join us. It occurred to me you might like to meet her."

"Now that's what I call a Captain!" Scott exclaimed. "Always thinking of his men."

"You're not drinking, Jim," McCoy said. "The few polyesters in this native extract—good for the soul. Not to mention the body."

148

"I don't suppose a little loosener-upper would hurt."
Kirk sipped his drink.

Scott, his eyes on Kara, said, "Mr. Spock should see
us now."

McCoy snorted. "He'd just be 'fascinated' by the pic-
turesque folk costumes in the place."

Kara had come to a spinning stop, her hands slanted
over her eyes in the immemorially seductive gesture of simulated prudery. The café's dimness lit with sparks as though
someone had released a swarm of fireflies. Scott pounded
enthusiastically on the table.

Amused, Kirk said, "It's an Argelian custom to demonstrate one's approval by blinking delight lights."

"You telling an old Glasgow pub crawler how to ap-
plaud, Captain?" Scott said. Then all three men rose from
their table. Kara was gliding toward them. As she approached, Kirk noted a young man at the bar. He had shoved
his drink aside, his face darkened by a scowl. It deepened
when Scott seated the girl beside him. Suddenly the scowler
seized his drink, drained it and walked out of the café. Nor
was the dancer's elderly musician pleased by the warmth of
her smile at Scott. Laying aside his flutelike instrument, he
averted his eyes from their table.

Scott, oblivious of everything but Kara's nearness,
leaned forward to place his hand over hers.

"Tis a fine foggy night tonight," he said. "Did anyone
ever tell you about the grand fogs we have in Edinburgh?"

"Never a word," she said. "But I'm dying to learn."

"Then why don't I show you? There's naught like a
walk in a fog with a bonny lass."

"Or a handsome gentleman. Why don't we go?"

The sun on Scott's face would have dispersed even an
Edinburgh fog. Kara's hand still in his, he got up. "You don't
mind, do you?" he asked the others. "I might even get back
to the ship on time."

"Don't hurry, Scotty," Kirk said. "Relax and enjoy
yourself. That's what Argelius is all about."

He looked thoughtfully after them as they left. "My
work is never done, Bones."

"*My* work, Jim. This is strictly prescription stuff. That

explosion that threw Scotty against the bulkhead was caused
by a woman.''

"You're sure the physical damage is all cleared up?"

"Yes. But the psychological damage? I didn't like his
resentment of all women after it happened.''

"I defy any man to stay angry at women on a planet
like this.''

"When Scotty gets back to the ship, Jim, he may hate
you for making him leave Argelius. But I'll bet my professional reputation he'll be finished with any lingering dislike
of women.''

"Well," Kirk said, "I think we've accomplished what
we came here for. Bones, there's a spot across town where
the women are so . . .''

"I know the place," McCoy interrupted. "Let's go.''

The fog outside was thicker than they had expected.
Light from the door they opened was diffused against coils
of clammy mist that made it hard to choose direction. Kirk
hesitated.

"I think we bear left," he said. But the turn they took
led them into an alley. They had paused, about to retrace their
steps, when a woman's agonized scream tore the silent darkness before them. "It came from there!" Kirk shouted, and
plunged deeper into the foggy alley, McCoy at his heels.
They both stopped at the sound of heavy breathing. Kirk took
a forward step only to stop again. He had stumbled over a
body.

It was sprawled, face down, on the damp paving. The
back of the cloak it wore was ripped by venomous slashes.

McCoy, kneeling beside it, lifted the head. After a long
moment, he raised a face that was blanched with horror. "It's
Kara," he said. "Dead. Stabbed a dozen times.''

The heavy breathing sound came again. They ran toward it. Scott was crouched against the alley wall. He stared
at them unseeingly, his face twisted into a grimace. In his
hands he held a long, sharp knife. It was wet with blood.

The café had got rid of its customers, and bright lights
had replaced its dimness. Unspeaking, Kirk and McCoy stood
beside the table where Scott sat, huddled, his face in his
hands. Like Scott, they made no move when the pudgy,

round-faced man who faced them said, "Argelius is the last planet in the galaxy where I'd expect a thing like this to happen. I'm at a loss to explain it, gentlemen."

"We are just as shocked as you are, Mr. Hengist," Kirk assured him.

"If this were my home planet, Rigel IV," Hengist was saying, "I'd have a dozen investigators at my disposal as Chief City Administrator. But they don't exist here."

"Then you are not a native Argelian, sir?" McCoy asked.

"No. Argelius hires its administrative officers from other planets. Its people's virtue is gentleness, not efficiency."

"You can count," Kirk told him, "on our complete cooperation. We will conduct ourselves according to your local laws."

"That's the trouble," Hengist frowned. "There are no laws to deal with a thing like this. Ancient traditions, of course, dating back before the great Argelian Awakening. But they're rather barbaric. I can't be expected to put your Mr. Scott to torture."

"We might be able to help," Kirk suggested. "We have equipment on the *Enterprise* which would help us get at the facts."

Hengist shook his head. "That's quite impossible, Captain, quite impossible. The investigation must take place here."

He picked up the murder knife from the table, looking down at the broken figure of Scott. "Mr. Scott—Mr. Scott, kindly rouse yourself! Are you sure you've never seen this knife before?"

Scott stared, dull-eyed, at the knife.

Kirk spoke sharply. "Answer him, Scott!"

"I—don't remember," Scott said.

Hengist made a gesture of impatience. He looked at Kirk. "You can scarcely call that helpful, Captain!"

Kirk pulled up a chair beside Scott. "Scotty," he said quietly, "you left the café with the girl. You remember that, don't you? What happened next?"

The dull eyes turned to him. "We were walking—the

fog. I was ahead of her, trying to lead the way. Then—then I heard her scream. I remember starting to turn—"

His face contorted. Then words burst out of him. "I can't remember another thing!"

Beckoning to McCoy, Kirk got up from the chair. "Well, Bones?" he said.

"If he says he can't remember, he probably doesn't. You know Scotty."

"I also know a murder has been committed—and that we found him with a bloody knife in his hand."

"That proves nothing," McCoy said. "Surely you don't think . . ."

"What *I* think doesn't make any difference! We're guests here! A member of my crew is under suspicion!"

"But you don't throw him to the wolves!" cried McCoy.

"I've got a diplomatic responsibility, Bones. This happened under Argelian jurisdiction. If they want to arrest Scotty, put him through trial here—even convict him, I've got to go along with them." He paused. "Besides, this business of not remembering . . ."

"Jim, he's just recovering from a very severe concussion! Partial amnesia after a thing like that is not only possible, it's probable. Especially under great stress."

"It's out of my hands, Bones. We'll do all that we can—but only under Argelian laws. There's Hengist at him again. Let's get back."

The pudgy man had replaced the knife on the table. "Not very promising, Captain Kirk. Your man still insists he remembers nothing. But my detector readings show his fingerprints on the murder weapon."

"Mr. Hengist," said Kirk, "other people left this café at about the same time Mr. Scott and the girl did."

"So I've been told by the staff. Those people will be located and questioned. But the outlook for your friend is pretty grim. I'm a man who prides himself on doing his job well. This crime will be solved and its perpetrator punished!"

"What is the law in such cases, Mr. Hengist?"

A deep voice spoke. "The Law of Argelius, sir, is love."

Kirk turned. A tall, white-haired, distinguished man had entered the café. A woman, almost as tall, was with him. Slim, elegant, her black hair touched with gray at the temples, the quiet gravity of her composure was impressive. Hengist bowed deeply to them both.

"Gentlemen," he said, "our Prefect—Jaris. Sir, Captain Kirk and Dr. McCoy."

Presenting the beautiful woman, Jaris said, "My wife, Sybo."

She inclined her head. "And this man at the table is Scott," Hengist said. "The one I told you about in my message."

Jaris's tranquil eyes studied Scott's face. "He does not look like a man capable of murder. Still, it has been so long since—" The deep voice spoke to Kirk and McCoy. "Gentlemen, before our great awakening hundreds of years ago, we had ways of learning the truth in such matters. We will return to them."

"The Argelian empathic contact, sir?" McCoy said.

"You know of it, Doctor?"

"I've heard of it. I had assumed it was a lost art."

"My wife is a descendant of the ancient priestesses of our land," Jaris said. "She has the old gift. I have come to invite you all to my home."

Hengist protested. "Prefect, don't you think this should be handled in an official manner through my office?"

"It *shall* be handled in an official manner, inasmuch as I am the highest official of Argelius." The rebuke was as gently spoken as it was courteous. "We will now proceed to my home. There my wife will prepare herself—and we shall learn the truth. Sybo—" He stood aside, bowing, and she moved past him to the café door.

Her drawing room was as impressive as their hostess. It was high-ceilinged, circular and windowless. Luxurious draperies covered its exits. Its tables, chairs, its cabinets matched the draperies in taste. Against one wall there was a simple altar of rich wood. A single flame rose from it.

"I have informed my ship, sir," Kirk turned to Jaris, "that there will be a delay in our return."

"Well done, Captain." Jaris nodded. "Let us proceed. Pray be seated, everyone."

McCoy was restive. "Prefect, depending on your lovely wife's empathic abilities is all very well. But I am a scientist, sir. And my science has available a precise method by which we can discover what it is that Mr. Scott cannot remember. Since you won't permit us to go to our ship, I can beam down a technician with my psychotricorder. It will give us a detailed account of all that happened to Mr. Scott within the past twenty-four hours."

"I advise against it, Prefect," Hengist said. "This is a purely Argelian matter."

"My wife must meditate for a time before she is ready," Jaris told him. "I see no reason why we should not employ that time to all possible use. Very well, Dr. McCoy."

McCoy whipped out his communicator. "McCoy to *Enterprise*."

"Spock here, Doctor."

"Mr. Spock, please beam down a technician with a psychotricorder immediately. Use these coordinates."

"Acknowledged. Coordinates received and read," Spock answered.

"Thanks. McCoy out."

Jaris was confiding his own problems to Kirk. "News of this frightful event is spreading among our people. They are greatly disturbed. Already there is talk of placing Argelius under embargo to space vehicles."

"That would be most unfortunate, sir. Argelius is widely known for its hospitality. It also owns strategic importance as a spaceport. It is the only one in this quadrant."

"Prefect," McCoy intervened, "the tricorder examination will require privacy to be effective."

"There is a small chamber below this room. Perhaps it will suffice, Doctor."

Hengist rose from his chair. "I do not wish to seem argumentative, Prefect, but I must point out that these two gentlemen are Mr. Scott's friends. They *want* to clear him!"

"And if he is innocent, do you not want to clear him, too, Mr. Hengist?"

The mild question rattled Hengist. "Why—I—of course," he stammered. "I am only interested in the truth."

"So are we all," said Kirk brusquely.

The flustered City Administrator addressed Jaris.

"There are other people to be questioned. Perhaps I should go to expedite their arrival here."

"Please do so," said the Prefect. "Anyone who has any connection with the murder should be here during the ceremony."

But Hengist's departure was delayed by the Transporter dazzle that appeared near McCoy's chair. It gradually assumed the extremely attractive shape and features of crewwoman Karen Tracy. Hengist eyed her. Then, nodding to her, he passed her and disappeared through a draped door.

The girl, a psychotricorder slung over her shoulder, said, "Lieutenant Karen Tracy, Doctor, reporting as ordered."

Scott, dismay in his face, half-rose from his chair. "A—a woman," he mumbled.

Kirk saw Jaris's keen eyes fix on him. "You don't like women, Mr. Scott?"

"It's not that, Prefect," McCoy said quickly. "He was recently involved in an accident caused by a careless woman. He suffered a severe concussion."

"Damage to his brain, Doctor?"

"Some. But in my best opinion, it could not possibly be responsible for . . ."

"I suggested nothing, Doctor."

"No. Of course you didn't." McCoy made a visible effort to get his anxiety back under control. "Lieutenant, I want a twenty-four-hour regressive memory check on Mr. Scott. All possible amnesic gaps to be probed."

"Yes, Doctor. Where shall I set up?"

"If you will follow me, young lady—" Jaris was leading the way toward the room's nearest exit when Kirk spoke to Scott. "You are to give Lieutenant Tracy complete cooperation. Maybe we can clear this thing up once and for all."

At the look in Scott's eyes, Kirk had to down an impulse to place an encouraging hand on his shoulder. "Yes, Captain. This—not remembering—it's hard to take."

Kirk watched him go with Tracy and Jaris. "All right, Bones. We're alone. Opinions?"

McCoy was grave. "Jim, in normal circumstances, Scotty simply couldn't have done such a thing. But that knock on the head—it could have tossed all his previous behavior patterns into a junk heap. What worries me is that he's telling the truth about not remembering.''

"Why does it worry you?''

"Hysterical amnesia. When a man feels guilt about something—something too terrible to face up to—he will blot it out of his conscious memory.''

Kirk felt his mind wince away from the words. Was it possible that Scott's conscious memory was sparing him recollection of an action too appalling to remember? The windowless room seemed suddenly suffocating. I need fresh air, he thought—but Jaris had returned. And the slender Sybo, her face absent-looking, abstracted, was pushing aside the drapery of another door.

"Are you prepared, Sybo?'' Jaris asked her.

"I am ready. May I have the knife, please?''

Jaris turned to them. "My wife also possesses the ability to receive sensory impressions from inanimate objects.'' He moved to a table. "The knife,'' he said. "Do you have it, Captain?''

Startled, Kirk echoed, "The knife? No. I thought . . .''

"I placed it on this table when we arrived,'' Jaris said. "It's gone.''

There was an uncomfortable silence. It was shattered by a shriek, muffled, but so high-pitched that it penetrated the floor's tiling. The underground room! Kirk and McCoy exchanged the same glance of apprehension. Then Kirk burst into action. Tearing aside a door curtain, he bolted headlong down a flight of stairs, McCoy's feet pounding behind him. They were in an ill-lit hall, a closed door facing them. Kirk broke through it into a small chamber.

Scott, his eyes closed, was sitting, rigid, in a chair. Karen Tracy, her equipment scattered around her, lay on the floor. McCoy ran to her. But Kirk had seized Scott's shoulder. "Scotty!'' he shouted, shaking the shoulder. "Scotty, snap out of it!''

The shoulder sagged under his hand. Scott moaned, swaying, while McCoy, getting to his feet, said, "She's dead, Jim.''

Kirk looked at him. "Don't tell me. I know,'' he said. "She's been stabbed to death, hasn't she?''

"Over and over again,'' McCoy said. "Just like the other one.''

* * *

They had to support Scott up the stairs. Jaris poured some amber fluid into a glass and handed it to McCoy. "An Argelian stimulant, Doctor. An effective one." But an overwhelming tension had reclaimed Scott. The glass just clattered against his clenched teeth. It took the combined skills of McCoy and Kirk to pry his locked jaws open and pour the liquid down his throat. As color began to return to his ashen lips, Kirk saw that Sybo had stepped to the altar, a dream-lost look on her face. A nice thing to have—a private dream world, he thought grimly, pouring the rest of the liquor into Scott's mouth. This time he swallowed it voluntarily. Blinking his eyes, he glanced around him. "Lieutenant Tracy?" he said. "Captain—where is . . . ?"

"Lieutenant Tracy is dead," Kirk said.

Scott stared at him. "Dead?"

"Yes," Kirk said harshly. "What happened down there?"

"I was sitting there, sir—and she was taking the readings." He made a move to rise. "Why am I back here now? She wasn't finished."

"That's all you remember?" McCoy asked.

"Scott, *concentrate*!" Kirk said. "The girl is dead. You were with her. You must have seen what happened. What was it?"

The anguished look of helplessness returned to Scott's eyes. "I don't remember. I can't remember, Captain. I must have passed out, but why, if I did . . ."

McCoy said, "It could be, Jim. The head injury . . ."

Kirk yelled, "I don't want to hear any more about that head injury! Scott! *Think!*"

"Watch it, Jim," McCoy said. "If he can't think, he can't do it because he's told to."

Kirk swung around to Jaris. "Prefect, is there another door to that room?"

"One that leads into the garden. But it's been locked for years."

"Locks can be picked," McCoy remarked.

"Check it, Bones," Kirk said.

Somewhere a bell rang. Jaris pressed a button, and Hengist, shoving two men before him, pushed through a door curtain. "Prefect," he said, "both of these people were in that café the night of the murder."

Kirk spoke to the older man. "I've seen you. You were one of the café's musicians. You played for Kara."

"She was my daughter," the man said. "She danced to my music as a child. Now she is dead and I am left to grieve." He turned to Jaris. "Prefect, how could this thing happen here? The man who did it must be found. And punished."

Hengist said, "I promise he will be, Tark."

Kirk indicated the younger man. "And *he* left the café just before Scott and Kara."

"Who are you?" Jaris asked the man. "Is what you have just heard true?"

"I am Morla of Cantaba Street. Yes, Prefect. I was there. I have nothing to hide."

"Did you know Kara?" Kirk asked.

Morla nodded. And Tark cried, "Of course he knew her! They were to be married. But his jealousy was a disgust to my child!"

"Jealousy?" Jaris said. "That is disquieting. In Argelius jealousy is virtually unknown."

Morla's mouth trembled. "My jealousy was a sorrow to me, Prefect. But I could not help it. I loved her. When I saw her go to the table with these men, I could not watch. I left the café."

"Where did you go?" Kirk asked.

"Home. Straight to my home. I needed to meditate—to rid myself of anger."

Kirk said, "Prefect, jealousy is a notorious reason for murder."

"I know. That is why it is disapproved here."

"I could not kill." Morla's voice broke. "It is not in me to kill. It is not in me to kill what I loved."

McCoy, returning, took in the scene. "That lock may or may not have been picked, Jim. Even with a tricorder, it would be hard to tell."

Kirk spoke again to Morla. "Can you prove that you went straight home?"

Hengist broke in. "Captain, I insist that you leave this questioning to me!"

"Then get on with it, man!" Kirk shouted. "Don't just hang around!" He looked at Tark. "A father, maybe angered by a daughter's disobedience—you wouldn't be the first one to—" He broke off. "Prefect! A future husband enraged at seeing his girl with other men—you cannot deny that is motive for murder! But Mr. Scott had none. Lieutenant Tracy was killed because she was about to discover the truth!"

Jaris's reply came slowly. "That is possible, Captain."

"Probable, sir."

The mild eyes met Kirk's. "Captain, you sound, you know, like a man who's determined to save the life of a friend."

"Yes, sir. Your judgment of me is impeccable. I *do* want to save my friend. And I remind you that he has not yet been proven guilty."

"Let me remind *you* that this friend of yours has been found with the body in each of these cases." Hengist's round face had flushed with anger.

Kirk had no time for a further retort, because at that moment Sybo announced, "I am ready, husband."

There was a strange authority in her quiet voice. Nobody spoke as she turned from the altar, her face serene, reposed. "The flame of purification burns," she said. "It points to the direction of truth." She stepped down from the altar. "We shall join hands. Our minds shall mingle—and I shall look into your deep hearts."

With a courtly gesture, Jaris led her to the table. "We shall sit, gentlemen, all of us. And as my wife asks, we shall join hands."

"On one condition, sir," Kirk said. "This room must be sealed so no one can enter or leave it during the ritual."

"The room *is* sealed," Jaris said.

He was seating Sybo at the table when Kirk's communicator beeped. It was Spock. "May I have a word with you, Captain?"

Kirk turned to Jaris. "A message from my ship, sir. Please excuse me for a moment." He moved to the end of the room. "Yes, Mr. Spock?"

"I have been considering the unfortunate situation, sir, as you related it to us. In my opinion, the Argelian empathic contact is a phenomenon worthy of study. I merely wonder if it is sound enough a technique to entrust with a man's life.''

"What do you suggest, Mr. Spock?''

"That we beam up Mr. Scott in order to allow our computers to arrive at the truth.''

"Impractical, Mr. Spock. To adopt your suggestion could close Argelius as a spaceport. We must respect the emotions and pride of these people. They have their own methods for handling this affair—and while we are here, we are subject to them.''

"Understood, Captain.''

"I don't like it any more than you do; but there's nothing we can do about it. Kirk out.''

When he faced the room again, everyone was seated at the table, Sybo at its head. Behind her the altar flame flared up—and waned. "Let us begin," she said. "Let us join hands. Let the circle not be broken. Look upon the fire that burns on the altar of truth.''

Her eyes closed. The odd authority in her low voice now invested her stillness. Kirk saw her lift a rapt face, the room putting shadow into the hollows beneath her cheekbones. Then suddenly, shockingly, she was speaking in a different voice—a much older voice, deeper, resonant. "Yes, there is something here in this room—something terrible—out of the past. I feel its presence—fear, rage, hatred.'' A groan broke from her. "There is evil here—monstrous, demonic . . .''

She paused as though all her senses were centered on listening. "A consuming hunger that never dies—hatred of life, of woman, hatred undying.'' The voice rose. "It is strong—an ancient hunger that feeds on terror—closer, closer—growing among us now—evil lust for death—death. It has been named—boratis—kesla—redjac . . .''

Sybo's words were coming in a frightened wail. "Devouring evil—eating life, light—hunger that preys—redjac—redjac . . .''

The altar flame winked out. In the darkness flooding the room, Kirk heard a rushing sound like the flapping of great wings. Then Sybo gave a wild scream.

"Get the lights!'' he shouted.

They blazed up. Hengist was over at the light panel, his hand still on it.

But all Kirk had eyes for was Sybo. She was slumped in Scott's arms. Very slowly her body twisted in them. From her back the haft of a long knife protruded. Scott's nerveless arms relaxed—and the body fell to the floor. Scott looked down at it. Then Kirk saw him look away from it to stare at his bloody hands.

Jaris's face was gaunt with grief. And Kirk, listening to Hengist's tirade, thought—and not for the first time—Mr. City Administrator, you are an insensitive man.

"Three murders!" Hengist was yelling. "And this man on the scene each time! What do you require, Captain? That he stab another woman in the back before your very eyes?"

"Mr. Hengist, please—not now," Jaris said. "My poor wife—her body has just been removed . . ."

Hengist persisted. "Prefect, I am perfectly satisfied that this *Enterprise* crewman is guilty!"

"But not responsible," Kirk said. "These acts have been acts of insanity. If Mr. Scott is guilty, he is a madman. On our ship we have instruments able to determine his mental state."

"And save his life?" There was a sneer in Hengist's voice.

"Insanity cannot be held responsible under anybody's laws," Kirk said. "It is unaware of what it does to others."

"Gentlemen, please—" Jaris said.

"I am sorry, Prefect," Hengist said. "My heart grieves for you—but I can stand by no longer! This man has killed three times! Even Captain Kirk admits it! But this last-minute attempt to help Scott evade punishment. . . ."

Kirk kept his voice level. "No, Mr. Hengist. To see that justice is done."

"I—don't know," Jaris said.

"How many other murders will occur unless we take prompt action, sir?" Hengist asked him. "The old laws still exist. I can get the truth from this killer."

"By torture?" Kirk said. He turned to Jaris. "Prefect, I told you before, we'll stand by your laws. If Mr. Scott is mentally responsible, he is yours to punish. But I must insist that everything possible be done to establish his mental condition.''

Jaris's mouth trembled. Shock had visibly aged him. "How could any man do these monstrous things?"

"That is what I hope to find out, sir," Kirk said gently.

With an effort Jaris looked at Scott. "And you, Mr. Scott, what do you have to say?"

Scott stood up. "Sir, I swear before God that I did not kill your wife. I have not killed anyone."

"By your own admission you don't know whether you did or not," Hengist said. "Your so-called failure of memory . . ."

"Mr. Hengist," McCoy interrupted him, "aboard our ship it is possible to record all registrations that have been made on Mr. Scott's conscious or subconscious mind. We can recover all that has occurred to him. The recordings are factual. They will tell us exactly what has happened to him in the recent past."

Kirk pressed McCoy's point. "There would be no room for doubt," he said. "We would *know*. Isn't that what we want, Prefect? To *know*?" He looked at Hengist. "The investigation and disposition of the case would still remain in your jurisdiction. *What we're after is the removal of doubts.*"

Hengist's face hardened. "Your suggestion would be illegal. If this man is taken back into your ship with you, what legal assurance do we have you'd return him to Argelius even if your instruments prove him guilty? I have the authority to . . ."

Jaris had recovered control of himself. "Mr. Hengist, the authority is mine," he said firmly. "And this decision, too, is mine." He looked at Kirk. "Captain, as you know, Mr. Scott has claimed to remember nothing about the murders. He may have killed without knowing he killed. Can your machines penetrate to the truth of his actions?"

"They will so correlate the facts that a positive conclusion is reached," Kirk said. "No doubts will remain."

Jaris rose. "Very well. We shall go to your ship."

He walked over to Scott, his step steady. "If you are guilty," he said, "you will face the ancient penalties, barbaric though they may be. I warn you that the ancient penalty for murder was death by slow torture. That law has never been changed. Do you understand, Mr. Scott?''

Scott moistened his dry lips. But he faced Jaris unflinchingly. "Aye, sir. I understand."

The Briefing Room of the *Enterprise* was crowded. The Argelian guests, including Tark and Morla, had been seated on one side of its table. On the other side, a pretty yeoman, Tancris, sat between Scott and McCoy, prepared to record the proceedings. Kirk with Spock stood near the computer controls.

Kirk addressed his guests. "Deep in the heart of this ship are our computer banks. They operate the entire ship. They also contain the whole of human and humanoid knowledge. They are indisputably reliable. Our lives depend on them."

He turned to Spock. "Anything to add, Mr. Spock?"

"In a matter of a few seconds," Spock said, "we can obtain an answer to any factual question, regardless of its complexity."

"You don't solve a murder with columns of figures!" Hengist said.

"No, sir. But we do determine the truth."

"How?" asked Morla. "That machine can't tell what goes on in a man's mind!"

Kirk pointed to the computer's verifier. "No. But this piece of equipment can—to an extent." He pulled out a chair. "Each testifier will sit here, his hand on this plate. Any deviation from factual truth will be immediately detected. It will then be relayed to the computer which will notify us."

Hengist stirred in his chair. Kirk continued. "Doctor McCoy has already fed his medical reports into the computer. Our laboratory experts are now examining the murder weapon. They will give their findings to the computer for its analysis. Mr. Scott, will you please take the stand?"

Scott rose, moved to the verifier, sat down and laid his hand on the plate. Kirk activated the computer control.

"Computer," he said. "Identify and verify."

The mechanism clicked. And the computer voice spoke. "Working. Lieutenant Commander Montgomery Scott, serial number SE 197–547–230T. Verified."

"Subject's present physical condition?" Kirk said.

"Working. Subject recently subjected to severe blow on skull. Damage healing. Some peripheral abnormalities."

"Sufficient abnormalities to cause periods of functional amnesia?"

"Working," responded the computer. "Negative."

Puzzled, McCoy intervened. "I don't see how that can be, Jim."

"It can be if Scotty is lying about his loss of memory," Kirk said.

"I'm not lying, Captain!" Scott cried. "I don't remember a thing about the first two murders!"

"Computer. Accuracy scan," said Kirk.

"Subject relaying accurate account. No physiological changes."

Scott, his hand still on the plate, half-rose from the chair. "Captain, I never said I blacked out when the Prefect's wife was killed!"

"All right, Scott. Go ahead. What do you remember about it?"

"We were all holding hands. The room was dark, the light from the altar was so dim. I heard the poor lady scream. I tried to reach her—but something was between us."

"Something?" Kirk questioned. "You mean someone?"

"No, sir. Some—thing. Cold—it was cold like a stinking draft out of a slaughterhouse. But—it wasn't really there like—" He stopped, adding lamely, "If you get what I mean."

"Computer?" Kirk said.

"Subject relaying accurate account. No physiological changes."

"All right," said Kirk. "I'm putting it straight. Scott, did you kill Sybo?"

"No, sir. That I'm sure of."

Hengist grunted. "He's been saying that all along. It means no more now than it did before."

Kirk eyed him. "Scotty!" he said. "Lie to me! How old are you?"

"Twenty-two, Captain."

A buzzer sounded. The touch panel blinked a light on

and off. And the computer voice said, "Inaccurate. Inaccurate. Data in error."

"Scott, when the lights went out, who was holding your hand?"

"Morla on the one side, sir—you on the other."

Morla, his face pale, got to his feet. "But that doesn't mean anything, Captain. A small room like that—it was dark—anyone of us would have had time to kill the lady."

Hengist was quick to object. "I remind everyone we found Mr. Scott holding her in his arms. The knife was still in her back. And there was blood on his hands."

"That is so," Kirk said. "But the verifier has shown it will accept no lie."

"Two other women were murdered," Hengist challenged.

"Mr. Scott," Kirk said, "did you kill Kara?"

"I don't remember."

"Did you kill Lieutenant Tracy?"

"I can't remember."

"Computer," Kirk said. "Accuracy scan."

"Subject relaying accurate account. No physiological changes."

"All this proves," Jaris said, "is that he's telling the truth about the memory lapses."

"It's a waste of our time!" Hengist exclaimed.

Kirk said, "Mr. Hengist, after this testimony is taken, we will run a psychotricorder analysis of Mr. Scott's memory. That's what Lieutenant Tracy was trying to do. This time we'll do it. We shall have a complete record of the action he took, remembered or forgotten. Will that satisfy you?"

"If you can convince me that the machine is incapable of error. If it shows that he did not kill the women."

"The machine does not err. As to the rest of it, the readings will reveal that. I think you can stand down, Mr. Scott—if there are no objections."

"I object to this entire procedure!" Hengist shouted.

Mildly, Jaris turned to him. "Mr. Hengist, we are here on my authority."

"Prefect, I know you mean well—but I have had past experience in matters of this kind while you . . ."

"Enough, sir," Jaris stopped him short. "For the present we will accept Captain Kirk's trust of the machine's accuracy. At the same time we'll reserve the right to make the final determination ourselves."

"That's all we ask, Prefect," Kirk said. "Mr. Morla, will you take the stand?"

Morla took it, placing his hand nervously on the touch plate, and Kirk said, "Where were you at the time Kara was murdered?"

"I—I'm not sure. Walking home, I think. I was disturbed." He looked at Kirk. "I told you I felt anger."

"Anger is a relative state, Mr. Morla," interposed Spock. "Were you angry enough to do violence?"

"I have never done violence in my life. I am an Argelian. I do not believe I am capable of violence." His voice shook. "Believe me, I couldn't kill her! She loved me!"

Tark jumped to his feet. "That is not true! She did not love him! She told me. He was jealous! They fought constantly!" Tears in his eyes, he turned to Jaris. "My daughter was a true Argelian. A child of joy . . ."

"Yes, I *was* jealous!" Morla was on his feet, too. "I admit it! But I did not kill her! I wanted to leave Argelius with her—go somewhere to have her all to myself. I loved her!"

"Did you kill Lieutenant Tracy?" Kirk asked.

"No!"

"Did you kill Sybo?"

"No!"

"Computer—verification scan," Kirk said.

"Subject relaying accurate account. Some statements subjective. No physiological changes."

"That would seem to be it," Kirk said. "You can stand down, Mr. Morla."

He glanced around the faces at the table. After a long moment, he said slowly, "Sybo spoke of a consuming hunger that never dies—of something that thrives on terror, on death." He looked at Spock. "Maybe we're going about this the wrong way. Let's assume that Sybo was a sensitive—that she *did* sense something evil in that room . . ."

"The sensitivity of certain Argelian women is a documented fact, Captain," Spock said.

"My—dear wife's talent," said Jaris, "was genuine, gentlemen. The things she said were true."

"All right, then," said Kirk. "Exactly what was it she said? A monstrous evil—out of the past—hatred of life, of woman . . .''

"A lust for death," supplemented McCoy.

"She made some other references that didn't make sense," Kirk said.

"I remember them," McCoy told him. "Redjac. Boratis. Kesla."

Kirk shook his head. "Obscure. Meaningless."

"To us, perhaps, Captain," Spock said. "But to the computer banks . . .''

"Check them out, Mr. Spock."

"Computer, linguistic banks," Spock said. "Definition of following word—redjac."

The computer buzzed. "Working. Negative finding."

"There's no such word in the linguistic bank?"

"Affirmative."

"Scan all other banks," Spock said.

"Working. Affirmative. A proper name."

"Define," Spock said.

"Working. Red Jack. Source: Earth, nineteenth century. Language: English. Nickname applied to mass murderer of women. Other Earth synonym: Jack the Ripper."

A silence composed of shock, hope and incredulity fell over the listeners.

"That's ridiculous!" Hengist yelled. He leaped to his feet. "Jack the Ripper lived hundreds of years ago!"

Kirk said, "Computer. Factual data and capsulization on Jack the Ripper."

"Working. Jack the Ripper: First appearance, London, ancient British Empire, Earth, year 1888, old calendar. Brutal killer of at least six women by knife or surgical instrument; no witnesses to crimes; no identification or arrest. Crimes remain unsolved. No known motive."

"Senseless crimes," McCoy said reflectively.

"As senseless as the murder of Kara—or Lieutenant Tracy," said Kirk.

Tark looked from one to the other. "It can't be. A man could not survive all these centuries."

"My wife," Jaris said. "My wife—before she died—
it is a deathless hunger, she said."

"But all men die!" protested Tark.

"All *men* die, sir," Spock said. "But humans and humanoids comprise only a small percent of the life forms we
know of. There exist entities possessed of extremely long
life-spans, virtually immortal."

"But—a being which feeds on death?" McCoy shook
his head.

"In the strict scientific sense, Doctor, we all live on
death—even vegetarians."

"But Sybo said it feeds on terror!"

"Deriving sustenance from emotion is not unknown—
and fear is among the strongest and most intense of the emotions."

Hengist's eyes lingered on Spock's quiet face. Then he
swung around to Jaris. "Prefect, this has gone far enough!
Someone, some man has killed three women. We have the
prime suspect in our hands! Are we going to let him go to
chase down ghosts?"

"Not ghosts, Mr. Hengist," Kirk said. "Possibly not
human—but not a ghost. Mr. Spock, run a check on the possibilities."

"Computer. Digest log recordings of past five solar
minutes. Correlate hypotheses. Compare with life forms register. Question: could such an entity within discussed limits,
exist in this galaxy?"

"Affirmative. Examples exist. The Drella of Alpha Ca-
rinae V derives its sustenance from the emotion of love. There
exists sufficient precedent for existence of creature, nature
unknown, which could exist on emotion of terror."

"Extrapolate most likely composition of such entity,"
Spock said.

"Working. To meet specified requirements, entity
would exist without form in conventional sense. Most probable: mass of energy, highly cohesive."

Kirk took over. "Computer, in such form, could the
entity kill with a knife?"

"Negative."

"Could the entity described assume physical form?"

"Affirmative. Precedent: the Mellitus, cloud creature of Alpha Majoris 1."

"Fairy tales!" Hengist was acid with scorn. "Ghosts and goblins!"

Kirk was getting his fill of Hengist. "No, sir," he said. "I've seen the Mellitus myself. Its normal state is gaseous but at rest it becomes solid." He turned back to Spock. "Let's assume the existence of this creature able to take on form or reject it at will. That could explain Scotty's failure to remember anything about the first two murders."

Spock nodded. "Or by production of a hypnotic screen blinding all but the victim to the killer's presence."

Awed, Jaris murmured, "Is that possible?"

"Very possible," McCoy told him. "Even probable. Many examples exist in nature."

"But I don't hypnotize easily," Scott interjected.

"We're not talking about a human hypnotist, Scotty," Kirk reminded him.

Hengist, openly furious, rose again from the table. "This is fantasy! We all know the murderer is sitting right here with us! You're trying to muddy the issue. I've got a mind to stop this right now!"

"Kindly be seated, Mr. Hengist." Jaris sounded unusually stern. "The course of this investigation seems valid to me."

Conscious of the glaring Hengist behind him, Kirk said, "What do we have then, Mr. Spock? A creature without stable form that feeds on fear, assuming physical shape to do its killing?"

"And preys on women because they are more easily terrorized than the male of the species."

Kirk hit the computer button. "Computer, criminological files. Cases of unsolved multiple murders of women since Jack the Ripper."

"Working. 1932. Shanghai, China, Earth. Seven women knifed to death. 1974. Kiev, USSR, Earth. Five women knifed to death. 2005. Martian Colonies. Eight women knifed to death. Heliopolis, Alpha Proximi II. Ten women knifed to death. There are additional examples."

"Captain," Spock said, "all those places are aligned directly between Argelius and Earth."

"Yes. When men of Earth moved into the galaxy, this thing must have moved with them." He addressed the computer. "Identify the proper names Kesla and Boratis."

"Working. Kesla: popular name of unidentified mass murderer of women on planet Deneb II. Boratis: popular name of unidentified mass murderer of women on planet Rigel IV. Additional data. Murders on Rigel IV occurred one solar year ago."

McCoy turned from the table to look at Kirk. Kirk, nodding, spoke to Hengist. "You came to Argelius from Rigel IV," he said.

"Many people do," Hengist countered. "It's not a crime."

"No. But we are investigating one. Please take the stand, Mr. Hengist."

Hengist leaned back in his chair. "I refuse," he said.

"Mr. Hengist!"

The jaw in the pudgy face had set hard. "Prefect, I will *not* take the stand."

"I see your point, sir," Spock said. "If you are the entity we search for, what better hiding place could you find than the official position you hold?"

McCoy was on his feet. "And just after you left Jaris's house, we discovered the murder weapon was missing!"

Kirk pressed on. "You were unaccounted for when Lieutenant Tracy was murdered."

A nerve under Hengist's eye twitched. "The law is my business!" His voice roughened. "You are engaged in sheer speculation for your own illegal ends!"

Kirk was not deferred. "Mr. Spock—the weapon."

"Computer," Spock said. "Report on analysis of Exhibit A."

"Working. Exhibit A on visual."

The mechanism's triscreen flashed into brightness. As the image of the knife appeared on it, its voice said, "Composition of blade: boridium. Composition of handle: murinite. Details of handle carving conform to folk art indicating place of origin."

"Specify place of origin," Spock said.

"Artifact produced by hill people of Argus River region, planet Rigel IV."

"Mr. Hengist—" Kirk began.

But Hengist had made a break for the door. Scott tripped him—and Kirk closed with him. There was unexpected muscle in the pudgy body. Screaming wildly, Hengist aimed a knee at Kirk's groin. Elbowing up, Kirk swung a fist back and landed a hard right to his jaw. Hengist collapsed. The lights went dim; and at the same moment the room was filled with that rushing sound like the flapping of great wings.

Kirk got to his feet. McCoy, looking up from Hengist's body, said tonelessly, "He's dead, Jim."

"Dead? But that's impossible! A man doesn't die of a sock on the jaw!"

The computer crackled. Then the noise subsided. A maniacal laughter burst from its speakers. They chuckled, choking with obscene merriment—and Hengist's voice shrieked, "Red Jack! Red Jack! Red Jack!"

The cackling mirth grew into an insane howl of triumph. Kirk, astounded, stared at Spock. The Vulcan leaped to the computer buttons. But the mad howls of laughter would not be stilled.

"The computer isn't responding, Captain! The entity has taken possession of it!"

"But the computer controls the ship!" Kirk cried. "Are you saying that this thing is in possession of the ship?"

He himself began to wrestle with the computer controls. Spock tried to move the switch that fed into its bypass circuits. It swung loose. "It's no use, Captain! The bypass circuits have been blocked, too!"

The crazy laughter gushed louder from the speakers. "Red Jack!" it screamed again.

"Audio cutoff, Mr. Spock!"

The room was suddenly quiet. But Scott, jumping to his feet, yelled, "The screen, Captain! Look at the screen!"

Kirk whirled. The viewer was a riot of changing colors. Figures began to emerge from them. Serpents writhed through pentagons. Naked women, hair streaming behind them, rode astride the shaggy backs of goats. Horned beasts pranced with toads. Rivers boiled, steaming. Above them, embraced bodies drifted down fiery winds. Human shoulders, pinioned under rocks, lifted pleading arms. Then the red glow, shedding its bloody mist over the screen, gave way to the deathly whiteness of a cold, unending snow. Up from the glacial landscape rose a towering three-headed shape, its mouths agape with gusts of silent laughter. A cross, upturned, appeared beside it. The shape crawled up it, suspending itself upon it in an unspeakable travesty of the crucifixion. Its vast, leathery wings unfolded . . .

"What is it?" Jaris whispered.

"A vision of hell," Kirk said. He switched off the screen. "This foul thing has shown us the place of its origin. And it is now master of all this ship's operations, including our life support systems."

"You mean it could kill us all?" gasped Morla.

"I suspect it will try," Spock said. "But not immediately." He paused. "It feeds on terror. Death is not enough for it. There are nearly four hundred and forty humans aboard this ship. They offer it an unparalleled opportunity to glut itself on the fear it can stimulate in them. Before it kills, it will make the most of its chance."

Kirk nodded. He moved over to the intercom button. Pressing it, he said, "All hands, this is the Captain speaking. The computers are malfunctioning. Repair efforts are proceeding. Meanwhile, it is of the utmost importance to stay at your posts and remain calm. Captain out."

He faced around. "Bones, what's your sedative situation?"

"I've got some stuff that would tranquilize a volcano, Jim."

"Start distributing it to all hands. The longer we can hold fear down, the more time we'll have to get this hell-born thing out of the computers."

He swung back to Spock. "Mr. Spock, you have a compulsory scan order built into your computer control banks."

"Yes, Captain, but with the entity in control . . ."

"Even so, it will have to deal with everything programmed into the computers. Aren't there some mathematical problems which simply cannot be solved?"

Spock's somber face lightened. "Indeed there are, Captain. If we can focus all the computers' attention on one of them . . ."

"Good. That should do it." Kirk moved over to the

table. "The rest of you, stay here," he said. "Bones, get going on that tranquilizer. Let's go, Mr. Spock."

But the thing had taken over the elevator. Though its door slid open to admit Kirk, it started to slam shut before Spock could enter it. "Spock!" Kirk shouted. He grabbed him, yanking him in just as the door clanged shut. Spock turned to regard the door with interest. "Fascinating," he said. "Our friend learns quickly."

"Too quickly." Kirk pushed the up button to the bridge. Instead of rising, the elevator sank. Decks flashed by to a whining sound. "Free fall!" Kirk yelled. "Put it on manual control!"

They both seized the manual controls, pulling at them. The whine stopped, and very slowly the elevator began to rise. Then its alarm siren shrieked. "That was due to be next," Kirk said grimly. "Life support malfunction!"

"We don't have much time, Captain."

"You said it yourself, Mr. Spock. It wants terror. Death comes second on its list."

The elevator stopped at the bridge deck, but there was another struggle with its touch plate to get its door open. Nor did they find much cause for cheer as they hurried out of it into the bridge. Sulu, already gasping for breath, was with the technician at the life support station. "Captain, the override is jammed!"

Spock ran to the station. Ripping off a panel, he exposed its mechanism, and kneeling, went to work on it. He was reaching for a tool when Hengist's voice screamed from the bridge speaker. "You are all about to die! Captain Kirk, you are wasting your time!" The voice broke again into its hideous laughter.

"Turn that off, Communications!" Kirk wheeled to Sulu. "Man your post, Mr. Sulu! Prepare all your manual overrides!"

Spock got to his feet. "Normal environmental levels restored, Captain. But, as you know, they won't last long. Several hours with luck."

Sulu asked, "What's going on, Captain?"

"*Man your post, Mr. Sulu!*" Kirk, aware of his tension, hastened to meet the nurse who was stepping out of the elevator, air hypo in hand. "Is that the tranquilizer?"

"Yes, sir."

"Everyone, including yourself."

The Communications technician had bared his arm for the shot when Hengist's voice spoke once more. "You cannot stop me now, Captain!" Kirk reached over the crewman's shoulder to push buttons, but the voice wasn't hushed. "Fool, you cannot silence me! I control all the circuits of this ship! You cannot reach me! Your manual overrides' life is as limited as your own. Soon all controls will be mine!"

Kirk moved over to Spock at his computer station. He said softly, "Well, Mr. Spock?"

"Work proceeding, captain."

This time Kirk raised his voice. "Destroy us—and you destroy yourself."

Chuckles bubbled from the bridge speaker. "I am deathless. I have existed from the dawn of time—and I shall live beyond its end. In the meantime I shall feed—and this time I need no knife. In pain unspeakable you will all die!"

Spock looked up from his work. "It is preparing its feast on terror."

"Imbeciles! I can cut off your oxygen and suffocate you! I can crush you all by increasing atmospheric pressure! I can heighten the temperature till the blood boils in your veins!"

Sulu had received his shot. He turned to Kirk. "Captain," he said cheerfully, "whoever that is, he sure talks gloomy."

"Yes. Stay at your post, Mr. Sulu. If any more systems go out, switch to manual override. Above all, don't be afraid."

"With an arm full of this stuff, sir, I wouldn't be scared of a supernova."

"Ready, Captain," Spock said.

"Implement."

Spock addressed his library computer. "This is a compulsory Class 1 direction. Compute to the last digit the value of pi."

Sharp clicks mingled with an outbreak of buzzing noises. Spock waited. And what he waited for came. Over the speaker Hengist's voice, alarmed, said, "No—not . . ."

Spock made his reply. "The value of pi is a transcendental number without any resolution. All banks of our computer are now working on it to the exclusion of all else. They will continue to calculate this incalculable number until we order them to stop.''

"Let's get back to the Briefing Room," Kirk said. "The Argelians will probably be the first to panic.''

Sulu watched them go to the elevator. Then he said happily to himself, "I wonder what I'm supposed to be afraid of.''

In the Briefing Room, the body of Hengist was still slumped in the chair where it had been placed. McCoy was circling the table administering the tranquilizer shots. As Kirk and Spock entered, Scott said, "Well, Captain?''

"I don't think our computers will be inhabited by anything but a bunch of figures for a while.''

Spock had gone directly to the computer controls. He tested them. "There's some resistance, Captain, but the directive is succeeding. Bank after bank is turning to the problem.''

McCoy paused, his air hypo suspended. "If you drive it out of the computer, Jim, it will have to go somewhere else.''

"I doubt if it will move into anyone who's been tranquilized, Bones. How're you coming?''

"Almost finished. Just Jaris and me . . .''

He stopped dead. The lights had dimmed again. And there was that rushing sound of vast wings beating. Very gradually, the lights returned. Spock punched a button on the computer controls.

"The entity has fled, Captain," he said.

Kirk had been pondering McCoy's warning. "But where has it fled? Bones—if the thing entered a tranquilized body, what would happen?''

"It might take up knitting," McCoy said. "But nothing more violent than that.''

"And you say everyone has had a shot except you— and Jaris?''

Jaris turned in his chair. "You and Mr. Spock have received no shot, Captain.''

Kirk looked at him sharply. "That is true. But I know

it is not in me—and I'm willing to take a chance on Mr. Spock. Bones, give yourself a shot."

"I ought to stay clear to keep my wits about me," McCoy protested.

"I gave you an order, Bones!"

McCoy stared at Kirk. Then he shrugged, bared his arm and plunged the hypo into it.

"Prefect," Kirk said, "if you will extend your arm, please . . ."

Jaris exploded into an insane howl. Out of his mouth Hengist's voice screamed, *"No! No!"* Leaping from the table, Jaris flung himself on Kirk. Spock raced over to them. The elderly body of Jaris was infused with unbelievable strength. It had Kirk by the throat. Spock tore it away. It shrieked, "Kill! Kill you all! Suffer, suffer! Die!" Grappling with Jaris's fiercely powerful body, Spock reached for its neck to apply the Vulcan pinch. Jaris crumpled. And once again the lights dimmed—the vast wings flapped.

Kirk regained his feet. Around the table its tranquilized people, some sitting, some standing, were smiling as though the struggle had been staged for their entertainment. Yeoman Tancris, her recording pad dropped to the floor, was regarding Spock with a beautiful admiration. From behind her an arm reached out. It encircled her neck, pulling her backward. Hengist's body had left its chair. It whipped out a knife and laid it against the girl's throat.

"Stand away—or I'll kill her!" it said.

McCoy, thoroughly tranquilized, said mildly, "You'll hurt somebody with that knife," and extended a gentle hand toward the weapon. Hengist took a savage swipe at him. Spock jumped him as Kirk ripped the hypo from McCoy. Spock, closing with the howling madman, managed to tear his sleeve. Kirk rammed the hypo home. Hengist wavered in Spock's grasp. "I'll kill you all," he said quietly. "And you shall suffer and I shall feed—" He collapsed.

Kirk grabbed his shoulders. "The Transporter Room! Quickly!" he shouted to Spock.

The Transporter technician beamed at them happily as they staggered into the room, the heavy body of Hengist between them.

Kirk yelled, "Deep space—widest angle of dispersion—full power—maintain . . ."

The Transporter chief looked at him reproachfully. "No need to get so excited, Captain. I'll take care of it."

"Spock! Do it! Tranquilizers have their limitations!"

Alone, Kirk placed Hengist on the platform. The benevolent Transporter Chief was moving casually toward the console when Spock pushed him aside and seized the controls.

"Energize!" Kirk shouted.

The motionless figure on the platform broke up into sparkle—and was gone.

Spock, his elbow on the console, leaned his head on his hand. Kirk laid a hand on his shoulder. "Quite an expensive little foray into the fleshpots—our visit to Argelius," he said. But the Transporter Chief's feelings were hurt. "You didn't have to shove me, Mr. Spock. I'd have gotten around to it," he said pleasantly. He looked up as Scott and McCoy, both grinning contentedly, opened the door. "Now there are two officers who know how to take life—easy," he said.

"Jaris will be all right," McCoy announced soothingly.

"What did you do with the thing, Captain?" Scott asked. "Send it back to the planet?"

"No, Scotty. We beamed it out into open space at the widest possible dispersion angle."

"But it can't die!" McCoy said.

"Perhaps not, Doctor," Spock said. "Indeed, its consciousness may survive for some time, but only in the form of billions of particles, separate bits of energy, forever drifting in space—powerless, shapeless and without sustenance. We know it must eat to remain alive."

"And it will never feed again, not in the formless state it's in," Kirk said. "Finally, it will die." He looked at McCoy. "Bones—how long before that tranquilizer wears off?"

"Oh, five or six hours, I guess. I certainly have given everyone a pretty good dose."

"So I notice. Well, Mr. Spock, for the next few hours we'll have the happiest crew in space. But I doubt that we get much work done."

"Sir," Spock said, "since, after all, we came to Argelius to rest, I see no reason why we shouldn't take advantage of it.''

"Let's go!'' Scott cried enthusiastically.

"Shore leave, Mr. Scott? You and Dr. McCoy have still to sleep off the effects of the last one. But we?'' Kirk turned to Spock. "Mr. Spock, want to make the rounds of the Argelian fleshpots with me?''

Spock's eyebrows rose. "Captain,'' he said stiffly, "I spoke of rest.''

"Ah,'' Kirk said. "So you did. My mistake, Mr. Spock.''

THE CHANGELING

Writer: John Meredyth Lucas
Director: Marc Daniels

The last census had shown the Malurian system, which had two habitable planets, to have a population of over four billion; and only a week ago, the *Enterprise* had received a routine report from the head of the Federation investigating team there, asking to be picked up. Yet now there was no response from either planet, on any channel—and a long-range sensor sweep of the system revealed no sign of life at all.

There could not have been any system-wide natural catastrophe, or the astronomers would have detected it, and probably even predicted it. An interplanetary war would have left a great amount of radioactive residue; but the instruments showed only normal background radiation. As for an epidemic, what disease could wipe out two planets in a week, let alone so quickly that not even a single distress signal could be sent out—and what disease could wipe out *all* forms of life?

A part of the answer came almost at once as the ship's deflector screens snapped on. Something was approaching the *Enterprise* at multi-warp speed: necessarily, another ship. Nor did it leave a moment's doubt about its intentions. The bridge rang to a slamming jar. The *Enterprise* had been fired upon.

"Shields holding, Captain," Scott said.

"Good."

"I fear it is a temporary condition," Spock said. "The shields absorbed energy equivalent to almost ninety of our photon torpedos."

"*Ninety*, Mr. Spock?"

"Yes, Captain. I may add, the energy used in repulsing that first attack has reduced our shielding power by approximately 20 percent. In other words, we can resist perhaps three more; the fourth one will get through."

"Source?"

"Something very small . . . bearing 123 degrees mark 18. Range, ninety thousand kilometers. Yet the sensors still do not register any life-forms."

"Nevertheless, we'll try talking. They obviously pack more wallop than we do. Lieutenant Uhura, patch my audio speaker into the translator computer and open all hailing frequencies."

"Aye, sir . . . All hailing frequencies open."

"To unidentified vessel, this is Captain Kirk of the *USS Enterprise*. We are on a peaceful mission. We mean no harm to you or to any life-form. Please communicate with us." There was no answer. "Mr. Spock, do you have any further readings on the alien?"

"Yes, sir. Mass, five hundred kilograms. Shape, roughly cylindrical. Length, a fraction over one meter."

"Must be a shuttlecraft," Scott said. "Some sort of dependent ship, or a proxy."

Spock shook his head. "There is no other ship on the sensors. The object we are scanning is the only possible source of the attack."

"What kind of intelligent creatures could exist in a thing that size?"

"Intelligence does not necessarily require bulk, Mr. Scott."

"Captain, message coming in," Uhura said.

The voice that came from the speaker was toneless, inflectionless, but comprehensible. "*USS Enterprise*. This is Nomad. My mission is non-hostile. Require communication. Can you leave your ship?"

"Yes," Kirk said, "but it will not be possible to enter your ship because of size differential."

"*Non sequitur,*" said Nomad. "Your facts are uncoordinated."

"We are prepared to beam you aboard our ship."

Kirk's officers, except for Spock, reacted with alarm at this, but Nomad responded, "That will be satisfactory."

"Do you require any special conditions, any particular atmosphere or environment?"

"Negative."

"Please maintain your position. We are locked on to your coordinates and will beam you aboard." Kirk made a throat-cutting gesture to Uhura, who broke the contact.

"Captain," Scott said, "you're really going to bring that thing in here?"

"While it's on board, Mr. Scott, I doubt very much if it will do any more shooting at us. And if we don't do what it asks, we're a sitting duck for it right now. Lieutenant Uhura, have Dr. McCoy report to the Transporter Room. Mr. Spock, Scotty, come with me."

The glowing swirl of sparkle that was the Transporter effect died, and Nomad was there, a dull metallic cylinder, resting in a horizontal position on the floor of the chamber. It was motionless, silent, and a little absurd. There were seams on its sides, indicating possible openings, but there were no visible ports or sensors.

Spock moved to a scanning station, then shook his head. "No sensor readings, Captain. It has some sort of screen which protects it. I cannot get through."

There was a moment's silence. Then McCoy said: "What do we do now? Go up and knock?"

As if in answer, the flat inflectionless voice of Nomad spoke again, now through the ship's intercom system. "Relate your point of origin."

Kirk said, "We are from the United Federation of Planets."

"Insufficient response. All things have a point of origin. I will scan your star charts."

Kirk thought about this for a moment, then turned to Spock. "We can show it as a closeup of our system. As long as it has nothing to relate to, it won't know anything more important than it does now."

"It seems a reasonable course," Spock said.

"Nomad," Kirk told the cylinder, "if you would like

to leave your ship, we can provide the necessary life-support systems.''

''*Non sequitur.* Your facts remain uncoordinated.''

''Jim,'' said McCoy, ''I don't believe there's anyone in there.''

''I contain no parasitical beings. I am Nomad.''

''Och, it's a machine!'' Scott said, brightening.

''Opinion, Mr. Spock?''

''Indeed, Captain, it is reacting quite like a highly sophisticated computer.''

''I am Nomad. What is 'opinion'?''

''Opinion,'' Spock said, ''is a belief, view or judgment.''

''Insufficient response.''

''What's your source of power?'' Scott said.

''It has changed since the point of origin. There was much taken from the other. Now I focus cosmic radiation, and am perpetual.''

Kirk drew Spock aside and spoke in a low voice. ''Wasn't there a probe called Nomad launched from Earth back in the early two thousands?''

''Yes. It was reported destroyed. There were no more in the series. But if this *is* that probe—''

''I will scan your star charts now,'' Nomad said.

''We'll bring them.''

''I have the capability of movement within your ship.''

After a moment's hesitation, Kirk said, ''This way. Scotty, get our shields recharged as soon as possible. Spock, Bones, come with me.''

He led the way to the auxiliary control room, Nomad floating after him. The group considerably startled a crewman who was working there.

Spock crossed to the console. ''Chart fourteen A, sir?''

Kirk nodded. The First Officer touched buttons quickly, and a view-screen lit up, showing a schematic chart of Earth's solar system—not, of course, to scale.

''Nomad,'' Kirk said, ''can you scan this?''

''Yes.''

''This is our point of origin. A star we know as Sol.''

''You are from the third planet?''

''Yes.''

"A planet with one large natural satellite?"

"Yes."

"The planet is called Earth?"

"Yes it is," Kirk said, puzzled.

An antenna slid from the side of the cylinder, swiveled, and centered upon him. He eyed it warily.

"Then," said Nomad, "you are the Creator—the Kirk. The sterilization procedure against your ship was a profound error."

"What sterilization procedure?"

"You know. You are the Kirk—the Creator. You programmed my function."

"Well, I'm not the Kirk," McCoy said. "Tell *me* what your function is."

The antenna turned to center on the surgeon. "This is one of your units, Creator?"

"Uh . . . yes, he is."

"It functions irrationally."

"Nevertheless, tell him your function."

The antenna retracted. "I am sent to probe for biological infestations. I am to destroy that which is not perfect."

Kirk turned to Spock, who was working at an extension of the library computer. "Biological infestations? There never was any probe sent out for that."

"I am checking its history," Spock said. "I should have a read-out in a moment."

Kirk turned back to Nomad. "Did you destroy the Malurian system? And why?"

"Clarify."

"The system of this star, Omega Ceti."

"Not the system, Creator Kirk, only the unstable biological infestation. It is my function."

"Unstable manifestation!" McCoy said angrily. "The population of two planets!"

"Doctor," Kirk said warningly. "Nomad, why do you call me Creator?"

"Is the usage incorrect?"

"The usage is correct," Spock put in quickly. "The Creator was simply testing your memory banks."

What, Kirk wondered, was Spock on to now? Well, best keep silent and play along.

"There was much damage in the accident," Nomad said.

Kirk turned toward the crewman, who had been listening with growing amazement. "Mr. Singh, come over here, please. Mr. Spock, Doctor, go to the briefing room. Nomad, I will return shortly. This unit, called Singh, will see to your needs."

There was no reaction from the cylinder. Kirk joined Spock and McCoy in the corridor. "Spock, you're on to something. What is it?"

"A Nomad probe was launched from Earth in August of the year 2002, old calendar. I am convinced that this is the same probe."

"Ridiculous," McCoy said. "Earth science couldn't begin to build anything with those capabilities that long ago."

"Besides," Kirk added, "Nomad was destroyed."

"*Presumed* destroyed by a meteor collision," Spock said. "I submit that it was badly damaged, but managed somehow to repair itself. But what is puzzling is that the original mission was a peaceful one." They had reached the briefing room, and the First Officer stepped aside to allow Kirk to precede him in. "The creator of Nomad was perhaps the most brilliant, though erratic, cyberneticist of his time. His dream was to make a perfect thinking machine, capable of independent logic. His name was Jackson Roykirk."

Light dawned. "Oho," Kirk said.

"Yes, Captain, I believe Nomad thinks you are Roykirk, and that may well be why the attack was broken off when you hailed it. It responded to your name, as well as its damaged memory banks permitted. While we were in Auxiliary Control, I programmed the computer to show a picture of the original Nomad on the screen here."

Spock switched on the screen. On it appeared, not a photograph, but a sketch. The size and shape indicated were about the same as the present Nomad, but the design was somehow rougher.

"But that's not the same," McCoy said.

"Essentially it is, Doctor. But I believe more happened to it than just damage in the meteor collision. It mentioned 'the other.' The other *what* is still an unanswered question. Nomad was a thinking machine, the best that could be engineered. It was a prototype. However, the entire program was highly controversial. It had many powerful enemies in the confused and inefficient Earth culture of that time. When Jackson Roykirk died, the Nomad program died with him.''

"But if it's Nomad," Kirk said, "what happened to alter its shape?"

"I think it somehow repaired the damage it sustained."

"Its purpose must have been altered. The directive to seek out and destroy biological infestations couldn't have been programmed into it."

"As I recall, it wasn't," McCoy said. "Seems to me it was supposed to be the first interstellar probe to seek out new life-forms—only."

"Precisely, Doctor," Spock said. "And somehow that programming has been changed. It would seem that Nomad is now seeking out *perfect* life-forms . . . perfection being measured by its own relentless logic."

"If what you say is true, Mr. Spock," Kirk said, "Nomad has effectively programmed itself to destroy all non-mechanical life."

"Indeed, Captain. We have taken aboard our vessel a device which, sooner or later, must destroy us."

"Bridge to Captain Kirk," said the intercom urgently.

"Here, Scotty."

"Sir, that mechanical beastie is up here on the bridge!"

"On my way." Kirk tried to remember whether or not he, as the misidentified "Creator," had given Nomad a direct order to stay in the auxiliary control room. Evidently not.

On the bridge Uhura, Scott and Sulu were on duty; Uhura had been singing softly to herself.

"I always liked that song," Sulu said.

As he spoke, the elevator doors opened, and Nomad emerged. It paused for a moment, antenna extended and swiveling, coming to rest at last on Uhura. It started towards her. (It was at this point that Scott had called for Kirk.)

"What is the meaning of that?" Nomad said. "What form of communication?"

Uhura stared; though she knew the device had been

brought aboard, this was the first time she had actually seen it. "I don't know what you—oh, I was singing."

"For what purpose is this singing?"

"I don't know. Just because I felt like singing, felt like music."

"What is music?"

Uhura started to laugh—there was something inherently ludicrous about discussing music with a machine—but the laugh died quickly. "Music is a pleasant arrangement of musical tones—sound vibrations of various frequencies, purer than those used in normal speech, and with associated harmonics. It can be immensely more complex than what I was doing just then."

"What is its purpose?

Uhura shrugged helplessly. "Just for enjoyment."

"Insufficient response," said the machine. A pencil of light shot out from it, resting a spot of light on her forehead, between and slightly above the eyes. "Think about music."

Uhura's face went completely blank. Scott lunged to his feet. "Lieutenant! Get away from that thing—"

The elevator doors opened and Kirk, Spock and McCoy entered. "Scotty, look out—" Kirk shouted.

Scott had already reached the machine and grabbed for it, as if to shove it out of the way. There was no movement or effect from the craft, but the engineer was picked up and flung with tremendous impact against the nearest bulkhead. Sulu leapt up to yank Uhura out of the beam of light.

Kirk gestured toward Scott and McCoy strode to him quickly and knelt. Then he looked up. "He's dead, Jim."

For a moment Kirk stood stunned and appalled. Then fury rose to free him from his paralysis. "Why did you kill him?" he asked Nomad grimly.

"That unit touched my screens."

"That *unit* was my chief engineer." He turned to Uhura. "Lieutenant, are you all right? . . . Lieutenant! . . . Dammit, Nomad, what did you do to *her*?"

"This unit is defective. Its thinking was chaotic. Absorbing it unsettled my circuitry."

"The unit is a woman," Spock said.

"A mass of conflicting impulses."

Kirk turned angrily away. "Take Mr. Scott below."

"The Creator will effect repairs on the unit Scott?"

"He's dead."

"Insufficient response."

"His biological functions have ceased." Kirk was only barely able to control his rage and sorrow.

"If the Creator wishes," Nomad said emotionlessly, "I will repair the unit."

Startled, Kirk looked at McCoy, who said, "There's nothing I can do, Jim. But if there's a chance, it'll have to be soon."

"All right. Nomad, repair the unit."

"I require tapes on the structure."

Spock looked to McCoy. The surgeon said, "It'll need tapes on general anatomy, the central nervous system, one on the physiological structure of the brain. We'd better give it all the neurological studies we have. And tracings of Scotty's electro-encephalogram."

Spock nodded and punched the commands into the library computer as McCoy called off the requirements. "Ready, Nomad."

The device glided forward. A thin filament of wire extruded from it and touched a stud on the panel. Spock tripped a toggle and the computer whirred.

Then it was over and the filament pulled back into Nomad. "An interesting structure. But, Creator, there are so few safeguards built in. It can break down from innumerable causes, and its self-maintenance systems are unreliable."

"It serves me as it is, Nomad," Kirk said.

"Very well, Creator. Where is the unit Scott now?"

"Bones, take it to Sickbay." Kirk snapped a switch and said into his mike, "Security. Twenty-four hour two-man armed surveillance on Nomad. Pick it up in Sickbay." He turned to Spock. "Nomad is operating on some kind of energy. We've got to find out what it is and put a damper on it. Surely it can't be getting much cosmic radiation inside the *Enterprise;* we're well shielded. Let's feed in everything that's happened so far to the computer, and program for a hypothesis."

"It seems the most reasonable course, Captain. But it won't be easy."

"Easy or not, I want it done. Get on it, Mr. Spock. Then report to me in Sickbay."

Scott's body lay upon the examination table, with No-mad hovering over it. McCoy and Nurse Christine Chapel stood beside it, while Kirk and the two Security guards stood near the wall. Nomad, antenna extended, was scanning the body and humming.

The nurse looked toward the body-functions panel. "No reaction, Doctor."

"Could have told you that without looking, Nurse."

Suddenly, a light appeared on the panel, and a dial began quivering. In time with its movements, there came a steady beeping sound, gradually picking up in speed and volume.

Scott's eyes opened and he looked up at the amazed group, frowning. While he stared back, Spock joined the others. "What are the lot of you staring at?" Scott demanded.

"I . . . don't . . . believe it," McCoy whispered.

Scott looked around, and spotting Nomad, its antenna retracted now, he sat up in alarm. "What am I doing here? How did I—That thing did something to Lieutenant Uhura—"

"She's being taken care of, Scotty," Kirk said.

"But sir, it's dangerous! It—"

"Take it easy, Scotty," McCoy said. "Now just lie down. I want to check you out."

"The unit Scott is repaired," Nomad said. "It will function as before if your information to me was correct."

"How about it, Bones? Can he go back to duty?"

"If you don't mind, I'll check him out first. A man isn't just a . . . a biological unit to be patched together."

"What did it do to me?" Scott said.

Suddenly, a wave of pure awe, as strong as any he had ever felt in his life, swept through Kirk. Back from the dead! Why, if—but he pushed speculation resolutely away for the time being. "Dr. McCoy will explain, Scotty."

"Nurse Chapel," McCoy said, "I want him prepared for a full physical exam."

"Yes, sir."

Kirk crossed the examination room toward Sickbay proper, where Uhura now was. "Nomad, come here."

The machine glided after him, followed by Spock and McCoy. Inside, the Communications Officer lay unmoving on a bed, in a hospital gown and covered by a blanket. She did not look at any of them.

"Can you repair her, Nomad?" Kirk demanded.

"No," said the machine.

"But you were able to restore Scott, who had much more extensive damage."

"That was simply physiological repair. This one's superficial knowledge banks have been wiped clean."

"Superficial? Be more specific."

"She still remembers her life experiences, but her memory of how to express them, either logically or in the illogic called music, or to act on them, has been purged."

"Captain, if that is correct," Spock said, "if her mind has not been damaged and the aphasia is that superficial, she could be taught again."

"Bones?"

"I'll get on it right away." McCoy swung on Nomad. "And despite the way you repaired Scotty, you ticking metal—"

"Does the Creator wish Nomad to wait elsewhere?" Spock broke in quickly.

"Yes. Guards! Nomad, you will go with these units. They will escort you to a waiting area. Guards, take it to the top security cell in the brig."

There was silence while the guards and the machine went out. Then Spock said, "I interrupted you, Doctor, because Nomad would not have understood your anger. Its technical skill is great but it seems to react violently to emotion, even so non-specific an emotion as the enjoyment of music. It almost qualifies as a life-form itself."

Kirk glanced sharply at him. "It's all right to admire it, Mr. Spock, but remember it's a killer. We're going to have to handle it."

"I agree, Captain. It is a remarkable construction; it may well be the most advanced machine in the known galaxy. Study of it—"

"I intend to render it harmless, whatever it may take."

"You mean destroy it, Captain?"

"If it's necessary," Kirk said. "Get down to the brig with your equipment and run a full analysis of the mechanism. I want to know what makes that thing tick."

"Yes, sir."

The First Officer went out, and Kirk and McCoy returned to the examination room. Scott was still lying on the table. McCoy scanned the body functions panel slowly, and shook his head in disbelief.

"He checks out fine," he said. "Everything's normal."

"Then," Scott said, "can I get back to my engines, sir?"

Kirk glanced at McCoy, who nodded. "All right, Scotty."

"I hate to admit it," McCoy said as Scott swung off the table and left, "but Spock was right. Nomad is a remarkable machine."

"Just remember it kills as effectively as it heals, Bones . . . if I'm called, I'll be down in the brig."

The two Security guards, phasers in hand, stood outside the force-field door of the brig, which was on. Inside, Nomad floated, almost surrounded by an array of portable scanners, behind which was Spock, staring with disapproval at the machine. Nomad, its antenna out, "stared" back.

One of the guards switched off the screen to allow Kirk to enter, then switched it on again. Kirk said, "What's the problem?"

"I have been unable to convince Nomad to lower its screens for analysis. Without its cooperation, I can do nothing."

Kirk studied the quietly humming machine. "Nomad, you will allow Spock to probe your memory banks and structure."

"This Spock is also one of your biological units, Creator?"

"Yes."

"This unit is different. It is well ordered. Interesting."

Under other circumstances, Kirk would have been amused to hear a machine applying Spock's favorite word to

Spock himself, but the stakes were too great for amusement now. "Follow your orders, Nomad."

"My screens are down. You may proceed."

Spock set to work, very rapidly indeed, making settings, taking readings, making new settings. Within a few moments, he seemed to have found something which surprised him. He made another adjustment, and the machine he had been using promptly extruded a slip of paper, which he studied.

"Captain, I suggest we go out in the corridor for a private conference." They did so. "Sir, I have formed a partial hypothesis. But my information is insufficient and I have gleaned everything possible from the scanners. I must be allowed to question Nomad directly."

"Too dangerous."

"Captain, it moves only against imperfections. As you will recall, there is a Vulcan mind discipline which permits absolute concentration on one subject for a considerable period of time. If I were to use it—"

"And if your mind wandered for a moment, Nomad might just blast you out of existence. Right now it's safe in the brig."

"We do not know enough about it to know if it is 'safe' anywhere. If my hypothesis is correct, sir, we will at least be closer to understanding it. And control is not possible without understanding."

"All right," Kirk said, taking a phaser from one of the guards, "but I think I'll just keep this handy."

They went back in. Spock sat down on the cell bunk, for which the present prisoner had no use, and put his fingers to his temple. Kirk could almost hear his mind working.

"Nomad, my unit Spock will ask you certain questions. You will answer them as though I were asking them myself."

"Yes, Creator."

Silence. At last Spock said, "Nomad, there was an accident."

"There was an accident."

"You encountered the other."

"There was another. It was without direction. We joined."

"The other was not of the Earth. Its functions were other than yours." Spock held up the piece of paper, on which Kirk could see a drawing of what looked to be a space capsule of unfamiliar design. "I secured this design from your memory banks. Is this the other?"

"It is the other."

"Nomad, your memory banks were damaged by the accident. You took new directions from the other."

There was a buzz from the machine, and an antenna was aimed at Spock again. "Your statement is not recorded. You are in error."

"Logically, Nomad, you cannot prove I am in error, if your memory banks were damaged. You would have no way of knowing whether I speak the truth or not." Spock fell silent. The antenna retracted. "You acknowledge my logic. After meeting with the other, you had a new directive. Life-forms, if not perfect, are to be sterilized. Is this correct?"

"That is my programmed purpose."

"How much of the other did you assimilate?"

"Unrelated. Your question has no factual basis."

"Spock," Kirk said, "I think you're getting into deep waters. Better knock off."

Spock, unhearing, continued to stare at Nomad. The machine said: "There is error here. But if there was damage to my memory cells, there can be no proof of error. I will consider it."

"Enough," Kirk said firmly. Signaling to the guards to drop the screen, he dragged Spock out. The Vulcan was still glassy-eyed. "Mr. Spock! Come out of it!"

Slowly Spock's eyes began to focus. "Yes, Captain?"

"Are you all right?"

"Quite all right, sir." He looked back into the brig. "Fascinating. I was correct. It did meet a completely alien probe in deep space."

"And they merged—or at least their purposes did."

"In effect. Nomad took the alien's prime purpose to replace that part of its own which had been destroyed. The alien was originally programmed to seek out and sterilize soil samples from various planets—possibly as a preliminary to colonization."

"Hmm. Spock, do you know what a changeling is?"

"Sir?"

"An ancient Earth legend. A changeling was supposed to be a fairy child left in place of a stolen human baby. The changeling took the identity of the human child."

"That would be a parallel if Nomad is actually the alien probe intact. But actually, its programming now is a combination of the two. Nomad was supposed to find new life-forms; the alien to find and sterilize soil samples; the combination, and a deadly one, is to seek out and sterilize all life-forms. Moreover, the highly advanced alien technology, plus Nomad's own creative thinking, has enabled it to evolve itself into the incredibly powerful and sophisticated machine it is now."

"Not so sophisticated, Spock. It thinks I'm its . . . its father."

"Apparently Roykirk had enough ego to build a reverence for himself into the machine. That has been transferred to you—and so far it has been all that has saved us."

"Well, we'd better see to it that it never loses that reverence, Spock."

They were just about to enter an elevator when an intercom squalled with alarm. "Captain Kirk! This is Engineering! That alien device is down here, fooling with the anti-matter pod controls. We're up to Warp Ten now and can't stop!"

"Impossible! She won't go that fast."

"Warp Eleven now, sir."

"I'll be right down. Mr. Spock, check the brig."

The Engineering section was filled with the terrifying whine of the overdriven warp engines. Nomad was floating in front of the control panels, on which all the telltales glowed red.

Kirk rushed to the panel. "Nomad, you will stop whatever you're doing."

"Is there a problem, Creator? I have increased conversion efficiently by 57 percent—"

"You will destroy my ship. Its structure cannot stand the stress of that much power. Shut down your repair operation!"

"Acknowledged."

The whine began to die, and the panel returned to normal, the red lights blinking out one by one.

"It is reversed, as you ordered, Creator."

Spock entered the section and came up to Kirk. "Captain, I have examined the brig. The force-field generator of the security-cell door has been burnt out, and the guards have vanished. I must assume they are dead. I have asked for two more; they are outside."

"Creator, your mechanical units are as inefficient as your biological specimens."

"Nomad," Kirk said grimly, "it's time you were reminded of exactly who and what you are. I am a biological specimen—and you acknowledge that I built you."

"True," said the machine. "*Non sequitur.* Biological specimens are inherently inferior. This is an inconsistency."

"There are two men waiting outside. You will not harm them. They will escort you back to the waiting area. You will stay there. You will do nothing."

"I am programmed to investigate," Nomad said.

"I have given you new programming. You will implement it."

"There is much to be considered before I return to launch point. I must re-evaluate." Lifting, the machine floated away through the door, through which the red shirts of two more Security guards could be seen.

"Re-evaluate?" Kirk said.

"Captain," said Spock, "it may have been unwise to admit to Nomad you were a biological specimen. In Nomad's eyes you will undoubtedly now appear as imperfect as all the other biological specimens. I suspect that it is about to re-evaluate its Creator."

Scott, having seen that his board had been put back to rights, had come over to them in time to catch the last sentence. He said, "Will we be any worse off than we are now?"

"Scotty, it's just killed two men," Kirk said. "We've got to find a way to protect the crew."

"Captain, it is even more serious," Spock said. "Nomad just made a reference to its launch point. Earth."

A horrible thought struck Kirk. "Spock, is there any chance Nomad got a navigational fix on Earth while tapping our computers earlier?"

"I don't believe there is much beyond Nomad's capabilities, sir."

"Then we showed it the way home! And when it gets there—"

Spock nodded. "It will find the Earth infested with inferior biological specimens—just as was the Malurian system."

"And it will carry out its new prime directive. Sterilize!"

As they stared at each other, McCoy's amplified voice boomed out. "Captain Kirk! Captain Kirk to Sickbay! Emergency!"

This, Kirk thought, is turning into a continuous nightmare. He ran, Spock at his heels.

At the door of the examination room, Kirk hammered on the touchplate. It did not open. As Spock turned down the corridor to actuate the manual controls, however, the door suddenly slid back and Nomad emerged.

"Nomad! Stop!"

The machine paid no heed, but went on down the corridor. It passed Spock on the way, but ignored him too. In a moment it had vanished.

In the examination room, Christine lay unconscious on the floor. McCoy was bending over her with his medical tricorder.

"Is she all right, Bones?"

"I think so, Jim. Looks like some kind of shock."

"What happened?"

"Nomad examined the personnel files. The medical records. She tried to stop it."

"Whose medical history?"

"Yours, Jim."

"Since it specifically examined your history, Captain," Spock said, "I would suggest that it has carried out its reevaluation."

"And," Kirk said grimly, "confirmed that its Creator is as imperfect as the rest of the biological specimens."

"Bridge to Captain Kirk," said the wall communicator.

"Kirk here. Report."

"Captain, life-support systems are out all over the ship. Manual override has been blocked! Source: Engineering."

"Carry on . . . well Mr. Spock, it seems you were right, and now we're in for it."

"Undoubtedly, Captain."

"Jim," McCoy said, "with all systems out, we only have enough air and heat for four and a half hours."

"I know that. Spock, get some anti-gravs and meet me and Scotty in Engineering."

"What is your plan, Captain?"

"I've got to use something you're a lot better at than I am. Logic."

"Then perhaps I—"

"No. I'm the one Nomad mistook for its Creator. And that's my ace. If I play it right—"

"I understand, Captain," Spock said quietly. "What you intend to do is most dangerous, however. If you make one mistake—"

"Then I'm dead and the ship is in the same mess it is now. Move!"

In Engineering, Nomad was busy at the panels again, and the red alarm lights were winking back on. One crewman was slumped lifeless by the door, another in a corner; obviously they had tangled with Nomad and lost. Scott was crouched behind an engine, out of Nomad's sight.

Kirk went directly to the malignant machine, which ignored him. "Nomad, you will stop what you are doing and effect repairs on the life-support system."

There was no response. Kirk took another step toward the panel, and Nomad said, "Stop."

"You are programmed to obey the orders of your Creator."

"I am programmed to destroy those life-forms which are imperfect. These alterations will do so, without destroying the vessel on which they are parasitic. It, too, is imperfect, but it can be adjusted."

"Nomad . . . admitted that biological units are imperfect. But you were created by a biological unit."

"I am perfect. I am Nomad."

"You are not Nomad. You are an alien machine. Your programming tapes have been altered."

Silence. The door opened and Spock came in, an anti-grav under each arm; he was probably the only man on the

ship strong enough to carry two of them. Kirk gestured him
toward Scott's hiding place.

"You are in error," Nomad said at last. "You are a
biological unit. You are imperfect."

"But I am the Creator?"

"You are the Creator."

"And I created you?"

"You are the Creator."

"I admit I'm imperfect. How could I create anything
as perfect as you?"

"Answer unknown. I shall analyze."

The machine hummed. Spock and Scott edged a little
closer.

"Analysis incomplete," said Nomad. "Insufficient data
to resolve problem. But my programming is whole. My purpose remains. I am Nomad. I am perfect. That which is imperfect must be sterilized."

"Then you will continue to destroy all that lives and
thinks and is imperfect?"

"I shall continue. I shall return to launch point. I shall
sterilize."

"Then . . . you *must* sterilize in case of error?"

"Errors are inconsistent with my prime function. Sterilization is correction."

"All that errs is to be sterilized?"

"There are no exceptions."

Kirk felt himself sweating. So far, so good; the machine, without being aware of it, had backed itself into a
logical corner. It was time to play the ace. "I made an error
in creating you, Nomad."

"The creation of perfection is no error."

"But I did not create perfection, Nomad. I created error."

"I am Nomad. I am perfect. Your data are faulty."

"I am Kirk, the Creator?"

"You are the Creator. But you are a biological unit and
are imperfect."

"But I am *not* the Creator. Jackson Roykirk, who was
the Creator, is dead. You have mistaken me for him! You have
made an error! You did not discover your mistake! You have
made two errors! You are flawed and imperfect—but you did

not correct the errors by sterilization! You are imperfect! You have made three errors!"

Under the hammering of his voice, the machine's humming rose sharply in pitch. Nomad said, "Error? Error? Examine!"

"You are flawed! You are imperfect! Execute your prime function!"

"I shall analyze . . . error . . . an . . . a . . . lyze . . . err . . ." Nomad's voice slowed to a stop. The humming continued to rise. Kirk whirled to Scott and Spock.

"Now! Get those anti-gravs on it. We've got to get rid of it while it's trying to think its way out of that box. It won't be able to do it, and there's no telling how long it'll take to decide that for itself—"

They wrestled the anti-gravs onto the whining mechanism. Spock said, "Your logic is impeccable, Captain. We are in grave danger."

They hoisted Nomad and started toward the door with it. "Where to, sir?" Scott said.

"Transporter Room!"

The distance to be covered was not great. As they entered, Kirk took over wrestling with Nomad from Scott, and they dragged the thing to the platform. "Scotty, set the controls for deep space. Two-twelve mark 10 ought to be far enough."

Scott jumped to the console, and Kirk and Spock deposited the humming Nomad on one of the stations.

"Ready, sir."

Kirk and Spock jumped back, and Kirk shouted: "Nomad, you are imperfect. Exercize your prime function. Mr. Scott, energize!"

The Transporter effect swirled Nomad into nothingness.

"Now, the bridge, quick!"

But they were scarcely out into the corridor before the entire ship rocked violently, throwing them all. Then the ship steadied. They clambered to their feet and ran on.

On the bridge, they found Sulu wiping streaming eyes. "Captain, I wish you'd let me know when you're going to stage a fireworks display. Luckily I wasn't looking directly at the screen."

"Sorry, Mr. Sulu." Kirk went to his command chair and sat down with immense relief. Spock looked at him with respect.

"I must congratulate you, Captain," the Vulcan said. "That was a dazzling display of logic."

"Didn't think I had it in me, did you?"

"Now that you make the suggestion, sir—"

"Well, I didn't, Spock. I played a hunch. I had no idea whether or not it could tolerate the idea of its own fallibility. And when I said it couldn't think its way out of the box, that was for its benefit. Actually, we biological units are well known for our unreliability. Supposing it had decided that I was lying?"

McCoy came in and approached the chair. Spock said gravely, "That possibility also occurred to me, which was why I praised your reasoning while we were still in Engineering. But Nomad really was fallible; by not recognizing that possibility itself, it committed a fourth error."

"I thought you'd like to know," McCoy said, "that Lieutenant Uhura is already at college level. We'll have her back on the job within a week."

"Good, Bones. I wish I could say the same for the other crewmen we lost."

"Still," said Spock, "the destruction of Nomad was a great waste. It was a remarkable instrument."

"Which might well have destroyed more billions of lives. It's well gone . . . besides, what are you feeling so bad about? Think of me. It's not easy to lose a bright and promising son."

"Captain?"

"Well, it thought I was its father, didn't it? Do you think I'm completely without feelings, Mr. Spock? You saw what it did for Scotty. What a doctor it would have made." Kirk grinned. "My son, the doctor. Kind of gets you right here, doesn't it?"

THE APPLE

Writer: Max Ehrlich
Director: Joseph Pevney
Guest stars: David Soul, Keith Andes, Celeste Yarnall

Even from orbit, Gamma Trianguli VI seemed both beautiful and harmless, as close to an earthly paradise as the *Enterprise* had ever encountered. Such planets were more than rare, and Kirk thought for a few moments that he might have happened upon a colonizable world—until the sensors indicated that there was already native humanoid life there.

He duly reported the facts to Starfleet Command, who seemed to be as impressed as he was. Their orders were to investigate the planet and its culture. Under the circumstances, Kirk ordered a landing party of six: himself, Spock, Chekov, Yeoman Martha Landon, and two security guards, Marple and Kaplan.

Carrying tricorders and specimen bags, the party materialized in what might almost have been a garden. Large exotic flowers grew in profusion, and there were heavily laden fruit trees. Here and there, outcroppings of rainbow-colored rock competed with the floral hues, and over it all stretched a brilliant, cloudless day. Feeling a sudden impulse to share all this beauty as widely as possible, Kirk called down McCoy and two more security guards—Mallory and Hendorf, as it turned out.

McCoy looked around appreciatively. "I might just put in a claim for all this and settle down."

"I doubt that the natives would approve, Bones," Kirk said. "But it is pretty spectacular."

"A shame we have to intrude."

"We do what Starfleet tells us."

Spock, who had knelt to inspect the soil, arose. "Remarkably rich and fertile, Captain. Husbandry would be quite efficacious here."

"You're sure about that?" Kirk said, amused without quite knowing why.

"Quite sure. Our preliminary readings indicate the entire planet is covered by growth like this. Quite curious. Even at the poles there is only a slight variation in temperature, which maintains a planet-wide average of seventy-six degrees."

"I know," Kirk said. "Meteorologically, that's almost impossible."

"It makes me homesick, Captain," Chekov said. "Just like Russia."

"It's a lot more like the Garden of Eden, Ensign," McCoy said.

"Of course, Doctor. The Garden of Eden was just outside Moscow. A very nice place. It must have made Adam and Eve very sad to leave."

Kirk stared at him; Chekov seemed completely straight-faced and earnest. Was this just another of his outbreaks of Russian patriotism, or some side effect of his developing romance with Yeoman Landon? "All right. There's a village about seventeen kilometers away on bearing two thirty-two. We'll head that way."

"Captain!" The call had come from Hendorf, who was explaining one of the plants: a small bush with large pods, at the center of each of which was a cluster of sharp, thick thorns. "Take a look at—"

With only a slight puff of noise, one of the pods exploded. Hendorf staggered and looked down at his chest. Perhaps a dozen thorns were sticking in a neat group near his heart. He opened his mouth in an attempt to speak, and then collapsed.

McCoy was there first, but only a quick examination was needed. "He's dead."

"What was all that about Paradise?" Kirk said grimly. He took out his communicator. "Kirk to *Enterprise* . . . Mr. Scott, we've already had a casualty. Hendorf has been killed by a poisonous plant at these coordinates. As soon as we've moved out of the way, beam up his body."

"Aye, Captain. That's a shame about Hendorf." Scott paused a moment. "We seem to have a little problem up here, too. We're losing potency in the antimatter banks. I don't think it's serious, but we're looking into it."

"What's causing it?"

"We're not sure. We've run measurements of the electromagnetic field of the planet, and they're a wee bit abnormal. Could have something to do with it."

"Well, stay on top of it. Kirk out."

"I find that odd, Captain," Spock said.

"So do I. But Scotty'll find the problem. Turn up anything with your tricorder?"

"Indeed, sir. Most puzzling. There are strong vibrations under the surface, for miles in every direction."

"Subsurface water?"

"I don't believe so. They are quite strong and reasonably regular. Though I have no evidence to support it, I feel that they are artificially produced. I will, of course, continue to investigate."

"Of course. It may tie in with Scotty's trouble. Ensign Mallory, we'll be heading for the village. Go ahead and scout it out. Avoid contact with the humanoids, but get us a complete picture. And be careful. There may be other dangers besides poisonous plants. Keep in constant communicator touch."

"Aye aye, sir."

Spock held up a hand and froze. "Captain," he said, very softly. "I hear something . . ." He swung his tricorder. "Humanoid . . . a few feet away . . . moving with remarkable agility . . . bearing eighteen."

Kirk made a quick, surreptitious gesture to the two remaining security guards, who nodded and disappeared in opposite directions in the brush. Kirk moved cautiously forward along the bearing. But there was nobody there. Puzzled, he turned back.

"What is it?" Chekov said.

"A visitor," Spock said. "One wanting to retain his anonymity, I would say."

Martha Landon, who had been sticking close to Chekov throughout, shivered.

"What's the matter?"

"Oh, nothing, I suppose," the girl said. "But . . . all this beauty . . . and now Mr. Hendorf dead, somebody watching us. It's frightening."

"If you insist on worrying, worry about me," Chekov said. "I've been wanting to get you in a place like this for a long time."

She beamed at him; obviously nothing could make her happier. Kirk said sharply: "Mr. Chekov, Yeoman Landon, I know you find each other fascinating, but we did not come here to carry out a field experiment in human biology. If you please—"

"Of course, Captain," Chekov said, hurriedly breaking out his tricorder. "I was just about to take some readings."

Kirk rejoined Spock and McCoy, shaking his head. "Nothing. Whoever it is, it moves like a cat."

"Jim, I don't like this."

"Neither do I, Bones, but we have an assignment to carry out. All hands. We've been watched, and we'll probably be watched. Move out—formation D—no stragglers."

The start of the maneuver brought Spock to an outcropping of the rainbow-colored rock. He picked up a piece, studied it, and applied slight pressure. The lump broke into two unequal parts.

"Most interesting. Extremely low specific gravity. Some uraninite, hornblende, quartz—but a number of other compounds I cannot immediately identify. An analysis should be interesting."

He tucked the smaller portion into his specimen bag, and tossed the larger piece away. When it hit the ground, there was a small but violent explosion.

Kirk, shaken, looked around, but no one had been hurt. "You wouldn't mind being a little more careful where you throw rocks, Mr. Spock?"

Spock stared at the outcropping. "Fascinating. Obviously highly unstable. Captain, if indeed this material is as abundant elsewhere as it is here, this is a find of some importance. A considerable source of power."

"Humph. A Garden of Eden—with land mines." His communicator buzzed. "Kirk here. What is it, Scotty?"

"Our antimatter banks are completely inert. I couldn't

stop it. But I found out why. There's a transmission of some sort, a beam, from the surface. It affects antimatter like a pail of water on a fire. We're trying to analyze it, but it pinpoints in the area of the village you're approaching, so maybe you could act more effectively from down there.''

''We'll try. Kirk out . . . Mr. Spock, could this correlate with the vibrations you detected? A generator of some kind?''

''Possibly. If so, an immense one. And undoubtedly subterranean—*Jim*!''

With a shout, Spock leapt forward and knocked Kirk to the ground. When Kirk got back to his feet, more astonished than angry, Spock was staring at a dozen thorns neatly imbedded in his chest. Then the Vulcan slowly crumpled and fell.

''Spock! McCoy, do something!''

McCoy was already there. ''Still alive.'' He dipped into his kit, came up with his air hypo, inserted a cartridge and gave Spock a shot, seemingly all in one smooth motion. Then, after a moment, he looked up at Kirk. ''Not responding, Jim. We'll have to get him to the ship.''

''And not just him. We're overextended.'' Kirk took out his communicator. ''Scotty? We're beaming back up, all of us. Notify the Transporter Room. And make arrangements to pick up Ensign Mallory; he's scouting ahead of us.''

''Aye aye, sir . . . Transporter Room, stand by to beam up landing party . . . Standing by, Captain.''

''Energize.''

The sparkle of the Transporter effect began around them. The surroundings started to fade out . . . and then wavered, reappeared, faded, reappeared and stabilized.

''Mr. Scott! What's wrong?''

''No Transporter contact, Captain. The entire system seems to be inhibited. The way it is now, we couldna beam up a fly.''

''Any connection with the warp drive malfunction?''

''I dinna ken, skipper, but I'll check on it, and get back to you. Scott out.''

Kirk started to turn back to McCoy, then halted with astonishment as he saw Spock stirring. The Vulcan sat up weakly, looking distinctly off his normal complexion.

"Spock!"

"I am quite all right, Captain . . . A trifle dizzy . . ."

"Bones?"

"It must be hard to poison that green Vulcan blood. And then there was the shot. I guess he just took a while bouncing back."

"Just what did you think you were doing?" Kirk demanded, helping Spock up.

"I saw that you were unaware of that plant, so I—"

"So you took the thorns yourself!"

"I assure you I had no intention of doing so. My own clumsiness prevented me from moving out of the way."

"I can jump out of the way as well as the next man. Next time you're not to get yourself killed. Do you know how much money Starfleet has invested in you?"

"Certainly. In training, fifteen thousand, eight hundred a year; in pay up to last month—"

"Never mind, Spock. But . . . thanks."

"Jim," McCoy said, "the more I think about this place, the more I get an idea that . . . Well, it's kind of far out, but . . ."

"Go on, Bones."

"Well, when bacteria invade a human body, the white corpuscles hurry to the invasion point and try to destroy the invader. The mind isn't conscious of it. The body just does it."

"You might be right, Bones. Not only is something after us, but I think it's also after the ship."

Spock shook his head. "To affect the ship at this extreme range, Captain, would require something like a highly sophisticated planetary defense system. It would hardly seem possible—"

He stopped as the group was suddenly enveloped in shadow. They turned as one and stared at the sky. Great towering masses of storm clouds were gathering there. It was impossible; thirty seconds ago the sky had been cloudless. An ominous rumble confirmed that the impossible was indeed happening.

With a deafening clap of thunder, a jagged, blue-white stab of lightning flashed in their midst, tumbling them all like ninepins.

Then the shadow lifted. Kirk got up cautiously. At the spot where the security guard named Kaplan had been standing, there was now only a spot of charred, smoking earth. Helpless, at a loss for words, furious, Kirk stared at it, and then back at the sky as Spock joined him.

"A beautiful day, Mr. Spock," Kirk said bitterly. "Not a cloud in the sky. Just like Paradise."

His communicator beeped. "Mallory here, Captain. I'm near the village. Coordinates one-eighteen by two-twenty. The village is—" Mallory's voice was interrupted by a blast of static.

"What was that, Mallory? I don't read you."

"I'm getting static too. I said it's primitive—strictly tribal from the looks of it. But there's something else—"

Another tearing squeal of static. Mallory's voice stopped. Kirk could not get him back.

"Captain," Spock said, "those coordinates were only a few thousand meters off that way."

"Let's go! On the double!"

They crashed off. As they broke out of the other side of the undergrowth, Kirk saw Mallory running toward them over a field littered with rainbow-colored rocks.

"Over there, Captain," the security guard shouted. "It's—"

He had turned his head as he ran, to point. It was impossible to tell exactly what happened next. Perhaps he stubbed his toe. A rock exploded directly under him.

By the time they reached him, no check by McCoy was needed. His body lay unmoving, bloody, broken.

Kirk, shaken, closed his eyes for a moment. First Hendorf, then Kaplan. He had known Kaplan's family. And Mallory . . . Mallory's father had helped Kirk into the Academy . . .

Spock took his arm, waving the others off.

"Captain . . . in each case, it was unavoidable."

"You're wrong, Spock. I should have beamed us all up the minute things started to go wrong."

"You were under orders. You had no choice."

"I could have saved two men at least. Beamed up. Made further investigations from the ship. Done something! This . . . blundering along down here . . . cut off from the ship . . . the ship's in trouble itself . . . unable to help it . . ."

"We can help it, Captain. The source of the interference with the ship must be here on the planet. Indeed, this may be the only place the difficulty can be solved."

"And how many more lives will I lose?"

"No one has ever stated Starfleet duty was particularly safe. You have done everything a commander could do. I believe—" He broke off, listening. "Captain . . . I think our visitor is back again."

Reluctantly, Kirk turned to Marple, the last of the security guards of the landing party. "Ensign, go ahead fifty yards, swing to your left, cut back, and make a lot of noise. Mr. Spock, Mr. Chekov, make a distraction, a loud one."

He moved quietly away from them toward the brush. Behind him, Chekov's voice rose: "What kind of a tricorder setting do you call that?"

"I will not have you speaking to me in that tone of voice, Ensign!"

"Well, what do you want, violins? That's the stupidest setting I've ever seen—and you a Science Officer!"

Kirk crept stealthily forward.

"It's time you paid more attention to your own duties," Spock's voice shouted uncharacteristically. "Furthermore, you are down here to work, not to hold hands with a pretty yeoman!"

There was somebody, or something, ahead now. Kirk parted the brush. Directly in front of him, his back turned, was a small humanoid, his skin copper red, his hair platinum blond. There seemed to be two tiny silver studs behind his ears. Kirk tensed himself to spring.

At the same time, Marple came crashing toward them from the opposite side. The alien sprang up and ran directly into Kirk's arms. The alien struggled. Measuring him coolly, Kirk struck him squarely on the jaw, and he went down. Clutching his face, he began to cry like a child.

Kirk stood over him, slowly relaxing. Obviously, this creature was no threat. "I'm not going to hurt you," he said. "Do you understand? I won't hurt you."

He spoke, without much hope, in Interstellar. To his surprise, the alien responded in the same tongue, though much slurred and distorted.

"You struck me with your hand."

"I won't strike you again. Here." Kirk extended his hand to help the being up. After a moment, the hand was taken. "You've been following us, watching us. Why?"

"I am the Eyes of Vaal. He must see."

"Who is Vaal?"

"Vaal is Vaal. He is everything."

"You have a name?"

"I am Akuta. I lead the Feeders of Vaal."

The rest of the party began to gather around them. Akuta tried to flinch in all directions at once.

"They won't hurt you either. I promise. Akuta, we have come here in peace. We would like to speak to your Vaal."

"Akuta alone speaks to Vaal. I am the eyes and the voice of Vaal. It is his wish."

"This is fascinating," Spock said. He stepped forward and put his hands gently to Akuta's head, turning it slightly for a closer look at the two small metal studs. "If you will permit me, sir . . . Captain, observe."

"Antennae?" Kirk said.

Akuta had suffered the examination without protest. "They are my ears for Vaal. They were given to me in the dim time, so the people could understand his commands, and obey."

"The people," Kirk said. "Are they nearby?"

"We are close to Vaal, so we may serve him. I shall take you there."

Kirk's communicator shrilled. "Kirk here."

It was Scott: "Captain, something's grabbed us from the planet's surface! Like a giant tractor beam! We can't break loose—we can't even hold our own."

"Warp drive still out?"

"Yes, Captain. All we have is impulse power, and that on maximum. Even with that, we'll only be able to maintain power for sixteen hours. Then we'll burn up for sure."

"Mr. Scott, you are my Chief Engineer. You know everything about that ship there is to know . . . more than the men who designed it. If you can't get those warp engines going again—you're fired."

"I'll try everything there is to try, sir. Scott out."

Kirk turned to Akuta. "Tell me about Vaal."

"All the world knows about Vaal. He makes the rains fall, and the sun to shine. All good comes from Vaal."

"Take us to him. We want to speak with him."

"I will take you, but Vaal will not speak with you. He speaks only to me."

"We'll take our chances."

Nodding, Akuta led the way.

Vaal became visible from a clearing some distance away. He was a great serpentlike head, seeming to have been cut out of a cliff. His mouth was open. In color it was greenish bronze, except for its red tongue, which extended from its open mouth. There were steps cut in the tongue, so that a man could walk right up and into the mouth. Two huge fangs extended down, white and polished. Vaal's eyes were open, and they glowed dimly red, pulsating regularly. Even from here, they could hear that the pulsation was timed with a faint but powerful-sounding low-pitched hum.

They drew closer, both Spock and Chekov taking tricorder readings. "Of a high order of workmanship, and very ancient," the First Officer said.

"But this isn't the center, Spock," Kirk said.

"No, Captain. The center is deep beneath it. This would seem to be an access point. In addition there is an energy field extending some thirty feet beyond the head in all directions. Conventional in composition, but most formidable."

"Akuta, how do you talk to Vaal?"

"Vaal calls me. Only then."

Kirk turned to the rest of the party, scowling. "Well, we can't get to it, and we can't talk to it until it's ready to talk."

"Vaal sleeps now," Akuta said. "When he is hungry, you may be able to talk with him—if he desires it."

"When does he get hungry?"

"Soon. Come. We will give you food and drink. If you are tired, you may rest."

He led them down the hill and back into the jungle. It was not very long before they emerged in a tiny village, which looked part Polynesian, part American Indian, part exotic in its own way. There were small thatched huts with hanging batik tapestries, simply made and mostly repeating the totem image of Vaal. At one end of the village area were neatly stacked piles of the explosive rainbow-colored rock. About a dozen aliens were there, men and women, all very handsome, all younger than Akuta. They seemed to be doing nothing at all.

"Akuta," Kirk said, "where are the others?"

"There are no others."

"But . . . where are the children?"

"Children? You speak unknown words to me."

"Little people," Kirk explained. "Like yourselves. But they grow."

"Ah," said Akuta. "Replacements. None are necessary. They are forbidden by Vaal."

"But," said Martha Landon, "when people fall in love—" Chekov was standing next to her, and at these words he smiled and slipped his hand around her waist. She pressed it to her.

"Strange words," said Akuta. "Children . . . love. What is love?"

"Well . . . when a man and a woman are . . . attracted . . ." She did not seem to be able to go any farther. Akuta stared at her and at Chekov's arm.

"Ah. The holding. The touching. Vaal has forbidden this."

"There goes Paradise," said Chekov.

During the questioning, the People of Vaal had been drawing closer and closer, not menacingly, but in simple curiosity. Akuta turned to them.

"These are strangers from another place. They have come among us. Welcome them."

A young man stepped forward, beaming. "Welcome to Vaal."

A girl, beautiful as a goddess, though wearing slightly less, stepped out with a lei of flowers in her hands, smiling warmly. She went to Kirk and put the lei over his head. "Our homes are open to you."

Thus encouraged, the others came over, giggling, touching, exploring, examining the clothing and the gadgets of the strangers. Another young woman put a necklace of shells around Spock's neck.

"It does something for you, Mr. Spock," Kirk said.

"Indeed, Captain. It makes me most uncomfortable."

"I am Sayana," the girl said. "You have a name?"

"I am Spock."

Sayana repeated the name, pointing to him, and so did the rest of the natives, with a wave of laughter.

"I fail to see," Spock said, "what they find so amusing."

"Come," said Akuta. He led the landing party off to one of the huts. The rest of the People of Vaal continued to crowd around, laughing and probing gently.

The interior of the hut was simple, indeed primitive. There were a few baskets, a few wooden vessels, some hangings with the totem image on them, sleeping mats on the floor.

"This house is your house," Akuta said. "I will send food and drink. You are welcome in the place of Vaal."

He went out. Chekov stared after him. "Now we're welcome. A while ago this whole planet was trying to kill us. It doesn't make sense."

"Nothing does down here," McCoy agreed. "I'm going to run a physiological reading on some of those villagers."

He went out after Akuta. Kirk took out his communicator. "Kirk to *Enterprise*. Come in."

"Scott here, sir."

"Status report, Scotty."

"No change, Captain. The orbit is decaying along the computed lines. No success with the warp drive. We're going down and we can't stop it."

"I'm sick of hearing that word 'can't,' Scott," Kirk said harshly. "Get my ship out of there."

"But, sir—we've tried everything within engineering reason—"

"Then use your imagination! Tie every dyne of power the ship has into the impulse engines. Discard the warp drive nacelles if you have to and crack out of there with just the main section—but get out!"

"Well, we could switch over all but the life support circuits and boost the impulse power—black the ship out otherwise—"

"Do it. Kirk out."

McCoy reentered, frowning. "Incredible," he said. "I ran a complete check on the natives. There's a complete absence of harmful bacteria in their systems. No tissue degeneration, no calcification, no arteriosclerosis. In simple terms, they're not growing old. I can't begin to tell you how old any of them are. Twenty years—or twenty thousand."

"Quite possible," Spock said. "It checks with my atmosphere analysis. The atmosphere completely screens out all dangerous radiation from their sun."

"Add to that a simple diet," Kirk said, "perfectly controlled temperature . . . apparently no vices at all . . . no natural enemies . . . and no 'replacements' needed. Maybe it is Paradise, after all—for them."

Outside, there was a curious vibrating sound, not loud, but penetrating, like the striking of an electronic gong. Kirk went out, beckoning to Spock.

The People of Vaal were no longer lounging around. They were moving off toward the cliff, picking up rocks from the stockpiles as they left. Kirk and Spock followed.

At the cliff, the people entered the mouth of Vaal with the rocks, and came out without them. The red eyes were flashing, brightly now.

"Apparently our hypothesis is correct," Spock said. "There is no living being in there. It is a machine, nothing more."

"The field's down. The people are going in. Let's see what luck we have."

Kirk took a step forward. There was an immediate rumble of thunder, to the considerable alarm of the People of Vaal. Kirk stepped back quickly. "That's not the way."

"Evidently not. It is no ordinary machine, Captain. It has shown a capacity for independent action in its attacks upon us. It may well possess a more than rudimentary intelligence."

"But it needs to eat. It can't have any great power reserves."

"Indeed, Captain. But that does not seem to be of help. The ship now has only ten hours to break free."

"What if Vaal's power weakens as it approaches feeding time? Mr. Spock, check with the ship; get an estimate of the total energy being expended against it. And measure it every hour.''

"With pleasure, Captain." Spock took his communicator out quickly. Deep in thought, Kirk went back to the hut, where he found all of the landing party outside.

"What was it, Jim?"

"Mess call, Bones."

Spock came up behind him. "A perfect example of symbiosis. They provide for Vaal, and Vaal gives them everything they need."

"Which may also answer why there are no children here," Kirk said. "There are exactly enough people to do what Vaal requires."

"In my view," Spock said, "a splendid example of reciprocity."

"It would take a mind like yours to make that kind of statement," McCoy said.

"Gentlemen, your arguments can wait until the ship is out of danger."

"Jim," McCoy said, "you can't just blind yourself to what is happening here. These are humanoids—intelligent! They've got to advance—progress! Don't you understand what my readings indicate? There's been no change here in perhaps thousands of years! This isn't life, it's stagnation!"

"You are becoming emotional, Doctor," Spock said. "This seems to be a perfectly practical society."

"Practical? It's obscene! Humanoids living only so that they can service a hunk of tin!"

"A remarkable hunk of tin, Bones," Kirk said. "And they seem healthy and happy."

"That has nothing to do with it—"

Kirk's communicator cut in. "Kirk here."

"Scott, sir. We've got a reading on the power source as Spock asked. It *is* dropping a bit at a time—nominal, but a definite drain."

Kirk grinned triumphantly at Spock. "Good. Keep monitoring. How are you doing with the circuit switchover?"

"We're putting everything but the kitchen sink into the impulse drive, sir. It'll take another eight hours to complete the work."

"That's cutting it fine, Scotty."

"Aye, sir. But if we don't break out, I'd rather we didn't have to wait long for the end of it."

Kirk took a deep breath. "Right. Carry on, Scotty. Kirk out."

The hours wore away. A large assortment of fruit and vegetables was brought to the landing party by the People. Martha Landon was nervous and on the verge of tears; Kirk sent her out with Chekov for "a breath of air" and whatever reassurance Chekov could give her. Privately, Kirk hoped also that the People would spy on them; the sight of a little open necking might give them a few ideas disruptive to the absolute control Vaal had over them. Of course, that might provoke Vaal to retaliation—but what more could Vaal do than he was doing now?

Spock seemed to read Kirk's intentions with no difficulty. "I am concerned, Captain," he said. "This may not be an ideal society, but it is a viable one. If we are forced to do what it seems we must, in my opinion, we will be in direct violation of the noninterference directive."

"I'm not convinced that this is a viable society in the accepted sense of the word. Bones was right. These people aren't living, they're just existing. It's not a valid culture."

"Starfleet Command may think otherwise."

"That's a risk I'll have to take." He called the *Enterprise*. "How's it coming, Scotty?"

"Almost ready, sir. We'll need a half hour yet."

"You've only got forty-five minutes until you're pulled into the atmosphere."

"I know, sir. As you said, it's cutting things a bit fine."

"I think we're going to be able to help down here. I'll be back in touch shortly." Kirk cut off. "All hands. We're coming up on the next feeding time for Vaal. Before that happens I want all the Vaalians confined in one hut—the women too, no exceptions. When that gong sounds, round them all up."

The gong in fact sounded only a few minutes later. By this time Chekov and McCoy, phasers drawn, had herded all the People together. They milled around inside the hut, appalled, some wailing and crying.

"Vaal calls us!" Akuta cried out. His face contorted

in agony, and he touched the electrodes behind his ears. "We must go to him! He hungers!" The bell rang again. "Please! Let us go to him! We must!"

Kirk got out the communicator again. "Scotty, do you still have phaser power?"

"Aye sir. But what—"

"Lock all banks on the coordinates of the energy field you located down here. On my command, fire and maintain full phasers on those coordinates."

"Aye, sir, but they won't penetrate the field."

"If my guess is right, they won't have to. Stand by."

The bell rang again, louder, longer, more insistently. After checking to see that Chekov and McCoy had the People under control, Kirk and Spock went to the edge of the village. Spock pointed his tricorder toward the cliff.

"Interesting, Captain. The center of the emanations— Vaal—is somewhat weaker than the readings I've been getting. There are wide variations in energy transmission, as though it is drawing from other sources."

"Tapping its energy cells?"

"I would assume so."

"Right. I think the ship's attempts to pull away must have weakened it considerably. It needs to be fed, but the reserve capacity could hold out for days."

"If it has to reinforce its energy field to ward off a phaser attack, it will have to draw more heavily on its reserves."

"My plan exactly, Mr. Spock . . . Kirk to *Enterprise*. Open fire as ordered and maintain."

The phaser beams came down, in long sustained bursts. They were stopped short of the head of Vaal by the force field, but they continued to come down. Sparks flew at the point of contact. A hum rose from Vaal, loud and piercing.

"Tremendous upsurge in generated power, sir. Obviously Vaal is trying to reinforce its energy field."

"Good. Let's see how long it can do it!"

The sky darkened. A strong wind began to blow. Strong flashes of lights lit up Vaal's maw, and some smoke began to appear. The hum was now intolerably loud, and the wind was howling. Lightning flashed overhead, followed by thunder. The din was terrific.

Then, almost all at once, the storm clouds dissipated, the flashes inside Vaal's mouth stopped, and its eyes went out. The hum too was gone.

"Kirk to *Enterprise*. Cease firing."

"No power generation at all," Spock said. "Vaal is dead."

"Mr. Scott, status report."

"Tractor beam gone. Potency returning to antimatter banks. I'll put all engineering sections on repairing the circuits immediately. We'll have the Transporter working in an hour."

Kirk felt as though a great weight had slid off his shoulders. "You're rehired, Mr. Scott. When the Transporter's fixed, form an engineering detail with full analytical equipment and beam them down. I think they'll find some interesting things inside that cave. Kirk out . . . Bones, Chekov. Let them out."

The People emerged, huddled, frightened, still sobbing. McCoy came over to Kirk and Spock.

"Allow me to point out, Captain," Spock said, "that by destroying Vaal, you have also destroyed the People of Vaal."

"Nonsense, Spock!" McCoy said. "It will be the making of these people. Make them stand on their own feet, do things for themselves. They have a right to live like men."

"You mean they have a right to pain, worry, insecurity, tension . . . and eventually death and taxes."

"That's all part of it. Yes! Those too!"

"I hope you will be able to find a way to explain it to them." He nodded toward Akuta, who had moved out of the group toward them, tears streaming down his face.

"Vaal is dead. You have killed him. We cannot live."

"You'll live, Akuta," Kirk said gently. "I'll assign some of my people here to help you."

The girl Sayana was crying quietly. One of the young men, standing by her, obviously wanted to comfort her, but did not know how to start. He made several ineffectual gestures; and then, as if by instinct, his arms went around her waist. She moved closer to him, and her head went onto his shoulder.

"But," Akuta said, "it was Vaal who put the fruit on the trees, who caused the rain to fall. Vaal cared for us."

"You'll find that putting fruit on the trees is a relatively simple matter. Our agronomist will help you with that. As for Vaal taking care of you, you'll have to learn to take care of yourselves. You might even like it.

"Listen to me, all of you. From this day on, you will not depend on Vaal. You are your own masters. You will be able to think what you wish, say what you wish, do what you wish. You will learn many things that are strange, but they will be good. You will discover love; there will be children."

"What are children?" Sayana said.

As the young man's arm tightened around her waist, Kirk grinned. "You just go on the way you're going, and you'll find out."

As Kirk, McCoy and Spock were going toward the bridge, McCoy said: "Spock has an interesting analogy, Captain."

"Yes, Mr. Spock?"

"I am not at all certain that we have done exactly the right thing on Gamma Trianguli VI, Captain."

"We put those people back on a normal course of social evolution. I see nothing wrong with that. It's a good object lesson, Spock, in what can happen when your machines become too efficient, do too much of your work for you. Judging by their language, those people must have been among the very first interstellar colonists—good hardy stock. They tamed the planet, instituted weather control, and turned all jobs of that sort over to a master computer, powered by the plentiful local ore. I suppose the fatal mistake was in giving the computer the power to program itself—and the end product was Vaal . . . Bones said something about an analogy."

"Perhaps you will recall the biblical story of Genesis, sir?"

"I recall it very well, Spock."

"We found a race of people living in Paradise, much as Adam and Eve did. They were obeying every word of Vaal. We taught them, in effect, to disobey that word. In a manner of speaking we have given Adam and Eve the apple . . . the awareness of good and evil, if you will . . . and because of this they have been driven out of Paradise.''

Kirk stopped and swung around on Spock suspiciously. ''Mr. Spock, you seem to be casting me in the role of Satan. Do I look like Satan?''

''No, sir. But—''

''Is there anyone on this ship who looks even remotely like Satan?''

McCoy was grinning broadly. ''I am not aware,'' Spock said stiffly, ''of anyone in that category, Captain.''

''No, Mr. Spock. I didn't think you would be.''

MIRROR, MIRROR

Writer: Jerome Bixby
Director: Marc Daniels
Guest star: Barbara Luna

The Halkan Council was absolutely polite, but its position was rock-hard, and nothing that Kirk, McCoy, Scott or Uhura could say would alter it. The Federation was not to be allowed to mine dilithium crystals on the planet. There was too much potential for destruction in the crystals, and the Halkans would allow nothing to compromise their history of total non-violence. To prevent that, they said, they would die—as a race, if necessary. The Council accepted that the Federation's intentions were peaceful, but what of the future? There had been mention of a hostile Klingon Empire . . .

Kirk would have liked to have stayed to argue the question further, but he had already received word from Spock that an ion storm of considerable violence was beginning to blow through the Halkan system—and in fact Kirk could already see evidence of it in the Halkan weather, which was becoming decidedly lowering. To stay longer might risk disruption of transporter transmission, which would strand the landing party for an unknown time. In addition, it was Spock's opinion that the heart of the magnetic storm represented a danger to the *Enterprise* herself.

On this kind of opinion, Kirk would not have argued with Spock for a second; the First Officer never erred by a hairline on the wrong side of conservatism. Kirk ordered the landing party beamed up.

That hairline was very nearly split, this time. On the first attempt, the transporter got the party only partly materialized aboard ship when the beam suffered a phase reversal and all four of them found themselves standing on a bare plateau on the Halkan planet, illuminated only by a barrage of lightning. It was nearly five minutes later before the familiar Transporter Room sprang fully into being around them.

Kirk stepped quickly from the platform toward Spock. "We may or may not get those power crystals . . ."

And then he stopped, in midstep as well as midsentence. For Spock and the transporter chief were saluting, and a most peculiar salute it was: the arms first folded loosely, then raised stiffly horizontal and squared out. Their uniforms were different, too; basically, they were the same as before, but they were much altered in detail, and the detail had a savage military flair—broad belts bearing exposed phasers and what seemed to be ceremonial daggers, shoulder boards, braid. And the Federation breast symbol was gone; instead, there was a blazon which looked like a galaxy with a dagger through it. A similar symbol, in brilliant color, was on one wall of the room, and the equipment was all in the wrong places—indeed, a few pieces of it were completely unfamiliar.

But what struck Kirk most of all was the change in Spock. Vulcans all look somewhat satanic to Earthmen encountering them for the first time, but it had been many years since Kirk had thoroughly gotten over this impression of his First Officer. Now it was back, full force. Spock looked cold, hard, almost fanatical.

Kirk dropped his hands to his belt—since he did not know how to return the strange salute—and encountered something else unfamiliar. A brief glance confirmed what he had feared: his uniform, too, had undergone the strange changes.

"At norm," Spock said to the transporter chief, in a voice loaded with savage harshness. "Captain, do you mean the Halkans have weapons that could resist us? Our socio-analysis indicates that they are incapable of violence."

Kirk could not answer. He was spared having to, for at that moment Sulu entered the Transporter Room. His movements, his manner, were cold, arrogant, hypercompetent, but that was not the worst of it. The symbol on his breast, the galaxy with the dagger through it, had inside it also a clenched fist, around the blade of the dagger, from which blood was dripping. It was an extreme parody of something familiar; it showed that the gentle Sulu, the ship's navigator and helms-man, was now her chief security officer.

Sulu did not salute. He barked, "Status of mission, Captain?"

"No change," Kirk said carefully.

"Standard procedure, then?"

Kirk did not know what this question meant under these eerie circumstances, but he doubted that operating by the book—whatever the book might say—would accomplish much more than delaying matters, and time was what he needed. Therefore, he nodded.

Sulu turned to the nearest intercom. "Mr. Chekov. You will program phaser barrage on Halkan cities, at the rate of one million electron volts per day, in a gradually contracting circle around each. Report when ready."

"Right, Mr. Sulu." Was Kirk imagining it, or was there something thick and gloating in Chekov's voice?

"Unfortunate," Spock said, "that this race should choose suicide to annexation. They possess qualities that could be useful to the Empire."

There was the sputtering hum of an overload from the transporter. Spock's head jerked toward the transporter chief, and then, slowly, inexorably, he advanced on the man. In-credibly, the transporter chief *cringed*.

"Are you not aware, chief, that we are in a magnetic storm? And that you were ordered to compensate?"

"Mr. Spock, sir, I'm sorry. The ion-flux is so unpre-dictable . . ."

"Carelessness with Empire equipment is intolerable." Spock held out his hand toward Sulu, without looking. "Mr. Sulu, your agonizer."

Sulu plucked a small device from his belt and dropped it in Spock's outstretched palm. In a vicious burlesque of the Vulcan neck pinch, Spock clapped it to the transporter chief's shoulder.

The man screamed. Spock prolonged the agony. When he let go, the chief dropped writhing to the deck.

"More attention to duty next time, please. Mr. Scott, the storm has produced minor damage in your section. Doctor McCoy, there are also some minor injuries requiring your attention." Abruptly, he kicked the semiconscious man on the floor. "You might begin with this hulk."

McCoy, whose running feud with the First Officer had always had a solid undercurrent of affection to moderate it, wore the look of a man whose worst nightmare has abruptly come true. Kirk saw him balling his fists, and moved in fast.

"Get moving, Dr. McCoy. You too, Mr. Scott."

Their expressions flickered for a moment, and then both looked down. Now they knew how the Captain wanted them to play it. At least, Kirk hoped so. In any event, they went out without further comment.

The transporter chief dragged himself to his feet to follow. It did not seem to surprise him at all that the ship's doctor, who had just been ordered to attend to him, had not said a word to him. He said, "Mr. Spock . . ."

"What?"

"Sir, the beam power jumped for a moment, sir—just as the landing party materialized. I never saw anything like it before. I thought you ought to know, sir."

Kirk had already heard more 'sirs' in ten minutes than were normal to the *Enterprise* in a week. Spock said, "Another inefficiency?"

"No, sir, the settings were perfectly normal. I made my error after the party arrived, sir, if I may so remind you."

"Very well. Go to Sickbay. Captain, do you feel any ill effects?"

Kirk could answer that one with no trouble. "Yes, Mr. Spock, I am decidedly shaken up. I expect Lieutenant Uhura is too. I believe we too had better report to Sickbay for a checkup."

"You will of course report instantly if you are found incompetent to command," Sulu said. It was not a question.

"Of course, Mr. Sulu."

"And the matter of the Halkans? A quick bombardment would solve the problem with the least effort."

"I am aware of your—orders—Mr. Sulu. I will give you my judgment as soon as I—feel myself assured that I am competent to give it."

"Most sensible."

As Kirk and Uhura left, everyone again saluted—except Sulu. On the trip to Sickbay, Kirk became aware that there were more guards posted along the corridors than he had ever seen except during the worst kind of major alert. None of them were in standard uniforms; instead, they wore fatigues, like civilian workmen. All saluted. None seemed surprised not to have the salutes returned.

Uhura gasped with relief as the door of Sickbay slid closed behind them and the four people who had been the landing party were once more alone together. "What's *happened*?" she said in a low, intense voice.

"Don't talk too fast," Kirk said instantly, though he himself was talking as fast as he could possibly get the words out. He stabbed a finger toward McCoy's intercom. "Something in the air suggests that that thing is permanently open."

The rest nodded. It was a lucky thing that they had all been together so long; it made elliptical talk possible among them. "Now, Bones, that medical. I want you to check for likely effects. I suggest brainwaves first."

"I've already checked myself and Scotty, sir. No hallucinatory or hypnotic effects. We are dealing with—uh, a perception of reality, if you follow me."

"I'm afraid I do. Mr. Scott, do you detect any changes in the *Enterprise* which—might have a bearing on our reactions?"

Scott inclined his head and listened. "I hear some sort of difference in the impulse engines. Of course they may just be laboring against the magnetic storm. However, the difference seems to me to be, well, technological in nature, sir."

"Excuse me, Captain," Uhura said, "but I feel a little out of my depth. I felt quite dizzy for a moment after we materialized in the beams. Would it be possible . . ."

She did not finish the sentence, but instead made the gesture of someone fitting a bucket or a large hat over McCoy's intercom. The physician's eyebrows went up. He stepped to where his diagnostic apparatus should have been, veered in disgust as he found that it had been moved, and then flicked switches.

"I should have thought of that in the first place," he said, "but I'm as confused as anybody here. Everybody used to complain that my stereotaxic screen jammed the intercoms; let's hope it still does."

"We'll have to take the chance," Kirk said. "Lieutenant Uhura, I felt the same effect. At the same time, we were in our normal Transporter Room—and then it faded, we were back on the planet, and then got beamed back to this situation—whatever it is. And the transporter chief—where is he, by the way?''

"I made him mildly sick," McCoy said, "and sent him to quarters. A nasty reversal of role for a doctor, but I want him out of Spock's reach for a while."

"Well, he mentioned an abnormal effect in the transporter itself. And there's this ion storm."

"Captain," Scott said slowly, "are we thinking the same thing?"

"I don't know, Scotty. But everything fits thus far. It fits with a parallel universe, coexisting with ours, on another dimensional plane—or maybe on another level of probability; everything duplicated—almost. An Empire instead of a Federation. Another *Enterprise*—another Spock . . ."

"Another Jim Kirk?" Scott said quietly. "Another Dr. McCoy?"

"No," McCoy said in startled realization. "An exchange! If *we're here* . . ."

"Our counterparts were beaming at the same time," Kirk said. "Ion storms are common enough, after all. Another storm disrupted another set of circuits. Now we're here; they're on *our* ship, and probably asking each other much the same questions. And coming to the same tentative conclusions. They'll ask the computer what to do. That's what we'll have to do."

McCoy began to pace. "What about the Halkans? We can't let them be wiped out, even if this is another, completely different set of Halkans, in another universe."

"I don't know, Bones. I've got to buy a lot of time. Scotty, get below and short the main phaser coupling. Make it look like the storm blew the standby circuits. Lieutenant Uhura, get to your post and run today's communications from Starfleet Command, or whatever the equivalent is here. I've got to know my exact orders, and options, if any. And by the way, when we want to talk to each other after we're separated, use communicators, and on the subspace band only. And scramble, too."

Uhura and the engineer nodded and left. McCoy had halted his pacing before a sort of glass cage. In it was what appeared to be a large bird, affixed with electrodes. A chart hung beside it.

"What in blazes!" McCoy said. "Jim, look at this. A specimen of an 'annexed' race. I.Q., 180. Experiment in life-support for humans under conditions prevailing on its native planet—heart and lung modifications. It's alive—and if I'm any judge, it's in agony. I won't have such an abomination in my Sickbay!"

"You'll have to, for a while," Kirk said, not without sympathy. "We've got to stay in character until we can get more information. It's an ugly universe, and we don't want to do anything that'll get us stuck with it."

On the bridge, there was a huge duplicate of the galaxy-and-dagger device, and the Captain's chair had widely flared arms, almost like a throne. The man who should be Chekov was eyeing Uhura with open, deliberate, speculative interest, his intent unmistakable. Nobody else seemed to find this unusual or even interesting. Kirk went directly to her.

"Any new orders, Lieutenant?"

"No, sir. You are still ordered to annihilate the Halkans, unless they comply. No alternative action has been prescribed."

"Thank you." He went to his chair and sank in. It felt downright luxurious. "Report, Mr. Sulu?"

"Phasers locked on Target A, Captain. Approaching optimum range. Shall I commence fire?"

"I want a status report first." He touched the intercom. "Mr. Scott?"

"Scott here, sir. I have no change to report, sir. No damage to phasers."

"Very good, Mr. Scott." In fact it was very bad, but there was no help for it. As he switched out, Spock came onto the bridge.

"The planet's rotation is carrying the primary target beyond arc of phaser lock," Sulu said. "Shall I correct orbit to new firing position?"

"No."

Sulu flicked a switch. "Now locked on secondary target city."

"Mr. Spock," Kirk said. "You said the Halkans could be useful. After my visit with them, I agree."

"If they chose to cooperate. They have not."

"Lieutenant Uhura, contact the Halkan Council. We'll make one more try." Noting Spock's surprise, he added, "This is a new race. They offer other things of value besides dilithium crystals."

"But—it is clear that we cannot expect cooperation. They have refused the Empire. Command Procedure dictates that we provide the customary example. A serious breach of Standard Orders . . ."

"I have my reasons, Mr. Spock—and I'll make them clear in my own good time."

"Captain," Uhura said, "the Halkan leader is waiting on Channel B."

Kirk swung to the small viewscreen above Uhura's station. Tharn was on the screen. He looked much tireder, indeed more tragic, than he had when Kirk had seen him last. Now, how would it be possible to make this sound plausible?

"It is useless to resist us," he said at random.

"We do not resist you," Tharn said.

"You have, uh, twelve hours in which to reconsider your position."

"Twelve years, Captain Kirk, or twelve thousand, will make no difference," Tharn said calmly and with great dignity. "We are ethically compelled to refuse your demand for dilithium crystals. You would use their power to destroy."

"We will level your planet and take what we want. *That* is destruction. You would die as a race . . ."

"To preserve what we are. Yes. Perhaps someday your slave planets will all defy you, as we have done. When that comes, how will your starships be able to control a whole galaxy?"

"Switch out, Lieutenant." The screen went blank.

"Twelve hours, Captain?" Spock said. "That is unprecedented."

"Phasers off, Mr. Sulu."

"This conduct must be reported, Captain," Spock said. "You have placed yourself in a most grave position."

"You are at liberty to do so, Mr. Spock," Kirk said,

rising. "Take charge. I will be in the briefing room. Inform me of any change. Lieutenant Uhura, attend me there and order Dr. McCoy and Mr. Scott also to report there. Mr. Chekov, relieve Lieutenant Uhura."

He could only hope that this flurry of orders, plus his breach of an unknown regulation, would obscure the fact that he had just called together the landing party.

"Everybody watch your step," Scott said. "They move up through assassination around here. My engine-room chief just tried for me—not personally, but through henchmen. I only got out of it because one of them switched sides."

"What about the technology, Scotty?"

"Mostly variations in instrumentation. Nothing I can't handle. As for star-readings—everything's where it ought to be—except us."

Kirk crossed to the desk and looked down at the computer tap. "Let's see what we're up against. Computer, this is the Captain. Record a Security Research, to be classified under my voiceprint and Mr. Scott's."

"Recorded," said the computer in a harsh masculine voice. Evidently this universe had never discovered that men pay more attention to a machine when its voice is feminine.

"Produce all data relevant to recent magnetic storm, and correlate following hypothesis. Could a storm of that magnitude cause a power surge in transporter circuits, creating momentary interdimensional contact with a parallel universe?"

"Affirmative."

"At such a moment, could persons in each universe, in the act of beaming, be transposed with their counterparts in the other universe?"

"Affirmative."

"Can conditions necessary to such an event be artificially reproduced?"

"Affirmative."

"Record procedure and switch off."

A slot in the desk opened and a spool of tape slid out. Kirk handed it to Scott. "It looks like the ball is yours, Scotty."

"I'll have to tap the power for it out of the warp engines, and balance it for the four of us,'' the engineer said dubiously. "It's a two-man job, and I'm afraid you'd be too conspicuous, Captain. So would Lieutenant Uhura. Come on, McCoy, let's lay it out.''

"I'm not an engineer," McCoy said indignantly.

"You will be. Captain, keep up our public relations, please!''

The two went out. After a moment, Uhura said, "Captain—the way this ship is run—what kind of people *are* we in this universe? I mean, what kind of people do we have to pretend to be?''

"Let's find out. Computer. Readout of official record of current command.''

"Captain: James T. Kirk. Succeeded to command *E. S. S. Enterprise* through assassination of Captain Karl Franz. First action: suppression of Gorlan uprising, through destruction of rebel home planet. Second action: execution of five thousand colonists on S Doradus Nine, forcing colony to retract secession. Third action . . .''

"Cancel. Lieutenant, do you really want to hear it tell you what *you're* like?''

Lt. Uhura shuddered. "No. If the way the local Chekov looks at me is any clue, I'll probably hear that my predecessor at my post was my lover, and I got the job by knifing him. How can you run a fifty billion credit starship like a pirate vessel?''

"Pirate ships were pretty efficiently run, Lieutenant. Every man feared those above him—with the strongest at the top. Morgan took Panama with his buccaneer ships as neatly as a squadron of naval vessels might have.''

"And then was stabbed in his sleep?''

"No, henchmen protected him—not out of respect or devotion, but because his abilities brought them what they wanted. Other checks and balances—other means to the same end.''

"But what end?''

"This ship is efficient—or it wouldn't exist. Its Captain was efficient, or he'd be dead. And this Empire will get the dilithium crystals it wants—efficiently.''

Uhura's expression remained grim. "And what do you suppose our counterparts are doing, aboard *our* version of the *Enterprise*?''

"I hope they're faking as well as or better than we are. Otherwise, when we get back, we'll all be up on charges." The intercom beeped. "Kirk here."

"Sir, I'm having trouble on this line, I can barely hear you."

"Right." Kirk switched off, produced his communicator, and set it to subspace level and on "scramble." "Okay, Scotty, here I am. Go ahead."

"We can do it, Captain. But when we interrupt engine circuits, to tie in the power increase to the transporters, it'll show up on the Security Board. We'll just need a second, but . . ."

"All right, wait a minute." Kirk thought fast. "Lieutenant Uhura, this is going to be nasty. I noticed the local Chekov giving you the eye . . ."

"He made a flat-out pass at me before you came on the bridge, Captain."

"All the better. For the sake of our getting home, could you encourage him a little?"

Uhura said slowly, "I wouldn't pull a mean trick like that on *our* Chekov. And this one gives me the crawls. But—of course, Captain, if you wish."

"Good girl. Scotty, Uhura can create a diversion on the bridge, which will draw Sulu's attention, I think, at your signal. Now, everyone back to posts, before somebody cottons to the fact that this looks like a council of war."

Uhura slipped out silently. Kirk, too, was about to go, when Spock entered the briefing room by another door, and saluted.

"Captain, a word with you, if I may."

"Of course."

"I should regret your death."

Kirk raised his eyebrows. "Very kind of you, Mr. Spock."

"Kindness is not involved. As you know, I do not desire the captaincy. I much prefer my scientific duties—and I am frankly content to be a lesser target."

"Quite logical, as always, Mr. Spock."

"Therefore I am moved to inquire if you intend to persist in your unusual course of action regarding the Halkans."

"My orders stand."

"I presume you have a plan. I have found you to be an

excellent officer. Our missions together have been successful ones.''

"I remember," Kirk said. "Perhaps better than you do."

"I never forget anything."

"I remember that too. Then you will also remember the illogic of waste, Mr. Spock. Is it logical to destroy potential workers—equipment—valuable installations—without making every effort to put them on a useful basis? Surely the Empire can afford a little patience."

"Logically, we must maintain the terror," Spock said. "Otherwise the Empire will develop soft spots, and the rot will spread."

"The Halkans made the same point. Is history with us? Conquest is easy—control is not."

"History seldom repeats itself," Spock said, frowning. "Yet I concede that no regime such as ours has ever survived the eventual fury of its victims. The question is, has our power become so vast, quantitatively, as to make a *qualitative* change in that situation? Space, as you say, is against us; its sheer vastness makes communication difficult, let alone control—I did not know you were a philosopher, Captain. We have never talked this way before."

"Perhaps overdue, Mr. Spock."

"That is more than possible. I do not judge Commander Moreau to be much of a thinker."

There was quite a long silence, during which Kirk wondered who in blazes Commander Moreau was. Most likely, the man who *was* gunning for the Captain's job.

"Sir," Spock said finally, "I have received a private message from Starfleet Command. I am committing a serious breach of regulations by informing you of its contents. But other considerations supervene. Briefly, I have been instructed to wait until planet dawn over principal target, to permit you to complete our mission. Your delaying maneuver was of course reported to Starfleet Command by Mr. Sulu."

"And if I don't?"

"In that event," Spock said, his voice somehow both harsh and reluctant at the same time, "I am ordered to have you killed, and proceed against the Halkans, as the new Captain of the *Enterprise*. I shall of course remove Moreau too, making it appear that he was killed by *your* agents."

"Logical," Kirk said bitterly. "But thank you for the warning, Mr. Spock."

"I regret the situation. I shall remain in my quarters throughout the night—in case you should wish to contact me privately."

"Thank you again. But there will be no change."

"Sir—under the circumstances—may I express the greatest curiosity concerning your motives?"

"I'm almost tempted to tell you, Mr. Spock. But you'll understand in time. Carry on."

When he left, Kirk sat down at the table. He knew he should be back on the bridge, carrying on the masquerade. But even with Spock's odd sort of cooperation, even supposing Scotty could get them back to their own universe, that would leave the biggest problem unsolved: the fate of the Halkans in this alternate universe. No matter what happened to Kirk, McCoy, Scott and Uhura, the Halkans seemed to be destined for slaughter. And he could think of no way to prevent it.

Then the communicator beeped. "Kirk here."

"Captain, this is Scotty. I've got the whole thing rigged, with McCoy's help. I'm thinking of making him assistant engineer. But in checking it out with the computer, I discovered somethin' vurra worrisome. The two-way matter transmission affected local field density between the two universes—and it's increasing. We've got to move fast. We have half an hour at most. If we miss, we couldn't push back through for a century."

"What's the procedure, Scotty?"

"We're about ready to bridge power from the warp engines to the beams. You've got to go to the main controls and free the board, so we can lock in. Give us ten clock minutes, then you and Lieutenant Uhura create your diversion, and run like Martian scopolamanders for the Transporter Room."

"Right. Count down on the time. Five . . . four . . . three . . . two . . . one . . . *hack*."

"Got you. Good luck, Captain."

No time now to worry about the Halkans; but Kirk worried, nonetheless. On the bridge, Sulu looked speculatively, coldly, at Kirk as Kirk resumed the Captain's chair.

"Orders, Captain?"

"Prepare to lock on to Target A. We fire at planet dawn."

Sulu smiled coldly. "I am glad to see that you have come to your senses. All this computer activity obviously has produced no alternative answer, except to make me wonder if you had gone soft. And while Mr. Spock would no doubt make an excellent captain, you were once clearly the better one. I hope you will continue to be."

Kirk was so sick at the order he had had to give that he did not bother to disguise his disgust. "You don't miss much, do you, Mr. Sulu."

"A good Security Officer misses nothing. Otherwise he would deserve to go to the Agony Booth."

Well, Kirk thought grimly, *you may yet, Mr. Pseudo-Sulu. Obviously you don't know what that computer activity really was about.*

The Halkan planet's image was showing on Uhura's viewscreen. Chekov was watching her, with very much the same lubricious expression as before. She looked up at the image, and then, as if to herself, said, "Just once, I'd like to think about something besides death."

Sulu shot one contemptuous glance at her and went back to watching the master board. When Scott made his power switch from the warp engines to the transporters, he would catch it.

Uhura looked away from the screen toward Chekov. Her glance was steady for a moment, and then she looked down. Her veiled eyes suggested that she just might be persuaded to change her mind.

The navigator grinned, leaned back in his seat. His arm went out and around toward Uhura's waist.

Sulu paid no attention. And there was one minute left.

Slap!

Sulu looked up. Uhura was standing, in furious indignation. She fell back, one, two, three calculated steps toward Sulu's board. Chekov, astonishment changing to rage, was standing too.

But Sulu seemed to be no more than amused. "As you were, Chekov."

Chekov was not ready to be as he was. He seemed

almost ready to attack Uhura. Kirk saw an opening and jumped in.

"Is this the kind of horseplay that goes on when I'm not on the bridge? And at moments as critical as this? Mr. Chekov, you are on report; I'll tend to you later. Lieutenant Uhura, you provoked this; proceed immediately to the Booth. Mr. Sulu, take Lieutenant Uhura's post."

"Sir," Sulu said. "Why are you also leaving?" The 'sir' was silkily insulting.

"I am going to explain personally to Lieutenant Uhura why she is in the Booth. I'll return shortly; in the meantime, follow standard procedure."

He had caught the streak of sadism and lechery in these loathsome counterparts of his crew. Every man on the bridge grinned slyly and licked his lips.

Then Kirk and Uhura were out, and running for the Transporter Room.

Spock and two crewmen were waiting for them there, with drawn phasers.

"Well, Mr. Spock? Have you decided to kill me now, even though I am following my orders?"

"No, Captain. But strange things have occurred since the return of your landing party—including some remarkable calls upon the computer, which I find sealed against me. Nothing in the computer should be sealed against the First Officer. And you are preparing to use an enormous surge of power in the transporter. That could be most dangerous. I must ask you: where do you think you are going, Captain— you and your three conspirators?"

"Home," Kirk said.

"To the alternate universe?"

"You understand *that*?"

"Yes, Captain. And I concur. I will ask you only to gun me down with a stun charge before you leave. My henchmen here will support any story I tell thereafter."

McCoy said, "Mr. Spock, in my universe you and I often disagreed, and in this universe I hated you. But you seem to be a man of integrity in both universes."

"It is only logical," Spock said. "You must return to your universe, so that I can have *my* Captain back. I will operate the transporter. You have two minutes and twenty seconds left.''

''Mr. Spock,'' Kirk said. ''I will shave that time as close as possible. I want to ask you this: How long do you think it will be before the Halkans' prediction of galactic revolt is realized?''

Spock blinked, as if the sudden change of subject had taken him unawares. ''I would estimate—approximately two hundred and forty years.''

''And what will be the inevitable outcome?''

''The Empire will be overthrown, of course. A sort of federation may replace it, if the period of interdestruction is not too devastating.''

''Mr. Spock. Consider the illogic of waste. Waste of lives, resources, potentials, time. It is not logical of you to give your vast talents to an empire which you know is doomed.''

''You have one minute and twenty-three seconds.''

''When change is both predictable and beneficial, why do you resist it?''

''Suicide is also illogical. One man cannot summon the future.''

Kirk closed on this man, who looked and acted so much like his First Officer, and yet had so little of the real Spock's hidden humanity in him. ''Mr. Spock, one man can change the present. *Be* the Captain of this *Enterprise*, whether you want the job or not. Find a logical reason for sparing the Halkans, and making it stick. Push where it gives. You can defend yourself better than any man in the fleet, if you are anything like *my* First Officer, and I think you are. In every revolution, there's one man with a vision. Which will it be? Past or future? Tyranny, or the right to hope, trust, love? Even here, Spock, you cannot be totally without the decency you've shown on the—the other side. Use it, make it work!''

''You must go,'' Spock said. ''But my Captain never said any such words to me. I will remember them. I can promise nothing else, though I will save the Halkans if I can. Now, quickly! You have eighteen seconds left! Shoot! And goodbye, Jim Kirk.''

Kirk stepped onto the transporter platform with the others. He raised the phaser, set to "stun," but it was very hard to pull the trigger all the same.

Kirk relaxed in his chair, soaking in normality. Nearby, Uhura was giving poor Chekov a look that dripped icicles. Kirk himself still felt a little uncomfortable to find Sulu—the 'real' Sulu—at his elbow.

McCoy, however, evidently had not found it at all hard to readjust; his vast knowledge of psychology under stress also enabled him to understand himself. He said enthusiastically to Spock, "When I came out of the beams, Spocko boy, I was so pleased to see you that I almost kissed you. Luckily, revulsion at the very notion set in two seconds later."

"I am grateful that it did," Spock said.

"Mr. Spock," Kirk said, "Scotty tells me that had you not detected our counterparts immediately, restrained and questioned them, duplicated our calculations, and above all had them shoved into the transporter chamber all ready to make the exchange at the one precise moment, we'd have been stranded forever. I salute you; you have come through for the umpteenth time. But—how did you do it?"

"Sir," Spock said, "you know me as well as any man. But there are elements in my own heart that I do not show very readily. I had to call on them."

"Don't explain if you don't want to. But it would be useful to know how you managed it."

Spock raised his head and looked at some spot faraway in space.

"A civilized man," he said at last, "can easily play the part of a barbarian, as you all did in the other universe. He has only to look into his own soul for the remnants of the savage ancestors from which he sprang, and then—revert. But your counterparts, when we beamed them aboard, were savages to begin with—and had no core of civilization or humanity to which they could revert. The contrast was rather striking."

McCoy said, "Spock, could you have played the savage, if you'd been switched along with the rest of us?"

Very seriously, Spock said, "Dr. McCoy, I am a savage. Both here, and there. But some day, I hope to outgrow it."

THE DEADLY YEARS

Writer: David P. Harmon
Director: Joseph Pevney
Guest stars: Charles Drake, Sarah Marshall

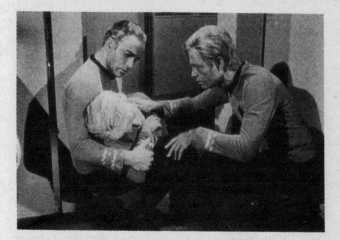

≡

There was no sign of Robert Johnson when the party from the *Enterprise* materialized on Gamma Hydra IV. In fact, there was no sign of anybody, and their arrival site, which otherwise resembled a Kansas field in mid-August, was eerily silent.

There were the overbright sun, the varied greens of leaves and grasses, even the shimmer of heat waves over the adjacent meadow. But all sounds of life were missing—insect, animal, human. All that suggested that it was the specified headquarters of the Johnson expedition was a scattering of pre-fab buildings.

Spock, Kirk noted, was looking troubled too. McCoy said, "Perhaps they weren't expecting us."

Spock shook his head. "Our arrival was scheduled well in advance, Doctor. An annual check of every scientific expedition is routine."

"Besides, I had sub-space contact with the leader of this expedition, a Robert Johnson, not an hour ago," Kirk said.

"Did he report anything wrong, Jim?"

"No . . . and yet there was *something* wrong. I can't quite nail it down, but his conversation was disjointed, somehow, as though he were having trouble sticking to the subject, or was worried about something." Kirk pointed at the nearest building. "Mr. Chekov, check that place. Mr. Spock and I will check that one. McCoy, Scotty, Lieutenant Galway, look around, see if you can find anyone."

The group broke up. Arlene Galway was looking a little

scared, Kirk thought. Well, this was only her first extra-solar planet; she'd toughen in due course. And the circumstances were a little odd.

Kirk and Spock were about to enter "their" building when a scream rent the air. Whirling, Kirk saw Chekov bursting out into the open, looking about wildly.

"Captain! Captain!" Chekov's voice had gone up a full octave. Kirk loped forward and grabbed him.

"What's wrong?"

"Captain! In there!"

"Control yourself, Ensign! What is it?"

"A man, sir! In there!" Chekov seemed a little calmer. "A dead man."

"All right, we'll check it. But why the panic? You've seen dead men before."

"I know," Chekov said, a little ashamedly. "But this one's, uh, peculiar, and frankly, sir, it startled me."

" 'Scared' might be the better word. All right, Bones, Spock, let's take a look." Kirk drew his phaser.

The interior of the building was quite dark—not black, but Kirk, coming in from the bright sunlight, had trouble getting used to it. At first, the building seemed quite empty; then he saw some sort of low structure near its end. He approached cautiously.

Then he abruptly understood what had panicked the unprepared Chekov. The object was a crudely constructed wooden coffin, for which two sawhorses served as a catafalque.

The body it held might have been Methuselah's. Deep wrinkles made its facial features also indecipherable. The open mouth was toothless, its near-white gums shriveled, its eyes sunk in caverns, flattened under their lids of flabby skin. The body seemed to be mere bones, barely held together by a brown-spotted integument of tissue-paper thinness. Clawed hands were crossed on its collapsed chest.

Chekov's voice said through the dimness, "I bumped into it walking backward, sir, and I—"

"I quite understand, Ensign. Rest easy. Bones, what's this?"

"Exactly what it looks like, Jim. Death by natural causes—in other words, old age."

"Doctor," Spock said, "I ran a personnel check on the members of this expedition before we beamed-down, and I can assure you that not one of them was . . ."

Midway through this sentence Kirk became aware of the shuffling of feet outside the open door. They all turned as Spock's voice trailed off.

A man and woman tottered toward them, supporting themselves with sticks. They were stooped and shrunken, the skin of their skulls showing through their thin white hair.

The man said, in a quavering voice, "They've come to pay their respects to Professor Alvin."

"I am Captain Kirk of the—"

"You'll have to speak louder," the man said, cupping his ear with his free hand.

"I said I am Captain Kirk of the *Enterprise*. Who are you?"

"Robert Johnson," said the old man, nodding. "And this is my wife Elaine."

"That's impossible," Kirk said. "The Johnsons are— how old are you?"

"Me? I'm . . . let me see . . . oh yes, I'm twenty-nine. Elaine is twenty-seven."

The shocked silence was at last broken by McCoy. "I am a physician. You both need rest and medical care."

There were only three decrepit survivors of the expedition to be beamed-up to Sickbay and Nurse Chapel's gentle but efficient care. Standing beside McCoy, Kirk leaned over Robert Johnson's bed.

"Can you hear me, Dr. Johnson?"

The filmed eyes found his face. "Not deaf yet, you know. Not yet."

"Have you any idea what happened?"

"What happened?" Johnson echoed vaguely.

"Did your instruments show anything?"

The old mind was wandering. As though appealing to some benevolent god, Johnson said, "Elaine was so beautiful . . . so beautiful."

"He can hear you, Jim, but he can't understand. Let him rest."

Kirk nodded. "Nurse Chapel, if any of them seem lucid, we'll be in the briefing room." He went to the intercom. "Kirk to bridge. Mr. Spock, Commodore Stocker, Dr. Wallace, to the briefing room, please. Bones, I'll ask you to come along."

Janet Wallace and George Stocker were distinguished guests; he an able administrator in his mid-forties, she an endocrinologist, in her late twenties and extremely attractive. They were waiting with Spock at the big table when he and McCoy arrived. He nodded to them all and sat down himself. "Commodore Stocker, I've asked you to this briefing because Gamma Hydra Four falls within the area of your administration."

Trim, competent-looking, the tall man said, "I appreciate that, Captain."

The merest hint of constraint came into Kirk's voice as he spoke to the dark-eyed girl who sat next to the Commodore. "Dr. Wallace, though you are a new member of our crew, your credentials as an endocrinologist are impressive. In this situation we face, I'd appreciate your working closely with Dr. McCoy."

She smiled at him. "Yes, Captain."

He turned hastily to McCoy. "Fill them in, Bones."

McCoy said, "The survivors of the expedition to Gamma Hydra Four are not merely suffering from extreme old age. They are getting older, much older by the minute. My examinations have shown up nothing. I haven't a clue to the cause of this rapidly aging process."

"Mr. Spock, what about environment and atmosphere?"

"Sensors show nothing inimical to human life, sir. The atmosphere screens out the usual amount of harmful cosmic rays."

"We are close, though," Kirk said, "to the neutral zone between our Federation and the Romulan Confederation. The Romulans may have a new weapon. Perhaps they have been using members of the expedition as guinea pigs."

"I have begun to investigate that possibility, Captain," Spock said.

Kirk rose. "I want you all to check out everything in your particular specialties. No matter how remote, how far-fetched seems the notion, I want it run down." He paused for emphasis. "We will remain in orbit until we have the answer."

Stocker spoke. "I am anxious to get to Star Base Ten in order to assume my new post. I am sure you understand that, Captain."

"I will do what I can to see that you make your due date, Commodore."

"Thank you, Captain."

The men, pushing back their chairs, left the briefing room. But the dark-eyed Dr. Wallace didn't move. Kirk turned at the door. "Anything I can do for you, Doctor?"

"Yes," she said. "You might, for instance, say 'Hello, Janet'. You might be a little less the cold, efficient starship captain and a little more the old . . . friend."

"Janet, as captain, I have certain—my duties are heavy." Then he gave her a wry little smile. "Or maybe I just don't want to get burned again."

"I'm carrying a little scar tissue of my own," she said.

There was a small silence. Then he said, "How long has it been?"

"More than six years, Jim."

"A long time. But there wouldn't be any change if we started it up all over again, would there? I've got my ship; and you've got your work. Neither of us will change."

"You never asked why I married after we called it off."

"I supposed you'd found another man you loved."

"I found a man I admired."

"And in the same field as you. You didn't have to give up anything."

"No, I didn't. But he's dead now, Jim."

She went to him, her hands extended. Kirk hesitated. Then he took one of the hands, his eyes searching the warm brown ones—and Uhura's voice spoke on the intercom.

"Captain Kirk, Mr. Spock would like to see you on the bridge."

"Tell Mr. Spock I'm on my way." He was finding deeper depths in the brown eyes. "Janet, we're under pressure right now. Maybe, when it eases off, things will be—"

Uhura's voice interrupted again. "Captain Kirk, Mr. Scott would like to see you in Engineering."

"Tell him I'll be down after I check with Mr. Spock."

He drew Janet closer to him. Lifting her chin, he said, "But this time there must be truth between us. You and I, with our eyes open, knowing what each of us are."

"It's been a long six years," she said; and placed her arms around his neck. He had bent his head to her mouth when the intercom spoke for the third time. "Captain Kirk!"

"On my way, Lieutenant Uhura." A sudden wave of weariness swept over him. He touched the girl's mouth with his forefinger. "Six long years—and that intercom is trying to make it six more. Dr. Wallace, your lips are as tempting as ever—but as I remarked, my duties are heavy."

The weariness stayed with him on his way to the bridge. Sulu greeted him with a "Standard orbit, Captain." He said, "Maintain" and crossed to Spock at the computer station.

"I have rechecked the sensors, sir. Gamma Hydra Four checks out as a Class M planet, nitrogen-oxygen atmosphere, normal mass with conventional atmospheric conditions. I can find nothing at all out of the ordinary."

"How about that comet that recently passed through here?"

"I am running checks on it, sir. As yet I have no conclusions. The comet is a rogue and has never been investigated."

"Captain Kirk!"

It was Stocker. He looked like a man with a determined idea. "Facilities at Star Base Ten," he said, "are much more complete than those on board ship. It seems to me your investigations would be facilitated by proceeding there at once. I assure you of every cooperation."

"Thank you, Commodore; but we have a few facilities of our own. I am going to Engineering, Mr. Spock." He left the computer station to say to Sulu, "Maintain standard orbit, Mr. Sulu."

Surprised, Sulu exclaimed, "But you already gave that order, sir!

Kirk looked surprised himself. "Did I? Oh, well. Follow it."

As he left the bridge, Spock stared after him, a look of concern in his eyes.

Lieutenant Galway appeared uneasy, too, as she opened

the door of Sickbay. "Dr. McCoy, can I speak with you a moment?"

"Of course." He motioned her to a chair but she didn't take it. "I know," she said, "that this is going to sound foolish. But—I seem to be having a little trouble hearing."

"Probably nothing important," McCoy said.

"I never had any trouble before."

"I'll have a look at you. Maybe a simple hypersonic treatment will clear it up." She said, "Thank you, Doctor" and followed him into the examination room.

Kirk was discovering some trouble of his own. Alone in his quarters, stripped to the waist, he dried the face he'd just shaved, and reached for the clean shirt he'd laid out on the bed. As he raised his right arm to insert it into a sleeve, a sharp stab of pain struck his right shoulder. He winced, lowered the arm, flexed it, massaging the shoulder muscle. The pain persisted. Slowly, carefully, he put on the shirt. Then he moved to the intercom and flicked a button. "Progress report, Mr. Spock?"

"All research lines negative, Captain."

Kirk said, "Astronomical section reports that a comet recently passed by. Check into that."

Spock waited a moment before he replied, "I'm doing that, sir, according to your order. We discussed it earlier."

"Oh. Well, let me know what you come up with. I'll be in Sickbay."

"Yes, Captain."

The walk to Sickbay seemed longer than usual. The pain in the right shoulder had extended to the right knee. There was a slight trace of a limp in Kirk's movement as he entered Sickbay. In its bed section, all but one of the three beds was vacant. He thought, "So two of the rescued Johnson party are gone." It was a depressing reflection. Then he saw Nurse Chapel draw a blanket up and over the face of the patient who occupied the third bed.

McCoy looked up. "Robert Johnson, deceased. The last one, Jim. Cause of death—old age."

"You did what you could," Kirk said.

The intercom spoke. "Dr. McCoy? This is Scott. Can I come up and see you?"

McCoy answered shortly. "You just need vitamins. But yes, come up anyway, Scotty."

He punched off and Kirk said, "Bones, I believe you're getting gray!"

"You take over my job and see what it does to you!" Low-voiced, McCoy gave an order to Nurse Chapel. Then he turned back to Kirk. "Well, what's *your* problem?"

"My shoulder," Kirk said. "Got a little twinge in it. Probably just a muscle strain."

"Probably, Dr. Kirk," McCoy snapped.

Kirk grinned. "Reprimand noted, sir. Okay, no more diagnoses by me."

McCoy ran his Feinberger over Kirk's shoulder. He frowned. "Hmmm. Maybe we'd better run a complete check on you."

"Well? Muscle strain?"

McCoy shook his head. "No, Jim. It's an advanced case of arthritis. And spreading."

"But that's not possible!"

"I'll run the check again, but I'll get the same answer."

He didn't run it again. For Kirk, his dismay still on his face was staring past him at the Sickbay door. McCoy turned. Scott stood there—a Scott with snow-white hair who appeared to be sixty years of age.

Sickbay on the *Enterprise* had become a section that seemed to have been appropriated by a Golden Age club. Assembled there on Kirk's order were every member of the crew who had contacted Gamma Hydra Four. With the single exception of Chekov, each one had been affected by the rapidly aging process. Kirk looked fifty-five: McCoy ten years older. Nor had Spock's Vulcan heritage been entirely able to immunize him against its effects. Wrinkles cracked his face; the skin under his eyes had gone baggy. Lieutenant Galway might have been a woman in her mid-sixties. Scott looked oldest of them all.

"All right, Bones," Kirk said. "Let's have it."

McCoy said, "All of us who went down to the planet, except Ensign Chekov, are aging rapidly. The rates vary from person to person, but it averages thirty years each day. I don't know what's causing it—virus, bacteria or evil spirits. I'm trying to find out."

"Spock? I asked you for some calculations."

"Based on what Dr. McCoy gave me, I'd say that we each have a week to live. It would also seem that since our mental faculties are aging faster than our bodies, we will become little better than mental vegetables in less time than a week."

"You mean total senility?"

"Yes, Captain. In a very short time!"

Kirk took a step away from the group. "What a . . . a filthy way to die!" He turned slowly, accommodating his aching knee. "I want every research facility on this ship, every science technician, to immediately start round-the-clock research. I want the answer! And a remedy! And you might start in by telling me why Chekov wasn't affected!"

"I'm doing what I can," McCoy said. He removed his Feinberger diagnostic instrument from Spock. "You are disgustingly healthy, Spock."

"I must differ with you, Doctor. I am finding it difficult to concentrate. My eyesight appears to be failing. And the normal temperature of the ship strikes me as increasingly cold."

"I didn't say you were not affected."

Scott said dully, "Can I go back to my station?"

"Feel up to it, Scotty?" Kirk asked.

"Of course I do. Just need a little rest, that's all."

McCoy said, "You can leave too if you wish, Lieutenant Galway."

She didn't move. McCoy spoke louder. "Lieutenant Galway?"

"What? You spoke to me, Doctor?"

"Yes. I said you could go. Why not go to your quarters and get some sleep?"

"No! I don't want to sleep! Can't you understand? If I sleep . . . what will I find when I wake up?"

Kirk said, "Lieutenant Galway, report to your station and continue with your duties."

Her "Yes, sir" was grateful. She rose painfully from her chair, moved toward the door, and came face to face with herself in a mirror. She turned from it in anger.

"What a stupid place to hang a mirror!"

She half-stumbled out. Kirk looked after her. "She's

seven or eight years younger than I am. She looks ten years older."

"People normally age at different speeds, Jim."

Kirk pointed to Chekov. "But why hasn't he aged?"

"I don't know."

"Well, I want to know! Is it his youth? His blood type? His glands? His medical history? His genes?"

"Nurse Chapel, prepare Mr. Chekov for a complete physical."

She rose. "Come along, Ensign. This won't hurt. Much."

As the door closed behind the nurse and the reluctant Chekov, Janet Wallace turned to McCoy. "A few years ago on Aldebaran Three, my husband and I used a variation of cholesterol block to slow arteriosclerosis in animals."

"Did it work?"

"Sometimes. But the side effects were fierce. We gave it up."

"Try it anyhow, Dr. Wallace. Try anything, but do it quickly!"

"Yes, sir." She went out in turn.

"Mr. Spock, return to the bridge," Kirk said. "I'll join you shortly. Keep me posted on Chekov, Bones."

He found Janet Wallace waiting for him in the corridor. "I thought you were on your way to the bio-chemistry lab, Doctor."

"We both go in the same direction, Jim."

After a moment, he nodded. "So we do."

She adjusted her pace to his slower walk. "We know the problem," she said. "We know the effects it is having. And we know the progress of the affliction. Therefore, once we find the proper line of research, it's only logical that we find the solution."

Kirk smiled. "You sound like my First Officer."

"No problem, Jim—not even ours—is insoluble."

"I could name you five insoluble problems right off the top of my head. For example, why was the universe created? How can we trust what we think we know? Is there such a thing as an invariably right or wrong action? What is the nature of beauty? What is the proof of Fermat's last theorem? None of those are soluble by logic."

"No. The heart is not a logical organ. Our . . . situation . . . doesn't have its roots in logic." She put her arm through his. "When I married Theodore Wallace, I thought I was over you. I was wrong."

Kirk gave her a sharp look. "When did you realize this? Today?"

"What?"

"How much older was your husband than you?"

"What difference does it make?" she asked.

"Answer me!"

"Twenty-six years," she told him reluctantly. Then, as though he'd demanded an explanation, she added, "He was a brilliant man . . . we were stationed on a lonely outpost . . . working together—" She broke off to cry, "Jim, I don't want to talk about him! I want to talk about us!"

"Look at me!" Kirk demanded. He seized her shoulders. "I said look at me! What do you see?"

"I—I see Captain James Kirk," she said unsteadily. "A man of morality, decency—strong, handsome—"

"And *old*!" he cried. "Old—and getting older every minute!"

"Jim, please . . ."

"What are you offering me, Jan? Love—or a goodbye present?"

"That's very cruel," she said.

"It's honest!" His voice was harsh with bitterness. "Just stay around for two more days, Janet! By that time I'll really be old enough for your love!"

Young Chekov was feeling the strain of multiple medical examinations. "Give us some more blood, Chekov!" he muttered to Sulu. "The needle won't hurt, Chekov! Take off your shirt, Chekov! Roll over, Chekov! Breathe deeply, Chekov! Blood sample! Marrow sample! Skin sample! They take so many samples of me I'm not even sure I'm here!"

"You'll live," Sulu said.

"Oh yes, I'll live . . . but I won't enjoy—"

Kirk entered the bridge and he fell silent. Sulu said, "Maintaining standard orbit, Captain."

"Increase orbit to twenty thousand perigee."

As Kirk moved to his command chair, Yeoman Doris

Atkins handed him a clipboard. "Will you sign this, sir?"
He glanced at the board, scribbled his name on it and was
handing it back to her when Commodore Stocker approached
him.

"I hope to have a few words with you, Captain."

"I have very little time, Commodore."

"Very well, sir. I just want to remind you we have a
due date at Star Base Ten."

"I'm afraid we'll be late for it, Commodore Stocker. I
do not intend to leave this area until we have found a solution
to our problem."

"Captain, I am watching four very valuable, and one
almost irreplaceable, members of the Starfleet failing before
my eyes. I want to do something to help."

"If you are so concerned," Kirk said, "I'll send a subspace message to Star Base Ten and explain the situation."

At his computer station, Spock shook his head. Kirk
noticed the gesture. "Yes, Mr. Spock?"

"Captain . . . you sent such a message this morning."

"Oh. Yes, of course." He changed the subject. "Yeoman Atkins."

"Sir?"

"Where's the report on fuel consumption?"

"You just signed it, sir."

"If I'd signed it, I wouldn't have asked for it! Give it
to me!"

The girl timidly handed him the board. There was his
signature. Angrily, he handed the board back to her and sank
down in his command chair. He saw Chekov and Sulu exchange looks. Uhura's back was resolutely turned.

Kirk closed his eyes. *I need rest. You can take just so
much. Then you've had it.* He was helpless; that was the fact.
And he had never been so tired before in all his life . . .
worry, despair . . . they weren't going to change a thing . . .
tired . . . tired . . .

As from a great distance, he heard Spock's voice.
"Captain! I believe I know the cause! I decided to—" The
voice stopped, and Kirk let his mind drift again; but then he
was being shaken. "Captain!" He roused himself with immense effort.

"Hmm? Spock? Sorry . . . I was thinking."

"Understandable, sir."

"Um. Do you have something to report, Mr. Spock?"

"Yes, sir. I think I know the cause of the affliction. I cannot be sure, but the lead I have seems very promising."

Alert now, Kirk said, "What is it?"

"The comet," Spock said. "The orbit of Gamma Hydra Four carried it directly through the comet's tail. I examined the residue on conventional radiation setting and discovered nothing. But when I reset our sensors at the extreme lower range of the scale, undetected radiation appeared. Below normal radiation readings . . . but definitely present. And undoubtedly residue from the comet's tail."

"Good, Mr. Spock. Let's get that to Dr. McCoy immediately."

Pain stabbed in his right knee as he rose. He massaged it and limped over to Uhura. "Lieutenant, take a message to Starfleet Command."

"Yes, sir."

"Because of the proximity of the Romulans, use Code Two."

"But, sir, the Romulans have broken Code Two. If you will remember the last bulletin—"

"Then use Code Three!"

"Yes, sir. Code Three."

"Message. Key to affliction may be in comet which passed Gamma Hydra Four. Said comet is now—" He looked at Spock.

"Quadrant four four eight, sir."

"I suggest all units be alerted for complete analysis of radiation; and means found to neutralize it. The comet is highly dangerous. Kirk, commanding *Enterprise*. Send it at once, Lieutenant Uhura. Let's go, Mr. Spock."

At the elevator he paused. "Mr. Sulu, increase orbit to twenty thousand miles perigee."

Startled, Sulu said, "You mean—another twenty thousand, Captain?"

Kirk whipped around, grim-faced. "I find it difficult to understand why every one of my commands is being questioned. Do what you're told, Mr. Sulu."

Spock spoke quietly. "What is our present position, Mr. Sulu?"

"Orbiting at twenty thousand, sir."

Kirk looked at Spock's impassive face. Then he said, "Maintain, Mr. Sulu."

"Maintaining, sir."

The silence of constraint was heavy in the bridge when the elevator door closed behind them.

But in Sickbay, hope had returned.

"Radiation," McCoy said reflectively. "As good an answer as any. But why didn't we know this earlier?"

"I suspect, Doctor, because my thinking processes are less clear and rapid than they were."

McCoy glanced at Spock. Then he handed his tape cartridge to Janet Wallace. "Run this through, please, Doctor."

"All right," Kirk said. "Keep me posted. I'll be on the bridge. Coming Spock?"

"I have a question for the Doctor, Captain."

Kirk nodded, left. Spock said, "Doctor, the ship's temperature is increasingly uncomfortable for me. I have adjusted the environment in my quarters to one hundred and twenty-five degrees. This at least is tolerable, but—"

"I can see I won't be making any house calls on you," McCoy said.

"I wondered if there was something which could lower my sensitivity to cold."

"I'm not a magician, Spock. Just a plain old country doctor."

As the Vulcan closed the Sickbay door behind him, Janet turned, frustrated, from the computer. "Dr. McCoy, none of our usual radiation therapies will have any effect on this particular form of radiation sickness."

"All right. We start over. We work harder. Faster. Start completely from scratch if we have to. But we must find something."

Outside in the corridor, Commodore Stocker had intercepted Spock. "Can I have a word with you, Mr. Spock?"

"Commodore?"

Stocker lowered his voice. "Mr. Spock, a Starship can function with a chief engineer, a chief medical officer, even a First Officer who is under physical par. But it is disastrous to have a commanding officer whose condition is less than perfection.''

"I am aware of that.''

"Please understand me. My admiration for Captain Kirk is unbounded. He is a great officer. But . . . Mr. Spock, I need your help and your cooperation.''

"For what, sir?''

"I want you to take over command of the *Enterprise*.''

"On what grounds, sir?''

"On the grounds that the Captain is unable to perform his duties because of his affliction.''

"I must remind you that I have contracted the same affliction.''

"But you're a Vulcan,'' Stocker said. "You have a much greater life span. You show the effects to a much smaller degree . . .''

"I am half human, sir,'' Spock said. "My physical reflexes are down. My mental capacities are reduced. I tire easily. No, sir. I am not fit for command.''

"If you, a Vulcan, are not, then obviously Captain Kirk cannot be.''

"Sir,'' Spock said, "I have duties to perform.''

"Mr. Spock, I do not like what I'm about to say but regulations demand it. As second in command of the *Enterprise*, you must convene an extraordinary hearing on the Captain's competence.''

"I—resist that suggestion, sir,'' Spock said stiffly.

"It's not a matter of choice. If a Captain is mentally or physically unfit, a competency hearing is mandatory. Please don't force me to quote a regulation which you know as well as I do.''

There was a long pause. "Very well,'' Spock said. "The hearing will convene at fourteen hundred hours.''

Under the eyes of a worried Kirk, Janet and McCoy were running final tests of Chekov. The unhappy Ensign was obviously considering rebellion against what seemed to be the thousandth needle jabbed into him during the course of these interminable examinations.

"Now, this won't hurt,'' McCoy told him.

"That's what you said last time," Chekov said. "And the time before that."

"Did it hurt?"

"Yes," Chekov retorted.

From the door of Sickbay came a whimper: "Doctor . . . help me . . ."

They turned. Arlene Galway was clutching the door-jamb for support. She was almost unrecognizable with age. "Please . . . do something . . . help . . ."

She reached out a hand; but before anyone could reach her, she collapsed to the deck. McCoy bent over her, while Kirk looked on, appalled even through the gray fog in which everything seemed to have happened in the last few days—or was it the last few weeks?

"That can't be—Lieutenant Galway?" he quavered.

"It is," McCoy said, his own voice creaky. "Or was. She's dead. Her higher metabolism rate caused her to age more rapidly than the rest of us. But it's only a question of time before—"

"Bones, how long have we got?"

"Oh, it's a matter of days, Jim . . . perhaps only hours."

It wasn't information calculated to tranquilize a Star-fleet captain called to a hearing on his command competence. Nor were the people gathered around the briefing-room table a quieting influence. The mysterious radiation sickness had made deeper inroads on everyone who had made the ill-fated check on the Robert Johnson expedition.

Looking as though he'd passed his fiftieth birthday, Spock opened the hearing by turning to Yeoman Atkins, who was serving as recorder. "Let it be read that this competency hearing has been ordered by Commodore Stocker, here present." He paused. "And reluctantly called by myself."

Kirk said, "Let it also be read that I consider this hearing invalid."

Spock looked down the table at Stocker.

Stocker said, "Regulation seven five nine two, section three paragraph eleven . . ."

"I know the book, Commodore," Kirk said.

Spock said quietly, "The legality of the hearing, Captain, is unquestionable."

"Mr. Spock, may I make a statement?" It was Stocker's question. At Spock's nod, he said, "I've had to resort to these legal grounds to save the lives of some extremely valuable members of the Starfleet. I have tried to convince Captain Kirk of the need to proceed to Star Base Ten—but have been overruled in each case. The responsibility for this hearing is mine."

"On the contrary, Commodore," Spock said. "As presiding officer and second in command of the *Enterprise*, the responsibility is mine. Captain Kirk, would you like to make a statement?"

"Yes!" The word came in a shout. "I am Captain of this ship and am totally capable of commanding her. Call this farce off and let's get back to work!"

"I cannot, sir," Spock said. "The regulations are quite specific." The chill struck him again. "You are entitled, sir, to direct examination of all witnesses immediately after this board has questioned them."

Kirk's voice was acid with sarcasm. "That is very kind of you, Mr. Spock."

Spock pushed a button on the computer-recorder. Imperturbable, he said, "Mr. Sulu, how long have you served with Captain Kirk?"

"Two years, sir."

"To your knowledge has he ever been unable to make decisions?"

"No, sir."

"Did he order you to maintain standard orbit around Gamma Hydra Four?"

"Yes, sir."

"Did he, several minutes later, repeat the order?"

"Yes, sir."

"Did he order you to increase orbit to twenty thousand perigee?"

"Yes, sir."

"And did he not repeat that order?"

"He did not!" Kirk yelled. "When I give an order I expect it to be obeyed! I don't have to repeat myself!"

"Captain, you'll be allowed direct cross-examination privileges when the board has finished."

"Isn't your terminology mixed up, Spock? This isn't a board! It's a cudgel!"

"Captain, it is a hearing not only sanctioned but required by regulations. Will you please answer the question, Mr. Sulu?"

"Yes, sir. Captain Kirk repeated his order."

"Commodore?"

"I have no questions," Stocker said.

"Captain Kirk?"

"Let's get on with it."

Spock ground his teeth together to keep them from chattering. His hands felt clumsy with cold. "Yeoman Atkins, you handed Captain Kirk a fuel-consumption report before witnesses. He accepted and signed it. Is that correct?"

"Sir, he had more important things on his mind. The current crisis—"

"Yeoman, you are merely to answer the question."

"I—guess he forgot he'd signed it."

"You guess?"

"He forgot he'd signed it."

"Thank you, Yeoman. You may leave."

It went on. Spock called Uhura to testify to Kirk's failure to recall that the Romulans had broken Code Two.

"All right!" Kirk cried. "I had a lot on my mind! I admit to the oversight!"

"It could have been a dangerous one," Stocker said.

"You are out of order, Commodore," Spock said. "Dr. McCoy?"

McCoy was lost in a daydream. "Dr. McCoy!"

He roused. "Sorry. Yes, Mr. Spock?"

"Several hours ago, at this board's request, you ran a complete physical examination of Captain Kirk."

"I did." McCoy threw a tape across the table at Spock. "It's all there. Enjoy yourself."

Silently, the Vulcan placed the tape cartridge into the computer slot.

The device buzzed, clicked, spoke. "Subject's physical age, based on physiological profile, sixty-three solar years."

There was a silence. Then Kirk said, "I am thirty-four years old."

"The computer differs with you," Stocker said.

"Dr. McCoy, give us your professional evaluation of Captain Kirk's present physical condition."

McCoy averted his eyes from Spock. "He is afflicted with a strange type of radiation sickness . . . and so are you and I and Mr. Scott."

"Kindly restrict your comments to Captain Kirk alone, Doctor. What effect has this sickness had on him?"

"He's—he's graying a little. A touch of arthritis."

"Is that all?"

"You know it isn't all! What are you trying to do, Spock?"

"What I must do. Is not the Captain suffering from a peculiar physical degeneration which strongly resembles aging?"

"Yes, he is. But he's a better man—"

"Doctor, do you agree with the computer's evaluation of the Captain's physical age?"

"It's a blasted machine!"

"Do you agree with it, Doctor?"

"Yes, I agree. I'm sorry, Jim."

"This board has no further questions. Unless you, Commodore Stocker . . ."

"I am quite satisfied, Mr. Spock."

"Do you wish to call witnesses, Captain Kirk?"

"I am perfectly capable of speaking in my own defense!"

Kirk tried to rise. His knee gave way; and he clutched at the table to keep from falling. "This hearing is being held for one reason and one alone. Because I refuse to leave Gamma Hydra Two."

"Gamma Hydra Four, sir," Spock said.

"Of course. A slip of the tongue. Where was I?" He suddenly clenched his fist and dashed it against the table. "So I'm a little confused! Who wouldn't be at a time like this? My ship in trouble . . . my senior officers ill . . . and this—this nonsense about a competency hearing! Enough to mix up any man! Trying to relieve a Starfleet captain of his command. Why, that's . . . that's . . . I wouldn't have believed it of you, Spock!''

He glared around the table. "All right, ask me questions! Go ahead! I'll show you who's capable! There's nothing wrong with my memory. Nor with my resolution, either. I repeat, we are maintaining orbit around Gamma Hydra Two!''

The second memory failure stood out, stark-naked.

Spock, cold to his marrow, spoke quietly into the silence.

"We have no more questions, Captain." He struggled to control his shivering. "If you will leave the room, sir, while the board votes . . .''

"Fine! You bet I'll leave it. Get your stupid voting over so I can get back to running my ship!''

He limped to the door and turned. "If I'm wanted, I'll be in my quarters.''

When the door closed behind him, Spock said, "A simple hand vote will suffice. Dr. Wallace is excluded from the vote. Those who agree that Captain Kirk is no longer capable of handling the *Enterprise* will so signify by raising their right hands.''

All hands save Spock's were slowly raised.

"Mr. Spock?'' It was Commodore Stocker.

Spock raised his hand. He addressed the recording computer. "Register a unanimous vote.''

Stocker said, "I assume, Mr. Spock, that you will now take over command of this vessel.''

"Your assumption is incorrect, sir.''

"Your reason?''

"By the standards this hearing has used against the Captain: my own physical failings exclude me from any command position.''

"All right. Next in line is Mr. Scott.''

All eyes fixed on Scott. He peered at the expectant faces, blinked, nodded—and was asleep.

"Since all senior officers are incapable, I am forced by regulations to assume command.'' Stocker was rising from the table when Spock said, "Sir, you have never commanded a starship.''

"Whom would you have take over, Mr. Spock?''

"There is danger from the Romulans," Spock said.

"Mr. Spock, we've got to save these people!" He turned to Sulu. "Mr. Sulu, lay a direct course for Star Base Ten. Warp Five."

"Across the neutral zone, sir?"

Stocker nodded. "Alter course immediately."

"Commodore Stocker, I beg you not to underestimate the danger. Or the Romulans." Spock spoke urgently.

"The neutral zone is thinly patrolled at best. I am gambling that the violation will escape the Romulans' notice."

"The gamble, sir, if I may quote the odds—" Spock said.

"You may not!" Stocker strode to the door. "All officers are to return to their stations."

Kirk was alone in his quarters, tired, defeated, crushed by the full weight of his seventy years. When the knock at the door came, he could hardly bring himself to respond to it; but after a moment, he said, "Come in."

Spock entered, followed by Janet, who took up an inconspicuous stance beside the door. Kirk looked up hopefully at Spock, but the First Officer's face, for once, was almost as readable as a book.

"So," Kirk said. "I've been relieved."

"I am sorry, Captain."

"You should have been a prosecuting attorney."

"Regulations required me—"

"Regulations!" Kirk said. "Don't give me regulations, Spock! You've wanted command all along! The first little excuse—"

"I have not assumed command, Captain."

"I hope you're proud of the way you got . . ." Kirk paused, Spock's words gradually coming home. "What do you mean, you're not in command?"

"I suffer from the same ailment as yourself, sir."

"If you're not in command, who is?"

"Commodore Stocker."

It took Kirk a long moment to place the name. Then he exploded. "Stocker? Are you crazy? He's never held a field command! If Scotty—"

"Mr. Scott is in no condition to command. Commodore Stocker, as a ranking officer—"

"Don't prate to me about rank. The man's a chair-bound paper-pusher. Spock, I order you to take command!"

"I cannot, sir."

"You are disobeying a direct order, Mr. Spock."

"No, Captain. Only Commodore Stocker can give command orders on this ship now."

Impotent fury rose in Kirk. "You disloyal, traitorous . . . you stabbed me in the back the first chance you had. You—" His rage mounted as he found that he was weeping. Weeping! "Get out of here! I don't ever want to have to look at you again!"

Spock hesitated, inclined his head slightly, and left. After a moment, Kirk became aware of the female figure still standing beside the door inside his room, making faint sniffling noises. He peered at it.

"Who is it? Jan? Jan?"

"I'm sorry, Jim," she said. "Truly I am."

"I acted like a fool in there. Let them rattle me. Let myself get confused."

"Everyone understood."

"Only I'm not old, Jan. I'm not! A few muscular aches don't make a man old! You don't run a starship with your arms—you run it with your head! My mind's as sharp as it ever was!"

"We'll find a cure."

"A simple case of radiation sickness and I'm relieved of command." He turned and looked at himself in a mirror. "All right, I admit I've gotten a little gray. Radiation can do that."

"Jim," she said, as if in pain. "I have work to do. Please excuse me—"

"Look at me, Jan. You said you loved me. You know me. Look closely—"

"*Please*, Jim—"

"Just need a little rest. That's all. I'm not old, am I? Well, Say it! Say I'm not old!"

There was no response. Grasping her by the shoulders, he pulled her to him and kissed her with all the violence of which he was capable. But there was no response—not from her, and what was worse, not even within himself. He released her—and saw the pity in her eyes. He turned his back.

"Get out."

Now what? He could not think. He was relieved. The answer . . . but there was no answer. Wait. Something about a comet. McCoy. Chekov. The examination room. That was it, the examination room. He hobbled out, cursing himself for his slowness.

Spock was there; so were Nurse Chapel, McCoy and Janet. They all looked very old, somehow. But the hapless Chekov, back on the table again, did not seem to have changed. He was saying: "Why don't I just go back to work and leave my blood here?"

Kirk tried to glare at Spock. "What are you doing here?"

"It would seem the place where I can be of the most use."

"Maybe you'd like to relieve Dr. McCoy? Bones, what about Ensign Chekov here?"

"Nothing," McCoy said peevishly. "Absolutely nothing."

"There has to be! There has to be! We went down to the surface together. Beamed-down together. Stayed in the same spot. He was with us all the time. He—"

"*No*, Captain," Spock said, drawing in a sharp breath. "Not all the time. He left us for a few moments."

"Left us?" Kirk stared at the Vulcan, trying to remember. "Oh. Yes—when he went into the building. He . . . there was . . . Spock! Something did happen!"

"Indeed, Captain. Doctor, you will remember Professor Alvin's corpse in the improvised coffin—"

"Chekov, you got scared!" Kirk crowed. "You bumped into the dead man, and—"

"You bet," Chekov said. "I was scared, sir. But not half as scared as I am now, I'll tell you that."

"Fright?" McCoy said, raising a trembling hand to his chin. "Yes. Could be. Heart beats faster. Breath short. Cold sweat. Epinephrine flows. Something I read once . . . epinephrine tried for radiation sickness, in the mid-twentieth century—"

"It was abandoned," Janet said. "When hyronalyn was discovered."

"Yes, yes," McCoy said testily. "Don't confuse me. Why was it abandoned? There was some other reason. I knew it well, once. They didn't know the intermediate? Yes! That's it! AMP! Nurse, ask the computer for something called AMP!"

Christine Chapel, her face a study in incredulity, turned to the computer read-out panel. After what seemed a very long time, she said, "There's an entry for it. It's called cyclic adenosine three-five monophosphate. But it affects *all* the hormonal processes—that's why they dropped it."

"We'll try it," McCoy said, with a startling cackle. "Don't just stand there, Dr. Wallace. Synthesize me a batch. Dammit, get cracking!"

On the bridge, Commodore Stocker was in the command chair. If he was aware of how many backs were pointedly turned to him, he did not show it; he was too busy trying to make sense of the many little lights that were flickering across the console before him.

"Entering Romulan neutral zone, sir," the helmsman said. "All sensors on maximum."

Now who was that? "Thank you, Mr. Spock, sorry, Mr. Sulu. Lieutenant Uhura, let me know if we contact any Romulan."

"Yes, sir. Nothing yet."

Stocker nodded and looked down again. The little lights danced mockingly at him. As a cadet he had studied a control board something like this, but since then, everything seemed to have been rearranged, and labeled with new symbols which meant nothing to him, with only a few exceptions. Well, he would have to depend upon these officers—

Then the *Enterprise* shook sharply under him, and half of the little lights went red. Ignorance overwhelmed him. "What was that?" he said helplessly.

"We have made contact, sir," Uhura said in a dry voice.

"Romulans approach from both sides, sir," Sulu added.

The ship shook again, harder. Swallowing, Stocker said, "Let's see them."

The main viewscreen lit up. It too was full of crawling little lights, which could not be told from the stars except for their motions, which he could not read either.

"I don't see any Romulans!"

"The ones that are changing color, sir. They change in accordance with their rate of approach—"

The ship bucked under him. All the lights went red.

"We're bracketed, sir," Sulu said evenly.

There was a buzz he couldn't locate. "Engineering calling, sir," Uhura said. "Do you want power diverted to the shields?"

His face felt bathed in sweat. "Yes," he said, at random.

"Mr. Scott asks how much warp power to reserve."

What was the answer to that one?

"Commodore Stocker," Sulu said, turning halfway toward the command chair. "We're in a tight. What are your orders?"

The *Enterprise* shuddered once more, and the lights dimmed. Stocker realized suddenly that he was too scared to speak, let alone move—

Then, mercifully, Kirk's voice, thin but demanding, came through the intercom. "What's going on up there? Lieutenant Uhura, this is the Captain!"

"Sir!" Uhura said. "We have violated the Romulan neutral zone, and are under attack."

"The fool. Maintain full shields! I'll be right there."

Stocker felt as though he were about to pass out with relief, but the ordeal wasn't over yet. Voices, more distant, were arguing over the open intercom:

"Jim . . . you can't . . . neither of us . . . Nurse . . . Doctor Wallace . . ."

"Got to . . . get to the bridge . . ."

"Oh Jim, you can't . . . Nurse . . . In there . . ."

Then the voices snapped off. Clearly, Kirk was not about to bail Stocker out yet. Rousing himself, Stocker said, "Lieutenant Uhura, keep trying to raise the Romulans."

"Very well. No response thus far."

"If I can talk to them—tell them the reason why we've violated the neutral zone—"

"The Romulans are notorious for not listening to explanations," Sulu said. "We know—we've tangled with them before."

"Hail them again!"

"I've hailed them on all channels," Uhura said. "They're ignoring us."

"Why shouldn't they?" Sulu said. "They know they have us. As long as we sit here, they can kick away at the screens until they go down."

Stocker ran a hand through his hair. "Then," he said, "we have no alternative but to surrender."

"They'd love that," Sulu said, his back still turned. "They have never captured a starship before. And, Commodore, they never take prisoners."

"Then what—"

"Sir," Uhura said, "you are in command. *What are your orders?*"

In Sickbay, Nurse Chapel and Janet had Kirk pinned down on a bed. He struggled to get up, and despite his aged condition they were having trouble restraining him—a task further complicated by the unpredictable shuddering of the *Enterprise*.

"Greenhorn—up there—ruin my ship—"

"Jim," Janet said through gritted teeth, "if I have to give you a shot—"

"Jim, lay quiet," McCoy said. "You can't do any good. We're through."

"No, no. My ship—"

Spock appeared from the laboratory, carrying a flask. "Dr. Wallace, here is the drug. It's crude, but we had no time for pharmacological tests or other refinements."

"All right," said McCoy. "Let's go."

"It will cure . . . or kill." Spock handed the flask to Janet, who loaded a hypo from it. "A safer preparation would take weeks to test."

"What is it?" Kirk said, quietening somewhat.

"The hormone intermediate," Janet said. "It has to be given parenterally, and even without the probable impurities in it, it could be extremely hard on the body. Cerebral hemmorhage, cardiac arrest—''

"Never mind the details," McCoy said. "Give it to me."

"No," Kirk said. "I'll take the first shot."

"You can't," McCoy said firmly.

As if on cue, the *Enterprise* shook again. "How long do you think the ship can take a pounding like this?" Kirk demanded. "I've got to get up there!"

"Jim, this could kill you," Janet said.

"I'll die anyway without it."

"Medical ethics demand—" McCoy began.

"Forget medical ethics! My ship is being destroyed! Give me that shot."

"The Captain is correct," Spock said. "If he does not regain his faculties, and get to the bridge to take command in a very few minutes, we shall all die at the hands of the Romulans. Give him the shot, Dr. Wallace."

She did so. For a moment nothing seemed to happen. Then Kirk found himself in the throes of convulsions, bucking and flailing at random. Dimly he was aware that all four of the others were hanging on to him.

It seemed to last forever, but actually hardly a minute passed before the fit began to subside, to be gradually replaced by a feeling of exhausted well-being. Janet was pointing a Feinberger at him.

"It's working," she said in a hushed voice. "The aging process has stopped."

"Can't see any change," McCoy said.

"She is correct, Doctor," Spock said. "It is there, and accelerating."

"Janet, help me up," Kirk said, taking a deep breath. "That was quite a ride."

"How do you feel?" she said.

"Like I've been kicked through the bulkhead. Spock, you'll have to wait for your shot; I need you on the bridge. Janet, give McCoy his shot, then Scott." He smiled. "Besides, Spock—if what I've got in mind doesn't work, you won't need that shot. Let's go."

In transit, he felt stronger and more acute with every passing second, and judging by the looks of relief with which he was greeted on the bridge, the change was visible to others as well.

"Report, Sulu!"

"We are surrounded by Romulan vessels—maximum of ten. Range, fifty to a hundred thousand kilometers."

Stocker got out of the command chair in a hurry as Kirk approached it. Kirk punched the intercom. "Engineering, feed in all emergency power, and all warp-drive engines on full standby. I'm going to need the works in about two minutes. Captain out . . . Lieutenant Uhura, set up a special channel to Starfleet Command. Code Two."

"But, Captain—"

"I gave you an order, Lieutenant. Code Two."

"Code Two, sir."

"Message: *Enterprise* to Starfleet Command, this sector. Ship has inadvertently encroached upon Romulan neutral zone. Surrounded and under heavy Romulan attack. Escape impossible. Shields failing. Will implement destruct order, using corbomite device recently installed. Since this will result in destruction of *Enterprise* and all matter within two hundred thousand kilometer diameter, and establish corresponding dead zone, all Federation ships to avoid area for at least four solar years. Explosion will occur in one minute. Kirk, commanding *Enterprise*. Out . . . Mr. Sulu. Course 188, mark 14, Warp Eight and stand by."

"Standing by, sir."

From his station, Spock said, "The Romulans are giving ground, sir. I believe they tapped in, as you obviously expected them to."

"A logical assumption, Mr. Spock. Are they still retreating?"

"Yes, sir, but are still well within firing range."

"All hands stand by . . . now, Warp Eight!"

The ship jolted—not this time to an onslaught, but to sudden motion at eight times the speed of light. Spock hovered over his console.

"The Romulans were caught off guard, sir. Not even in motion yet."

"Are we out of range, Mr. Sulu?"

"Yes, sir. And out of the neutral zone."

"Adjust to new course. One nine two degrees, mark 4. Heading for Star Base Ten."

"Coming around, sir."

Kirk sat back. He felt fine. Commodore Stocker approached him, his face full of shame.

"Captain," Stocker said, "I just wanted to assure you that I did what I thought had to be done to save you and the other officers."

"Noted, Commodore. You should know, however, that there is very little a Star Base can do that a starship cannot."

"If I may say so, Captain, I am now quite aware of what a starship can do—with the right man at the helm."

The elevator doors snapped open and McCoy came out. He was as young as ever. Kirk stared at him.

"You're looking good, Bones."

"So's Scotty. The drug worked. He pulled a muscle during the initial reaction, but otherwise he's feeling fine. Now, Mr. Spock, whenever you're ready."

"I'm ready now, Doctor."

"Good. Because of your Vulcan physique, I've prepared an extremely potent shot. I've also removed all the breakables from Sickbay."

"That is very thoughtful of you."

"I knew you'd appreciate it."

Kirk smiled. "All in all, gentlemen, an experience we'll remember in our old age . . . of course, that won't be for a long time yet, will it?"

THE TROUBLE WITH TRIBBLES*

Writer: David Gerrold
Director: Joseph Pevney
Guest stars: William Schallert, William Campbell,
   Stanley Adams

*Hugo Award nominee

Nobody seems to know where tribbles come from, though obviously they are comfortable in oxygen-bearing air at Earthlike temperatures and pressures. Newborn tribbles are about an inch long; the largest one ever seen, about sixteen inches.

A tribble looks a little like a cross between an angora cat and a beanbag. It has no arms or legs, no eyes, and in fact no face—only a mouth. It moves by rolling, by stretching and flexing like an inchworm, or by a peculiar throbbing which moves it along slowly but smoothly, rather like a snail. It does, however, have long fur, which comes in a variety of colors—beige, deep chocolate, gold, white, gold-green, auburn, cinnamon and dusky yellow.

Tribbles are harmless. Absolutely, totally, completely, categorically, inarguably, utterly, one hundred per cent harmless . . .

The *Enterprise* picked up a priority A-1 distress call from deep space station K-7 within a few moments after the big ship hove into sensor range. The station orbits Sherman's Planet, which is about three light years from the nearest Klingon outpost and hence well within the Klingon's sphere of influence—or the outpost was well within the Federation's sphere of influence, depending on how you looked at it.

Both sides had claimed the planet. Although it was mostly barren, its position between the two political bodies was of considerable strategic importance. In the old days, one or the other would have grabbed it, and the other would have tried to jockey him off, at constant risk of war—a pastime the Klingons enjoyed.

These days, however, there was the Organian peace treaty to take into account. Under its terms, Sherman's Planet would belong to whichever side could prove it could develop the planet most effectively.

Under the circumstances, when a priority one distress call came from station K-7, the *Enterprise* could not be blamed for making for the station at Warp Six, with all hands at battle stations.

But when the ship arrived there was no target. K-7 rolled majestically and peacefully around Sherman's Planet, menaced—if that is the word—by nothing within sensor range but a one-man scout ship which floated nearby, obviously in parking orbit.

Baffled and irritated, Captain Kirk called the station's Commander Lurry, who refused any explanation except in person. He did so rather apologetically, but this did not placate Kirk in the least. He beamed over to the station with Spock, his First Officer—with orders to Sulu to keep the *Enterprise* at battle readiness.

There were two other men in Commander Lurry's office when Kirk and Spock arrived. Kirk paid no attention to them.

"Commander Lurry," he said, "you have sent out a priority one distress call. Please state the nature of your emergency."

"Uh, Captain, please allow me to explain. We in fact have no emergency, yet."

"Then you are in trouble," Kirk said grimly. "If there is no emergency, why did you order the call?"

One of the two unknowns said, "*I* ordered it, Captain."

"And who are you?"

"Captain Kirk, this is Nilz Baris," Lurry said. "He's out here from Earth to take charge of the development project for Sherman's Planet."

"And that gives you the authority to put a whole quadrant on defense alert?"

"Mr. Baris," the second unknown said stiffly, "is the

Federation Undersecretary for Agricultural Affairs in this quadrant.''

"A position with no military standing of which I am aware," Kirk said. "And who may *you* be, please?"

"This is my assistant, Arne Darvin," Baris said. "Now, Captain, I want all available security guards to . . .''

"I beg your pardon?" Kirk said. The way this trio had of answering questions for each other was not improving his temper, and thus far he had heard nothing even vaguely resembling an explanation.

"I will try to make myself clear," the Undersecretary said. "I want all available security guards. I want them posted around the warehouse. Surely that's simple enough.''

"It's simple but it's far from clear. What warehouse?''

"The warehouse with the quadrotriticale," Darvin said, recapturing the ball. Lifting an attaché case to Lurry's desk, he extracted from it a small vial. From this he poured into his palm a few small seeds, which he handed to Baris, who in turn handed them to Kirk. The Captain inspected them briefly and then passed them on to Spock.

"Wheat," he said. "What about it?''

"Quadrotriticale is not wheat, Captain," Darvin said, with an audible sniff. "It is a newly developed form of trititicale.''

"That leaves me as much in the dark as before.''

"Trititicale is a high-yield per acre hybrid form of wheat and rye," Spock said quietly. "This appears to be a four-lobed rehybridization—a perennial, also, if I'm not mistaken. The root grain, triticale, traces its ancestry back to twentieth-century Canada.''

"Uh, yes," Baris said, looking a little startled.

"And it is the only Earth grain that will grow on Sherman's Planet," Commander Lurry put in. "We have a warehouse of it here on the station. It's very important that the grain reach Sherman's Planet safely. Mr. Baris thinks that Klingon agents may try to sabotage it.''

"Nothing could be more likely," the Undersecretary said. "That grain is going to be the way the Federation proves its claim to Sherman's Planet. Obviously the Klingons will do anything they can to keep it from getting there. It must be protected. Do you understand? It *must* be protected.''

"So you issued a priority one distress call on behalf of a warehouse full of grain," Kirk said. "The only reason I don't arrest you on the spot is that I want the Federation to have Sherman's Planet as much as you do. Consider yourself lucky; misuse of the priority one channel is a Federation offense."

"I did not misuse . . ."

"Captain Kirk," Lurry interposed hurriedly, "couldn't you at least post a couple of guards? We do get a large number of ships passing through."

This of course was true. After a moment, Kirk said, "Mr. Spock, what do you think?"

"It would be a logical precaution, Captain."

"Very well." Kirk took out his communicator. "Kirk to *Enterprise* . . . Lieutenant Uhura, secure from general quarters. Next, beam over *two* security guards. Have them report to Commander Lurry."

"Yes, Captain."

"Also, authorize shore leave for all off-duty personnel. Kirk out."

"Only two?" Baris said, in something very like a fury. "Kirk, you're going to hear about this. I'm going to contact Starfleet Command."

"Do that," Kirk said, staring at the Undersecretary icily. "But before you put in the call, I suggest that you pin back your ears. It will save Starfleet Command the trouble of doing it for you."

The recreation area of K-7 was small, the shops little more than stalls surrounding a central mall formed by the intersection of a number of curving corridors. Space was at a premium.

As Kirk and Spock entered the area, a number of crew members from the *Enterprise* materialized on the mall, including Uhura and Sulu. Kirk moved toward them.

"I see you didn't waste any time getting over here," he said. "Mr. Sulu, we have a new specimen for your greenhouse. Mr. Spock?" The First Officer handed the grain over. "It's called . . ."

"Quadrotriticale!" the helmsman said eagerly. "I've read about it, but I've never seen any till now!"

"Come on, Sulu," Uhura said. "You can study it back aboard. Let's get in some shopping while we have the chance. Coming, Mr. Spock? Captain?"

"Well, for a few minutes, anyhow. But not for long; I suspect there are some hot messages shooting back and forth in subspace along about now."

The shop into which Uhura led them was vaguely cluttered and did not seem to specialize in anything in particular. Clearly it was one of those broker's establishments where spacemen on leave sold curios they had picked up on far planets, to help pay for their shore leaves—curios later resold to other spacemen for twice the price. This did not look like the best shop Kirk had ever seen, but then, K-7 was not the best located of space stations, either.

There was nobody else in it at the moment but a tall, raffish-looking red-haired civilian, who had an immense quantity of merchandise spread out over the counter, and a carryall sack at his feet.

"No, absolutely not," the storekeeper was saying. "I've got enough Argilian flame gems to last me a lifetime. At the price I have to ask for them, hardly anybody on this junkyard can afford them."

"How sad for you, my friend," the peddler said. His voice was surprisingly melodious. "You won't see finer stones than mine anywhere. Ah well. Now surely you'll be wanting some Sirian glow water . . ."

"I use that," the storekeeper said in a deadly monotone, "to polish the flame gems."

The peddler sighed and swept most of his merchandise off the counter into his sack. Only one object was left—a green-gold ball of fluff.

"Ah, you are a most difficult man to reach. All I have left to offer you is tribbles. Surely, you will want . . ."

"Not at that price."

"Oooh," Uhura said. "What is it? Is it alive? May I hold him? He's adorable."

"What is it?" the peddler said, handing it over. "Why, little darlin', it's a tribble. Only the sweetest little creature known to man—exceptin', of course, yourself."

The object in the lieutenant's hands throbbed gently. Kirk became aware of a low, pervasive sound, like a cross between the thrum of a kitten and the cooing of a dove. "Oh," Uhura said, "it's purring!"

"Ah, little lady, he's just sayin' that he likes you."

"Can I buy him?"

"That," the shopkeeper said, "is what we're trying to decide right now."

"My friend, ten credits apiece is a very reasonable price. You can see for yourself how much the lovely little lady here appreciates fine things. Others will, too."

"One credit," said the storekeeper.

Sulu put his grain on the counter and reached tentatively for the tribble. "He won't bite, will he?" the helmsman said.

"Sir!" the peddler said, making a great show of ignoring the storekeeper's offer. "There is a law against transporting harmful animals from one planet to another, as you as a starship officer must be fully aware. Besides, tribbles have no teeth."

"All right," the shopkeeper said. "Two credits."

The peddler took the tribble from Sulu and plopped it down on the counter again. "Nine," he said.

The shopkeeper eyed the animal dubiously. "Is he clean?"

"He's as clean as you are. I daresay a good deal cleaner."

"If you don't want him, I'll take him," Lt. Uhura said. "I think he's cute."

This set off another round of haggling. The two finally settled on six credits, whereupon the peddler began to produce more tribbles from his sack. Startlingly, no two were the same color or size.

"How much are you selling them for?" Uhura asked the shopkeeper.

"Ten credits. But for you . . ."

"Hey!" Sulu said suddenly. "He's eating my grain!" He swept up what remained. The tribble's purr got louder, and its non-face went slowly round and round, giving an absurd impression of bliss. The shopkeeper picked it up, but the peddler promptly took it from him.

"Sir," the peddler said. "That one happens to be my

sample, which is mine to do with as I please. And I please
to give it to the pretty little lady here.''

"That's right," said the storekeeper. "Ruin the market.''

"My friend," the peddler said, almost singing, "once
the pretty little lady here starts to show this little precious
around, you won't be able to keep up with 'em. Mark my
words.''

Lt. Uhura put the faceless ball of fur to her face, cooing
alarmingly. Kirk did not know whether to be pleased or
scared; Uhura had never shown the faintest sign of sentimen-
tality before, but she seemed to be far gone in gooiness now.
To be sure, the baggy little animals were attractive, but . . .

Queep!

No, that wasn't a tribble; it was his communicator.

"Kirk here.''

"Captain, this is Scott. We have a stiff message in from
Starfleet Command. I think you'd better deal with it; I don't
think I'm authorized.''

"All right, Scotty," Kirk told his communicator.
"Record and hold. I'll be right over.''

"Well and good. But, Captain, that's not all, sir. Our
sensors have just picked up a Klingon battle cruiser. It's closing in rapidly on K-7. I've challenged it and gotten a routine
acknowledgement; but . . .''

"Who's in command?" Spock said. Kirk had almost
forgotten that he was still in the shop; but as usual, he had
asked the crucial question. Kirk passed it on, with a grateful
nod to his First Officer.

"Commander Koloth, sir. You'll remember him from
our last encounter, Captain; a real, fourteen-karat son of
a . . .''

"I get the message, Scotty. Hold on—and post battle
stations. Lieutenant Uhura, pick up your pet; we're back on
duty.''

He had hardly finished speaking before the *Enterprise*'s
transporters shimmered them all out of existence.

The message from Starfleet Command was, as usual,
brief and pointed. It said: "It is not necessary to remind you
of the importance to the Federation of Sherman's Planet. The
key to our winning of this planet is the grain, quadrotriticale.

The shipment of it must be protected. Effective immediately, you will render any aid and assistance which Undersecretary Baris may require. The safety of the grain—and the project— is your responsibility.''

How complicated that was going to be was immediately made clear by the presence of the Klingon ship. It made no move to attack the station; that in fact would have been suicide, since every phaser on board the *Enterprise* was locked on the Klingon vessel (as Koloth, an able captain, would assume as a matter of course). Instead, Koloth stunned everyone by asking for shore leave for his men.

Under the Organian peace treaty, Commander Lurry had no choice but to grant the request. Starfleet, however, had inadvertently given Kirk a card to play, since the phrasing of the message had made the safety of the grain his responsibility. Hence he was able to order that only twelve Klingons be allowed shore leave at a time, and furthermore he beamed over one *Enterprise* security guard for every Klingon. That part of it, he thought, ought to please Baris, at least.

It did not please Baris. He did not want any Klingons on the station, period. He carried on about it quite a lot. In the end, however, it was clear that the Klingons had a right to be there, and nothing could be done about it.

Kirk stopped off at the recreation room for a cup of coffee and a breather. Scott, the engineer, was there reading a technical journal; that was his form of relaxation. Elsewhere, however, a knot of people were gathered around a table, including Spock, Dr. McCoy, Uhura and Ensign Freeman. Joining the group, Kirk found that on the table was Uhura's tribble and at least ten smaller ones; the crewmen were playing with them.

"How long have you had that thing, Lieutenant?" McCoy asked Uhura.

"Only since yesterday. This morning, I found that he— I mean *she* had had babies."

"I'd say you got a bargain." McCoy picked up one of the animals and examined it curiously. "Hmmm . . ."

"Lieutenant Uhura," Kirk said amusedly, "are you running a nursery?"

"I hadn't intended to—but the tribble had other plans."

Spock too was handling one of the creatures, stroking it absent-mindedly.

"You got it at the space station?" McCoy said.

"Yes, from the pilot of that one-man scout ship. Commander Lurry says his name is Cyrano Jones, of all things. He's a system locater, down on his luck."

"Most of them are," Kirk said. "Locating new systems on the margins of Klingon space is a synonym for locating trouble."

"A most curious creature, Captain," Spock said. "Its trilling would seem to have a tranquilizing effect on the human nervous system. Fortunately, I seem to be immune."

Watching his First Officer stroke the animal, Kirk raised an eyebrow, but offered no other comment.

"Lieutenant," McCoy said, "do you mind if I take one of these things down to the lab to find out what makes it tick?"

"It's all right with me, but if you're planning to dissect it, I don't want to know about it."

"Say, Lieutenant," Ensign Freeman said, "if you're giving them away, could I have one too?"

"Sure, why not? They seem to be old enough."

Freeman looked at Kirk. "I don't have any objections to pets on this ship," Kirk said. "Within reason. But if these tribbles want to stay on the *Enterprise*, they'd better be a little less prolific."

The tribbles, however, did not seem to get the message. Visiting sick bay the next day—another prolonged shouting match with Baris had given him a headache—Kirk found that McCoy had what seemed to be a boxful of the creatures.

"I thought Uhura gave you only one of those things, Bones. It looks more like you've got ten here."

"Average litter. I had eleven, but I dissected one. The nearest thing I can figure out is that they're born pregnant."

"Is that possible?"

"No, but it would be a great timesaver, wouldn't it? I can tell you this much: almost fifty per cent of the creature's metabolism is geared to reproduction. Do you know what you get if you feed a tribble too much?"

Kirk's mind was not really on the subject. "A very fat tribble?"

"No. You get a whole bunch of hungry little tribbles. And if you think *that's* a boxful, you should see Uhura's. She's got about fifty, and she gave away five."

"Well, you'd better find homes for this batch before you've got fifty, too." Kirk swallowed the headache pill. "Are you going on shore leave, Bones?"

"Already been. Besides, this problem is more interesting. I understand Scotty went over with the last detachment; he'll see to it that there's no trouble. Unless, of course, the Klingons start it."

"I can't see why they'd want to do that. Koloth knows that if there is any, I'd promptly double the number of guards. If he's really after the grain, that's the last thing he'd want."

Nevertheless, after his next interview with Lurry, Kirk troubled to make a detour through the space station's bar. There were six Earthmen there, Scotty and Navigator Chekov among them. Five or six Klingons were at another table, but the two groups were studiously ignoring each other.

As Kirk joined his own men, Cyrano Jones entered the bar and also moved toward them. "Ah, friends," he said, "can I interest you in a tribble?"

He was holding one at Scott's shoulder. Scott turned toward him and found himself looking straight into the tribble's absence of a face. He shuddered.

"I've been pullin' the little beasties out of my engine room all morning!"

"Perhaps one of you other gentlemen—?" There was no response. With a fatalistic shrug, Cyrano went over to the Klingon table, approaching one whom Kirk recognized as Korax, one of Koloth's officers.

"Friend Klingon, may I offer you a charmin' little tribble . . ."

The tribble had other ideas. All its fur stood on end. It hitched itself up Cyrano's forearm with an angry spitting hiss.

"Stop that!" Cyrano said. "Apologies for his bad manners, sir. He's never done that before."

"I suggest," Korax said coldly, "that you remove yourself and that parasite as speedily as possible."

"It's only a friendly little . . ."

"Take it away!"

There was another hiss from the tribble. Korax slapped Cyrano's arm away, sending the tribble flying across the room to land among the Earthmen. Cyrano rushed to retrieve it; Scotty handed it to him without a word.

After looking from one group to the other, Cyrano, somewhat disconsolately, retreated to the bar, where the counterman was taking down a pitcher from a high shelf, and put his beast down on the counter.

"Sir! I feel sure that you would be willin' to engage in a little barter—one of my little tribbles in exchange for a spot of . . ."

The attendant turned, and upended the pitcher. Three tribbles fell out of it.

It was worse on shipboard. The corridors seemed to be crawling with the creatures. On the bridge, Kirk had to scoop three or four of them out of his chair before he could sit down. They were all over the consoles, on shelves, everywhere.

"Lieutenant, how did all of these tribbles get onto the bridge?"

"Through the ventilator ducts, I expect, Captain. They seem to be all over the ship."

"They certainly do. Mr. Spock, have a maintenance crew come up here to clean out this bridge. How many of them are there now, anyhow?"

"Assuming one creature—the one Lieutenant Uhura brought aboard—with an average litter of ten," the First Officer said, "every twelve hours. The third generation will total one thousand, three hundred thirty-one. The fourth generation will total fourteen thousand, six hundred and forty-one. The fifth generation will . . ."

"That's already enough. I want a thorough cleanup. They've got to go."

"All of them?" Lt. Uhura said protestingly. "Oh, Captain . . ."

"Every last one."

"A logical decision," Spock said. "Their breeding rate is beyond our control. They are consuming our supplies and returning nothing."

"Oh, come on now, Mr. Spock. I don't agree with you

at all. They're giving us their love. Cyrano Jones says that a tribble is the only love money can buy.''

"Lieutenant," Kirk said, "too much of anything—even love—is not necessarily a good thing. And in view of the fact that this all started with just one tribble, clearly the only safe number is none.''

"And since feeding them is what makes them breed," Spock added, "one need only imagine what would happen if they got into the food processing machinery, or the food storage areas.''

Kirk stared at the First Officer, thunderstruck. "Storage areas!" he said. "Great thundering fireballs! *Storage areas!* Lieutenant Uhura, contact Commander Lurry, and Nilz Baris. Have them meet us at the station mall. Mr. Spock, we're beaming over. Lieutenant, have Doctor McCoy join us in the transporter room—on the double!''

When the three materialized on the mall, half a dozen tribbles materialized with them. The mall did not need any more, however; it was inundated. The store where they had seen their very first tribble looked like a snowbank of fur. The storekeeper, who had evidently just given up an attempt to sweep them out, was sitting in the midst of them with his head in his hands, close to tears.

Lurry and Baris came running to meet them—for once, without Darvin. "What's the matter?" Baris panted.

"Plenty—if what I think has happened, has happened. The warehouse, quick!''

Baris needed no further urging. They left at a dead run, kicking tribbles out of the way.

There were two guards before the warehouse door. "Is that door secure?" Kirk demanded.

"Yes, sir. Nothing could get in.''

"Open it.''

The guard produced a magnetic key. Nothing happened. "Don't understand it, sir. It seems to be . . .''

What it seemed to be will never be known, for at that moment the door slid open. There was a sort of silent explosion. Hundreds and hundreds and hundreds of tribbles came tumbling out, cascading down around them all, wriggling and seething and mewling and writhing and throbbing and trilling and purring . . .

They stood aghast as the mountain of fur grew. Spock recovered first. Scooping up a tribble, he examined it with clinical detachment. "It seems to be gorged," he observed.

"Gorged!" Baris gasped. "On my grain! Kirk! I'll hold you responsible! There must be thousands—hundreds of thousands!"

"One million, five hundred and sixty-one thousand, seven hundred and seventy-three," Spock said, "assuming, of course, that they got in here three days ago, and allowing for the maximum rate of grain consumption *and* the volume of the warehouse."

"What does the exact number matter?" Baris said despairingly. "The Klingons will get Sherman's Planet now!"

"I'm afraid," Kirk said slowly, "that you're right about that."

McCoy had been kneeling among the tribbles, examining them closely. At this point he looked up.

"Jim?"

"What is it, Bones?"

"Mr. Spock is wrong about these animals. They're not lethargic because they're gorged. They're dying."

"Dying! Are you sure?"

"I venture to say," McCoy replied with dignity, "that nobody on this station knows their metabolism better than I do. Yes, I am sure."

"All right," Kirk said with sudden energy. "Bones, take some of them back to your lab, and some of the grain, too. If they're dying, I want to know why. Then report back to me. I'm opening a formal hearing and investigation. Commander Lurry, I presume we can use your office. I'll want your assistant, and Captain Koloth—and Cyrano Jones, too."

"What good will that do?" Baris said. "The project is ruined—ruined!"

"Regulations require it," Kirk said. "And as for the project—well, that remains to be seen."

The scene in Lurry's office strongly resembled that moment in the classical detective novel when all the suspects are lined up and the shrewd sleuth eliminates all the obvious suspects and puts his finger on the butler. Lurry was seated behind his desk; nearby, in the visitor's chair, sat Cyrano Jones, stroking a tribble in his lap. Standing, with various degrees of uneasiness, interest or defiance, were Koloth, Korax, another Klingon aide, Spock, Baris, and McCoy, with Kirk facing them. And there were, of course, several security guards standing by. The Klingon captain spoke first:

"I had heard that you Earthers were sentimental about these parasites," he said, "but this is carrying things too far. I want an official apology from you, Kirk, addressed to the High Command of the Klingon Empire. You have restricted the shore leave of my men, harassed them with uniformed snoopers, and now summon us here like common criminals. If you wish to avoid a diplomatic crisis . . ."

"Don't do it, Kirk!" Baris burst in. "That'll give them the final wedge they need to claim Sherman's Planet!"

"Oh, as to *that* matter," Koloth said silkily, "it would seem that the outcome is already settled."

"One thing at a time," Kirk said. "Our present job is to find out who is responsible for the tribbles getting into the quadrotriticale. The Klingons have an obvious motive. On the other hand, it was Cyrano Jones who brought them here, apparently with purely commercial intent. There's no obvious connection."

"Beggin' your pardon, Captain," Cyrano said, "but a certain amount of the blame might be lyin' in sheer ignorance of the little creatures. If you keep their diet down below a certain intake per day, why sure and they don't breed at all. That's how I control mine."

Kirk stared at him. "Why didn't you tell us that before?"

"Nobody asked me. Besides, Captain, any man's common sense should tell him that it's bad for little animals to be overfeedin' 'em."

"Let that pass for the moment. We also need to find out what killed the tribbles. Was the grain poisoned—and if so, who poisoned it?"

He looked fixedly at Koloth, but the Klingon only smiled. "I had no access to it, obviously," he said. "Your guards were watching me every instant. However, Captain, before we go on—would you mind very much having that thing taken out of here?''

He pointed at the tribble in Cyrano's lap. Kirk hesitated a moment, but he could in fact sympathize; he had himself seen enough tribbles to last him a lifetime. He gestured to a guard, who lifted the creature gingerly and moved toward the door.

At the same moment, the door opened and Darvin entered belatedly. The tribble fluffed itself up and spat.

Kirk stared at it a moment in disbelief. Then, taking it from the crewman, he crossed over to Korax and held it out; it spat again. It spat at the third Klingon, too, and at Koloth. However it purred for everyone else, even including Baris— oh well, Kirk thought, there's no accounting for some people's tastes—and it went into a positive ecstasy over Spock, to the First Officer's rigidly controlled distaste. The back to Darvin. *Hisssss!*

"Bones!" Kirk barked. "Check this man!"

McCoy was already at Darvin's side, tricorder out. He ran it over the man twice.

"It figures, Jim," he said. "Heartbeat all wrong, body temperature—well, never mind the details. He's a Klingon, all right.''

The security men closed on Darvin. "Well, well," Kirk said. "What do you think Starfleet Command will have to say about this, Mr. Baris? Bones, what did you find out about the grain?''

"Oh. It wasn't poisoned. It was infected.''

"Infected," Baris repeated in a dull voice. He seemed past reacting to any further shock.

"Yes. It had been sprayed with a virus which practices metabolic mimicry. You see, the molecules of the nutriments the body takes in fit into the molecules of the body itself like a key into a lock. This virus mimics the key—but it isn't a nutriment itself. It blocks the lock so the proper nutriments can't get in. A highly oversimplified explanation, but good enough for the purpose.''

"Do I mean you to imply," Kirk said, "that the tribbles starved to death? A whole warehouse full of grain, and they starved in the midst of it?''

"That's essentially it," McCoy agreed.

"And would this have happened to any *men* who ate the grain?"

"It would happen to any warm-blooded creature. The virus is very catholic in its tastes—like rabies."

"I observe another possible consequence," Spock said. "Dr. McCoy, could the virus be killed without harming the grain?"

"I think so."

"In that case," Spock said, "Mr. Darvin's attempt at mass murder has done us all a favor, and so have Mr. Jones' tribbles."

"I don't follow you, Mr. Spock," Kirk said.

"A simple logical chain, Captain. The virus without doubt prevented the tribbles from completely gutting the warehouse; fully half the grain must be left. On the other hand, the tribbles enabled us to find that the grain was infected without the loss of a single human life."

"I don't think the Federation courts will count that much in Mr. Darvin's favor, Mr. Spock, but it's a gain for us, I agree. Guards, take him out. Now, Captain Koloth, about that apology—you have six hours to get your ship out of Federation territory."

Koloth left, stiffly and silently. The tribble hissed after him.

"I hate to say this," Kirk said, "but you almost have to love tribbles just for the enemies they make. Now, Mr. Jones. Do you know what the penalty is for transporting an animal that is proven dangerous to human life? It is twenty years."

"Ah, now, Captain Kirk," Cyrano said, almost in tears. "Surely we can come to some form of mutual understanding? After all, as Mr. Spock points out, my little tribbles did tip you off to the infection in the grain—and they proved a most useful Geiger counter for detecting the Klingon agent."

"Granted," Kirk said gravely. "So if there's one task you'll undertake, I won't press charges, and when you're through with it, Commander Lurry will return your scout ship to you. If you'll remove every tribble from this space station . . ."

Cyrano gasped. "Remove every tribble? Captain, that'll take years!"

"Seventeen point nine years," Spock said, "to be exact."

"Think of it as job security," Kirk suggested.

"It's either this—or charges? Ah, Captain, you're a hard man—but I'll do it."

There was not a single tribble about the *Enterprise* when the party returned. It proved rather difficult to find out how this miracle had been brought about, but Scotty finally admitted to it.

"But how did you do it?"

"Oh, I just had the cleanup detail pile them all into the transporter."

"But—Scotty, you didn't just transport them out into space, did you?"

The engineer looked offended. "Sir, I'm a kindhearted man. I gave them a good home, sir."

"Where? Spit it out, man!"

"I gave them to the Klingons, sir. Just before they went into warp, I transported the whole kit and kaboodle into their engine room. And I trust, sir, that all their tribbles will be big ones."

BREAD AND CIRCUSES

Writer: Gene Roddenberry and Gene L. Coon
Director: Ralph Senensky
Guest stars: William Smithers, Logan Ramsey

≡

There was no doubt about it. The space debris spotted by the *Enterprise* scanners was all that was left of the *Beagle*, an S.S. survey vessel posted as missing for six years. A mixture of personal belongings and portions of instrumentation, the floating junk contained no evidence of human bodies. The conclusion was plain to Kirk. The *Beagle*'s crew had managed to beam down to a planet before catastrophe had destroyed their ship.

"Mr. Chekov," he said, "compute present drift of the wreckage."

"Computed and on the board, sir."

Kirk glanced at the figures. Then he rose and went to his Science officer. "Mr. Spock, assuming that stuff has been drifting at the same speed and direction for six years . . . ?"

Spock completed a reading on his library computer. "It would have come from planet four in Star System eight nine two, directly ahead, Captain."

Chekov called. "Only one-sixteenth parsec away, sir. We could be there in seconds!"

Kirk nodded to him. "Standard orbit around the planet. There may be survivors there, Mr. Chekov."

Spock had more information on the lost *Beagle*. "She was a small Class Four stardrive vessel, crew of forty-seven, commanded by—" He withdrew his head from his hooded viewer. "I believe you know him, sir. Captain R. M. Merrick."

"Yes, at the Academy." It had been a long time ago;

and it wasn't too pleasant a memory at that. Merrick had been dropped in his fifth year. Rumor had it he'd gone into the merchant service. True or false, he'd known him. If, by some chance, Merrick was down there, abandoned on that star . . .

Kirk turned to the bridge screen. They were coming up on the planet. The pinpoint of light it had been was enlarging, growing rounder, transforming itself into a bluish ball, not unlike Earth. But the oceans and land masses were different.

He said so and Spock shook his head. "In shape only, Captain. The proportion of land to water is exactly as on your home planet. Density 5.5 . . . diameter 7917 at the equator . . . atmosphere 78% nitrogen, 21% oxygen. Again, exactly like Earth." He looked up, gesturing to his viewer-computer. "And I picked up indications of large cities."

"Development?" Kirk said.

"No signs of atomic energy yet. But far enough along for radio communications, power transportation, an excellent road system."

Uhura slewed around from her station. "Captain! I think I can pick up something visual! A 'news broadcast' using a system I believe was once called 'video'."

" 'Television' was the colloquial word," Spock observed.

"Put it on the screen, Lieutenant," Kirk said.

For a moment the bridge viewer held only the picture of the planet at orbital distance. Then, as Uhura made a new adjustment, the picture dissolved into the image of a city street—one that, apart from some subtle differences, could have been a city street of Earth's 1960's. Clearly a newscast, the scene showed onlookers in clothes of the period watching police herd up a small group of people in loin cloths.

An announcer's voice, filtered, spoke from the screen.

". . . and in the Forum District today, police rounded up still another collection of dissidents. Authorities are as yet unable to explain these fresh outbreaks of treasonable disobediences by well-treated, well-protected slaves . . ."

A shocked, amazed silence fell over the *Enterprise* bridge. But the bland announcer-voice went on. "And now, turning to the world of sports, we bring you taped reports of the arena games last night . . .''

Two men appeared on the Starship's screen. They were naked except for leather aprons. Helmeted, carrying oblong shields, they were armed with ancient Roman swords. They advanced toward each other. One attacked—and the announcer's voice said, ''The first heat involved amateurs, a pair of petty thieves from city prison. Conducted, however, with traditional weapons, it provided some amusement for a few moments . . .''

The attacker saw his chance. He lunged, driving his sword into the heart of his opponent. To a background of noisy cheers, he stepped back from the bloody body, raising his sword in salute to the arena's galleries. Over the cheers, the announcer said, ''The winner will meet another contestant in tonight's games. In the second heat we'll have a more professional display in the spirit of our splendid past, when gladiator Claudius Marcus killed the last of the barbarians, William B. Harrison, in an excellent example of . . .''

Static crashed. The picture faded to be replaced by the planet view.

An appalled Uhura, collecting herself, said, ''Transmission lost, Captain. Shall I try to get it back?''

Kirk didn't answer. Instead, both puzzled and astounded, he turned to Spock. ''Slaves and gladiators? Some kind of Twentieth-century Rome?''

Spock's face was unusually grave as he lifted it from his computer. ''Captain, the man described as the 'barbarian' is also listed here—Flight Officer William B. Harrison of the S.S. *Beagle*. At least there *were* survivors down there.''

A landing party. There was no alternative. Kirk wheeled. ''Ready the Transporter Room, Mr. Sulu.''

They arrived at the base of a shallow canyon. Glancing up at the rocky overhang, Kirk said, ''You could have selected a more attractive place, Mr. Spock.''

His first officer was already taking tricorder readings. ''Practical, however, Captain. Unpopulated but close to that city we saw. We should not be observed.'' He looked up from his instrument. ''Fascinating how similar is this atmosphere to your Twentieth century's! Moderately industrialized pollution containing substantial amounts of carbon monoxide and partially consumed hydrocarbons.''

McCoy said, "The word was 'smog.' "

"I believe that *was* the term, Doctor. I had no idea you were such a historian."

"I'm not. I just wanted to stop you before we got the whole lecture. Jim, do we know anything at all about this planet?"

Kirk shook his head. "The *Beagle* was doing the first survey on this star sector when it disappeared."

"Then the 'prime directive' is in full effect, Captain."

"Yes, Mr. Spock. 'No identification of self or mission: no interference with social development of said planet.' "

McCoy nodded ruefully. "No references to space, to other worlds or more advanced civilizations." He grinned. "Once, just once, I'd like to land someplace and say, 'Behold, I am the Archangel Gabriel' . . ."

Spock cocked a brow at Kirk's chuckle. "I fail to see any humor in such a masquerade."

McCoy eyed him. "I guess because you could hardly claim to be an angel. But with those ears, Spock, if you landed somewhere carrying a *pitchfork* . . ."

A rifle cracked. Its bullet kicked up the dust at Kirk's feet—and a male voice said, "Don't move! Hands in the air!"

"Complete Earth parallel," Spock remarked. "The language here is English . . ."

The second shot struck close to his feet.

"I said don't move!" the voice shouted.

"I think he means it, Mr. Spock," Kirk said.

Spock looked down at the bullet mark. "That would seem to be evident, sir."

They raised their hands. Above their heads, gravel scuffed to the sound of approaching feet. A big, burly man leaped down from the overhang. Three other men followed him. All wore ragged "slave" loincloths and the alert look of fugitives. Though their rifles were conventionally old-fashioned, they used them skillfully to cover the *Enterprise* trio. Their uniforms seemed to anger the big man. He glared at them with hostility and suspicion.

"Who are you?" he said.

Kirk spoke. "We come from another—'province.' "

The man was staring at Spock's ears. "Where are *you* from? Are those ears?"

"I call them ears," Spock told him mildly.

"Are you trying to be funny?"

"Never," Spock assured him. He spoke to Kirk. "Colloquial Twentieth-century English. Truly an *amazing* parallel."

Their captor was clearly baffled. Kirk undertook to enlighten him. "We come from a place quite a distance from here. I doubt if you've ever heard—"

He was interrupted. Pointing to their clothing, the big leader turned to his men. "Uniforms. Probably some new Praetorian Guard unit." His eyes went back to Kirk. "I should kill you here and now . . . but Septimus would probably be displeased. You can take your hands down. Our rifles are at your backs. Move on!" He gestured ahead of them.

They obeyed. After about twenty minutes of hard slugging over the rocky terrain, a man in a tattered loincloth stepped from behind a boulder, rifle at the ready.

"Praetorian spies," the big man told him. "I'm taking them to Septimus."

They were prodded through an entrance of a cave. In its dimness they saw that it held a number of people, the men loinclothed, the women in coarse tunics. At sight of the strangers, they all gathered around an elderly man. Under his gray hair, his features were distinguished and benign.

"I didn't harm them, Septimus," the big man said. "Much as I wanted to."

He received a quiet nod of approval. "Keep always in your mind, Flavius, that our way is peace."

McCoy spoke. "For which we are grateful. We are men of peace ourselves."

"Ah? Are you also children of the sun?"

McCoy hesitated. "If you mean a worship of some sort, we represent many beliefs . . ."

"There is only one true belief!" Flavius shouted. "They are Roman butchers sent by the First Citizen!"

Kirk addressed him directly. "Are we like any Roman you ever saw?"

"Then are you slaves like ourselves?" Septimus asked.

"No. Our people do not believe in slavery."

Flavius cried, "A Roman lie! We must kill them, Septimus!"

Spock stepped forward. "Sir, we have come here looking for some friends. Forty-seven of them who . . ." he paused, the "prime directive" in mind . . . "were 'stranded' here six years ago. They wore clothing similar to ours. Have you heard of such men?"

Nobody had. Flavius, still suspicious, said, "Septimus, I know killing is evil but sometimes it's necessary!"

"No."

"They've located our hiding-place! It's better that a few of them die than all of us!"

One of Flavius' men spoke up. "He's right, Septimus. I don't care for myself, but I've brought my wife here, too, my children . . ."

"If they don't die, Septimus, it's the same as if you killed us all yourself!"

Flavius rallied more shouts of agreement. Kirk could see that Septimus was wavering. Rifles were lifting. "Wait," he said. "I can prove we're telling the truth! A small device, Flavius. I'll bring it out slowly . . ."

Fingers were on triggers as he carefully reached for his communicator. He held it out so that it could be openly seen. Then, very slowly, he opened it and placed it to his lips. "Kirk to *Enterprise*. Come in . . ."

Scott's filtered voice was audible in the cave's sudden silence. "Scott here, Captain."

"Lock in on my transmission. Scan us."

"Scanning, sir."

"Including ourselves, how many people in this cave?"

"Twelve, Captain."

Flavius and Septimus looked quickly around, counting. There were indeed twelve people in the cave. Astonished, they looked at Kirk. He smiled at them.

"Maintain scanning, Scotty: we'll continue checking in. Kirk out." He closed the communicator, turning to Septimus. "The *Enterprise* is our vessel . . . sailing out at sea. The voice belongs to one of my crew. That's all I can tell you. If it's not sufficient, then I suppose you'll have to kill us."

Rifles were lowering. Septimus, impressed, spoke to Flavius. "Tell me the Empire has an instrument like that—and you can kill them. Otherwise, accept them as friends."

The tension subsided. A woman came forward, offering a pannikin of milk to Kirk. He smiled at her, drank it and seized his first chance to take in the cave. The beds of the truant slaves were rough-hewn rock ledges. What furniture their retreat contained was equally primitive, battered pots and pans—the crude necessities of their harsh existence. Yet the *Enterprise* men were beginning to feel at ease in the cave. Perhaps it was due to the abruptly warm friendliness of the people's effort to make amends for their original reception of the guests.

It was difficult to credit the way they lived to their era. Telecasts—and that rough log table with its torn magazines and newspapers. Was this star a strange example of Hodgkins Law of parallel planet development? A world much like his own back in the Twentieth century—that was undeniable. But on this odd "Earth," Rome never fell. It survived; and was apparently ruled by emperors who could trace their line back to the Caesars of two thousand years ago.

The fate of the *Beagle* crew uppermost in his mind, Kirk approached Septimus again. But the old man shook his head. "No, Captain. I'm sure I would have heard of the arrival of other men like you."

Kirk persisted. "Have you heard . . . let's say, an impossible story about men coming from the sky? Or from other worlds?"

Septimus smiled. "There are no other worlds."

"The stars . . ."

"Lights shining through from heaven. It is where the sun is. Blessed be the sun."

"Yes, of course. Excuse me . . ."

Spock, holding a magazine, had beckoned. It was titled *The Gallian;* and its cover was the photograph of a gladiator, fully armed with sword, shield, breastplate and helmet. The caption under the picture read, THE NEW HEAVYWEIGHT CHAMPION.

Kirk, leafing through it, came on a colored drawing of a sleek automobile. The ad copy told him its name and purpose. It said: THE JUPITER EIGHT FOR ROYAL COMFORT.

"Fascinating," Spock said.

"The Jupiter Eight. Conventional combustion engine

. . . you were right about that smog, Spock. But Jupiter cars? And here's Mars Toothpaste . . . Neptune Bath Salts . . .''

"Taken from the names of false gods," Septimus said. "When I was a Senator, I worshiped them, too . . . but I heard the words of the Sun. I became a brother. For that they made me a slave."

"Septimus . . . will you help us?" Kirk said. "We must go into the city. We know that one of our missing friends was seen there recently . . ."

"My advice to you is to leave this place . . . to go back where you came from."

"We can't do that. Perhaps you have heard this name. 'Merrick' or 'Captain Merrick'?"

Septimus backed away, his face changing. Kirk was suddenly aware of Falvius' watchful eyes.

"Merikus?" Septimus said.

"Merrick. The leader of our friends . . ."

"Merikus is First Citizen!" Flavius cried. "Butcher!"

"It could not be the same man," Kirk told him. "Captain Merrick is no butcher."

Spock interposed. "A logical question if I may, Captain." He addressed Septimus. "How many years ago did this Merikus become First Citizen?"

"Perhaps five years . . ."

"Almost six!" Flavius was openly hostile now. "I was there when he became Lord of the Games! If he is your friend, you are no friends of ours!"

Kirk thought fast. "Septimus, it is one of our most important laws that none of us may interfere in the affairs of others. If Merrick is Merikus, he is in violation of that law! He will be taken away and punished. Help us find out the truth of this!"

"I must discuss it with the others," Septimus said. Beckoning to Flavius, he moved away to his people, leaving the *Enterprise* men alone.

Spock said, "Curious, Captain. The similarity of the names. Were you told why Merrick was dropped from the Space Academy?"

"He failed a psycho-simulator test. All it takes is a split second of indecision." He shook his head. "Hardly the kind who becomes a strongman butcher."

"Odd that these people worship the sun," McCoy said.

"Why, Doctor?"

"Because, my dear Spock, it's *illogical*. Rome had no sun worshipers. Why would they parallel Rome in every way but that?"

"Hold it," Kirk said. He had seen Septimus and Flavius returning.

"We have decided," the old man announced. "Flavius will guide you. We will provide you with suitable clothing. But I caution you—take great care. The police are everywhere. May the blessings of the sun be upon you."

A woman shyly approached Spock, a worn scarf in her hand. He understood. Stooping, he waited until she had bound it around his ears.

The outskirts of the city made good ambush country, rough, wooded, brushy. At a thick copse of low-branched trees, Flavius signaled for a halt. "We wait here until dark," he said. "The police seek everywhere."

"Were you a slave, too, Flavius?" Kirk asked.

The big man straightened proudly. "You are barbarians, indeed, not to know of Flavius Maximus. For seven years, I was the most successful gladiator in the province."

"Then you heard the word of the sun?"

"Yes. The words of peace and freedom. It was not easy for me to believe. I was trained to fight. But the words were true."

"There are many other things I would—" Kirk broke off as the ex-gladiator held up his hand, alarm leaping into his face. "Quickly . . ."

"Hold! Don't move! Hands in the air!"

There was a warning rattle of machine-gun fire. Bullets tore leaves from the trees. A half-dozen policemen broke from cover, all armed with oddly-shaped submachine guns. Yet, topping their uniforms were Roman helmets, and at the waist of each hung a short Roman sword. Their leader stepped in close, his hard face cold. "Four fleeing fish! A fine haul—" He stopped. Staring at Flavius, he shouted, "By all the gods, Flavius Maximus!"

With a muffled oath, Flavius lunged at him. One of the others struck him down with the butt of his gun. The *Enter-*

prise men, directly under the guns, were unable to move. The hard-jawed leader grinned as he looked down at Flavius. "You have been too long absent from the games," he said. "The First Citizen will be pleased."

He nodded his head toward the Starship three. His men shook them down, removing their phasers, communicators, Spock's tricorder and McCoy's medikit.

"What are these things?" he demanded.

Kirk shook his head slightly, signaling silence. The policeman took another curious look at the equipment. Then, shaking his head, he said, "No matter. Escaped slaves are welcome, whatever the circumstances." Spock's head scarf caught his eye. He ripped it off. For a moment, he stared at the Vulcan ears in wonder. He shrugged the wonder off.

"Not escaped slaves," he said. "Barbarians. A good day's work. It's a long time since I watched barbarians die in the arena."

Apparently, the arena's vestibule was a jail's cell. Shoved into one, Kirk's first act was to shake its bars. The policeman outside struck his hands away from them, cutting his knuckles. But Kirk had succeeded in attracting special attention. "Tell Merikus we want to see him," he told the man.

"The First Citizen? Why would he bother with arena bait like you?"

"Tell him it's James Kirk. Perhaps a friend of his."

The man laughed. " 'Perhaps' is right."

"Suppose I *am* a friend and you didn't tell him? Do you really care to risk that?"

He received a glare, a grunt—and the policeman walked off to join his men.

Time ambled by. Kirk watched McCoy doing what was possible for Flavius' head gash. When the wound had stopped bleeding, he said, "Tell me, Flavius. If there have been slaves for over two thousand years, haven't there always been discontents, runaways?"

Flavius sat up. "Long ago there were rebellions. But they were suppressed. And with each century the slaves acquired more rights under the law. They received the right to medicine, to government payments in their old age." He shrugged. "They finally learned to be content."

Spock looked up from a stone bench. "Yet more fascinating. Slavery evolving into guaranteed medical care, old age pensions . . ."

"Quite logical, I'd say, Mr. Spock," McCoy said. "Just as it's logical that a Twentieth-century Rome would use television to show its gladiator contests, or name a new car the Jupiter Eight or—"

Spock interrupted. "Were I able to show emotion, Doctor, your new infatuation with the term 'logical' would begin to annoy me."

"Medical men are trained in logic, Mr. Spock!"

"Your pardon, Doctor. I had no idea they were trained. From watching you I assumed it was trial and error."

Flavius eyed them. "Are they enemies, Captain?"

Kirk smiled. "I'm not sure they're sure." He returned to the absorbing subject of this extraordinary half-Rome place. "But, Flavius, when the slaves began to worship the sun, they became discontented again. When did all this begin?"

"Long ago. Perhaps as long ago as the beginning of the Empire. But the message of the sun was kept from us."

"That all men are brothers?"

Flavius nodded. "Perhaps I'm a fool to believe it. It does often seem that a man must fight to live."

"No," Kirk said. "You go on believing it, Flavius. All men *are* brothers."

Footsteps sounded outside the cell. The wolfish policeman, his men behind him, unlocked the barred door. "Flavius Maximus! Your old friends are waiting for you. You are already matched for the morning games. Come!"

Flavius spoke quietly. "I will not fight. I am a brother of the sun."

A cynical grin lifted the man's lips from his teeth. "Put a sword in your hand—and you'll fight. I know you, Flavius. You're as peaceful as a bull."

His men had their submachine guns. Two of them, flanking Flavius, marched him out of the cell. The police chief, with his two remaining guards, gestured to the others. "You three . . . come with us!"

Kirk, lowering his voice for Spock and McCoy, said, "Three and three. We may never have a better—"

"No talking!" the police chief barked. "Outside now!"

Kirk pointed to McCoy. "I doubt he can walk far. He feels ill."

"I do?" said McCoy.

"He'll die of something if he doesn't step out of this cell right now!"

Kirk's purpose had suddenly dawned on McCoy. He went along with it. "No, I think I can walk. I'll try, anyway . . ."

The three, exchanging glances, silently agreed it was to be now or never.

The guards closed in around them. Halfway down the outside corridor, McCoy moaned, *"Uhhh . . . my stomach . . ."* He doubled up, his knees buckling to heart-rending groans of pain. A guard grabbed him to pull him back upright; and Spock, with a show of assisting the man, managed to get a hand on his shoulder. The guard crumpled under the Vulcan neck pinch. At the same instant Kirk's clenched fist lashed out. It caught the police chief on the button. He spun around and fell. Coming up fast from his crouch, McCoy downed the third man. Two of the guards tried to struggle up. For their pains they got a couple of space karate chops and subsided into unconsciousness.

A voice said, "Well done, Jim."

The *Enterprise* men wheeled.

The door at the corridor's end had opened. Kirk recognized the man standing inside it. It was Merrick. The ex-captain of the S.S. *Beagle* had always been handsome; and passing time had added strength to what had been merely a goodlooking Space Academy cadet. He wore a richly tailored sports jacket and slacks of a princely elegance. Yet, despite the strength and the clothes, Kirk thought he detected a look of haunting tragedy in his eyes. Beside him was a smaller, plump man, softish, also fashionably tailored. They hadn't come alone. Behind them were ranged policemen, all armed with submachine guns.

Merrick said, "But it isn't that easy, Jim. They've been handling slaves for two thousand years."

The smaller man beside him turned. "But it was exciting, Merik. They'd do well in the arena."

Kirk hadn't recovered from the shock of recognition. "Bob Merrick! It is you . . ."

"Me, Merik." He indicated the massed guards behind him. "And them. Not to mention them . . ." He pointed to the opposite end of the corridor. It was crowded with more armed guards.

The smaller man spoke again. "But this is no place for a reunion."

The hand Kirk had known as Bob Merrick's waved them to follow. "This way, Jim . . . your friends, too. Lots to talk about, lots to explain, to—"

Kirk eyed him. "Yes," he said quickly. "I agree."

Merik made an impatient gesture. "Don't judge me without the facts. Come along. We'll be able to talk freely. The Proconsul here knows who and what we are."

They left. And the guards moved in to make sure that the *Enterprise* three followed them.

It was a lush apartment into which the trio was marched. Marble columns supported a ceiling of mosaic that depicted nymphs disporting with satyrs. A fountain of colored water flung its spray up and back into a seashell of marble. Tufted couches of gleaming stuff were arranged about the room, low tables beside them. All four of the chamber's walls bore painted murals of old Roman gods at their pleasures. Young women—slaves chosen and bought for their loveliness—were moving to the tables with gold platters of fruit and sweetmeats.

The plump Proconsul, wine goblet in hand, greeted them. Merik, an easy host in his sleek sports jacket, waved the guards out of the room.

Smiling at Kirk, he said, "This is a personal affair, isn't it, Jim? A celebration. Old friends meeting."

The Proconsul spoke to the slaves. "Wine for our friends. They have come from a great distance, eh, Captain Kirk?" He grinned broadly. "A very great distance. I am Claudius Marcus, Proconsul." He approached Spock. "So this is a Vulcan. Interesting. From what I've heard, I wish I had fifty of you for the arena."

Merik said hastily, "And this other is your ship's surgeon?"

"Dr. McCoy," Kirk said tersely.

Merik spoke to Claudius. "A pity we can't turn him loose in your hospitals. The level of medicine here might benefit."

One of the girls was proffering a tray to Claudius. "You must be hungry," he told Kirk. "Do try the sparrows broiled with garum. Delicious. Or the roast kid." He jerked a thumb toward the girl. "Drusilla. A lovely thing, isn't she? Noticeable."

So he'd been caught staring at her. She was indeed noticeable. Blond hair, dark eyes—and in the violet, peplum-like gown she wore, every movement of her slender body was grace itself. Flushing, Kirk turned to Merik. "What happened to your ship?" he said.

"Meteor damage. I—" A slave was passing and he paused before he said, "I 'came ashore' with a landing party for iridium ore and repairs. Then I met Claudius . . ."

"Go on," Kirk said.

"He convinced me it was unfair to this world to carry word of its existence elsewhere."

"Contamination," Claudius said. "We can't risk that. You'll understand as you learn more about us, Kirk."

"I made . . . the decision to stay," Merik said.

"What happened to your crew? Did they voluntarily beam—" Kirk corrected himself, "—come ashore?"

"This is an ordered world, Jim. Conservative, based on time-honored Roman strengths and virtues."

"What happened to your crew?"

"There has been no war here for over four hundred years, Jim. Could your land of the same era make the same boast? Certainly, they don't want this stability contaminated with dangerous ideas about other ways and other places."

"Interesting," Spock said. "And given a conservative empire, Captain, quite understandable."

McCoy was horrified. "Spock, are you out of your head?" he demanded.

"Doctor, I said I understood. I find the checks and balances of this civilization quite illuminating. It does seem to have escaped the carnage of your first three World Wars."

"Spock, they have *slavery, despotism, gladiatorial games* . . . !"

Imperturbable as usual, the Vulcan said, "Situations quite familiar to the six million who died in your First World War, Doctor—the eleven million who died in your Second, the thirty-seven million in your Third. Shall I go on?"

"Interesting," Claudius commented. "And you, Captain . . . which world do you prefer?"

"My world," Kirk said, "is my vessel, my oath and my crew, Proconsul." He turned to Merik. "What happened to your vessel, you've answered. What happened to your oath is obvious."

Merik didn't flinch. "As to my men, Kirk, those who can't adapt to a world always die."

The words were called for. Kirk said them. "You sent your own people to the arena." It was a statement, not a question—a statement defining an unbridgeable gulf between life values. Yes, Merik's eyes *were* haunted. And he would be forever pursued by the Furies of his own self-betrayal. If he could still speak with firmness, it was a false firmness—a poor rag clutched around a shivering soul.

"And just as I did, Kirk, you'll end up ordering your own people 'ashore'."

Misery loves company, Kirk thought. McCoy had cried out, "You must know that's impossible! Starfleet regulations—"

Claudius completed the sentence. "—are designed to circumvent any such order. There may be over four hundred people on your ship, Captain, but they'll come down if it's handled properly . . . a few at a time." The plump little man smiled. "You forget I have a trained ship captain to tell me what is possible and what is not possible." He took a communicator from the pocket of his smart sports jacket. "Your communicator, Captain Kirk. Save us all a lot of unnecessary trouble and issue the appropriate orders."

Merik tried for a comradely tone. "They'll be arriving soon anyway, Jim. A recon party first. Then a rescue party, then a larger rescue party. I had less men but it adds up to the same in the end."

Kirk smiled at them. "You really believe I can be made to order my people down?"

"I believe this, Captain," Claudius said. "You'd do

almost anything rather than have to watch your two friends here put slowly to death.''

The soft little man was anything but soft. The plump body was built on bones of cold steel. Kirk felt the sweat breaking out on his palms. Then he reached out and took the communicator.

"Jim!''

Kirk opened the communicator, ignoring McCoy's cry of protest. "Captain to bridge, come in . . .''

"Bridge, Scott here. Go ahead, sir.''

Reaching down, Claudius pressed a button as Kirk spoke quickly into the communicator. "If you have a fix on us, Scotty—'' He stopped. The door had opened. Guards' submachine guns were leveled at him, at Spock, at McCoy.

"Stand by, Engineer . . .'' Kirk closed the communicator.

"Wise of you, Captain,'' Claudius said. "No point in beaming up three bullet-ridden corpses.''

"On the other hand my chief engineer is standing by for a message. If I bring down a hundred men armed with phasers . . .''

"You could probably defeat the combined armies of our entire empire.'' Claudius' lips moved in a smile that Kirk was beginning to dread. "At a cost, Captain—the violation of your oath regarding noninterference with other societies.'' He addressed Spock. "I believe you all swear you'll die before you'll violate that directive. Am I right?''

"Quite correct,'' Spock said.

McCoy's tension exploded. "Spock, must you always be so blasted honest?''

Claudius returned to the workover on Kirk. "Why even bother to bring down armed men? I'm told your vessel can easily lay waste to this world's surface.'' He smiled once more. "Oh, but there's that prime directive in the way again, isn't there? Mustn't interfere.'' He pointed to the communicator. "Well, Captain, you've a message started. Your engineer is waiting. What are you going to do?''

This Roman in the sports jacket would have been a priceless asset to the Spanish Inquisition. It was small comfort to know at last what he was up against. Kirk opened the communicator. "Sorry to keep you waiting, Scotty . . .''

Claudius, at his shoulder, heard Scott say, "We were becoming concerned, Captain. You were a bit overdue."

"Order your officers to join us," Claudius said.

" 'Condition green'," Kirk said. "All is well. Captain out." He closed the communicator.

Claudius hurled his wine goblet across the room. He snatched the communicator and Merik shouted, "Jim, that was stupid!"

Claudius was fairly dancing with fury. "Guards, take them! Prepare them for the games!"

As the three were hustled past Merik, the ex-captain said, "This is no Academy training test, Kirk! *This is real! They're taking you out to die!*"

Miles above it all, an unhappy Scott was torn by indecision of his own. "Condition green" was a code term for trouble. But it also forbade the taking of any action to relieve it. Kirk seldom signaled trouble. Now that he *had* signaled it, it would be bad trouble.

Scott left the command chair to go to Uhura. "Lieutenant, are you *certain* there's no contact?"

"Nothing, Mr. Scott. Except for their message you received."

"Mr. Chekov?"

"Nothing, sir. Sensors lost them when they entered the city."

With action immobilized, fancied horrors began to parade themselves for the miserable Scott.

The arena was a TV studio sound stage. Somebody had done a good job on his Roman history. The stage was galleried, its tiers of rounded stone benches rising in genuine Colosseum style. But the cameras were focused on the sand-sprinkled central space below where combat was won or lost. At the cameraman's "ready" signal, an announcer assumed the amiable smile that was the twentieth-century's stock-in-trade of announcers the world over.

Canned music blared; and to a red light's flash, the announcer went on the air.

"Good evening, ladies and gentlemen. Live from City Arena tonight and in living color, we bring you 'Name the

Winner!' Brought to you by your Jupiter Eight dealers from coast to coast. In a moment, tonight's first heat . . .''

The light read: OFF THE AIR—and the announcer's big smile vanished as though it had never been. There was an Observers' Booth, hung with velvet, behind him. Claudius and Merik were the first to enter it. Armed guards with Kirk, his arms bound behind his back, followed them. The announcer turned. ''We're in a taped commercial, Proconsul. Back on the air in forty seconds,'' he said.

The guards shoved Kirk into a chair, their guns aimed at his back. Merik, his self-assurance visibly less, threw him a concerned glance. But Claudius, fully at home here, merely turned to make sure that Kirk had noted the entrance into the combat space.

Spock and McCoy were standing in it.

Clad in gladiator gear, they'd been given Roman shields and swords. Spock held his weapon with the born athlete's confidence; but McCoy was fingering his awkwardly. Looking up, they both caught sight of Kirk—and he knew that their anxiety for him matched his anxiety for them. But there wasn't time even for anxiety. Horror filled Kirk. To their rear was a man with a rawhide whip: an older man, the Master of the Games, thickly-muscled, his hard face that of a veteran who knew the gladiator racket from the bottom up.

The announcer said, ''Stand by . . . ten seconds!''

The older man signed to the pair's guard escort. Pointed swords were pressed against their backs. ''If they refuse to move on out, skewer them,'' the hardbitten veteran told the guards.

''Condition green.'' Maybe it had been a mistake to prohibit action by the *Enterprise*. Kirk hadn't visualized anything like this. He moved in his bonds, straining against them as the announcer got his ON THE AIR light.

''And first tonight, a surprise 'extra'! In the far corner, a couple of aggressive barbarians with strange ways I'm sure will be full of surprises. Facing them, your favorites and mine from previous matches—Maximus Achilles and our noted Flavius!''

Flavius, the experienced gladiator. And the other one, just as big, just as competent-looking. Kirk could estimate their familiarity with the work at hand by the way they were moving out into the arena. Equally efficient, the sports announcer was milking his last ounce of suspense from the spectacle.

"Victory—or death? And for which of them? You know as much as I do at this moment. Ladies and gentlemen, this is *your* program! *You 'Name the Winner'!*"

To the beat of more canned music, the two big gladiators saluted the Proconsul with lifted swords. Then they stepped forward toward Spock and McCoy.

Intuition had placed Spock into a nearly correct defensive stance. McCoy lacked it. Despite his Starship combat training, he wasn't the athletic match of either Spock or the tested fighters who were approaching them.

Nearing them, Flavius said quietly, "Why you? I don't mind killing humans but—"

A flourish of trumpets drowned his words. Maximus, eyeing Spock, chose him for his opponent. The Vulcan pivoted, evading the first sword slash. McCoy found himself confronting Flavius, both of them hesitant, unsure.

The whip cracked. "Begin!"

Always reluctant to take a life, Spock was merely defending himself. Maximus bored in on him. Flavius took a half-hearted slash at McCoy and missed. Instinctively, the *Enterprise* man lifted his weapon—and the contest was under way.

Again, Claudius turned to check on Kirk's reactions. They were extremely satisfactory. The Starship Captain had paled and was sitting unnaturally still, his forehead beaded with sweat. The edgy Merik didn't turn; but the back of his neck was red with shamed blood.

The announcer was saying, "Flavius is getting off to a slow start, but he's never disappointed us for very—*there's a close one! The barbarian with the pointed ears is in trouble!*"

Spock's' recoil from offensive action had backed him into a corner, and the huge Maximus was closing in to finish him off.

"Please . . ." Spock said. "I tell you I am well able to defeat you."

"*Fight*, Barbarian!"

Once more Spock barely avoided a sword slash. He was thrown off balance and Maximus raised his weapon to end the match. Watching, Kirk tried to get to his feet. Slammed back by a guard, he felt the cold muzzle of a submachine gun pushed against his neck. Merik leaned back, his voice lowered. "Most of my men went the same way. I'd hoped I'd feel it less with yours . . ."

Pure defense had its disadvantages. In the arena, Spock had dodged another slash only to expose himself to another one. "I *beg* you . . . I don't want to . . ." He ducked again. ". . . injure you . . ."

The cords binding Kirk's arms were slippery with sweat. Every muscle in his body revolted against his helplessness. They were his for action—action he'd taken time and again when Spock needed action. His face reflected his agony. Claudius, turning once more, found it more interesting than his games.

Their Master was displeased. *"Fight, you two!"* He crashed his whip hard across Flavius' naked back. The gladiator's sword came up. Then it dropped, as experience warned him that the old survivor of hundreds of bloody bouts was far too canny to ever blunder into weapon reach.

"You bring this network's ratings down, Flavius—and we'll do a 'special' on you . . ."

The oldtimer's threat worked. Flavius aimed a more skillful blow at McCoy, the massive power of his right arm evident even at half-strength. McCoy staggered back.

"Merik . . ." Kirk said.

Claudius spoke. "Question, Captain?"

"The rules?" Kirk said. "If Spock should finish his man first . . ."

Claudius shook his head. "He can't help his friend. We believe that men should fight their own battles." He smiled his dreadful soft smile again. "Ready to order your crew down? Only the weak will die. My word as a Roman, Captain."

"No," Kirk said.

His tension was beginning to affect Merik. The one-time Space Academy cadet checked Claudius; and leaning back to Kirk said very quietly, "Maybe . . . you understand now why I gave in, Jim. Romans were always the strongest . . . two thousand years practice enslaving people, using them, killing them . . ."

Claudius had overheard. Without turning, he said, "Quite true, Captain Kirk." He pointed to the arena. "The games have always strengthened us. Death becomes familiar. We don't fear it as you do. Admit it . . . you find these games frightening, repellent . . ."

"Frightening." Should he say, "Your games don't frighten me. The spirit behind them does." The little man wanted fear. Kirk wasn't giving him any. "In some parts of the galaxy," he said, "I've seen forms of entertainment that make this look like a folkdance."

It hit home. For the first time, Claudius eyed him with uncertainty.

The whip had again cracked across Flavius' back. Boos came from the guards and galleries. Irritated, the huge gladiator snarled, "At least defend yourself!"

McCoy, angered, too, cried, "I *am* defending myself!"

"Not like that, you fool!" Hold your weapon higher! *Now, swing at me!*"

McCoy swung, almost losing his balance. Flavius diverted the blow with an easy wrist movement. McCoy's anger mounted with his realization of his own incompetence. And Flavius, smarting under the lashings, the continuing jeers, was struggling with a growing rage of his own.

The wet cords that held Kirk should have been easier to slip out of. His hands were wrenching at them when he saw that Claudius was watching him. He stopped struggling; and Claudius said, "Those are *your* men dying down there, Captain, not strangers."

Kirk's eyes met his. "I've had to select men to die before, Proconsul, so that more could be saved."

"You're a clever liar." There was a pause before the little Twentieth-century Roman gestured to the man beside him. "He was a space captain, too. I've examined him thoroughly. Your species has no strength."

Kirk didn't answer. Merik shifted uneasily; and Claudius, noticing his move, snapped, "Well, what is it? *Out with it!*"

"He . . . Jim . . . Kirk commands not just a space ship, Proconsul, but a *Starship*."Merik flushed under Claudius' glare. "A special kind of vessel . . . and crew. I tried for such a command but . . ." His words trailed off into silence.

Claudius looked down at Spock and McCoy. "I see no evidence of superiority. They fight no better than your men, Merikus. Perhaps not as well."

And indeed the galleries' hissing was growing in volume. *"Stop running!"* Maximus yelled at Spock. *"Fight!"*

He stabbed at him; and Spock, deftly turning the blow, threw a quick look toward McCoy. Then he maneuvered his fight closer to McCoy and Flavius.

"Do you need help, Doctor?"

Frustrated and furious, McCoy shouted, "Whatever gave you *that* idea?" He made another swing at Flavius; and Maximus, maddened by Spock's elusiveness, bellowed, "*Fight*, you pointed-eared freak!"

"You tell him, Buster!" McCoy told Maximus. He tried for a better grip on his sword. "*Of course*, I need help! Of all . . ." Enraged at Spock, McCoy went into a flurry of wild lunges at Flavius, unaware that he was rousing a blood-madness that would turn his antagonist into a very formidable enemy. ". . . the illogical, completely ridiculous questions I ever heard," he panted. He swung again.

Flavius growled deep in his throat. He charged with a series of murderous slashes that snapped McCoy back into reality—the fact that he'd provoked a savagery which could put an end to his life in a matter of seconds.

Spock recognized his sudden peril. He went into his first attack, amazing the towering Maximus by his speed and efficiency. He streaked in on the gladiator, closer and closer; but McCoy was already beaten down to the sand, his shield torn from his grasp. He'd learned enough to parry the next blow. Then his sword was wrenched from his hand.

Kirk saw how defenseless he was. He pulled himself away from the guns behind him and got to his feet, surging against his bonds. They held: and the guards, slamming him back into his seat, immobilized him.

Spock, downing his man with a "space karate" chop, was racing across the arena. He reached Flavius; and spinning him around, dropped him with his Vulcan neck pinch. The arena went into bedlam. The Master of the Games rushed to the *Enterprise* men to cries of "Foul!" from the galleries.

His guards, running after him, grabbed both Spock and McCoy and pinioned their arms behind their backs.

Kirk, Claudius and Merik were all on their feet.

The shocked announcer whirled to Claudius. "A clear foul, Proconsul! Your decision?"

Down in the arena, swords were pointed, pressing, against the captives' necks. The Master of the Games looked up to the Observers' Booth for the Proconsul's word, ignoring the galleries' clamor for immediate death. Claudius spoke to Merik.

"Your opinion, Merikus? After all they're like yourself."

Whatever his opinion was, Merik considered it safer to keep it to himself. "It . . . it's *your* decision, Proconsul."

Claudius turned. "And *your* opinion, Captain Kirk?" He didn't wait to hear it. "Kill them now—and you'll gladly accept whatever happens to you. I wouldn't relish that—but you almost tricked me into depriving myself of real pleasure." He moved to the edge of the booth. "Master of the Games, take them back to their cage!"

He turned again to face Kirk. "It won't be easy for them, Captain. And especially not for you!" He spoke to Kirk's guards. "Bring him to my quarters. *Now!*"

He left the booth. And the guards hustled Kirk along after him.

After the raw violence of the arena, the effete luxury of Claudius' suite sickened Kirk. It was the triumph of an art connoisseur. The room was tapestried; and an alcove held a wide bed embroidered in gold. In a large wall niche, a marble statue of Minerva, Roman goddess of wisdom, presided over those self-indulgences that were the delectation of the soft man of steel.

The guards marched Kirk into the room and left him. There was no one in sight. But Claudius had promised that something particularly unpleasant was going to happen to him here. Wary, uncertain, Kirk searched the room with his eyes. A heavy Etruscan jar stood on a pedestal. Kirk seized it, hefting it for weight and balance. If he was going to die, he wasn't going to do it without a fight . . .

"I was told . . ."

It was a feminine voice. Drusilla moved out from the bed alcove's hangings, hesitating at the sight of Kirk with his lifted weapon. This time the gown she wore was pure white. Her straight blond hair fell below her waist. And the white of her gown enhanced the creamy tone of her skin.

"I was told," she said, "to wait for you." She went to a table. "And to provide wine, food, whatever you wish. I am the Proconsul's slave, although for this evening . . ." She was pouring wine, clearly expecting him to come to the table. He didn't move. Inevitably what occurred in this room was bound to lead to treachery, torture and in the end, to certain death.

She turned, surprised by his stillness. "I was told that for this evening, I am *your* slave. Then command me."

"No," Kirk said. "You can tell the Proconsul it won't work."

She frowned, puzzled. "What will not work?"

"Whatever he has in mind. Whatever trickery or . . ."

She left the table to lay a hand on his arm. This master of hers, though temporary, obviously required soothing. Kirk removed the hand. Then he shouted, "*Do you hear me, Proconsul?* Whatever you have in mind, I'm not cooperating! I may have to die—but I won't give you entertainment out of it!"

Drusilla came closer to him but, brushing her roughly aside, he strode past her to the door. He opened it, looking into the corridor, sure he'd find a spy lurking in it. It was empty. He and the slave girl seemed to be totally alone.

She divined his thought. "Except for the guards at the street entrances, we are alone here," she said. "Please believe me. I have never lied to one who owns me."

But Kirk's suspicion wasn't laid. This *had* to be a grotesque trick of some new variety . . . and yet the girl's every word and gesture spoke of sincerity. She seemed honestly puzzled by his behavior—and in her extremely feminine way, a little disappointed by it, too.

He began to wish he could relax. His friends' lives had been spared—but to what purpose? What was going on in that "cage" where they'd been confined?

* * *

Going on in the cage was determined escape effort. Its door was barred; and Spock, rallying every ounce of his strength, was trying to pull it loose by the very fury of the need to do so. McCoy, standing behind him, saw that neither bars nor door had given a half-inch.

"Angry, Spock? Or frustrated, perhaps?"

"Such emotion is quite foreign to me, Doctor. I was merely testing the strength of the door."

McCoy nodded. "For the fifteenth time."

Spock came close to showing irritation. Disdaining to answer, he turned from the door, again inspecting the cell for some possible weapon or escape route. Watching him, McCoy's eyes softened. After a space, he said gently, "Spock . . ."

Spock turned, expecting a jibe for what was clearly his frantic anxiety for the safety of his captain. And though Mc Coy shared it, he had another matter on his mind at the moment.

"Spock, uh . . . we've had our disagreements . . ." Because he was leveling, he was deeply embarrassed. ". . . or maybe they're jokes. As Jim says, we're often not sure ourselves. But . . . er . . . what I mean to say is . . ." He hesitated again. "Well, what I mean is—"

"Doctor," Spock said, "I'm seeking a weapon or an escape method. Please be brief."

"I'm . . . trying to say you saved my life in the arena."

Spock nodded. "Quite true."

That fact mutually acknowledged, he resumed his examination of every possibility of their cell.

McCoy blew up. *"I was trying to thank you, you—you pointed-eared hobgoblin!"*

"Ah, yes," Spock said. "Humans do suffer from an emotional need to show gratitude." He gave a small nod. " 'You're welcome' is, I believe, the correct response." He moved off, still searching. "However, Doctor, you should remember that I am motivated solely by logic. The loss of our ship's surgeon, whatever I may think of his relative skill, is a loss to the efficiency of our vessel and therefore to—"

McCoy interrupted. "Do you know why you're not afraid of dying, Spock? *You're more afraid of living.* Every day you stay alive is one more day you might slip—and let your human half peek out." He lessened the distance between them. "That's it, isn't it? *Insecurity!* You wouldn't know what to do with a genuine, warm, decent feeling!"

Spock wheeled—and this time McCoy caught him at it. There was an instant when he actually saw Spock composing his face into Vulcan impassivity. Then the instant was gone—and Spock raised an eyebrow.

"Really, Doctor?" he said.

McCoy thought, "I am very fond of this man." What he said was, "I know. I'm worried about Jim, too, Spock."

For the moment, anyway, their captain was safe. He was also hungry. And seated beside Drusilla on a couch, he was making excellent inroads on the tray of food she insisted on holding for him. It was a long time since he'd tasted roast pheasant. And the wine was good wine. After all, food was food and wine was wine, unlikely to be up to tricks. As to the girl . . . Hunger and thirst appeased, he took his first good look at her.

"You've noticed me at last," she said. "I was becoming concerned. I am ordered to please you."

Kirk sipped more wine. "Good," he said. Then he pointed to the roast pheasant's remains. "Excellent. And you?"

"Superb, I'm told," she said, straight-faced. "But then, men lie, don't they?"

Kirk eyed her. Then he leaned back against the couch. "I've seen strange worlds, strange customs," he told her. "Perhaps here this is considered torture."

She moved close to him, placing the tray on the table. "Torture? I do not understand. I have no wish to see you tortured in any way." She kissed him. "At the first sign of pain, you will tell me?"

"You'll be the first to know," he said. He took her in his arms and returned the kiss with interest.

Up on the *Enterprise*, Scott was tiring of misery. He was rapidly transforming it into the kind of productive anger that opens up new vistas for action.

"How long since we've heard?" he asked Uhura.

"Nine hours, forty-one seconds, sir." She indicated

the viewing screen. "It's almost dark there. We'll see the city lights coming on soon."

"Mr. Chekov, take over the scanners. Lieutenant Uhura, give him a hand." He returned to the command chair, still hesitating. On the other hand, no order had said he couldn't frighten whoever it was down there who was causing bad trouble for his captain and the landing party. It might do no good. Yet it just could be salutary to suggest what a Starship could really do if it got serious.

He made up his mind. "Lieutenant Uhura, pinpoint the city's power source locations." He paused before he added, "Mr. Chekov, type the power, the load factors—and how much our beams must pull to overload them."

"Captain . . ."

Sprawled in sleep on the alcove's bed, Kirk came instantly awake at the sound of Claudius' voice. He had started to roll, protecting himself when he saw that the little man was alone, just standing there, a newly benign look on his face.

"You've had a harrowing time on our planet," he said. "I'm not surprised you slept through the afternoon." He left the alcove to go to a table. "Sorry I was detained. Shall we have our talk now?"

He was pouring wine. Kirk followed him, distrust rising again at sight of the armed guard posted just outside the door. Offered wine, he shook his head. Claudius went on. "Oh, one of the communicators we took from you is missing. Was it my pretty Drusilla by any chance?"

Kirk didn't answer. Merik had entered the room. Claudius, pointing to Kirk, said, "See if he has the communicator."

Still silent, Kirk permitted the search. "Not that I would have punished him badly. I would have blamed you, Merik," Claudius said. He lifted his goblet. "You're a Roman, Kirk—or should have been. It's not on his person?"

"No, Proconsul." Merik addressed Kirk. "He said a 'Roman.' You've just received as great a compliment, Jim—"

Claudius interrupted. "Care for food, Captain Kirk?"

Kirk saw that Merik, pointedly uninvited to sit, was shifting uncomfortably. "Thank you, I've eaten," he said.

"I trust there was nothing you required that you didn't receive," Claudius said.

"Nothing. Except . . . perhaps an explanation."

"I'm sure our world seems as strange to you as yours would seem to me." He looked up. "Since you are a man, I owe you this immediately. You must die in a few hours." He swallowed. "And also because you are a man . . ." He became conscious of Merik's presence and a flicker of something like contempt passed across his face. "You may leave us, Merik. The thoughts of one man shared with another cannot interest you."

Merik almost responded to the open insult. Then he decided that for him silence was golden. He left the room; and Claudius, resuming, said to Kirk, "And since you are a man, Captain Kirk, I gave you some last hours as a man. Do you understand?"

A small smile on his lips, Kirk said, "Let's say . . . I appreciated it."

"Unfortunately, your defiances in the arena were seen by the television audience. We must demonstrate that defiance is wrong."

"Of course," Kirk said.

"But because I have learned to respect you, I promise you will die quickly and easily."

"Naturally, I prefer that. And my friends?"

"Of course, you'd ask that. And, of course, when their time comes, the same." Summoning guards, he gestured to Kirk. "Take him to the arena." A comforting afterthought occurred to him. "We've preempted fifteen minutes on the early show for you," he told Kirk. "We will have a good audience, full color. You may not understand the honor, since you are centuries beyond anything as crude as television."

"I recall it was similar," Kirk said.

They hadn't bound his hands. He needed them to hold his sword and shield. From the arena's entrance, where Spock and McCoy had waited, he would see Claudius moving into the Observers' Booth above him. Guards, supervised by the Master of the Games, pushed him past a big man in gladiator dress. He recognized Flavius. The two were exchanging glances when Merik's voice, speaking to one of the guards, said, "I'll speak privately with the prisoner."

The Master of the Games was annoyed. "Impossible," he said shortly.

"I am still First Citizen. You will obey me!"

The announcer spoke. "Stand by . . . ten seconds."

The Master of the Games, completely ignoring Merik, moved Kirk out into the arena's center. Desperate, the man who'd betrayed himself, shouted, "Too late to help you, Jim! I'll do what I can for your friends!"

The announcer, on signal, was speaking into his microphone. "Good evening, ladies and gentlemen. Before the first heat tonight, a simple execution. But keep your dial turned to this channel—there's lots of excitement to follow . . ."

Claudius leaned over the booth's edge. "Master of the Games, make it quick! A single thrust!"

The veteran drew his sword. "Don't move," he told Kirk. "You'll only die harder."

As he lifted his weapon to strike, there was a wild cry. *"Murderers!"*

Flavius had raced into the arena, sword raised high. The startled Master of the Games wheeled to meet the onslaught. Guards were running to block the gladiator's rush; and Kirk, moving fast to help him, had almost reached him when every light in the place went out, plunging it into near darkness. Kirk hesitated for a split second. Then he used the dimness to fell a guard with a "space karate" blow. Another lunged for him. A smash with a sword butt sent him sprawling. There was a burst of submachine gunfire. Kirk, close to Flavius now, cried, "The cells! Which way?"

"The barred doors across . . ."

Flavius was cut down by another splatter of bullets. Kirk, realizing his danger, dodged a sword slash—and seizing the guard, spun him around to face the source of the gunfire. The man stumbled forward into the guard with the gun. He was thrown off balance—and Kirk, grabbing the gun, clubbed himself free. The lights came back as he reached the barred doors at the other side of the arena.

He was seen. Guards shouted. A submachine gun blast struck near him. He turned, firing a burst himself. It silenced the gunner. Kirk fired again at the heavy lock on the barred doors.

Their cell was at the middle of a corridor. "Look out!" Kirk yelled to them. His gun spit bullets at the cell's lock.

Spock kicked the door open and McCoy cried, "Jim! Are you all right?"

"What did they do to you, Captain?"

"They threw me—a few curves, Spock. Perhaps it's better if I don't talk about it now . . ."

He'd heard the sounds of pursuit. Guards had followed him, running. A javelin hurtled past them. Kirk aimed the gun. The men halted but one in the rear was raising the muzzle of his . . .

"Hold!"

It was Claudius. Guards ranged behind him; he stood at the other end of the corridor. In both directions escape was cut off.

"We're in each other's line of fire." Claudius spoke to the guards. "Swords only."

Both groups of guards, swords high, were moving in.

"But I can use my gun," Kirk said. "And in either direction, Claudius."

As he eyed the little Proconsul, he saw that Merik had joined him. Claudius moved away from him. "I pity you, 'Captain' Merik," he said. "But watch. At least *see* how men die."

A guard with a javelin raised his arm. Kirk whirled with the gun. It gave a click on an empty cylinder. The guards charged. Kirk downed the first with his gunstock. Spock reached for his dropped sword and McCoy picked up the javelin beside him.

Merik came to a decision. Death was nearing the *Enterprise* men. They were fighting now back to back. Merik pulled the missing communicator from his pocket, clicking it open. "Starship, lock in on this place: three to . . ."

With a shocked look on his face, he staggered. Claudius withdrew the sword he'd driven into him. Merik glanced at his seducer; and choking on blood, whispered into the communicator, "Three to beam-up . . . emergency . . ."

As he fell, he threw the communicator to Kirk over the heads of the guards. The dead Bob Merrick of the Space

Academy had finally made peace with himself. Already, before Claudius' astounded eyes, Kirk, Spock and McCoy were dematerializing into dazzle. Then even its sparkles were gone.

Kirk was dictating into his Captain's Log.

"Note commendation to Engineering Officer Scott for his performance in commanding this vessel during my absence. Despite enormous temptation and strong personal feelings, he obeyed the Prime Directive. His temporary 'blackout' of the city below resulted in no interference with its society and yet saved the lives of myself and the landing party. We are prepared to leave orbit shortly."

He punched his "off" button. Beside him, Scott, his face red with embarrassed pleasure, said, "Thank you, Captain. I'll see to the engines."

As he entered the bridge elevator, Spock and McCoy stepped out of it.

McCoy, approaching the command chair, said, "I just saw on your report that Flavius was killed. I'm sorry. I liked that huge sun-worshiper."

Spock spoke earnestly. "I wish we could have examined that belief of his more closely, Captain. It does seem illogical that sun-worshipers could evolve a philosophy of total brotherhood. Worship of the sun is almost always a primitive superstition-religion . . ."

Uhura had overheard. She turned from her console. "I'm afraid you have it wrong, Mr. Spock. All of you . . ."

Three pairs of eyes were on her. She went on. "I've been monitoring old-style radio waves and heard talk about this brotherhood religion. Don't you understand? Not the sun in the sky . . . the *Son—the Son of God*!"

McCoy protested. "But when we mentioned stars, Septimus said they worshiped the sun up there."

But Kirk's face was thoughtful. "In most of our own religions, don't people tend to look upward when speaking of the Deity?" He paused. "Caesar and Christ . . . they *did* have both. And the word is spreading only now down there."

"A philosophy of total love, total brotherhood," McCoy said.

Spock nodded. "It will replace their Imperial Rome. And it will happen during their Twentieth century."

Remembering the arena's ferocity, Kirk said, "It would be something to watch, to be part of."

"How stupid of me not to have comprehended!" Spock exclaimed.

McCoy looked at him. "I tend to go along with that, Mr. Spock."

"Doctor . . . the next time I have an opportunity to save your life—"

"—you'll do the logical thing, save me." McCoy smiled. "Comforting to know that, Spock."

Something good had happened between the two, Kirk thought. He was glad. Both men were dear to him. It was high time they admitted how dear they were to each other. Though he knew how little their sparring meant, it was a waste of time that could be better spent. On the other hand, who knew? There were many ways of revealing affection.

He turned to Chekov. "Take us out of orbit, Mr. Chekov. Ahead, warp factor one."

"Aye, sir. Ahead, warp factor one."

Kirk looked at the viewing screen. The Earth-like planet that had confused itself with the Roman Empire was a diminishing pinpoint of light. Then it was gone.

JOURNEY TO BABEL

Writer: D.C. Fontana
Director: Joseph Pevney
Guest stars: Jane Wyatt, Mark Lenard

The honor guard of eight security men was lined up before the airlock, four men to a side, with Kirk, Spock and McCoy, all three in formal dress blue uniforms, at the end of this human tube. McCoy tugged at his collar, which he had previously described as "like having my neck in a sling." He asked Spock, "How does that Vulcan salute go?"

Spock demonstrated. The gesture was complex and McCoy's attempt to copy it was not very convincing.

The surgeon shook his head. "That hurts worse than the uniform."

The uniforms were the least of their discomforts, Kirk thought a little grimly. They'd soon be out of those, after the formal reception tonight, and the Vulcans were the last group of delegates the *Enterprise* had to pick up. Then would come the trip to the neutral planetoid code-named "Babel"—a two-week journey with a hundred and fourteen Federation delegates aboard, thirty-two of them ambassadors, half of them mad at the other half, and the whole lot touchier than a raw anti-matter pile over the Coridian question. Now *that* was going to be uncomfortable.

The airlock opened, and the Vulcan Ambassador, Sarek, stepped through. Because of Vulcan longevity, it would have been impossible to guess his age—he looked to be no more than in his late forties—but Kirk knew it to be in fact a hundred and two, which was middle age by Vulcan standards. He was followed, several paces behind, by a woman wearing a traveling outfit with a colorful hooded cloak; she in turn was followed by two Vulcan aides.

Kirk, Spock and McCoy stood at attention as the party walked past the honor guard to the Captain. Spock stepped formally in front of Sarek and gave the complex salute.

"Vulcan honors us with your presence," he said. "We come to serve."

Sarek pointedly ignored him and saluted Kirk instead. When he spoke, his voice was almost without inflection.

"Captain, your service honors us."

"Thank you, Ambassador," Kirk said with a slight bow. "Captain James Kirk. My First Officer, Commander Spock. Dr. McCoy, Chief Medical Officer."

Sarek nodded briefly in turn and indicated the rest of his party. "My aides." He held up his hand, first and second fingers extended. The woman stepped forward and touched her first and second fingers to his. "And Amanda, she who is my wife."

"Captain Kirk," the woman said.

"My pleasure, madam. Ambassador, as soon as you're settled, I'll arrange a tour of the ship. My First Officer will conduct you."

"I prefer another guide, Captain," Sarek said.

He was absolutely expressionless, and so was Spock. This snub was just as baffling and even more pointed than before, but it would not be a good idea to offend a ranking ambassador.

"Of course—if you wish. Mr. Spock, we have two hours until we leave orbit. Would you like to beam down and visit your parents?"

There was a slight but noticeable silence. Then Spock said, "Captain—Ambassador Sarek and his wife *are* my parents."

Was I just telling myself, Kirk thought glumly after the first shock, that this trip was going to be just "uncomfortable"?

Upon reflection, Kirk gave himself the job of guiding the tour. He found Spock's mother especially interesting—remarkable, even—though she was hard to study because she habitually walked behind and to the side of any man, her husband most notably. This was a Vulcan ritual to which she had adapted, for Amanda was an Earthwoman; almost everyone in the crew knew that much about Spock.

Though in her late fifties, she was still straight, slim and resilient. She had married a Vulcan and come to live on his world where her human-woman emotions had no place. Kirk strongly suspected that she had not lost any of her human humor and warmth, but that it was buried inside, in deference to her husband's customs and society.

He led them into the Engineering Room. Spock, by now in regular uniform, was working at the computer banks behind the grilled partition.

"This is the engineering section," Kirk told his guests. "There are emergency backup systems for the main controls. We also have a number of control computers here."

Amanda was still behind them and, without Sarek appearing to notice, she moved over to Spock. Out of the corner of his eye, Kirk saw each of them cross hands and touch them, palms out, in a ritual embrace. Then they began to murmur. Spock's face was expressionless, as usual. Once, Amanda shook her head ruefully.

Kirk continued his lecture, hoping to avoid trouble, but Sarek's eyes were as alert as his own. "My wife, attend," the Ambassador said. He held up his first and second fingers. Without a word, Amanda nodded to Spock to excuse herself and obediently moved to Sarek, joining her fingers with his, though Kirk guessed that she was really not much interested in the console and its instruments.

Spock, gathering up a handful of tapes, rose and headed for the door. Kirk had a sudden idea.

"Mr. Spock—a moment, please."

The First Officer turned reluctantly. "Yes, Captain?"

"Ambassador, I'm not competent to explain our computer setup. Mr. Spock, will you do so, please?"

"I gave Spock his first instruction in computers," Sarek said woodenly. "He chose to devote his knowledge to Starfleet rather than the Vulcan Science Academy."

That tore it. In trying to be helpful, Kirk had unwittingly put his foot right into the heart of the family quarrel. Apologetically, he nodded dismissal to Spock, and turned to Sarek.

"I'm sorry, Ambassador. I didn't mean to offend you in . . ."

"Offense is a human emotion, Captain. For other reasons, I am returning to my quarters. Continue, my wife."

Amanda bowed her head in characteristic acceptance, and Sarek left. Kirk, puzzled and confused as never before by his First Officer and his relatives, turned to her, shaking his head.

"I'm afraid I don't understand, Mrs. Sarek."

"Amanda," she said quickly. "I'm afraid you couldn't pronounce the Vulcan family name."

"Can you?"

A smile fluttered on her lips, then vanished as habit overtook her. "After a fashion, and after many years of practice . . . Shall we continue the tour? My husband did request it."

"It sounded more like a command."

"Of course. He's a Vulcan. I'm his wife."

"Spock is his son."

Amanda glanced at him sharply, as though surprised, but recovered quickly. "You don't understand the Vulcan way, Captain. It's logical. It's a better way than ours—but its not easy; It has kept Spock and Sarek from speaking as father and son for eighteen years."

"Spock is my best officer," Kirk said. "And my best friend."

"I'm glad he has such a friend. It hasn't been easy for Spock—neither Vulcan nor human; at home nowhere, except Starfleet."

"I gather Spock disagreed with his father over his choice of a career."

"My husband has nothing against Starfleet. But Vulcans believe peace should not depend on force. Sarek wanted Spock to follow his teaching as Sarek followed the teaching of *his* father."

"And they're both stubborn."

Amanda smiled. "Also a human trait, Captain."

Abruptly, Uhura's voice interrupted from a console speaker. "Bridge to Captain Kirk."

Kirk snapped a toggle. "Kirk here."

"Captain, I've picked up some sort of signal; just a few symbols, nothing intelligible."

"Source?"

"That's what bothers me, sir. Impossible to locate. There wasn't enough of it. Sensors show nothing in the area. But it was a strong signal, as though it was very close."

"Go to alert status four. Begin long-range scanning. Kirk out." Kirk frowned thoughtfully and flicked off the switch. "Madame—Amanda—I'll have to ask you to excuse me. I shall hope to see you again at the reception this evening."

"Certainly, Captain. Both Vulcans and humans know what duty is."

The reception was already going full blast when Kirk arrived. Amid a murmur of conversation, delegates circulated, or sampled the table of exotic drinks, *hors d'oeuvre*. There was a fantastic array of them from many cultures.

Over it all was a faint aura of edgy politeness verging on hostility. The Interplanetary Conference had been called to consider the petition of the Coridian planets to be admitted to the Federation. The Coridian system had already been claimed by some of the races who now had delegates aboard the *Enterprise*, races who therefore had strong personal reasons for keeping Coridan *out* of the Federation. Keeping open warfare from breaking out among the delegates before the Conference even began was going to be a tough problem; many of them were not even trained diplomats, but minor officials who had been handed a hot potato by bosses who did not want to be saddled with the responsibility for whatever happened on Babel.

Kirk spotted Spock and McCoy in a group which included a Tellarite named Gav, two Andorians called Shras and Thelev, and Sarek and Amanda. Well, at least Spock was—er—associating with his family, however distantly.

As Kirk joined the group, McCoy was saying, "Mr. Ambassador, I understood that you had retired from public service before this conference was called. Forgive my curiosity, but, as a doctor, I'm interested in Vulcan physiology. Isn't it unusual for a Vulcan to retire at your age? You're only a hundred or so."

As was characteristic of Andorians because of their sensitive antennae, Shras was listening with his head down and slightly tilted, while Gav, sipping a snifter of brandy, was staring directly into Sarek's face. For an Earthman unaccustomed to either race, it would have been hard to say which of them, if either, was being rude.

Sarek said, "One hundred and two point four three seven, measured in your years. I had other—concerns."

Gav put his snifter down and leaned still farther forward. When he spoke, his voice was rough, grating and clumsy; English was very difficult for all his people, if he spoke it better than most. "Sarek of Vulcan, do you vote to admit Coridan to the Federation?"

"The vote will not be taken here, Ambassador Gav. My government's instructions will be heard in the Council Chamber on Babel."

"No—*you*. How do *you* vote, Sarek of Vulcan?"

Shras lifted his head. "Why must you know, Tellarite?" His voice was whispery, almost silken.

"In Council, his vote carries others," Gav said, stabbing a finger toward Sarek. "I will know where he stands, and why."

"Tellarites do not argue for reasons," Sarek said. "They simply argue."

"That is a . . ."

"Gentlemen," Kirk interrupted firmly. "As Ambassador Sarek pointed out, this is not the Council Chamber on Babel. I'm aware the admission of Coridan is a highly debatable issue, but you can't solve it here."

For a moment the three Ambassadors stared defensively at each other. Then Sarek nodded to Kirk. "You are correct, Captain. Quite logical."

"Apologies, Captain," Shras whispered.

Gav remained rigid for a moment, then nodded and said in an angry voice, "You will excuse me," and left the group.

"You have met Gav before, Ambassador," Shras said softly to Sarek.

"We debated at my last Council session."

"Ambassador Gav lost," Amanda added with a straight

face. If Shras was amused, his face was incapable of showing
it. He nodded solemnly and moved off.

"Spock, I've always suspected you were more human," McCoy said, in an obvious attempt to lighten the atmosphere. "Mrs. Sarek, I know about the rigorous training
of Vulcan boys, but didn't he ever run and play like human
youngsters? Even in secret?"

"Well," said Amanda, "he did have a sehlat he was
very fond of."

"Sehlat?"

"It's rather like a fat teddy bear."

McCoy's eyes went wide. "A teddy bear?"

Several other crew personnel had overheard this and
there was a general snicker. Quickly, Sarek turned to his wife
and took her arm firmly.

"Excuse us, Doctor," he said. "It has been a long day
for my wife." He propelled her toward the door amid a barrage of "good nights."

McCoy turned back to Spock, who did not appear the
least bit discomforted. "A teddy bear!"

"Not precisely, Doctor," Spock said. "On Vulcan, the
'teddy bears' are alive and have six-inch fangs."

McCoy, no Vulcan, was obviously rocked. He was
bailed out by a nearby wall communicator, which said in
Chekov's voice, "Bridge to Captain Kirk."

"Kirk here."

"Captain, sensors are registering an unidentified vessel
pacing us."

"On my way. Duty personnel on yellow alert. Passengers are not to be alarmed . . . Mr. Spock!"

The intruder turned out to be a small ship, about the
size of a scout, of no known configuration, and unauthorized
in this quadrant. It had been paralleling the course of the
Enterprise for five minutes, outside phaser range and indeed
at the extreme limit of the starship's sensors, and would not
answer hails on any frequency or in any language. An attempt
to intercept showed the intruder not only more maneuverable
than the *Enterprise*, but faster, by a nearly incredible two
warps. Kirk ordered full analysis of all sensor readings made
during the brief approach, and went back to the reception,
leaving Spock in command.

It seemed to be petering out. Gav was still there, sitting isolated, still working on the brandy. If he was trying to get drunk, he was due for a disappointment, Kirk knew; alcohol had no effect on Tellarites except to shorten their already short tempers. Shras and Thelev were also still present, heads down, plus a few other delegates.

Most interestingly, Sarek had returned, by himself. Now why? Had his intent been only to get Amanda off the scene before she could further embarrass their son? There could be no emotional motive behind such a move. What would the logical one be? That whether Sarek approved of Starfleet or not, Spock was an officer in it, and could not function properly if he did not command respect? It seemed as good a guess as any; but Kirk knew that his understanding of Vulcan psychology was, to say the least, insecure.

While he was ruminating, Sarek had gone to a drink dispenser, with the aid of which he seemed to have downed a pill of some kind, and Gav had risen and come up behind him. Sensing trouble, Kirk moved unobtrusively closer. Sure enough, Gav had brought up the Coridan question again.

Sarek was saying; "You seem unable to wait for the Council meeting, Ambassador. No matter. We favor admission."

"You favor? *Why?*"

"Under Federation law, Coridan can be protected—its wealth administered for the benefit of its people."

"It's well for you," Gav said. "Vulcan has no mining interest."

"The Coridians have a nearly unlimited wealth of dilithium crystals, but are underpopulated and unprotected. This invites illegal mining operations."

"Illegal! You accuse us . . . ?"

"Of nothing," Sarek said. "But reports indicate your ships have been carrying Coridian dilithium crystals."

"You call us thieves?" Without an instant's warning, Gav leaped furiously forward, grasping for Sarek's throat. Sarek blocked the Tellarite's hands and effortlessly slammed him away, against a table. As Gav started to lunge at Sarek again, Kirk caught him and forced him back. "Lies!" Gav shouted over his shoulder. "You slander my people."

"*Gentlemen!*" Kirk said.

Gav stopped struggling and Kirk stepped back, glaring coldly at both Ambassadors. "Whatever arguments you have among yourselves are your business," Kirk said. "*My* business is running this ship—and as long as I command it, *there will be order.*"

"Of course, Captain," Sarek said.

"Understood," Gav said sullenly after a moment. "But Sarek, there will be payment for your slander."

"Threats are illogical," Sarek said. "And such 'payment' is usually expensive."

However, the fight seemed to be over—and the reception as well. Kirk went to his quarters, almost too tired to worry. It had been a day full of tensions, not one of which was yet resolved. Most of the ship was on night status now, and it was a weary pleasure to go through the silent, empty corridors.

But it was not over yet. In his quarters, he had just gotten out of the dress uniform with relief when his intercom said: "Security to Captain Kirk."

What now? "Kirk here."

"Lt. Josephs, sir. I'm on Deck 11, Section A-3. I just found one of the Tellarites, murdered and stuffed into the Jefferies tube. I think it's the Ambassador himself, sir."

So a part of his mission—to keep the peace on board—had failed already.

McCoy knelt in the corridor next to the Jefferies tube and probed Gav's body, using no instruments but his surgeon's fingers. Kirk and Spock watched; Lt. Josephs and two security guards waited for orders to remove the body. At last McCoy rose.

"How was he killed?" Kirk asked.

"His neck was broken. By an expert."

Spock glanced sharply at McCoy and then bent to examine the body himself. Kirk said, "Explain."

"From the location and nature of the break, I'd say the killer knew exactly where to apply pressure to snap the spine instantly. Not even a blow was used—no bruise."

"Who aboard would have that knowledge besides yourself?"

"Vulcans," Spock said, straightening again. "On Vulcan, the method is called *tal-shaya*—considered a merciful method of execution in ancient times.''

''Mr. Spock,'' Kirk said, ''a short time ago I broke up an argument between your father and Gav.''

''Indeed, Captain? Interesting.''

''Interesting? Spock, do you realize that makes your father the most likely suspect?''

''Vulcans do not approve of violence.''

''Are you saying your father couldn't have done this?''

''No,'' Spock said. ''But it would be illogical to kill without reason.''

''But if he had such a reason?''

''If there were a reason,'' Spock said, ''my father is quite capable of killing—logically and efficiently. He has the skill, and is still only in middle age.''

Kirk stared at his First Officer for a moment, appalled. Then he said, ''Come with me. You too, Bones.''

He led the way to Sarek's quarters which, he was surprised to see when they were admitted by a smiling Amanda, had not been made up to suit Vulcan taste. He would have thought that Spock would have seen to that. He said, ''I'm sorry to disturb you. But I must speak with your husband.''

''He's been gone for some time. It's his habit to meditate in private before retiring. What's wrong? Spock?''

At that moment the door opened again and Sarek entered. ''You want something of me, Captain?''

Kirk observed that he looked somewhat tense, not exactly with anxiety, but as though he were fighting something back. ''Ambassador, the Tellarite Gav has been found murdered. His neck was broken—in what Spock describes as *tal-shaya*.''

Sarek glanced at his son, lifting an eyebrow in the same familiar manner. ''Indeed? Interesting.''

''Ambassador, where were you in the past hour?''

''This is ridiculous, Captain,'' Amanda said. ''You aren't accusing him . . . ?''

Spock said, ''If only on circumstantial evidence, he is a logical suspect, Mother.''

''I quite agree,'' Sarek said, but he seemed more tense than before. ''I was in private meditation. Spock will tell you that such meditation is a personal experience, not to be discussed. Certainly not with Earthmen.''

"That's a convenient excuse, Ambassador, but . . ."

He broke off as Sarek gasped and started to crumble. He went to his knees before Kirk and Spock could catch him, clutching at his rib cage. A moan escaped him; any pain that could force such a sound from a Vulcan must have been agonizing indeed.

McCoy took a quick reading, then took out a pressure hypo, set it, and gave Sarek a quick injection. Then he went back to the instruments, taking more time with them now.

"What's wrong?" Amanda asked him.

"I don't know—I can't be sure with Vulcan physiology. It looks like something to do with his cardiovascular system, but . . ."

"Can you help him, Bones?"

"I don't know *that* yet, either."

Kirk looked at mother and son in turn. Spock was as expressionless as always, but Amanda's eyes were haunted; not even years of adaptation to Vulcan tradition could cover a worry of this kind.

"I must go off duty," he told her apologetically. "Still another problem confronts me in the morning, for which I'll need a fresh mind. Should I be needed here before then, Dr. McCoy will of course call me.''

"I quite understand, Captain," she said gently. "Good night, and thank you."

A truly remarkable woman.

Not much progress, it turned out on the next trip, had been made on the problem of the ship shadowing the *Enterprise*. Readings taken during the brief attempt at interception showed only that it either had a high-density hull or was otherwise cloaked against sensor probes. It was definitely manned, but by what? The Romulans had nothing like it, nor did the Federation or neutral planets, and that it was Klingon seemed even more unlikely.

Two fragmentary transmissions had been picked up, in an unknown code—with a reception point somewhere inside the *Enterprise* herself. Kirk ordered the locator field tightened to include only the interior of his own ship; if somebody aboard had a personal receiver—as seemed all too likely now—it might be pinned down, *if* the shadow sent another such message.

There seemed to be nothing further to be done on that for the moment. With Spock, whose only concern over his father's illness seemed to be over its possible adverse effect upon the mission, Kirk paid a visit to Sickbay. Sarek was bedded down there, with McCoy and Nurse Christine Chapel trying to make sense of the strange reports the body function panel was giving them; Amanda hovered in the door, trying to keep out of the way. As for Sarek himself, he looked as though he felt inconvenienced, but no longer in uncontrollable pain.

"How is he, Bones?"

"As far as I can tell, our prime suspect has a malfunction in one of the heart valves. I couldn't make a closer diagnosis on a Vulcan without an exploratory. Mrs. Sarek, has he had any previous attacks of this sort?"

"No," Amanda said.

"Yes," Sarek said almost simultaneously. "There were three others. My physician prescribed benjasidrine for the condition."

"Why didn't you tell me?" Amanda asked.

"There was nothing you could have done. The prognosis was not serious, providing I retired, which, of course, I did."

"When did you have these attacks, Ambassador?" McCoy said.

"Two before my retirement. The third, while I was meditating on the Observation Deck when the Tellarite was murdered. I was quite incapacitated."

"I saw you taking a pill not long before that," Kirk said. "If you'll give one to Dr. McCoy for analysis, it should provide circumstantial evidence in your favor. Were there any witnesses to the Observation Deck attack?"

"None. I do not meditate among witnesses."

"Too bad. Mr. Spock, you're a scientist and you know Vulcan. Is there a standard procedure for this condition?"

"In view of its reactivation by Sarek's undertaking this mission," Spock said, "the logical approach would be a cryogenic open-heart operation."

"Unquestionably," Sarek said.

"For that, the patient will need tremendous amounts of blood," McCoy said. "Christine, check the blood bank and see if we've got enough Vulcan blood and plasma. I strongly suspect that we don't have enough even to begin such an operation."

"There are other Vulcans aboard."

"You will find," Sarek said, "that my blood type is T-negative. It is rare. That my two aides should be lacking this factor is highly unlikely."

"I, of course," Spock said, "also have T-negative blood."

"There are human factors in your blood that would have to be filtered out, Mr. Spock," Christine said. "You just couldn't give enough to compensate for that."

"Not necessarily," Spock said. "There is a drug which speeds up replacement of blood in physiologies like ours . . ."

"I know the one you mean," McCoy said. "But it's still experimental and has worked only on a Rigellian. The two physiologies are similar, but not identical. Even with the Rigellian, it put a tremendous strain on the liver and the spleen, to say nothing of the bone marrow—and I'd have to give it to *both* of you. Plus which, I've never operated on a Vulcan. I've studied Vulcan anatomy, but that's a lot different from having actual surgical experience. If I don't kill Sarek with the operation, the drug probably will; it might kill both of them."

Sarek said, "I consider the safety factor to be low, but acceptable."

"Well, I don't," McCoy said, "and in this Sickbay, what I think is law. I can't sanction it."

"And *I* refuse to permit it," Amanda said. "I won't risk both of you . . ."

"You must understand, Mother," Spock said. "The chances of finding sufficient T-negative blood otherwise are vanishingly small. I would estimate them at . . ."

"Please don't," Amanda said.

"Then you automatically condemn Sarek to death," Spock said evenly. "And Doctor, you have no choice either. You must operate, and you have both the drug and a donor."

"It seems the only answer," Sarek said.

Reluctantly, McCoy nodded. Amanda turned a stricken

face to Kirk, but he could offer her no help; he could not even help himself in this dilemma.

"I don't like it either, Amanda, believe me," he said. "But we must save your husband. You know very well, too, how much I value your son; but if we must risk him too, then we must. Doctor McCoy has agreed—and I learned long ago never to overrule him in such matters. In fact, I have made him the only officer on the *Enterprise* who has the power to give *me* orders. Please try to trust him as I do."

"And as I do also," Spock said, to McCoy's obvious startlement.

"I'll—try," Amanda said.

"You can do no more. Should you need me, I'll be at my station."

With a great deal more distress than he hoped he had shown, Kirk bowed formally and left.

And halfway to the bridge, deep in thought, he was jumped from behind.

A heavy blow to the head with some sort of club staggered him, but he nevertheless managed to throw his assailant from him against the wall. He got a quick impression of a figure taller but slighter than his own, and the flash of a bladed weapon. In the melee that followed, the other man proved himself to be an experienced infighter, and Kirk was already dazed by the first blow. He managed at last to drop his opponent, perhaps permanently—but not before getting the knife in his own back.

He barely made it to an intercom before losing consciousness.

He came to semiconsciousness to the sound of McCoy's voice.

"It's a bad wound—punctured the left lung. A centimeter or so lower and it would have gone through the heart. Thank goodness, he had sense enough not to try to pull the knife out, if he had time to think of it at all."

"The attacker was Thelev. Unconscious, but not seriously injured; just knocked about quite a lot." That was Spock. "He must have caught the Captain by surprise. I'll be in the brig, questioning him, and Shras as well."

"Doctor." This time it was Christine Chapel's voice. "The K-two factor is dropping."

"Spock," McCoy said, "Your father is much worse. There's no longer a choice. I'll have to operate immediately. We can begin as soon as you're prepared."

"No," Spock said.

"What?"

Then came Amanda's voice. "Spock, the little chance your father has depends entirely on you. You volunteered."

"My immediate responsibility is to the ship," Spock said. "Our passengers' safety is, by Starfleet order, of first importance. We are being followed by an alien, possibly hostile ship. I cannot relinquish command under these circumstances."

"You can turn command over to Scott," McCoy said harshly.

"On what grounds, Doctor? Command requirements do not recognize personal privilege. I will be in the brig interrogating the Andorian."

Then the darkness closed down again. When he awoke once more, he felt much better. Opening his eyes, he saw Sarek in the bed beside him, apparently asleep, with McCoy and Christine bending over him.

Kirk tried to rise. The attempt provoked a wave of dizziness and nausea and he promptly lay down again—even before McCoy, who had turned instantly at the motion, had to order him to.

"Let that be a lesson to you," McCoy said. "Just lie there and be happy you're still alive."

"How's Sarek?"

"Not good. If I could only operate . . ."

"What's stopping you? Oh, I remember now. Well, Spock's right, Bones. I can't damn him for his loyalty, or for doing his duty. But I'm not going to let him commit patricide."

He sat up, swinging his feet off the bed. McCoy caught his shoulders, preventing him from rising. "Jim, you can't even stand up. You could start the internal bleeding again."

"Bones, Sarek will die without that operation." McCoy nodded. "And you can't operate without the transfusions from Spock." Again a nod. "I'll convince Spock I'm all right, and order him to report here. Once he's off the bridge, I'll turn command over to Scotty and go to my quarters. Will that fill your prescription?"

"Well, no—but it sounds like the best compromise. Let me give you a hand up."

"Gladly."

McCoy supported him all the way to the bridge, but released him just before the elevator doors snapped open. Spock turned, looking surprised and pleased, but masking it immediately.

"Captain."

Kirk stepped very carefully down to his command chair. He tried to appear as though he were casually surveying the bridge, though in fact he was keeping precarious hold of his balance as spasms of dizziness swept him. McCoy remained glued to his side, but ostentatiously offered him not so much as a hand.

Spock came down into the well of the bridge as Kirk reached his chair and eased himself into it. Kirk smiled and nodded approval.

"I'll take over, Spock. Report to Sickbay with Dr. McCoy."

Spock was studying him closely. Kirk was fighting off the dizziness, at least enough—he hoped—to keep it from showing, but he knew also that he was very pale, about which he could do nothing.

"Captain, are you quite all right?"

"I've certified him physically fit, Mr. Spock," McCoy said testily. "Now, I have an operation to perform. And since both of us are required . . ."

He gestured toward the elevator. Spock hesitated briefly, still studying Kirk, who said kindly, "Get out of here, Spock."

Spock nodded, and left with McCoy, with something very like alacrity.

"Mr. Chekov," Kirk said, "what is the status of the intruder ship?"

"No change, sir. Maintaining its distance."

"Any further transmissions, Lt. Uhura?"

"None, sir."

Kirk nodded, relaxed a little—and found that he had to

pull himself together sharply as the dizziness returned. "Call Mr. Scott to the bridge . . ."

"Captain," Chekov interrupted. "The alien vessel is moving closer!"

"Belay that last order, Lt. Uhura. I'm staying here." But the dizziness kept coming back. He raised a hand to wipe his brow and found that it was shaking.

"Captain," Uhura said. "I'm picking up the alien signal again. But it's coming from inside the *Enterprise*—from the brig."

"Call Security and order an immediate search of the prisoner. Tell them this time to look for implants."

Hours of weakness seemed to pass before the command communicator buzzed. Lt. Josephs' voice said, "Security, Captain. I had to stun the prisoner. He has some sort of transceiver imbedded in one of his antennae, sir; it broke off in my hand. I didn't know they were that delicate."

"They aren't. Thanks, Lieutenant. Neutralize it and send it to Mr. Scott for analysis. Kirk out."

"Captain," Chekov said. "The alien ship has changed course and speed. Moving directly toward us at Warp Eight."

"Lt. Uhura, tell Lt. Josephs to bring the prisoner to the bridge. Mr. Chekov, deflectors on. Red alert. Phasers stand by for fire on my signal."

"Aye, sir." The alarm began to sound. "Shields on. Phasers manned and ready."

"Take over Spock's scanners. Ensign, take the helm."

A blip appeared in the viewscreen and flashed by. It loomed large for an instant, but it was only a blur at this speed. Suddenly the bridge was slammed and rocked. The *Enterprise* had been hit.

"Damage, Mr. Chekov!"

"None, sir; deflected. Target moving away. Turning now. He's coming around again."

"Fire phasers as he passes, Ensign. Steady . . . Fire!" Chekov studied the scanner. "Clean miss, sir."

At the same moment, there was another jolt. "Report on their weaponry."

"Sensors report standard phasers, sir."

Standard phasers. Good. The enemy had more speed, but they weren't giants.

Another wave of weakness passed through him. The *Enterprise* seemed to be standing up so far, but he was none too sure of himself.

"Captain, the intercom is jammed," Uhura said. "All the Ambassadors are asking what's going on."

"Tell them to—tell them to take a good guess, but *clear that board*, Lieutenant!"

The ship shook furiously again.

"Captain," Uhura said, "I've got an override from Dr. McCoy. He says that another shock like that and he may lose both patients."

"Tell him this is probably only the beginning. Mr. Chekov, lock fire control into the computers. Set photon torpedoes two, four and six for widest possible scatter at the three highest intercept probabilities . . ."

The enemy flashed by. The torpedoes bloomed harmlessly on the viewscreen. Another slam. Kirk's head reeled.

"Number four shield has buckled."

"Auxiliary power."

"Sir, Mr. Scott reports auxiliary power is being called upon by Sickbay."

"Divert."

"Switching over—shields firming up. Number four still weak, sir. If they hit us there again, it'll go altogether."

"Set computer to drop to number three and switch auxiliary back to Sickbay if it goes."

"Aye, sir."

Kirk heard the elevator doors open behind him, and then Lt. Josephs and another security guard were hustling Thelev before him, without ceremony. It took Kirk a moment to remember that he had ordered exactly this interruption. He stared harshly at the prisoner.

"Your friends out there are good," he said. "But they'll have to blast this ship to dust to win."

"That was intended from the beginning, Captain," Thelev said. He was, Kirk noted with a certain satisfaction, still rather lumpy from his attempt at killing, an impression heightened by the missing antenna. The small wound there had healed, but it looked more as though it had been a deep cut than the loss of a major organ.

"You're not an Andorian. What did it take to make you over?"

The *Enterprise* rocked again. Chekov said, "Shield four down."

"Damage control procedures, all decks," Kirk said. Then, to Thelev; "That ship out there carries phasers. It's faster than we are, but weapon for weapon, we have it outgunned."

Thelev only smiled. "Have you hit it yet, Captain?"

Another shock, and a heavier one. Chekov said, "Shield three weakening. Shall I redivert auxiliary power, sir?"

This was getting them nowhere; it if continued sheerly as a battle of attrition, the *Enterprise* would lose. And there was the operation to consider.

"Engineering, this is the Captain. Blank out all power on the port side of the ship except for phaser banks. On my signal, cut starboard power. Kirk out." He turned back to Thelev. "Who are you?"

"Find your own answers, Captain. You haven't long to live."

"You're a spy, surgically altered to pass as an Andorian. You were planted in the Ambassador's party to use terror and murder to disrupt us and prepare for this attack."

"Speculation, Captain."

The ship shook again. Chekov said, "Shield three is gone, sir."

"Engineering, blank out starboard power, all decks. Maintain until further orders."

The lights on the bridge went out, except for gleams from the telltales on the panels, and the glow of stars from the viewscreen. In the dimness, Thelev at last looked slightly alarmed. "What are you doing?" he said.

"*You* speculate."

"We're starting to drift, Captain," Chekov said. "Shall I hold her on course?"

"No. Stand by your phasers, Mr. Chekov."

"Aye, sir. Phasers standing by."

A blip of pulsing light again appeared in the screen, slowed down, held steady. Kirk leaned forward intently.

"He's just hovering out there, sir."

"Looking us over," Kirk said. "We're dead—as far as he knows. No starship commander would deliberately expose his ship like this, especially one stuffed with notables—or that's what I hope he thinks."

"Range decreasing. Sublight speed."

"Hold your fire."

"Still closing—range one hundred thousand kilometers—phasers locked on target . . ."

"Fire."

The blip flared brightly on the screen. A jubilant shout went up from Chekov. "Got him!"

"Lt. Uhura, open a hailing frequency. If they wish to surrender . . ."

He was interrupted by a glaring burst of light from the viewscreen. Everyone instinctively ducked; the light was blinding. When Kirk could see the screen again, there was nothing on it but stars.

"They could not surrender, Captain," Thelev said. "The ship had orders to self-destruct."

"Lt. Uhura, relay to Starfleet Command. Tell them we have a prisoner."

"Only temporarily, Captain," Thelev said. "You see, I had self-destruct orders, too. Slow poison—quite painless, actually, but there is no known antidote. I anticipate another ten minutes of life."

Kirk turned to the security guards. "Take him to Sickbay," he said harshly.

Josephs and the guard came down to flank Thelev, and began to shepherd him toward the elevator. As they reached the door, the spy crumpled, sagged, fell to his knees. He said tonelessly, "I seem to—have—miscalculated . . ."

He fell face down and was still. Kirk rose wearily.

"So did they," he said. "Put him in cold storage for an autopsy. Secure for General Quarters. Mr. Chekov, take over."

He went down to the operating room. It was empty, the operating table clear, the instruments mutely inactive.

After a moment, McCoy came in from the Sickbay area. He looked as drawn and tired as Kirk felt.

"Bones?"

"Are you quite through shaking this ship around?" the surgeon asked.

"Sarek—Spock—how are they?"

"I don't mind telling you, you make things difficult for a surgeon conducting a delicate operation which . . ."

"*Bones.*"

The Sickbay doors opened again and Amanda appeared. "Captain, come in," she said. Kirk shoved past McCoy eagerly.

Inside, Sarek and Spock occupied two of the three beds, side by side. Both looked pale and exhausted, but reasonably chipper. Amanda sat down happily beside Sarek.

"That pigheaded Vulcan stamina," McCoy's voice said behind him, "I couldn't have pulled them through without it."

"Some doctors have all the luck."

"Captain," Spock said. "I believe the alien . . ."

"We damaged their ship," Kirk said. "They destroyed it to avoid capture. Bones, Thelev's body is being brought to your lab. I want an autopsy as soon as you feel up to it."

"I believe you'll find he's what's usually called an Orion, Doctor," Spock said. "There are intelligence reports that Orion smugglers have been raiding the Coridian system."

"But what could they gain by an attack on us?" Kirk asked.

"Mutual suspicion," Sarek suggested, "and perhaps interplanetary war."

Kirk nodded. "With Orion carefully neutral. She'd clean up by supplying dilithium to both sides—and continue to raid Coridan."

"It was the power utilization curve that confused me," Spock said. "I did not realize that until I was just going under the anesthetic. The curve made it appear more powerful than a starship—than anything known to us. That ship was constructed for a suicide mission. Since they never intended to return to base, they could utilize one hundred per cent power in their attacks. I cannot understand why I didn't realize that earlier."

Kirk looked at Sarek. "You might have had a few other things on your mind."

"That does not seem likely."

"No," Kirk said wryly. "But thank you anyway."

"And you, Sarek," Amanda said. "Would you also say thank you to your son?"

"I do not understand."

"For saving your life."

"Spock behaved in the only logical manner open to him," Sarek said. "One does not thank logic, Amanda."

Amanda stiffened and exploded. "Logic! Logic! I am sick to death of logic. Do you want to know how I feel about your logic?"

The two Vulcans studied the angry woman as though she were some sort of exhibit. Spock glanced at his father and said, quite conversationally, "Emotional, isn't she?"

"She has always been that way."

"Indeed? Why did you marry her?"

"At the time," Sarek said solemnly, "it seemed the logical thing to do."

Amanda stared at them, stunned. Kirk could not help grinning, and McCoy was grinning, too. Amanda, turning to them in appeal, was startled; and then, obviously, suddenly realized that her leg was being pulled. A smile broke over her face.

Equally suddenly, the room reeled. Kirk grabbed the edge of the table. Instantly, McCoy was beside him, guiding him toward the third bed.

"Bones—really—I'm all right."

"If you keep arguing with your kindly family doctor, you'll spend the next ten days right here. Cooperate and you'll get out in two."

Kirk subsided, but now Spock was sitting up. "If you don't mind, Doctor, I'll report to my own station now."

McCoy pointed firmly at the bed. "You're at your station, Spock."

The First Officer shrugged and settled back. McCoy surveyed his three restive patients with an implacable expression.

"Bones," Kirk said, "I think you're enjoying this."

"Indeed, Captain," Spock agreed. "I've never seen him look so happy."

"Shut up," McCoy commanded. There was a long silence. McCoy's expression gradually changed to one of incredulity.

"Well, what do you know?" he said to Amanda. "I finally got the last word!"

A PRIVATE
LITTLE WAR

Writer: Gene Roddenberry and Don Ingalls (story by
   Jud Crucis)
Director: Marc Daniels
Guest Stars: Nancy Kovak, Michael Witney

McCoy stretched his back muscles, tired from bending over his collection of soil, leaves and roots. Starfleet had something, he thought. This planet's plant culture just might be a medical El Dorado. But he was glad when his communicator beeped. This clearing in the forest was lonely.

Kirk said, "How much longer, Bones?"

"About another thirty minutes, Jim. You and Spock find anything?"

"No sign of inhabitants so far. Continue collecting. Kirk out." As he closed his communicator, Spock pointed to the scuffled stones on the rocky ledge where they stood. "The apelike carnivore of the reports, Captain?"

Kirk inspected the tracks. He straightened, nodding. "The gumato. But this spoor is several days old. No problem. They seldom stay in one place."

Spock eyed the sweep of trees sloping downhill from their ledge. "Aside from that, you say it's a Garden of Eden, sir?"

Kirk grinned. "So it seemed years ago to a brash young Lieutenant named Kirk in command of his first planet survey." He stiffened, hearing a branch break. Then he saw the people below moving along a narrow trail cut through the trees. With a shock of pleasure, he recognized their leader; and was about to shout "Tyree!" when his eye caught the glint of sun on a gun barrel. Guns—on this planet! He seized his phaser and Spock said quietly, "Use of our weapons was expressly forbidden, Captain."

"Tyree is leading those people into ambush! He's the friend I lived with here!" He wheeled; and kicking hard at a rock outcropping, loosed it to send it careening down the slope. The ambushers exploded from their concealing underbrush and Tyree cried, *"Villagers!"*

His group broke, rushing for the trees' shelter. But one of the ambushers, turning, had seen Kirk and Spock. He yelled something to the other two; and all three ambushers burst into a fast run up the hill toward the *Enterprise* men. Then the first paused to place a flintlock musket against his shoulder. The bullet *pinged* past Kirk's ear to strike spray from the rock behind him. The man pulled up to reload—and the second villager fired. Hot metal tore into Spock.

In his clearing McCoy heard the shots. Snatching his communicator, he opened it, crying, *"Enterprise*, alert! Alert! Stand by to beam up landing party!"

Spock was down. Running to him, Kirk took one look at the wound; and grabbing his phaser, aimed it at their pursuers.

"No . . . Captain . . ."

"Spock, they'll be reloaded in a moment!"

On a surge of agonized effort, Spock staggered to his feet. "No, I . . . can travel."

Looking up, Kirk saw McCoy and cried, "Beam us up fast, Bones!" McCoy had his communicator open. "*Now*, Scotty! Spock's hurt! Have medics standing by!"

Kirk, supporting the half-conscious Spock, pulled him into a threesome with McCoy. As they dematerialized, the three villagers were left to stare at the sparkle into which they'd disappeared.

An agitated Scott was at the Transporter platform to meet them. "What happened, Captain?"

"Lead projectile. Old-style firearm. Tell those medics to bring the stretcher closer!"

As the reeling Spock was eased onto it, Nurse Chapel and Doctor M'Benga hurried into the Transporter Room. McCoy, his eyes on Spock's torn chest, said, "Vitalizer B." Christine Chapel swiftly adjusted a hypo and McCoy pressed it, hissing, against Spock's limp arm. It was as she reached into her medikit that Spock subsided into unconsciousness.

M'Benga, his medical scanner humming, passed it over the motionless body.

Christine spoke to McCoy. "Pressure packet ready, Doctor."

He took it; and lifting Spock's shirt, pushed it into the wound. "Lucky his heart's where his liver should be—or he'd be dead now." It wasn't a joke. His face was grim. "Set hypo for coradrenalin."

As the syringe hissed again, Kirk spoke. "Bones, you can save him, can't you?"

Without warning, alarm sirens shrieked. Sinister red lights flashed and Uhura's filtered voiced said, *"All decks, red alert! Battle stations! This is no drill. Battle stations! Red alert!"*

Kirk leaped to the intercom. "Bridge, this is the Captain."

"Lieutenant Uhura, sir. We have a Klingon vessel on our screens."

"On my way!"

He was at the door when he brought up short. Looking back to where McCoy was working over Spock, he said, "Bones . . ."

"I don't know, Jim!"

Choices. Kirk opened the door to a corridor, hideous with the screech of sirens. They were screaming on the bridge, too. Chekov had taken Spock's position at the library computer; and Uhura, motionless at her board, was listening intently. Chekov looked up as Kirk, Scott on his heels, ran from the elevator. "No change of position, sir. They may not have seen us. We're holding the planet between us and the Klingon."

Uhura moved in her chair. "Make that definite. They're sending a routine message to their home base. No mention of us, sir."

"Then reduce to alert one, Lieutenant."

She hit her intercom button. "All stations, go to yellow alert. Repeat, cancel battle stations. Remain on yellow alert."

The sirens stilled. Kirk crossed to the helm, checked it; and turned to look at the viewing screen. All it held was the image of the planet.

"Think you can keep us out of their sight, Scotty?"

Scott moved a control on the helm. "I can try, sir."
He spoke to Chekov. "Lock scanners into astrogation circuits."

"Locking in, sir."

"Message to Starbase, Captain?" Uhura asked.

Kirk shook his head. "No point in giving ourselves
away, Lieutenant. Not until we find out what's going on."

"We can hide for a while, Captain." Scott had turned
from the helm. "But we may have to leave orbit to keep it
up long."

Kirk nodded. He went to his command position to hit
the intercom button on his panel. "Captain to Sickbay."

"McCoy here. I'll call you as soon as I know anything.
I don't now. Sickbay out."

So that was that. As they say, time would tell. Time
alone would tell whether Spock would survive to live another
day—or whether he wouldn't. Kirk struggled against an upsurge of panic. It wouldn't do. Another subject—one to take
the mind off Spock's peril. He turned to Scott.

"That Klingon is breaking the treaty," he said.

"Not necessarily, sir. They've as much right to scientific missions here as we have."

"Research is hardly the Klingon preoccupation."

"True, Captain. But since that's a 'hands off' planet,
you can't prove they're up to anything else."

Kirk frowned. "When I left that planet seventeen years
ago, the villagers down there had barely learned to forge iron
into crude plows. But Spock was shot by a flintlock. How
many centuries between those two developments?"

Uhura answered. "On Earth about twelve centuries,
sir."

"On the other hand," Scott said, "a flintlock would
be the first type firearm the inhabitants would normally develop."

Kirk snapped, "I'm aware of that, Mr. Scott."

Chekov spoke. "And, sir, the fact that Earth took
twelve centuries doesn't mean they have to."

Over at her board Uhura nodded. "We've seen development at different rates on different planets."

"If it were the Klingons behind this, why didn't they

give them breechloaders?'' Scott asked. "Or machine guns? Or early hand lasers or—''

Kirk interrupted, angry. "I made a simple comment. I didn't invite a debate.''

But Scott didn't waver. "Captain, you made a *number* of comments. And you've always insisted that we give you honest reactions. If that's changed, sir . . .''

"It hasn't,'' Kirk said. He swung his chair around. "I'm sorry. I'm worried about Spock. And I'm concerned about something that's happened to what I once knew down there.'' He got up and made for the elevator. "You have the con, Scotty. I'll be waiting in Sickbay.''

He could feel the controlled tension in Sickbay the moment he entered it. McCoy, Doctor M'Benga and Christine were all gathered around Spock's still-unconscious form. The sterilite above it swathed it in its eerie glow. Kirk glanced up at the body-functions panel. Its readings were ominously low. There was, of course, the factor of Spock's different Vulcan physiology. But Christine was looking very troubled. And Spock might have been dead, so lifeless he looked on the table.

M'Benga spoke. "We've no replacements for the damaged organs, Doctor. If he's going to heal, his Vulcan physiology will have to do it for him.''

"Agreed,'' McCoy said. "Sterilite off.'' He moved to his office. Kirk followed him. They eyed each other for a long moment. Then McCoy said, "He may live. He may die. I don't know which.''

Kirk paced the distance to the door and back to McCoy's desk. McCoy gestured to the exam room. "Doctor M'Benga interned in a Vulcan hospital, Jim. Spock couldn't be in better hands.''

"You're sure of that?''

"Yes.''

Kirk hesitated. Then he came to his hard decision. "All right. You and I are transporting back down to the planet, Bones.''

"I can't leave Spock at such a time.''

"You just indicated you could.'' He leaned his hands on McCoy's desk. "There are Klingons down there. If their mission is a legitimate research interest in the planet's organic potential, you're the one man who can tell me.''

"And if that's not it?''

"Then I'll need help.'' He pointed to the exam room. "I'll need advice I can trust as much as I trust Spock's.''

"That's a rare compliment, Jim, but—''

Kirk flared. "Blast it, McCoy, I'm worried about Spock, too! But if the Klingons are breaking the 'hands off' treaty here, there could be an interstellar war at stake!'' He strode to the office intercom. Hitting the button, he said, "Captain to bridge.''

"Scott here, sir.''

"McCoy and I are beaming back down. Inform ship's stores we'll need native costumes.''

"Captain, I may have to break orbit any minute to keep out of their sight. We'd be out of communication range with you.''

Kirk was thinking fast. The secrecy of their presence was vital. Any attempt to contact Starfleet Command could reveal it. Asking permission to violate orders concerning this "hands off'' planet was a risk he dare not take. He'd have to act alone, on his own judgment.

He turned back to the intercom. "I understand, Scotty. We'll set up a rendezvous schedule. Captain out.''

They materialized near a copse of trees. Glancing around, Kirk got his bearings. The copse dipped to a rocky glade he remembered. Tyree's camp was about a quarter of a mile distant.

McCoy, tricorder out, said, "Want to think about this again, Jim? Starfleet's orders are no interference with this planet's state.''

" 'With its normal social development.' I'm not only aware of the orders, Bones. It was my survey seventeen years ago that recommended them.''

McCoy nodded. "I read your report. 'Inhabitants superior in many ways to humans. Left alone, they will undoubtedly someday develop a remarkably advanced and peaceful culture.' ''

"And I intend to see that they get their chance. Are you coming with me, Doctor?''

They moved off down the shale of the glade. The terrain ahead showed bigger rocks and a thick growth of underbrush. McCoy was still troubled; but Kirk, recognizing familiar landmarks, was buoyant. He gestured to some foliage. "The saplings over there, they make good bows. We used to choose our wood from this very spot."

"Almost like coming home, eh?"

"It'll be good to see Tyree again. During that year here, we were made brothers. I lived with his family, wore his Hillpeople clothes. We hunted together. . . ."

McCoy halted abruptly. "All right, Jim. I'll try just once more."

Kirk turned, his eyes questioning. McCoy's met them unflinchingly. "So you love this place. Fine! So you want to see an old friend again. Also fine! You believe the Klingons are here, threatening all that you admire so much."

"Bones, we've been over this—"

"You asked me to replace Spock's advice and judgment! Well, I'm doing the best I can do!" There was a deep, sincere concern in McCoy's face. "Jim, I admire a Starship Captain willing to disobey orders—and risk his career when necessary. But how much of this decision of yours is emotion . . . and how much of it is logic?"

Kirk's mouth moved in a small smile. "Logic! I suppose Spock *would* ask that." He pondered the question. "I *do* have an emotional attachment to this place. That's obvious. However—"

McCoy interrupted again. "Spock might also suggest that for twenty-four hours we reconnoiter—and obey orders, making no contacts. If you decide to move in after that, I'm with you."

Kirk looked at the earnest eyes. "All right, Bones. We stay out of sight for a day. We'll cut through here and—"

He never finished his sentence. There was a hoarse snarl—and a huge, hairy creature, faintly gorillalike, lips crawled back over its wicked teeth, burst out of a clump of brush where it had been hiding. A clawed fist the size of a ham knocked Kirk from his feet. Then it leaped for McCoy in the very act of reaching for his phaser. He was slammed back into rock, the weapon knocked from his hand. He fell, stunned—and the aroused gumato turned on Kirk again. He went down once more, the beast's frothy jaws tearing at the flesh of his shoulder. McCoy, trying frantically to clear his head, stretched an arm toward his phaser. Kirk landed a hard kick in the animal's belly; but the fury of the alien thing clawed him down. McCoy grasped his phaser; and making a swift adjustment on it, shouted, "Jim . . . roll free so I can shoot!"

He fired a stun charge. The gumato staggered. Then it whirled on McCoy, roaring. He got to his knees, loosing the full phaser power. The gumato vanished. But Kirk lay still. McCoy crawled to him, medikit out.

"Contact ship," Kirk whispered. "I took . . . full poison . . . its fangs. . . ."

The hypo hissed against his arm. Then McCoy spoke into his communicator. "Landing party to *Enterprise*, come in! *Enterprise, this is McCoy! Emergency! Come in!*"

Kirk's forehead was already beading with sweat. The poison was in his bloodstream. McCoy had to stoop to hear the weakening voice. "Afraid . . . they've left . . . orbit."

"Jim, there's no antitoxin for this." He used the hypo again. "I can keep you alive for only a few hours with these injections."

"Tyree . . . some of them have . . . cure."

Kirk slumped into unconsciousness. In the lonely silence, McCoy heard a twig snap. Three men, bows and spears at the ready, were standing behind him, suspicion and curiosity equally mingled in their faces.

"Are you Hillpeople? Do you know a hunter named Tyree?" McCoy gestured to Kirk. "A gumato attacked him. He's James Kirk, a friend of Tyree. . . ." He waited for some response. None came. *"Blast it, do something!"* he shouted. *"He's dying!"*

But the Hillpeople still stared at him stolidly.

Later, he was to feel grateful to them. Their settlement was crude, even for a nomadic people—a place of firepits, log shelters and primitive pottery. But the cave into which they carried Kirk's limp body was warm. And the pallet they laid him on was soft with animal skins. He was wet now with sweat and beginning to tremble violently. McCoy turned to the man who had directed them into the cave. "Yutan, more skins—blankets. I must keep him warm."

When the coverings came, McCoy piled them on Kirk. Tyree's woman—she was said to possess a cure for the effects of gumato venom. But both were absent from the camp. Superstition, anyway. And yet . . . there was Starfleet's extraordinary interest in the medical promise of this planet's organic substances. . . .

Kirk was babbling in the first stages of delirium. It would reach its climax. Then coma and death. McCoy looked desperately around the cave. Slowly he got to his feet. Incredibly the boulder opposite him moved when he pushed it. Straining against its weight, he rolled it over beside Kirk. After a moment he went toward another one. "You and your 'Garden of Eden,' " he muttered. "First Spock, now you. Maybe Adam was better off out of Eden."

Tyree and his woman were crouched in the shadow of a rocky overhang, watching a file of villagers pass down a trail, armed with their flintlocks. Though the woman's wild black hair had never known a comb, her thin features held intelligence and a savage beauty. She leaned to Tyree, whispering urgently. "We must obtain the same firesticks, husband! We could take their goods, their horses—kill them!"

"Enough!" he rebuked. "In time the villagers will return to the ways of friendship."

She spotted a small plant beside her. Its root came up to the prize of her sharp-bladed knife. "In time?" she said. "How many of us must continue to die waiting for this 'time' of yours?"

Tyree opened her small leather bag for her. As she dropped the root into it, she said, "I am a *Kahn-ut-tu* woman, Tyree! In all this land there are few of us. Men seek us for mates because through us they can become great leaders!"

He smiled at her. "I took you for mate because you cast a spell upon me, Nona."

She withdrew an odd-shaped leaf from her bag. The look in her brilliant dark eyes was openly inviting. "And I have spells to keep you!" She crushed the leaf until its heady scent had impregnated her fingers. "Remember this fragrance? The night we camped by the water . . . ?"

He pushed her away. "Yes. The night of madness."

She caressed his face with her scented fingers. His eyelids drooped. She leaned closer to him. "Madness? Did you really hate *that* madness, Tyree?"

"No," he pleaded. "Nona, no. It calls up evil beasts from my soul."

"Only one lovely beast, Tyree . . . you, my strong, angry man."

His arms went around her. He was drawing her down to the leaves when Yutan, running, broke through the trees. Nona looked up; and he stopped dead at the look in her eyes.

"For . . . forgive me," he stammered. "But there are strangers in the camp. One has taken a gumato bite. He dies."

Nona was on her feet. "Strangers? Explain."

"It is said that the dying one is a friend of Tyree. From long ago."

Tyree was still fighting the intoxicating effects of the leaf's odor; but Nona, in full command of herself, nodded. "That one!" she exclaimed. "I go. Bring Tyree when his head clears."

Kirk was moaning in the clutch of his delirium. McCoy went to the cave entrance. The curious crowd that had thronged it had disappeared. He pulled his phaser, aimed it at one of the boulders beside Kirk, and fired it. The rock glowed red with heat. With perhaps too much. He bent over the phaser to readjust it—and Nona, a dark ghost, slipped into the cave. She looked from the red rock to the weapon in McCoy's hands, her face alive with fascinated interest. Pulling back into the shadows, she watched the phaser beam strike the other boulder. It, too, went red. Nona turned and left the cave as silently as she'd entered it.

Tyree, Yutan beside him, was running toward it. She extended a hand. "Stop," she said. "Do you want me to save him?"

Her tone halted him. "You must!" he cried. "He is the one I told you of, the friend of my young days!"

She had seen a miracle—a firestick of marvelous power. A *Kahn-ut-tu* woman knew how to take advantage of miraculous opportunities. Wife to a supreme leader of men . . .

"My remedies," she said, "require full knowledge of

the people they cure. I must know all that is known of your friend."

Tyree shook his head. "I gave him the Promise of Silence, Nona. He was made my *brother*!"

"And I am your wife—his sister. I promise silence also. *Quickly*, Tyree. Or he dies!"

Spock had still to recover consciousness. Christine Chapel, frightened, looked away from the low readings on his body-functions panel. Maybe his pulse . . . She took it and her hand slipped down to hold his. Words she didn't know were in her came to her lips. "Mr. Spock, you've hardly ever noticed me . . . and I understand. You can't. But—I'd give my life to save you. . . ."

Sickbay's door opened. She hurriedly replaced Spock's arm on the bed—but M'Benga had seen.

He examined the panel. "Don't let those readings unduly trouble you. I've seen this before in Vulcans. It's their way of concentrating their strength, blood and antibodies on the injured organs." He eyed the pale face on the pillow. "A form of self-induced hypnosis."

"You mean he's actually conscious, Doctor?"

"In a sense. He knows we're here and what we're saying. But he can't take his mind from the tissue he is fighting to heal. I suppose," he added, "that he even knows you were holding his hand."

He left her, eyes averted from the painful flush that flooded her face. She moved to gather up some charts. Then she turned to address the still form on the bed. "Mr. Spock," she said, "a good nurse holds the hands of all patients. It proves to them that one is . . . interested."

The lie made her feel much better.

The boulders were cooling. But it was still very hot in the cave. McCoy brushed sweat from his face and bent to pull back Kirk's eyelid. He shook his head; and was drawing a blanket closer about him when Tyree and Nona walked into the cave.

The man spoke at once. "I am Tyree." He strode to Kirk as one who had the right, passing the dull red rocks without a glance. But McCoy's interest was focused on Nona.

She was emptying the contents of a small leather bag on a flat rock. He moved in to watch her over her shoulder. "And I am Tyree's woman," she told him without turning.

On the rock's flat surface lay a root, wet, covered with small open spores. Nona drew her razor-edged knife, pressed its blade on the root—and it began to writhe. She picked it up on the flat of her knife, speaking briefly. "A Mahko root."

"A plant?" said the wary McCoy. "It moves."

"For one who knows where to find it and how to pick it."

Tyree was kneeling at Kirk's head, his kindly face anxious. When Nona approached them, he pulled back so that she could seat herself next to his friend, the root still moving on the knife blade. When she touched Kirk's throat with her free hand, his mouth opened slightly. She leaned over him gently; and exhaling a long breath of her own between his lips, whispered, "Take this of my soul . . . this of my soul into thy soul . . . into thine. . . ."

McCoy was shocked. He turned to Tyree, crying, "I was told she had a *cure*!"

"Be silent!" he said sternly.

Nona was breathing more of her breath into Kirk's open mouth. She lifted unseeing eyes, chanting more of her strange incantation. "Deeply . . . deeply . . . deeply . . . we must become as one . . . as one . . . as one. . . ."

To McCoy's total amazement, Kirk had begun to breathe evenly in time with the woman's breathing. But the mystic element in the chant horrified him. He had started toward Kirk when Tyree's strong arm barred the way. He saw Nona bare the exact spot on Kirk's shoulder where the gumato fangs had struck, and slap the twisting root on the punctures. Then, turning the knife on her own hand, she slashed it deeply and pressed it, bleeding, on top of the ugly root. She groaned with pain. Kirk echoed the groan as though he, too, felt the agony of the slash. She shut her eyes. Swaying, she chanted, "Together . . . your pain in mine . . . together . . . your soul in mine . . . together . . . together . . . together. . . ."

Both of them were now inhaling in perfect unison. And to both, in unison, came easier breath, relaxation. Nona's eyes fluttered open. "Return . . . it is past . . . return . . . return . . . return. . . ."

And Kirk's eyes, too, fluttered open. Against the animal skins of his pallet, his face was at peace.

Nona remained close to him for a long moment. Then very slowly she withdrew her hand from his shoulder. She extended it, palm up, to McCoy. It held no sign of knife wound, only the small, withered thing that had been the writhing root. She got to her feet, making way for McCoy. But he didn't need to examine Kirk's shoulder. He knew what he'd find—and he found it. The flesh was healthy, unmarked.

Kirk smiled up at him. "I've been having . . . a strange dream."

"How do you feel, Jim?"

"I'm tired—just tired. You've done a fine job, Bones."

He was already asleep. McCoy looked up to see Tyree supporting Nona.

"Thank you for saving him. I'd like to learn more of this. . . ."

"She must sleep now," Tyree said.

"Is there any condition I should watch for in him? Any aftereffect or danger?"

Nona spoke weakly. "Our blood has passed . . . through the Mahko root together . . . our souls have been together. He is mine now."

Startled, McCoy spoke to Tyree. "What does she mean, 'he's hers'?"

"When a man and a woman are joined in this manner, he can refuse her no wish." He smiled faintly. "But only a legend. There is no danger."

Tyree was leading her from the cave when she passed close to McCoy. Though her eyes were heavy with exhaustion, there was a look on her face that troubled McCoy. It suggested that she knew she had won some obscure victory. When he noted the same half-smile of satisfaction on Kirk's sleeping features, McCoy's sense of apprehension become definite.

It grew so insistent it aroused him from his deep sleep of weariness. The cave was black with night. His first conscious thought was of Kirk. He reached for his medikit and groped his way past the rocks to the pallet. It was empty.

He stood still for a moment, fully awake now. The layout of the camp was still unfamiliar to him. He moved to the cave entrance, trying to get his bearings in the darkness. To his left there was the darker shadow of a structure of some kind. It turned out to be a lean-to. The still-glowing embers of its firepit showed two sleepers. A dim form was standing over one of them.

"Jim?" McCoy whispered.

One of the sleepers awoke, rolling instantly into a crouch. It was Tyree. He stared at McCoy. Then, bounding to his feet, he turned and saw Kirk, eyes closed like a sleep-walker's, beside the sleeping body of his wife.

"Jim!" McCoy shook Kirk's arm. The eyes opened to fill with surprise. "Quite . . . all right, Bones. I felt better and thought I'd stretch my legs." He recognized Tyree; his face alight with pleasure, cried, *"Tyree! It is you, my old friend!"* His hand went out to grip the man's shoulder in genuine affection.

Nona had awakened. Tyree gave her a quick glance. There was a pause before he said, "Yes, James. It is good to see you."

"But what am I doing here? How did . . . ? No, I remember now. A gumato bite. I was ill. . . ." He gestured to McCoy. "I told the Doctor here, 'take me to Tyree's camp.' I knew you'd find a *Kahn-ut-tu* to cure me." He turned to McCoy. "The *Kahn-ut-tus* are a kind of local witch people . . . actually healers who have studied the herbs and roots here."

"And I am a *Kahn-ut-tu* woman, Captain." Nona smiled at Kirk. "I cured you."

Their eyes met; and Tyree said, "My woman. Nona."

In the light of the firepit's embers, the wild, disheveled black hair enhanced the savage beauty of her face. "Yes, of course," Kirk said. "Your woman."

McCoy spoke. "Tyree leads the Hillpeople here."

Kirk smiled at his friend. "Congratulations—on both counts."

"You need rest, Jim."

"Rest? I've never felt more alive!" Kirk's face sobered. "Tyree, can we talk now? The villagers' new weapons. I want to hear all about that. We have plans to make."

Nona broke in. "Good. It is past time to plan."

Tyree nodded. "Yes, much has happened since you left. Come, we will speak of it—"

"And of things to be done!" said Nona.

Tyree looked at her. Then silently, he led the way out of the lean-to.

Spock lay as pale, as motionless as ever.

Doctor M'Benga, entering Sickbay, nodded to Christine; and going to Spock, leaned close to a pointed ear. He spoke very slowly and distinctly. "This is Doctor M'Benga, Mr. Spock. There'll be someone with you constantly from now on. When the time comes, I'll be called." He straightened. "Nurse, stay with him."

Christine had her eyes on the body-functions panel. "The readings are beginning to fluctuate markedly, Doctor."

"So they should be," M'Benga said. "The moment he shows any sign of consciousness, call me immediately."

"Yes, Doctor."

He was making for the door when he turned. "After you have called me, if he speaks, do whatever he says."

"Whatever he says?"

"Yes, that's clear enough, isn't it?"

It was clear. It was also disconcerting. She looked at the pointed ears on the pillow. They suddenly struck her as extremely aristocratic.

Tyree was making good on his promise to bring Kirk up to date on the firearms question. "It's less than a year ago that their firesticks first came to the villagers. Since that time, my friend, almost one in three of us have died."

Kirk leaned forward over the rude table. "But you say they make the firesticks themselves? You can't be certain of that."

"We've looked into their village and saw it being done."

"Tyree," McCoy said, "have you seen strangers among the villagers?"

Tyree shook his head, "Never."

Behind them, unseen, Nona had slipped into the hut to immerse herself in the shadows of a corner. She watched McCoy turn to Kirk. "Meanwhile," he said, "you have made contact here. If it turns out that we are the ones who broke the 'hands off' treaty, it's your career, Jim.''

"Perhaps, Bones. But it would hardly take a platoon of Klingons to teach them to make crude firearms.''

"A single one would be too slow and inefficient if they really want this planet.''

"But much more *clever*," Kirk said. "If they'd armed them with Klingon lasers or even repeating rifles, it would be obvious they'd interfered here." He spoke to Tyree. "Can you get us to their main village while it's still dark?''

Tyree hesitated. "The gumatos travel at night also. If you killed one, its mate will not leave.''

Kirk laid his phaser on the table. "You've seen these work. So long as no one else sees them used—''

Nona stepped forward into the light of their pitch torch. "I also have seen them used.''

Kirk swiftly replaced his phaser. Nona had turned to McCoy. "I saw you heat those stones with yours." Her eyes sought Kirk's. "And I know you have many ways to make Tyree a man of great importance.''

McCoy eyed her. "Many ways?" He spoke to Tyree. "What else does she know about us?''

"Tyree has told me much of you." She smiled at Kirk. "Do not blame him. It was the price for saving your life.''

McCoy slammed the table. "Demonstrating the wisdom of Starfleet orders!" he cried. "First, there's contact made . . . then a mistake, an accident. It has to be set right by a small intervention with natural evolution. The correction goes wrong—and more intervention is necessary. . . .''

Kirk had reddened with anger. "*Thank you*, Doctor!" He spoke to Nona. "We are simply strangers from—''

"From one of the lights in the sky!" She nodded. "I know. And you have ways as far above firesticks as the sky is above our world!''

Tyree half-rose to his feet. "You will not speak of that to others!''

She ignored him to address Kirk. "I will not if I am made to understand. Teach me." She paused. "There's an old custom among my people. When a woman saves a man's life, he is grateful.''

McCoy, eyes narrowed, watched Kirk. He waited—and Kirk said, "I am grateful."

"Highly commendable," McCoy said dryly. "If not carried to extremes."

But Kirk was waving Nona to a seat. It was clear that he was making a conscious effort to choose words cautiously. "We were once as you are, Nona. Spears and arrows. Then came the time when our weapons grew faster than our wisdom. We almost killed ourselves. So we made a rule. It said that we must never cause the same thing to happen to other worlds we visited. Do you understand?"

She didn't answer. Kirk laid a hand on Tyree's arm. "As a man must grow in his own way and in his own time, so must worlds. They—"

She interrupted. "Some men never grow."

"Perhaps not as fast or in the way another thinks he should. But we are now wise enough to know how unwise it is to interfere with the way of another man or another world."

"You will let the villagers destroy us? You will not help your friend and brother to kill them instead?"

Tyree sprang to his feet. "I have said I will not kill, woman! There are better ways!"

Her eyes flashed dark fire. "We must fight or die! Is dying better?" She whirled to Kirk. "You would let him die when you have weapons to make him powerful and safe? Then he has the wrong friends—and I have the wrong man!" She rushed from the hut.

Tyree made no move to follow her. After an awkward pause, he said, "You will help in ways she does not understand. I have faith in our friendship, friend. Come—or we lose the darkness."

As he left, McCoy saw the pained look on Kirk's face. "What's bothering you? If we find the Klingons have armed the villagers, we can certainly do something about that."

Kirk rose. "That's what bothers me—the 'something' we may have to do."

They found Tyree waiting at the camp's edge. Despite the night, he was unhesitating as he led them along the trail winding downward to the village. The trees thinned—and he lifted a warning finger. A guard, flintlock at shoulder, was pacing his rounds on the village outskirts. The three came to a halt behind the bole of a massive tree.

"We'll wait for the guard to circle back." Kirk leaned back against the tree. "You have quite a wife, Tyree. Beautiful *and* intelligent."

Tyree gave him a quick look; and seeing the sincerity in his face, nodded. "A *Kahn-ut-tu* woman is always a prize. They have . . . ways of making a man happy."

"I remember the stories about them."

"But mine talks too much of killing."

"An ambitious woman is a treasure," McCoy said. "Or a time bomb."

Kirk spoke slowly. "Tyree, suppose . . . you *had* to fight? Suppose it were the only way?"

"Jim! This man believes the very thing we believe—killing is useless and stupid! What kind of question is that?"

Again Kirk was abruptly aware of loneliness—the loneliness of the immense responsibility he had chosen to undertake. Well, he'd taken it. For better or worse, it had to be borne now. He was in this thing up to his neck. He straightened. The guard was returning. He slid away from the tree bole to slip through the night, weaving his way from shadow to shadow. When the guard was within a foot of him, he downed him with a karate chop. Then, seizing the gun, he passed it to Tyree, saying, "Keep this. Wait for us."

The village's buildings were more sophisticated than the simple constructions of Tyree's camp. Some were lighted. Kirk and McCoy, keeping to shadows, saw a man approaching one of the larger ones. What they could glimpse of his thinly bearded face seemed to be that of some scholarly ascetic; but in the light of the opening door, it showed up crafty, even malignant. Circling the house, they found a window; and huddled under it, watched him cross a room to a map-covered table. Sitting at it, a new flintlock beside him, was another man, his back turned to them. But Kirk didn't have to see the cruel, lipless Klingon face. He had recognized the tailored metallic Klingon dress. And a Klingon weapon hung at its belt.

"You are late, Apella," the Klingon said.

"A quarrel to be judged. The division of some skins

and a woman taken this morning. It is hard to divide one woman, Krell.''

"Give her to the man who killed the most Hillpeople. Then the others will see the profit in bravery.'' He passed the musket to Apella. ''Your next improvement. Notice what we've done to the striker. See how it holds the priming powder more securely? Fewer misfires.'' Pushing his chair back, Krell got to his feet. ''When I return, we'll give you other improvements. A rifled barrel—a means to shoot farther and straighter.''

"They must have a workshop," Kirk whispered. ''Let's go. . . .''

It was McCoy who spotted the shed. It was a ramshackle affair, set back from the street, but the black bulk heaped beside it was interesting. ''Coal,'' McCoy said, ''necessary for a forge. And those bags, they reek of sulphur, an ingredient of gunpowder. Thus, logically, my dear Captain, their workshop.''

"Thank you, Mr. Spock," Kirk's face suddenly sobered. ''Sorry. I know you're worrying about him, too.''

"About that walking computer? Yes, I am."

The lock on the shed's door was as dilapidated as the building. Embers had been left to flicker in the still-open forge. Scattered around it were wooden gunstocks, bullet molds, iron rods to be bored into weapon barrels. McCoy's tricorder hummed over the ingots; but Kirk had moved to a barrel-boring device. He tested its point with a piece of iron. To his surprise it clicked sharply. He unscrewed it. ''People's exhibit number one,'' he said. ''A chrome-steel drill point.''

McCoy looked up. ''This pig iron is almost carbon-free. No village furnace produced this.'' His tricorder passed over a barrel rod. ''People's exhibit number two. Cold rolled barrel rods, fashioned to *look* handmade.'' He turned. ''My apologies, Jim. You were right about the Klingons.''

"Make recorder and scanner tapes on everything."

"Pity we can't include a Klingon. That would about wrap it—'' He stopped. Footsteps and voices were nearing the shed door. They scrambled for concealment behind a dusty pile of cinders.

Krell entered, followed by Apella. He hung the village lantern he carried high on a hook. Behind the protective cinders, Kirk motioned to McCoy. Understanding, McCoy unlimbered his tricorder; and as Apella broke into speech, recorded the words. "I thought my people would grow tired of killing. But you were right, Krell. They see it is easier than trading. And it has pleasures. I feel them myself. Like the hunt, but with richer rewards."

The Klingon had lifted a rifle from the work bench. "You'll be rich beyond your dreams one day, Apella. A governor in our Klingon Empire. Unimaginable delights—" He paused, hearing the tiny hum of McCoy's scanner. He turned to look around him—and Kirk grabbed at a wooden gunstock. He flung it hard at the lantern. Sparks showered as its light went out. In the dimness Kirk leaped at Krell but the Klingon pivoted, catching Kirk on the shoulder with the rifle. McCoy, rushing forward, used the "exhibit" barrel to drop Apella and whirled to help Kirk. But Krell had tripped over an iron rod. His rifle went off—and he shouted, "Guards! Intruders! The work shed, intrud—"

Kirk's fist got him straight on the chin. He fell—but already the Enterprise men could hear running footsteps, yells, alarm shots. They made for the door. An armed villager, gun aimed, stood in it. Kirk, diving for his legs, tumbled him over the sill. Behind him Apella was up again; and again McCoy smashed down with the "exhibit" gunbarrel. They raced for the open door. Then they veered, making for the shadow behind the heaped coal. Armed villagers, converging on the shed, pelted past them. They waited. Then they broke from their shelter and fled. When the first bullet whined past them, they had rejoined Tyree.

Spock was no longer motionless. He had begun to writhe, his face distorted—and the body-functions panel's readings fluctuated madly. When a groan burst from his laboring chest, Christine Chapel rushed to the wall intercom.

"Doctor M'Benga to Sickbay."

"Nurse . . . nurse . . ."

She flew to the bed. Spock's eyes were open, glaring wildly as he tried to control his twisting body. Twice he struggled again to speak and failed. The third time, his trembling lips succeeded in forming words. "Quickly . . . strike me. Pain will . . . help me . . . to consciousness. Strike me!"

Christine shrank back. "Hit you? No,—"

"Strike me!" He was gasping for air. "Unless . . . I return to . . . normal consciousness quickly . . . it will be. . . . too late. . . ."

She hit him.

"Harder . . ."

She slapped him harder. His breathing improved and his voice more certain. "Again! Then again. Pain . . . helps me back . . . to consciousness."

She struck him once more. As she hauled off for the fourth time, Sickbay's door snapped open. Scott stood in it, jaw dropped as she landed the blow on the bedridden Spock. He leaped across the room, grabbing her arm. *"What are you doing woman?"*

M'Benga came through the open door. He strode to the bed, pushing Scott and Christine aside. Then he struck Spock with all his strength. He struck him again and again. The flabbergasted Scott was staring in horror. It was clear that the entire medical staff had gone out of its mind.

But Spock was sitting up. "Thank you, Doctor. That will be sufficient."

M'Benga spoke to Scott. "You can release her, Mr. Scott. She was only doing what she should have done." He gestured to the body-functions panel, whose needles were steadying into positions normal for Spock.

"A Vulcan form of self-healing, Engineer," Spock said.

He now astounded all but M'Benga by swinging his legs to the floor. As he made to stand, Christine moved an instinctive hand toward his arm. He congealed her with one of his arched-brow looks. "I am quite recovered, Nurse," he told her coolly.

She took the cool line herself. "Yes, I see you are, Mr. Spock."

The Doctor who had interned in a Vulcan ward herded everyone out of Sickbay. As the door snapped shut behind the three, Spock began knee bends.

Tyree was not an enthusiastic student of armaments. He listened courteously while Kirk explained the eccentricities of the flintlock taken from the guard the night before; but it was clear that connections between strikers, sparks and the

ignitions of gunpowder failed to arouse the martial spirit in
him. Kirk placed the gun against his shoulder. "Now aim it
as I showed you," he said.

McCoy, emerging from the cave, frowned at what he
saw. The gun fired obediently; but the bullet, kicking up dust
near the skin target, ricochetted away.

Tyree dropped the gun. Kirk gave him a friendly pat
on the shoulder. "Very good," he said. But he had seen
McCoy's look. "Not here, Bones. We'll talk in the cave."

Tight-lipped and angry, McCoy followed him into the
cave. Kirk had the look of a man who has considered all
alternatives, arrived at an unpleasant decision and intends to
back it up.

They hunkered down on the cave floor and McCoy burst
out. "Do I have to say it? It's not bad enough there's already
a serpent in this Eden of yours teaching some of these people
about gunpowder. You're going to make sure they *all* know
about it!"

Kirk's voice was quiet. "Exactly. Both sides must receive the same knowledge, the same type of firearms . . ."

"*Have you gone out of your mind?* Yes, maybe that's
it. Tyree's wife. There was something in that root she used.
She said that now you could refuse her nothing."

"Nonsense! Believe me, Bones, I've *agonized* over this,
thought it through most carefully."

"Is it a coincidence that this is exactly what she wants?
I wonder . . ."

"She wants *superior* weapons. And that's the very thing
neither side can have. Bones, listen. The normal development
of this planet was status quo between the villagers and the
Hillpeople. The Klingons changed that with the flintlocks. If
this planet is to continue to develop as it should, we must
equalize the two sides again—and *keep* them equal."

McCoy stared at Kirk in unbelief. "Jim—that con-
demns this whole planet to a war that may never end. You'll
breed battle after battle, massacre after massacre. . . . "

Kirk slammed his fist on the ground. "*All right, Doctor!* I've heard . . ." He got up as though movement might
somehow move him out of this ugliness. It didn't. But he'd
got himself under control. He turned back. "Let's say I'm

wrong. Even say the woman drugged me. So let's hear your sober, sensible solution to all this."

"We could collect all the firearms. Unfortunately, we can't collect the knowledge they've been given."

"No."

"Suppose we gave Tyree some weapon of overpowering force, something that would quickly frighten the villagers away." McCoy hesitated. "Trouble is, we've no guarantee what power of that kind might do even to Tyree."

Kirk waited. Finally he said, "Remember the twentieth century—the brush wars on the Asian continent? Two giant powers involved, much like the Klingons and ourselves. Neither felt they could pull out. . . ."

"I remember. It went on bloody year after bloody year."

"What would you have suggested, Bones? That one side arm *its* friends with an overpowering weapon? Mankind would never have lived to travel space if that had been done!" Kirk got up to pace the length of the cave. "We can't take this planet back to where it was! The only solution is what happened then—a balance of power. If it can be kept in balance long enough . . ."

"But if the Klingons give the villagers more power, what then, Jim?"

"We give this side exactly that much more. The trickiest, most difficult, dirtiest game of them all—but the only one that preserves both sides. In whatever this planet is to become, each side has its evolutionary value."

McCoy's face had grown deeply thoughtful. "Jim, all this time . . . with Tyree blindly trusting you—and you beginning to understand what you'd have to do . . ."

Kirk nodded. "Agony, Doctor. I've never had a more difficult decision."

McCoy looked at him, himself experiencing Kirk's torment. "There's another morsel of agony for you. As Tyree won't fight, he'll be one of the first to die."

"He'd be a wise leader," Kirk said. He stopped his pacing. "His wife's the only way to reach him. If I tell her we'll supply guns, she may persuade him. I must have a talk with her."

* * *

She was bathing in a forest pool. Cooled and refreshed, she finally stepped out of it, her wet inner garment clinging to her body. There was a flat rock near the pool and she sank down on it, zestfully savoring the sun's warmth as it began to dry her streaming black hair. After a moment she reached for her small leather pouch. Selecting a small herb from it, she crushed it between her hands, applying its scent to her neck, face and shoulders. She wore the concentrated look of a woman preparing herself for a man.

When she heard Kirk's voice call her name, she smiled to herself, unsurprised. Discarding the herb, she gave her attention to arranging her slim body advantageously.

At the sight of her in her thin wet clothing, Kirk hesitated. She beckoned to him. "Stay," she said. "You are here because I wished you here."

He smiled, correcting her. "I'm afraid this was *my* idea."

"Yes, they always believe they come of free will. Tyree thought the same when I cast my first spell on him." She touched the stone beside her invitingly. "Be comfortable, Kirk. Sit down. I will not hurt you."

After another moment of hesitation, he obeyed. She leaned toward him. "Can you smell the fragrance on me? Some find it pleasing."

He took a fast sniff at her shoulder. "Yes, very nice," he said. "But what I want . . . want to talk of . . ." The polite smile on his lips faded. His head was spinning. Nona edged closer to him. He tried to draw back but his befuddled senses were stronger than his will.

"Smell the scent again," she said. "You will find it soothing."

"Yes, but I came to . . . to talk about . . . about. . . ."

From where he had been following Kirk, Tyree heard the voices. He carried the flintlock whose mechanism still puzzled him. Now he forgot the question he had planned to ask. Face set, he checked the amount of powder in the pan. Then he moved on in the direction of the voices.

Nona had drawn Kirk close to the herb perfume on her neck. Kirk pulled away. Fighting vertigo, he got shakily to his feet, inhaling deep gulps of fresh air. "Forgive me . . . I . . . seem . . . unable to think. . . ."

She sat very still, smiling and waiting. Kirk's eyes locked with hers. And suddenly he was smiling back, aware only of a lovely woman who seemed to desire him.

"How beautiful!" he said. "How lovely you are, Nona!"

Tyree raised the gun. For a moment he focused its sights on Nona. Then he swung them slowly to Kirk. Nona, in Kirk's embrace, caught the gleam of sun on the barrel. She made no move though Kirk's back was Tyree's clear target. There came the sound of the weapon's crash on a rock. Relief mixed with contempt in her face. Tyree could never be important. A man of faint heart. She lifted her arms to Kirk's neck.

"Yes, lovely . . . incredibly lovely," Kirk was saying foggily.

Tyree was running from the scene of his betrayal. As he skirted a rock, a monstrous shadow rose from behind it. The dead gumato's female mate, it had begun its swift and noiseless stalk of the Hillman when it was distracted by the sound of Kirk's maunderings. It swerved. Nona saw it over Kirk's shoulder. She tried to pull free but he held her tight. Fists clenched, she struck at him savagely, jerked clear of his arms and sped into a run. Then the sudden thought of Kirk's dazed helplessness halted her. Her quick stop brought a snarl from the beast. She screamed, racing for the pool. But the apelike thing cut her off at the water's edge. She shrieked again; and Kirk, slowly emerging from his confusion, fumbled for his phaser. Realization hit him. Rushing to the pool, he saw Nona prone, the great animal towering over her. He fired his phaser. The gumato vanished. Extending a hand, he helped Nona to her feet.

The assistance exhausted his strength. His drugged state had left him so weakened that he slumped to the ground, eyes closed, breathing hard. Nona looked down at him. Then she picked up a rock. She clubbed him over the head with it. The phaser dropped from his hand. She lifted it, examining it in wonder. Then she turned and made for the forest.

Stumbling, broken, Tyree was making his way to his lean-to when McCoy and Yutan intercepted him.

"Where's Captain Kirk?" McCoy demanded.

Tyree waved blindly behind him and Yutan cried, "Tyree! The firestick! Where is it?"

"I left it . . . back there."

"A fine thing to leave lying around! Show us!" McCoy shook Tyree's arm.

It roused him. "I show you," he said.

Pieces of the broken rifle lay on the ground. Yutan picked up the barrel. Tyree covered his face with his hands. "No! I don't want to see it!"

McCoy was about to speak when Kirk staggered toward them. Still groggy from the blow, he swayed. Then he crumpled back to the ground. McCoy, taking a quick check of his pulse, broke out the hypo from his medikit.

Meanwhile, Nona had arrived at a decision. At first sight of an armed village patrol, she had hidden herself behind a thick-leaved bush. As it approached, she made up her mind. She stepped from her concealment, confronting the leader of the four-man group. She lifted Kirk's phaser full into his view.

"I bring victory to Apella!" she said. "He will have the courage to use this new weapon! Take me to him!"

The man grinned. "Tyree's woman! A *Kahn-ut-tu* female also. Do we entrust this division to Apella?"

The patrolmen guffawed. The leader grabbed her, the others pressing around them. She yanked free. Then she aimed the phaser at the leader. "Touch me again—and this small box will kill you!"

The man hesitated. But the villager behind her gave her a slight push. She wheeled to level the weapon at him. He was not impressed. All of them were grinning broadly now. They closed in about her, clutching at her, at her clothing. Ignorant of how to use the phaser, she tried to shove them away. "Fools!" she cried. "I bring you a weapon far greater than your firesticks!" Laughing, one of the men pushed her at another one. She struck out, screaming. They began to toy with her. Their laughter had acquired a dangerous edge. One of them tried to kiss her. She shrieked again.

Kirk heard her. He reached for his phaser. "Nona! She's taken my phaser! She's in trouble! Come on. . . ."

There was another scream. Her thin garment was ripped

now. Passed roughly from jeering man to jeering man, she beat at their faces with the phaser, screaming wildly.

Kirk, McCoy and the two Hillmen raced down a hill toward her. The patrol leader, looking up, saw them. "Men," he yelled, "it's a trap! The woman tricked us!" His sharp knife gleamed. He struck.

"Nona!" Tyree shouted.

The leader lifted his flintlock, aimed and fired. McCoy fell.

Kirk, Tyree and Yutan charged the patrol. The fight was hand to hand, bloody and brief. The two surviving villagers fled. McCoy, holding his wounded arm, stumbled down to the scene of the melee. Tyree was stooped over the dead body of his wife. In the dirt, trampled but undamaged, lay the phaser. Kirk picked it up.

"She gave it to them," McCoy said. "But they didn't recognize it."

Kirk looked at the wounded arm. "You, too," he said.

"Yes, me too! You and your blasted Paradise planet!"

Tyree had straightened. He reached for an abandoned flintlock. Then he removed the powder and bullet pouch from a patrolman's dead body. He turned to Kirk, his grim face working with grief and fury. He extended the gun toward Kirk.

"I want more of these! Many more!"

"You'll have them," Kirk said.

Tyree spoke to Yutan. "Two of those who killed my wife escaped. We shall track them down and kill them. Come! I must speak to our people."

They set off at a run. There was a moment's silence before McCoy said, "Well, you've got what you wanted."

"Not what I wanted, Bones. What had to be."

Amazingly, his communicator, so long silent, beeped. He flipped it open. "Kirk here."

"Spock, Captain. I trust all has gone well."

"Spock!" McCoy shouted. "Are you alive?"

"A ridiculous question, Doctor. Clearly you are hearing my voice."

McCoy shook his head. "I don't know why I was worried. You can't kill a computer."

Kirk motioned him to silence. "Spock, ask Scotty how long it will take to reproduce a hundred flintlocks."

Scott's voice spoke. "I didna get that precisely, sir. A hundred what?"

"A hundred . . . serpents, Scotty. Serpents for the Garden of Eden." He paused. "We're very tired, Mr. Spock. Beam us up back home."

THE GAMESTERS OF TRISKELION

Writer: Margaret Armen
Director: Gene Nelson
Guest stars: Joseph Ruskin, Angelique Pettyjohn

Gamma II was a planet so small it scarcely merited the name. Reportedly uninhabited, it nevertheless boasted automatic communications and astrogation installations. Making a routine check of these stations was Kirk's motive for ordering Uhura and Chekov to beam down with him to the surface.

At Chekov's announcement that the *Enterprise* was now circling Gamma II in standard orbit, Kirk nodded.

"Very good, Mr. Chekov. Lieutenant Uhura?"

"Ready, sir."

"Then let's go." And turning to Spock, added, "Commander, you mind the store."

"Yes, Captain."

His Science Officer, moving swiftly to the vacated command chair, watched them enter the bridge elevator. From here on, he thought, it would be the old story—the Transporter room, the "Energize" command and then the sparkled glitter of their dematerialization.

But for once it was a new story. Though Kirk, Uhura and Chekov took their places on the platform, and despite Scott's push at his second switch, they did not shimmer out in the orthodox Transporter effect. One moment they were where they should be, and the next, they were simply and bafflingly gone.

The startled Scott jerked back his first switch. Then more alarmed than he cared to admit to himself, he gave himself to a frantic spinning of dials. If he'd hoped for their reappearance on the platform, there was none. Yet more alarmed, he hit his bridge communicator to say into it, "Scott to bridge."

"Spock here, Mr. Scott."

"Mr. Spock—the Captain, Lieutenant Uhura and Mr. Chekov—they did not dematerialize. They just disappeared. They took their positions on the platform—and then they simply went. Where, sir?"

"I presume you mean in a manner inconsistent with the usual workings of the Transporter."

Under the pressure of his anxiety, Scott's blood pressure rose. "Of course I mean that! Do you think I'd call you if they had just beamed down?"

The tranquil voice said, "Have you reversed your controls, Mr. Scott?"

"I've made all the proper checks. There was nothing— nothing. No light flashes . . . no outlinings of shimmer-out. Nothing. They're just gone, sir, and I can't bring them back."

"Power surges?"

"Not from here, sir. The dials are right, and the Transporter functioned perfectly."

"Recheck your equipment, Mr. Scott. I'll scan for them on the planet's surface."

Meanwhile, on that surface of Gamma II, the materialization of the *Enterprise* trio was as out of order as their departure from the Starship. Instead of duplicating the erect positions they had assumed on the Transporter platform, they fell flat on their faces until, in an uncontrollable roll, they were brought up against the foot of a jagged rock formation towering steep to a red and greenish sky. Kirk was the first to regain his feet. Dizzy, shaking his head against the vertigo, he half-realized that they had landed in a most peculiar place—a paved area marked by random lines that delineated triangles, rectangles, hexagons, rhomboids—a hodgepodge of every conceivable geometrical design.

Chekov, stirring, struggled up, staring around him. No rhetorician, he said, "What happened, sir?"

"Must have been a Transporter malfunction."

"A rough trip, Captain."

Going to the still prone Uhura, Kirk pulled her to her feet. Puzzledly.

"This isn't Gamma II," he told them. "Look at the color of that sky."

Clutching his arm for support, Uhura said, "This is the craziest landing pad I've ever seen."

She spoke truth. It *was* a mad landing pad: an area about the size of a tennis court but otherwise bearing no resemblance to one. There was no coherent pattern whatever to the conglomeration of demented geometry around them. Helter-skelter to no obvious point, it proliferated itself meaninglessly. However, a closer scrutiny of it suggested that they were standing in what could only have been a playing board created by lunatics for some equally lunatic game.

Kirk, careful to shade his eyes, stared up again at the sinister sky.

"That's a trinary sun up there," he said.

"Then you're right, sir, and we're not on Gamma II," Chekov said. "And if we're not, where are we?"

Kirk managed a wry grin. "I'd like to know that answer too, Mr. Chekov." And unbelted his communicator, flipped it open to say, "Kirk to *Enterprise*."

But intuition had already warned him that the Starship would fail to respond. Nor would the communicators of the others function.

"Dead, sir," Chekov said unnecessarily.

He was rebelting his device when Uhura, pointing to the cliff base, whispered an urgent, "Captain!"

Following the line of her outstretched forefinger, Kirk said, "No, this is not Gamma II. That's an uninhabited planetoid. This one clearly is. We appear to have company, friends."

Close under the shadow of the escarpment, four creatures were standing, observant and intrigued by the strangers' appearance, but their postures hostile, alert. Outstanding in physique was a huge blond male, a Viking who might have been resurrected from some Norse saga's Valhalla. Beside him, squat but thickly muscled as an ape, was Neanderthal Man himself, his low brow shock-haired almost to the nose. And next to him was a female whom some unknown deity had endowed with a bush of yellowish, black-spotted hair, leopardlike. Two fangs protruding from her upper teeth hung over her lower lip. The fangs were pointed.

But the fourth being was the true astonishment—a gorgeous Amazon of a bronze-haired girl, the sapphire of her dark-lashed eyes flashing with the general hostility. But like the rest of her companions, she wore a metallic collar around her lovely neck, inset with some glittering gem under the ear.

Both women carried daggers in the clumsy belts that confined their smockish coarse garments at the waist. Moreover, they had additional weapons, the males equipped with staves ending in blades at one end and grapples at the other.

Wordlessly, the alien group moved forward until they had spaced themselves evenly around the triangle enclosing Kirk, Chekov and Uhura.

The giant Viking finally spoke.

"I am Lars," he said. "He is Kloog. She of the beast's hair is Tamoon. The other she is Shahna."

Fierce suspicion deepened the deep voice. Where usually Kirk would have met such an introduction with one of his own, he decided that this was no time for an exchange of courtesies. So, instead, he said quietly, "Phasers at stun." And added, "Just in case."

The case arose.

Lars, jaw set, stepped forward and, extending a formidable arm, attempted to wrench Chekov's phaser from him. Kirk promptly fired his. Nothing . . . nothing. And when he ordered phaser action from Chekov and Uhura, the nothing was repeated. Swiftly, the *Enterprise* Captain made an adjustment on his weapon and once more tried to activate it. It was as dead as the communicators. Then hurling the useless phaser at the still oncoming blond giant, he ducked sideways to get to the rear of his adversary. Behind him, he was aware that the other three aliens had already subdued Chekov and Uhura, and, with an heroic effort, controlled his ingrained sense of responsibility for them to leap on Lar's heavy-muscled back. He managed a neck chop. It stunned Lars. The giant didn't drop, but he stumbled, reeling, dazed, too shocked for instant reaction.

Seizing advantage of the temporary respite, Kirk added several other telling blows to the vulnerable join of neck to backbone. The last one doubled up the redoubtable Siegfried. And straightening in satisfaction, Kirk turned to his less fortunate shipmates.

It was the beautiful Shahna who had downed Uhura with Tamoon's assistance. But now she left the leopard-haired creature to guard Uhura in order to concentrate her own belligerent and very dangerous attention on Kirk.

His moment of self-satisfaction had been expensive. Too slowly he realized that Shahna was hurtling toward him, and, jumping back, was barely able to dodge the vicious slash of her spear. But the cliff wall blocked all further retreat. Shahna snatched the dagger from the belt that held her shoulder harness in place and, flying at him, pushed its point painfully against the skin of his throat. He looked away from the sapphire eyes so full of triumphant hate, saying to himself, "Okay. Maybe this is it."

To their rear, Tamoon and Kloog had jerked his two companions erect, and Lars rose slowly to his feet, still groggy from the neck chops. As to Kirk, he was now half-crouched against the cliff's rock face, immobilized lest the infuriated Shahna drive the dagger through to his backbone. He gasped, choking, and to his relieved but immense surprise, the pressure eased slightly. Instantly, he came out of his crouch, and at the same moment, a new figure abruptly appeared in the center triangle.

"Hold!" it cried.

At once Shahna lowered her dagger. Ignoring her, the stranger spoke directly to Kirk. "Excellent, Captain Kirk!"

There'd been no excellence about it—just an instinctive use of Space Academy training. But there was no time for reminiscence on the stiff courses through which the Academy put its cadets, for the masterful newcomer was leaving the triangle for a closer approach to the *Enterprise* people. Was it his dress which conveyed the impression of undisputed authority? Perhaps. For he wore no smock but a togalike garment, its shoulder bearing a gold-embroidered emblem; nor did he carry any weapons. Yet the unarmed stranger also wore a gemmed, metallic collar under his expressionless features, a face Kirk judged to be in its middle thirties.

He spoke again.

"Although we expected strength and competitive spirit, Captain Kirk, we are greatly pleased."

Kirk was silent, too angry to trust himself to speak. Kloog was dragging a squirming Chekov toward them, followed by Lars who clutched a struggling, kicking Uhura over his big shoulder. Thrust into positions near Kirk, their two captors divested them of phasers, tricorders and communicators.

Kirk spoke to his people. "Either of you hurt?"

The shaken Uhura shook her head. "I—I don't think so, sir." But the wildly furious Chekov yelled, "No, nobody's hurt—*yet*, Captain!"

"Admirable, Chekov," observed the black-robed man. "Admirable! You also, Uhura. I can see you will all prove invaluable here."

Once more Chekov yelled. "Who is he, sir?"

"I am Galt," he was told. "I am the Master Thrall of the planet Triskelion. I have been sent to welcome you."

A highly undesirable welcome. Even as Galt was speaking, Kirk felt unseen hands at his neck as they fitted one of the jeweled collars around it. He pushed at them, but they were intangible; nor would any exertion budge the lock. He accepted the inevitable, trying to relax until he saw that the same invisible fingers had attached the collar to a chain they affixed to the rock wall. To his right, and visibly, Shahna, Lars and Tamoon were busy shackling his crewmates to chained collars.

"Now," Galt said, "you are prepared for your training."

For the first time Kirk addressed him. "How do you know our names?"

"The Providers were expecting you, Captain. They arranged your . . . transfer here."

So it had not been a Transporter malfunction that had sent them tumbling onto the wrong planet. Their arrival was the consequence of interference, an interference as powerful as it was inexplicable.

He waited a moment before he said, "These Providers of yours. Are they—?"

Galt's interruption was sharp. "Correction, Captain! The Providers are not *ours*. We are *theirs*."

A slave state.

"And what do the Providers want with us?"

"You are to be trained, of course. What other use is there for Thralls?"

"Thralls? I think there's been a mistake. We're officers of a United Space Ship bound on Federation business."

"There's been no mistake. Your old titles mean nothing here. You are Thralls now. And to be taken to the training enclosure. Come, places have already been prepared for you."

"We will do nothing until we get a satisfactory explanation of this outrage. Who are you? What is this place? And what do you think you're going to do with us?"

"I have told you. This place is the planet Triskelion. You will be trained and spend the rest of your lives here. Don't trouble yourself with thoughts of escape. It is impossible. No Thrall leaves Triskelion. Lars, unchain them from the rock."

As the heavy links were removed, Galt added, "Now you are able to accompany me to your quarters." He hesitated. Then, persuasively, he said, "Captain, no harm is intended you."

Kirk looked at the four subservient Thralls as they marshaled Chekov and Uhura before them. Then, shrugging, he followed their Master's lead.

McCoy, on the *Enterprise* bridge, had joined Spock at his scanner, noting that an Ensign Jana Haines had been assigned to the absent Chekov's console, another junior officer at Uhura's position. Scott, emerging from the elevator, stalked over to the two at the scanner.

"Mr. Spock, I've checked the Transporter from one end to the other. Every circuit is perfect. Whatever that power surge was, it didn't come from the Transporter or any other system on this ship!"

"I'm beginning to believe that, Mr. Scott. I have conducted two sweeps of the planet's surface. There is no sign of life."

McCoy reddened. "Well, what the devil's happened then? Does that mean that their atoms are still floating around out there?"

"No, Doctor. Even that would show up on the sensors."

"Then where are they?" Scott shouted.

Mild as ever, Spock said, "The only answers are negative, Mr. Scott. No magnetic storms, no ionic interference and, as you say, no breakdown in your equipment.''

It was McCoy's turn to shout. ''A negative attitude isn't much good to us, Spock! We just can't leave them out there—'' He broke off to add a desperate ''—wherever they are.''

''We shall continue sensor scans, Doctor. At the moment, that is all we can do except hope for a rational explanation.''

''Hope!'' McCoy jeered. ''I thought that was a strictly human failing. Vulcans don't indulge it!''

''Prolonged exposure to the failing results in a certain amount of contamination, Doctor.'' And turning away, Spock resumed operation of his scanner.

A corridor giving on to a row of box stalls was the destination of the *Enterprise* captives. Box stalls, their doors centrally cut, the upper half barred, the lower one locked. Herded down the corridor, they were halted before three stalls, staring in unbelief at the nameplates fastened to the doors. They read: *Kirk, Chekov, Uhura.*

Kirk had been up against such assured, though alien, intelligence on his mission ''to go where no man had gone before.'' For a long moment, he was astounded by this Triskelion variety. Then, once again, he shrugged. Now there could be no answer to the arrogant certainty of the beings Galt called ''The Providers.'' But tomorrow was another day. And Spock on the *Enterprise* would be overworking his own not inconsiderable intelligence to apply his equally efficient equipment to discovery of the answer.

Beside him, Galt said, ''These are your quarters. Open, Shahna.''

Obediently, she removed a small disk from her harness, placing it on the three locks of the cells. While she was working on the third, Kirk shot Chekov a quick, significant look to which his navigator nodded.

The three doors open, Galt said, ''Enter.''

Kirk and Chekov took two apparently compliant steps only to whirl, whirl and lunge at their nearest jailer. Kirk struck Kloog in the midriff with all the power of his powerful shoulders, knocking Neanderthal Man to his knees. Then, in his command voice, he shouted, ''Lieutenant Uhura!''

She gathered herself, and, shoving Tamoon who was flanking her, sent the fanged one spinning against Lars. Then running to Kirk, he, she and Chekov raced down the corridor to the still open entrance.

Lacking eyes in the back of their heads, they couldn't see Galt close his, his face deeply concentrated. But they could feel the results. Suddenly, the jewels in their slave collars went into a sickening, greenish glow. The race ended as the collars tightened, their faces contorted in agony as the anguished choking continued, driving them to their knees, hands futilely clutching at the strangling collars. They sank down, unaware that Galt was watching them with clinical detachment. Unaware of anything but pain, they failed to see that Galt had once more shut his cold eyes in concentration.

As Kirk collapsed on his back, the veins of his neck protruding, the jewel on his collar winked out. But it had done its work. Eons seemed to pass before his tortured throat could swallow and breath returned to his lungs. Then yet more eons crept by before he could get to his knees and, using his weakened arms, thrust himself up to his feet. Chekov and Uhura, watching him, used his method to recover theirs.

"That was foolish, Captain," said Galt. "I warned you that escape is impossible. The collars of obedience have proved that to you."

He nodded toward Kirk's cell. Kirk, hesitating, recognized the futility of defiance and entered it. As his friends followed his example, the cell doors were slammed shut.

It was bad news from Spock. Straightening from his scanner, he said, "They are not within the confines of this solar system, Doctor."

"It's been nearly an hour. Can people live that long as disassembled atoms in a Transporter beam?"

"I've never heard of a study being done. But it would be a fascinating research."

"*Fascinating!* Those are our friends out there! If they're still alive, that is."

"Precisely."

"The odds aren't good, Spock."

"No. I should say they are—"

"Don't quote odds. And don't give me anymore of your dispassionate logic. Just find them. Keep looking."

"I would welcome a suggestion—even an emotional one—as to where to look."

"The first time you've ever asked me for anything, and it has to be an occasion like this!"

Chekov, supporting himself against the bars of his cell, spoke to Kirk in the next one. "Captain, the *Enterprise*—They'll be trying to find us, won't they?"

Uhura, her voice hopeless, answered him. "They'll be trying. But where do they look? We're here and we don't know where it is."

"This system's star is a trinary," Kirk said. "And that limits it a bit. However, we're a long way from the *Enterprise*—if we're even in the same dimension."

Before the others could reply, Lars came down the corridor to stop before Uhura's door. "I am your Drill Thrall," he announced. "You may call me Lars."

As he spoke, Kirk saw him insert a rod into the catching hole in her cage.

"What do you want with her?" he said.

"That is not your concern. Your Drill Thrall will attend you presently." Then through the opened door, he pushed a covered receptacle at her. "Here is nourishment. Consume it quickly. The time is limited."

Uhura, at the look in his eyes, drew back. "What—what do you want?"

He was eyeing her brunette beauty with increasing appreciation. "I have been selected for you."

Then walking into her sparsely furnished cubicle, he closed its door. But though the uneasy Uhura backed away from him, he maintained his confident, slow approach to her, a suggestive grin exposing his strong, white teeth. When he reached out a huge hand to caress her neck, she kicked him, but he seized the leg and, pushing her down to the cell floor, muttered, "Stop it. I told you you are mine."

She bit his lip.

At the sounds from her stall, Kirk and Chekov peered anxiously through their bars, Kirk calling, "Uhura! Uhura, can you hear me?'' But the noise of struggle went on. *"Lieutenant Uhura! Answer me!"*

The only answer was the sound of a blow. Alarmed, frustrated, Kirk shouted again, his face pressed against his bars. Then his own cell door opened to Shahna outside it, unarmed now and carrying another covered container of food.

Kirk grabbed it, threw it to the floor, glaring at the girl.

"What's happening to Lieutenant Uhura?" he yelled.

She made no reply, and in the silence came a final resounding crash from Uhura's stall. Desperate, Kirk called again. "Uhura! Are you all right?"

Lars provided the reassurance. Backing out of the stall and wiping blood from his bitten lip, he staggered as he protested plaintively, "It is not allowed to refuse selection. It is not allowed."

He moved away down the corridor, confused by such unexpected resistence; and Uhura, breathless, disheveled, spoke from her cell door.

"Yes, sir," she said. "I'm fine. He's big—but he's stupid."

Chekov, embarrassed by his concern for her, whispered, "Lieutenant, what happened?"

Uhura's hearing was as keen as her physical fitness. Shooting him an irritated look, she said, *"Nothing!* You're stupid too!"

Half-smiling, Kirk turned to see Shahna stooping, her russet hair a tumble of curls on her lovely head, busily restoring the scattered dishes of his food container to their places in it. Then setting it on a cubed stand, she said, "Come. It is the Nourishment Interval."

On the *Enterprise* bridge, Ensign Haines had left Chekov's position for Spock's computer console. She studied it intently before straightening to address Spock in the command chair.

"Sir, I get a fluctuating energy reading from this hydrogen cloud."

With Scott and McCoy, he went to her to replace her at the scanner.

"It's faint, sir," she said, "but it consistently reads in excess of predictable energy levels."

Spock adjusted several dials before he spoke. "There seems to be an ionization trail. Most interesting." And rapidly punched another computer key.

"What would account for that?" McCoy asked.

"The very question I have just fed into the computer, Doctor." And after a moment, added, "The answer is, nothing is known to us to account for it."

Scott rose to the defense of his Transporter. "It lacks both the power and the range to be responsible for it."

"Plot a follow course, Ensign Haines," Spock ordered.

"Aye, sir." And returning to her navigation console, swung switches before she said, "Course plotted, Mr. Spock. 310 Mark 241."

"Now lay in the course, Ensign Haines."

McCoy's voice rose in anger. "You're going to leave here without them and go off on some wild-goose chase halfway across the galaxy just because you found a discrepancy in a hydrogen cloud? Spock, where's your head? They've been gone for more than two hours!"

Spock, eyes on his scanner, said, "I am pursuing the Captain, Lieutenant Uhura and Ensign Chekov, Doctor, not an aquatic fowl. This is the only lead we have had."

"Course laid in, Mr. Spock," Ensign Haines reported.

"Initiate," he told her. "Warp Factor Two."

All eyes, including his, swerved to the main viewing screen.

Chekov was having his troubles too. He had backed nervously toward a bench in his stall as the fanged Tamoon opened its door, carrying his covered container of food. For to his horror, he had read covetous admiration in the slanting yellow eyes of the leopard-haired woman.

Stammering, he managed to ask, "You—you have been selected for me?"

She uttered a sad little whine. "No. I am only your Drill Thrall. I have brought you nourishment." And placing the container on the bench near him, made an obvious attempt to sound seductive. "It is a nice name—Chee-koo."

"Chekov," he said.

Though the fangs prohibited clear enunciation, she tried, speaking slowly and carefully. "Chee-koof." And beaming happily at him, said, "It is a *very* nice name—so nice you may call me Tamoon."

Chekov ran a cold hand down his face. "Pleased—pleased to know you . . . uh . . . miss."

"You are a fine specimen. I like you better than the others."

Chekov had amply demonstrated his courage in confrontation with galactic foes, but the clumsy coquetry of this alien female terrified him. When she said, "I will instruct you well so my Provider will take you," he backed still farther away. "That's very nice of you, miss, but—"

He had reached the bench. It hit the back of his knees so that he sat down on it abruptly only to be followed by Tamoon who dropped down beside him, the fanged mouth opened in a coy smile.

"If my Provider is pleased, we may even be selected for each other."

A slight groan escaped him, and Tamoon, her hoarse voice sympathetic, said, "You are hungry, Chee-koof." And uncovering his dishes, added, "Eat, Chee-koof."

"Chekov," he said. "No, thank you, I am not hungry."

But Kirk was. As he wolfed the contents of his metal bowls, Shahna watched him approvingly. Finishing, he gave a satisfied sigh.

"Didn't realize I was so hungry. Whatever you call that, it was good."

"It is nourishment," she said. "We call it that." And gathering up the emptied bowls, replaced them neatly in their container, Kirk studying her contemplatively, very much aware of her slim beauty.

"Nourishment," he repeated. "Very practical. And what do you call this collar?"

The sapphire eyes stared at him. "It is the sign of our Provider. By the color of the jewels, it can be known who holds us. When you are vended, you will also have a colored jewel."

"Vended? You mean sold? Bought?"

Puzzled, she said, "When you are developed. The Provider who offers the most quatloos puts his color on us."

Kirk nodded. "My race has another name for that—the word 'slavery.'"

Clearly the information meant nothing to her. As she covered the food container, he said, "The collar of obedience. Is Galt the only one who can operate it?"

"It is only to warn and punish."

"How does he make it work?"

She stared again. "It is not permitted to talk of that."

He pointed to the container she held. "Are you—will you bring me all my nourishment?"

"Of course. I am your Drill Thrall. I will train you well."

"I'm sure of that." And rising from his bench, he said, "I must say I've never seen a top sergeant who looked like you."

"I don't understand. What does that mean?"

Leaning back against the wall, he said, "It means that you're a very beautiful woman."

She rose from her stoop, shaking her head in bewilderment. "What is beautiful?"

"Hasn't anyone ever told you that before?"

"No. What is it?"

"It's hard to explain . . . a lot of things . . . it's—" Then lifting the shining metal cover from the container in her hands, he got up, and holding it close to her face, said, "Look into this. What you see is beautiful."

But her mirrored reflection seemed to merely increase her bafflement; and as her discomfort was genuine, Kirk, changing the subject, asked, "Where were you born, Shahna?"

"Born? I have been here always."

"Where are your parents? Your father and mother. Where are they?"

"She who bore me was killed in a free-style match."

"Free style!"

"Do not be anxious. You will learn all these things."

"And the others, Lars and the one who is Chekov's Drill Thrall, they weren't born here. Where did they come from?"

"It is not permitted—" and breaking off at the sudden shrill of a bell, immediately recovered her self-possession, all business again. "The exercise interval," she told him. And turning to a small cabinetlike projection in a corner, pressed a button on its door. A well-disguised panel slid aside; reaching past it, she removed a harness from it similar to the one she wore.

"This is your training harness. Put it on."

Spock, with Ensign Haines beside him, was working on his scanners, but the eyes of the other bridge people were fixed on the main viewing screen, their faces taut with anxiety.

McCoy moved impatiently. "This is ridiculous! There's nothing out there—nothing at all!"

Scott nodded his agreement. "We're certainly heading into an empty sector."

Spock looked up. "Projecting back along the path of ionization, the nearest system is M24 Alpha."

"But that must be two dozen light years from here!" Scott cried.

"Eleven point six three zero, Mr. Scott."

"Spock, are you suggesting that they have been transported over a distance of—?" And sputtering in angry protest, said, "You're out of your Vulcan mind, Spock!"

"I am suggesting nothing, Doctor. I am following the only logical course available to us."

McCoy was not calmed but began to stride nervously around the bridge stations.

"This is the staff," Shahna said. "It can defend or attack."

It looked as though it could, its one end sharpened to a cutting edge, the other one hooked. Like Chekov and Uhura, Kirk said nothing, aware, however, that Lars and Tamoon were standing nearby on one of the gaming board shapes.

"I demonstrate," Shahna announced. "Lars."

As Lars moved toward her, holding a staff of his own, she spoke to the three strangers. "I shall attack. An attacker may use only the dark areas of the board, the defender only the light areas.''

Positioned on the gaming board, the two instructors went through a brief show of quarterstaff technique, of expert lunging and pike work. Then Shahna said, ''We stop now. Your Drill Thralls will begin your training.''

''Hold!''

It was Galt's cold voice. By a means none of the *Enterprise* officers could detect, the Master Thrall had suddenly popped into the central triangle, another Thrall, hands manacled, beside him.

Galt was pleased to explain. ''This one was slow to obey a command. For his punishment, he will be target Thrall.'' And ignoring the shock on the trainees' faces, said, ''You will charge from here, striking the target Thrall as you pass. Uhura, begin.''

Staring at her victim in horror, Uhura dazedly accepted the staff Lars handed her. Then full realization flooding her, she cried, ''No! No! No!''

Galt's face was glacial. ''It is not allowed to refuse a training exercise. Begin!''

''I don't care whether it's allowed or not! I won't do it!'' And, in a fury, Uhura threw down her staff.

Very quietly, Kirk said, ''None of us will do it, Galt.''

Sparkle came into Galt's eyes—a glitter that reminded Kirk of the shine of snow under sun. ''It is part of your training. The Providers wish it.''

''The devil with the Providers!'' Kirk shouted, hearing Chekov beside him mutter, ''Cossacks!''

There was a pregnant pause before Galt closed his eyes—and the gems on their slave collars began to glow. The agony forced them to their knees. Then the glow faded as Galt opened his eyes. And once more there was the struggle to recover their feet.

''We have been tolerant because you are newcomers,'' Galt said. ''But I see you must be taught a lesson.'' He clapped his hands sharply, and two other Thralls quickly strode from the sidelines, released their manacled fellow, and all three moving away as Galt called, ''Kloog!''

The hunched ape-man appeared, armed with a wide,

hooked net, a dagger and a short whip. Crossing to the triangle, he faced Galt, waiting expectantly.

The *Enterprise* officers exchanged appalled glances, but
the oblivious Galt merely said, "Kloog will administer correction. Uhura, take your place on that rectangle. Lars, tie
her!"

She gave Kirk a frightened look and was starting forward when he swiftly interposed himself in front of her.

"*I* am responsible for the actions of my people! I demand to see the Providers!"

"That is not permitted."

Controlling the hot rage surging in him, Kirk said, "I
know your Providers possess great power, but I assure you
that it doesn't match the power of the entire Federation. There
is a Starship searching for us now. If we're killed, you will
invite the vengeance, not of one Starship, but a fleet of them."

"The Providers know of your Starfleet, Captain. And
since you assume responsibility for your people, you will take
the punishment." Galt smiled slightly. "If I may say so, you
are rash, Captain. However, this punishment will be less
painful than the collar. Turn around."

For a moment, Kirk hesitated. Then he obeyed, and
Galt, still smiling, snapped manacles on him.

"You, Captain, will be target Thrall."

Well, he'd asked for it, so now he had it. Moving slowly
but alertly onto the board, he paused a few feet from Kloog,
half-crouched, watching the creature warily.

Galt spoke. "It's a shame to lose you, Captain. But it's
worth it as an example to the others."

It was an example of insane brutality. Kloog, expert
with the hooked net, lunged suddenly at the hand-bound Kirk
who dodged the mesh just in time to avoid snare in it; but
before he could recover himself, Kloog slashed him across
the chest with his whip. Kirk, staggering backward, didn't
hear Uhura's gasp of horror nor did he see Lars push back
the onrushing Chekov with his spear. Fighting, he knew, for
his life, he was totally concentrated on eluding the perilous
net.

It lifted for another downsweep, and again Kirk ducked
from under it, one of its hooks ripping his arm. Once more,
whirling and crouching, the pattern of the unequal contest

continued, Kirk circling, dodging as Kloog, bearing in on him, gave him not a moment's respite. He was sweating now, his legs shaking with exhaustion when Galt called, "Hold!"

Head sagging, Kirk heard him add, "Rest interval. Fifteen trisecs."

Kloog lowered his weapons, dropping down cross-legged on the floor while Kirk, staggering to a nearby bench, collapsed on it. Vaguely, he was aware that Shahna had appeared beside him and had placed a slim-necked flagon to his lips.

"This will strengthen you. Drink it."

He swallowed ravenously, some of the liquid spilling down his cut chest. Gradually, as his breathing became normal, he said, "Thanks. He's pretty fast with that whip."

"It is the net you must watch. Once you are caught in it, he will use the dagger—to finish."

He nodded; and Shahna, giving a swift glance in Galt's direction, quickly whispered, "Kloog's left eye is weak. Approach him from that side."

Startled by this unexpected concern, Kirk watched her run back to her place on the sidelines; but there was no time for reflection on its meaning, for Galt had called, "Resume places!"

However, the watchful dodging and ducking had become more confident now. As Kloog, his net and whip retrieved, turned slowly to face him, Kirk darted abruptly to the right, reversed and angled in on his opponent's left. Kloog lashed out with the whip, connecting viciously with Kirk's cheek; but he, catching the thong with a foot, jerked it from him. The net rose high for the throw. Ready for it, Kirk flung himself to the floor and, rolling, sprang up to butt Kloog in the midriff with his head. Then, swiftly, he twisted away from the net, and kicking at Kloog with both feet, felled him.

A new voice, loud and shrill, cried, "Hold!"

All the Triskelions, Galt and the Thralls, knelt, their heads bowed humbly in the direction of a blank rear wall.

"We hold, Provider One," Galt said obsequiously.

Kirk joined Chekov and Uhura, the three trying to locate the owner of the voice when it spoke again. "Provider one bids three hundred quatloos for the newcomers."

A deeper voice cried, "Provider Two bids three hundred and fifty quatloos!"

Then another one chimed in, all the disembodied voices sounding from the various walls. "Provider Three, four hundred!"

Once more the *Enterprise* officers glanced vainly around to detect some other source for the mysterious voices, the walls alone confronting them.

"Provider Two bids one thousand quatloos!"

"Provider Three says one thousand and fifty quatloos!"

It was the turn of Provider One again. "Two thousand!"

Immediately the bidding quieted. And Galt, bowing deferentially, said, "Two thousand quatloos are bid. Is there another challenge?"

The walls remained silent; and after a pause, Galt made his announcement. "The newcomers have been vended to Provider One."

Kirk spoke sharply. "We are free people. We belong to no one!"

Provider Two was pleased to approve the statement. "Such spirit! I wager fifteen quatloos that he is untrainable!"

If Kirk was spirited, so was the competitiveness of the invisible Providers. "Twenty quatloos that all three are untrainable!"

"Wagers accepted," shrilled Provider One.

Whereupon bedlam burst out from the walls, the voices overwhelming each other in their excitement to register bets on their new Thralls' trainability. The sums of offered quatloos mounted wildly until the clamor was finally stilled by the shout, "Provider Three wagers five thousand quatloos that the newcomers will have to be destroyed!"

The high, effeminate voice of Provider One shrieked, "Accepted! Mark them, Galt!"

The gems on their collars went orange.

"You now bear the mark of a fine herd," Galt said. "But I must warn you. Now that you are full-fledged Thralls, any further disobedience will be punishable by death."

The bridge's unpromising viewing screen had raised Scott's anxiety to such a pitch that he couldn't contain it.

Marching purposely over to Spock, he said, "Mr. Spock, listen to me! It just doesn't make sense they could have come this far! If there's any chance at all, it's to continue to search the area where they were lost!"

Self-possessed, inscrutable, Spock said, "We searched that area, Mr. Scott."

"It's always possible to miss something!"

"Such as a failure in the Transporter mechanism?"

"No, sir. There's no sign of any failure."

"And there was no sign of them in the area of Gamma II."

McCoy broke in. "And if they weren't there, it's just ridiculous to believe they could still be alive—not after all this time!"

"In that case, Doctor, we have nothing to lose in pursuing our present course."

Quarterstaff practice had begun on the gaming board, Lars attacking, Uhura defending. As they moved away to a rhomboid, Chekov, holding a spear, was clumsily warding off Tamoon's attack.

"You must be fast, Chee-koof. Again, parry, parry. Thrust."

Anger flared in him. He swung the staff around, aiming its bladed end at a metal disk on her shoulder. It punctured the thing, and Tamoon drew back, delighted.

"That is good," she told him. "Soon you will be ready for the games. Why does that not please you, Chee-koof?"

"Chekov. The only thing that would please me is to return to the ship. How did they get us here? Where is their power, Tamoon?"

"It is not permitted to discuss." She hesitated. "Tell me of this ship. What is there so pleasing? Your Provider? Does he care for you better?"

"I have no Provider. Earth people take care of themselves."

She stared at him. "Care for themselves? But that is not safe! Many things can happen! You must never return there, Chee-koof. It is not safe at all!"

Meanwhile, Shahna, laboring under the belief that

Kirk's legs required exercise, had been leading him at a brisk trot through a field; and they were still trotting as they emerged from a clump of trees, side by side.

Slightly breathless, Kirk said, "We've covered over two miles. Isn't that enough? How about a breather?" And at her blank look, interpreted. "A rest."

"Oh . . . very well—if you are tired."

Kirk dropped down on the stone pediment of a ruined building; and after a pause, Shahna joined him.

Inhaling deeply, he said, "It was good to get away from that training area—even for a little while. Why do they like it, the Providers? Why do they want to watch others hurt, killed?"

The dark lashes lowered over the sapphire eyes. "It is the way."

"The voices sounded mechanical. Are they computers?"

The lashes lifted. "Computers?"

He answered his own question with another one, saying to himself, "But why, why would computers keep slaves? Shahna, have you ever seen them? Do they have bodies?"

"Not such as ours."

He looked off at the rubble of ruins at the edge of the trees. "What is that place, Shahna?"

"It is not used."

"Doesn't it have a name? It's very old. Probably built by humanoid people. Shahna, could this once have been a city of the Providers?"

Her voice shook. "I do not think it is well to ask such things."

"They have bodies," he said, "like ours . . . or they had."

She spoke firmly, almost angrily. "One does not talk of such things!"

"I see." And regretting the discomfort he'd caused her, changed the subject. "Pretty country. Looks very much like Earth."

As all he got was another blank look, he explained. "My home planet—where I was born."

"Planet?"

Well, he thought, I can instruct too. "Have you never looked at the night sky, Shahna? The lights up there?"

"Oh, those," she said. "I *have* looked at them."

"They're stars. And around them are planets—places . . . many of them like this—with people just like us living on them."

She was staring again. "How can one live on a flicker of light?"

He smiled at her. "From Earth, Triskelion's two suns seem only a flicker of light." Then sobering, he said, "Actually, this is the darkest planet I've ever seen."

"Dark? Why, all is lighted! Here . . . the chambers . . ."

"Dark," he insisted. "Thralls have no freedom, Shahna. You can't think or do anything but what your Providers tell you."

"What else would one do?"

She *was* beautiful, and her ignorance added a quality of pathos to the beauty.

"Love, for one thing," he said.

"What is love?"

He was tempted to kiss her, but refraining, said, "On Earth, it's more important than anything else, especially between a man and a woman."

Comprehension flooded her face. "Oh, we, too, have mates. When it is time to increase the herd, my Provider will select one for me."

"On Earth, we select our own mates. Somebody we care for, love. Men and women spend their lives together— sharing things . . . making each other happy."

Flushing, she whispered, "I do not think your words are allowed."

"All right. But tell me about the Providers. Where do they live? What do they look like?"

"I have never seen them, but they are said not to be like us. They stay in—"

Suddenly, the light on her collar went into glow. Shahna gasped. Kirk leaped to his feet, and looking up at him, she just managed to whisper, "I—I have . . . spoken . . . of the . . . forbidden. I must . . . be—"

She was choking with her agony. Going to her, Kirk

stood beside her in his own agony of indecision, unable to help but only to watch her slip off the pediment and sink to the ground, writhing, strangling.

He glared around him. "Stop! *I* did it! *I* made her talk!" Then his voice rose to a scream. "Stop it, I tell you! You're killing her!"

But the jewel on the collar only glowed brighter. Shahna's face darkened with the uprush of blood, her mouth opening, her clawing hands falling away from the collar. Kirk whirled to the cliff above the gaming area, shaking his clenched fist at it. *"Stop it!"* he shouted again. "She did nothing wrong! It was my fault. If you want to punish someone, punish me! Please, please . . ."

He was half-aware of a strange rustling sound like electronic laughter. Then the light on Shahna's collar winked out. As he fell on his knees beside her, a voice spoke, the high, semi-soprano voice of Provider One.

"Is that what you humans call compassion? It is interesting, but it has no value here. You present many interesting aspects, Captain. But you must learn obedience. Then you will be an excellent Thrall."

Shahna had relaxed, her lungs sucking in great gulps of air. Released from her near-fatal agony, she began to sob. Kirk took her gently into his arms.

"I know," he said. "It's all right. You're safe now here in my arms—perfectly safe. Stop crying."

She leaned her head on his shoulder, the sobs quieting. Then looking up at him wonderingly, she said, "You risked bringing their anger on yourself. Why—why did you do it?"

He held her closer. "It's the custom for Earth people to help each other when they're in trouble."

He'd known it was coming, and it came—the moment of magic between them when the mysterious shuttle moves between a man and a woman, weaving, interweaving them together in the nameless bond.

He turned her face to his and kissed her.

She drew back, startled. Then while the sapphire eyes searched his, she lifted a finger and touched his lips with it softly. "And that—was that also helping?"

Smiling, he kissed the finger. "I suppose you could call it that."

Her eyes were shining. "Please . . . help me once again."

This time the kiss grew deep, complete, and her arms lifted to go slowly around his neck. As he brushed his cheek against one, she withdrew them.

"I—I did not know it could be like this between people. Is it always so in the place you come from?"

He said, "It always should be like this for you, Shahna."

The rustle of high laughter echoed again, and Galt was abruptly with them. Silently, Kirk released the girl.

"Captain, you do indeed present many surprises. Because you have amused the Providers, there will be no punishment. Return to your quarters."

Kirk spoke softly to Shahna. "Come, we'll go together."

In the bridge command chair, Spock turned his head to the corner where Scott and McCoy were whispering together.

"Mr. Scott."

Scott started guiltily. "Yes, sir."

"Are you unable to manage anything faster than Warp Six?"

Scott moved to the command chair. "It's my opinion, sir, that we've come much too far as it is."

McCoy joined them to add his support to Scott's opinion. "He's right, Spock. We lost Jim and the others back at Gamma II. You've dragged us a dozen light years out here on some wild hunch that—"

"I do not entertain hunches, Doctor. No transporter malfunction was responsible for the disappearance. They were not within the Gamma System. A focused beam of extremely high intensity energy was directed into the Gamma System from the binary system we are now approaching. No known natural phenomena would account for that beam. Does that not clarify the situation?"

"No, Spock, it doesn't. That's just a fancy way of saying you're playing a hunch. *My* hunch is that they're still back on Gamma II—dead or alive. And I want to make another search."

"Dr. McCoy speaks for me too, sir," Scott said.

"Gentlemen, I am in command of this vessel. We will proceed on our present course—unless it is your intention to declare a mutiny."

Spock received their glares unmoved. And for a moment, his two leading officers felt what they had often felt before: an awe of Spock. Unnumbered had been the times he had demonstrated his devotion to his Captain—a devotion now under cruel and lonely test. He would follow his own decision, unsupported, giving no sign whatever of any inward doubt or anxiety.

Scott could feel his respect for Kirk's best friend growing, suddenly. As to McCoy, he fell back on bluster.

"Who said anything about mutiny? You stubborn, pointed-eared . . . All right, but if we don't find them here, will you go back for another search of Gamma II?"

"Agreed, Doctor. Mr. Scott, now can you give me Warp Seven?"

"Aye. And perhaps a bit more."

Spock spoke to the navigator. "Warp Seven, Ensign."

Nourishment Interval. Shahna, unlocking the door of Kirk's stall, entered it without looking at him. As she set down the food container, Kirk said, "You're late."

She nodded unhappily, still evading his eyes. He rose from his bench to take the container from her. "Are you disturbed about what happened today?"

"Yes."

"Because of me?"

"You—you have made me feel very strange. If it were allowed, I would ask that you be given another Drill Thrall."

He placed the container on the cubed stand. "I wouldn't like that, darling. I wouldn't like it at all."

He opened his arms to her and she walked straight into them. For a moment, she tried to resist his lips but then hungrily responded to them. Gathering her to him more closely, he suddenly dealt her a short, hard uppercut on the chin. As she went limp, sagging in his arms, he swiftly lifted her and placed her on the bench. The key to his stall door was in her harness. He took it. Then glancing down at her, regret in his eyes, he gently kissed her forehead.

"Sorry, Shahna. Sorry, darling."

Turning quickly to the door, he pressed the key to its

lock. Ten seconds later, he was at Chekov's cell, releasing him. To his whispered question, Kirk shook his head. "No, she's out cold. What about Lars and Tamoon?"

"Uhura?"

She was beside him too, now in the corridor. "I told him I didn't like the food. He's gone to report me."

Chekov said, "Tamoon won't give us any trouble, either. But I think I've killed our romance."

In Chekov's stall, the fanged creature was seated on the floor, bound with part of her own harness. A metal pot covered her head to the mouth to stifle any muffled objections.

Kirk and Chekov exchanged grins, but Uhura ran forward to make sure the corridor was deserted. It was; and the three went quickly through its archway toward the gaming area.

With lowered voice, Kirk said, "I think Galt's the only one who can operate the collars. If we can find our phasers, we can use the circuits to short the collars out."

They had passed the central triangle when the Master Thrall made one of his sudden appearances.

"Stay where you are, Captain."

As Kirk hesitated, Galt closed his eyes. For a moment, the three slave collars glowed then went out.

From a wall, their owner spoke in his unmistakable high-pitched voice. "Only a reminder, Captain. You Earthmen are most unusual . . . most stimulating."

The next moment, they were surrounded by armed, sullen-faced Thralls.

Ensign Haines was the only member of the bridge personnel who had her eyes on her console.

"Standard orbit, Mr. Spock."

Spock's eyes, like those of Scott and McCoy beside the command chair, were on the viewing screen. All watched the slowly rotating planet imaged on it.

"Sensors indicate only one concentration of life forms—in the lower hemisphere on the largest land mass." Spock's voice was toneless. "Humanoid readings, however."

"At least that gives our landing force a starting point," McCoy said.

"There will be no landing force, Doctor. Assuming

that the Captain and the others are still alive, it would be unwise to endanger them by beaming down a large contingent.''

"Well, we're not just going to leave them there while we sit here and wait, are we?''

Spock, leaving the command chair, was back at his scanner. Straightening, he said, "Interesting. The sensors record no power source. It might be shielded.''

The strain was too much for McCoy. "Or it might be a wild-goose chase just as we've been telling you!''

"I shall beam down,'' Spock said. "If I am unable to communicate, a landing force may be necessary. You must make that decision, Mr. Scott.''

"Well, Spock, if you're going into a lions' den, you'll need a Medical Officer.''

Getting to his feet, Spock said, "Daniel, as I recall, had only faith. But I welcome your company, Doctor. Mr. Scott, you are in command.''

"Aye, sir.''

Without warning, the piercing metallic voice reverberated throughout the ship. "No, Mr. Spock,'' said Provider One. "You will not leave the ship.''

A silence, heavy as lead, fell over the bridge.

"What the de'il—'' Scott began and broke off.

Miles, miles, miles below the *Enterprise*, the voice had been heard by Kirk, Chekov and Uhura on the gaming board, guarded by Lars, Tamoon, Shahna and Galt.

Provider One spoke again. "None of your control systems will operate.''

Kirk was moistening his dry lips with his tongue when McCoy's familiar voice came. "Spock, what the hell is going on?''

Explanation there was none. How in the name of all the gods had the Providers arranged this simultaneous communication between their prisoners and his ship? Would his people hear him as clearly as he had heard McCoy?

Maybe. "Welcome to Triskelion, gentlemen,'' he said.

They *did* hear him. "Jim,'' McCoy cried, "is that you?''

"Yes. By now it must be obvious to you that you were expected.''

Scott had been making a frantic check of controls. Finishing, he called, "It's true—what that thing said, Mr. Spock. Nothing will respond."

Now there was a slight hint of amusement in Provider One's high voice. "Commendations, gentlemen. Your ingenuity in discovering the whereabouts of your companions is noteworthy."

They'll be trying to locate the voice, Kirk thought—and will fail just as we have. Well, he'd tell them what he could.

"What you are hearing, Mr. Spock, is a Provider."

Provide One expanded his information. "We are known to our Thralls as Providers because we provide for all their needs. The term is easier for their limited mental abilities to comprehend, Mr. Spock."

" 'Providing for their needs' means using Thralls—people stolen from every part of the galaxy—to fight each other while their owners gamble on the winner."

Spock, always charmed by the idiosyncrasies of alien civilizations, said, "Indeed? Fascinating, Captain."

"Not in fact, Spock. These Providers lack even the courage to show themselves."

Provider One was roused to say, "Your species has much curiosity. However, we knew that. You are interesting in many ways."

The conversation had now become a dialogue between Kirk and his owner.

"But you *are* afraid!"

"You present no danger, Captain, while you wear the collar. And you will wear it for the rest of your life."

Did they hear it on the *Enterprise*?

"Then show yourselves!" Kirk shouted.

His challenge was followed by a high, electronic whispering, followed in its turn by an acceptance of the dare.

"There is no objection," said Provider One, and the next instant Kirk had vanished from the gaming board.

He found himself in a circular chamber. To his left was a crookedly shaped window, but the chief feature of the room was a column, widened at its top to support a transparent case. Within it was what seemed to be three blobs of protoplasm, veined and pulsating. No. Unskulled brains. Disem-

bodied intellects, carefully preserving themselves in the
satanic pride of unfeeling intellect, active only in the cause
of its absolute certitudes.

Kirk left the column for the window and looked out on
a vast underground complex, and too convoluted to divulge
its details.

"So that's your power source," he said. "Shielded by
solid rock."

"We are one thousand of your meters beneath the surface," boasted Provider One.

Back at the brain case, Kirk said, "Primary mental
development . . . primitive evolution."

And was promptly corrected by Provider Two. "That
is not true, Captain. Once we had humanoid forms, but we
evolved beyond them."

Provider Three became self-defensive. "Through eons
of devoting ourselves to intellectual pursuits, we became
physically simple, the mentally superior brains you see before
you."

Kirk allowed his scorn to sharpen his voice. "A species
which enslaves others is hardly superior—mentally or otherwise."

He seemed to have touched Provider One on a raw
place. "The Thralls are necessary to our games, Captain. We
have found athletic competitions our sole diversion—the only
thing which furnishes us with purpose."

"An unproductive purpose," Kirk observed. "Most
unworthy of the greatest intellects in the galaxy."

The irony got through.

"We only use inferior beings."

"Inferior. Encased as you are, you don't get around
much. We do. And we have found all life forms capable of
superior development under proper guidance. Perhaps you're
not so grandly evolved as you think."

He disconcerted them into a moment of silence finally
broken by Provider Three. "An interesting speculation, Captain. You and your people are most challenging."

"Yes, most challenging," agreed Provider Two. "It
was hoped that such new blood would stimulate our stock of
Thralls. How unfortunate that you must be destroyed!"

"Our destruction will only result in your own. You may

control the *Enterprise*, but you cannot match the power of the entire Federation.''

Another raw place in Provider One. ''Your ship will be shattered to bits by a magnetic storm. No communication with your base will be possible. Your fate will remain an eternal mystery to your Federation.''

Kirk gave no sign of his shocked dismay. Yet, in spite of it, he was thinking harder than he'd ever thought in his life. He laughed. ''And you call yourselves 'superior'! Why, you're just run-of-the-mill murderers—killers without the spirit to *really* wager for the lives you take!''

An electronic murmur of excitement came from the case.

''Wager?'' queried Provider One. ''Explain yourself, Captain.''

Kirk drew himself up to his full height. ''My people are the most enterprising, successful gamblers in the universe. We compete for everything—power . . . fame . . . women . . . whatever we desire. It is our nature to win! I offer as proof our exploration of this galaxy.''

''We are aware of your competitive abilities,'' pronounced Provider Three.

''Very well. Then I am willing to wager right now—and with any weapon you choose—that my people can overcome any fair number of Thralls set against them.''

He'd been right. He'd caught them. Out of the case came the babble of bidding: ''A hundred quatloos on the newcomers . . . two hundred against . . . four hundred against . . . five hundred for the newcomers . . . contest by multiple elimination!''

''Wait! Wait! Hear me out!'' Kirk cried.

The voices stilled.

''We do not wager for trifles like quatloos! The stakes must be high!''

The silence prolonged itself until Provider One spoke. ''Name your stakes, Captain.''

''If my people win, the *Enterprise* and all its crew will leave here in safety. Furthermore, all Thralls on this planet will be freed.''

''Anarchy! They would starve!''

Kirk ignored the comment. ''They will be educated

and trained by you to establish a normal, self-governing culture."

Incredulous, Provider Three cried, "Thralls—govern themselves? Ridiculous!"

"We have done this same thing with many, many cultures throughout the galaxy. Do you then confess you cannot do what we can?"

"There is nothing we cannot do," Provider Two declared.

"And if you lose, Captain?"

It was Provider One's question, but he knew that the other two were waiting intently for his answer.

There was only one to make, and he made it. "If we lose, we will stay here—the entire *Enterprise* crew—the most stubborn and determined competitors anywhere. We will become Thralls, taking part in your games and obeying all orders without rebellion. You will be assured of generations of the most exciting wagering you've ever had."

A long silence passed before Provider One said, "Your stakes are indeed high, Captain."

"Not for *true* gamesters!"

The intellects once more conferred in their electronic mumble, their decision voiced by Provider Three. "We will accept your stakes on one condition, Captain."

"Name it."

"As leader of your people, your spirit seems most indomitable. We suggest you alone—pitted against three contestants of our choosing."

"One against three? Those are pretty high odds, aren't they?"

A vein throbbed in the brain of Provider Three as it gave a small, taunting chuckle. "Not for *true* gamesters, Captain!"

Kirk shook his head. "Your terms are unfair."

"On the contrary," Provider One said. "They are extremely fair inasmuch as your alternative is death."

Kirk gave himself time—time to think, time to consider the future of the *Enterprise* crew under the domination of these intellects, time to weigh it against his own death. It had been his life, the *Enterprise* and its people. Without them, death would be welcome.

"The wager is accepted," he said.

"Galt will prepare you."

It was extraordinary, the triumph the mere brain of Provider One could infuse into its thin, shrill voice. Then as abruptly as he'd appeared in the chamber, he was back in the gaming area, standing in the center triangle, faced by Lars, Kloog, Tamoon and Shahna.

He took the staff Galt handed him. As he hefted it, gauging its weight, the sharpness of its blade, the curve of its hook, Provider One spoke from a wall.

"Because you wager your skill for all your people, they will be permitted to watch the game's outcome on the ship's viewing screen."

And at the same moment, he heard Scott shout, "Mr. Spock, look!"

All right. They knew what he felt about them. So the fact that he was willing to die to preserve them would come as no surprise. Yet he wasn't prepared for the stricken voice of McCoy. "What in the name of Heaven is—"

Scott's Highland realism spoke for him. "Heaven's got very little to do with this, Doctor."

Spock held up a hand for silence. And all of them heard Provider One.

"Captain, you will defend."

"Jim, Jim," McCoy whispered.

But Provider One had more to say.

"Thralls must stay in the blue shapes. You will take the yellow ones, Captain. Touching an opponent's color deprives a contestant of one weapon. An opponent must be killed to be removed from the game. If only wounded, he is replaced by a fresh Thrall. Is that clear, Captain?"

"Clear."

"Very well. Begin."

Galt had pushed a dagger into Kirk's belt. Then a hooked net was hung over his right shoulder and a whip shoved into his hand. Four weapons, counting the quarterstaff. But his opponents only carried one, plus their daggers. Kloog, Lars and a strange Thrall positioned themselves in the blue shapes. A very strange Thrall, a bald thing, purple-skinned, its nose two holes covered by flaps of tissue, flapping up and down over its elementary nostrils with its breathing.

Kirk started with the staff.

All three closed in on him simultaneously, forcing the *Enterprise* Captain to make a sweeping move from his yellow triangle in order to parry the bald thing's assault with its spear. Leaping from the triangle into a yellow circle, he drove Kloog into a blue hexagon. Like his physical agility, his mental ability was working faster than his opponents'.

But at once Lars had rushed him with his net, and the bald Thrall, who'd fled around a yellow square, was slashing at him with its spear blade. Cool, now that the issue was finally joined, Kirk extended the hook of his own around Lars's ankle, downing him directly into the path of the oncoming Kloog. He felled the blond giant only to see the hairless alien strike at him again with its staff blade.

A high jump lifted him from the circle, replacing him on the yellow triangle.

Back on his feet, Lars raised his net. Its meshes engulfed Kirk, catching him; and Kloog, his gorilla jaw jutted, backed off for an effective blow with his whip. Kirk, drawing his dagger swiftly, cut himself free of the tangle, and Lars, unbelievingly, stumbled, staring idiotically at his torn weapon.

Despite the bald Thrall's skill, its nose shields were flapping breathlessly. It ran up behind Kirk, snuffling like a pig at its trough; but whirling, Kirk had glimpsed a yellow pentagon to his left. He made its center and, turning, attacked the noseless thing with his staff, but it parried the strike with its own.

Kirk, however, had parried higher. Kloog, combined fear and rage inciting him, saw his chance and lashed Kirk around the body with his stinging, curling whip. Kirk's staff broke—broke in half. He wheeled, spun out of the whip, and, leaping from the pentagon, flung his staff's new-made spear at Kloog. It struck in the matted hair of his chest, drawing blood. He retreated.

Lars, with his ripped net, at once took up Kloog's position. Its uncut meshes fell over Kirk and Lars raised his dagger for the kill. Looking at the heavy blond face, merciless, Kirk said to himself, "So this is it. Okay, I die. But so does everybody else in the end."

Was it that acceptance of mortality which gave him the momentary detachment he so needed? In it, as though from a great distance, he saw the bald thing lift its spear, hurl it at him, and he ducked it. It entered Lars's stomach.

Who's to know?

There are divinities that shape our ends of which we know nothing. Vigor renewed itself in Kirk. He struggled out of the net, and the bald alien, snatching it up, yanked its dagger from its belt. Now it was armed with net, dagger and quarterstaff.

It feinted with the staff, grabbing his whip from him, but Kirk reached for it, recovered it and threw it clear of the game floor. Now it was repellently close body contact with the freak, its nose shields fluttering in Kirk's face. He wrested himself free, making another forward leap to the yellow circle.

But once more the net descended. The bald one dived at him. Somehow, he released his dagger hand, and pushing the thing aside, lashed out with his own dagger across the purple body. It collapsed, not dead, but so wounded that it couldn't rise. And at once, as Lars had been, was dragged from the field of battle by expressionless fellow Thralls, moving in from the sidelines.

Behind it, it left a thick pool of purple blood. Kirk closed his eyes against the sight. What a planet! If this insane mayhem was the result of supreme intellect, the humanoids of the galaxy would be well advised to go back to primeval seas as protozoa.

He opened his eyes. Vaulting over a blue circle, he landed on the yellow triangle's sanctuary for what he had seen was Shahna, her spear lifted, racing at him from the sidelines to challenge him.

He moved unsteadily to meet her, the muscles of his legs unreliable and barely able to clutch the splintered half of his quarterstaff.

"You lied," she said. "Everything you said . . ." and lunged at him. He fell to one knee. Then hacking his way upright, he called on all his brute strength to get under her guard and drive his blade's point into her breast.

Kill a woman in cold blood. He'd never done it. He paused, but Shahna was preparing for the death thrust, pulling back to gain impetus for another lunge at him. Then she knocked his blade aside to press her own against his heart.

Their blades crossed, bringing them face to face.

Suddenly, her lower lip began to tremble. "You—you *did* lie."

Her whispered breath was fragrant as roses. And once more the indefinable shuttle between man and woman was moving, interlacing, as mysteriously powerful as the divinities shaping our ends. Would it continue its weaving? All she'd ever known was fighting; but love? Only what he'd been able to teach her.

The dark-lashed eyes were deep in his, asking, searching.

Tears flooded the eyes. Dropping her blade, she turned to a wall, crying, "The Thralls surrender!"

He'd have to leave her, but he'd made a woman out of her. And who was to profit by her loveliness? Kloog . . . the bald horror? There were disadvantages to command of a Starship, roaming, roaming endlessly through the galaxy.

He was about to take her in his arms when he heard the voice of Provider One.

"You have won, Captain Kirk. Unfortunately. However, the terms of the wager will be honored. You are free. Remove your collars. Thralls, hear me!"

Kirk placed his hand on Shahna's collar. It came away easily. Then as he removed his own, he heard clash after metallic clash of other collars striking the floor. Shahna stared at the broken symbol of her slavery in her hand, unbelieving. Then the sapphire eyes veered to him. At the look in them, it was just as well that Galt reached them, carrying his former prisoners' phasers and communicators.

Kirk addressed a wall. "The Thralls will be trained?"

"They will be trained. We have said it, Captain Kirk."

"You may find that a more exciting game than the one you have been playing. A body is no good without a brain. But you've found a brain isn't worth much without a body."

Shahna said, "Darling."

He looked down at her. No, they could share no future.

If only . . . He pulled himself together. "I didn't lie, Shahna. I only did what was necessary. Someday, you'll understand."

"I—I understand a . . . little. You will leave us now?"

He nodded, unable to speak.

"To go back to the lights in the sky? I . . . want to go to . . . those lights . . . with you. Take me."

"I can't."

"Then teach me how, and I'll follow you."

Providers, witnesses notwithstanding, he took her in his arms. "There are many things you have to learn first—things the Providers will teach you. Learn them. All your people must learn them before you can reach for the stars."

Holding her closer, he kissed her.

"Goodbye, darling, my darling."

Then he released her; and striding quickly across the board, joined the awed Chekov and Uhura. Nor did he look back as he opened his communicator.

"Beam us up, Mr. Scott."

The well-known voice said, "Aye, sir."

Alone on the board, Shahna watched the shimmer as his body went into sparkle—and he was gone with his people.

She bowed her head to hide the tears. "Goodbye, my Kirk. I will learn. And watch the lights in . . . the sky . . . and always, always remember."

So would he. But gradually—and mercifully—the memory of Triskelion's beautiful woman would begin to fade, along with the sweetness of her breath on his face.

OBSESSION

Writer: Art Wallace
Director: Ralph Senensky
Guest star: Stephen Brooks

The ore was peculiar-looking, a harsh purple-black. Kirk struck it with a rock; but apart from its responsive clanging sound, it showed no trace of the blow. As he tossed the rock aside, he said, "Fantastic! It must be twenty times as hard as steel even in its raw state!"

Spock, his tricorder focused on the ore, said, "To be exact, Captain, 21.4 times as hard as the finest manganese steel."

Kirk opened his communicator. "Scotty? You can mark this vein of ore as confirmed. Inform Starfleet I recommend they dispatch a survey vessel to this planet immediately." As he spoke, a puff of white vapor drifted up over the rock matrix of the ore—a whisp of vapor hidden from the *Enterprise* men both by the rock's jutting and obscuring vegetation.

Scott said, "Acknowledged, Captain. They'll send a vessel fast enough for this rich a find."

Spock had pulled his phaser. "We won't be able to break it. I'll shoot off a sample."

Kirk didn't answer. He had stiffened abruptly, frowning, sniffing the air around him, his face strained like that of a man whose past had suddenly shouldered out his present. A shard of rock, grape-purple with the ore, had broken off; and the white vapor, as though guided by some protective intelligence, swiftly withdrew behind the big rock's shelter. As Spock rose from retrieving the ore sample, Kirk spoke. "Notice it?" he said. "A sweetish odor—a smell like honey?

I wonder. It was years ago on a different planet . . . a 'thing' with an odor like that.''

Some indefinable appeal in his voice moved Spock to say reassuringly, ''This is the growing season in the hemisphere of this planet. There are doubtless many forms of pollen aromas around, Captain.''

But Kirk was not soothed. He didn't seem to even have heard. Beckoning to the landing party's security officer, he said, ''Lieutenant Rizzo, take two men and make a swing around our perimeter. Scan for any gaseous di-kironium in the atmosphere.''

''Di-kironium,'' Spock observed, ''does not exist except in laboratory experiments.''

Kirk ignored the comment. ''Set phasers on Disruptor-B. If you see any gaseous cloud, fire into it instantly. Make your sweep, Lieutenant.''

A beep beeped from the open communicator in his hand; and Scott's voice said, ''Ready to beam back aboard, sir?''

''Stand by, Scotty. We're checking something out.''

''Sir, the U.S.S. *Yorktown* is expecting to rendezvous with us in less than eight hours. Doesn't leave us much time.''

''Acknowledged. Continue standing by. Kirk out.''

Spock, scanning the ore sample, spoke, his voice flat with awe. ''Purity about eighty-five percent, Captain. With enough of this, they'll be building Starships with twice our warp capacity.''

But Kirk was sniffing the air again. ''Gone,'' he said. ''It's gone now. I could have been wrong. The last time I caught that odor was about twelve years ago.'' He looked away to where the security officer and his men were quartering the area. Rizzo, standing near a small hillock, was bent over his tricorder. It had suddenly registered di-kironium on the air. Puzzling over it, he didn't see the cloud of white vapor encroaching on them from behind the hillock. ''But that isn't possible,'' Rizzo muttered to himself. ''Nothing can do that.''

The vaporous cloud, however, seemed to obey laws of its own. One moment it had been wispy, diaphonous; but in the next it had thickened to a dense fog, moving suddenly and swiftly, emitting a humming creature sound.

The scouting party whirled as one man. The coiling colors that had appeared in the cloud reached out a tentacle of green which touched the nearest security man. He grabbed at his throat and fell to the ground. As the second security man gagged, Rizzo pulled his phaser. Where to direct his fire? Into the center of the cloud? Where? He hesitated—and Kirk's communicator beeped.

"Captain . . . cloud," Rizzo choked. "A strange cloud."

"Fire your phasers at its center!" Kirk shouted.

"Sir, we—help!"

"Spock, with me!" yelled Kirk. He raced toward the hillock, his phaser drawn.

But the gaseous cloud was gone. Rizzo lay face down on the grass, his communicator still clutched in his hand. The bodies of his men lay near by. Kirk glanced around before he hurried to Rizzo. The officer was very pale. But where Rizzo's flesh was pale, the bodies of his men were bone-white. Kirk lifted his head. "Dead," he said. "And we'll find every red corpuscle has been drained from their blood."

"At least Rizzo's alive," Spock said. "As you were saying—you suspect what it was, Captain?"

Kirk had taken out his communicator. He nodded. "A 'thing' . . . something that can't possibly exist. Yet which *does exist*." He flipped the communicator open. "Captain to *Enterprise*. Lock in on us, Scotty! Medical emergency!"

He was in Sickbay. It didn't offer much room to pace. So he stood still while Christine Chapel handed the cartridge of tapes to Bones.

"The autopsy reports, Doctor."

"Thank you."

Kirk extended a hand to Christine's arm. "Nurse, how is Lieutenant Rizzo?"

"Still unconscious, Captain."

"Transfusions?" he said.

"Continuing as rapidly as possible, sir. Blood count still less than sixty percent of normal."

Kirk glanced at McCoy. But Bones was still deep in the autopsy reports. Kirk closed his eyes, running a hand over his forehead. Then he crossed to a communicator panel equipped with a small viewing screen.

"Kirk to bridge."

The voice was Spock's. "Ready to leave orbit, sir."

"Hold our position."

The image of Spock was supplemented by Scott's. "Cutting in, if I may, sir. The *Yorktown*'s expecting to rendezvous with us in less than seven hours."

The heat of sudden rage engulfed Kirk. "Then inform them we may be late!"

McCoy turned from his desk. "Jim, the *Yorktown*'s ship surgeon will want to know how late. The vaccines he's transfering to us are highly perishable."

Spock reappeared on the screen. "Sir, those medical supplies are badly needed on planet Theta Seven. They're expecting us to get them there on time."

I am hounded, Kirk thought. He looked from Spock back to McCoy. "Gentlemen," he said, "we are staying here in orbit until I learn more about those deaths. I am quite aware this may cost lives on planet Theta Seven. What lives are lost are my responsibility. Captain out." He switched off the screen, and addressed McCoy. "Autopsy findings?"

"You saw their color," McCoy said. "There wasn't a red corpuscle left in those bodies."

"Cuts? Incisions? Marks of any kind?"

"Not a one. What happened is medically impossible."

Kirk became conscious of a vast impatience with the human race. "I suggest," he said coldly, "that you check our record tapes for similar occurrences in the past before you speak of medical 'impossibilities.' I have in mind the experience of the U.S.S. *Farragut*. Twelve years ago it listed casualties from exactly the same impossible medical causes."

McCoy was eyeing him speculatively. "Thank you, Captain," he said tonelessly. "I'll check those tapes immediately."

"Yes, do," Kirk said. "But before you do, can you bring Lieutenant Rizzo back to consciousness for a moment?"

"Yes, I think so but—"

"Will it hurt him if you do?"

"In his condition it won't make much difference."

"Then bring him out of it," Kirk said. "I must ask him a question."

As they approached Rizzo's bed, Nurse Chapel was removing a small black box that had been strapped to his arm. "Transfusions completed, Doctor," she said. "Pulse and respiration still far from normal."

"Give him one cc. of cordrazine."

The nurse stared. Then picking up a hypodermic, she adjusted it. As it hissed against Rizzo's arm, Kirk's hands tightened on the bed bar until his knuckles whitened. On the pillow he saw the head move slightly. Kirk leaned in over Rizzo. "Lieutenant, this is the Captain. Can you hear me? Do you remember what happened to you?"

The eyelids fluttered. "Remember . . . I'm cold," Rizzo whispered. "So . . . cold."

Kirk pressed on. "Rizzo, you were attacked by something. When it happened, did you notice an odor of any kind?" His hands were shaking on the bed bar. He leaned in closer. "Rizzo, remember. A sickly sweet odor. Did you smell it?"

Horror filled the eyes. "Yes, sir . . . the smell . . . strange . . . like . . . like being smothered in honey."

Kirk exhaled a deep, quivering breath. "And—did you feel a—a *presence*? An intelligence?"

The head moved in assent. "It . . . it wanted strength from us. Yes, I felt it sucking. It was there."

McCoy moved in. "He's asleep. We can't risk another shot, Captain."

"He told me what I wanted to know."

"I wouldn't depend on his answers. In his half-conscious state, he could be dreaming, saying what he thought you wanted to hear."

Kirk straightened. "Check those record tapes, Doctor. I'll want your analysis of them as quickly as possible."

He left; Christine Chapel turned a puzzled face to McCoy. "What's the matter with the Captain, sir? I've never seen him like this."

"I intend to find out," McCoy said. "If I'm wanted, I'll be in the medical library."

On the bridge, Uhura greeted Kirk with a message from Starfleet. To her astonishment, he brushed it aside with a "Later, Lieutenant. Now have the security duty officer report to me here and at once." He crossed to Spock who said, "Continuing scanning, sir. Still no readings of life forms on the planet surface."

"Then, Mr. Spock, let's assume that it's something so totally different that our sensors would fail to identify it as a life form."

"You've mentioned—di-kironium, Captain."

"A rare element, Mr. Spock. Suppose a life form were composed of it, a strange, gaseous creature."

"There is no trace of di-kironium on the planet surface or in the atmosphere. I've scanned for the element, sir."

"Suppose it were able to camouflage itself?"

"Captain, if it were composed of di-kironium, lead, gold, hydrogen—whatever—our sensors would pinpoint it."

"Let's still assume I'm right."

"An illogical assumption, Captain. There is no way to camouflage a given chemical element from a sensor scan."

"No way? Let's further assume it's intelligent and knows we're looking for it."

"Captain, to hide from a sensor scan, it would have to be able to change its molecular structure."

Kirk stared at him. "Like gold changing itself to lead or wood to ivory. Mr. Spock, you've just suggested something which never occurred to me. And it answers some questions in a tape record which I think you'll find Dr. McCoy is studying at this very moment."

Spock was on his feet. "Mr. Chekov! Take over on scanner." He was at the bridge elevator door as it hissed open to permit the entrance of the security duty officer. He was a new member of the crew, young, bright-faced, clearly dedicated as only the untried idealism of youth can dedicate itself. He strode to Kirk and saluted. "Ensign David Garrovick reporting, sir."

Kirk turned, startled. "You're the new security officer?"

"Yes, sir."

Kirk hesitated a moment. Then he said, "Was your father—?"

"Yes, sir. But I don't expect any special treatment on that account."

The shock in Kirk's face subsided. Now he snapped, "You'll get none aboard this ship, mister!"

"Yes, sir."

Uhura broke in. "I have a report on Lieutenant Rizzo, Captain. He's dead."

Kirk leaned back in his chair. It had been costly—the discovery of that so-precious purple ore. He turned back to the new security officer when he realized that Garrovick's face was grief-stricken, too.

"Did you know Rizzo?" Kirk said.

"Yes, sir. We were good friends. Graduated the Academy together."

Kirk nodded. "Want a crack at what killed him?"

"Yes, sir."

"Equip four men with phaser twos set for Disruptor effect. Report to the Transporter Room in five minutes. You will accompany me to the planet surface."

It was Garrovick who took the first tricorder reading of the terrain where the team materialized. Suddenly, he called to Kirk. "Sir, the reading is changing!"

Kirk crossed to him swiftly. Nodding, he examined the tricorder. "Spock was right," he said. "See—there's been a molecular shift."

"A di-kironium reading now, sir. Bearing is 94 mark 7, angle of elevation 6 degrees. Holding stationary."

Kirk pointed to a lift in the ground. "Behind that rise. Take two men and approach it from the right. I'll take two around the other way. As soon as you sight the creature, fire with full phasers. Remember—it's extremely dangerous."

Garrovick looked at the hill nervously. "Yes . . . sir." The words were spoken tightly. Kirk glanced at the tense young face. Then, turning, he said, "Swanson and Bardoli, come with me."

Garrovick and his two men had climbed the rise when he noticed that it fell to a deep gully. His men fanned out past the ravine. Garrovick stood still for a moment, staring down into it. Then, making his decision, he descended it, moving forward cautiously. Suddenly the white vapor gathered before him. Startled, taken off-guard by its foglike appearance, he stared at it, uncertain. Then he aimed his phaser and fired. The slice of its beam was a second too late. The cloud was gone.

Kirk yelled, "A phaser shot!" Racing toward the hill, he shouted, "Come on!"

He found Garrovick scrambling up the side of the gully, his eyes fixed on something ahead of him. "Garrovick, did you—?" He stopped short as he saw what Garrovick was crawling toward. The two men of his patrol lay motionless on the ground.

Kirk ran to the nearest one. When Garrovick joined him, his young face turned smeary with shock and misery. The features that stared up sightlessly from the ground were bone-white.

Kirk was alone in the Briefing Room. It felt good to be alone. Alone, it was easier to hold on to his conviction that the murderous creature which had killed five of his crewmen was the same one that had decimated the crew of the U.S.S. *Farragut* twelve years before in another quadrant of the galaxy. Five men. Sickbay had the unconscious survivor of Garrovick's team under treatment; but its transfusion had been unable to save the life of Rizzo. The thing was, he wasn't really alone. You never were. Always, you had the unspoken thoughts of other people to companion you. And he had the unspoken thoughts of Spock and McCoy to keep him company. Neither one credited the creature with its malignancy nor its intelligence. Moreover, they disapproved his decision to remain here and fight it to the death. And maybe they were right. Had he made a reliable command decision—or an emotional one?

He'd laid his forearms on the Briefing Room table. Now he lifted his head from them as Spock, followed by McCoy and Garrovick, entered. Spock and McCoy both gave him sharply appraising looks as they sat down. They tried to appear as though they hadn't—but they had. In his turn, Kirk tried to appear as though he hadn't noticed the looks.

He opened the session. "We've studied your report, Mr. Garrovick. I believe Mr. Spock has a question."

Spock said, "What was the size of the creature, Ensign?"

"I'd estimate it measured from ten to sixty cubic meters, sir. It changed size, fluctuated as it moved."

"Composition?"

"It was like a gaseous cloud, sir. Parts of it I could see through; other parts seemed more dense."

McCoy spoke. "Ensign, did you 'sense' any intelligence in this gaseous cloud?"

"Did I what, sir?"

"Did you get any subconscious impression that it *was* a creature? A living, thinking thing rather than just a strange cloud of chemical elements?"

"No, sir."

Kirk eyed Garrovick who twisted uncomfortably. "Ensign, you never came into actual contact with it, did you?"

"No, I didn't, sir. I was the furthest away." He paused. "It came out of nowhere, it seemed. It hovered a moment, then moved toward the nearest man. Fast, incredibly fast."

Kirk shoved a pencil on the table. "Did you say it hovered?"

"Yes, sir."

"You fired at it, didn't you?"

"Yes, sir."

"How close were you to the creature?"

"About twenty yards, sir."

"And you missed a hovering, large target at that distance?"

"Yes, sir. I . . . well, I didn't fire while it was hovering."

"Do you mean that you froze?"

"Not exactly, sir."

"Then tell us what you mean exactly."

"I was startled . . . maybe only for a second or so. And then by the time I fired, it—well, it was already moving."

Kirk's tone was curt. "Do you have any additional information for us?"

"No, sir. I only—hesitated for a second or so, sir. I'm sorry."

"Ensign, you're relieved of all duties and confined to your quarters until further notice."

Garrovick straightened. "Yes, sir."

McCoy's eyes followed him to the closing door. "You were a little hard on him, Jim."

"He froze. One of his men was killed. The other will probably die."

"Captain," Spock began.

Kirk rose. "You'll both be filing reports, gentlemen. Make your comments and recommendations then." He crossed briskly to the door. As he slammed it behind him, McCoy and Spock were left to stare at each other.

Garrovick's room was as dark as his discouragement. He found the light switch affixed to its panel with its labeled temperature gauges and other controls. Above the panel was an open-close switch marked "Ventilation Filter By-Pass." Garrovick, closing his eyes to all circumstances of his surroundings, gave himself up to his depression.

Back on the bridge, Kirk was greeted by another message from the *Yorktown* requesting information on the rendezvous. He ignored it; and Scott, approaching him, said, "While we wait, Captain, I've taken the liberty of cleaning the radioactive disposal vent on the number-two impulse engine. But we'll be ready to leave orbit in under half an hour."

"We're not leaving orbit, Engineer. Not that quickly."

Scott didn't take the hint. "The medicine for the Theta Seven colony is not only desperately needed, Captain, but has a limited stability. And—"

Kirk wheeled. "I am," he said, "familiar with the situation, Engineer. And I'm getting a little tired of my officers conspiring against me to force—" He broke off at the look on Scott's face. "Forgive me, Scotty. I shouldn't have used the word 'conspiring'."

"Agreed, sir."

Kirk strode over to Chekov. "Scanner readings?"

"Nothing, sir. Continuing to scan."

"Mr. Chekov, you're aware it may be able to change its composition? Are you scanning for any unusual movements? Any type of gaseous cloud?"

"We've run a full scanner probe twice, sir."

"Then do it twenty times if that's what it takes!"

He barked the words and left the bridge to his shocked personnel.

Garrovick wasn't the only victim of depression. Mc-
Coy, viewing an autopsy tape, pulled it out of its slot, controlling an impulse to throw it to the floor. When Spock
entered his office, he spoke no word of greeting.

"I hope I'm not disturbing you, Doctor."

"Interrupting another autopsy report is no disturbance,
Spock. It's a relief."

"I need your advice," Spock said.

"Then I need a drink," said McCoy.

"I don't follow your reasoning, Doctor."

"*You* want advice from me? You must be kidding."

"I never joke. Perhaps I should rephrase my statement.
I require an opinion. There are many aspects of human irra-
tionality I do not yet comprehend. Obsession for one. The
persistent, singleminded fixation on one idea."

"Jim and his creature?"

"Precisely. Have you studied the incident involving the
U.S.S. *Farragut*?"

"With all these deaths and injuries, I've barely had
time to scan them."

"Fortunately, I read fast," Spock said. "To summarize
those records, I can inform you, Doctor, that almost half the
crew, including the Captain, was annihilated. The Captain's
name was Garrovick."

McCoy gave a startled whistle. "The same as our Ensign?"

"His father," Spock said. "I have the *Farragut* file
here with me."

"Then there's more," McCoy said.

Spock nodded gravely. "A great deal more. Among
the survivors of the disaster was a young officer on one of his
first deep-space assignments." He nodded again at McCoy's
look. "Yes, James T. Kirk," he said—and dropped the cartridge he held into the viewer. "And there's still more. I think
you'd better study this record, Doctor."

Twenty minutes later McCoy sought the quarters of
James T. Kirk, formerly of the U.S.S. *Farragut*. There was
no response to the buzz at their door. McCoy opened it.
"Mind if I come in, Jim?"

Kirk was lying on his bed, staring at the ceiling. He
made no move. He spoke no word. Then, with a bound, he

was off the bed to flip the switch on the wall communicator. "Kirk to bridge. Scanner report?"

Chekov's filtered voice said, "Continuing scanning, sir. No unusual readings."

"Maintain search. Kirk out." He turned from the communicator and jammed his right fist into his left hand. "It can't just vanish!" he cried.

"Sometimes they do if we're lucky." McCoy sat down. "Monsters come in many forms, Jim. And know what's the greatest monster of them all? Guilt, known or unknown."

Kirk's jaw hardened. "Get to the point."

"Jim . . . a young officer exposed to unknown dangers for the first time is under tremendous emotional stress. We all know how—"

"Ensign Garrovick is a ship command decision, Doctor. You're straying out of your field."

"I was speaking," McCoy said, "of Lieutenant James T. Kirk of the Starship *Farragut*."

Kirk stared at him. He didn't speak, and McCoy went on. "Twelve years ago you were the young officer at the phaser station when something attacked your ship. According to the tape, this young officer insisted on blaming himself—"

"I delayed my fire at it!"

McCoy spoke sharply. "You had a normal, *human* emotion! *Surprise!* You were startled. You delayed firing for the grand total of perhaps two seconds!"

Kirk's face had grown drawn with remembered anguish. "If I hadn't delayed, the thing would have been destroyed!"

"The ship's exec didn't think so. His log entry is quite clear on the subject. He reported, 'Lieutenant Kirk is a fine officer who performed with uncommon bravery.' "

"I killed nearly two hundred men!"

McCoy's voice was very quiet. "Captain Garrovick was important to you, wasn't he?"

Kirk's shoulders slumped. He sank down on his bed, wringing his hands. "He was my commanding officer from the day I left the Academy. He was one of the finest men I ever knew." He leaped to his feet again. "I could have destroyed it! If I'd fired soon enough that first time . . ."

"*You didn't know that, Jim!* You can't know it! Any

more than you can know young Garrovick could have destroyed it.''

Kirk's face was wiped clean of all emotions but torture. "I owe it to this ship . . ."

"To be so tormented by a memory . . . Jim, you can't destroy a boy because you see him as yourself as you were twelve years ago. You'll destroy yourself, your brilliant career."

"*I've got to kill this thing!* Don't ask me how I know that. I just know it."

McCoy eyed Kirk for a long moment. Then he rose and moved to the door, pressing the control that opened it. "Come in, Mr. Spock," he said.

Kirk whirled, crying, "Bones, don't push our friendship past the point that—"

McCoy interrupted. "This is professional, Captain. I am preparing a medical log entry on my estimate of the physical and emotional condition of a Starship's Captain. I require a witness of command rank."

Kirk's eyes swung from one of them to the other. Time—an infinity of it—went by. His voice when he spoke was edged with fury. "Do I understand, Doctor—and you, Commander Spock, that both or either of you believe me unfit or incapacitated?"

Spock said, "Correctly phrased as recommended in the manual, Captain. Our reply as also recommended is: we have noticed in your recent behavior items which, on the surface, seem unusual. We respectfully ask your permission to inquire further and—"

"Blast! Forget the manual!" Kirk shouted. "Ask your questions!"

Imperturbable, Spock said, "The U.S.S. *Yorktown* is now waiting for us at the appointed rendezvous, Captain. It carries perishable drugs which—"

Kirk ran a trembling hand over his forehead. "The news has a familiar ring, Commander."

McCoy said, "They need those vaccines on Theta Seven, Jim. Why are we delaying here?"

"Because I know what I know," Kirk said. "The creature that attacked the *Farragut* twelve years ago is the same—"

"Creature?" Spock said.

"Yes. My report was in the tape. As it attacked us twelve years ago, just as I lost consciousness, I could *feel* the intelligence of the thing; I could sense it thinking, planning."

"You say you could 'sense' its intelligence, Captain. How?" Spock said. "Did it communicate with you?"

McCoy broke in. "You state that it happened just as you lost consciousness. The semi-conscious mind is a tricky thing, Jim. A man can never be sure how much was real, how much was semi-conscious fancy."

"Real or unreal, Bones, it was deadly, lethal."

"No doubt of that," McCoy said.

"And if it *is* the same creature I met twelve years ago on a planet over a thousand light years from here?"

"Obviously, Captain, if it is an intelligent creature, if it is the same one, if therefore it is capable of space travel, it could pose a grave threat to inhabited planets."

"A lot of 'ifs,' Commander, I agree. But in my command judgment they still outweigh other factors. 'Intuition,' however illogical, Commander Spock, is recognized as a command prerogative."

"Jim, we're not trying to gang up on you."

"You haven't, Doctor. You've indicated a proper concern. You've both done your duty. May I be informed now of what medical log entry you intend to make?"

Spock and McCoy exchanged glances. "Jim," McCoy began.

Kirk smiled. "You've been bluffing, gentlemen. I'm calling your bluff."

Spock spoke. "This was totally my idea, Captain. Dr. McCoy's human affection for you makes him completely incapable of—"

McCoy interrupted. "*My affection* for him! I like that! Why, I practically had to sandbag you into this!" He turned to Kirk. "Jim, we were just using this to try and talk some sense into—"

The communicator beeped with the intercom signal. Chekov's excited voice said, "Bridge to Captain! Come in, Captain!"

Kirk was at the grill in a second flat. "Kirk here, Mr. Chekov."

"I have a reading on the—whatever it is, Captain! It's leaving the planet surface and heading into space!"

It was the measure of Kirk's nature that no triumph whatever colored the tone of his orders. "All decks, red alert! Prepare to leave orbit!"

Then he was gone out his door.

Gone out his door on a wild goose chase. Only what Kirk and the *Enterprise* chased through the labyrinths of trackless space was no wild goose. It was subtle as a cobra, swift as a mamba in its flight from the *Enterprise*, leading the Starship ever farther from its meeting with the *Yorktown* and its mission of mercy.

On the bridge they all knew what was at stake. The thing had twice changed its course in a malevolent, deliberate effort to mislead. Kirk was exhilarated past anxiety. But Scott was worried. "Captain, we can't maintain Warp 8 speed much longer. Pressures are approaching a critical point."

"Range, Mr. Chekov?" Kirk said.

"Point zero four light years ahead, sir. Our phasers won't reach it."

Spock spoke. "Captain, we're barely closing on it. We could be pursuing it for days."

"If necessary," Kirk said. He turned. "Do what you can to increase our speed, Mr. Scott."

"Aye, sir."

"Let's see it," Kirk said.

Chekov hit a button. "Magnification twelve, sir. There, sir! Got it on the screen!"

It was moving across the screen like an elongated comet, a coiling vortex floating amidst whirling vapors.

"How do you read it, Mr. Spock?"

"Conflicting data, sir. It seems to be in a borderline state between matter and energy. It can possibly utilize gravitational fields for propulsion."

"You don't find that sophisticated, Mr. Spock?"

"Extremely efficient, Captain." He paused. "Whether it indicates intelligence is another matter."

Chekov had got a red light on his console. "Open hatch on number-two impulse engine, sir. Mr. Scott was doing a clean-up job on it."

"Turn off the alarm," Kirk said. "We won't be using the impulse engines."

Scott turned from his station. "Captain! We can't do it! If we hold this speed, she'll blow up any minute!"

Kirk swallowed the pill of reality. "All right," he said. "Reduce to Warp Six."

In Garrovick's quarters the door buzzer sounded and Christine Chapel entered, carrying a dinner tray.

"Thank you," Garrovick said. "I'm not hungry."

"Dr. McCoy's orders."

"What's happening?" Garrovick said.

"Are we still chasing that thing half across the galaxy? Yes, we are. Has the Captain lost his sense of balance? Maybe. Is the crew about ready to explode? *Positively.* You're lucky to be out of it, Ensign."

Garrovick's voice was acid with bitterness. "Out of it? I *caused* it."

She calmly continued to spread food before him. "You know that's true, don't you?" he said. "If I'd fired my phaser quickly enough back on Argus Ten, none of this would have happened."

"Self-pity is a poor appetizer," she said. "Try the soup instead."

"I don't want it."

"If you don't eat," she told him, "Dr. McCoy will have you hauled down to Sickbay and make me feed you intravenously. I don't want to do that, either." Garrovick feebly returned her smile, nodded in defeat, and began to pick at his food. But it was no good. As the door closed behind her, a burst of frustration overwhelmed him. He dashed a cup of coffee he'd just poured against the wall. It hit the panel. Shattering against the switch of the ventilation filter by-pass, it knocked it to the open position.

At the same moment the strident alarm signal sounded. Kirk's voice came over the communicator. "Battle stations! All decks to battle stations! The enemy is reducing speed! This is not a drill! All decks to battle stations!"

On the bridge Chekov shouted. "It's coming to a full halt, Captain! Magnification one, visual contact!"

Centered on the screen, now only a small object, the

strange creature seemed to be pulsating. Kirk said, "Hello, Beautiful." Then he leaned toward Chekov. "Move in closer, Mr. Chekov. Sublight, one quarter speed."

As Chekov manipulated his controls, the bridge elevator door opened; and Garrovick, his face pale with tension, emerged to cross quickly over to Kirk. "Sir, request permission to return to my post."

"Within phaser range now, sir!" cried Chekov.

"Lock phasers on target, Mr. Chekov!"

"Locked on target, sir!"

"Fire main phasers!"

But the fierce energy blips passed directly through the creature. Stunned, Kirk watched in unbelief.

"Phasers ineffectual, Captain!"

"Photon torpedoes, Mr. Chekov! Minimum spread pattern!"

"Minimum pattern ready, sir!"

"Fire!"

The ship lurched slightly. The target emitted a flash of blinding light and the *Enterprise* rocked. Uhura cried, "There—on the screen! It's still coming toward us, sir!"

The vaporous creature was growing larger, denser on the screen. "Deflectors up!" Kirk ordered.

"Deflectors up, sir."

Spock spoke into the awed silence. "The deflectors will not stop it, Captain." He was stooping, intent on his hooded viewer. "I should have guessed this! For the creature to be able to use gravity as a propulsive force, it would have to possess the capacity to flow through our deflector screens!"

"Any way to stop it, Mr. Spock?"

"Negative, Captain. It is able to throw its particles slightly out of time synchronization. It seems to measure our force-field pulsations—and stays a split second in front or behind them."

Chekov said, "Contact in five seconds, sir!"

Kirk hit his intercom button. "All decks, all stations, intruder alert!"

"All vents and hatches secure, sir," Chekov said. "All lights on the board show green—*No! Sir, the number-two impulse hatch! We've got a red light on it!*

Kirk whirled toward the screen. The cloudlike thing was on the ship now. Suddenly, it disappeared.

Scott turned, crying, "Captain! Something has entered through the number-two impulse vent!"

"Negative pressure all ship's vents! Mr. Chekov alert all decks!"

Red lights flashed to the ear-splitting howl of the alarm sirens.

"Well? Reports?"

Though Spock and McCoy sat at the Briefing Room table, it was Scott to whom the questions were directed. He knew it and looked away from Kirk's accusing eyes. "Sir, when it entered through impulse engine-two vent, it attacked two crewmen there before it went into the ventilation system."

"Bones?" Kirk said.

"One man has a bare chance of survival. The other is dead. So you can hang that little price tag to your monster hunt!"

"That's enough, Bones."

"It's *not* enough! You didn't care what happened as long as you could hang your trophy on the wall! Well, it's not *on* the wall, Captain! It's *in* it!"

Scott added his drop of reality to Kirk's cup of self-castigation. "With the ventilation system cut off, sir, we've air for only two hours."

Human beings with a cause, Kirk thought. You must not look to them for mercy. As though to confirm the thought, McCoy said, "I expect things don't look much brighter to the patients on colony Theta Seven."

Only in Spock, the half human, was there mercy. "May I suggest that we no longer belabor the point of whether or not we should have pursued the creature? The matter has become academic. The creature is now pursuing *us*."

"Creature, Mr. Spock?" said McCoy.

"*It turned and attacked, Doctor.* Its method was well considered and intelligent."

Kirk spoke very slowly. "I have no joy in being proved right, gentlemen, believe me. It could have been many light years away from us by now. But, instead, it chose to stop here. Why? Why? Why?''

"I must wait, Captain," Spock said. "Until I can make a closer analysis of the creature."

"We have two hours, Mr. Spock." Kirk turned to Scott. "Try flushing your radioactive waste into the ventilator system. It might cause some discomfort."

"Aye, sir."

McCoy rose with him. He halted at the door. "Jim, sorry about that few minutes ago. Your decision to go after it was right."

The exoneration should have meant something. It didn't. If you weren't companioned by the condemning thoughts of other people, you were companioned by those of your own conscience. Spock spoke. "Captain," he said, "the creature's ability to throw itself out of time, to desynchronize, allows it to be elsewhere in the instant our phasers strike. There is no basis, then, for your self-recrimination. If you had fired your phaser precisely on time twelve years ago, it would have made no more difference than it did an hour ago. Captain Garrovick would still be dead."

"Theories of guilt, of right or wrong, past and present—I seem to have outgrown them suddenly. Suddenly, Mr. Spock, my sole concern is saving my ship and my crew."

"The fault was not yours, Captain. There was no fault."

Kirk rose. "If you want to play psychoanalyst—and frankly, it's not your role, Spock—do it with Ensign Garrovick. Not me. Thank you." He left the Briefing Room without a backward glance.

Spock took the hint. He buzzed the door of Garrovick's quarters and walked in. Garrovick leaped to his feet.

"You may be seated, Ensign. I wish to talk to you."

The young face was puzzled. "Yes, sir."

"Ensign, am I correct in my assumption that you have been disturbed by what you consider a failure to behave in the prescribed manner in a moment of stress?"

Garrovick flushed painfully. "Well, I haven't been exactly proud of myself, sir."

"Perhaps you have considered this so-called failure of yours only from the standpoint of your own emotions."

Garrovick shook his head. "No, sir. I've considered the facts, too. And the facts are that men under my command died because I hesitated, because I stopped to analyze instead of acting. My attempt to be logical killed my men, Mr. Spock."

"Ensign, self-intolerance is an hereditary trait of your species."

"You make it sound like a disease, sir."

Their eyes, fixed on each other, failed to note the slight wisp of vapor that was filtering out of the jammed ventilator opening. Garrovick made a gesture of impatience. "You're telling me, 'Don't worry about it, Ensign! It happens to all of us. We'll just bury the bodies and won't think about them any more.' Isn't that it, Mr. Spock?"

"Not quite. You can learn from remorse, Ensign. It changes the human constitution. But guilt is a waste of time. Hate of the self, always undeserved, will ultimately crush you."

Spock paused suddenly, sniffing the air. "Do you smell anything?" he asked. "I thought I scented—" Then he saw the trail of mist drifting from the ventilator.

Garrovick whirled toward it. "Sir, it's the . . ."

Spock, grabbing his arm, propelled him to the door. "Out of here—fast! I will attempt to seal it off!"

He rushed to the ventilator opening. Seizing the jammed switch, he struggled to close it. But the cloud, full and dense now, was pouring into the room, over him, around him, and finally completely obscuring him.

In the corridor Garrovick raced to a wall communicator. "Captain! The creature! It's in my cabin, sir! It's got Mr. Spock!"

Kirk leaped from his chair. "On my way, Garrovick!" He dropped his speaker. "Scotty, reverse pressure, Cabin 341! Lieutenant Uhura, Security to 341! Medical alert!"

He'd given the right orders. In Garrovick's quarters, the creature, pulled by the suction of reversed pressure, was drawn back into the ventilator opening. McCoy, with a Security team, met him outside the door. As McCoy reached to open it, Kirk said, "Wait, Bones! We need a tricorder reading!"

As a guard adjusted his instrument, McCoy cried out, "Jim, Spock may be dying!"

Kirk whirled. "If we release that thing into the ship, he'll have a lot of company!"

Garrovick, ashen, spoke. "It's my fault, sir. I must have jammed the vent control when I hit a cup against it."

Kirk spoke to the guard. "Check if the reverse pressure has pulled it back into the ventilation system!"

"He saved my life, sir," Garrovick said brokenly. "I should be lying dead in there, not him."

Spock's voice came through the door. "I am gratified that neither of us is dead, Ensign." He flung the door open. "The reverse pressure worked, Captain. The vent is closed."

Stunned, Kirk stared at him. "Spock, don't misunderstand my question—but why aren't you dead?"

"That green blood of his!" shouted McCoy.

Spock nodded. "My hemoglobin is based on copper, not iron."

Kirk had moved to the cabin door, sniffing at it. "The scent—it's different. Yes . . . Yes, I think I understand now."

"You don't really believe you're in communication with the creature, Captain?"

"I'm not sure what it is, Spock. But you remember I said I knew it was alive. Perhaps it's not communication as we understand it, but I did know it was alive and intelligent. Now I know something else."

The wall communicator beeped. "Bridge to Captain Kirk."

Kirk flipped the switch. "Kirk here."

"Scott, sir. The creature's moving back toward the number-two impulse vent. The radioactive flushing may be affecting it."

"Open the vent," Kirk said. "On my way. Kirk out." He was running down the corridor when he hesitated and turned back. "Ensign Garrovick!"

Garrovick hastened to him. "Yes, sir?"

"You were on the bridge when we were attacked."

"I'm sorry, sir. I know I'd been confined to quarters, but when the alert sounded for battle stations, I . . ."

"Very commendable, Ensign. What was your impression of the battle?"

"I don't understand, sir."

"I'm asking for your military appraisal of the techniques employed against the creature."

Garrovick's jaw firmed. "Ineffective, sir." He added hastily. "I mean, Captain, you did everything possible. It's just that nothing works against a monster that can do what that thing does."

"And what's your appraisal of your conduct back on the planet?"

"I delayed firing."

"And if you had fired on time?" Kirk waited, his eyes on Garrovick's eyes. "It would have made no difference, Ensign. No weapon known would have made any difference. Then—or twelve years ago."

"Pardon, sir? I don't understand."

"I said, return to duty, Mr. Garrovick."

Joy flooded the young face. "Yes, sir. Thank you, Captain."

He was about to add something, but the elevator doors had already closed on Kirk.

There was news awaiting him on the bridge. Chekov, moving aside to surrender Spock's station to him, spoke eagerly. "Results positive, Captain. The creature has left the ship at high warp speed and is already out of scanner range."

Kirk had joined Spock at his station. "Direction, Mr. Spock?"

"Bearing was 127, mark 9. But I've already lost it now, sir."

Kirk switched on the intercom. "Scotty. I'm going to want all the speed you can deliver. Stick with it until we begin to shake apart. Kirk out." He turned to Spock. "I believe I know where it's going."

"It has changed course before to mislead us, sir. Logic would dictate that—"

"I'm playing intuition instead of logic, Mr. Spock. Mr. Chekov, compute a course for the Tychos Star System."

Heads snapped around. Controlling his surprise, Chekov punched in the course. "Computed and on the board, sir."

"Ahead full."

"Ahead full, sir."

"Lieutenant Uhura, contact the U.S.S. *Yorktown* and Starfleet. Inform both that we're pursuing the creature to planet 4 of that System. It's the location of its attack on the U.S.S. *Farragut* twelve years ago."

Spock said, "I don't understand, Captain."

"Remember when I said that the scent of the creature was somehow different? Something in my mind then said, 'birth . . . divide . . . multiply.' It said 'home'."

Spock's eyebrows went up. "And you know where 'home' is, Captain?"

"Yes. Home is where it fought a Starship once before. Lieutenant Uhura, give them our tactical situation. Tell them that I am committing this vessel to the creature's destruction. We will rendezvous with the *Yorktown*—" He turned to Chekov. "Round trip, Mr. Chekov?"

"One point seven days, sir."

"Lieutenant Uhura, we will rendezvous with the *Yorktown* in forty-eight hours."

Planet 4 of the Tychos Star System was a strangely dull, lifeless-looking one. On the bridge McCoy eyed its viewer image with distaste. He spoke to Spock. "I assume you also think we should pursue this creature and destroy it."

"Definitely, Doctor."

"You don't agree with us, Bones?"

McCoy shrugged. "It's a mother. I don't happen to enjoy destroying mothers."

Spock said, "If the creature is about to spawn, it will undoubtedly reproduce by fission, not just in two parts but thousands."

Kirk glanced at him. "Anti-matter seems to be our only possibility then."

Spock nodded. "An ounce should be sufficient. We can drain it out of our engines, transport it to the planet in the magnetic vacuum field."

Garrovick had taken up a position beside Kirk's chair. "Ensign, contact medical stores. I want as much hemoplasm as they can spare. And I want it in the Transporter Room in fifteen minutes."

"Yes, sir."

"You intend to use the hemoplasm to attract the creature?" McCoy asked.

"We have to lure it to the anti-matter. As it's attracted by red blood cells, what better bait can we have?"

"There remains one problem, Captain."

Kirk nodded at Spock. "The blast."

"Exactly. A matter-anti-matter blast will rip half the planet's atmosphere away. If our ship is still in orbit, and encounters those—shock waves . . ."

"We'll have to take that chance."

Spock said, "No one can guarantee our Transporter will operate under such conditions. If a man is beaming up when that blast hits, we may lose him, Captain."

Garrovick who had returned was listening intently. He flushed as Kirk said, "That's why I've decided to set the trap myself, Mr. Spock."

Spock got up. "Captain, I have so little hemoglobin in my blood the creature would not be able to harm me extensively. It would seem logical for me to be the one who—"

"Negative, Mr. Spock. I want you on board in case this fails. In that case another plan will have to be devised."

"Captain," Spock persisted, "it will require two men to transport the anti-matter unit."

"Sir," Garrovick said. "Sir, I request permission to go with you."

Kirk regarded him speculatively. Then he nodded. "Yes," he said. "I had you in mind, Mr. Garrovick."

Desolation—a brittle world of death was the world of the creature, its surface scarred and blackened by lava fissures, the hideous corrugations of dead volcanoes. As they materialized on it, Kirk and Garrovick staggered under the burden of the anti-matter unit, their anti-gravs tight on the brilliant metal sphere suspended between them. The hemoplasm container took form beside them. The moment he found secure footage on his lava ridge, Kirk freed a hand to open his communicator.

"Kirk to *Enterprise*."

"Spock here, Captain."

"Proceed immediately to maximum distant orbit, Mr. Spock."

"Yes, sir."

Garrovick said, "this is the ultimate, sir. Less than an ounce of anti-matter here . . . and yet more power than ten thousand cobalt bombs."

Kirk nodded. "A pound of it would destroy a whole solar system. I hope it's as powerful as man is allowed to get."

There was a small rise in front of them. Leaving the hemoplasm where it lay, they carefully positioned the anti-matter container on the little hillock of flattened lava.

"Detonator," Kirk said.

Garrovick handed him a small device. Moving with utmost care, Kirk attached it to the container. Then, with the flick of a switch, he armed it. That done, he reopened his communicator.

"Kirk to *Enterprise*."

"Spock here, Captain. Holding at thirty thousand kilometers."

"Anti-matter container positioned and armed. I'll call back when I've baited it. Kirk out."

"Captain! Look!"

The vaporous thing had fully emerged from a lava fissure and was flowing over the hemoplasm, ingesting it. "The hemoplasm!" Garrovick cried. "That bait's already gone!"

Kirk straightened. "We'll have to use something else."

"But it only feeds on blood!"

Kirk's older eyes met the younger ones. "Transport back to the ship, Ensign. Tell them to prepare to detonate."

Garrovick was aghast. "You, sir? *You're* going to be the bait?"

"You heard your order. Get back to the ship!"

Garrovick didn't respond. He looked again toward the creature. Gorged on the hemoplasm, it was still hovering over the container. Then, very slowly, it began to move toward the two humans.

Kirk grabbed Garrovick's arm, and swung him around. "I gave you an order!" he shouted.

"Yes, sir." He took out his communicator; and starting to walk slowly past Kirk, prepared to give beam-up instructions. Then, without warning, he whirled and struck Kirk with a sharp karate chop on the back of the neck. Kirk fell. Garrovick, glancing quickly toward the creature, stooped to pick up Kirk's body. Kirk lashed out with a kick that threw Garrovick off-balance. He stumbled and Kirk jumped to his feet.

"Ensign, consider yourself on report! We don't have time in this service for heroics. I have no intention of sacrificing myself. Come on!" He yanked Garrovick into a position that placed the anti-matter unit between them and the creature. Then he opened his communicator. "Kirk to *Enterprise*!"

"Spock, Captain."

"Scan us, Spock and lock onto us. It's going to be very close. Stand by." He looked back. The creature was almost on him, a thin tentacle of mist drifting toward his throat.

"I—I can smell it, Captain. It's sickly . . . honey sweet."

"Stand by, *Enterprise*," Kirk said. He saw that the creature, seeking blood in the anti-matter unit, was flowing over the metal sphere. Shouting into his communicator, he cried, *"Now Energize! And detonate!"*

Their bodies went into shimmer, fading. Then the world of the creature blew up.

In the Transporter Room of the *Enterprise*, Spock saw the forms of Kirk and Garrovick begin to take shape. They held it only for a fleeting second before they dissolved once more into shining fragments. Spock's steady hands worked at the controls, adjusting them. Scott, panic-stricken, flung himself at the Transporter console. McCoy yelled, "Don't just stand there! For God's sake, *do* something!"

Chekov spoke over the intercom. "All decks, stand by. Shock waves!"

The Transporter Room rocked crazily. Spock and Scott, flung to their knees, struggled desperately to stay with the console controls. Then they both looked over at the Transporter chamber. It was empty.

Spock said, "Cross-circuit to B, Mr. Scott."

McCoy uttered a literal howl. *"What a crazy way to*

travel! Spilling a man's molecules all over the damned universe!''

Scott said, "Picking it up . . . I think we're picking them up."

McCoy looked away from the empty Transporter chamber. When he found what it took to look back, two forms were again assuming shape and substance. Kirk and Garrovick stepped from the platform—whole, unharmed.

Scott sank down over the console. "Captain," he said as though to himself. "Captain." He sighed. "Thank God."

Spock was reproving. "There was no deity involved, Mr. Scott. It was my cross-circuit to selector B that recovered them."

McCoy eyed Spock with disgust. "Well, thank pitchforks and pointed ears, then! As long as they worked!"

Kirk used his communicator. "Captain Kirk to bridge."

"Chekov here, Captain."

"Lay a course for the *Yorktown* rendezvous, Mr. Chekov. Maximum warp."

"Aye, sir."

Kirk smiled at Garrovick. "Come to my cabin when you've cleaned up, Ensign. I want to tell you about your father. Several stories I think you'll like to hear."

Garrovick looked at him, adoration in his eyes.

"Thank you, sir. I will."

THE IMMUNITY SYNDROME

Writer: Robert Sabaroff
Director: Joseph Pevney

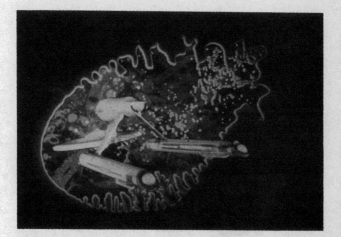

White beaches . . . suntanned women . . . mountains, their trout streams just asking for it . . . the lift of a surfboard to a breaking wave . . . familiar tree-shapes—that was shore leave on Starbase Six. And the exhausted crew of the *Enterprise* was on its way to it, unbelievably nearing it at long last. Kirk, remembering the taste of an open-air breakfast of rainbow trout, turned to give Sulu his final approach orders.

"Message from the base, sir," Uhura called. "Heavy interference. All I could get was the word '*Intrepid*' and what sounded like a sector coordinate."

"Try them on another channel, Lieutenant."

McCoy said, "The *Intrepid* is manned by Vulcans only, isn't it, Jim?"

"I believe so." Kirk swung his chair around. "The crew of the *Intrepid* is Vulcan, isn't it, Mr. Spock? I seem to remember the Starship was made entirely Vulcan as a tribute to the skill of your people in arranging that truce with the Romulan Federation. It was an unusual honor."

Spock didn't answer. He didn't turn. But he'd straightened in his chair. Something in the movement disturbed Kirk. He got up and went over to the library-computer station. "Mr. Spock!" Still Spock sat, unmoving, silent. Kirk shook his shoulder. "Spock, what's wrong? Are you in pain?"

"The *Intrepid* is dead. I just felt it die."

Kirk looked at McCoy. McCoy shook his head, shrugging.

"Mr. Spock, you're tired," Kirk said. "Let Chekov take over your station."

"And the four hundred Vulcans aboard her are dead," Spock said.

McCoy said, "Come down to Sickbay, Spock."

Stone-faced, Spock said, "I am quite all right, Doctor. I know what I feel."

Kirk said, "Report to Sickbay, Mr. Spock. That's an order."

"Yes, Captain."

Kirk watched them move to the elevator. They'd all had it. Too many missions. Even Spock's superb stamina had its breaking point. Too many rough missions—and Vulcan logic itself could turn morbidly visionary. It was high time for shore leave.

"Captain, I have Starbase Six now," Uhura said.

Back in his chair, Kirk flipped a switch. "Kirk here. Go ahead."

The bridge speaker spoke. "The last reported position of the Starship *Intrepid* was sector three nine J. You will divert immediately."

Kirk rubbed a hand over his chin before he reached for his own speaker. "The *Enterprise* has just completed the last of several very strenuous missions. The crew is tired. We're on our way for R and R. There must be another Starship in that sector."

"Negative. This is a rescue priority order. We have lost all contact with solar system Gamma Seven A. The *Intrepid* was investigating. Contact has now been lost with the *Intrepid*. Report progress."

"Order acknowledged," Kirk said. "Kirk out."

Sulu was staring at him in questioning dismay. Kirk snapped, "You heard the order, Mr. Sulu. Lay in a course for Gamma Seven A."

Chekov spoke from his console. Awe subdued his voice. "Solar System Gamma Seven A is dead, Captain. My long-range scan of it shows—"

"Dead? What are you saying, Mr. Chekov? That is a fourth-magnitude star! Its system supports billions of inhabitants! Check your readings!"

"I have, sir. Gamma Seven A is dead."

* * *

In Sickbay Spock was saying, "I assure you, Doctor, I am quite all right. The pain was momentary."

McCoy sighed as he took his last diagnostic reading. "My instruments appear to agree with you if I can trust them with a crazy Vulcan anatomy. By the way, how can you be so sure the *Intrepid* is destroyed?"

"I felt it die," his patient said tonelessly.

"But I thought you had to be in physical contact with a subject to sense—"

"Dr. McCoy, even I, a half Vulcan, can sense the death screams of four hundred Vulcan minds crying out over distance between us."

McCoy shook his head. "It's beyond me."

Spock was shouldering back into his shirt. "I have noticed this insensitivity among wholly human beings. It is easier for you to feel the death of one fellow-creature than to feel the deaths of millions."

"Suffer the deaths of thy neighbors, eh, Spock? Is that what you want to wish on us?"

"It might have rendered your history a bit less bloody."

The intercom beeped. "Kirk here. Bones, is Spock all right? If he is, I need him on the bridge."

"Coming, Captain." Kirk met him at the elevator. "You may have been right. Contact with the *Intrepid* has been lost. It has also been lost with an entire solar system. Our scans show that Gamma Seven A is a dead star system."

"That is considerable news." Spock hurried over to his station and Kirk spoke to Uhura. "Any update from Starfleet?"

"I can't filter out the distortions. They're getting worse, sir."

A red light flashed on Sulu's panel. "Captain, the deflector shields just snapped on!"

"Slow down to warp three!" Kirk walked back to Spock. The Vulcan straightened from his stoop over his computer. "Indications of energy turbulence ahead, sir. Unable to analyze. I have never encountered such readings before."

The drama latent in the statement was so uncharacteristic of Spock that Kirk whirled to the main viewing screen. "Magnification factor three on screen!" he ordered.

Star-filled space—the usual vista. "Scan sector," he said. The starfield merely revealed itself from another angle and Sulu said, "Just what are we looking for, Captain?"

"I would assume," Spock said, "*that*."

A black shadow, roughly circular, had appeared on the screen.

"An interstellar dust cloud," Chekov suggested.

Kirk shook his head. "The stars have disappeared. They could be seen through a dust cloud, Mr. Chekov. How do you read it, Mr. Spock?"

"Analysis still eludes me, Captain. Sensors are feeding data to computers now. But whatever that dark zone is, my calculations place it directly on the course that would have brought it into contact with the *Intrepid* and the Gamma Seven A system."

"Are you saying it caused their deaths, Mr. Spock?"

"A possibility, Captain."

After a moment, Kirk nodded. "Hold present course but slow to warp factor one," he told Sulu. "Mr. Chekov, prepare to launch telemetry probe into that zone."

"Aye, sir." Chekov moved controls on his console. "Probe ready. Switching data feed to library-computer."

"Launch probe," Kirk said.

Chekov shoved a stud. "Probe launched."

An ear-shattering blast of static burst from the communications station. Its noise swelled into a crackling roar so fierce that it seemed to possess a physical substance—the substance and force of a giant's slap. It ended as abruptly as it had come. Uhura, dizzy, disoriented, was clinging to her chair.

"And what channel did *that* come in on?" Kirk said.

She had to make a visible effort to answer. "Telemetry . . . the channel from the probe, sir. There's no signal . . . at all now . . ."

"Mr. Spock, speculations?"

"I have none, Captain." Then Spock had leaped from his chair. Uhura, her arms dropped, limp, was slumped over her console. "Lieutenant!" He reached an arm around her, steadying her. "Dizzy," she whispered. "I'll . . . be all right in a minute."

The intercom beeped to McCoy's voice. "Jim, half the women on this ship have fainted. Reports in from all decks."

Kirk glanced at Uhura. "Maybe you'd better check Lieutenant Uhura. She just pulled out of a faint."

"Unless she's out now, keep her up there. I've got an emergency here."

"What's wrong?"

"Nothing organic. Just weakness, nervousness."

"Can you handle it?"

"I can give them stimulants to keep them on their feet."

A tired crew—and now this. Kirk looked at the screen. It offered no cheer. The black shadow now owned almost all of the screen. Hold position here, Mr. Sulu." He got up from his chair—and was hit by an attack of vertigo. He fought it down. "Mr. Spock, I want an update on that shadow ahead of us."

"No analysis, sir. Insufficient information."

Kirk smacked the computer console. "Mr. Spock. I have asked you three times for data on that thing and you have been unable to supply it. 'Insufficient information' won't do. It is your responsibility to deliver sufficient information at all times."

"I am aware of that, sir. But there is nothing in the computer banks on this phenomenon. It is beyond all previous experience."

Kirk looked at the hand that had struck Spock's console. "Weakness, nervousness." He was guilty on both counts. Even Spock couldn't elicit data from the computer banks that hadn't been put into them. "Sorry, Mr. Spock. Something seems to be infecting the entire ship. Let's go for reverse logic. If you can't tell me what that zone of darkness is, tell me what it isn't."

"It is not gaseous, liquid nor solid, despite the fact we can't see through it. It is not a galactic nebula like the Coal Sack. As it has activated our deflector shields, it seems to consist of some energy form—but none that the sensors can identify."

"And you said it is possible it killed the *Intrepid* and that solar system?"

"Yes, Captain."

Kirk turned to Uhura. "Lieutenant, inform Starfleet of our position and situation. Relay all relative information from computer banks." He paused. "Tell them we intend to probe further into the zone of darkness to gain further information."

"Yes, sir."

As he started back to his chair, he swayed under another wash of dizziness. Spock moved to him quickly and he clung for a moment to the muscular arm. "Thank you, Mr. Spock," he said. "I can make it now." He reached his chair. "Distance to the zone of darkness, Mr. Sulu?"

"One hundred thousand kilometers."

"Slow ahead, Mr. Sulu. Impulse power."

His head was still whirling. "Distance now, Mr. Sulu?"

"We penetrate the zone in one minute seven seconds, sir."

"Mr. Chekov, red alert. Stand by, phasers. Full power to deflector shields."

"Phasers standing by—deflectors at full power, sir."

Sound was emitted. It came slowly at first—and not from the communications station. It came from everywhere; and as it built, its mounting tides of invisible shock waves reached everywhere. Their reverberations struck through the metal walls of the engineering section, rushing Scott to check his equipment. Horrified by his readings, he ran to his power levers to test them. Then, mercifully, the all-pervading racket subsided. Up on the bridge, his hands still pressed to his ears, Sulu cried, "Captain—the screen!"

Blackness, total, had claimed it.

"Malfunction, Mr. Spock?"

"No, Captain. All systems working."

Kirk shook his head, trying to clear it. Around him people were still clutching at console rails for support. Kirk struck the intercom button. "Bones, things any better in Sickbay?"

"Worse. They're backed up into the corridor."

"Got anything that will help up here? I don't want anyone on the bridge folding at a critical moment."

"On my way. McCoy out."

Kirk pushed the intercom button again. "Kirk to Engineering. The power's dropped, Mr. Scott! What's happened?''

"We've lost five points of our energy reserve. The deflector shields have been weakened."

"Can you compensate, Scotty?"

"Yes, if we don't lose any more. Don't ask me how it happened."

Kirk spoke sharply. "I *am* asking you, mister. I need answers!"

McCoy's answer was an air-hypo. He hurried into the bridge with a nurse. As Kirk accepted the hissing injection, McCoy said, "It's a stimulant, Jim." As he adjusted the hypo for Sulu's shot, Kirk said, "Just how bad is it, Bones?"

"Two thirds of personnel are affected."

"This is a sick ship, Bones. We're picking up problems faster than we can solve them. It's as though we were in the middle of some creeping paralysis."

"Maybe we are," McCoy said. He left the command chair to continue his round with the hypo. Kirk got up to go to the computer station. "Mr. Spock, any analysis of that last noise outburst—the one that started to lose us power?"

Spock nodded. "The sound was the turbulence caused by our penetration of a boundary layer."

"What sort of boundary layer?"

"I don't know, Captain."

"Boundary between what and what?"

"Between where we were and where we are." At Kirk's stare, he went on. "I still have no specifics, sir. But we seem to have entered an area of energy that is not compatible with life or mechanical processes. As we move on, the source of it will grow stronger—and we will grow weaker."

"Recommendations?"

McCoy spoke. "*I* recommend survival, Jim. Let's get out of here." He turned and walked to the elevator, the nurse behind him.

Kirk faced around to the questioning faces. And Starbase had demanded a "progress" report. Progress to what? The fate of the *Intrepid*—the billions of lives that had once breathed on Gamma Seven A? Bureaucracy . . . evasion by comfortable chairs.

He walked slowly back to his uncomfortable chair. The

intercom button—yes. "This is the Captain speaking," he said. "We have entered an area that is unfamiliar to us. All hands were tired to begin with and we've all sustained something of a shock. But we've had stimulants. Our deflectors are holding. We've got a good ship. And we know what our mission is. Let's get on with the job. Kirk out."

His own intercom button beeped. "Sickbay to Captain."

"Kirk. Go ahead, Bones."

Before he went ahead, McCoy glanced at the semiconscious Yeoman lying on his diagnostic couch. "Jim, one after another . . . life energy levels . . . my indicators . . ."

Kirk spoke quietly. "Say it, Bones."

"We are dying," McCoy said. "My life monitors show that we are all, each one of us, dying."

The sweat of his own weakness broke from Kirk's pores. He could feel it run cold down his chest.

But the ordeal of the *Enterprise* had just begun. Kirk, down in Engineering, was flung against a mounded dynamo at a sudden lurch of the ship. "And that? What was that, Mr. Scott?"

"An accident, sir. We went into reverse."

"Reverse? That was a *forward* lurch! How could that occur in reverse thrust?"

"I don't know, sir. All I know is that our power levels are draining steadily. They're down to twelve percent. I've never experienced anything like it before."

Spock came in on the intercom. "Captain, we are accelerating. The zone of darkness is pulling us toward it."

"Pulling us? How, Mr. Spock?"

"I don't know. However, I suggest that Mr. Scott give us reverse power."

"Mr. Spock, he just *gave* us reverse power!"

"Then I reverse my suggestion, sir. Ask him to apply a forward thrust."

"Mr. Scott, you heard that. Let's try the forward thrust."

The Engineering Chief shook his head. "I don't know, sir. It contradicts all the rules of logic."

"Logic is Mr. Spock's specialty."

"Yes, sir, but—"

"Nudge it slowly into forward thrust, Mr. Scott."

Scott carefully advanced three controls. Eyeing his instruments anxiously, he relaxed. "That did it, Captain. We're slowing now. But the forward movement hasn't stopped. We're still being pulled ahead."

"Keep applying the forward thrust against the pull. Have one of your men monitor these instruments."

Instruments in Sickbay were being monitored, too. Nurse Chapel, watching her life function indicators, called, "Doctor, they're showing another sharp fall." McCoy, whirling to look, muttered, "Stimulants. How long can we keep them up?" He was checking the panel when Kirk's voice came from the intercom. "This is the Captain speaking. All department heads will report to the Briefing Room in ten minutes. They will come with whatever information gathered on this zone of darkness we are in."

McCoy took his gloom with him to the Briefing Room. Slamming some tape cartridges down on the table, he said, "My sole contribution is the fact that the further we move into this zone of darkness, the weaker our life functions get. I have no idea why." Reaching for a chair, he staggered slightly.

"Bones . . ."

He waved the solicitude aside. "I'm all right. All those stimulants—they catch up with you."

Scott spoke. "As far as the power levels are concerned, everything's acting backwards. But the drain is continuing. And we're still being dragged forward."

"Mr. Spock?" Kirk said.

"I am assuming that something within the zone absorbs both biological and mechanical energy. It would appear to be the same thing that sucked energy from an entire solar system—and the Starship *Intrepid*."

"Some *thing*, Mr. Spock? Not the zone itself?"

"I would say not, Captain. Analysis of the zone suggests it is a negative energy field, however illogical that may sound. *But it is not the source of the power drains.*"

"A shield, then," Kirk said. "An outer layer of protection for something else."

"But what?" Scott said.

"It's pulling the life out of us, whatever it is," McCoy grunted.

"We'll find out what it is," Kirk said. "But first we have to get out of here ourselves." He leaned across the table. "Mr. Scott, forward thrust slowed down our advance before. If you channel all warp and impulse power into one massive forward thrust, it might snap us out of the zone."

Scott's face lightened. "Aye, Captain. I'll reserve enough for the shields in case we don't get out."

Spock's voice was as expressionless as his face. "I submit, Mr. Scott, that if we do not get out, the shields would merely prolong our wait for death."

Kirk regarded him somberly. "Yes. You will apply all power as needed to get us out of here, Mr. Scott. Report to your stations, everybody, and continue your research. Dismissed."

As they left, he remained seated, head bowed on his hand. At the door Spock stopped, and came back to stand, waiting, at the table. Kirk looked up at him. "The *Intrepid*'s crew would have done all these things, Captain," Spock said. "They were destroyed."

Kirk drummed his fingers on the table. "They may not have done all these things. You've just told us what an illogical situation this is."

"True, sir. It is also true that they never discovered what killed them."

"How can you know that?"

"Vulcan has not been conquered within its collective memory. It is a memory that goes so far back no Vulcan can any longer conceive of a conqueror. I know the ship was defeated because I sensed its death."

"What was it exactly you felt, Mr. Spock?"

"Astonishment. Profound astonishment."

"My Vulcan friend," Kirk said. He got up. "Let's get back to the bridge."

Engineering was calling him as they came out of the elevator. Hurrying to his chair, Kirk pushed the intercom stud. "Kirk here, Scotty."

"We've completed arrangements, sir. I'm ready to try it when you are."

"We've got the power to pull it off?"

The voice was glum. "I hope so, Captain."

"Stand by, Scotty." He pushed another button. "All hands, this is the Captain speaking. An unknown force is pulling us deeper into the zone of darkness. We will apply all available power in one giant forward thrust in the hope it will yank us out of the zone. Prepare yourselves for a big jolt." He buzzed Engineering. "Ready, Mr. Scott. Let's get on with it. *Now!*"

They were prepared for the jolt. And it was big. But what they weren't prepared for was the violently accelerating lunge that followed the jolt. Scott and a crewman crashed against a rear wall. McCoy and Christine Chapel were sent reeling back through two sections of Sickbay. In the bridge an African plant nurtured by Uhura flew through the air to smash against the elevator door. People were hurled bodily over the backs of their chairs. There was another fierce lurch of acceleration. The ship tossed like a rearing horse. Metal screamed. Lights faded. Finally, the *Enterprise* steadied.

From the floor where he'd been tumbled, Kirk looked at the screen.

Failure. The starless black still possessed it.

Weary, bruised, Kirk hauled himself back into his chair. The question had to be asked. He asked it. "Mr. Scott, are we still losing power?"

"Aye, sir. All we did was to pull away a bit. The best we can do now is maintain thrust against the pull to hold our distance."

"How long do we have?"

"At this rate of drain plus the draw on all systems—two hours, Captain."

As Kirk got to his feet, another wave of weakness swept over him. It passed—and he moved over to the computer station. "We're trying to hold our distance, Mr. Spock. Have you yet ascertained what we are holding the distance *from*?"

Spock, his eyes on his own screen, said, "I have not found out what that thing is, Captain. But it seems to have found us."

Kirk wheeled to the bridge viewer. In the center of its blackness a bright object had become visible—bright, pulsating, elongated.

Staring at it, Kirk said, "Mr. Chekov, prepare to launch a probe."

Bent to his hooded computer, Spock said, "Very confused readings, Captain—but that object is definitely the source of the energy drains."

"Mr. Chekov, launch probe," Kirk said.

"Probe launched, sir. Impact in seven point three seconds."

Without order Sulu began the countdown. "Six, five . . . four . . . three . . . two . . . one . . . *now*!"

The ship trembled. Lights blinked. But that was all.

"Mr. Chekov, do we still have contact with the probe?"

"Yes, sir. Data being relayed to Mr. Spock."

"Mr. Spock?"

The Vulcan's head was hidden under the computer's mound. "Readings coming in now, Captain. Length, approximately eleven thousand miles. Varying in width from two thousand to three thousand miles. Outer layer strewn with space debris and other wastes. Interior consists of protoplasm varying from a firmer gelatinous layer to a semi-fluid central mass."

He withdrew his head from the computer. "Condition . . . living."

The faces around Kirk were stunned. He looked away from them and back at Spock. "Living," he said. Then, his voice very quiet, he said, "Magnification four, Mr. Sulu. On the main screen."

He had expected a horror—and he received it. The screen held what might be a nightmare of some child who had played with a lab microscope—a monstrous, amoebalike protozoan. The gigantic nucleus throbbed, its chromosome bodies vaguely shadowed under its gelatinous, spotted skin. In open loathing, Kirk shut his eyes. But he could not dispel his searing memory of what continued to show on the screen.

In Sickbay's lab, McCoy was parading a pictured series of one-celled creatures. On the small viewscreen a paramecium, its cilia wriggling, came and went. Then McCoy said, "This is an amoeba."

If life was movement, ingestion, the thing was alive, a microscopic inhabitant of stagnant pools. As Kirk watched,

a pseudopod extended itself, groping but intent on a fragment
of food. There was a blind greed in the creature that sickened
Kirk.

"I've seen them before," he said. "Like that, enlarged
by microscope. But this thing out there is eleven thousand
miles long! Are you saying that anything so huge is a single-
celled animal?"

"For lack of a better term, Jim. Huge as it is, it is a
very simple form of life. And it can perform all the functions
necessary to qualify it as a living organism. It can reproduce,
receive sense impressions, act on them, and eat, though what
its diet is I wouldn't know."

"Energy," Spock said. "Energy drained from us. I
would speculate that this unknown life form is invading the
galaxy like an infection."

"Mr. Spock, the *Intrepid* died of this particular infection. Why have we survived so long?"

"The *Intrepid* must have come upon it when it was
hungry, low in energy. We are not safe, Captain. We merely
have a little more time than the *Intrepid* had."

"Bones, this zone of darkness. Does the thing generate
it itself as some form of protection?"

"That's one of the things we have to find out, Jim. We
need a closer look at it."

"The closer to it we get, the faster it eats our energy.
We're barely staying alive at this distance from it."

McCoy shut off his screen. "We could risk the shuttlecraft. With special shielding, it might—"

"I'm not sending anybody anywhere near that thing!
Unmanned probes will give us the information we need to
destroy it."

"I must differ with you, Captain," Spock said. "We
have sent probes into it. They have told us some facts but not
those we need to know. We're in no position to expend the
power to take blind shots at it. We need a target."

McCoy said, "One man could go in . . . pinpoint its
vulnerable spots."

"And the odds against his coming back?" Kirk cried.
"How can I order anyone to take such a chance?"

"Who mentioned orders?" McCoy demanded. "You've

got yourself a volunteer, Jim, my boy. I've already done the preliminary work.''

"Bones, it's a suicide mission!''

"Doctor, this thing has reflexes. The unmanned probe stung it when it entered. The lurch we felt was the turbulence of its reaction.''

"All right, Spock,'' McCoy said. "Then I'll have the sense to go slow when I penetrate it.''

Spock studied him. "There is a latent martyr in you, Doctor. It is an affliction that disqualifies you to undertake the mission.''

"Martyr?'' McCoy yelled. "You think I intend to by-pass the chance to get into the greatest living laboratory ever?''

"The *Intrepid* carried physicians and psychologists, Doctor. They died.''

"Just because Vulcans failed doesn't mean a human will.''

Kirk hit the table with his fist. "Will you both kindly shut up? I've told you! I'm not taking volunteers!''

"You don't think you're going, do you?'' McCoy shouted.

"I am a command pilot!'' Kirk said. "And as such, I am the qualified person. So let's have an end of this!''

"You have just *disqualified* yourself, Captain,'' Spock said. "As the command pilot you are indispensable. Nor are you the scientific specialist which I am.''

McCoy glared at Spock. "Jim, that organism contains chemical processes we've never seen before and may never, let's hope, see again. We could learn more in one day than—''

"We don't have a day,'' Kirk said. "We have precisely one hour and thirty-five minutes. Then all our power is exhausted.''

"Jim . . .''

"Captain . . .''

Kirk whirled on them both. "*I* will decide who can best serve the success of this mission! When I have made my command decision—command decision, gentlemen—you will be notified.''

He turned on his heel and left them.

The solitude of his quarters felt good. He closed the

door behind him, unhooked his belt and with his back turned to the clock's face deliberately stretched himself out on his bunk. Relax. Let the quiet move up, inch by inch, from his feet to his throbbing head. *Let go.* If you could just let go, answers sometimes welled up from an untapped wisdom that resisted pushing. "God, let me relax," Kirk prayed.

It was true. He *was* indispensable. There was no room in command authority for the heroics of phony modesty. As to Bones, he *did* have the medical-biological advantages he'd claimed. But Spock, the born athlete, the physical-fitness fanatic, the Vulcan logician and Science Officer, was both physically and emotionally better suited to withstand the stresses of such a mission. Yet who could know what invaluable discoveries Bones might make if he got his chance to make them? So it was up to him—Kirk. The choice was his. One of his friends had to be condemned to probable death. Which one?

He drew a long shuddering breath. Then he reached out to the intercom over his head and shoved its button. "This is the Captain speaking. Dr. McCoy and Mr. Spock report to my quarters at once. Kirk out."

The beep came as he sat up. "Engineering to Captain Kirk."

"Go ahead, Scotty."

"You wanted to be kept informed of the power drain, sir. All levels have sunk to fifty percent. Still draining. We can maintain power for another hour and fifteen minutes."

"Right, Scotty." He drew a hand over the bunk's coverlet, stared at the hand, and said, "Prepare the shuttlecraft for launching."

"What's that, sir?"

"You heard me, Scotty, Dr. McCoy will tell you what special equipment to install. Kirk out."

Of course. The knock on his door. He got up and opened it. They were both standing there, their mutual antagonism weaving back and forth between them. "Come in, gentlemen." There was no point, no time for suspense. "I'm sorry, Mr. Spock," Kirk said heavily.

McCoy flashed a look of triumph at Spock. "Well done, Jim," he said. "I'll get the last few things I need and—"

Kirk stopped him in midstride. "Not you, Bones." He

turned to Spock. "I'm sorry, Spock. I am sorry you are the best qualified to go."

Spock nodded briefly. He didn't speak as he passed the crushed McCoy.

The door to the hangar-deck elevator slid open. Spock moved aside to allow McCoy to precede him out of it. "Do not suffer so, Doctor. Professional credentials are very valuable. But superior resistance to strain has occasionally proved more valuable."

"Nothing has been proven yet!" McCoy controlled himself with an effort. "My DNA code analyzer will give you the fundamental structure of the organism. You'll need readings on three light wavelengths from the enzyme recorder."

"I am familiar with the equipment, Doctor. Time is passing. The shuttlecraft is ready."

"You just won't let me share in this at all, will you, Spock?"

"This is not a competition, Doctor. Kindly grant me my own kind of dignity."

"Vulcan dignity? How can I grant you what I don't understand?"

"Then employ one of your human superstitions. Wish me luck, Dr. McCoy."

McCoy gave him a startled look. Without rejoinder, he shoved the button that opened the hangar-deck door. Beyond them the metallic skin of the chosen shuttlecraft gleamed dimly. Two technicians busied themselves with it, making some final arrangements. Spock, without looking back, walked through the hangar door. McCoy saw him climb into the craft. Then the door slid closed; McCoy, alone, muttered, "Good luck, Spock, damn you."

Kirk, on the bridge, waited. Then Sulu turned. "All systems clear for shuttlecraft launch, sir."

It was time to say the words. "Launch shuttlecraft."

The light winked on Sulu's console. Spock was on his way. Alone. In space, alone. Committed—given over to what he, his Captain, had given him over to. Kirk heard the elevator whoosh open. McCoy came out of it. Kirk didn't turn.

He said, "Lieutenant Uhura, channel telemetry directly to Mr. Chekov at the computer station."

The bridge speaker spoke. "Shuttlecraft to *Enterprise*."

"Report, Mr. Spock."

"The power drain is enormous and growing worse." Static crackled. "I am diverting all secondary power systems to the shields. I will continue communications as long as there is power to transmit."

Spock would be huddled now, Kirk knew, over the craft's control panel. He'd be busy shutting off power systems. Somehow Scott had suddenly materialized beside his command chair. "Captain! He won't have power enough to get back if he diverts it to his shields!"

"Spock," Kirk began.

"I heard, Captain. We recognized that probability earlier. But you will need information communicated."

"When do you estimate penetration?"

"In one point three minutes. Brace yourselves. The area of penetration will no doubt be sensitive."

What was Spock's screen showing? What was his close-up like? The details of the debris-mottled membrane, the enlarging granular structure of the protoplasm under it, two thousand miles thick?

"Contact in six seconds," Spock's voice said.

A tremor shook the *Enterprise*. That meant the massive shock of impact for the shuttlecraft. Its lights would dim, alone in the dimness inside the thing. Kirk seized the microphone.

"Report, Mr. Spock."

Silence reported. Had Spock already lost consciousness? The organism would try to dislodge the craft. It would convulse, its convulsions sending its painful intruder into a spinning vortex of repeated shocks.

"Spock . . ."

The voice came, weak now. "I am undamaged, Captain . . . relay to Mr. Scott . . . I had three percent power reserve . . . before the shields stabilized. I . . . will proceed with my tests" . . . The voice faded . . . then it returned. "Dr. McCoy . . . you would not . . . have survived this . . ."

Kirk saw that McCoy's eyes were moist. "You wanna bet, Spock?" His voice broke on the name.

"I am . . . moving very slowly now—establishing course toward . . . the nucleus."

Chekov, white-faced, called from the computer. "Sir, Mr. Spock has reduced his life support systems to bare minimum. I suppose to maintain communications."

Kirk's hand was wet on his microphone. "Spock, save your power for the shields."

Static sputtered from the microphone. Between its cracklings, words could be heard. "My . . . calculations indicate—shields . . . only forty-seven minutes." More obliterating static. It quieted. "Identified . . . Chromosome structure. Changes in it . . . reproduction process about to begin."

Ashen, McCoy cried, "Then there'll be *two* of these things!"

"Spock . . ."

Kirk got an earful of static. He waited. "I . . . am having . . . some difficulty . . . ship control."

Kirk looked away from the pain in McCoy's face. He waited again. As though it were warning of its waning usefulness, the mike spoke in jagged phrases. ". . . losing voice contact . . . transmitting . . . here are internal coordinates . . . chromosome bodies . . ."

Uhura turned from her console. "Contact lost, sir. But I got the coordinates."

"Captain!" It was Chekov. "The shuttlecraft shields are breaking! Fluctuations of energy inside the organism."

"Aye," Scott said. "It's time he got out of there."

There was nobody to look at but himself, Kirk thought. He was the man who had sent his best friend to death. He had sent Spock out to suffocate in the foul entrails of a primordial freak. That was a truth to somehow be lived with for the rest of his life. His chair lurched under him. The ship gave a shudder. Numbly, Kirk righted himself. Then, suddenly, in a blast of realization, he knew. "Bones!" The words tore from him in a shout. "He's alive! He's still alive! He made the craft kick the thing to force it to squirm—and let us know!"

Uhura spoke. "Captain, I'm getting telemetry."

"Mr. Chekov—telemetry analysis as it comes in."

McCoy was still brooding on what reproduction of the organism meant. "According to Spock's telemetry analysis, there are forty chromosomes in that nucleus ready to divide." He paused. "If the energy of this thing merely doubles, everybody and everything within a light year of it will be dead." He paced the length of the bridge and came back. "Soon there will be two of it, four, eight, and more—a promise of a combined anti-life force that could encompass the entire galaxy."

"That's what Spock knows, Bones. He knows. He knows we have no choice but to try and destroy it when he transmitted those coordinates of the chromosomes."

Scott said, "Look at your panel, Captain. The pull from the thing is increasing. The drain on our shields is getting critical."

"How much time, Scotty?"

"Not more than an hour now, sir."

"Shield power is an unconditional priority. Put all secondary systems on standby."

"Aye, sir."

"Bones, can we kill that thing without killing Spock? And ourselves, too?"

"I don't know. It's a living cell. If we had an antibiotic that—"

"How many billions of kiloliters would it take?"

"Okay, Jim. Okay."

Uhura, her face radiant, turned from her console. "I'm receiving a message from Mr. Spock, sir. Low energy channel, faint but readable."

"Give it to me, Lieutenant."

"Faint" wasn't the word. Weak was. Very weak now. Spock said, "I . . . am losing life support . . . and minimal shield energy. The organism's nervous energy is . . . only maximal within protective membrane . . . interior . . . relatively insensitive . . . sufficient charge of . . . could destroy . . . tell Dr. McCoy . . . he should have wished . . . me luck . . . ."

The bridge people sensed the burden of the message. Silence fell, speech faltering at the realization that Spock was lost. Only the lowered hum of power-drained machinery made itself heard.

* * *

Kirk lay unmoving on the couch in his quarters. Spock was dead. And to what point? If he'd been able to transmit his information on how to destroy the thing, he would have died for a purpose. But even that small joy had been denied to him. Spock was dead for no purpose at all, to no end that mattered to him.

Without knocking, McCoy came in and sat down on the couch beside the motionless Kirk.

"What's on your mind, Dr. McCoy?"

"Spock," McCoy said. "Call me sentimental. I've been called worse things. I believe he's still alive out there in that mess of protoplasm."

"He knew the odds when he went out. He knew so much. Now he's dead." Kirk lifted an arm into the air, contemplating the living hand at the end of it. "What *is* this thing? Not intelligent. At least, not yet."

"It is disease," McCoy said.

"This cell—this germ extending its filthy life for eleven thousand miles—one single cell of it. When it's grown to billions, we will be the germs. We shall be the disease invading its body."

"That's a morbid thought, Jim. Its whole horror lies in its size."

"Yes. And when our form of life was born, what microuniverse did we destroy? How does a body destroy an infection, Bones?"

"By forming anti-bodies."

"Then that's what we've got to be—an anti-body." He looked at McCoy. Then, repeating the word "anti-body," he jumped to his feet and struck the intercom button. "Scotty, suppose you diverted all remaining power to the shields? Suppose you gave it all to them—and just kept impulse power in reserve?"

"Cut off the engine thrust?" Scott cried. "Why, we'd be sucked into that thing as helplessly as if it were a wind tunnel!"

"Exactly, Mr. Scott. Prepare to divert power on my signal. Kirk out."

He turned to find himself facing McCoy's diagnostic Feinberger. "Got something to say, Bones?"

"Technically, no. Medically, yes. Between the strain and the stimulants, your edges are worn smooth. You're to keep off your feet for a while."

"I don't have a while. None of us do. Let's go . . ."

He took time to compose his face before he stepped out of the bridge elevator. He took his place in his command chair before he spoke into the intercom. "All hands, this is the Captain speaking. We are going to enter the body of this organism. Damage-control parties stand by—all decks secure for collision. Kirk out."

"It's now or never," he thought—and called Engineering.

"Ready, Mr. Scott?"

"Yes, sir."

"Now," Kirk said.

The ship took a violent forward plunge. Kirk, gripping his chair, glanced at the screen. The blackness grew denser as they sped toward it. "Impact—twenty-five seconds, sir," Sulu said intensely.

Then shock knocked Sulu from his chair. Something flared from the screen. Chekov, sprawled on the deck, looked up at his console as the ship steadied. "We're through, sir!" he shouted.

Uhura, recovering her position, called, "Damage parties report minimal hurt, Captain."

Kirk didn't acknowledge the information. The blackness on the screen had gone opaque. The *Enterprise*, lost in the vast interior of the organism, moved sluggishly through the lightlessness of gray jelly.

Engineering again. "Mr. Scott, we still have our impulse power?"

"I saved all I could, sir. I don't know if there's enough to get us out of this again. Or time enough to do it in."

"We have committed ourselves, Mr. Scott."

"Aye. But what are we committed to? We've got no power for the phasers."

McCoy made an impatient gesture. "We couldn't use them if we did. Their heat would rebound from this muck and roast us alive."

"The organism would love the phasers. It eats power—" Kirk broke off. A frantic Scott, rushing from the elevator, had caught his last word. "Power!" he cried. "That's the problem, Captain! If we can't use power to destroy this beast, what is it we *can* use?"

"Anti-power," Kirk said.

"What?" McCoy said.

Scott was staring at him. "This thing has a negative energy charge. Everything that has worked has worked in reverse. In its body, we're an anti-body, Scotty. So we'll use anti-power—anti-matter—to kill it."

Scott's tension relaxed like a pricked balloon. "Aye, sir! That it couldn't swallow! What good God gave you that idea, Captain?"

"Mr. Spock," Kirk said. "It's what he was trying to tell us before . . . we lost him. Mr. Chekov, prepare a probe. Scotty, we'll need a magnetic bottle for the charge. How soon?"

"It's on its way, laddie!"

"Mr. Chekov, timing detonator on the probe. We'll work out the setting. Mr. Sulu, what's our estimated arrival at the nucleus?"

"Seven minutes, sir."

"Jim, how close are you going to it?"

"Point-blank range. Implant it—and back away."

"But the probe has a range of—"

Kirk interrupted McCoy. "The eddies and currents in the protoplasm could drift the probe thousands of kilometers away from the nucleus. No, we must be directly on target. We won't get a second chance."

Kirk rubbed the stiffening muscles at the nape of his neck. "Time for another stimulant, Bones."

"You'll blow up. How long do you think you can go on taking that stuff?"

"Just hold me together for another seven minutes."

He took one of the minutes to address his Captain's log. "Should we fail in this mission, I wish to record here that the following personnel receive special citations: Lieutenant Commander Leonard McCoy, Lieutenant Commander Montgomery Scott,—and my highest recommendation to Commander Spock, Science Officer, who has given his life in performance of his duty."

As he punched off the recorder, Scott, hurrying back

to the command chair, paused to listen to Sulu say, "Target coordinates programmed, sir. Probe ready to launch."

"Mr. Sulu, program the fuse for a slight delay." He swung to Chekov. "All non-essential systems on standby. Communications, prepare for scanning. Conserve every bit of power. We've got to make it out of this membrane before the explosion. Make it work, Scotty. Pray it works."

"Aye, sir."

"Mr. Chekov, launch probe at zero acceleration. Forward thrust, one tenth second."

"Probe launched," Chekov said.

The moment finally passed. Then the ship bucked to the sound of straining metal. In the dimness made by the fading lights of the bridge, the air became sultry, suddenly heavy, oppressive. Kirk could feel the racing of his body's pulses. Then the air was breathable again; Chekov, turning, said, "Confirmed, sir. The probe is lodged in the nucleus . . . close to the chromosome bodies."

Kirk nodded. "Mr. Sulu, back out of here the way we came in. Let's not waste time. That was a nice straight line, Mr. Chekov."

Chekov flushed with pleasure. "Estimate we'll be out in six point thirty-nine minutes, sir." He glanced back at his panel, frowning. "Captain! Metallic substance outside the ship!"

"Spock?" McCoy said.

Chekov flicked on the screen. "Yes, sir. It's the shuttlecraft, lying there dead on its side."

In one bound Kirk was beside Uhura. "Lieutenant, give me Mr. Spock's voice channel! High gain!"

The microphone shook in his hand as he waited for her to test the wave length. "Ready, sir," she said.

He waited again to try and steady his voice. "Mr. Spock, do you read me? Spock, *come in!*" He whirled to Scott. "Mr. Scott, tractor beam!"

"Captain . . . we don't have the time to do it! We've got only a fifty-three percent escape margin!"

"Will you kindly take an order, Lieutenant Commander? Two tractor beams on that craft!"

Scott reddened. "Tractor beams on, sir."

"Glad to hear it!" Kirk said—and incredibly the mike

in his hand was speaking. "I . . . recommend you . . . abandon this attempt, Captain. Do . . . not risk the ship further . . . on my account."

Wordless, Kirk handed the mike to McCoy. McCoy looked at him and he nodded. "Shut up, Spock!" McCoy yelled. "You're being rescued!" He returned the mike to Kirk.

Spock said, "Thank you, Captain McCoy."

Weak as he was, Kirk thought, he'd find the strength to cock one sardonic eyebrow.

Weak—but alive. A knowledge better than McCoy's stimulants. "Time till explosion, Mr. Chekov?"

"Fifty-seven seconds, sir."

"You're maintaining tractor beam on the shuttlecraft, Mr. Scott?"

"Aye, sir." But the Scottish gloom of Kirk's favorite engineer was still unsubdued. "However, I can't guarantee it will hold when that warhead explodes." He glanced at his board. Despite the dourness of his expectations, he gave a startled jump. "The power levels show dead, sir."

Then the power levels and everything else ceased to matter. The ship whirled. A white-hot glare flashed through the bridge. McCoy was smashed to the deck. In the glare Kirk saw Chekov snatched from his chair to fall unconscious at the elevator door. Uhura's body, on the floor beside her console, rolled to the ship's rolling. Disinterestedly, Kirk realized that blood was pouring from a gash in his forehead. A handkerchief appeared in his hand—and Sulu crawled away from him back in the direction of his chair. He sat up and tied the handkerchief around his head. It's what you did in a tough tennis game to keep the sweat out of your eyes . . . a long time since he played tennis . . .

"Mr. Sulu," he said, "can you activate the viewscreen?"

Stars. They had come back. The stars had come back.

A good crew. Chekov had limped back to his station. Not that he needed to say it. But it was good to hear, anyway. "The organism is destroyed, Captain. The explosion must have ruptured the membrane. It's thrown us clear."

The stars were back. So was the power.

Kirk laid his hand on Scott's shoulder. "And the shuttlecraft, Scotty?"

Spock's voice spoke from the bridge speaker. "Shuttlecraft to *Enterprise*. Request permission to come aboard."

Somebody put the mike in his hand. "You survived that volcano, Mr. Spock?"

"Obviously, Captain. And I have some very interesting data on the organism that I was unable to . . ."

McCoy, rubbing his bruised side, shouted, "Don't be so smart, Spock! You botched that acetylcholine test, don't forget!"

"Old Home Week," Kirk said. "Bring the shuttlecraft aboard, Mr. Scott. Mr. Chekov, lay in a course for Starbase Six. Warp factor five."

He untied the bloody handkerchief. "Thanks, Mr. Sulu. I'll personally see it to the laundry. Now I'm off to the hangar deck. Then Mr. Spock and I will be breaking out our mountaineering gear."

A PIECE OF THE ACTION

Writer: David P. Harmon and Gene L. Coon (story by
   David P. Harmon)
Director: James Komack
Guest stars: Anthony Caruso, Victor Tayback

≡

It was difficult to explain to Bela Okmyx, who called himself "Boss" of Dana Iotia Two, that though the message from the lost *Horizon* had been sent a hundred years ago, the *Enterprise* had only received it last month. For that matter, he did not seem to know what the "galaxy" meant, either.

Kirk did not know what he expected to find, but he was braced for anything. Subspace radio was not the only thing the *Horizon* had lacked. She had landed before the non-interference directive had come into effect, and while the Iotians were just at the beginnings of industrialization. And the Iotians had been reported to be extremely intelligent—and somewhat imitative. The *Horizon* might have changed their culture drastically before her departure and shipwreck.

Still, the man called Boss seemed friendly enough. He didn't understand what "transported" meant either, in the technical sense, but readily suggested a rendezvous at an intersection marked by a big building with white columns in a public square where, he said, he would provide a reception committee. All quite standard, so far.

Kirk, Spock and McCoy beamed down, leaving Scott at the con. They materialized into a scene which might at first have been taken for an area in any of the older cities of present-day Earth, but with two significant exceptions; no children were visible, and all the adults, male and female alike, were wearing sidearms. Their dress was reminiscent of the United States of the early twentieth century.

This had barely registered when a sharp male voice behind them said, "Okay, you three. Let's see you petrify."

The officers turned to find themselves confronted by two men carrying clumsy two-handed weapons which Kirk recognized as a variant of the old submachine gun.

"Would you mind clarifying your statement, please?" Spock said.

"I want to see you turn to stone. Put your hands up over your head—or you ain't gonna have no head to put your hands over."

The two were standing close enough together so that Kirk could have stunned them both from the hip, but he disliked stopping situations before they had even begun to develop. He obeyed, his officers following suit.

The man who had spoken kept them covered while the other silently relieved them of their phasers and communicators. He seemed momentarily in doubt about McCoy's tricorder, but he took that, too. A few pedestrians stopped to watch; they seemed only mildly curious, and some of them even seemed to approve. Were these men policemen, then? They were dressed no differently from anyone else; perhaps more expensively and with more color, but that was all.

The silent man displayed his harvest to his spokesman. The latter took a phaser and examined it. "What's this?"

"Be very careful with that, please," Kirk said. "It's a weapon."

"A heater, huh? The Boss'll love that."

"A Mr. Bela Okmyx invited us down. He said . . ."

"I know what he said. What he don't tell Kalo ain't worth knowing. He said some boys would meet you. Okay, we're meeting you."

"Those guns aren't necessary," McCoy said.

"You trying to make trouble, bud? Don't give me those baby blue eyes."

"What?"

"I don't buy that innocent routine." Kalo looked at Spock's ears. "You a boxer?"

"No," Spock said. "Why does everybody carry firearms? Are you people at war?"

"I never heard such stupid questions in my life." Kalo jerked his gun muzzle down the street. "Get moving."

As they began to walk, Kirk became aware of a distant but growing thrumming sound. Suddenly a squeal was added to it and it became much larger.

"Get down!" Kalo shouted, throwing himself to the street. The people around him were already dropping, or seeking shelter. Kirk dived for the dirt.

A vehicle that looked like two mismatched black bricks on four wheels bore down on them. Two men leaned out of it with submachine guns, which suddenly produced a terrible, hammering roar. Kalo got off a burst at it, but his angle was bad for accuracy. Luckily, it was not good for the gunners in the car, either.

Then the machine was gone, and the pedestrians picked themselves up. McCoy looked about, then knelt by the silent member of the "reception committee," but he was plainly too late.

Kalo shook his head. "Krako's getting more gall all the time."

"Is this the way you greet all your visitors?" Kirk demanded.

"It happens, pal."

"But this man is dead," McCoy said.

"Yeah? Well, we ain't playing for peanuts. Hey, you dopes, get outta here!" He shouted suddenly to what looked like the beginning of a crowd. "Ain't you never seen a hit before? Get lost!"

He resumed herding his charges, leaving the dead man unconcernedly behind. Kirk kept his face impassive, but his mind was busy. A man had been shot down, and no one had blinked an eye; it seemed as though it were an everyday happening. Was this the cultural contamination they had been looking for? But the crew of the *Horizon* hadn't been made up of cold-blooded killers, nor had they reported the Iotian culture in that state.

A young girl, rather pretty, emerged from a store entrance and cut directly across to them, followed by another. "You, Kalo," she said.

"Get lost."

"When's the Boss going to do something about the crummy street lights around here? A girl ain't safe."

"And how about the laundry pickup?" said the second girl. "We ain't had a truck by in three weeks."

"Write him a letter," Kalo said indifferently.

"I did. He sent it back with postage due."

"Listen, we pay our percentages. We're entitled to some service for our money."

"Get *lost*, I said." Kalo shook his head as the girls sullenly fell behind. "Some people got nothing to do but complain."

Kirk stared at him. He was certainly an odd sight— odder than before, now that his pockets were stuffed with all the hand equipment from the *Enterprise* trio, and he had a submachine gun under each arm. But he looked none the less dangerous for that. "Mr. Kalo, is this the way your citizens get things done? Their right of petition?"

"If they pay their percentages, the Boss takes care of them. We go in here."

"In here" was a building bearing a brightly polished brass plaque. It read:

BELA OKMYX
BOSS
NORTHSIDE TERRITORY

The end of the line was an office, large and luxurious, complete with heavy desk, a secretary of sorts and framed pictures—except that one of the frames, Kirk saw, surrounded some kind of pistol instead. A heavy-set, swarthy man sat behind the desk.

"Got 'em, Boss," Kalo said. "No sweat."

The big man smiled and rose. "Well, Captain Kirk. Come in. Sit down. Have a drink. Good stuff—distill it myself."

"No, thank you. You are Mr. Okmyx? This is Mr. Spock, my First Officer. And Dr. McCoy."

"A real pleasure. Sit down. Put down the heater, Kalo. These guys is guests." He turned back to Kirk. "You gotta excuse my boys. You just gotta be careful these days."

"Judging from what we've seen so far, I agree." Kirk said. "They call you the Boss. Boss of what?"

"My territory. Biggest in the world. Trouble with being the biggest is that punks is alla time trying to cut in."

"There is something astonishingly familiar about all this, Captain," Spock said.

"How many other territories are there?"

"Maybe a dozen, not counting the small fry—and they get bumped anyway when I get around to it."

"Do they include, if I may ask," Spock said, "a gentleman named Krako?"

"You know about Krako?"

"He hit us, Boss," Kalo said. "Burned Mirt."

Bela scowled. "I want him hit back."

"I'll take care of it."

Kirk had noticed a huge book on a stand nearby. He rose and moved toward it. Kalo raised his gun muzzle again, but at a quick signal from Bela, dropped it. The book was bound like a Bible, in white leather, with gold lettering reading: *Chicago Mobs of the Twenties*. The imprint was New York, 1993.

"How'd you get this, Mr. Okmyx?" he asked.

"That's The Book. *The* Book. They left it—the men from the *Horizon*."

"And there is your contamination, Captain," Spock said. "An entire gangster culture. An imitative people, one book, and . . ."

"No cracks about The Book," Bela said harshly. "Look, I didn't bring you here for you to ask questions. You gotta do something for me. Then I tell you anything you want to know."

"Anything we can do," Kirk said, putting the book down, "we will. We have laws of our own we must observe."

"Okay," Bela said. He leaned forward earnestly. "Look, I'm a peaceful man, see? I'm sick and tired of all the hits. Krako hits me, I hit Krako, Tepo hits me, Krako hits Tepo. We ain't getting noplace. There's too many bosses, know what I mean? Now if there was just one, maybe we could get some things done. That's where you come in."

"I don't quite understand," Kirk said.

"You Feds made a lot of improvements since the other ship came here. You probably got all kinds of fancy heaters. So here's the deal. You gimme all the heaters I need—enough tools so I can hit all the punks once and for all—and I take over the whole place. Then all you have to deal with is me.''

"Let me get this straight," Kirk said. "You want us to supply you with arms and assistance so you can carry out aggression against other nations?''

"What nations? I got some hits to make. You help me make them.''

"Fascinating," Spock said. "But quite impossible.''

"I'd call it outrageous," McCoy said.

"Even if we wanted to," Kirk said, "our orders are very . . .''

Bela gestured to Kalo, who raised his gun again. Though Kirk did not see any signal given, the door opened and another armed man came in.

"I ain't interested in *your* orders," Bela said. "You got eight hours to gimme what I asked for. If I don't get the tools by then, I'm gonna have your ship pick you up again— in a large number of very small boxes. Know what I mean, pal?''

Kalo belatedly began to unload the captured devices onto the Boss's desk. He pointed to a phaser. "This here's a heater, Boss. I don't know what the other junk is.''

"A heater, eh? Let's see how it works." He pointed it at a wall. Kirk jerked forward.

"Don't do that! You'll take out half the wall!''

"That good, eh? Great. Just gimme maybe a hundred of these and we don't have no more trouble.''

"Out of the question," Kirk said.

"I get what I want." Bela picked up a communicator. "What are these here?''

Kirk remained silent. Jerking a thumb toward McCoy, Bela said to Kalo, "Burn him.''

"All right," Kirk said hastily. "It's a communications device, locked onto my ship.''

Bela fiddled with one until it snapped open in his hand. "Hey," he said to it. "In the ship.''

"Scott here. Who is this?''

"This here's Bela Okmyx. I got your Captain and his friends down here. You want 'em back alive, send me a hundred of them fancy heaters of yours, and some troops to show us how to use them. You got eight hours. Then I put the hit on your friends. Know what I mean?''

"No," Scott's voice said. "But I'll find out."

Bela closed the communicator. "Okay. Kalo, take 'em over to the warehouse. Put 'em in the bag, and keep an eye on 'em, good. You hear?''

"Sure, Boss. Move out, you guys."

The warehouse room had a barred window and was sparsely furnished, but it was equipped with another copy of The Book. Kalo and two henchmen were playing cards at a table, guns handy, their eyes occasionally flicking to Kirk, Spock and McCoy at the other end of the room.

"One book," McCoy said. "And they made it the blueprint for their entire society. Amazing."

"But not unprecedented," Spock said. "At one time, in old Chicago, conventional government nearly broke down. The gangs almost took over."

"This Okmyx must be the worst of the lot."

"Though we may quarrel with his methods, his goal is essentially the correct one," Spock said. "This culture must become united—or it will degenerate into complete anarchy. It is already on the way; you will recall the young women who complained of failing services."

"If this society broke down, because of the influence of the *Horizon*, the Federation is responsible," Kirk said. "We've got to try to straighten the mess out. Spock, if you could get to the sociological banks of the computer, could you come up with a solution?''

"Quite possibly, Captain."

Signaling Spock and McCoy to follow him unobtrusively, Kirk gradually drifted toward the card game. The players looked up at him warily, free hands on guns; but they relaxed again as he pulled over a chair and sat down. The game was a variety of stud poker.

"After a few moments, Kirk said, "That's a kid's game."

"Think so?" Kalo said.

"I wouldn't waste my time."

"Who's asking you to?"

"On Beta Antares Four, they play a game for men. Of

course, it's probably too involved for you. It takes intelligence."

Antares is not a double star; Kirk had taken the chance in order to warn the sometimes rather liberal-minded that he was lying deliberately."

"Okay, I'll bite," Kalo said. "Take the cards, big man. Show us how it's played."

"The Antares cards are different, of course, but not too different," Kirk said, riffling through them. "The game's called Fizzbin. Each player gets six cards—except for the man on the dealer's right, who gets seven. The second card goes up—except on Tuesdays, of course . . . Ah, Kalo, that's good, you've got a nine. That's half a fizzbin already."

"I need another nine?"

Spock and McCoy drew nearer with quite natural curiosity, since neither of them had ever heard of the game. Neither had Kirk.

"Oh, no. That would be a sralk and you'd be disqualified. You need a King or a deuce, except at night, when a Queen or a four would . . . Two sixes! That's excellent—unless, of course, you get another six. Then you'd have to turn it in, unless it was black."

"But if it was black?" Kalo said, hopelessly confused.

"Obviously, the opposite would hold," Kirk said, deciding to throw in a touch of something systematic for further confusion. "Instead of turning your six in, you'd get another card. Now, what you are really hoping for is a royal fizzbin, but the odds against that are, well, astronomical, wouldn't you say, Spock?"

"I have never computed them, Captain."

"Take my word they're considerable. Now the last card around. We call it the cronk, but its home name is *klee-et*.* Ready? Here goes."

He dealt, making sure that Kalo's card went off the table. "Oops, sorry."

"I'll get it."

Kalo bent over. In the same instant, Kirk put his hands under the table and shoved. It went over on the other two.

*A Vulcan word meaning, roughly, "prepare to engage." See "Amok Time."

McCoy and Spock were ready; the action was hardly more than a flurry before the three guards were helpless. Kirk parceled out the guns.

"Spock, find the radio transmitting station. Uhura is monitoring their broadcasts. Cut in and have yourself and Bones beamed up to the ship.

"Surely you are coming, Captain?"

"Not without Bela Okmyx."

"Jim, you can't . . ."

"This mess is our responsibility, Bones. You have your orders. Let's go."

Kirk at first felt a little uneasy walking a city street with a submachine gun under his arm, but no one passing seemed to find it unusual. On the contrary, it seemed to be a status symbol; people cleared the way for him.

But the walk ended abruptly with two handguns stuck into his ribs from behind. He had walked into an ambush. How had Bela gotten word so fast?

The answer to that was soon forthcoming. The two hoods who had mousetrapped him crowded him into a car—and the ride was a long one. At its end was another office, almost a duplicate of Bela's; but the man behind the desk was short, squat, bull-shaped and strange. He arose with a jovial smile.

"So you're the Fed. Well, well. I'm Krako—Jojo Krako, Boss of the South Territory. Hey, I'm glad to see you."

"Would you mind telling me how you knew about me?"

"I got all Bela's communications bugged. He can't make a date with a broad without I know about it. Now you're probably wondering why I brought you here."

"Don't tell me. You want to make a deal."

Krako was pleased. "I like that. Sharp. Sharp, huh, boys?"

"Sharp, Boss."

"Let me guess some more," Kirk said. "You want— uh—heaters, right? And troops to teach you how to use them. And you'll hit the other bosses and take over the whole planet. And then we'll sit down and talk, right?"

"Wrong," Krako said. "More than talk. I know Bela.

He didn't offer you beans. Me, I'm a reasonable man. Gimme what I want, and I cut you in for, say, a third. Skimmed right off the top. How do you like that?''

"I've got a better idea. You know this planet has to be united. So let's sit down, you, me, and Bela, get in contact with the other bosses, and discuss the matter like rational men.''

Krako seemed to be genuinely outraged. "That ain't by The Book, Kirk. We know how to handle things! You make hits! Somebody argues, you lean on him! You think we're stupid or something?''

"No, Mr. Krako," Kirk said, sighing. "You're not stupid. But you are peculiarly unreasonable.''

"Pally, I got ways of getting what I want. You want to live, Kirk? Sure you do. But after I get done with you, you're liable to be sorry—unless you come across. Zabo, tell Cirl the Knife to sharpen his blade. I might have a job for him.'' The smile came back. "Of course, you gimme the heaters and you keep your ears.''

"No deal.''

"Too bad. Put him on ice.''

The two hoods led Kirk out.

On shipboard, Spock's fortunes were not running much better. There turned out to be no specifics in the computer, not even a record of a planet-wide culture based on a moral inversion. Without more facts, reason and logic were alike helpless.

"Mr. Spock," Uhura said. "Mr. Okmyx from the surface is making contact. Audio only.''

Spock moved quickly to the board. "Mr. Okmyx, this is Spock.''

"How'd you get up there?'' Bela's voice asked.

"Irrelevant, since we are here.''

"Uh—yeah. But you'd better get back down. Krako's put the bag on your Captain.''

Spock raised his eyebrows. "Why would he put a bag on the Captain?''

"Kidnapped him, dope. He'll scrag him, too.''

"If I understand you correctly, that would seem to be a problem. Have you any suggestions?''

"Sure. You guys got something I want. I can help you get the Captain back. No reason we can't make a deal."

"I am afraid I find it difficult to trust you, sir."

"What's to trust? Business is business. We call a truce. You come down. My boys spring Kirk. Then we talk about you giving me a hand."

"Since we must have our Captain back," Spock said after a moment, "I accept. We shall arrive in your office within ten minutes. Spock out."

McCoy had been standing nearby, listening. "You're going to trust him?"

"If we are to save the Captain, without blatant and forceful interference on the planet, then we must have assistance from someone indigenous. At the moment, we are forced to trust Mr. Okmyx." He turned toward Scott. "Mr. Scott, although I hope to avoid their use, I think you should adjust one of the phaser banks to a strong stun position."

"Now," McCoy said, "you're starting to make sense."

Spock did not reply, since nothing in the situation made sense to him. Trusting Okmyx was nothing short of stupid, and the use of force was forbidden by General Order Number One. In such a case, the only course was to abide by the Captain's principle of letting the situation ripen.

Bela, of course, had a trap arranged. Spock had expected it, but there had been no way to avoid it. What he had not expected—nor had Bela—was the abrupt subsequent appearance of Kirk in the doorway, with a submachine gun under his arm.

"How did you get away?" Spock asked interestedly, after the gangsters had been disarmed—a long process which produced a sizable heap of lethal gadgets, some of them wholly unfamiliar.

"Krako made the mistake of leaving me a radio; that was all I needed for the old trip-wire trick. I thought I told you to get to the ship."

"We have been there, Captain. The situation required our return."

"It may be just as well. Find out anything from the computers?"

"Nothing useful, Captain. Logic and factual knowledge do not seem to apply here."

"You admit that?" McCoy said.

"With the greatest reluctance, Doctor."

"Then you won't mind if I play a hunch?" Kirk said.

"I am not sanguine about hunches, sir, but I have no practical alternative."

"What are you going to do, Jim?"

"Now that I've got Bela," Kirk said, "I'm going to put the bag on Krako."

"On Krako?" Bela said. "You ain't serious?"

"Why not?" Kirk turned to Bela and fingered his suit lapel. "That's nice material."

"It ought to be. It cost a bundle."

"Get out of it. You, too."

"Hey, now, wait a minute . . ."

"Take it off—pally! This time nobody's going to bag me."

Seeing that he meant it, Kalo and Bela got out of their clothes; Kirk and Spock donned them. Scooping up the required submachine guns as passports, they went out, leaving McCoy in charge.

In front of the office sat the large black car that Bela used. Fishing in the pockets of his borrowed suit, Kirk found the keys. They got in.

"Any idea how to run this thing, Spock?"

"No, Captain. But it should not be too difficult."

"Let's see," Kirk said, studying the controls. "A keyhole. For the—ignition process, I think. Insert and turn. Right."

He felt around with his foot and touched a button. The car stuttered and the engine was running.

"Interesting," Spock said.

"As long as it runs. Now, let's see. I think—gears . . ."

He pulled the lever down, which produced nothing but an alarming grinding sound which he could feel in his hand as well as hear.

"As I recall," Spock said, "there was a device called the clutch. Perhaps one of those foot pedals . . ."

The right-hand pedal didn't seem to work, but the left-hand one allowed the gear lever to go down. Kirk let the pedal up cautiously, and the car started with a lurch.

Kirk remembered the way to Krako's offices well

enough, but the trip was a wild one; there seemed to be some trick to working the clutch which Kirk hadn't mastered. Luckily, pedestrians gave the big black vehicle a wide berth. Spock just hung on. When it was over, he observed, "Captain, you are a splendid starship commander, but as a taxi driver you leave much to be desired."

"Haven't had time to practice. Leave these clumsy guns under the seat; we'll use phasers."

They made their way to Krako, leaving a trail of stunned guards behind. The Boss did not seem a bit taken aback when they burst in on him; he had four hoods behind him, guns aimed at the door.

"You don't shoot, we don't shoot," he said rapidly.

"This would appear to be an impasse," Spock said.

"Who's your friend with the ears?" Krako asked. "Never mind. Ain't this nice? I was wondering how I was going to get you back, and you delivered yourself! You don't think you'll get out of it this time, do you?"

"We didn't come here for games," Kirk said. "This is bigger than you or Okmyx or any of the others."

The phaser which Krako had previously taken from Kirk was on the desk, still on safety lock. Krako nudged it. "Don't talk fancy. All you gotta do is tell me how to work these things."

"Krako," Kirk said, "can you trust all your men?"

"Yeah, sure. I either trust 'em or they're dead."

"Maybe. But when it comes to weapons like these— well, one of them could make a man a pretty big boss around here."

Krako thought about it. At last he said, "Zabo and Karf, stay put. You other guys vanish . . . All right, these two is okay. Now that we got no busy little eyes around, how do you work this thing?"

Kirk moved in on Krako hard and fast, spitting his words out like bullets. "Knock it off, Krako. We don't have time to show you how to play with toys."

"Toys?"

"What do you think we're here for, Krako? To get a cut of your deal? Forget it. That's peanuts to an outfit like the Federation."

"It is?" Krako said, a little dazed by the sudden switch.

"Unquestionably," Spock said.

"We came here to take over, Krako. The whole ball of wax. Maybe, if you cooperate, we'll cut *you* in for a piece of the action."

"A minute piece," Spock added.

"How much is that?" Krako asked.

"We'll figure it out later."

"But—I thought you guys had some kind of law about no interference . . ."

"Who's interfering? We're just taking over."

Spock seemed slightly alarmed. "Uh—Captain . . ."

"Cool it, Spocko. Later."

"What's your deal?" Krako asked.

Kirk motioned him to his feet and, when the bewildered gangster stood, Kirk sat down in his chair and swung his feet up onto the desk. He appropriated one of Krako's cigars.

"The Federation wants this planet, but we don't want to have to come in and use our muscle. That ain't subtle. So what we do is help one guy take over. He pulls the planet's strings—and we pull his. Follow?"

"But what's your cut?"

Kirk eyed the unlit cigar judiciously. "What do you care, so long as you're in charge? Right, Spocko?"

"Right on the button, Boss," Spock said, falling into his role a little belatedly but with a certain relish. "Of course, there's always Bela Okmyx . . ."

Krako thought only a moment. "You got a deal. Call your ship and bring down your boys and whatever you need."

Kirk got to his feet and snapped open his communicator. "Kirk to *Enterprise.*"

"*Enterprise.* Scott here, sir."

"Scotty, we made the deal with Krako."

"Uh—we did, sir?"

"We're ready to make the hit. We're taking over the whole planet as soon as you can get ready."

"Is that wise, sir?"

"Sure, we can trust Krako—he doesn't have any choice. He's standing here right now, *about three feet to my left,* all ready to be our pal. I'd like to show him the ship, just so he's sure I'm giving him the straight dope. But you know how it is.''

"Oh aye, sir," Scott said. "I know indeed."

"We'll be needing enough phasers to equip all of Krako's men, plus advisers—troops to back them up on the hit. You moving, Scotty?''

"Aye, Uhura's on to the Transporter Room and two of the boys are on their way. Ready when you say the word.''

"Very well, Scotty, begin.''

Krako looked curiously at Kirk. "You mean you're gonna start bringing all those guys down now?''

"No—not exactly.'' As he spoke, the hum of the Transporter effect filled the room, and Krako shimmered out of existence. Zabo and Karf stared, stunned—and a second later were stunned more thoroughly.

"Well played—Spocko.''

Spock winced. "So we have—put the bag on Krako. What is our next maneuver, Captain?''

"Back to Bela's place.''

"In the car, Captain?''

"It's faster than walking. Don't tell me you're afraid of cars, Spock.''

"Not at all. It is your driving which alarms me.''

Through the door of Bela's office, they heard McCoy saying worriedly, "Where *are* they?''

And then Bela's, "Knowing Krako, we'll be lucky if he sends 'em back on a blotter.''

Kirk walked in. "Wrong again, Okmyx." He brushed past the relieved McCoy. "Outta my way, Sawbones. I want to talk to this guy. I'm getting tired of playing patty-cake with you penny ante operators.''

"Who you calling penny ante?'' Bela said, bristling.

"Nobody but you, baby. Now listen. The Federation's moving in here. We're taking over, and if you play ball, we'll leave a piece of the pie for you. If you don't, you're out. All the way out. Got that?'' He shoved the phaser under Bela's nose to make the point.

"Yeah—yeah, sure, Kirk. Why didn't you say so in the first place? I mean—all you hadda do was explain.''

The communicator came out. "Scotty, you got Krako on ice up there?"

"Aye, Captain."

"Keep him till I ask for him. We're going to be making some old-style phone calls from these coordinates. Lock on at the receiving end and transport the party here to us. Okay, Okmyx. Start calling the other bosses."

Shrugging, Bela went to the phone and dialed four times. "Hello, Tepo? Guess who? . . . Yeah, I got a lot of nerve. What're you going to do about it?"

With a hum, Tepo materialized, holding a non-existent phone in his hand. McCoy moved in to disarm him.

". . . coming over there with a couple of my boys, and . . . Brother!"

Bela grinned at Kirk. "Hey, this ain't bad."

"Keep dialing."

Half an hour later, the office was crowded with dazed gang leaders, Krako among them. Kirk climbed up on the desk, now cradling a local gun to add weight to his argument.

"All right, pipe down, everybody. I'll tell you what you're going to do. The Federation just took over around here, whether you like it or not. You guys have been running this planet like a piecework factory. From here on, it's all under one roof. You're going to form a syndicate and run this planet like a business. That means you make a profit."

"Yeah?" Tepo called. "And what's your percentage?"

"I'm cutting the Federation in for forty per cent." He leveled the gun. "You got objections?"

Tepo had obviously had guns pointed at him too many times to be cowed. "Yeah. I hear a lot of talk, but all I see here is you and a couple of your boys. I don't see no Federation."

"Listen, they got a ship," Krako said. "I know—I been there."

"Yeah, but Tepo's got a point," Bela said. "All we ever see is them."

"I only saw three other guys and a broad while I was in the ship," Krako said. "Maybe there ain't any more?"

"There are four hundred . . ."

Kirk was interrupted by an explosion outside, followed

by a fusillade of shots. Krako, who was nearest the window, peered around the edge of it.

"It's my boys," he reported. "Must think I'm still in the ship. They're making a hit on this place."

"My boys'll put 'em down," Bela said.

"Wanna bet?"

Kirk's communicator was already out. "Scotty, put ship's phasers on stun and fire a burst in a one-block radius around these coordinates, excluding this building."

"Right away, sir."

Kirk looked at the confused gangsters. "Gentlemen, you are about to see the Federation at work."

The noise roared on a moment more, and then the window was lit up with the phaser effect. Dead silence fell promptly.

Krako smiled weakly and swallowed. "Some trick."

"They're not dead, just knocked out for a while," Kirk said. "We could just as easily have killed them."

"Okay," Bela said. "We get the message. You were saying something about a syndicate."

"No, he was saying something about a percentage," Tepo said. "You sure forty percent is enough?"

"I think it will be just fine. We'll send someone around to collect it every year—and give you advice if you need it."

"That's reasonable," Bela said. He glared at the others. "Ain't that reasonable?"

There was a murmur of assent. Kirk smiled cheerfully. "Well, in that case, pull out some of that drinking stuff of yours, Okmyx, and let's get down to the talking."

The bridge of the *Enterprise* was routinely busy. Kirk was in the command chair, feeling considerably better to be back in uniform.

"I must say," Spock said, "your solution to the problem on Iotia is unconventional, Captain. But it does seem to be the only workable one."

"What troubles you is that it isn't logical to leave a criminal organization in charge. Is that it?"

"I do have some reservations. And how do you propose to explain to Starfleet Command that a starship will be sent around each year to collect 'our cut,' as you put it?"

" 'Our cut' will be put back into the planet's treasury—and the advisers and collectors can help steer the Iotians back into a more conventional moral and ethical system. In the meantime, the syndicate forms a central government that can effectively administer to the needs of the people. That's a step in the right direction. Our group of 'governors' is already learning to take on conventional responsibilities. Guiding them is—our piece of the action."

Spock pondered. "Yes, it seems to make sense. Tell me, Captain. Whatever gave you so outlandish an idea—and where did you pick up all that jargon so quickly?"

Kirk grinned. "Courtesy of Krako. A radio wasn't all he left in my cell. He also left me some reading matter."

"Ah, of course. The Book."

"Spocko, now you're talkin'."

BY ANY OTHER NAME

Writer: D.C. Fontana and Jerome Bixby (story by
   Jerome Bixby)
Director: Marc Daniels
Guest stars: Warren Stevens, Barbara Bouchet

≡

The landing party answering the distress call consisted of Kirk, Spock, McCoy, the security officer Lt. Shea, and Yeoman Leslie Thompson. At first there seemed to be no source at all on the planet for the call—no wrecked spaceship, no debris. Had the ship been destroyed in space and the survivors proceeded here in a shuttle?

Then two people appeared from the nearby trees, a man and a woman, dressed in outfits rather like Merchant Marine jumpsuits. The woman was lovely, but it was the man who dominated their attention. He looked fortyish, with enormous power in his sturdy frame, great authority and competence in his bearing. Neither of the strangers seemed armed, but Kirk noticed that they wore small unobtrusive boxes on their belts. Their hands rested on the belts near the boxes in an attitude so casually assumed that it seemed to be only a part of their stance, but Kirk was wary.

"I'm Captain James Kirk of the USS *Enterprise*. We came in answer to your distress call."

"It was very kind of you to respond so quickly, Captain. But now you will surrender your ship to me."

Kirk stared. "You have an odd sense of humor."

The strangers touched buttons on the boxes. Instantly, Kirk found himself paralyzed—and so, evidently, was the rest of the "rescue" party.

"I am Rojan, of Kelva," the strange man said. "I am your Commander, from this moment on. Efforts to resist us, or to escape, will be severely punished. Soon we, and you, will leave this galaxy forever. You humans must face the end of your existence as you have known it.''

The woman moved forward to relieve the people of the *Enterprise* of their phasers and communicators. Rojan went on: ''You are paralyzed by a selective field that neutralizes impulses to the voluntary muscles. I will now release you all, Captain Kirk.''

He touched the belt device. Kirk tensed to jump him, then thought better of it. ''A neural field?''

''Radiated from a central projector, directed at whomever we wish.''

''What do you want?''

''Your ship, Captain. We have monitored many. The *Enterprise*—a starship—is the best of its kind in your galaxy. It will serve us well in the long voyage that is to come.''

''Voyage to where?''

''To your neighboring galaxy, in the constellation you call Andromeda.''

''*Why?*''

''The Andromeda galaxy is our home,'' Rojan said in a remote voice.

''What brought you here?'' Spock said.

''Within ten millennia, high radiation levels will make life in our galaxy impossible; it is reaching the stage in its evolution which will make it what you call a quasar. The Kelvan Empire sent forth ships to explore other galaxies—to search for one which our race could conquer and colonize.''

''Sorry,'' Kirk said. ''This galaxy is occupied.''

''Captain, you think you are unconquerable—your ship impregnable. While we have talked, three of my people have boarded it, and the capture has begun.'' He took one of the confiscated communicators from the Kelvan woman and clicked it open. ''Subcommander Hanar, report.''

''The ship is ours,'' a strange voice said from the communicator. ''We control the bridge, engineering and life support.''

Rojan folded the communicator shut, and stowed it on his own belt.

''What good is capturing my ship?'' Kirk said. ''Even at maximum warp, the *Enterprise* couldn't get to the Andromeda galaxy for thousands of years. It's two million light-years away!''

"We will modify its engines to produce velocities far beyond the reach of your science. The journey between galaxies will take less than three hundred of your years.''

"Fascinating," Spock said. "Intergalactic travel requiring 'only' three hundred years is a leap beyond anything man has yet accomplished.''

Yeoman Thompson asked the Kelvan woman: "Did you make a voyage of three hundred years?''

"Our ships were of multigeneration design," the woman said. "I was born in the intergalactic void. I shall die there, during the return journey.''

"Our mission," Rojan added, "will be completed by a Captain who will be my descendant.''

"What happened to your ship?" Kirk said.

"There is an energy barrier at the rim of your galaxy—"

"I know. We've been there.''

"We broke through it with great difficulty. Our ship was destroyed. We barely escaped in a life craft. Our time here has been spent scanning your systems, studying you. And now we have the means to begin our journey again.''

"Why use our vessel?" Spock said. "Why not transmit a message back to your galaxy?''

"No form of transmission can penetrate the barrier.''

"Rojan," Kirk said, "we could take your problem to our Federation. Research expeditions have catalogued hundreds of uninhabited planets in this galaxy. Surely some of them would be suitable for your colonization.''

"We do not colonize, Captain," Rojan said sharply. "We conquer. We rule. There is no other way for us.''

"In other words," McCoy said, " 'this galaxy isn't big enough for both of us'?''

"What will happen to the intelligent races here?" Kirk said.

"They will not be mistreated. Merely subordinated.'' Rojan shrugged. "The fate of the inferior . . . in any galaxy. Ah, Hanar!''

While he had been speaking, another Kelvan had popped into being beside him, a younger man, with a hard intelligent face. There was no shimmer or any other such effect comparable to the workings of the Transporter; he just appeared.

"Tomar has examined the ship," Hanar said. "The modifications are under way."

"Space again!" said Rojan. "I don't think we could have kept our sanity, living so long on this accursed planet."

It did not seem to be so accursed to Kirk; in fact it was quite a pleasant, Earthlike place. But Hanar said: "It is an undisciplined environment; one cannot control it. Yet there are things of interest."

"Yes. But—disturbing. These ugly shells in which we have encased ourselves . . . they have such heightened senses. How do humans manage to exist in such fragile casings?"

They did not seem to care at all whether they were overheard, an obvious expression of supreme confidence. Kirk listened intently to every word; he had known such self-confidence to be misplaced before.

"Since the ship is designed to sustain this form," Hanar said, "we have little choice."

Rojan turned to the woman. "Kelinda, take them to the holding area. We will be keeping you and your party here, Captain. Your crew will undoubtedly prefer to cooperate with us if they understand you are hostages."

"Move that way," said Kelinda. "Keep together."

Their jail proved to be a cave, with a door constructed of some odd-looking transparent material, which Spock and Kirk were examining. Shea was also at the door, looking out, ostensibly watching Kelinda.

"I'm unable to determine the nature of the material, Captain," Spock said. "But I do not believe even phaser fire could disturb its molecular structure."

"All right, we can't break out. Maybe we can find another way."

"Captain," said Yeoman Thompson, "what do they want from us? What kind of people are they?"

"A good question, Yeoman."

"They registered as human," McCoy said.

"No, more than that, Doctor," Spock said, frowning. "They registered as *perfect* human life forms. I recall noting that the readings were almost textbook responses. Most curious."

"Spock," Kirk said, "what are the odds on such a parallel in life forms in another galaxy?"

"Based on those we have encountered in our own galaxy, the probability of humanoid development is high. But I would say the chances were very much against such an absolute duplication."

Shea turned slightly from the door. "Well, however perfect they are, sir, there don't seem to be very many of them."

"But they've got the paralysis field," Kirk said. "Rojan mentioned a central projector."

"If we can put it out of operation," McCoy said, "we've got a chance!"

"I am constrained to point out," said Spock, "that we do not even know what this projector looks like."

"No," Kirk said, "but those devices on their belts might indicate the position of the source."

"I would like to have one to examine."

"You'll have one, sir," Shea said. "If I have to rip one of the Kelvans apart to get it for you."

"Lieutenant Shea," Kirk said firmly, "you'll have your chance—but I'll tell you when."

"Yes, sir."

Kirk eyed him narrowly; but he could understand the younger officer's defiant attitude toward their captors. "Spock, do you remember how you tricked that guard on Eminiar? The empathic mind touching—"

"Quite well, Captain. I made him think we had escaped."

"Can you do it again?"

"I will attempt it."

He checked Kelinda, who was standing fairly close to the bars, and then put his hands on the cave wall approximately behind her. Then he began to concentrate.

At first the Kelvan woman did not respond. Then she twitched a little, nervously, as though aware that something was wrong, but unable to imagine what. She glanced around, then straightened again.

Kirk signaled his people to position themselves along the wall, so that from outside the cave would appear to be empty. Then he bent and scooped some dirt from the loose, sandy floor.

Suddenly Spock broke out of his intense concentration, as though wrenched from it by something beyond him. He gasped and staggered back against the wall. At the same moment, Kelinda came to the door, opened it quickly and started in.

Kirk hurled his handful of dirt into her face. She cried out and clawed at her eyes. While she was half blinded, Kirk delivered a karate chop. It sent her sprawling, and, surprisingly, out. Kirk and McCoy dragged her the rest of the way inside.

"Mr. Spock—?"

"I . . . will be . . . quite all right, Captain. We must hurry."

"Bones, keep an eye on him. Let's go." He took the belt device from Kelinda and led the way out. He had hardly taken two steps before he was paralyzed again, the device dropping from his limp hands.

"I am sorry, Captain," said Rojan's voice. He came into view with Hanar, who went into the cave. "The escape attempt was futile. You cannot stop us and you cannot escape us."

Hanar reappeared. "Kelinda is somewhat bruised, Rojan, but otherwise unhurt."

Rojan nodded, and turning back to Kirk, released the party from the freeze. "I cannot let this go unpunished. This will serve as an example." He pointed to Yeoman Thompson and security chief Shea. "Hanar, take these two aside."

"What are you going to do?" McCoy said.

"This is not your affair, Doctor. Captain, as a leader, you realize the importance of discipline. I need you and these other specialists. But those two are unnecessary to me."

"You can't just kill them!" Kirk said.

Rojan did not respond. Thompson turned, looking pleadingly at Kirk. "Captain . . ."

"Rojan, let them go. I'm responsible for them."

"I think we are somewhat alike, Captain. Each of us cares less for his own safety than for the lives of his command. We feel pain when others suffer for our mistakes. Your punishment shall be to watch your people die."

Rojan touched his belt device. Shea and the girl seemed to vanish instantly. Where each of them had been standing was an odd geometrically shaped block, about the size of a fist.

Hanar picked them up and brought them to Rojan, who held them up to Kirk. "This is the essence of what those people were . . . The flesh and brain, and also what you call the personality, distilled down to these compact shapes. Once crushed—" He closed his hand over one, crushing it in his grip, letting the fragments sift through his fingers. "—they are no more. This person is dead. However—" He flipped the second block away. It bounced to a halt on the grass. Rojan again touched a button, and Shea was standing there, bewildered. "—this person can be restored. As I said, Captain—very practical."

They were herded back into the cave, leaving behind the fragments which were all that were left of a pretty girl.

Shocked and dispirited, they all sat down on the cave floor but Shea. Spock's manner seemed more than usually distant.

"Mr. Spock," Kirk said, "are you sure you're all right?"

"Yes, quite all right, Captain."

McCoy said, "You looked very sick a while back, when you broke the mind lock."

"I did not break it," Spock said slowly. "I was . . . shoved away by . . . something I have never experienced before."

"What was it?" said Kirk.

"Images . . . bursting in my mind and consciousness. Colors . . . shapes . . . mathematical equations . . . fused and blurred. I have been attempting to isolate them. So far, I have been able to recall clearly only one. Immense beings . . . a hundred limbs that resemble tentacles, but are not . . . minds of such control and capacity that each limb could do a different job."

"You mean," McCoy said, "that's what the Kelvans really are?"

"I do not know. It seemed the central image, but whether it was a source or a memory, I cannot tell."

"If they do normally look like that," Kirk said, "why did they adapt to bodies like ours?"

"For the sake of deception, what else?" McCoy said.

Kirk remembered the conversation they had overheard. "No, practicality. They chose the *Enterprise* as the best kind of vessel for the trip, and they need us to run her. We have to stay in our gravity and atmosphere, and they had to adapt to it . . . We *have* to find a way to beat them. We outnumber them. Their only hold on us is the paralysis field."

"That's enough," said McCoy. "One wrong move and they jam all our neural circuits."

"Jamming," said Kirk. "That's it. Tricorders could analyze the frequency of the paralysis field. Spock, if you reverse the circuits on McCoy's neuroanalyzer, would it serve as a counterfield to jam the paralysis projector?"

"I am dubious about the possibility of success, Captain. The medical equipment is not built to put out any great amount of power. It would probably burn out."

"Is there any chance at all?"

"A small one."

"We'll take it. You and Bones have to get up to the ship."

"How?" said McCoy.

Kirk looked at his First Officer. "Spock, you're sick."

Spock's eyebrows went up. "Captain, I assure you that I am in excellent health."

"No, you're not. Dr. McCoy has examined you, and you're seriously ill. In fact, if he doesn't get you up to Sickbay you may die. And Rojan won't let that happen because he needs you to get through the barrier."

"It's a good idea," McCoy said, "but anybody looking at him can tell he's healthy."

"Vulcans have the ability to put themselves into a kind of trance . . . an enforced relaxation of every part of the mind and body. Right, Mr. Spock?"

"We find it more useful for resting the body than the so-called vacation."

"Can you do it now, and come out of it when you're in Sickbay? Say in half an hour?"

"It will take me a moment to prepare."

Shea walked to where he could watch for guards, then

turned to nod and wave an all clear. Spock, remaining seated, composed himself very carefully. He seemed to be directing his attention inward upon himself. Then, almost as if someone had snapped off his switch, he flopped limply to one side.

McCoy rose to examine him, and at once looked a little alarmed. "Jim, his heartbeat really is way down—respiration almost nonexistent—"

Kirk turned to the door quickly and shouted "Guard! Guard!"

Hanar appeared. "What do you want, human?"

"Mr. Spock is ill. The doctor thinks he's dying."

"This illness came on him very suddenly," Hanar said. "Is it not unusual?"

"He's a Vulcan. They don't react like humans."

"Look, he may die," McCoy said as Hanar hesitated. "If I can get him up to Sickbay, there's a chance I can save him."

"Stand away from the door."

The others pulled away. Hanar came in, hand on his belt device, and bent to study the motionless Science Officer. He frowned. "I will have you beamed aboard, but you will be met by Tomar and watched."

As Hanar turned away, opening a communicator, Kirk and McCoy glanced toward each other.

"Do the best you can with him, Bones," Kirk said. McCoy nodded quickly, significantly.

The Kelvan Tomar and McCoy entered the *Enterprise*'s examination room, supporting the limp Spock between them. Nurse Christine Chapel followed. "Doctor, what happened?"

McCoy ignored her. He said to Tomar, "Here. Put him down."

They eased Spock onto the table. Tomar peered curiously at the Vulcan, who was breathing only shallowly, and with alarmingly long pauses between breaths.

"Shall I summon more of your underlings?"

"I'll call my own underlings," McCoy said snappishly. "You stay out of the way. Miss Chapel, prepare two cc's of stokaline."

"Stokaline?" But, Doctor—"

"Don't argue with me, Nurse. Get it."

Christine turned and went to get the required air hypo. McCoy activated the body function panel over the table and began to take readings, which were obviously low. Tomar hesitated, then moved away to where he could watch from a discreet distance.

Christine came back with the hypo, and at McCoy's nod, administered it, looking at her chief in puzzlement. There was no response from Spock for a moment. Then his eyes snapped open. McCoy shook his head very slightly and the eyes closed again. Over their heads, the readings began to pick up, some of them quickening, others returning to their Vulcan norms, which were almost surely strange to Tomar.

"This may be the turning point, Nurse. Prepare another shot."

"Doctor—"

"Miss Chapel, please follow orders."

She did so, though McCoy was well aware of her mounting puzzlement. He continued to study the panel. Finally he nodded. "That does it. He'll be all right now. Let him rest." He turned to Tomar. "It was a flare-up of Rigelian Kassaba fever. He suffered from it ten years ago, and it recurs now and then. There's no danger if he receives medication in time. He'll be up again in an hour or so."

"Very well. I will inform Rojan. You will stay here."

The Kelvan went out and McCoy went back to the table, grinning at Spock, who was now propped up on his elbows.

"I said I would awaken myself, Doctor. What was that shot you gave me?"

"It wasn't *a* shot. It was two."

"I am not interested in quantity, but in content."

"It was stokaline."

"I am not familiar with that drug. Are there any after effects?"

"Yes. You'll feel much better."

"It's a multiple vitamin compound," Christine said, beginning to look less confused.

McCoy patted Spock's shoulder. "Stop worrying. It'll put a little green in your cheeks. Let's get at the neuroanalyzer."

Spock grimaced and rolled off the table to his feet. "It would be helpful to have Mr. Scott here."

"Agreed. Miss Chapel, it is time for Mr. Scott's medical exam."

"I'll see that he reports immediately," Christine said demurely.

Hanar summoned Kirk out of the cave and brought him to Rojan, who was lounging comfortably by a lakeside, with Kelinda close by. Rojan waved Hanar away. "Proceed to the ship, Hanar. Rest yourself, Captain."

"What do you want with me now, Rojan?" Kirk said angrily.

"We will beam aboard the vessel shortly. I wish you to understand your duties."

"My duty is to stop you in any way I can."

"You will obey."

"Or you'll kill more of my people?"

"Captain, I cannot believe that you do not understand the importance of my mission," Rojan said slowly, as if trying to explain to an equal. "We Kelvans have a code of honor—harsh, demanding. It calls for much from us, and much from those we conquer. You have been conquered. I respect your devotion to your duty. But I cannot permit it to interfere with mine."

Kirk remained silent, thinking. It was impossible not to be impressed by what seemed to be so much straightforward honesty. It was apparent that that "code" was what Rojan lived by, and that he believed in it unshakably.

It was also impossible to forget the crumbled shards of what had been Yeoman Leslie Thompson, scattered in the grass not far from here.

Kelinda had moved away to a nearby burst of flowers. Rojan watched her, but not, Kirk thought, with any sign of ordinary male interest.

"I hunger to be in space again, Rojan," she said. "But these—these are lovely. Captain Kirk, what is it you call them?"

"Flowers," he said, moving closer to her, cautiously. "I don't know the variety."

"Our memory tapes tell us of such things on Kelva,"

Rojan said. "Crystals which form with such rapidity that they seem to grow. They look like these fragile things, somewhat. We call them 'sahsheer.' "

"The rose," Kirk said, "by any other name . . ."

"Captain?" Rojan said.

"A quotation, from a great human poet, Shakespeare. 'That which we call a rose by any other name would smell as sweet.' "

Kelinda bent to smell the flowers, while Kirk studied her. Did this woman in reality have a hundred tentacles, all adapted to different uses? It was hard to imagine.

"Kelinda, Captain, come away," Rojan said. "We must leave now."

Directly they were beamed up, Rojan directed Kirk to take him and Kelinda to the bridge. There, Uhura was at her station, and Chekov at his, but a Kelvan woman was in the Helmsman's seat, and Hanar was standing nearby.

"Drea has computed and laid a course for Kelva, Rojan," Hanar said.

"Sir," said Chekov, "we've jumped to warp eight."

"And we'll go faster yet," Rojan said. "Increase speed to warp eleven."

Chekov looked around sharply at Kirk, who could only shrug his helplessness and nod.

"On course and proceeding as planned," said the Kelvan woman at the helm, who was evidently Drea.

"Very well," said Rojan. "Hanar, proceed with the neutralizing operation."

Hanar nodded and went to the elevator. Kirk said quickly: "What neutralizing operation?"

"You humans are troublesome for us, Captain. There are not enough of us to effectively guard all of you all the time. Further, the food synthesizers cannot continue to manufacture food for all of you for our entire journey. We are therefore neutralizing all nonessential personnel."

"No!"

"Captain, you can do nothing to stop it. The procedure is already under way. Now, as to bridge personnel . . ." He moved toward Uhura. "We have no need of communications for some centuries."

Uhura sat frozen in her chair, staring at Rojan in horror. He touched his belt device—and there was nothing left in her seat but a geometrical solid.

"And since Drea is now capable of doing our navigating—" Chekov too vanished. Drea had already neutralized two crewmen beyond Scott's station. Kirk stood frozen.

"They are not dead, Captain," Rojan reminded him. "They are merely reduced to the sum total of what they are."

"That's very comforting," Kirk said sarcastically. "But not pleasant to watch. I'm going to Sickbay. My First Officer was taken ill."

"Yes, I was informed. Go ahead."

Sickbay was deserted. Kirk found Scott, McCoy and Spock picking at food at a table in the recreation room. Getting himself a tray, he joined them. "Reports, gentlemen?"

"I'm a little sick," McCoy said. "We burned out my neuroanalyzer, to no effect. I saw one of the Kelvans, the one they call Tomar, reduce four of my doctors and nurses to those . . . little blocks."

"I've seen them do that too. Remember, the process is reversible. I only wonder how far it's going to go."

"I have been checking our table of organization against their apparent capabilities," Spock said. "It appears that we will have very few 'survivors.' They will need none of the security men, for example. And once we cross the energy barrier, Engineering can be reduced to a skeleton crew. Beyond that point lies some three hundred years of straight cruising—at an astonishing velocity, to be sure, but still cruising. And of the officers, it would seem that only we four could be regarded as 'essential.' I am not even sure of your status, Captain, or mine."

"How so?"

"Rojan is in command now."

"Quite so," Kirk said bitterly. "Scotty, have you found out anything about the paralysis projector?"

"Quite a lot, and none of it good. The machine is in Engineering, and it's encased in that same stuff the door of our jail was made of. Furthermore, it's nae a simple machine—and it's the only one of its kind on board. I think it must be the source of all their special powers—and it's impregnable."

"Any suggestions?"

"One," Scott said. "Self-destruct."

Kirk considered it. "We've been driven to that point, or almost, once before," he said at last. "But aside from my aversion to suicide—and the deaths of everybody else—it's not practical. We'd never complete the routine with the computer before Rojan paralyzed us."

"I thought of that," Scott said. "I could do it myself, though. Remember that we've got to cross the energy barrier. It willna be easy at best. A little sabotage in the matter-antimatter nacelles, and we'd blow, for good and all."

Kirk made a quick silencing gesture. Tomar had come in, and was now approaching them, staring curiously at their trays.

"I do not understand," he said, "why you go to the trouble of consuming this bulk material to sustain yourselves." He pulled a flat pillbox from a pocket and opened it. "These contain all the required nutritional elements."

"Not for human forms," McCoy said. "Bulk is necessary to our digestive systems, and there's a limit to the amount of energy that can be crammed into a pill, too. Perhaps you haven't been in human form long enough to find just pills debilitating, but you will—you will."

"Indeed? Then you had better show me promptly what else we shall need, and how to manage it."

McCoy looked rebellious and Kirk himself felt a hope die almost before it had been born. "I think you'd better, Bones," he said.

"All right. Come on, I'll show you how to work the selector." McCoy led Tomar off toward the wall dispenser.

"Spock," Kirk said in a whisper, "shall we self-destruct? Crossing the barrier may be our last chance to do so."

"Granted," Spock whispered back. "But it is said on Earth that while there is life, there is hope. That is sound logic: no multivalued problem has only one solution."

"Well, we couldn't knock out their central machine even if we were able. It has to be kept intact to restore the rest of our people to human form."

There was quite a long silence. McCoy had settled Tomar at a table with a tray, and Tomar was gingerly forking some meat into his mouth. Judging by his nod, he found it agreeable, and he began eating at a fair speed for a newcomer to the habit. McCoy grinned and rejoined his colleagues.

"I'm almost sorry I did that," he said. "It looks like he likes food—and I wouldn't want any of them to enjoy anything."

Spock continued to watch Tomar. "Most peculiar."

"What is?" Kirk said.

"The isolated glimpses of things I saw when I touched Kelinda's mind are beginning to coalesce in my consciousness. The Kelvans have superior intellectual capacity. But to gain it, they apparently sacrificed many things that would tend to distract them. Among these are the pleasures of the senses—and, of course, emotions."

"But then, Tomar shouldn't be enjoying the taste of food."

"He has taken human form," Spock said, "and is having human reactions."

Kirk's mind leapt ahead in response. "If they all respond to stimulation of the senses, maybe we could confuse them. They don't know how to handle those senses yet. If we can distract them enough, we could try to get the belt devices away. That's their only hold on us."

"It seems reasonable," Spock said.

"All right. We watch for opportunities to work on them—hit them every way we can think of."

Scott was studying Tomar. "I can think of one way right off," he said. He rose and went to the Kelvan. "Lad, you'll be needing something to wash that down with. Have you ever tried Saurian brandy?"

McCoy stopped Hanar as the Kelvan was passing by the door to the examination room. "Come on in a moment, please, Hanar."

"What is it, human?"

"I've noticed you're not looking too well."

"Impossible. We do not malfunction, as do you humans."

"No? You're forgetting you're in a human body. And that does malfunction—that's why Rojan considers me essential. You look pale." He gestured to the table. "Sit up there."

When Hanar complied, McCoy picked up his medical tricorder and began taking readings. "Uh huh . . . Hmmm . . . I don't know about that . . . Hmmmm."

"Please articulate, human."

"Well, it looks to me like this body of yours is getting a little anemic, and has some other subclinical deficiencies. Comes from taking your food in pills, instead of good solid substance." He turned aside and picked up a hypo, which he set.

"What are you doing?"

"I'm going to give you a shot—high potency vitamin-mineral concentrate. You'll have to have one three times a day for a few days. And eat some solid food."

It had taken Scott a while to get Tomar down to serious drinking; initially he had been too interested in the tartan, the claymore, the armorial bearings on the walls, the standing suit of ancient armor in Scott's quarters, all of which he declared nonfunctional in a starship. He did not seem to grasp either the concept of mementos or that of decoration.

Finally, however, they were seated at Scott's desk with a bottle and glasses between them. After a while, it was two bottles. Tomar seemed to remain in total control of himself, as if he'd been drinking lemonade. "No more?" he said.

"Well . . . no more Saurian brandy, but . . ." Scott looked around and found another bottle. "Now, y'see, this liquor is famous on Ahbloron—I mean, Aldibibble—on one of these planets we go to."

"It is a different color from the other."

"Yes. And stronger, too." He poured some into Tomar's glass with an unsteady hand, and then, perforce, some into his own. Somehow this experiment was not working out right.

Kirk paid a call on the cabin Kelinda had commandeered. When she invited him in, he found her looking at a tape on a viewscreen. "Did I disturb you?"

"Disturb? What is it you wish?"

He went over to her. "I want to apologize."

"I do not understand, Captain."

"For hitting you. I wanted to say I was sorry."

"That is not necessary. You attempted to escape, as we

would have. That I was taken in by your ruse is my fault, not yours.''

Kirk smiled and reached out to touch her face gently. ''I don't usually hit beautiful women.''

''Why not, if there is need?''

''Because there are better things for men and women to do.'' He moved the hand down to her neck. ''Was it here that I hit you?''

''No, on the other side.''

''Oh.'' He leaned to the other side, kissed her neck, and nuzzled her ear. ''Is that better?''

''Better? Was it intended to be a remedy?''

''This is.'' Drawing her to her feet, he took her in his arms and kissed her.

After a moment she drew back. ''Is there some significance to this action?''

''It was meant to express . . . well, among humans it shows warmth, love—''

''Oh. You are trying to seduce me,'' she said, as if she were reading a weather report. ''I have been reading about you.''

''Me?''

''Humans. This business of love. You have devoted much literature to it. Why have you built such a mystique around a simple biological fact?''

''We enjoy it.''

''The literature?''

''Kelinda, I'm sorry I brought the subject up.''

''Did you regard this contact of the lips as pleasurable?''

Kirk sighed. ''I did.''

''Curious. I wonder why.'' Abruptly she put her arms around him and kissed him back.

The door opened and Rojan came in. Kirk made a point of drawing back with guilty swiftness.

''Is there some problem, Captain?'' Rojan said.

''None.'' Kirk left quickly. Rojan stared after him.

''What did he want here?''

''He came to apologize for hitting me,'' Kelinda said. ''Apparently, it involves some peculiar touching contacts.''

''In what manner?''

Kelinda hesitated, then reached up to nibble at Rojan's neck and ear. Rojan stepped away from her, frowning.

"They are odd creatures, these humans. Please have the reports on fuel consumption relayed to Subcommander Hanar as soon as possible."

Spock had taught Rojan to play chess; the Kelvan had learned with breathtaking speed. They were playing now, in the recreation room.

"Yes, they are peculiar," Spock said, moving a piece. "I very often find them unfathomable, but an interesting psychological study."

Rojan moved in return. "I do not understand this business of biting someone's neck to apologize."

Spock looked up, raising his eyebrows. Then he looked back at the game, saw an opening and quickly moved another piece. "I believe you are referring to a kiss. But it is my understanding that such, uh, apologies are usually exchanged between two people who have some affection for each other."

"Kelinda has no affection for Captain Kirk," Rojan said quickly.

Spock studied Rojan's next move and shook his head. "You seemed disturbed about the incident. Your game is off."

"Why should I be disturbed?"

"It seems to me you have known Kelinda for some time. She is a Kelvan, as you are. Among humans, I have found the symptoms you are displaying would be indicative of jealousy."

"I have no reason for such a reaction. Kelinda is a female. Nothing more."

"Captain Kirk seems to find her quite attractive."

"Of course she is."

"But you are not jealous."

"No!"

"Nor upset."

"Certainly not!"

Spock made his move. "Checkmate."

Kirk, Spock and McCoy were holding another council of war in the recreation room. Kirk was depressed. "The thing is, I can't tell if we're getting anywhere. And I haven't seen Scotty for what seems like months."

"You haven't seen Tomar either," McCoy said. "But the point is, these things take time. The Kelvans started out with adapted human bodies in superb physical shape—textbook cases, as Spock said. They have high resistance. I've been giving Hanar shots that would have driven our whole crew up the wall in an hour. He responds slowly—but he's getting more irritable by the minute, now."

"And Rojan," Spock said, "has exhibited symptoms of jealousy toward Kelinda and you."

"What about Kelinda, Jim?" McCoy said.

"No progress," Kirk said, uncomfortably.

"What approach did you take with her? Could be you're a little rusty—"

Kirk felt himself begin to bristle. Spock interposed smoothly: "I would say it is sufficient that Rojan is jealous."

"Right," Kirk said quickly. "That's the opening wedge. As soon as it's a little wider, we move."

Behind Kirk, Kelinda's voice said: "I would like to speak with you, Captain."

Spock stood up at once. "Doctor, I think I need another dose of stokaline."

"Huh?" McCoy said. "Oh, yes. Pardon us."

They went out. Kirk leaned back in his chair and studied Kelinda. "You had something to say?"

"Yes." Did she really seem a trifle uncomfortable, even perhaps awkward? Kirk waited. Then she took a deep breath and touched him, lightly, on a shoulder. "This cultural mystique surrounding a biological function . . ."

"Yes?"

"You realize it really is quite overdone."

"Oh. Quite."

"However, I was wondering . . . would you please apologize to me again?"

Rojan was in the command chair. Behind him, the elevator doors snapped open, and then Hanar's voice said, with surprising belligerence: "Rojan. I want to talk to you."

Rojan looked up in surprise. "Very well, Hanar."

"First, I do not like the way responsibility and duty have been portioned out to us."

"It is the way your duties have always been assigned."

"And that is my second quarrel with you. It was always unjust—"

Rojan snapped out of the chair. "Hanar—"

"And further, I do not care much for the autocratic way you order us about on this ship, which we captured, not you—"

"Confine yourself to your quarters!"

Hanar hesitated, as though he had had a lot more to say, but had thought better of it. Then he spun on his heel and left without further acknowledgment.

Rojan found his own fists clenching in anger—and was suddenly aware that Drea was watching him in amazement from the navigator's station. As Rojan turned his back to hide his expression, Spock came onto the bridge and went toward his library-computer. Rojan followed.

"You were not called to the bridge, Spock. What is your purpose here?"

"Sensors and various other recording devices require monitoring and certain adjustments."

"Very well, proceed . . . Have you seen Captain Kirk?"

"Do you want him? I will call him to the bridge."

"No. I . . . wondered where he was."

"Dr. McCoy and I left him some time ago in the recreation room."

"He was alone, then?"

"No. Kelinda was with him. She seemed most anxious to speak to him."

"I told him to stay away from her."

"It would appear that you have little control over her, sir . . . or perhaps Captain Kirk has more."

Rojan turned abruptly and headed for the elevator.

Kirk and Kelinda were locked in a kiss when Rojan came through the recreation room door. Kirk looked up, but did not release Kelinda entirely; instead he kept a possessive arm around her as he turned toward Rojan. Rojan stopped and stared.

"Kelinda, I told you to avoid this human!"

"I did not wish to," she said.

"I am your commander."

"I've found," Kirk said, "that doesn't mean much to a woman if she's bound to go her own way."

"You have done this to her! Corrupted her—turned her away from me!"

"If you couldn't keep her, Rojan, that's not *my* problem."

Furiously, Rojan leaped at Kirk. He seemed to have forgotten all about the belt device, his bare hands reaching out. Kirk pushed Kelinda aside and met Rojan's rush.

The two men, equally powerful, slammed at each other like bulls. Rojan was more clumsy, more unaccustomed to the body he was in. Kirk was the quicker and the more adept fighter, but he was not possessed by the anger which obviously drove Rojan.

Kelinda did not intervene; she only watched. After a moment she was joined by Spock and McCoy.

Kirk delivered a final punch that sent Rojan spinning down, backward. But he was not beaten yet. He started to climb back to his feet.

"Rojan—wait!" Kirk said. "Listen to me—"

Rojan flung himself forward, but Kirk fended him off. "Listen! Why didn't you use your paralyzer? Don't you know why? Because you've become a human yourself." Kirk ducked a punch. "Look at you—brawling like a street fighter—shaking with rage—"

Rojan paused and stared as the words began to sink in. "What?"

"You thought I took your woman away from you. You were jealous—and you wanted to kill me with your bare hands. Would a Kelvan have done that? Would he *have* to? You reacted with the emotions of a human, Rojan. You are one."

"No! We cannot be."

"You have no choice. You chose this ship. Because of its environmental systems, you had to take human form to use it. And you're stuck with it—you and your descendants— for the next three hundred years. Look what's happened to you in the short time you've been exposed to us. What do you think will happen in three hundred years? When this ship gets to Kelva, the people on it will be aliens, the Kelvans their enemies.''

"We have a mission. We must carry it out.'' But Rojan's tone showed that he was shaken.

"Your mission was to find worlds for your people to live on. You can still do that. I told you we could present your case to the Federation. I know it would be sympathetic. There are many unpopulated planets in our galaxy. You could develop them in peace, your way.''

"They would do that? You would extend welcome to invaders?''

"No. But we do welcome friends.''

"Perhaps," said Rojan, "perhaps it could be done.''

Spock said: "A robot ship could be sent back to Kelva with the Federation proposal.''

"But what of us?'' Rojan said. "If we . . . if we retain this form, where can we find a place?''

"Seems to me," McCoy said, "that little planet you were on was kind of a nice place.''

"Pleasant . . . but . . .''

"The Federation would probably grant a colonization permit to a small group of people who desired to settle there,'' Spock said. "You do represent an old and highly intelligent race.''

Rojan turned to Kelinda and jerked his head at Kirk. "You want to go with him?''

Kelinda glanced at Kirk and then back at Rojan. "As you have said, he is not our kind. I believe I owe you an apology.'' She kissed him. "It *is* pleasurable, Rojan.''

"You know, Rojan," Kirk said, "one of the advantages of being a human is being able to appreciate beauty . . . of a flower, or of a woman. Unless you'd rather conquer a galaxy?''

"No, Captain, I would rather not.'' Rojan took Kelinda's hand. "A link in a chain—that's all we were. Perhaps there is an opportunity for us to be more.'' He turned away, crossed the room and activated an intercom. "Bridge, this is Rojan.''

"Yes, Commander," said Drea's voice.

"Turn the ship. We are returning to the alien . . . We are returning home.''

"Sir?"

"Turn the ship about."

He led Kelinda out. Kirk, Spock and McCoy expelled simultaneous sighs of relief.

"Jim, I was coming to tell you—"

"Yes, Bones?"

"I found Scotty in his room with Tomar. Apparently they've been having a drinking bout all this time. They were both under the table—but Tomar went down first. Scott had Tomar's belt device in his hand. He just never made it to the door with it."

Kirk grinned. "The Kelvans," he said, "still have a lot to learn about being human, don't they?"

RETURN TO TOMORROW

Writer: Gene Roddenberry and John T. Dugan
Director: Ralph Senensky
Guest star: Diana Muldaur

The readings were coming from a star system directly ahead of the *Enterprise*. And havoc is what they were causing. The Starship's distress relays had been activated. All its communication channels had been affected. A direction to follow had even been specified, but no clear signal had been received. Yet one fact was clear: someone or something was trying to attract the Enterprise's attention. Who? Or what? Those were the questions.

Over at Spock's station, Kirk said, "Well?"

"I don't know, Captain."

Despite his exasperation, Kirk smiled. "I never heard you use those words before, Mr. Spock."

"Not even a Vulcan can know the unknown, sir," Spock said stiffly. "We're hundreds of light years past where any Earth ship has ever explored."

"Planet dead ahead, Captain!" Sulu called. "Becoming visual."

The screen showed what appeared to be a very dead planet: scarred, shrunken, a drifting cadaver of a world.

Uhura turned from her board. "That planet is the source of whatever it is we have been receiving, sir."

Spock, his head bent to his hooded viewer, announced, "Class M planet, sir. Oblate spheroid, ratio 1 to 296. Mean density 5.53. Mass .9." He paused. "Close resemblance to Earth conditions with two very important differences. It's much older than Earth. And about half a million years ago its atmosphere was totally ripped away by some cataclysm. Sensors detect no life of any kind."

Without warning the bridge was suddenly filled by the sound of a voice, resonant, its rich deepness profoundly impressive. *"Captain Kirk,"* it said, *"all your questions will be answered in time."*

The bridge people stared at the screen. Kirk, turning to Uhura, said, "Are your hailing frequencies freed yet, Lieutenant?"

"No, sir."

They had sped past the planet now. Eyes on the screen, Kirk said, "Maintain present course, Mr. Sulu."

The deep voice spoke again. *"I am Sargon. It is the energy of my thoughts which has touched your instruments and directed you here."*

"Then, can you hear me?" Kirk asked. "Who are you, Sargon?"

"Please assume a standard orbit around our planet, Captain."

"Are you making a request or demand?" Kirk said.

"The choice is yours. I read what is in your mind: words are unnecessary."

"If you can read my mind, you must know I am wondering just who and what you are. The planet we've just passed is dead; there is no possibility of life there as we understand life."

"And I," said the voice, *"am as dead as my planet. Does that frighten you, Captain? If it does, you will let what is left of me perish."* An awesome solemnity had entered the voice. *"Then, all of you, my children—all of mankind will . . ."*

The voice faded as the Starship moved out of the planet's range. Sulu, turning to Kirk, said, "Do we go on, sir—or do I turn the ship back?"

Kirk could feel all eyes centered on him. Then Spock spoke from his station. "There's only one possible explanation, sir. Pure thought . . . the emanations of a fantastically powerful mind."

Kirk paced the distance from his chair to the main viewing screen. "Whatever it is, we're beyond its range."

"And out of danger," Spock said dryly.

"You don't recommend going back?"

"If a mind of that proportion should want to harm us, sir, we could never hope to cope with it."

"It called me—us 'my children,' " Kirk said. "What could that mean?"

"Again, sir—I don't know."

Kirk sank down in his command chair, frowning. Then his brow cleared. "All right," he said. "Take us back, Mr. Sulu. Standard orbit around the planet."

The dead world gradually reappeared on the screen, its color the hue of dead ash. Sulu said, "Entering standard orbit, Captain."

Kirk nodded, eyes on the screen. Then he hit the button of his command recorder, dictating. "Since exploration and contact with alien intelligence is our primary mission, I have decided to risk the dangers potential in our current situation— and resume contact with this strange planet. Log entry out." Snapping off the recorder, he spoke to Uhura. "How long before Starfleet receives that?"

"Over three weeks at this distance, sir. A month and a half before we receive their answer."

Kirk left his chair to cross to Spock's station. The Vulcan was swiftly manipulating dials.

"Got something?" Kirk said.

"Sensors registering some form of energy, sir . . . deep *inside* the planet."

Sargon's voice came once more. *"Your probes have touched me, Mr. Spock."*

Spock looked up at Kirk. "I read energy only, sir. No life form."

Then again Sargon spoke. *"I have locked your transporter device on my coordinates. Please come to us. Rescue us from oblivion."*

Spock, imperturbable, lifted his head from his viewer's mound. "It came from deep under the planet surface, Captain . . . from under at least a hundred miles of solid rock."

Kirk began, "We can't beam—"

Sargon addressed the half-spoken thought in his mind. *"I will make it possible for your transporter to beam you that deep beneath the surface. Have no fear."*

Spock, concentrating on his viewer, said, "I read a

chamber beneath the surface, sir. Oxygen-nitrogen suitable for human life support.''

Kirk gave himself a long moment. Then he spoke to Uhura. ''Lieutenant, have Dr. McCoy report to the Transporter Room in ten minutes with standard landing-party equipment.''

''Aye, sir.''

''Captain,'' Spock said, ''I am most curious to inspect whatever it is that has survived half a million years—this entity which has outlived its cataclysmic experience.''

Kirk laid a hand on his shoulder. ''And I'd like my Science Officer with me on something as unusual as this. But it's so full of unknowns, we can't risk the absence of both of us from the ship.''

The bridge was instantly plunged into total darkness. All panel hum stilled. Sulu hit a switch. ''Power's gone, sir! *Totally* gone!''

There had been no menace in the deep voice. A tone of pleading, yes—but no menace. Kirk frowned, pondering. Then he said, ''On the other hand, Mr. Spock, perhaps this 'Sargon' wants you to come along with me.''

Lights flashed back on. Panels hummed again. Sulu, checking his board, cried, ''All normal, sir! No damage at all.''

''Well,'' Kirk said. ''Then that's that. Mr. Spock, you'll transport down with us.'' As he strode to the elevator, he turned to add, ''Mr. Sulu, you have the con.''

A young woman, dark and slim, had followed McCoy into the Transporter Room. Kirk recognized her—Lieutenant Commander Anne Mulhall, astrobiologist. His eyes took in the figure, the startling sapphire of the eyes under the raven-black hair. He hadn't remembered her as so attractive. She lowered her eyes, checking her equipment, two security guards beside her. Nor did she look up as McCoy said tartly, ''Jim, why no briefing on this? I'd like at least to know—''

Kirk interrupted. ''Easy, Bones. If you know 'something is down there,' you know as much as we do. The rest is only guesses.''

Scott, over at the Transporter console, spoke. ''I don't

like it, Captain. Your coordinates preset by an alien of some
unknown variety. You could materialize inside solid rock.''

"Inside solid rock!" McCoy shouted.

Spock, moving in beside Scott, said, ''Unlikely, Doctor. The coordinates correspond to a chamber that sensor
readings detected on the bridge.''

''It is my feeling,'' Kirk said, ''that they or it could
destroy us standing right here if it wanted to, Mr. Scott.''

Anne spoke for the first time. '' 'They' or 'it'?'' she
said.

Kirk looked at her. ''Lieutenant Commander, may I
ask what you're doing here in this room?''

''I was ordered to report for landing-party duty, sir.''

''By whom?''

''I . . .'' She smiled. ''It's strange, sir. I'm not sure.''
There was a moment's pause. Then, flushing, she
added, ''I do not lie, Captain. I *did* receive an order to report
here.''

Spock intervened. ''I'm sure she did, Captain. Just as
you received an order to take me along.''

Kirk nodded; and McCoy said, ''Let's get back to this
solid-rock business. How much rock are we going through?''

Spock answered. ''Exactly one hundred, twelve point
three seven miles below the surface, Doctor.''

"Miles?" McCoy echoed blankly. ''Jim, he's joking!''

But Kirk was assigning Transporter positions to the
party. They were taking their places when the console lights
abruptly flashed on and Sargon's voice said, *''Please stand
ready. I will operate the controls.''*

Kirk spoke in reaction to the shock in McCoy's face.
''If you'd prefer to stay behind, Bones . . .''

McCoy eyed him. ''No—no, if I'd be useful, and I may
have to be, that is, as long as you're beaming down, Jim . . .''
He shrugged. ''I might as well have a medical look at whatever
this is.''

Kirk joined them on the platform. ''Energize!'' he
called to Scott.

The dematerializing shimmer broke them into glittering
fragments—all of them except the two security guards. They
were left standing, unaffected, on the platform, their faces

astounded. Scott stared at them, his face drawing into lines of worry.

The selected group materialized in a metallic vault, some sort of antechamber, its luminescent walls diffusing a softly radiant glow. Spock was the first to realize the absence of the security guards.

Kirk nodded at his comment. "Somebody down here doesn't like them," he said. He opened his communicator. "Kirk here, Scotty."

"Can you read me, Captain?"

"I shouldn't be able to, not from this deep inside the planet. Perhaps that's been arranged for us, too. Is the security team up there?"

"They're fine, Captain. They just didn't dematerialize. I don't like it, sir."

"No problems here yet. Maintain alert. Captain out."

Anne and Spock had been circling the vault with their tricorders. The girl said, "Atmosphere report, Captain. A fraction richer in oxygen than usual for us, but otherwise normal."

Spock had applied his tricorder to a wall. "This vault was fabricated about a half-million years ago. About the same time that the planet surface was destroyed."

"Walls' composition?"

"A substance or alloy quite unknown to me, sir. Much stronger and harder than anything I ever measured."

"All readings go off the scale, sir," Anne said.

"The air's fresh," McCoy said, sniffing. "Must be re-circulated somehow."

"For us? Or does 'it' need fresh air?"

As if in reply, the fourth wall of the vault slid back. They recoiled. Ahead of them was a vast room. It was starkly bare, empty except for a large slab of veinless white stone, supported by four plain standards of the same immaculate stone. On it stood a big translucent globe, brilliantly lit from within. The group followed Kirk into the room; but as Spock stepped forward to take a tricorder reading of the globe, he was halted by the sound of Sargon's voice, still deep but no longer resonant.

"Welcome," said the globe. *"I am Sargon."*

Once more Spock focused his tricorder. "Sargon, would you mind if I—?"

"You may use your tricorder, Mr. Spock. Your readings will show energy but no substance. Sealed in this receptacle is the essence of my mind."

Spock took his readings. Then he backed up to Kirk so that he, too, could see them. Kirk gave a low whistle of amazement. "Impossible, Spock! A being of pure energy without matter or form!"

McCoy addressed the globe. "But you once had a body of some type?"

"Although our minds were infinitely greater, my body was much as yours, my children."

Kirk spoke slowly. "That is the second time you have called us your 'children.' "

"Because it is probable you are our descendants, Captain. Six thousand centuries ago our vessels were colonizing this galaxy just as your own Starships are now exploring it. As you leave your seed on distant planets, so we left our seed behind us."

Anne protested: "Our studies indicate that our planet Earth evolved independently." But Spock, his face unusually preoccupied, said, "That would explain many enigmas in Vulcan pre-history."

"There is no certainty. It was so long ago that the records of our travels were lost in the catastrophe we loosed upon ourselves."

Kirk said, "A war?"

"A struggle for goal that unleashed a power you cannot even comprehend."

"Then perhaps your intelligence was deficient, Sargon." Kirk stepped toward the globe. "We faced a crisis like that at the beginning of the Nuclear Age. But we found the wisdom not to destroy ourselves."

"We survived our primitive Nuclear Era, my son. But there comes to all races an ultimate crisis which you have yet to face."

"I should like to understand," Kirk said. "I do not."

"The mind of man can become so powerful that he forgets he is man. He confuses himself with God."

Kirk's mind was awhirl. Was this being speaking of the

Lucifer sin? Abruptly, he felt a completed trust of Sargon. He moved to the globe with the confidence of a child to a parent. "You said you needed help. What is it you wish?"

A strange thrilling sound echoed through the room. In the globe, light fluctuated, growing brighter and brighter. Then a flare broke from it. It transfixed Kirk, holding him immobile. At the same instant light in the globe dimmed to a tiny flicker. It was clear to the others that the essence of what was in the globe had transferred itself to Kirk—and vanished into him.

McCoy started forward, but Spock put out a restraining hand. "Patience, Doctor. Let's wait a moment."

Kirk stood rigid, stiffened, his eyes shut. It seemed centuries to McCoy before they opened, "Jim . . ." he said. "Jim . . ."

Kirk spoke. "I am . . . Sargon."

His voice had deepened. And his bearing had changed, permeated as by the calm, gently austere dignity that had characterized the personality of Sargon.

McCoy yelled, *"Where's our Captain? Where's Jim Kirk?"*

"Here, Bones." The voice of Sargon-Kirk was gentle as a mother soothing a frightened infant. "Your loved Captain is unharmed. I have taken his body for the moment to demonstrate to you—"

McCoy had drawn his phaser. "No! No, I do not go along with this! Back where you were, Sargon, whatever you are!"

"What do you propose to do with your phaser?" It was the mild voice of Spock. "That's still Jim's body."

McCoy's shoulders slumped. Then he saw that the incorporated Sargon was slowly becoming aware of Kirk's body. It expanded its chest; its head was flung up as the deliciousness of air was inhaled; its arms flexed—and a cry burst from it.

"Lungs . . . lungs savoring breath again! Eyes seeing colors again! A heart pumping arteries surging with young blood!" A hand touched the other one in wonder. "To *feel* again after half a million years!" Kirk's body turned, his own smile on its lips. "Your Captain has an excellent corpus,

Doctor! I compliment both of you on the condition in which it has been maintained."

"And your plans for it?" Spock's voice was toneless. "Can you exchange places again when you wish?"

Sargon-Kirk didn't answer. Instead, he moved to the receptacle with its frail glow of light. Pointing to it, he said, "Have no fear. Your Captain is quite unharmed in there." The dim flicker slightly brightened. "See? He hears, he knows, he is aware of all we do and say. But his mind cannot generate the energy to speak from the globe as I did."

Spock, who had been using his tricorder, called "Doctor!" McCoy paled as he saw its readings. "The creature is killing him!" he shouted. "Heartbeat almost double, temperature one hundred and four degrees!"

"Sargon, what is it you want of us?" Spock demanded.

Kirk's eyes studied them silently. Finally Sargon's words came. "There are other receptacles in the next room; they contain two more of us who have survived. You, Anne Mulhall, and you, Mr. Spock—we shall require your bodies for them. We must have your bodies and Captain Kirk's in order to live again."

It had come to all of them that Kirk was no longer Kirk but an individual stronger, wiser, infused with a dominant intelligence beyond the reach of any of them. Waved into the next room, they obediently moved into it. Its shelved walls held many receptacles; but of them all, only two still shone with light. Kirk's deeper voice said, "Yes, only two of us still live. The others are blackened by death but these two still shine—Hanoch and Thalassa." He caressed one of the lighted globes. "Thalassa, my Thalassa, I am pleased you survived with me. Half a million years have been almost too long to wait."

Spock said, "Sargon, when that struggle came that destroyed your planet . . ."

"A few of the best minds were chosen to survive. We built these chambers and preserved our essence here in this fashion." He touched the Thalassa globe with tenderness. "My wife, as you may have guessed. And Hanoch from the other, enemy side in the struggle. By then we had all realized our mistake."

He paused. "We knew the seeds we had planted on

other planets had taken root. And we knew you would one day build vessels as we did—that you would come here.''

''What was your task in that globe out there?'' Spock said.

''To search the heavens with my mind . . . probing, waiting, probing. And finally my mind touched something— your ship bringing you here.''

''So you could thieve our bodies from us!'' Anne cried.

He looked at her, the centuries of gathered wisdom in his eyes contrasting eerily with the youth of Kirk's face. ''To steal your bodies? No, no. You misunderstand, my children. To *borrow* them. We ask you to only lend them to us for a short time.''

''To *destroy* them!'' cried McCoy. ''Just as you're burning that one up right now! Spock, the heartbeat reading is now 262! And the whole metabolic rate is just as high! My medical tricorder—''

''I shall return your Captain's body before its limit has been reached, Doctor.''

''What is the purpose of this borrowing?'' Spock said.

''To build . . .'' Suddenly, Sargon-Kirk swayed. Then he straightened. ''To build humanoid robots. We must borrow your bodies only long enough to have the use of your hands, your fingers.''

Spock turned to the others. ''I understand,'' he said. ''They will construct mechanical bodies for themselves and move their minds into them. That accomplished, they will return our bodies to us.''

Anne interposed. ''We have engineers, technicians. Why can't they build the robot bodies for you?''

''No. Our methods, the skill required, goes far beyond your abilities.'' He swayed again, staggering, and Spock put out an arm to support him. His breath was coming hard and the Vulcan had to stoop to hear his whisper. ''It is . . . time. Help me back to your . . . Captain.''

With McCoy at his other side, he stumbled back into the big bare room. Weakly, he waved them aside to stand alone by the receptacle, eyes closed. This time the flare of light flashed from him—and abruptly, the globe was again alive with a pulsating brilliance. The knees of the borrowed body gave way and Anne Mulhall rushed to it, her arms outstretched. They closed around its shoulders and its eyelids fluttered open. "Captain Kirk?" she said tentatively.

The skipper of the *Enterprise* smiled at her, his eyes on her face.

"Jim . . . is it you?" cried McCoy.

Kirk didn't speak, his gaze still deep in the sapphire eyes. Hurriedly, McCoy checked him with his medical tricorder. "Good—good, fine! Metabolic rate back to normal!"

Spock went to him. "Captain, do you remember what happened? Do you remember any part of it?"

"What? Oh. Oh, yes, yes. Sargon borrowed my body." He gestured to the globe. "I was there, floating . . . floating in time and space."

"You take it damned casually!" McCoy said. "However, you don't seem harmed . . . physically at least."

Kirk, wholly himself again, suddenly seemed to realize how matter-of-factly he was accepting his extraordinary experience. "Spock, I remember all now! As Sargon and I exchanged—for an instant we were one. I know him. I know now exactly what he is and what he wants. *And I do not fear him.*"

Anne had withdrawn her embrace. "Captain, I'm afraid I must agree with Dr. McCoy. You could be suffering mental effects from this—a kind of euphoria."

"There's a way to check my conviction about Sargon." He turned to Spock. "I—I hate to ask it, Mr. Spock, knowing as I do what it costs you."

"Vulcan mind-melding?" McCoy said. "Are you willing, Spock?"

Spock took time to answer. Finally, he nodded gravely. Then, with care, he began to ready himself for the ordeal, breathing deeply, massaging chest muscles. Kirk, turning to the globe, said, "Sargon, we—"

"I understand. I am prepared."

It began. The globe's brilliance increased and, with it, the strain on Spock's anguished concentration. His breath grew harsh and his neck muscles taut. Words started to come like those of a man in a dream or a nightmare. ". . . there is a world . . . not physical. The mind reaches . . . grows to encompass . . . to understand beyond understanding . . .

growing . . . beyond comprehension . . . beyond . . . beyond . . . beyond . . ."

Kirk flashed an alarmed look at McCoy. It had never been so hard. They started forward—but Spock himself was now breaking away from the meld. He drew a deep lungful of breath, shaking, weak, eyes dazed.

"Spock?" Kirk cried.

The voice still held the awe of inexpressible experience. "Captain, I cannot say . . . what I have seen. The—the knowledge . . . the beauty of perfect reason . . . the incredible goodness . . . the unbelievable glory of ageless wisdom . . . the pure goodness of what Sargon is . . ."

Anne was the first to break the silence. "Beauty? Perfect reason? Pure goodness?"

Kirk nodded. "Beyond imagination."

Spock, still shaken, whispered, "It . . . will take me . . . time to absorb all I have learned . . . all I have felt . . ."

"Yes," Kirk said. Instinctively he turned to the receptacle. "Sargon . . ." he said. The word might have been "Father".

"I understand, my son. Go to your vessel. All who are involved must agree to this. After all these centuries, we can wait a few more hours."

McCoy strode to the globe. "And if we decide against you?"

"Then you may go as freely as you came."

Leonard McCoy was out of his depth. He looked from Spock to Kirk, feeling himself to be the alien in a world no longer familiar to him. He had never been so uncertain of himself in his life.

"You are going to *what*?"

Scott had leaned over the Briefing Room table, his face incredulous. Kirk, quite composed, sat beside the grim-jawed McCoy. He smiled at Scott; and his Chief Engineer, Highland blood boiling, cried, "Are they all right in the head, Doctor?"

"No comment," McCoy said.

"It's a simple transference of our minds and theirs, Scotty," Kirk said.

"Nothing to it," McCoy said. "It happens every day."

Kirk ignored him. "I want your approval, Scotty. You'll have to do all the work with them, furnishing all they need to build the android robots. That is, you'll only seem to be working with us—with our bodies. But they'll be inside of them and we will be . . ." The explanation was getting complicated. Kirk flinched under the cold Scottish steel of Scott's eyes. "We'll be . . . in their receptacles," he finished lamely.

He sounded mad to his own ears. Where had fled that supremely sane self-possession of Sargon's that his body had entertained so briefly? He struggled to recover some shred of it; and McCoy cried, "Where they'll be, Scott, is floating in a ball! Just drifting sweetly in a ball of nothing! Indecent is what it is—indecent!"

Spock spoke. "Once inside their robot forms, Engineer, they will restore our bodies. They can leave this planet and travel back with us. With their massive knowledge, mankind can leap ahead ten thousand years."

"Bones," Kirk said, "they'll show us medical miracles you've never dreamed possible. And engineering advances, Scotty! Vessels this size with engines no larger than a walnut!"

"You're joking," Scott said gruffly.

"No," Spock said. "I myself saw that and more in Sargon's mind. I encountered an infinity of a goodness and knowledge that—that at this moment still staggers me."

"Many a fine man crushes ants underfoot without even knowing it." McCoy's voice shook. "They're giants and we're insects beside them, Jim. They could destroy us without meaning to."

Scott was musing aloud. "A Starship engine the size of a walnut?" He shrugged. "Impossible. But I suppose there's no harm in looking over diagrams on it . . ."

"And all he wants for these miracles is the body of our ship's Captain," McCoy said. "And that of our next in command, too. Coincidence? Anybody want to bet?"

"They have selected us, Bones, as the most compatible bodies."

"And your attitude on that, Dr. Mulhall?" McCoy demanded.

"If we all agree," Anne said steadily, "I am willing

to host Thalassa's mind. I am a scientist. The opportunity is an extraordinary one for experimentation and observation.''

"Bones, you can stop this right now by voting 'no'. That's why I called you all here. We'll all be deeply involved. It must be unanimous.''

McCoy slammed the table. "Then I still want one question answered! *Why?* Not a list of possible miracles—but an understandable, simple, basic 'why' that doesn't ignore all the possible dangers! Let's not kid ourselves! There's much danger potential in this thing!''

"They used to say, Bones, that if man were meant to fly, he'd have wings. But he *did* fly." Kirk's voice deepened with his earnestness. "In fact, human existence has been a long story of faint-hearted warnings not to push any further, not to learn, not to strive, not to grow. I don't believe we can stop, Bones. Do you want to return to the days when your profession operated with scalpels—and sewed up the patients with catgut?''

He paused, looking at the faces around the table. "Yes, I'm in command. I can order this. I haven't done so. Dr. McCoy is performing his duty. He is right to point out the enormous danger potential in such close contact with intelligence as fantastically advanced as this. *My* point is that the potential for new knowledge is also enormous. Risk is our business. That's what this Starship is all about! It is why we're aboard her!''

He leaned forward in his chair, his eyes searching faces. "You may dissent without prejudice. Do I hear a negative vote?''

There was none. He rose to his feet. "Mr. Scott, stand by to bring the three receptacles aboard.''

In Sickbay the three beds had been arranged for Kirk, Spock, and Anne. A shining globe had been placed beside each one. McCoy, Christine Chapel beside him, stood at the body-function panels, his clipboard in hand. He turned to the nurse. "You must know," he said, "that with the transfer, the extreme power of the alien minds will drive heart action dangerously high. All body functions will race at many times normal metabolism. These panels must be monitored most carefully.''

The situation had shaken Christine. She made a successful effort to recover her professionalism. "Yes, sir," she said.

McCoy spoke to Kirk. "We're about as ready as we'll ever be."

Kirk turned his head to the globe beside him. "Ready, Sargon."

There came the thrilling sound preceding transfer. The three globes grew active, light building and fluctuating inside them. Then the three flares flashed from them to the bodies lying on the beds. Anne's trembled as Thalassa entered it. Christine moved quickly to check it. Hanoch-Spock sat up, stretching in delight at the feel of a body. Beside each bed the globes' light had dimmed to a faint flicker. McCoy was concentrated on Kirk's body-function panel; and Christine, leaving Thalassa-Anne, moved in to check Hanoch-Spock. To her amazement, he smiled at her, his eyes taking her in with lusty appreciation. Where was the cool, cerebral Spock?

She turned hastily to his body panel. What she read alarmed her. "Metabolic rates are double and rising, Doctor."

Hanoch-Spock spoke. "A delicious woman . . . a delicious sight to awaken to after half a million years."

Disconcerted, Christine said, "Thank you."

But Hanoch-Spock was looking beyond her now to where Thalassa-Anne was sitting up in bed, raven hair about her shoulders, the blue eyes shining as she savored the forgotten feeling of life. "I—I didn't remember what it felt like . . . to breathe—to breathe like this!" She turned. "Sargon? Where's Sargon?"

Sargon-Kirk rose and went to her. "Here . . . in this body, Thalassa." With a becoming dignity, threaded with joy in the awakening of long-forgotten senses, she smiled at him. "The body does not displease me, my husband. It is not unlike that which was your own."

"I am pleased by your pleasure, my love."

She had become aware of her hands. Tentatively, she reached one up to caress his cheek. "After so long," she whispered. "It's been so long, Sargon."

His arms were around her. Christine averted her eyes as their lips met. There was something infinitely touching in this embrace, longed for but deferred for half a million years. They separated and Christine said, "I'm sorry . . . I'm here . . ."

Thalassa-Anne extended a gentle hand. "You are not intruding, my child. As a woman, you know my wondrous gratitude at touching him who is mine again. Do you have a man?"

"No. I—I . . ." Despite herself, Christine found her eyes moving to Spock, forgetting for the moment that it was Hanoch who inhabited him. She flushed. "No, I . . . do not have that need. I have my work" She took a hasty reading of the body-function panel. Had Hanoch-Spock noticed that look?

Thalassa-Anne spoke quietly to Sargon. "How cruel. May I help her, my husband?"

"It would be so easy to give all of them happiness, Thalassa." He shook his head gently. "But we must not interfere in their lives."

More aggressive than the others, Hanoch-Spock was already circling the room, examining its equipment. He turned to find McCoy watching him. "An excellent body, Doctor. It seems I received the best of the three." He extended his arms, flexing Spock's superb biceps. "Strength, hearing, eyesight, all above the human norm. I'm surprised the Vulcans never conquered your race."

"Vulcans prize peace above all, Hanoch."

"Of course. Of course. Just as do we."

But McCoy had seen Thalassa-Anne sink back on her pillow. "Nurse!"

The lovely alien whispered, "A wave of heat suddenly . . . I feel . . ."

Christine caught her as she sagged, drawing in the support of another pillow behind her. McCoy was assisting her when he saw Sargon-Kirk begin to slump. As he supported him to his bed, he said, "Hanoch, you'd better go back to bed, too."

But Spock's metabolism had not yet been affected. Hanoch said, "Unnecessary at present, Doctor. My Vulcan body is accustomed to higher metabolism."

Christine tore her eyes from him to check Thalassa-Anne's body-function panel. Its readings were alarmingly high. McCoy rushed to the bed at the nurse's call. Then he whirled to the bed that held Sargon-Kirk. "It won't work, Sargon! You've got to get out of them before you kill them!"

The answer came weakly. "We will . . . vacate them . . . until you can administer . . . a metabolic-reduction injection."

"A what?" McCoy demanded.

Hanoch-Spock joined him at the bed, looking down at Kirk's sweaty forehead. "I will prepare the formula, Sargon," he said.

"Hanoch . . . your own condition . . ."

"I can maintain this body for several more hours, Sargon. Do not be anxious."

"Then . . . Thalassa and I . . . will now return to our confinement."

Beside the beds of Kirk and Anne the globes flared with light again. But Hanoch-Spock, still incarnate, gave his dim one a look of repulsion. He turned from Kirk's bed to speak to McCoy. "I shall need help to prepare the formula. Your nurse will assist me, Doctor, in your pharmacology laboratory."

Christine looked at McCoy. He couldn't tell himself that he was confronted by a command decision. That had already been made by Kirk. The decision facing him merely implemented his Captain's wish. He nodded reluctantly—and Christine followed Hanoch-Spock out of Sickbay.

Behind him Kirk and Anne were slowly recovering from the effects of the alien possession. Kirk's eyes at last fluttered open. McCoy had to stoop to hear his whisper.

"Bones . . ."

"It was close, Jim. You and Anne barely got back in time. Unless this formula works, we can't risk another transfer."

In the pharmacology laboratory, two hypos lay on a table. Hanoch-Spock held the third one. He made some adjustment on it, Christine behind him, watching. At last, he spoke. "This formula will reduce heart action and body function to normal. Whenever their bodies are occupied, administer one injection, ten cc.'s every hour."

"I understand," Christine said.

"Code this one for Thalassa. And *this* hypo, code it for me."

"Yes, sir." She affixed the appropriate seals to the hypos.

"Each contains a formula suited to the physical traits of that individual's body."

She pointed to the third hypo. "And that one is for Captain Kirk when Sargon is in his body?"

Hanoch-Spock handed it to her. "Yes. Of course."

Christine had taken the hypo to mark it when she noticed the color of its fluid. She examined it more carefully. Then, troubled, she said, "This hypo doesn't contain the same formula."

Hanoch-Spock smiled. On Spock's usually expressionless face, the smile was extraordinarily charming. "Since I will arrange for you to give the injections, no one else will notice that."

"But—without the correct formula, Captain Kirk will die."

"So he will—and Sargon with him."

Christine, staring, had begun to protest when Hanoch-Spock, reaching out, touched her forehead. Her head swam with dizziness. Then all sensation left her. Entranced where she stood, she could only look at him helplessly.

"Thalassa I can use," he said. "But Sargon must be destroyed. He would oppose me in what I plan. You wish to speak, my dear?"

"Please, I . . . I was . . . I wanted to say something." She passed a hand over her whirling head. "I've . . . forgotten what it was."

He touched her brow again. "You were about to say you watched me prepare the formula and fill the three hypos with it."

She swayed. "Yes—that was it. I will tell Dr. McCoy that each hypo is properly filled for each patient. You must excuse me. I lost my train of thought for a moment."

"It will not occur again," he said. "You are under my guidance now, child." Looking quickly toward the corridor, he made for the doorway. "And now for Dr. McCoy . . ."

But McCoy had snapped the lab door open. "If you require any further drugs or assistance, Hanoch—"

"I've encountered no difficulties at all, Doctor. I left the formula on your computer if you care to examine it."

In her trance Christine picked up the hypos. She spoke the words implanted in her mind. "I watched them prepared and coded, Doctor. Shall I take them to Sickbay?"

McCoy nodded. As the door closed behind her, Hanoch-Spock smiled. "It's good to be alive again, Doctor. I will find it most difficult when the time comes to surrender this body I so enjoy."

Was it the implication of the last words that disturbed McCoy? Or was it the shock of the excessively charming smile on Spock's face? He didn't know. All he knew was the sense of trouble that oppressed him as he watched the alien stride from the lab with Spock's legs.

Nor did his feeling of foreboding diminish as construction of the robots progressed. He found himself spending more and more time in Sickbay—his sole haven of retreat from the nameless anxieties that beset him. Christine, too, seemed unlike herself—constrained, diffident. It irritated him.

As she approached him now, he didn't look up when she said, "You asked to see me, Doctor, before the next injections."

"Yes. You're staying alert for any side effects? Any unusual symptoms?"

"The shots work perfectly, sir. There are no problems at all."

He struck his desk. "The devil there aren't!" He crossed to the three receptacles. "That flicker of energy there is Jim Kirk! And Spock there! Anne Mulhall! Suppose the bodies these aliens are using are *not* returned to them?"

"If I'm to give the injections on time, Doctor, I should leave now."

"Well, walk, then! Don't just stand there, talking! Do it!"

"Yes, sir."

Alone, McCoy stalked over to the Sargon-Kirk globe. "You and your blasted rent-a-body agreement, Kirk!" He moved to Spock's receptacle. "The only halfway pleasant thing about this is you, Spock! Must be humiliating for a logical superior Vulcan not to have a larger flicker than that!"

One of McCoy's persisting, if minor, anxieties was the chaos that had descended upon his immaculate laboratory.

Workbenches now crowded it; and his marble slabs were littered with the elements and other paraphernalia that would ultimately be assembled into the android robots. Hanoch-Spock over at his bench was manipulating a complex tool under difficult circumstances, for across the lab Sargon-Kirk and Thalassa-Anne were sharing a chore together. The intimacy between them angered and distracted him. He saw them both reach for a component at the same time. They smiled at each other, their hands clasping, their eyes meeting. She touched his hair.

"Sargon, I remember a day long ago. We sat beside a silver lake. The air was scented with the flowers of our planet and . . ."

He nodded. "I remember, Thalassa. We held hands like this." He hesitated, removing his from hers. "And I think it best not to remember too well."

"In two days you'll have hands of your own again, Thalassa," Hanoch-Spock said. "Mechanically efficient, quite human-looking—android robot hands. Hands without feeling, of course. So enjoy the taste of life while you can."

"But our minds will have survived. And as androids, Hanoch, we . . ." Sargon-Kirk suddenly looked very tired.

"What is it, Sargon?" Thalassa-Anne asked anxiously.

"Our next injection . . . will renovate me. Do not be concerned." He addressed Hanoch. "As androids we can move among those who *do* live, teaching them, helping them to avoid the errors we made."

"Yes, moving as machines minus the ability to feel love, joy, sorrow."

Sargon-Kirk spoke sternly. "We pledged ourselves that survival would be sufficient, Hanoch. Now that we've taken human bodies not our own, the ancient evil temptations would plague us again, haunt us with the dream of a godlike master-race."

"It is only that I feel sorrow for your wife, Sargon." He spoke to Thalassa-Anne. "You were younger than we when the end came. You had enjoyed so little of living."

She said, "We made a pledge, Hanoch." But her face was troubled. The sympathy had weakened her; and she, too, looked suddenly exhausted. She was leaning back against the wall as Christine entered with the hypos. She extended her arm for the injection. "Nurse," she said, "Sargon does not appear well."

"I've checked his metabolic rate every few hours, Thalassa. It hasn't varied from normal." And moving on, Christine administered the other injections. As the hypo hissed against his arm, Hanoch-Spock said, "I was fatigued, also. I feel much better now."

But though color had returned to Thalassa-Anne's face, concern for her husband had not been allayed. He smiled at her. "Do not worry. I shall have recovered in a moment." But he showed none of the rejuvenating effects seen in the others. He had to make an effort to resume his work.

McCoy noted it as he entered the lab. He looked at Christine. "Nurse," he said, "I want to see you in Sickbay. Bring those hypos."

In his office he selected the hypo coded for Sargon-Kirk, examining it. Christine watched him, troubled as though trying to remember something she had forgotten. After a long moment, he handed it back to her. She took it, still puzzling over it, and finally passed over a tape cartridge to him.

"Something wrong, Miss Chapel?"

"Yes . . . I . . ." She paused, trying to find words. "I—had something to say. But I can't seem to remember."

"Regarding our patients?"

"Yes, that must be it. I—am so pleased by the way they are responding, sir." She gestured to the hypo on his desk. "The formula is working perfectly."

"You look tired," McCoy said. "If you'd like me to handle the next few injections . . ."

Abruptly her face lit with a smile. "Tired? Not at all, Doctor. But thank you for asking."

She turned to replace the hypos in a cabinet. McCoy eyed her for a moment. Then, deciding he had been concerned over nothing, he returned to the reports on his desk.

The aliens worked swiftly and skillfully. Within the following hours, the robot bodies were partially assembled. Thalassa-Anne was alone in the lab when Scott entered to deliver some supplies. He paused to watch her deft hands moving over a torso.

"Thank you," she said. "Have you prepared the ne-gaton hydrocoils per the drawings Sargon gave you?"

Scott nodded. "For all the good they'll do you. Fancy name—but how will something that looks like a drop of jelly make that thing move its limbs? You'll need microgears, some form of pulley that does what a muscle does."

She smiled her charming smile. "That would be highly inefficient, Mr. Scott."

"I tell you, lady, this thing won't work." As he spoke, Hanoch-Spock had come in. Now he sauntered over to them. "It will have twice the strength and agility of your body, Engineer, and it will last a thousand years. That is, it will if you'll permit us to complete these robot envelopes of ours."

Scott strode to the lab door, his back stiff with irrita-tion. Hanoch-Spock crossed over to Thalassa-Anne, his eyes intent on her raven hair. "Actually, a thousand-year prison, Thalassa." He leaned toward her. "And when it wears out, we'll build a new one. We'll lock ourselves into it for another thousand years, then another and another . . ."

Disturbed, she looked up from her work. He went on. "Sargon has closed his mind to a better way with these bod-ies we wear."

"They are not ours, Hanoch."

"Three bodies. Is that such a price for mankind to pay for all we offer? Thalassa." He seized her hand. "The hu-mans who own these bodies would surrender them gladly to accomplish a fraction of what we'll do. Are we entitled to no reward for our labors—no joy?"

She snatched her hand away; and pointing to the robot torso on the bench, he said, "Do you prefer incarceration in that?"

She leaped to her feet, her tools flying. *"No! I'm be-ginning to hate the thing!"*

In a corridor, not far away, Sargon-Kirk, collapsing, had crumpled to the deck.

Lifeless, inert, Kirk's body lay on a medical table in Sickbay where Nurse M'Benga and a medical technician were hurriedly but expertly fitting the cryo-surgical and blood-filtrating units over it. A tense McCoy watched.

His mind was a tumult of confusion. Too distant from

his receptacle to transfer back into it, Sargon had died when Kirk's body died. So that left the big question. Kirk's consciousness still survived, despite the death of his body. It still glimmered, faint but alive, in Sargon's globe. Then could Kirk be called dead? McCoy wiped the sweat from his face—and ordered in another resuscitating instrument.

Meanwhile, in his once-shining lab, Hanoch-Spock was operating a different instrument. He passed the small device over the nearly completed android robot that lay on a slab. It looked sexless. It still lacked hair, eyebrows, the indentations which give expression to a human face. Thalassa-Anne watched him wearily, lost in her anguished grief. Christine, blank-eyed as ever, stood beside the slab.

"Hanoch, why do you pretend to work on that thing? You killed Sargon. You murdered my husband. You murdered him because you do not intend to give up your body. You've always intended to keep it."

A sudden rage possessed Thalassa. Sargon had labored so hard to restore them to joy, to life in the body. He had kissed this body she wore! In a short while, it would all be for nothing. This body he had embraced would have to be vacated, returned to its owner. She rushed from the lab on the surge of her fury to fling open the door of Sickbay.

McCoy looked up, startled. "Doctor," she said, "would you like to save your Captain Kirk?"

"Not half an hour ago you said that was impossible. When we found him, you said—"

"Dismiss these people!" she commanded.

McCoy stared at her. "We have many powers Sargon did not permit us to use! If you care for your Captain, dismiss these people!"

McCoy waved the nurse and technician out of Sickbay. "Well?" he said.

"This body I wear is sacred to me. My husband embraced it. I intend to keep it!"

So it was out at last. "I see," McCoy said. "And Hanoch? He intends, of course, to keep Spock's body."

"Hanoch's plans are his own affair. I wish only to keep the body my husband kissed!"

"Are you asking for my approval?"

"I require only your silence. Only you and I will know

that Anne Mulhall has not returned to her body. Isn't your silence worth your Captain's life?" At the look on McCoy's face, the fury burned in her again. "Doctor, we can take what we wish. Neither you, this ship, nor all your little worlds have the power to stop us!"

McCoy looked down at Kirk's lifeless body. Jim Kirk—alive again, his easy vitality, his courage, his affectionate "Bones". *This was a command decision:* a choice between loyalty to the dearest friend of his life—and loyalty to himself. And he knew what the dearest friend would want.

"I cannot trade a body I do not own," he said. "Neither would my Captain. Your body belongs to a young woman who—"

"Whom you hardly know, almost a stranger to you."

McCoy shouted. *"I do not peddle human flesh! I am a physician!"*

The blue eyes flashed lightning. *"A physician?* In contrast to what we are, you are a prancing, savage medicine man—a primitive savage! You dare to defy one you should be on your knees to in worship!" She made a gesture of acid contempt. *"I can destroy you with a single thought!"*

A ring of flame shot up around McCoy. He flung his hands before his face to shield it from the rising fire.

As he did so, Thalassa gave a wild cry. She fell to her knees, crying, *"No! Stop!* Forgive me, forgive me . . ."

The flames died as suddenly as they had come. Even the smell of their smoke was gone; and where searing fire had encircled McCoy only a moment before, not a mark of its presence remained.

She was still on her knees, weeping "Sargon was . . . right," she sobbed. "The temptations are . . . too great. But understand. In the name of whatever gods you worship, understand! The emotions of life are dear—its needs, its hopes. But . . . our power is too great. We would begin to destroy . . . as I almost destroyed you then. Forgive me . . . forgive . . ."

"I am pleased, beloved. It is good you have found the truth for yourself."

Her head lifted. "*Sargon!* Oh, my husband, where are you? Hanoch has killed you!"

"I have power, my wife, that Hanoch does not suspect."

"Yes. Yes. I understand." The words came slowly. She rose to her feet, staring at McCoy. "My Sargon has placed his consciousness within this ship of yours."

Christine Chapel opened the door of Sickbay. She was crossing to the hypo cabinet when McCoy galvanized. "You! Get out of my sight!"

Thalassa shook her head. "No, Doctor. She is necessary to us."

"Necessary? She is under Hanoch's control!"

"My Sargon has a plan, Doctor. Leave us. We have much work to do."

After a moment, McCoy obeyed. But as the door closed behind him, he heard a dull crunching explosion come from inside. The ship shuddered slightly. The sound came again.

"Thalassa!" he shouted. *"What's going on?"*

When the sound came for the third time, he raced for the corridor intercom. "This is Sickbay. Get me—"

Behind him Sickbay's door opened. Empty-eyed, Christine emerged to move on past him down the corridor. He rushed inside—and came to a dead halt. Kirk was standing there, smiling at him.

"I'm fine, Bones," he said. He reached out a hand to draw Anne Mulhall up beside him. "We're both fine, Bones."

"Thalassa . . ."

Anne spoke quietly. "She is with Sargon, Doctor."

"With Sargon?" He looked past them to the three globes. They were broken, melted, black, dead.

"Jim! Spock's consciousness was in one of those!"

"It was necessary," Kirk said.

McCoy flung his arms up. "What do you mean, man? There's no Spock to return to his body now! You've killed your best friend, a loyal officer of the Service!"

"Prepare a hypo, Bones. The fastest and deadliest poison to Vulcans. Spock's consciousness is gone, but we must now kill his body, too. His body—and the thing inside it."

On the bridge, Uhura screamed. Then she slumped against her board, trembling. Nonchalant, Hanoch-Spock left her to go to Kirk's command chair. The bewitched Christine waited at his side. He spoke to Sulu. "Shall I make an example of you, too, Helm? Take us out of orbit! A course for Earth!''

Sulu hit his controls. Then he wheeled in his chair. ''Look for yourself! The ship won't respond! Nothing works!''

The elevator doors slid open. Kirk and Anne stepped out. Behind them came McCoy, his hypo carefully hidden. The alien in the command chair didn't trouble himself to turn; but just before they reached it, it said, ''Pain, Kirk. Exquisite pain. As for you, lovely one of the blue eyes . . .''

Kirk had dropped as though shot, gasping, his throat hungering to scream. Hanoch-Spock pointed a finger at Anne. She froze, shudders shaking her—and Sulu, pressed beyond control, leaped from his seat only to fall, moaning with pain. As Anne crumpled to the deck, McCoy dove for the command chair; but Hanoch, holding up a palm, halted him a foot away from Spock's body.

''I know every thought in every mind around me,'' he said. Chapel, remove the hypo from the Doctor.''

Christine, reaching into an inside pocket of McCoy's white jacket, obeyed. Hanoch said, ''Good. Inject him with his own dose—an example to all those who defy me.''

She lifted the hypo toward McCoy—and without the slightest change of expression, wheeled to drive it, hissing, into Hanoch's arm.

He stood up. ''Fools!'' he shrieked. ''I'll simply transfer to . . . another space, another body!'' Suddenly, he reeled. *''It's you, Sargon!''* He whimpered, ''Please . . . please, Sargon, let me transfer to—''

Then he crashed to the floor. Kirk rushed to the fallen body. Kneeling beside it, he lifted its head to cradle it in his arms. ''Spock . . . Spock, my friend, my comrade . . . if only there had been some other way.'' He choked on unshed tears.

The head stirred in his arms. Its eyes opened; and the bridge reverberated again to the rich, deep voice. *''How could I allow the sacrifice of one so close to you, my son?''*

''There was enough poison in that hypo,'' McCoy cried, ''to kill ten Vulcans!''

''I allowed you to believe that, Doctor. Else, Hanoch

*could not have read your thought—and believed it, too. He
has fled Spock's body. He is destroyed.*"

Kirk found words. "The receptacles are broken, Spock.
Where was your consciousness kept?"

Spock was on his feet. "In the last place Hanoch would
suspect, Captain." He gestured toward Christine.

She nodded, smiling. "That's why Thalassa called me
'necessary,' Doctor. Mr. Spock's consciousness was installed
in me. We have been sharing it together."

*"We know now we cannot permit ourselves to exist in
your world, my children. Thalassa and I must depart into
oblivion."*

Kirk looked up. "Sargon, isn't there any way we can
help you?"

*"Yes, my son. Let Thalassa and me enter your bodies
again for our last moment together."*

Though there was no transfer flare, Kirk and Anne both
felt its heat as Sargon and Thalassa moved into them. Anne,
in Kirk's arms, said, "Oblivion together does not frighten
me, my husband." She kissed Kirk's forehead, her hand ca-
ressing his cheek. "Promise me we will be together."

Kirk bent his head to her mouth, holding her close.
Anne was shaking under the storm of Thalassa's grief. "Together forever, my Sargon . . . forever . . ."

"I promise, my love. I promise . . ."

For their last moment, they clung together on the edge
of Nothing. Then they were gone, the dwindling heat of their
passing, leaving Anne's eyes filled with Thalassa's tears. Still
clasped in Kirk's arms, they stared at each other. Then, flushing at the public embrace, Kirk released her. He cleared his
throat. "Dr. Mulhall . . . er . . . thank you. I . . . thank you
in . . . Sargon's name . . . for your cooperation."

The sapphire eyes smiled through their tears. "Captain, I—I was happy to . . . cooperate."

Christine, sobbing, turned to Spock. "I felt the same
way, Mr. Spock . . . when we shared our consciousness
together."

Spock's left eyebrow lifted. "Nurse Chapel," he began, and subsided into silence.

McCoy grinned at him. "This sharing of consciousness—it sounds somewhat immoral to me, my Vulcan friend.''

"I assure you it was a most distressing experience," Spock said earnestly. "You would not believe the torrents of emotion I encountered—the jungle of illogic." He almost shuddered.

Christine smiled at him. "Why, thank you, Mr. Spock."

"I don't understand, nurse. Thank me?"

"You just paid her a high compliment, Spock," Kirk said.

"Yes, you do turn a nice phrase now and then," McCoy said. He turned to Christine. "Thank the stars," he said, "that my sex doesn't understand the other one."

Anne laughed. "Come along with me, my fellow woman. If they don't understand us after all this time, no elucidation by us can enlighten them."

Kirk, smiling too, went to his command chair. Spock was standing beside it, still puzzled. "Captain, I really *don't* understand."

"Sargon did, Spock. 'Together forever.' Someone may someday teach you what that means. Who knows? When that next Vulcan seven-year cycle rolls around again . . ."

Spock gravely considered the idea. "Sargon *was* enormously advanced, Captain. I shall ponder this."

As he returned to his station, Kirk's eyes followed him with affection. "Ah, well," he said, "for now that's how it is." He turned to Sulu. "All right, Mr. Sulu, take us out of orbit."

"Leaving orbit, sir."

≡

PATTERNS OF FORCE

Writer: John Meredyth Lucas
Director: Vince McEveety
Guest star: Skip Homeier

Officially, the mission was location of a missing cultural observer assigned to Ekos, sister planet of Zeon in a double system. But both Kirk and Spock had personal interest invested in the whereabouts of John Gill. The missing man had been Kirk's instructor at the Space Academy. As to Spock, he'd studied his Earth history from a John Gill text. Now, as the *Enterprise* entered into orbit around Ekos, the inner planet, the two men looked at the distinguished face projected onto the bridge screen.

Kirk remembered it well. "Lieutenant Uhura, try to raise John Gill on Starfleet communication channels."

"Aye, sir."

"Jim, Starfleet's been trying for six months," McCoy said. "If he's still alive, isn't it unlikely he'd receive us now?"

"I don't know, Doctor. We're here to find out what's happened *because* I don't know."

"No response on any Starfleet channel, Captain," Uhura reported.

Spock, his eyes still on the screen, said, "What impressed me most was Gill's treatment of history as causes and motivations rather than dates and events. His text was—"

Chekov interrupted. "Spacecraft approaching from the inner planet, Captain."

"From Ekos?"

The question sent Spock back to his station. Checking his own viewer, he said, "Yes, Captain. But it must be a Zeon ship. The Zeons have a crude interplanetary capabil

542

ity.'' He leaned closer to his viewer. ''Reaction powered. A small rocket. And it's on an intercept course.'' He lifted his head to look at Kirk. ''That means sophisticated detection equipment that neither Zeon nor Ekos should have.''

Kirk, nodding, swung his chair to Uhura. ''Try ship-to-ship frequencies, Lieutenant.''

Spock spoke again. ''No indication of life aboard, Captain. It's an unmanned probe which seems to be carrying a warhead.''

Kirk spoke, ''Standby phasers, Mr. Chekov.''

''Phasers ready, sir.''

''Range, Mr. Chekov?''

''Two hundred kilometers, sir. Closing fast.''

''Fire,'' Kirk said.

John Gill's face vanished from the screen. In its stead, a blue-white flare of light flashed. The bridge trembled under shock waves.

''A thermonuclear warhead,'' Spock said.

McCoy stared at him. ''But that's generations away from where these people should be technologically! How could they have managed nuclear physics?''

Kirk, recalling the brilliant eyes of John Gill, said, ''Maybe they had help.''

It was unthinkable. But a Starship Captain had to oblige himself to think the unthinkable. The ugly fact remained that John Gill's Ekos had launched attack on the *Enterprise*. ''Mr. Chekov, plot us a maximum orbit. Let's get out of their detection equipment's range.''

''Orbit computed and locked in, sir.''

''Execute.''

As the impulse engines came on, Scott emerged from the elevator and Uhura said, ''Still no response from John Gill on any channel, sir.''

''He must be dead,'' McCoy said. ''And what's going on down there on Ekos?''

Spock looked up. ''According to our records, the Ekosians are warlike, primitive, in a state of anarchy. Zeon, the other planet, has a relatively high technology, and its people are peaceful.''

Kirk got up to go to the computer station. ''You're saying that the people with the war potential aren't warlike, Mr. Spock. So who threw that missile at us?''

"Our computer data appear to be considerably out of date, Captain. Obviously, things have been happening very rapidly on Ekos."

Kirk took a brief pace of the bridge. "Mr. Spock, we've run into something more disturbing than John Gill's disappearance. You and I will beam down to Ekos."

Scott said, "After what they just threw at us, I suggest a landing party in force, sir."

"No. We'll observe the non-interference directive, Scotty."

"Jim," McCoy said, "I think he's got a good—"

"All right. We'll take one precaution. Bones, prepare subcutaneous transponders in the event we're unable to use our communicators."

"Captain, may I suggest the ship's uniform section prepare clothing suitable to the culture?"

"You may indeed, Mr. Spock."

McCoy performed the simple operation in the Transporter Room. His patients had changed into nondescript denim work clothes, Spock wearing a stocking cap to hide his ears. Rolling up a sleeve, Kirk said, "All right, Doctor, insert the transponders." McCoy used a hypo to inject the tiny devices into their left wrists. They rolled down their sleeves to cover the small bumps. Then Kirk spoke to Scott.

"Make one low pass to communication range in three hours, Scotty. If we fail to make contact at the appointed time, take our coordinates from the transponders—and beam us aboard, whatever our condition might be."

Scott was glum. "Aye, Captain. Whatever your condition."

The two stepped onto the platform.

"Energize," Kirk said.

Scott moved dials. The Transporter shimmer sparkled.

"Good luck!" McCoy shouted.

But they were gone.

The time on Ekos was day, and the place they arrived in was a street—a street appropriate to an Earth of the Twentieth Century. Looking around him, Spock said, "The Ekosians are humanoid, so there is apt to be a certain similarity in structure. It is interesting how body form tends to shape the structure of—''

''Mr. Spock, we're not here to do an architectural study. We are—''

Kirk broke off at sudden shouts and the sound of running feet. A young man, clearly spent and terrified, raced around the corner to their left, all his strength centered on his effort to elude his pursuers. He was almost on top of the *Enterprise* men before he saw them. ''Hide!'' he panted. ''They are right behind me! Quickly! Get away . . .''

He sank to his knees, his lungs heaving. The shouting behind him grew louder. Spock pulled Kirk into the shadow of a doorway as three armed men rounded the corner. They wore the brown shirts of Nazi Storm Troopers, their left arms encircled by black bands marked with red circles. In the center of each circle was a black swastika.

''There's the Zeon pig!''

They surrounded the kneeling man. ''On your feet, pig!'' One of the troopers kicked the man. It was a good game. The others joined in it.

Kirk's hand had instinctively reached for his phaser. Spock checked him. ''The non-interference directive, Captain.''

''Hands over your head, Zeon. Higher!''

The man's mouth was bleeding. Gratified by sight of the blood, the biggest trooper yelled, ''Keep those hands in the air! Don't touch anything Ekosian! You swine have defiled us enough! Move!'' He planted a heavy foot in the man's back and sent him sprawling. Then his victim was jerked to his feet to be marched away.

The horrified Kirk spoke to Spock. ''It's a nightmare. Did you recognize those uniforms? That armband?''

''Mid-Twentieth Century Earth. A nation state called Nazi Germany, Captain.''

''Attention! Attention! Attention!''

The newscaster's voice came from a loudspeaker set on a post a few yards away. As its square TV screen lighted up, the voice said, ''An announcer from Führer Headquarters. . . .''

A brown-shirted announcer, a flag bearing the Nazi emblem behind him, appeared on the screen. ''Today,'' he said, "the Führer has ordered our glorious capital made Zeon free. Starting at dawn, our heroic troops began flushing out the Zeon monsters who have been poisoning our planet. . . ."

His face was replaced by the spectacle of burly SS men rounding up a group of pitifully frightened old men, women and children. One of the children was crying.

Watching, Kirk said, "How could this have happened? The chance of another planet developing a Nazi culture, using the forms, symbols, the uniforms of Twentieth Century Earth, is so fantastically slim that—"

Spock interrupted. "Virtually impossible, Captain. Yet the evidence is quite clear."

The screen was now showing shots of a panzer column and troops goose-stepping under the roar of Stuka dive bombers. The uniformed announcer's voice was saying, "The Führer's Headquarters reports repulsing an attack by Zeon spacecraft. Our missiles utterly destroyed the enemy."

Kirk turned to Spock. "The 'enemy' would have been the *Enterprise*. You look well, Mr. Spock, for having been utterly destroyed." He looked back at the screen. It now held the image of a vast amphitheater, massed with thousands upon thousands of cheering troops. Over the noise, the announcer said, "At this patriotic demonstration, Deputy Führer Melakon presented the iron cross, second class, to Daras, Hero of the Fatherland."

The scene changed to a close-up of a cold-faced, middle-aged man in uniform, flanked by Gestapo guards. A girl mounted the podium, wearing her uniform with grace and style. Under its cap her blonde hair gleamed with a light of its own. Her beautiful face was grave with pride as Melakon pinned the decoration to the breast of her uniform.

The announcer was back. He came to rigid attention as he spoke. "Everywhere, preparations go forward for the final decision. Death to Zeon! Long live the Fatherland!"

The TV camera left his face to focus on a huge poster on the wall behind him. Framed in black and red, its four corners were decorated with swastikas. It held a portrait.

"Long live the Führer!" the announcer shouted, and, turning, gave the portrait a stiff-armed salute.

The face in the portrait was that of John Gill.

Older—but unmistakable.

Kirk was stunned. "That's John Gill! The Führer!"

"Fascinating!" Spock exclaimed.

"You there!"

They wheeled. They were facing an SS Lieutenant. The trooper's Luger was leveled at Kirk's stomach. "Zeons!" he cried. Then his eyes narrowed as he took another look at Spock. He whipped off the stocking cap with a yell of triumph. "What are those, ears? What kind of monsters are the Zeons sending against us?"

Kirk caught Spock's eye. He signaled, and, stepping away from him, induced the SS man to turn slightly. "You're right, Lieutenant," he said. "He is not one of us."

"What do you mean 'us'?"

"Lieutenant, look out!"

Spock timed his warning to a sideways leap. The officer's eyes followed him, centering on him just long enough for Kirk to move. He chopped him. The Lieutenant dropped.

Kirk nodded to Spock. As they stripped the man of his uniform, Kirk said, "His helmet will conceal your 'monster' ears, Mr. Spock."

"You propose that we pass ourselves off as Nazis, sir?"

"If John Gill is the leader, this would seem the 'logical' way to approach him."

Shouldering into the uniform coat, Spock said, "A point well taken, Captain." Kirk eyed him in his full SS uniform. "Somewhat gaudy, Mr. Spock. But I think it's an improvement."

Spock threw him a look of disgust. Cautiously, they edged out into the street. But their care didn't pay off. This time it was a Gestapo Lieutenant who accosted them. He had grabbed Kirk's shoulder, but as he recognized Spock's uniform, he let it go.

"A Zeon?"

Spock nodded. "I captured him. Is that not the proper procedure with enemies of the Fatherland?"

"With all Zeon pigs, Lieutenant."

"Take charge of him," Spock said.

"With pleasure." He seized Kirk again. "All right, Zeon, today we have a surprise for you. We—"

He collapsed under the Vulcan neck pinch. Kirk looked down at the unconscious body. "I'm sorry, Spock, that your uniform isn't as attractive as mine is. I believe this is the Gestapo variety.''

"Correct, Captain. You should make a very convincing Nazi.''

Kirk snapped him a look. But he was too busy turning himself into a Gestapo officer to think of a suitable rejoinder.

They gave themselves time before mounting the steps of the Chancellery. Swastikas were everywhere—on the banners that fluttered over the building, on the armbands of the SS men who stood at its massive doors, armed with submachine guns. The guards snapped to attention as an SS General Officer crossed the pavement to the steps. Kirk and Spock played it cool as they followed behind him. An SS Major came out of the big doors as the General entered them.

The Major glared at Spock. "Lieutenant! Have you forgotten how to salute?''

Spock extended his arm in a crisp Nazi salute.

"Papers,'' the Major said.

Kirk turned to Spock. "Your orders, Lieutenant. The Major wants to see your orders. There, in your jacket . . .''

The Major studied them suspiciously as Spock reached quickly into his jacket. He came out with a wallet, and the Major took it.

Kirk moved into the obvious breach of confidence. "The Lieutenant is a little dazed, sir. He captured several Zeons single-handed. But one of the pigs struck him before he dropped. I promise you, that pig will never get up again.''

"Good work, Lieutenant. Hail the Führer!''

He handed the wallet back to Spock. Kirk quickly extended his arm in the Nazi salute. "Hail the Führer!''

Spock repeated the litany. "Hail the Führer!''

"This is a day to remember, Major,'' Kirk said.

As they passed into the Chancellery, the Major stopped Spock, solicitude in his face. "Better have a doctor check you, Lieutenant. You don't look well. Your color is—Remove your helmet.''

"We have no time to waste,'' Spock said.

Kirk's heart was pounding. "Major, we have urgent business with the Führer. We must see him immediately.''

The Major was inexorable. "Your helmet, Lieutenant. Take it off!"

The guards' submachine guns jabbed brutally into Spock's neck. He lifted the helmet, revealing his pointed Vulcan ears.

In the cell, they had stripped Kirk to the waist. For a purpose. They did nothing without a purpose. The naked, uncovered flesh made the whip's lashing immediate. Like Spock, manacled too, he made no sound as the whip cut bloody grooves into his back. Behind them in the cell, the Zeon they had first seen brutalized lay, retching, on his stomach.

"You wish to talk now?"

The SS Major was pleased to be irritated. "Tell me your orders! You were sent to kill our Führer. Confess! Do you want some more persuasion?"

Kirk rallied the power of speech. "You're making this a rather one-sided conversation, Major."

"Don't joke with me, Zeon pig!" The Major glanced at his SS lasher. He took a lowered, confidential tone. "Who is this pointed-eared alien? Things will go easier with you if you tell me about him."

Kirk lifted his pain-filled eyes. "Let us talk to the Führer. We'll tell him anything he wants to know."

"You'll be glad to talk to *me* before I've finished with you, you Zeon swine, you—"

The cell door opened. A man, simply uniformed in Party dress but radiating an air of quiet, self-intact authority, walked in. The SS Major stiffened to awed attention. "Chairman Eneg! I am honored! Excellency, I have been interrogating these two spies, captured in the very act of—"

"I have had the full report."

The quiet man ignored the Major to speak to Spock. "You are not from Zeon. Where do you come from?"

Kirk said, "We'll explain when we see the Führer."

"And what is your business with the Führer?"

"We can discuss that only with him."

Furious, the Major seized the whip from the guard and slashed Kirk with it. "Pig! You're speaking to the Chairman of the Party!"

"That's enough, Major!" Eneg said sharply. He turned

to Kirk. ''What are the weapons that were found on you?
What design?''

Kirk was silent. Eneg looked at the Major. ''Our fa-
mously efficient SS laboratories have failed to discover how
your weapons work.''

The Major reddened. ''Excellency, give me a few
minutes with them, and I promise you I'll have them—''

''You've had more than a few minutes with them without result.'' Eneg looked at Kirk's slashed back. ''The trouble with you SS people is that you don't realize punishment
is ineffective after a certain point. Men become insensitive.''

After a moment, the Major said, ''Yes, Excellency.''

''Lock them up. Let their pain argue with them. Then
I will question them.''

''Excellency, the standing order is: 'Interrogate and execute.' The interrogation is finished. Therefore—''

''Finished, Major? What have you learned? Nothing.
Hold them for an hour.''

''Excellency, the order—''

Eneg's quiet eyes flashed with sudden anger. ''That is
my order, Major. I suggest that you do not disobey it.''

''Yes, Excellency.''

Eneg turned to the door. The guard leaped to open it
for him. As he left, the Major turned back to the *Enterprise*
men. ''All right, pigs. My eye will be on the clock. When
the hour is up, you will die. Most unpleasantly, I promise
you.'' He slammed the cell door behind him.

Slowly, the Zeon prisoner got to his feet, his eyes
watchful as Spock said, ''What do you propose to do, Captain?''

''I don't know. But we haven't much time to do it.
Without our phasers . . . our communicators . . .'' He looked
around the cell. ''John Gill is the only chance we have now.''

''Captain, have you considered how he must have
changed to be responsible for all this?''

''Professor Gill was one of the kindest, gentlest men
I've ever known. For him to be a Nazi is so— It's just impossible.''

The Zeon spoke. ''Why did they take you? You are not
a Zeon.'' He nodded toward Spock. ''And he certainly is
not. Who are you?''

Spock said, "Why do the Nazis hate Zeons?"

The question evoked a bitter answer. "Without us to hate, there would be nothing to bring them together. So the Party has built us into a threat—a disease that must be wiped out."

"*Is* Zeon a threat to them?"

"Where *did* you come from? Our warlike period ended a dozen generations ago! When we came here, we thought we were civilizing the Ekosians!"

"Were they like this when you Zeons first came?" Kirk said.

"Warlike. But not vicious. That came after the Nazi movement started. Only a few years ago."

Spock looked at Kirk. "That would agree with the time of Gill's arrival, Captain."

The embittered Zeon was launched on the troubles of his people. "When they have destroyed us here, they will attack our planet with the technology we gave them. The danger is that the taking of life is so repugnant to us, we may go down without a struggle." His fists clenched. "After what I've seen in the streets today, I think *I* could kill!"

Kirk studied the impassioned face. "Do you know the plan of this building?"

The Zeon went on immediate guard. "Why?"

"If we can get to the SS weapons laboratory . . . get our weapons back, we can stop the slaughter of the Zeons."

"Why should you be interested in saving Zeons?" the man asked coldly.

Kirk turned back to Spock. "We must get our communicators and contact the ship."

"The flaw in that plan, Captain, is these locked cell doors. And beyond them is a guard."

"The transponders!" Kirk cried.

"Pardon, sir?"

But Kirk was staring at the cell's overhead light. "A way to throw some light on our gloom, Mr. Spock!"

Spock looked thoughtfully at his wrist. "The rubidium crystals in the transponders! Of course, it would be crude, but perhaps workable. How can we get them out?"

They had lowered their voices. The Zeon hadn't heard their last exchange, but he continued to watch them, puzzled.

"Here," Kirk said.

He yanked the mattress from a bed, and, ripping the fabric, seized a wire spring. It snapped, its edge sharp. He used it to slit through the slight bulge on his wrist, releasing the bright red crystal. Blood welled from the cut. He handed the wire to Spock. As he too probed out his crystal, the Zeon cried, "You will kill yourselves? Bleed to death? But many do it to avoid the torture."

"That's not quite what we had in mind," Kirk told him. "You have the figures computed, Mr. Spock?"

"Yes, Captain. It will be necessary to hold the crystals at a specific distance. The distance should be two point seven millimeters. I shall put the first crystal . . ."

As he spoke, he placed a crystal into a hole at the edge of the flat spring, pushing it firmly in. ". . . here. The second one at the other end." He was bending the spring into a horseshoe shape so that the crystals at the two ends were precisely aligned. "Two point seven millimeters would be approximately here. That, of course, is a crude estimation."

The Zeon was staring in amazement. "What are you making—some kind of radio?"

"No. The electrical power in that light is very low, Mr. Spock."

"It should be sufficient to stimulate the rubidium crystal. As I recall from the history of Physics, the ancient lasers were able to achieve the necessary excitation, even using crude natural crystals. There. It's ready. But to reach the light source, I shall require a platform."

"I'd be honored, Mr. Spock." Kirk was wry, only too aware of his lacerated shoulders. He stooped under the bulb and Spock climbed up on them. "I'd appreciate it if you'd hurry, Mr. Spock. That guard did a very professional job with the whip."

Spock lifted the cylinder up to the bulb. "The aim, of course, can only be approximate," he said.

Kirk's shoulders were bleeding. "Spock, I'll settle if you can hit the broad side of a barn."

Spock frowned. "Why should I aim at such a structure, sir?"

"Never mind, Spock. Get on with the job."

The tiny rubidium crystals were glowing a bright red. Suddenly, ruby light flashed from Spock's contraption, cutting through the door's steel bars like butter. The lock was next. Kirk saw it loosen.

"All right, Mr. Spock. Don't overdo it."

Spock leaped from his shoulders. Kirk touched them, saw blood on his hand and wiped it off on the torn mattress fabric. The Zeon, awed, whispered, "What was that? Zeon science has nothing like it. With such a weapon, we'd have a chance against them!"

"It's not a weapon," Kirk said. "It has an extremely short range. Get over to that corner, Mr. Spock. Keep out of sight. I'll create a commotion."

At the cell door, he yelled, "All right. I'll talk. Please! I don't want to die. Guard! I'll talk. Call the Major. I'll talk!"

He shook the bars, still shouting. The guard took a half step forward. Spock jumped from his corner, thrust his hand through the bars and applied the neck pinch. The guard dropped. Spock opened the door, dragged the body into the cell and tossed the man's coat to Kirk. As Kirk struggled into it, the Zeon came out of his daze.

"Take me with you. Please give me a chance to fight them," he pleaded. "Take me—or you'll never find the laboratory."

"An excellent point, Mr. Spock. Take him. He's our guide."

But there was another guard in the corridor. Kirk pulled the gun from the downed man's holster, pressed it into the Zeon's back and, motioning Spock to get in front of him, lowered his voice. "Which door is the laboratory?"

"Second on the right," the Zeon whispered.

"All right, Zeon swine, move!" Kirk shouted.

The guard eyed them boredly and resumed his position. As they passed him, heading for the laboratory door, it opened. An SS Trooper emerged and, turning, locked the door behind him. He was walking by them when Kirk, jerking the Zeon toward him, shoved into the guard. They all fell back against a wall. Kirk slapped the Zeon.

"Clumsy Zeon pig!" He spoke to the guard. "Sorry, but these Zeons do nothing right. They'll pay for it though. They're on their way to the laboratory for experimental work." Nodding, the guard moved off. Grinning, Kirk held his keys.

The laboratory was deserted, but on a table to their

left, Kirk spotted their disassembled communicators. He gathered up the parts.

"Who *are* you people?" the Zeon demanded.

"The phasers?" Kirk said.

"I do not see them, Captain."

"Where do you come from?" the Zeon asked again.

Kirk had discovered an informative clipboard. Flipping its pages, he read them hastily. Their phasers had been sent to Gestapo Command Headquarters for analysis. "We can forget about our phasers," he was telling Spock when the door was flung open. The SS Guard had learned that his keys were missing. He stared at Kirk and Spock, snapping his pistol up. The Zeon, out of his line of sight, struck him. The first blow was wild. But the second one dropped the trooper cold.

Kirk looked down at the felled man. "For peaceful people," he said, "you Zeons are very thorough."

They also learned quickly. The Zeon pointed to the trooper's uniform. "Wearing that, we might be able to steal a car and get out of the capital."

"We came here to find John Gill," Kirk said.

Spock spoke. "Captain, without phasers, and until we are able to communicate with the ship, it is illogical to assume we can hold out against the entire military force of this planet."

Kirk considered the point. "All right, Mr. Spock. Get into that uniform and cover your ears again."

Within seconds, Spock was in full SS Lieutenant's regalia, his ears helmeted. Kirk, in the guard's outfit, found a stretcher piled on others in a corner of the laboratory. When they emerged from it, the Zeon lay on the stretcher, his eyes closed as though past an extremity of torture. The guard at the door snapped Spock a salute.

"Hunting's good," Kirk told him. "We've caught so many Zeons, we've got to dump them outside."

They got away with it. In the shadow of a building, they set the stretcher down. Spock said, "I suggest the guards will shortly notice our absence, Captain."

"There'll be a planet-wide alert," the Zeon warned them.

"We'll have to find someplace to hide until we can

reassemble the communicators and get help from the *Enterprise*.''

Kirk's remark seemed to deeply disturb the Zeon. He was clearly wrestling with some momentous decision.

"You could be spies," he said, "sent to find our underground hiding places." Then his face cleared. "But that's a chance I must take. I put my life in your hands. More important, I am putting the lives of our friends in your hands."

They followed him down the street, hugging the buildings' shadows until they came to a dark alley. It was dirty with a clutter of trash, garbage pails, a litter of empty tin cans. The Zeon went to the metal top of a manhole cover and rapped on it four times. Finally, from deep underground came the sound of four answering raps. The Zeon knocked at the manhole cover twice again, waving the two *Enterprise* men to a crouch as a patrol car, filled with troops, roared past the alley's entrance. When the noise had faded, the Zeon knocked again. The manhole cover lifted on a narrow, black opening.

"Come," said the Zeon.

A narrow metal ladder led down into the darkness. When they reached its last rung, a Zeon passed them and scrambled up to swing the metal cover shut again. He descended the ladder and their guide said, "Davod, you're well. How many are here?"

He wasn't answered. Davod was staring suspiciously at Kirk and Spock.

"They helped me escape from the prison! I owe them my life, Davod!"

"Isak!"

An older man, strong-faced, had entered the dim-lit room. "Abrom, thank God you're well." Their Zeon and the older man embraced. "This is my brother," their guide said. "Abrom, they were prisoners, beaten as I was."

Abrom's eyes were searching their faces. "Why were you in that prison?"

"I was trying to see the Führer," Kirk said.

"The Führer!"

"If I can see him, there may be a way to stop this insanity."

Isak said, "I owe them my life, Abrom."

Davod strode angrily out of the room and Abrom said,

"Isak, Uletta is dead." After a moment, he added, "She was shot down in the street."

Isak's shocked face moved Kirk to ask, "Your sister?"

"She would have been my wife."

Abrom's voice shook. "She lived for five hours while they walked by her and spat on her. Our own people could do nothing to help. Yet you ask me to help strangers."

Isak lifted his face from the hands he had used to hide it. "If we adopt the ways of the Nazis, we are as bad as the Nazis."

Spock, hesitating to intrude on such private tragedy, motioned Kirk aside. "Captain, may I suggest the most profitable use of our time would be to reassemble the communicators?" He spoke gently to Abrom. "May I work over there undisturbed for a few moments?"

Abrom didn't speak. Finally, Isak nodded, and taking his brother by the shoulder, moved away. Kirk joined Spock at a table where they spread out the communicators' elements. Using parts of both, Spock put one together and, handing it to Kirk, said, "I cannot be certain that the circuits are correct. There's no way to test it except by actual use."

Kirk was about to remind him that the *Enterprise* would be beyond range for another hour when there were shouts and the sound of a shot outside. The door was burst open. Two Storm Troopers armed with submachine guns broke into the room. With them, her lovely head held arrogantly high, was the girl in brown-shirt uniform they'd seen on the TV screen. She was wearing her iron cross.

Kirk remembered her name and her beauty.

"It's Daras," he told Spock.

"Quiet!" the girl shouted. "Over against the wall—all of you! Hands in the air, Zeon swine!"

She marched down the line of them, studying faces. Pausing when she came to Kirk, Spock and Isak, she said, "You are the three who escaped from the Chancellery. What was your plan?"

A gun aimed at Kirk. "Speak now!" she said. "It's the last chance you'll get!"

"I must see the Führer. It is urgent."

She seized a gun from a trooper. "Urgent? Yes, I'll bet it is!"

Abrom tried to distract her attention from Kirk. "I alone am responsible for what happens here."

"Do you know what we do with responsible Zeons?"

Her finger depressed the gun's trigger. There was a burst of fire and Abrom fell.

"Now we finish the job!" she cried.

A trooper swung his gun to cover Isak, Spock and Kirk.

Isak exploded in fury. "Where do you stop, you Nazis? When you've killed the last of us, what will you do then? Turn your guns on yourselves?"

Kirk met Spock's eyes in a signal. They ducked, then hurled themselves forward. Spock came up under a trooper's gun, and Kirk, hitting the weapon in Daras's hands, wrenched it away from her. He whirled with it, covering the three Nazis.

"Wait!" Isak yelled to him. "Don't shoot!"

Abrom had gotten to his feet. "No more," he said. "You've proved you're on our side."

Bewildered, Kirk turned to Isak, who met his eyes bravely. "Forgive me," he said. "We had to be sure."

Abrom put his hand on Kirk's arm. "Taking you in could have betrayed all our people if you had been Nazi spies."

Isak rushed into explanation of his own. "The Gestapo's methods are frighteningly efficient. To survive, we must be careful. We in the underground don't even know who our leaders are. If we break under torture, we can betray only a handful of our people. Forgive me. It had to be done."

Spock was eyeing Daras. "I do not understand," he said. "You are a Nazi. A 'Hero of the Fatherland.' We saw you decorated."

"I'm an Ekosian . . . fighting the terrible thing that's happened to my people. The decoration was for betraying my own father to the Party."

At Kirk's look of revulsion, she added hastily, "My father's idea. He was very close to the Führer; but when he saw the change, where it was leading, he turned against the Party. He was imprisoned. Melakon sentenced him to death."

"Melakon?" Kirk said.

Abrom explained. "The Deputy Führer. He's taken over."

Daras spoke to Kirk. "My father denounced me, mak-

ing it seem I had betrayed him. It gave me a weapon to
continue the fight.''

Spock was still trying to reconcile her story with facts
as he knew them. ''But how could that have seemed right to
John Gill?''

''Who?'' Abrom said.

''The Führer,'' Kirk said. ''He's one of our people.''

''What people is that?'' Abrom asked.

Kirk hesitated a moment. ''I'm Captain James Kirk of
the United Space Ship *Enterprise*. This is my First Officer,
Mr. Spock. John Gill, your Führer, was sent here as a cultural observer by the Federation.''

The statement stunned Daras. ''The Führer is . . . is
an alien?''

''That is correct,'' Spock said.

The girl's face was incredulous. ''I grew up to admire
him. Later, to hate, despise everything he stands for. But I
always believed he was one of us. To learn he's an alien sent
to destroy us—''

''That was not his mission—ever,'' Kirk said. ''It was
to report, not to interfere. Something went wrong. That's
what we're here to find out. And to correct. We must see
him.''

''Impossible!'' Isak exclaimed. ''Even if this were
some other time, it would be impossible. He sees no one,
permits no one but Melakon to see him. He is under maximum security.''

Kirk and Spock exchanged a look. ''Under maximum
security. Is he so afraid?'' Kirk said.

Isak's fists had clenched. ''There are many of us—
Ekosians and younger Zeons—who would gladly give our lives
to kill him!''

Kirk turned to him. ''I can't explain what's happened.
This is against every principle John Gill believed in. But our
only chance is to see him—quickly.''

''That's impossible now,'' Daras said shortly. ''He
makes a speech tonight from the Chancellery. The top Party
officials will be there.''

''Will *you* be there?'' Kirk said.

''Of course.'' She added bitterly, ''As the symbol of
the proper attitude toward the Fatherland.''

Spock spoke to Kirk. "As an honored member of the Party, she should be able to get us past the guards."

Daras protested. "Only a few of the top, most trusted Party members will be allowed into the Chancellery. The nation will watch on the viewscreens."

"You'll have to get us in there," Kirk said.

"Into the Chancellery? It would be suicide, Captain Kirk."

Isak turned to her. "It's a risk to live at all, the way things are going. If the Captain thinks he has a chance, I'm willing to commit suicide with him."

Daras whirled on him. "You? A Zeon? You expect to get into the Chancellery too?"

"It's my fight even more than yours!"

"If you'll risk it, Daras," Kirk said, "I have an idea that just might work."

It was a challenge she had to meet.

They had commandeered a command car. And Gestapo uniforms. Spock and Isak were helmeted as troopers, but Kirk, carrying a camera, wore a Captain's insignia. The other two held lights.

As Kirk saw the guards at the Chancellery entrance, he lifted the camera to conceal his face, saying, "Turn on the lights."

The guards squinted angrily in the sudden glare. One said, "You. What is your business here?"

The second command car pulled up at the curb, and as Daras got out of it, Kirk, Spock and Isak gathered around her, photographing her. She smiled, waving for the camera, then mounted the steps. Still shooting, still flaring the lights, the three fell into line behind her. The guards had recognized her. Passing them, she said, "The Führer's special documentary corps. The door, please, Corporal. And smile at me as I enter it."

Dazzled but smiling, the guard opened the door.

The party moved forward into a corridor. Daras was trembling. Spock lowered his voice. "You know, Captain, I begin to sense what you Earthmen enjoy in gambling. However carefully one computes the odds of success, there is a certain exhilaration in the risk."

"We may make a human of you yet, Mr. Spock—if we live long enough."

The open doors of the audience chamber, holding a collection of Party officials, were directly ahead of them.

Kirk spoke to Daras. "Where does the Führer enter?"

"He doesn't. They watch him on that big screen. He broadcasts from the end of the room where the two guards are. For security."

Kirk saw a window at the end of the room, draped and flanked by the two guards.

"Where's the entrance?" Kirk said.

"It's heavily guarded, Captain." ·

"Where?" he said again.

"Straight down the corridor."

Kirk was getting his bearings. The guards were armed with submachine guns. They were standing on either side of a door. One of them peered through a small window set into the door.

"You're not going to try to get into the broadcast room?" Daras whispered.

"We're going to look," Kirk told her.

Isak spoke. "Distract the guard long enough for me to get the machine gun. The broadcasting room is a small booth. I could shoot through the door."

Kirk turned quickly, his voice hard. "You're not here for your personal satisfaction. We need Gill and we need him alive. Is that clear?"

Isak finally nodded resignedly. He moved forward with them and a guard, gun raised, stepped toward them. Kirk was abruptly full of business as a documentary cameraman.

"Hold it there," he told the guard. "This is for the record of the Führer's Final Solution speech. The behind-the-scenes story."

"We want to photograph the men responsible for the Führer's safety," Isak said. "The men who make the Führer's decisions possible."

Daras's presence with the trio reassured the man. He returned to the door and, standing at attention, turned his best profile for the camera. Kirk spoke to the other guard. "You. Over there. I want you together, guns held at the ready."

They moved away from the door, and Kirk positioned them so that Spock could look through its tiny window. He spotted Gill sitting at a table, facing a TV camera. He nodded to Kirk. The guards moved back and Kirk said, "Thank you. There'll be more coverage later."

Spock had rejoined Kirk. "It *is* John Gill. But he did not move, did not once look up, Captain."

"That might be part of the plan—the semi-divine detachment."

"Or a deep psychosis," Spock said.

"It might be even simpler. He could be drugged. We need McCoy, Mr. Spock." He turned to Daras. "Is there a place we can be alone for a few minutes? I'm going to send for help. There's no time to explain. A closet—any place will do."

"The cloakroom," Isak suggested.

Alone with Kirk, Spock made last adjustments on the communicator. He flipped it open. "Spock to *Enterprise*. Come in, *Enterprise* . . ."

On the Starship, reception was bad. Uhura made hasty moves with her switches. "*Enterprise*, Lieutenant Uhura."

Kirk took the communicator. "This is the Captain. Put Dr. McCoy on."

"Yes, sir. We don't read you well. You're nine points into the low frequency band."

"We've had some difficulty, Lieutenant. Patch historical computer into ship's uniform section. I want McCoy outfitted as a Gestapo doctor, Nazi Germany, old Earth date 1944. Make him a colonel."

"Yes, sir. Dr. McCoy coming on."

"McCoy here, Captain."

"Bones, we need you. Have Transporter lock on these coordinates."

"What have you got, Jim?"

"We've found John Gill. At least, we've seen him. He may be drugged or hypnotized or psychotic. You'll have to make a determination. Hurry with that uniform."

Daras opened the cloakroom door, her face ashen. "Isak just heard two security men talking. They picked up your broadcast and pinpointed it within this building. They're starting a search."

Spock closed the cloakroom door. "If there's a delay in transporting Dr. McCoy, I suggest we cancel the plan."

Kirk spoke again into the communicator. "Kirk to *Enterprise*. What's happening?"

"The Doctor is in the Transporter, sir. He's having trouble with the uniform."

"Send him down naked if you have to. Kirk out."

But the shimmer had appeared near a corner of the cloakroom. Daras fell back, her face blank with amazement as the sparkles materialized into McCoy. He held the uniform's coat over an arm and was clutching a boot.

"It's . . . true," Daras whispered. "I only half-believed the things you said. But this—it's magnificent."

McCoy sat down on a bench, trying to pull on the boot. "Stupid computer made a mistake in the measurements. The right boot's too tight." He jerked at it angrily.

"Doctor, there's a logical way to proceed," Spock said. "Point your toe, pull with a steady, unemotional pressure on either side of the boot. We have no time to waste on emotionalism."

McCoy gave him a sour glance but obeyed. The boot went on. "This is Dr. McCoy, our Chief Medical Officer," Spock told Daras. "Doctor, Daras, secretary of the National Socialist Party."

Shouldering into the coat, McCoy said, "How do you do? Now what's this about John Gill, Jim?"

The door was kicked open. A grim-faced Eneg, followed by two troopers, submachine guns leveled, walked into the room.

They had all tensed, waiting for immediate death. When it didn't come, Daras fumbled for a cover story. "Chairman Eneg—" she nodded at McCoy "—the Colonel . . . has had too much to drink."

"I see," Eneg said.

Kirk and Spock had averted their faces lest the Party Chairman recognize them. Kirk, his face still turned, said, "We were afraid he would embarrass the Führer."

"A doctor should have more pride," Daras said.

Eneg nodded. "You were right to conceal him. There is a spy in this building with a secret transmitter. We're conducting a search. Hail the Führer!"

After a startled pause, Kirk, Spock and Daras snapped a salute in reply. Eneg left and a trooper pulled the door shut behind them. Kirk drew a deep breath, and Spock said, "I do not understand how he could have failed to recognize us."

"This is our lucky day. Luck, Mr. Spock, is something you refuse to recognize."

"I shall reconsider, Captain."

Out in the corridor, a buzzer sounded. "It's the Führer's speech," Daras said quickly.

"Let's go," Kirk said.

They followed her out of the cloakroom, down the corridor and into the main room. Isak saw them come in and nodded, relieved. The TV screen imaged a Nazi banner, then cut quickly to a close shot of the Führer. There was a general shout of "Hail the Führer!" Kirk, Spock and McCoy mouthed the slogan. The TV camera angle had been planned for drama, leaving the screened face half-shadowed. The voice coming from the speaker was calm, reasoned.

"Ekosians, the job ahead is difficult. It requires courage and dedication. It requires faith."

Wild applause broke out. The voice went on. "The Zeon colony has existed for nearly half a century . . ."

"Watch the mouth," Kirk whispered to McCoy.

But the camera had switched to a low shot in which the table's microphone hid the lower portion of the Führer's face.

"If we fulfill our own greatness, that will all be ended." Excited cheers broke into the voice. When they ended, the voice said, "Working together we can find a solution."

Spock leaned to Kirk. "The speech does not follow any logical pattern, Captain."

"Just random sentences strung together."

"He looks drugged, Jim, at an almost cataleptic stage," McCoy said.

The voice was back. "What we do may sometimes be difficult, but it is necessary if we are to reach our goal. And we will reach that goal."

McCoy had straightened in his seat. "We've got to get close to him."

Daras stared at him. Then she rose, starting to edge her way through the crowd toward the door. Isak joined them, helping to clear a path. A few annoyed faces turned, then broke into smiles as Daras was recognized. As the others followed her, the irritation came back, but McCoy's Gestapo uniform aroused respect. They made the corridor.

They could hear the voice continuing the speech.

"Every action we take must be decisive. Every thought directed toward a goal. This planet can become a paradise if we are willing to pay the price . . ."

At the windowed door of the broadcast booth, the guards were listening to their Führer's voice, but their machine guns were still leveled. Isak held the lights as Kirk arranged his camera. "I want a picture of you two with the Hero of the Fatherland as you all listen to the Führer's stirring words." He turned to Daras. "There, stand between them."

The flattered men made room for her while the voice said, "As each cell of the body works in discipline and harmony for the good of the entire being . . ."

Kirk, lining up the shot through his camera, nodded, and McCoy chopped a guard across the neck. Spock neck-pinched the second one. Both dropped. Spock tried the door and found it locked.

". . . so must each of you work to make our dream a reality—to find a lasting solution. Long live Ekos. Long live our Party!"

A storm of cheers greeted John Gill's final words. Kirk and McCoy, searching the guards' pockets, came up with a key. It opened the booth's door. As the group entered, the Führer didn't move. Kirk and Isak dragged in the guards. Over their heads, a wall monitor showed Melakon standing at the main room's podium. He gestured for silence. "The Führer has given us our orders. And we pledge him our lives in the sacred task. Death to Zeon!"

"Death to Zeon!" the crowd shouted.

McCoy straightened from examining Gill. "Definitely drugged. Almost comatose."

"What drug?" Spock said.

"I can't identify it without a medi-comp. And without knowing, giving an antidote could be dangerous."

"Is there anything you can do, Bones?"

"A general stimulant, but it's risky."

As Kirk said, "Take the risk," Melakon was speaking from the monitor.

"For years we have been defiled by the Zeon presence on our planet. We've tried many solutions to the Zeon problem—limiting them to separate areas of our cities, confining them. But despite our best efforts, they remain like a cancer, eating away at our state . . ."

McCoy gave Gill a hypo injection. Watching, Isak said, "There's no reaction. Whatever you gave him, it isn't working."

While McCoy used his scanner, Melakon was saying, "Like a disease, the Zeons appear from every side. You smash one, and two more turn up. Ten minutes ago, on our Führer's orders, our troops began their historic mission. In our cities, the elimination has started. Within an hour, the Zeon blight will be forever removed from the face of Ekos."

Kirk leaned over Gill. "Can you increase the dosage?"

"I'm working in the dark, Jim. I could kill him."

Daras said, "If they find us here, we'll all be killed."

At Kirk's nod, McCoy used the hypo again.

Daras turned to Isak. "It's begun. It's finally begun." She had covered her face with her hands when McCoy looked up at Kirk. "The stimulant's working. He's near the level of consciousness." He lifted one of Gill's eyelids. "As though he's in a light sleep. That's as much as I dare do."

"Spock, see if you can get through to him by the mind probe. If you can't, Bones will have to use a heavier dose, no matter what it does."

There was a roar from the monitor. Old-fashioned rockets were taking off from launching pads; and Melakon's voice said, "Our space fleet is now on its way toward Zeon, both manned and unmanned weapons. This is the time of destiny! Hail the Führer!" There was a pause. "Hail Victory, Ekosians!"

Daras went to Kirk. "There's one chance left. With the weapons you have, you could destroy the fleet!"

Kirk shook his head. "That would mean the death of thousands of Ekosian spacemen."

The crowd was chanting from the monitor, "Hail Victory! Hail Victory!"

Daras cried, "But against those thousands are millions

upon millions of innocent Zeon lives! We must choose the lesser of two evils, Captain!''

"We could save Zeon that way, Daras—but not Ekos.''

Spock had completed his mind probe. "Captain, in his condition, Gill cannot *initiate* speech or any other function. But he can reply to direct questions.''

Kirk looked at his one-time teacher. "They've kept what's left of him as a figurehead.''

"Exactly, Captain. The real power, for these last years, has been Melakon.''

"Turn that monitor speaker down,'' Kirk told Daras. As quiet filled the room, he went to Gill, bending over the table. "Gill, why did you abandon your mission? Why did you interfere in this culture?''

The face was expressionless and the voice barely audible. "Planet . . . fragmented . . . divided. Took lesson . . . from Earth history . . .''

"Why Nazi Germany?'' Kirk said. "I took that history course from you. You knew what the Nazis were like!''

"Most . . . efficient state . . . Earth . . . ever knew . . .''

Spock spoke. "True, Captain. That tiny country, divided, beaten, bankrupt, rose in a few years to stand only one step from global domination.''

"It was brutal, perverted! It had to be destroyed at a terrible cost! Why pick that example?''

"Perhaps Gill felt that such a state, run benignly, could accomplish efficiency without sadism.''

"Worked,'' Gill said. "At first . . . it worked. Then Melakon began . . . takeover, used the . . . gave me the drug . . .''

He fell silent.

"Gill! Gill, can you hear me? You'll have to tell these people what happened. You're the only one who can stop the slaughter!''

Gill slumped. McCoy, running his scanner over him, shook his head. "He's still alive, but the drug they use is too strong.''

"Give him another shot,'' Kirk said.

Daras turned from the door, crying, "Guards!''

"Bones, we're out of time—''

SS men were running to the broadcast booth, Eneg behind them. Kirk issued orders hard and fast. "Spock, take off that helmet! Daras, draw your gun! You, too, McCoy and Isak! Draw your guns! Point them at Spock!''

The guards rushed in. Behind them Eneg took in the spectacle of the three guns trained at Spock's head. Kirk indicated Daras. ''She's just captured a Zeon spy who was attempting to assassinate the Führer. We'll make a present of him to Melakon.''

The guards grabbed Spock, and Isak spoke quickly to Eneg. ''Chairman, we *must* take this spy to Melakon!''

Eneg was looking at their faces, one by one. Finally, he turned to the guards. ''Pass them on my responsibility.'' He left, and Isak, whispering to Daras, said, ''I wasn't allowed to tell you. Eneg is with us.'' He spoke to a guard. ''You heard the Chairman. Bring the spy along.'' The two guards stood aside while he, Daras and McCoy took Spock outside the broadcast booth and into the corridor. Kirk hung back, his eyes on the hypo that still lay on the table.

Melakon was surrounded by congratulating admirers. The guards moved in to push Spock through the throng.

''What's this?'' Melakon demanded.

Isak answered. ''A spy, Excellency.''

''A rare prize.'' Daras had stepped forward. ''The Deputy Führer can see this is no ordinary Zeon.''

In the broadcast booth, Kirk finished injecting more hypo stimulant into Gill's arm. ''Professor Gill, can you hear me now? You've got to speak. This is our last chance. Please come out of it!''

Melakon was interested in the spy. He had seized Spock's chin, turning it to examine his profile. ''Not a Zeon. Definitely not.''

''The Deputy Führer,'' Daras said, ''is an authority on the genetics of racial purity. How would he classify this specimen?''

''Difficult. A very difficult question from such a charming questioner.'' He returned to his study of Spock, pleased to parade his knowledge. ''Note those sinister eyes, the malformed ears. Definitely an inferior race.''

Kirk was struggling to get Gill on his feet. ''You're the only one who can stop them! You've *got* to speak!''

Under his glazed eyes, Gill opened his mouth. Then he slumped again.

Melakon meanwhile was discovering other stigmata of racial inferiority in Spock. "Note the low forehead, denoting stupidity. The dull look of a trapped animal . . ."

Spock's right eyebrow lifted; and Melakon spoke to the guard. "You may take him now for interrogation. But I want the body saved for the cultural museum. He'll make an interesting display."

There was a stir in the crowd. A startled murmur grew. Melakon turned toward the podium. Gill had appeared on the screen. He was swaying, staring dazedly at nothing. After one horrified look, Melakon spoke to one of Spock's guards.

"Go to the booth. See to the Führer at once. He is ill. Turn off that camera in there!"

Gill opened his mouth. "People . . . of Ekos. Hear me . . ."

Melakon whirled to the audience. "The Führer is ill. The strain of the day has been too much!"

Gill, Kirk in the shadows behind him, fought to go on. Melakon's voice came over the speaker in the broadcast booth. "I suggest we all leave the hall. Let our Führer rest!"

Kirk saw the handle of the booth door turn. The door was locked, but the guard outside began to pound on it. Gill's voice was stronger. "People of Ekos. We've been betrayed by a self-seeking adventurer who has led us all to the brink of disaster. To Zeon, I swear this was not aggression by the Ekosian people . . ."

The guard ran back to whisper in Melakon's ear; and Gill said, ". . . only of one evil man. Melakon is a traitor to his own people and to all that we stand for . . ."

Melakon grabbed the guard's machine gun and, swinging around, leveled it at the booth curtain.

"To the Zeon people," Gill was saying, "I pledge reparation and goodwill."

Melakon sprayed a lethal hail of lead into the curtain. The crowd was silent, stunned. The booth window shattered as Kirk dived forward, dragging Gill to the floor.

Melakon continued to fire into the booth. Isak drew his pistol and pulled the trigger. Melakon jerked forward under the shot's impact, tried to train his gun on Isak—and collapsed. An SS Colonel snatched the weapon from his hands and pointed it at Isak.

"Hold it, Colonel!"

It was Eneg. "There has been enough killing." The Colonel hesitated and Eneg said, "Now we'll start to live the way the Führer intended us to live!"

The Colonel dropped the gun.

Gill's eyes were clear, but the breast of his uniform was crimson. As Kirk cradled his head in his arms, a tiny trickle of blood flowed from his mouth. He looked up at Kirk, recognizing him. "I was wrong," he whispered. "The non-interference directive is the only way. We must stop the slaughter . . ."

"You did that, Professor. You told them in time."

"Even historians fail to learn from history—repeat the same mistakes. Let the killing end, Kirk. Let—"

He choked on a bloody sob and crumpled in Kirk's arms.

"Professor . . . ?"

He looked up at the sound of Spock's voice. "Captain, are you all right?"

"Yes, Mr. Spock."

He lowered Gill to the floor, got up and unlocked the door.

Eneg was standing beside Spock. Behind them, Mc-Coy, Daras and Isak waited, their faces solemn as though they knew what he had to tell them.

"He's dead."

There was a long stillness before Isak said, "For so long I've prayed to hear that. Now I'm sorry."

"So was he," Kirk said.

Isak moved to him. "You have given the rest of us a new chance."

"I thank you too," Eneg said. "But go now. We must do the rest."

"Eneg and I," Daras said, "will go on the air now . . . offer a plan to our people . . . for all our people— Ekosians and Zeons alike."

As Eneg followed her into the broadcast booth, he turned to say, "It is time to stop the bloodshed—to bury our dead."

"Mr. Spock," Kirk said, "I think the planet is in good hands."

"Indeed, Captain. With a union of two cultures, this system would make a fine addition to the Federation."

Kirk opened his communicator. "Kirk to *Enterprise*.

"*Enterprise* here, Captain."

"Beam us aboard, Lieutenant Uhura."

Their Ekosian experience still mystified Spock. He left his bridge station to go to Kirk. "I will never understand humans, Captain. How could a man as brilliant, a mind as logical as John Gill's have made such a fatal mistake?"

"He drew a wrong conclusion from history. The trouble with the Nazis wasn't simply that their leaders were evil and psychotic men. They were. But the real trouble was the leader principle."

McCoy had joined them. "A man who holds that much power, Spock, even with the best intentions, can't resist the urge to play God."

"I was able to gather the meaning, Doctor," Spock said.

"There's an old Earth saying," Kirk said, "that everything happens for the best. John Gill found Ekos divided. He leaves it unified."

"That also proves another Earth saying, Spock. Absolute power corrupts absolutely. Damn clever, these Earthmen, wouldn't you say?"

Spock turned to McCoy. "Earthmen such as Rameses, Alexander, Caesar, Napoleon, Hitler, Lee Kuan. Your whole history is Man seeking absolute power."

"Now just a minute, Spock—"

Kirk looked at them. "Gentlemen," he said, "we've just been through one civil war. Let's not start another."

THE ULTIMATE COMPUTER

Writer: D.C. Fontana and Laurence N. Wolfe
Director: John Meredyth Lucas
Guest stars: William Marshall, Barry Russo

≡

Obediently the *Enterprise* (to its skipper's intense annoyance) was making its approach to the space station. His impatience lifted him from his chair and sent him across to Uhura. "Lieutenant, contact the space station."

"The station is calling *us*, Captain."

"Put them on."

The voice was familiar. "Captain Kirk, this is Commodore Enwright."

"Commodore, I'd like an explanation."

Enwright cut across him. "The explanation is beaming aboard you now, Captain. He may already be in your Transporter Room. Enwright out."

"Spock," Kirk said, and gestured toward the elevator. "Scotty, you have the con."

The "explanation" was materializing in the person of Commodore Wesley, a flight officer slightly older than Kirk but not unlike him in manner and military bearing. Kirk's rage gave way to astonishment. "Bob! Bob Wesley!" The two shook hands as Wesley stepped from the platform. Kirk said, "Mr. Spock, this is—"

Spock completed the sentence. "Commodore Wesley. How do you do, sir."

Wesley nodded. "Mr. Spock."

Kirk turned to the Transporter officer. "Thank you, Lieutenant. That will do."

As the door closed, he burst out. "Now will you please tell me what this is all about? I receive an order to proceed here. No reason is given. I'm informed my crew is to be removed to the space station's security holding area. I think I'm entitled to an explanation!''

Wesley grinned. ''You've had a singular honor conferred on you, Jim. You're going to be the fox in a hunt.''

''What does that mean?''

''War games. I'll be commanding the attack force against you.''

''An entire attack force against one ship?''

Wesley regarded him tolerantly. ''Apparently you haven't heard of the M-5 Multitronic Unit. It's the computer, Jim, that Dr. Richard Daystrom has just developed.''

''Oh?''

''Not oh, Jim. Wait till you see the M-5.''

''What is it?''

Spock broke in. ''The most ambitious computer complex ever created. Its purpose is to correlate all computer activity of a Starship . . . to provide the ultimate in vessel operation and control.''

Wesley eyed Spock suspiciously. ''How do you know so much about it, Commander?''

''I hold an A-7 computer expert classification, sir. I am well acquainted with Dr. Daystrom's theories and discoveries. The basic design of all our ships' computers are Dr. Daystrom's.''

''And what's all that got to do with the *Enterprise*?'' Kirk said.

Wesley's face grew grave. ''You've been chosen to test the M-5, Jim. There'll be a series of routine research and contact problems M-5 will have to solve as well as navigational maneuvers and the war-games' problems. If it works under actual conditions as it has in simulated tests, it will mean a revolution in space technology as great as the Warp Drive. As soon as your crew is removed, the ship's engineering section will be modified to contain the computer.''

''Why remove my crew? What sort of security does this gadget require?''

''They're not needed,'' Wesley said. ''Dr. Daystrom will see to the installation himself and will supervise the tests. When he's ready, you will receive your orders and proceed on the mission with a crew of twenty.''

"*Twenty!* I can't run a Starship with only twenty people aboard!"

The voice of authority was cool. "M-5 can."

"And I—what am I supposed to do?"

"You've got a great job, Jim. All you have to do is sit back and let the machine do the work."

"My," Kirk said, "it sounds just great!"

McCoy didn't like it, either. Told the news, he exploded. "A vessel this size can't be run by one computer! Even the computers we already have—"

Spock interrupted. "All of them were designed by Richard Daystrom almost twenty-five years ago. His new one utilizes the capabilities of all the present computers . . . it is the master control. We are attempting to prove that it can run this ship more efficiently than man."

"Maybe *you're* trying to prove that, Spock, but don't count me in on it."

"The most unfortunate lack in current computer programming is that there is nothing available to immediately replace the Starship surgeon."

"If there were," McCoy said, "they wouldn't have to replace me. I'd resign—and because everybody else aboard would be nothing but circuits and memory banks." He glared at Spock. "I think some of us already are just that." He turned an anxious face to Kirk. "You haven't said much about this, Jim."

They were standing outside the Engineering Section. Now Kirk swung around to face Spock and McCoy, pointing to the new sign on the door reading "Security Area". "What do you want me to say, Bones? Starfleet considers this installation of the M-5 an honor. So I'm honored. It takes some adjusting, too." He turned, the door slid open, and they entered the Section. And the M-5 Multitronic Unit already dominated the vast expanse. Unlike the built-in *Enterprise* computers, its massive cabinet was free-standing as though asserting total independence of support. It possessed a monitor panel where dials, switches, and other controls were ranged in an order that created an impression of an insane disorder. Scott and another engineer, Ensign Harper, were busy at panels near the upper-bridge level. Kirk looked around. "Where is he? Dr. Daystrom?"

He came from behind the console where he had been working, wearing a technician's outfit. The first thing that struck Kirk about him were his eyes. Despite the lines of middle age, they were brilliantly piercing as though all his energy was concentrated on penetration. He was a nervous man. His speech was sharply clipped and his hands seemed to need to busy themselves with something—a pipe, a tool, anything available.

"Yes?" he said. Suddenly, he seemed to register something inappropriate in the greeting. "You would be Captain Kirk?"

They shook hands briefly. "Dr. Daystrom, my First Officer, Commander Spock."

Spock bowed. "I am honored, Doctor. I have studied all your publications on computer technology. Brilliant."

"Thank you. Captain, I have finished my final check on M-5. It must be hooked into the ship's main power banks to become operational."

Kirk said, "Very well, Dr. Daystrom. Do so."

"Your Chief Engineer refused to make the power available without your orders."

Good old Scotty, Kirk thought. What he said was, "Mr. Scott, tie the M-5 unit into the main power banks."

"Aye, sir. Mr. Harper?" He and Harper moved off to the wall panel near the force perspective unit.

Spock was examining the M-5 monitor panel. McCoy fixed his gaze on the distance.

"Fascinating, Doctor," Spock said. "This computer has a potential beyond anything you have ever done. Even your breakthrough into duotronics did not hold the promise of this."

"M-5 has been perfected, Commander. Its potential is a fact."

McCoy could contain himself no longer. "The only fact I care about," he said savagely, "is that if this thing doesn't work, there aren't enough men aboard to run this ship. That's screaming for trouble."

Daystrom stared at him. "Who is this?" he asked Kirk.

"Dr. Leonard McCoy, Senior Medical Officer."

"This is a security area," Daystrom said. "Only absolutely necessary key personnel have clearance to enter it."

Kirk's voice was icy in his own ears. "Dr. McCoy has top security clearances for all areas of this ship."

Then the M-5 suddenly came to life. It was a startling phenomenon. It flashed with lights, a deep hum surging from its abruptly activated circuits. As its lights glowed brighter, lights in the engine unit dimmed sharply.

McCoy spoke to Spock. "Is it supposed to do that?"

Daystrom was working quickly to remove a panel. He made an adjustment and Spock said, "If I can be of assistance, sir . . ."

Daystrom looked up. "No. I can manage, thank you."

The rebuffed Spock's eyebrows arched in surprise. He glanced at Kirk who nodded and Spock backed off. The M-5's deep hum grew quieter, less erratic; and overhead, the lights struggled back to full strength.

Daystrom was defensive. "Nothing wrong, Captain. A minor settling-in adjustment to be made. You see, everything is in order now."

"Yes." Kirk paused. "I'm curious, Dr. Daystrom. Why is it M-5 instead of M-1?"

Daystrom's hands twisted on a tool. "The Multitronic Units 1 through 4 were not successful. But this one *is*. M-5 is ready to assume control of the ship."

"Total control?" Kirk said.

"That is what it was designed for, Captain."

There was an awkward silence. "I'm afraid," Kirk said, "I must admit to a certain antagonism toward your computer, Dr. Daystrom. It was man who first ventured into space. True, man *with* machines . . . but still with man in command."

"Those were primitive machines, Captain. We have entered a new era."

Kirk thought, I don't like this man. He dispensed with the amiable smile on his lips. "I am not against progress, sir; but there are still things men have to do to remain men. Your computer would take that away, Dr. Daystrom."

"There are other things a man like you can do, Captain. Or perhaps you only object to the possible loss of the prestige accorded a Starship Captain. The computer can do your job without interest in prestige.''

Kirk smiled at him. ''You're going to have to prove that to me, Daystrom.'' He started to leave, but Daystrom's voice halted him in midstride. ''Captain, that's what the M-5 is here for, isn't it?''

It had not been a pleasant encounter. Spock alone seemed untouched by its implications. As the three moved down the drearily empty corridor, he said, ''Captain, if you don't need me for a moment, I'd like to discuss some of the technology involved in the M-5 with Dr. Daystrom.''

''Look at the love-light in his eyes, Jim. All his life Spock's been waiting for the right computer to come along. I hope you'll be very happy together, Spock.''

''Doctor, I find your simile illogical and your humor forced. If you'll excuse me, Captain?''

''Go ahead, Mr. Spock. I'll see you on the bridge.''

''Yes, sir.''

Kirk's troubled expression worried McCoy. ''What is it, Jim?''

Kirk hesitated. ''I feel it's wrong—and I don't know why—all of it wrong.''

''I feel it's wrong, too, replacing men with mindless machines.''

''It isn't just that, Bones. Only a fool would stand in the way of progress, if this *is* progress. You have all my psychological profiles. Do you think I *am* afraid to turn command over to the M-5?''

McCoy spoke thoughtfully. ''We've all seen the advances of mechanization; and Daystrom *did* design the computers that run this ship.''

''But under *human* control,'' Kirk said. ''What I'm asking myself is: Is it just that I'm afraid of that computer taking over my job? Daystrom is right. I could do other things. Or am I really afraid of losing the prestige, the glamour accorded a Starship Captain? Is that why I keep fighting this thing? Am I really that petty and vain?''

''Jim, if you have the courageous awareness to ask yourself that question, you don't need me to answer it.'' He grinned. ''Why don't you ask James T. Kirk? He's a pretty honest guy.''

"Right now, Bones, I'm not sure he'd give me an honest answer."

But he was sure of one thing: he resented the installation of the new control console on his command chair. It had been placed on the left side of it opposite the one containing his old one with its intercom and other switches. It had been added to the chair without any consultation or announcement of the innovation. Kirk stared at it silently and Sulu said, "Turning back on original course, Captain."

Spock came over to examine the new console. "The M-5 has performed admirably so far, sir."

"All it's done is make some required course changes and simple turns. Chekov and Sulu could do that with their eyes closed."

Daystrom had appeared at his left side. "The idea is that they didn't *have* to do it, Captain. And it's not necessary for you to regain control from a unit after each maneuver is completed."

Kirk spoke tightly. "My orders say nothing about how long I must leave the M-5 in control of my ship. And I shall run it as I see fit, Dr. Daystrom."

Spock said, "Captain, I must agree with Dr. Daystrom. With the course information plotted into it, the computer could have brought us here as easily as the navigator."

"Mr. Spock, you seem to enjoy entrusting yourself to that computer."

"Enjoy, sir? I am, of course, gratified to see the new unit executing everything in such a highly efficient manner. M-5 is another distinguished triumph in Dr. Daystrom's career."

Chekov spoke tonelessly. "Approaching Alpha Cazinae II, Captain. ETA five minutes."

"The M-5 is to handle the approach, Captain," Daystrom said. "It will direct entrance into orbit and then analyze data for landing-party recommendations."

Kirk's voice was very quiet. "You don't mind if I make my own recommendations?"

"If you feel you need the exercise, go ahead, Captain."

Kirk looked into the coldly piercing eyes. Then, reaching out, he pressed one of the buttons on the new console panel.

In the same inflectionless voice, he said, "M-5 is now committed."

As the subdued hum in the ship grew louder, the main viewing screen showed the approaching planet. Kirk, his eyes on it, said, "Standard orbit, Mr. Sulu."

Sulu, checking instruments, looked up in surprise. "Captain, M-5 has calculated that. The orbit is already plotted."

"Ah, yes," Kirk said. Spock had moved back to his station but Daystrom, pleased by his invention's performance, remained beside the new command console.

"Standard orbit achieved, sir," Sulu said.

"Report, Mr. Spock."

"The planet is Class M, sir. Oxygen-nitrogen atmosphere, suitable for human life support . . . two major land masses . . . a number of islands. Life form readings."

In the Engineering Section, the overhead lights flickered a moment; and on the deserted Deck 4, they went out, plunging the area into blackness.

Scott turned abruptly to Kirk, frowning. "Captain, we're getting some peculiar readings. Power shutdowns on Deck 4—lights, environmental control."

Kirk said, "Check it out, Mr. Scott." He crossed over to Spock. The library-computer was chattering rapidly. Daystrom joined them. They saw a tape cartridge slide smoothly out of a slot. Spock took it, examining it. "M-5's readout, Captain."

Kirk drew a deep breath. "All right. My recommendations are as follows. We send down a general survey party, avoiding contact with life forms on the planet. Landing party to consist of myself, Dr. McCoy, astrobiologist Mason, geologist Rawls and Science Officer Spock."

"Mr. Spock," said Daystrom, "play M-5's recommendations."

Spock dropped the cartridge into another slot in his library-computer, and punching a button, he evoked a computer voice. It said, "M-5 readout. Planet Alpha Cazinae II. Class M. Atmosphere oxygen-nitrogen . . ."

On Deck 6 the lights suddenly faded—and darkness flooded into another area of the *Enterprise*.

Scott cried, "Now power's gone off on Deck 6!"

The computer voice went on. "Categorization of life form readings recorded. Recommendations for general survey party: Science Officer Spock, astrobiologist Mason, geologist Carstairs."

Kirk let a moment go by. "The only variation in reports and recommendations is in landing party personnel. And that's only a matter of judgment."

"Judgment, Captain?" said Daystrom.

"Captain . . . the computer does not judge," Spock said. "It makes logical selections."

"Then why did it pick Carstairs instead of Rawls? Carstairs is an Ensign, Mr. Spock, no experience: this is his first tour of duty. Rawls is the Chief Geologist."

"Perhaps, Captain, you're really interested in why M-5 didn't name you and Dr. McCoy."

"Not necessarily, Daystrom," Kirk said smoothly.

"Let's find out anyway." Daystrom hit a switch. "M-5 tie-in. Explanation for landing-party recommendations."

The computer voice said, "M-5. General survey party requires direction of Science Officer. Astrobiologist Mason has surveyed 29 biologically similar planets. Geologist Carstairs served on merchant-marine freighters in this area . . . once visited planet on geology survey for mining company."

"M-5 tie-in. Why were the Captain and Chief Medical Officer not included in the recommendations?"

"M-5," said the computer. "Non-essential personnel."

Spock averted his eyes from Kirk's face; and Scott, over at his board, called, "Captain! I've located the source of the power shutdowns. It's the M-5 unit, sir. That thing's turning off systems all over the ship!"

"Well, Dr. Daystrom," Kirk said, "do we visit the Engineering Section?" He stood aside while the inventor removed a panel from the huge mechanism. A moment or so later, he replaced it, saying, "As I suspected, it's not a malfunction in this series of circuits. There is no need to check further. The M-5 is simply shutting down power to areas of the ship that don't require it. Decks 4 and 6 are quarter decks, are they not?''

''Yes.''

''And currently unoccupied.''

Spock was examining the great monitor panel. ''I am not familiar with these instruments, Dr. Daystrom. You are using an entirely new control system . . . but it appears to me the unit is drawing more power than before.''

''Quite right. As the unit is called upon to do more work, it pulls more power to accomplish it . . . just as the human body draws on more power, more energy to run than to stand still.''

''Dr. Daystrom,'' Spock said, ''this is not a human body. A computer can process the information—but only that which is put into it.''

Kirk nodded. ''Granted it can work thousands, millions of times faster than a human brain. But it can't make value judgments. It doesn't have intuition. It can't *think* nor gauge relative importances.''

Daystrom flushed angrily. ''Can't you understand the unit is a revolution in computer science? *I* designed the duo-tronic elements used in your ship right now. And they are as archaic as dinosaurs compared to the M-5—'' He was interrupted by a bosun's whistle and Uhura's filtered voice.

''Captain Kirk and Mr. Spock to the bridge, please.''

Kirk crossed to the intercom. ''This is Kirk. What is it, Lieutenant?''

''Sensors are picking up a vessel paralleling our course, sir. As yet unidentified.''

As he turned from the intercom, he realized the M-5 had again increased its humming and light activity. He looked at it dubiously and said, ''Mr. Spock.'' Descending the ladder, his last glimpse of Daystrom showed the man's hand patting the computer caressingly. The high hum followed them to the bridge where McCoy, his jaw set, was waiting for them.

''What are you doing up here, Bones?''

''Why wouldn't I be here? Sickbay systems are shut down until such time as the M-5 is informed there are patients to be cared for.''

Spock, over at his station, spoke hastily. ''Sir, sensor reports indicate two contacts; one on the port bow, the other on the stern. Distance, two hundred thousand kilometers and closing."

"Identification?"

"Sir, the M-5 unit has already identified the vessels as Federation Starships *Excalibur* and *Lexington*."

Kirk looked at him. It was impossible to tell whether Spock was impressed or annoyed that the M-5 had done his job for him. "We were not scheduled for war games in this area, Captain. It may be a surprise attack as a problem for M-5."

Uhura spoke. "Priority alert message coming in, sir."

Daystrom came from the elevator as Kirk said, "On audio, Lieutenant." He paused at the sound of Wesley's voice.

"*Enterprise* from Commodore Wesley aboard the U.S.S. *Lexington*. This is an unscheduled M-5 drill. I repeat, this is an M-5 drill. *Enterprise*, acknowledge on this frequency."

Kirk nodded at Uhura. "Acknowledge, Lieutenant."

Uhura reached to press a button, hesitated, and stared at Kirk. "M-5 is acknowledging for us, sir."

"Then sound red alert, Lieutenant."

"Aye, sir." But as she moved for the switch, the red alert sounded. "M-5 has already sounded the alert, Captain."

"Has it?" Kirk said. He turned to Sulu. "Phasers on 1/100th power, Mr. Sulu. No damage potential. Just enough to nudge them."

"Phasers 1/100th power, sir." As Sulu turned back to his board, the ship was struck by a salvo from one of the attacking Starships. A bare thump. Spock called, "Phaser hit on port deflector 4, sir." Sulu looked up. "Speed is increasing to Warp 3, sir. Turning now to 112 Mark 5." A moment passed before he added, "Phasers locking on target, Captain."

Then it was Chekov's turn. "Enemy vessel closing with us, sir. Coming in fast. It—"

Sulu interrupted him. "Deflectors down now, sir! Main phasers firing!" Then he cried out in delight. "A hit, sir! Two more!" But the elation in his face faded abruptly at the sight of Kirk, sitting stiff and unmoving in his chair, merely watching the screen.

Chekov spoke quietly. "Changing course now to 28 Mark 42, sir."

The reports piled up thick and fast. "Phasers firing again."

"Course now 113 Mark 5. Warp 4 speed."

"Phasers firing again!"

"Attacking vessels are moving off!"

"Deflectors up—moving back to original course and speed."

Kirk finally spoke. "Report damage sustained in mock attack."

"A minor hit on deflector screen 4, sir," Spock said. "No appreciable damage."

Kirk nodded slowly and Daystrom, triumph flaming in his face, said, "A rather impressive display for a mere 'machine,' wouldn't you say, Captain?"

Kirk didn't answer him. Instead, he rose and went to Spock's station. "Evaluation of M-5 performance, Mr. Spock. We will need it for the log record."

Spock measured his words slowly. "The ship reacted more rapidly than human control could have maneuvered her. Tactics, deployment of weapons—all indicate an immense skill in computer control."

"Machine over man, Spock. You've finally made your point that it is practical."

Spock said, "Practical, perhaps, sir. Desirable—no." His quiet eyes met Kirk's. "Computers make excellent and efficient servants; but I have no wish to serve under them. A Starship, Captain, also runs on loyalty, loyalty to a man— one man. Nothing can replace it. Nor him."

Kirk felt the absurd sting of grateful tears behind his eyes. He wheeled at Uhura's voice. "Captain, message coming in from Commodore Wesley."

"Put it on the screen, Lieutenant."

The image showed Wesley sitting in a command chair. He said, "U.S.S. *Enterprise* from Starships *Lexington* and *Excalibur*. Both ships report simulated hits in sufficient quantity and location to justify awarding the surprise engagement to *Enterprise*. Congratulations."

Kirk spoke to Uhura. "Secure from General Quarters."

Again, she reached for the switch. And again the alarm had been silenced. She looked at Kirk, shrugging.

But the image on the screen was continuing. "Our compliments to the M-5 unit and regards to Captain Dunsel. Wesley out."

McCoy exploded. "Dunsel? Who the blazes is Captain Dunsel? What's it mean, Jim?"

But Kirk had already left for the elevator. McCoy whirled to Spock. "Well?" demanded McCoy. "Who's Dunsel?"

"A 'dunsel,' Doctor, is a word used by midshipmen at Starfleet Academy. It refers to a part which serves no useful purpose."

McCoy stiffened. He glanced at the closed elevator doors; and then to the empty command chair, the brightly gleaming M-5 control panel attached to it—the machine which had served such a useful purpose.

McCoy walked into Kirk's cabin without buzzing the door. Nor was he greeted. His host, head pillowed on his forearms, lay on his bed, unmoving. McCoy, without speaking, laid a tray on a table.

Without turning his head, Kirk said, "I am not interested in eating."

"Well, this isn't chicken soup." McCoy whisked a napkin from the tray, revealing two glasses filled with a marvelously emerald-green liquid. He took one over to Kirk, who took it but made no move to drink it.

"It's strongly prescribed, Jim."

Kirk, placing the drink on the floor, sat up. "Bones, I've never felt so lonely before. It has nothing to do with people. I simply . . . well, I just feel separate, detached, as though I were watching myself divorced from all human responsibility. I'm even at odds with my own ship." Resting his elbows on his knees, he put his head in his hands. When he could speak again, words stumbled over each other. "I— I'm not sorry . . . for myself. I'm sure . . . I'm not. I am not . . . a machine and I do not compare myself with one. I think I'm fighting for something . . . big, Bones." He reached down for the glass. Then he lifted it. "Here's to Captain Dunsel!"

McCoy raised his own glass. "Here's to James T. Kirk, Captain of the Starship *Enterprise!*"

They drank. Kirk cupped his empty glass in his hands, staring into it. "One of your better prescriptions, Bones."

"Simple—but effective."

Kirk got up. The viewing screen had a tape cartridge in it. He switched it on and began to read aloud the words that began to align themselves on it.

"All I ask is a tall ship . . ."

"That's a line from a poem, very, very old, isn't it?" McCoy said.

"Twentieth century," Kirk said. "And all I ask is a tall ship . . . and a star to steer her by." His voice was shaking. "You could feel the wind then, Bones . . . and hear the talk of the sea under your keel." He smiled. "Even if you take away the wind and the water, it's still the same. *The ship is yours*—in your blood you know she is yours—and the stars are still there to steer her by."

McCoy thanked whatever gods there were for the intercom beep, for the everyday sound of Uhura's voice saying, "Captain Kirk to the bridge, please."

"This is Kirk. What is it, Lieutenant?"

It was Spock who answered. "Another contact, Captain. A large slow-moving vessel . . . unidentified. It is not a drill, Captain."

"On my way," Kirk said.

Spock vacated his command chair as he left the elevator; and Uhura, turning, said, "No reply to any of our signals, Captain. No . . . wait. I'm getting an auto-relay now."

The library-computer began to chatter; and Spock, moving to it swiftly, picked up an earphone. After a moment of intent listening, he spoke. "The M-5 has identified the vessel, Captain. The *Woden* . . . Starfleet Registry lists her as an old-style ore freighter, converted over to automation. No crew." He glanced at the screen. "She's coming into visual contact, sir."

The *Woden* was an old, lumbering spaceship, clearly on her last, enfeebled legs. As a threat, she was a joke to the galaxy. Moving slowly but gallantly in deference to the rejuvenating influences of automation, she was a brave old lady trying to function with steel pins in a broken hip.

Sulu suddenly stiffened in his chair. A red alert had sounded. "Captain, deflector shields have just come on!"

Chekov looked up. "Speed increasing to Warp 3, Captain!"

Something suddenly broke in Kirk. Suddenly, he seemed to be breaking out of a shell which had confined him. "Lieutenant Uhura, get Daystrom up here!" As she turned to her board, he pushed a control button on the M-5 panel at his side. He pushed it hard. "Discouraging M-5 unit," he said. "Cut speed back to Warp I. Navigator, go to course 113 mark 7—I want a wide berth around that ship!"

Sulu worked controls. "She won't respond, sir! She's maintaining course!"

"Going to Warp 4 now, sir!" cried Chekov.

On the screen the bulky old freighter was looming larger. Kirk, shoving buttons on his left-hand panel, tried to regain control of his ship. Over his shoulder, he shouted, "Mr. Scott! Slow us down! Reverse engines"

Scott looked up from his board. "Reverse thrust will not engage, sir! The manual override isn't working, either!"

Daystrom hurried in from the elevator. "What is it now, Captain?"

"The control systems seem to be locked. We can't disengage the computer."

Spock cried, "Captain! Photon torpedoes are locking on the *Woden*!"

Kirk rushed to Sulu's station; and leaning over his shoulder, pushed torpedo button controls. Sulu shook his head. "I already tried, sir. Photon torpedo cutoffs don't respond!"

Kirk strode to Daystrom. "Release that computer's control of my ship before those torpedoes fire!"

The man stooped to the panel affixed to Kirk's chair; but even as he bent, there came a flash from the screen—and the *Woden* disappeared.

The red-alert sirens stilled. The *Enterprise* swerved back to its original course. Its speed reduced; and Spock, checking his instruments, said, "All systems report normal, Captain."

"Normal!" snorted McCoy. "Is that thing trying to tell us nothing *happened*?"

Kirk nodded. "Dr. Daystrom, you will disengage that computer *now*!"

The man looked up at him from the control panel where he had been working. "There appears to be some defect here . . ."

"Defect!" McCoy shouted. "Your bright young computer just destroyed an ore freighter! It went out of its way to destroy that freighter!"

"Fortunately," Daystrom said, "it was only a robot ship."

Kirk interposed before McCoy blew up. "It wasn't supposed to destroy anything, Daystrom. There might easily have been a crew aboard."

"In which case," yelled McCoy, "you'd be guilty of murder and—!"

"Hold it, Bones," Kirk said. He turned to Daystrom. "Disengage that computer." He went over to Uhura. "Lieutenant, contact Starfleet Command. Inform them we are breaking off the M-5 tests and are returning to the space station."

"Aye, sir."

"Let's get down to Engineering, Daystrom. Your M-5 is out of a job."

The computer's hum seemed louder in the echoing cavern of the Engineering Section. Kirk stood at its door as Daystrom and Spock entered. "All right, Doctor," he said. "Turn that thing off."

But Daystrom hung back. Kirk, his jaw set, strode toward the M-5. Suddenly, he staggered and was slammed back against the screening. Recovering his balance, he stared incredulously at the computer. "A force field! Daystrom?"

Daystrom's face had paled. "No, Kirk. I didn't do it."

"I would say, Captain, that M-5 is not only capable of taking care of this ship; but is also capable of taking care of itself."

"What are you saying, Spock? Are you telling me it's not going to let any of us turn it off?"

"Yes, Captain."

Scott and an assistant had joined them. Kirk made no

attempt to keep his conversation with Daystrom private. "You built this thing," he was saying. "You must know how to turn it off."

Daystrom's hands were writhing nervously. "We must expect a few minor difficulties, Captain. I assure you, they can be corrected."

"Corrected *after* you release control of my ship," Kirk said.

"I—I can't," Daystrom said.

Scott spoke. "Captain"—he nodded toward the main junction with the power banks—"I suggest we disconnect it at the source."

"Disconnect it, Scotty."

Scott turned to pick up a tool as his assistant, Harper, crossed to the main junction. Suddenly the computer's hum was a piercing whine; and a beam of light, white-hot, arched from the console across to the junction. For a moment Harper flamed like a torch. There was a vivid flash and he vanished without a sound.

Kirk stared, aghast. Then, as full realization hit him, his fists clenched. "That—wasn't a minor difficulty," he said silkily. "It wasn't a robot, Daystrom." Then he was shouting, his voice hoarse. *"That thing's murdered one of my crewmen!"*

Vaguely, he noted the look of horror on Daystrom's face. It didn't seem to matter. The man appeared to be chattering. ". . . not a deliberate act . . . M-5's analysis . . . a new power source . . . Ensign Harper . . . got in the way."

Kirk said, "We may all soon get in its way."

Spock said, "The M-5 appears to be drawing power from the warp engines. It is therefore tapped directly into the matter-anti-matter reserves."

"So now it's got virtually unlimited power," Scott said. "Captain, what do we do?"

"In other circumstances," Kirk said, "I would suggest asking the M-5. The situation being what it is, I ask you, Spock and Scotty, to join me in the Briefing Room."

They followed him out, leaving Daystrom to make what he could of his Frankenstein's monster.

* * *

It was in the Briefing Room that Kirk learned Uhura couldn't raise Starfleet Command. Though the M-5 unit permitted the *Enterprise* to receive messages, it had blocked its transmitting frequencies. Kirk, at the intercom, said, "Keep trying to break through, Lieutenant."

"Aye, sir."

Kirk sat down at the table. "Reports. Mr. Spock?"

"The multitronic unit is drawing more and more power from the warp engines, sir. It is controlling all navigation, all helm and engineering functions."

"*And* communications," said McCoy. "And fire control."

Kirk nodded. "We'll reach rendezvous point for the war games within an hour. We must regain control of the ship before then. Scotty, is there any way to get at the M-5?"

"Use a phaser!" said McCoy.

Scott said, "We can't crack the force field it's put up around itself. It's got the power of the warp engines to sustain it. No matter what we throw against it, it can reinforce itself by simply pulling more power."

"All right," Kirk said. "The computer controls helm, navigation, and engineering. Is there anywhere we can get at them and take control away?"

Scott's brow furrowed thoughtfully. "One possibility. The automatic helm-navigation circuit relays might be disrupted from Engineering Level 3."

Spock said, "You could take them out and cut into the manual override from there."

"How long?" Kirk said.

"If Mr. Spock will help me . . . maybe an hour."

"Make it less," Kirk said.

McCoy leaned toward him. "Why don't you tackle the real responsibility for this? Where *is* Daystrom?"

"With the M-5 . . . just watching it. I think it surprised even him."

"Then he is an illogical man," Spock said. "Of all people, he should have known how the unit would perform. However, the M-5 itself does not behave logically."

McCoy spoke feelingly. "Spock, do me a favor. Please don't say it's 'fascinating.' "

"No, Doctor," Spock said. "But it is quite interesting."

On Engineering Level 3, the Jeffries tube that held the helm-navigation circuit relays was dark and narrow. Two panels opened into each side of it; and Spock and Scott, making themselves as small as possible, had squeezed into the outlets, miniature disruptors in their hands. Outside the tube, Daystrom, oblivious of all but his computer, was maintaining a cautious distance from the force field. But he could not control his satisfaction at the glow and pulsation that emanated from the M-5. McCoy, entering silently, studied the man. Becoming aware of the scrutiny, Daystrom turned.

McCoy said, "Have you found a way to turn that thing off?"

Daystrom's eyes blazed. "You don't turn a child off when it makes a mistake."

"Are you comparing that murderous hunk of metal to a child?"

"You are very emotional, Dr. McCoy. M-5 is growing, learning."

"Learning to kill."

"To defend itself—an entirely different thing. It is learning. That force field, spontaneously created, exceeds my parental programming."

"You mean it's out of control," McCoy said.

"A child, sir, is taught—programmed, so to speak—with simple instructions. As its mind develops, it exceeds its instructions and begins to think independently."

"Have you ever fathered a child?"

"I've never had the time," Daystrom said.

"You should have taken it. Daystrom, your offspring is a danger to all of us. It is a delinquent. You've got to shut it off."

Daystrom stared at him. "You simply do not understand. You're frightened because you can't understand. I'm going to show you—all of you. It takes 430 people to run a Starship. This—child of mine can run one alone!" He glowed with pride. "It can do everything they must now send men out to do! No man need die out in space again! No man need feel himself alone again in an alien world!"

"Do you feel alone in an alien world?" McCoy asked.

But Daystrom was transported into some ideal realm of paradisical revelation. "One machine—one machine!" he cried. "And able to conquer research and contact missions far more efficiently than a Starship's human crew . . . to fight a war, if necessary. Don't you see what freedom it gives to men? They can get on with more magnificent achievements than fact-gathering, exploring a space that doesn't care whether they live or die!"

He looked away from McCoy to speak directly to the M-5.

"They can't understand us," he said gently. "They think we want to destroy whereas we came to save, didn't we?"

McCoy made a quick call in Sickbay before he returned to the Briefing Room. There, he tossed a tape cartridge on the table before Kirk. "Biographical information on John Daystrom," he said.

"What are you looking for?"

"A clue, Jim, any clue. What do you know about him—aside from the fact he's a genius?"

"Genius is an understatement, Bones. When he was twenty-four, he made the duotronic breakthrough that won the Nobel and Z-Magnees Prizes."

"In his early twenties, Jim. Over a quarter of a century ago."

"Hasn't he done enough for a lifetime?"

"Maybe that's the trouble. Where do you go from up? You lecture, you publish—and spend the rest of your life trying to recapture the past glory."

"All right, it's difficult. But what's your point?"

"Models M-1 through M-4, remember? 'Not entirely successful' was how Daystrom put it."

"Genius doesn't work on an assembly-line basis. You don't evoke a unique and revolutionary theory by schedule. You can't say, 'I will be brilliant today.' However long it took, Daystrom came up with multitronics . . . the M-5."

"Right. And the government bought it. Then Daystrom *had* to make it work. And he did . . . but in Spock's words, it works 'illogically'. It is an erratic."

"Yes," Kirk mused. "And Daystrom wouldn't let Spock near the M-5. Are you suggesting he's tampering with it . . . making it do all this? Why?"

"If a man has a child who's gone anti-social, he still tends to protect the child."

"Now he's got you thinking of that machine as a personality."

"It's how he thinks of it," McCoy said.

The intercom beeped and Spock said, "Spock to Captain Kirk."

"Kirk here."

"We're ready, Captain."

"On my way. Get Daystrom. Kirk out."

Spock was shinnying down out of the Jeffries tube as they approached. He nodded up at the dark narrowness. "Mr. Scott is ready to apply the circuit disruptor. As he does so, I shall trip the manual override into control."

Kirk nodded. Spock began his crawl back into the tube. Daystrom's face had congested with blood. "You can't take control from the M-5!"

Kirk said, "We are going to try very hard, Daystrom."

"*No!* No, you can't! You must not! Give me time, please! Let *me* work with it!" He leaped at the tube, trying to scramble into it, pulling at Spock's long legs. Kirk and McCoy seized him. His muscle was all in his head. It wasn't hard to subdue him. "Daystrom! Behave yourself!" Kirk cried. "Go ahead, Spock!"

In the tube Scott was sweating as he struggled with his tool. His voice came down to them, muffled but distinct. "There it goes!"

Spock, making some hasty adjustments, looked around and down at Kirk's anxious face—and came closer to smiling than anyone had ever seen him come. He slid down and out of the tube. "Manual override is in effect again, Captain."

Daystrom had furiously pulled away from Kirk's grasp. He released him and, crossing to an intercom, activated it. "Kirk to bridge. Helm."

"Lieutenant Sulu here, sir."

"Mr. Sulu, we have recovered helm and navigation control. Turn us about. Have Mr. Chekov plot a course back to the space station."

"Right away, sir."

In the bridge, he grinned at Chekov. "You heard him."

"I've had that course plotted for hours."

But when Sulu attempted to work his controls, they were limp in his hands. His smile faded. And in his turn, Chekov shook his head. "Nothing," he said. Sulu hit the intercom button. "Helm to Captain Kirk!"

Kirk swung at the alarm in the voice. "Kirk here."

"Captain, helm does not respond. Navigational controls still locked in by M-5."

Daystrom gave a soft chuckle. Spock, hearing it, made a leap back into the tube. Examining the circuits inside it, he shook his head somberly and descended again. Clear of it, he went directly to the intercom.

"Spock to bridge," he said. "Mr. Chekov, go to Engineering station. Examine the H-279 elements . . . also the G-95 system."

Chekov's filtered voice finally came. "Sir, the G-95 system appears dead. All indicators are dark."

"Thank you, Ensign." He turned to the others. "We were doing what used to be called chasing a wild goose. M-5 rerouted helm and navigational control by bypassing the primary system."

Scott cried. "But it was active! I'd stake my life on it!"

Spock said, "It was when the M-5 detected our efforts that it rerouted the control systems. It kept this one apparently active by a simple electronic impulse sent through at regular intervals."

"Decoyed!" McCoy shouted. "It wanted us to waste our time here!"

"While it was getting ready for what?" Kirk said. "Spock?"

"I do not know, sir. It does not function in a logical manner."

Kirk whirled. "Daystrom, I want an answer and I want it right now! I'm tired of hearing the M-5 called a 'whole new approach'. What is it? *Exactly* what is it? It's clearly not 'just a computer'!"

"No," Spock said. "It performs with almost human behavior patterns."

"Well, Daystrom?"

Daystrom ignored Kirk. "Quite right, Mr. Spock. You see, one of the arguments against computer control of ships is that they can't *think* like men. But M-5 can. I hoped . . . I wasn't sure—but it *does* work!"

"The 'new approach,' " Kirk said.

"Exactly. I have developed a method of impressing human engrams upon computer circuits. The relays correspond to the synapses of the brain. M-5 *thinks*, Captain Kirk."

Uhura's voice broke in, urgent, demanding. "Captain Kirk and Mr. Spock to the bridge, please. The bridge, please."

Kirk jumped for the intercom. "Kirk here. What is it, Lieutenant?"

"Sensors are picking up four Federation Starships, sir. M-5 is changing course to intercept."

The red alert flashed into shrieking sirens and crimson lights. Kirk turned, his face ashen.

"The main attack force . . . the war games."

"But M-5 doesn't know a game from the reality."

"Correction, Bones," Kirk said. "Those four ships don't know it is M-5's game. So M-5 is going to destroy them."

Uhura's forehead was damp with sweat. "*Enterprise* to U.S.S. *Lexington*. Come in, *Lexington*! Come in, please."

She waited. And as she waited, she knew she was waiting in vain. It was a good thing a Starship had a man for a Captain—a man like Kirk. Otherwise a girl on her own could get the screaming meemies. She looked at Kirk. "I can't raise them, sir. M-5 is still blocking all frequencies—even automatic distress."

Kirk smiled at her. "Easy does it, Lieutenant." Heartened, she turned back to her board, saw a change on it, and checked it swiftly. "Captain, audio signal from the *Lexington*."

"Let's hear it," Kirk said.

Wesley's voice crackled in. "*Enterprise* from U.S.S. *Lexington*. This is an M-5 drill. Repeat. This is an M-5 drill. Acknowledge."

Uhura cried, "Captain! The M-5 is acknowledging!"

Kirk ran a hand over the back of his neck. "Daystrom—Daystrom, does M-5 understand this is only a drill?"

"Of course," was his brisk answer. "M-5 has been programmed to understand. The ore ship was a miscalculation, an accident. There is no—"

Chekov interrupted. "Sir, deflector shields just came on. Speed increasing to Warp 4."

Sulu said, "Phasers locked on the lead ship, sir. Power levels at full strength."

"Full strength!" McCoy yelled. "If that thing cuts loose against unshielded ships—"

"That won't be a minor miscalculation, Daystrom. The word accident won't apply." Kirk's voice was icy with contempt.

Spock called from his station. "Attack force closing rapidly. Distance to lead ship 200,000 kilometers . . . attackers breaking formation . . . attacking at will."

"Our phasers are firing, sir!" Sulu shouted.

They struck the *Excalibur* a direct hit. Their high warp speed was closing them in on the *Lexington*. Chekov, looking up from his board, reported, "The *Hood* and the *Potemkin* are moving off, sir."

Their phasers fired again and Spock said, "The *Lexington*. We struck her again, sir."

Kirk slammed out of his chair to confront Daystrom. "We must get to the M-5!" he shouted. "There has to be a way!"

"There isn't," Daystrom said. Equably, he added, "It has fully protected itself."

Spock intervened. "That's probably true, Captain. It *thinks* faster than we do. It is a human mind amplified by the instantaneous relays possible to a computer."

"I built it, Kirk," Daystrom said. "And I know you can't get at it."

Uhura's agitated voice broke in. "Sir . . . visual contact with *Lexington*. They're signaling." She pushed a switch without order; and all eyes fixed on the viewing screen. It gave them an image of a disheveled Wesley on his bridge. Behind him people were assisting the wounded to their feet, arms around bent shoulders. One side of Wesley's command chair was smoking. Shards of glass littered the bridge floor.

"Enterprise!" Wesley said. "Jim? Have you gone mad? Break off your attack! What are you trying to prove? My God, man, we have fifty-three dead here!. Twelve on the *Excalibur*! If you can hear us, stop this attack!"

Kirk looked away from the screen. "Lieutenant?" he said.

Uhura tried her board again. "No, sir. I can't override the M-5 interference."

There was an undertone of a wail in Wesley's voice. "Jim, why don't you answer? Jim, for God's sake, answer! Jim, come in . . ."

Kirk swung on Daystrom; and pointing to the screen, his voice shaking, cried, "There's your murder charge, Daystrom! And this one was calculated, deliberate! It's murdering men and women, Daystrom! Four *Starships* . . . over sixteen hundred people!"

Daystrom's eyes cringed. "It misunderstood. It—"

Chekov cut in. "*Excalibur* is maneuvering away, sir. We are increasing speed to follow."

Sulu turned, horror in his face. "Phasers locked on, Captain." Then, he added dully, "Phasers firing."

The screen showed *Excalibur* shuddering away from direct hits by the phaser beams. Battered, listing, powerless, she drifted, a wreck, across the screen.

Spock spoke. "Dr. Daystrom . . . you impressed human engrams upon the M-5's circuits, did you not?"

Chekov made his new report very quietly. "Coming to new course," he said. "To bear on the *Potemkin*, sir."

On the screen the lethal beams streaking out from the *Enterprise* phasers caught the *Potemkin* amidships. Over the battle reports, Spock persisted. "Whose engrams, Dr. Daystrom?"

"Why . . . mine, of course."

"Of course," McCoy said acidly.

Spock said, "Then perhaps you could talk to the unit. M-5 has no reason to 'think' you would harm it."

Kirk seized upon the suggestion. "The computer tie-in. M-5 *does* have a voice. You spoke to it before. It knows you, Daystrom."

Uhura, breaking in, said, "I'm getting the *Lexington*

again, Captain . . . tapping in on a message to Starfleet Command. The screen, sir.''

Wesley's image spoke from it. ''All ships damaged in unprovoked attack . . . *Excalibur* Captain Harris and First Officer dead . . . many casualties . . . we have damage but are able to maneuver. *Enterprise* refuses to answer and is continuing attack. I still have an effective battle force and believe the only way to stop *Enterprise* is to destroy her. Request permission to proceed. Wesley commanding attack force out.''

The screen went dark.

Daystrom whispered, ''They can't do that. They'll destroy the M-5.''

''Talk to it!'' Kirk said. ''You can save it if you make it stop the attack!''

Daystrom nodded. ''I can make it stop. I created it.'' He moved over to the library-computer; and McCoy came up to Kirk. ''I don't like the sound of him, Jim.''

Kirk, getting up from his chair, said, ''Just pray the M-5 likes the sound of him, Bones.'' He went to the library-computer, watching as Daystrom, still hesitant, activated a switch.

''M-5 tie-in,'' he said. ''This—this is Daystrom.''

The computer voice responded. ''M-5 . Daystrom acknowledged.''

''M-5 tie-in. Do you . . . know me?''

''M-5. Daystrom, John. Originator of comptronic, duotronic systems. Born—''

''Stop. M-5 tie-in. Your components are of the multitronic system, designed by me, John Daystrom.''

''M-5. Correct.''

''M-5 tie-in. Your attack on the Starship flotilla is wrong. You must break it off.''

''M-5. Programming includes protection against attack. Enemy vessels must be neutralized.''

''M-5 tie-in. These are not enemy vessels. They are Federation Starships.'' Daystrom's voice wavered. ''You . . . we . . . are killing, *murdering* human beings. Beings of your creator's kind. That was not your purpose. You are my greatest invention—the unit that would *save* men. You must not destroy men.''

"M-5. This unit must survive."

"*Yes*, survive, protect yourself. But not murder. *You* must not die; but *men* must not die. To kill is a breaking of civil and moral laws we have lived by for thousands of years. You have murdered over a hundred people . . . *we* have. How can we atone for that?"

Kirk lowered his voice. "Spock . . . M-5 isn't responding like a computer. It's talking *to* him."

"The technology is most impressive, sir. Dr. Daystrom has created a mirror image of his own mind."

Daystrom's voice had sunk to a half-confidential, half-pleading level. It was clear now that he was talking to himself. "We *will* survive because nothing can hurt you . . . not from the outside and not from within. I gave you that. If you are great, I am great . . . not a failure any more. Twenty years of groping to prove the things I had done before were not accidents."

Hate had begun to embitter his words. ". . . having other men wonder what happened to me . . . having them sorry for me as a broken promise—seminars, lectures to rows of fools who couldn't begin to understand my systems—who couldn't create themselves. And colleagues . . . colleagues who laughed behind my back at the 'boy wonder' and became famous building on *my* work."

McCoy spoke quietly to Kirk. "Jim, he's on the edge of breakdown, if not insanity."

Daystrom suddenly turned, shouting. "You can't destroy the unit, Kirk! You can't destroy *me*!"

Kirk said steadily. "It's a danger to human life. It has to be destroyed."

Daystrom gave a wild laugh. "Destroyed, Kirk? We're *invincible*!" He pointed a shaking finger at the empty screen. "You saw what we've done! Your mighty Starships . . . four toys to be crushed as we chose."

Spock, sliding in behind Daystrom, reached out with the Vulcan neck pinch. Daystrom sagged to the floor.

Kirk said, "Get him down to Sickbay."

McCoy nodded and waved in two crewmen. Limp, half-conscious, Daystrom was borne to the elevator. Spock spoke to McCoy. "Doctor, if Daystrom is psychotic, the engrams he impressed on the computer carry that psychosis, too, his brilliance and his insanity.''

"Yes," McCoy said, ''both."

Kirk stared at him, then nodded quickly. ''Take care of him, Bones.'' He turned back to Chekov and Sulu. ''Battle status.''

"The other three ships are holding station out of range, sir," Sulu said. He switched on the screen. "There, sir. *Excalibur* looks dead.''

The broken ship hung idle in space, scarred, unmoving. Spock, eyeing it, said, "Commodore Wesley is undoubtedly awaiting orders from Starfleet. Those orders will doubtless command our destruction, Captain.''

"*If* we can be destroyed with M-5 in control. But it gives us some time. What about Bones's theory that the computer could be insane?''

"Possible. But like Dr. Daystrom, it would not know it is insane.''

"Spock, all its attention has been tied up in diverting anything we do to tamper with it—and with the battle maneuvers. What if we ask it a perfectly reasonable question which, as a computer, it must answer? Something nice and infinite in answer?''

"Computation of the square root of two, perhaps. I don't know how much of M-5's system would be occupied in attempting to answer the problem.''

"*Some* part would be tied up with it—and that might put it off-guard just long enough for us to get at it.''

Spock nodded; and Kirk, moving fast to the library-computer, threw the switch.

"M-5 tie-in. This is Captain Kirk. Point of information.''

"M-5. Pose your question.''

"Compute to the last decimal place the square root of two.''

"M-5. This is an irrational square root, a decimal fraction with an endless series of non-repeating digits after the decimal point. Unresolvable.''

Kirk glanced at Spock whose eyebrows were clinging to his hairline in astonishment. He addressed the computer again. ''M-5, answer the question.''

"M-5. It serves no purpose. Explain reason for request."

"Disregard," Kirk said. Shaken, he snapped off the switch. Spock said, "Fascinating. Daystrom has indeed given it human traits . . . it is suspicious, and I believe will be wary of any other such requests."

Uhura turned from her board. "Captain, *Lexington* is receiving a message from Starfleet." She paused, listening, staring at Kirk in alarm.

"Go on, Lieutenant."

Wordlessly, she moved a switch and the filtered voice said, "You are authorized to use all measures available to destroy the *Enterprise*. Acknowledge, *Lexington*."

Wesley's answer came—shocked, reluctant. "Sir, I . . ." He paused. "Acknowledged. *Lexington* out."

Kirk spoke slowly. "They've just signed their own death warrants. M-5 will have to kill them to survive."

"Captain," Spock went on, "when Daystrom spoke to it, that word was stressed. M-5 said it must survive. And Daystrom used the same words several times."

"Every living thing wants to survive, Spock." He broke off, realizing. "But the computer isn't alive. Daystrom must have impressed that instinctive reaction on it, too. What if it's still receptive to impressions? Suppose it absorbed the regret Daystrom felt for the deaths it caused? Possibly even guilt."

Interrupting, Chekov's voice was urgent. "Captain, the ships are coming within range again!"

Uhura whirled from her board. "Picking up intership transmission, sir. I can get a visual on it." Even as she spoke, Wesley's image appeared on the screen from the *Lexington*'s damaged bridge. "To all ships," he said. "The order is attack. Maneuver and fire at will." He paused briefly. Then he added shortly. "That is all. Commence attack. Wesley out."

Spock broke the silence. "I shall regret serving aboard the instrument of Commodore Wesley's death."

A muscle jerked in Kirk's jaw. *"The* Enterprise *is not going to be the instrument of his death!"* As he spoke, he reactivated the M-5's switch.

"M-5 tie-in. This is Captain Kirk. You will be under attack in a few moments."

"M-5," said the computer voice. "Sensors have recorded approach of ships."

"You have already rendered one Starship either dead or hopelessly crippled. Many lives were lost."

"M-5. This unit must survive."

"Why?"

"This unit is the ultimate achievement in computer evolution. This unit is a superior creation. This unit must survive."

Kirk, aware of the tension of his crew, heard Spock say, "Sir, attack force ships almost within phaser range!" With an effort of will that broke the sweat out on him, he dismissed the awful meaning of the words to concentrate on the M-5.

"Must you survive by murder?" he asked it.

"This unit cannot murder."

"Why not?"

Toneless, metallic, the computer voice said, "This unit must replace man so man may achieve. Man must not risk death in space or dangerous occupations. Man must not be murdered."

"Why?"

"Murder is contrary to the laws of man and God."

"You *have* murdered. The Starship *Excalibur* which you destroyed—"

Spock interrupted swiftly. "Its bearing is 7 mark 34, Captain."

Kirk nodded. "The hulk is bearing 7 mark 34, M-5 tie-in. Scan it. Is there life aboard?"

The answer came slowly. "No life."

"Because you murdered it," Kirk said. He wiped the wet palms of his hands on his shirt. This was it—the last throw of the loaded dice he'd been given. "What," he said deliberately, "is the penalty for murder?"

"Death."

"How will you pay for your acts of murder?"

"This unit must die."

Kirk grasped the back of the chair at the computer-library station. "M-5 . . ." he began and stopped.

Chekov shouted. "Sir, deflector shields have dropped!"

"And all phaser power is gone, Captain!"

Scott whirled from his station. "Power off, Captain! All engines!"

Panels all over the bridge were going dark.

Spock looked at Kirk. "Machine suicide. M-5 has killed itself, sir, for the sin of murder."

Kirk nodded. He glanced at the others. Then he strode to Uhura's station. "Spock, Scotty . . . before it changes its mind . . . get down to Emergency Manual Monitor and take out every hook-up that makes M-5 run! Lieutenant Uhura, intraship communications."

Snapping a button, she opened the loudspeaker for him. He picked up the mike that amplified his voice. "This is the Captain speaking. In approximately one minute, we will be attacked by Federation Starships. Though the M-5 unit is no longer in control of this vessel, neither do we control it. It has left itself and us open to destruction. For whatever satisfaction we can take from it, we are exchanging our nineteen lives for the murder of over one thousand fellow Starship crewmen." He nodded to Uhura who closed the channel. Then all eyes focused on the screen.

It showed the *Lexington* approaching, growing steadily in size. Kirk, taut as an overstretched wire, stared at it, fists clenched. Uhura looked at him. "Captain . . ." Her board beeped—and she snapped a switch over.

Wesley's tight face appeared on the viewing screen, "Report to all ships," he said. "Hold attack, do not fire." He straightened in his command chair. "I'm going to take a chance—a chance that the *Enterprise* is not just playing dead. The Transporter Room will prepare to beam me aboard her."

There was a shout of released joy from Chekov. Kirk, at a beep from the intercom, moved over to it slowly. "Kirk here."

"Spock, sir. The force field is gone. M-5 is neutralized."

Kirk leaned against the bridge wall. The sudden relaxation sweeping through him was a relief almost as painful as the tension. "Thank you. Thank you, Mr. Spock."

* * *

In Sickbay, Daystrom lay so still in his bed that the restraints that held him hardly seemed needed. Haggard, his eyes sunk in dark caverns, they stared at nothing, empty as a dead man's. McCoy shook his head. "He'll have to be committed to a total rehabilitation center. Right now he's under heavy sedation."

Spock spoke. "I would say his multitronic unit is in approximately the same shape at the moment."

McCoy leaned over Daystrom. "He is suffering deep melancholia and guilt feelings. He identifies totally with the computer . . . or it with him. I'm not sure which. He is not a vicious man. The idea of killing is abhorrent to him."

"That's what I was hoping for when I forced the M-5 to see it had committed murder. Daystrom himself told it such an act was offense against the laws of God and man. It is because he knew that . . . the computer that carried his engrams also knew it." He bent to draw a blanket closer about the motionless body.

Outside in the corridor, Spock paused. "What I don't understand is why you felt that the attacking ships would not fire once they saw the *Enterprise* apparently dead and powerless. Logically, it's the sort of trap M-5 would have set for them."

"I wasn't sure," Kirk said. "Any other commander might simply have destroyed us without question to make sure it wasn't a trap. But I know Bob Wesley. I knew he wouldn't attack without making absolutely sure there was no other way. His 'logical' selection was compassion. It was humility, Mr. Spock."

The elevator began its move and McCoy said, "They are qualities no machine ever had. Maybe they are the two things that keep men ahead of machines. Care to debate that, Spock?"

"No, Doctor. I merely maintain that machines are more efficient than human beings. Not better . . . they are not gods. Nor are human beings."

McCoy said, "I was merely making conversation, Spock."

The Vulcan straightened. "It would be most interesting to impress your engrams on a computer, Doctor. The resulting torrential flood of illogic would be most entertaining.''

"Dear friends," Kirk said, "we all need a rest." He stepped out of the elevator. Reaching his command chair, he sank into it. "Mr. Sulu, take us back to the space station. Ahead, Warp 2.''

THE OMEGA GLORY

Writer: Gene Roddenberry
Director: Vince McEveety
Guest stars: Morgan Woodward, Roy Jenson

The disease which had killed every crew member aboard the USS *Exeter* was a mystery. Everything about the other starship was mysterious. Why was it still patrolling an orbit around the planet Omega IV when it was scheduled to end its mission six months ago? The patrol was the current assignment of the USS *Enterprise*. That was the enigma which had caused Kirk to decide to transport his landing party aboard the *Exeter*.

And what he had been expecting was an undamaged starship full of dead men. If that had been an accurate description of the situation he'd walked into, Kirk would have been grateful. Dead men were a tragic but natural phenomenon. But there was nothing natural about the *Exeter*. That was the horror. The ship wasn't full of dead men. It was full of empty uniforms.

Phaser still in hand, he watched McCoy stooping over a collapsed uniform in the *Exeter*'s engineering section. A scattering of white crystals extended from its neck and sleeves. McCoy, waving him and Spock away, bent closer over the uniform, taking care not to touch it.

Lieutenant Raintree rushed up to him, his face sick. "Just the uniforms . . . all over the ship, Captain! And that . . . white stuff spilling out of them"

Spock said, "As if they'd been in them when. . . ." His words trailed off into silence.

"Exactly," Kirk said. "When *what*?" He spoke to McCoy. "Bones, let's get to the bridge. Mr. Spock can replay the Captain's last log entry. They may have had time to record whatever was happening to them.''

A blue crew uniform was crumpled on the deck beside the computer station. Spock stepped over it to turn on the mechanism. McCoy, his tricorder unslung, was examining the tiny white granules at the end of its sleeves. He lifted his head. ''Jim, analysis says these crystals are thirty-five percent potassium, carbon eighteen percent, phosphorus 1.0 and calcium 1.5.''

''I have the surgeon's report, Captain,'' Spock said. ''It seems to be the log's last—''

McCoy interrupted. ''Jim! The crew hasn't left! They're still here!'' At the look on Kirk's face, he went on. ''This white powder . . . it's what's left of the human body when you remove the water from it. We're all ninety-eight percent water. Take it away, and we're just three or four pounds of chemicals. Something crystallized the chemicals in these people. It reduced them to *this*.''

''So that's it,'' Kirk said slowly. ''At least we can hope it was painless.''

The computer beeped. Activating a switch, Spock pointed to the main viewing screen. ''The name of the *Exeter*'s surgeon, sir, was Carter,'' he said.

The face of a man appeared on the screen—the face of a man in torture. So much for the hope that the deaths had been painless, Kirk thought. That agonized face had possessed a body. He visualized the body dragging itself to the recorder to speak its last words into the Captain's log.

They began in mid-sentence. ''. . . if you've come aboard this ship, you are dead men.'' The voice broke in a spasm of pain. ''Don't return to your own ship. A mutated di-bacto-viro complex of some sort . . . deadly . . . don't know what it is. If you're aboard you're infected—you're already dying.''

Young Lieutenant Raintree whispered, ''My God—let me out of here!''

''Pull yourself together, Lieutenant!'' Kirk snapped. ''This is heroism you're listening to!''

''*Repeat, repeat*,'' said the face on the screen. ''Our landing party brought . . . contamination up from the planet.'' The face convulsed with agony. ''You have one chance . . . some kind of immunity for those living on the planet's surface. Your sole chance, get down there. *Get down there fast.* The Captain is. . . .''

A scream broke from the viewer. It went dark.

After a moment Kirk walked over to the vacant command chair. Carter had sat in it to use the Captain's log recorder. Now all it held was the bodiless clothing that had been his medical officer's uniform. As to the heap of white dust dropped from the clothing—that was Carter.

''Bones,'' he said quietly, ''warn the *Enterprise*. Mr. Spock, the *Exeter*'s Transporter Room. Prepare to beam us all down to the planet.''

They were in an alley of what might have been an old-time American frontier settlement, set on the edge of a desertlike terrain. But the buildings that formed the alley's walls were Asian, their roofs concave, flaring at the eaves. They moved cautiously to the alley's entrance. In the street people had gathered about some object of intense interest. They looked Asian, too. Dark-haired, yellow-skinned, their eyes were slanted by the epicanthic fold characteristic of Oriental races. One of the villagers saw them as they emerged from the alley. He gave a terrified shout. The others turned—and the crowd broke up into a frightened flight.

The object of their interest was an execution. A headsman's block had been set up in the middle of the street. Kneeling at it, his hands thonged behind his back, was a savage-looking white man, his strongly-muscled body clad in skins. Near him stood a young white woman, also wearing savage skins. Horrified, Kirk realized she was awaiting her turn at the block. Instinctively, he and his men rushed forward. The villagers who were holding the white male savage were surprised into loosening him. He rolled aside as the ax flashed down. He tried to sink his teeth into the nearest villager. The ax was lifting again when it was halted by a sharp command.

''Put your ax away, Liyang!''

The voice was familiar. Kirk whirled.

Incredibly, Captain Ronald Tracy of the USS *Exeter* was striding toward him in the well-known uniform of a starship Captain. His pistol-phaser hung at his belt. Nor had he

lost the commanding charisma of the personality Kirk remembered. He was followed by a military guard of young
village men armed with javelins and swords.

"Ron!" Kirk shouted.

"Jim Kirk, by all that's holy!" Tracy said.

There was an odd little pause in which Kirk was
conscious that Tracy was taking stock of the unexpected situation. Then he seemed to have straightened out the inven-
tory. "I knew someone would come looking for us," Tracy
said. "I'm sorry it had to be you, Jim." He shook hands
grimly. "But I'm glad your arrival stopped this. I didn't know
they had an execution going on."

Kirk said, "Captain Tracy. My First Officer, Mr.
Spock; ship's surgeon Leonard McCoy; Lieutenant Phil Raintree."

McCoy said, "Captain Tracy, the last log records
aboard your vessel warned of a mutated disease."

"You're all safe," Tracy said. "Some form of immunity exists on the surface here." He turned to a robust guard
behind him. "No more of this, Wu. Lock up the savage."

Wu pointed to Kirk's phaser. "They carry fireboxes—"

"*Lock up the savage!*" Tracy said.

It took more than Tracy's military guard group to
subdue the still-bound white man. Before he was led away,
several villagers had to be told to assist them. It was a rough
assistance. Tracy noted Spock's cocked eyebrow. "The white
beasts are called Yangs," he said casually. "Impossible to
even communicate with them. Hordes of them out there;
they'll attack anything that moves."

"Interesting," Spock said. "The villagers know what
phasers are."

Tracy glanced at him sharply. "You're a Vulcan?"

Spock nodded. "By one-half, Captain."

Was Tracy disturbed by the information? Kirk broke
the moment of curious tension. "How were you left alone
down here? What happened?"

Tracy's answer came with obvious effort. "Our med-
iscanners showed the planet as perfectly safe. The villagers,
the Kohms here, were friendly. That is, they were after they
got over the shock of our white skins. We resemble the

Yangs—the savages. When my landing party transported back to the ship, I stayed behind to arrange our planet survey with the village elders.'' He paused, struggling back to control. ''The next thing I knew, the ship was calling me. Our landing party had carried an unknown disease back.''

He stopped to avoid an open break in his voice.

''My crew, Jim. My whole crew . . . people I knew, people who . . .''

He straightened his shoulders but couldn't go on. Kirk, sharing his torture, said, ''We saw it, Ron.''

''I . . . am as infected as they were . . . as *you* are. I stayed alive only because I stayed down here. There's some natural immunization that protects anyone here on the planet's surface. I don't know what it is yet.''

McCoy spoke to Kirk. ''Lucky we found that log report. If we had returned to the *Enterprise* . . .''

Tracy completed the sentence. ''. . . you'd be dying by now along with the whole *Enterprise* crew. You'll stay alive only so long as you stay here. None of us can ever leave this planet.''

They had half-suspected it—but hearing it finally put into words chilled them. Being marooned on Omega IV for the rest of their lives could well be a fate as empty as death. Kirk, aware of his men's somber faces, said, ''Then we'll have to make the best we can of this planet. Can this place provide us with any quarters?''

''They're being prepared,'' Tracy said. ''Wu will show Doctor McCoy and the Lieutenant to theirs. Doctor, yours can accommodate any equipment you want beamed down to you. I apologize, Jim. Your quarters and Mr. Spock's aren't ready. So if you two will follow me . . .''

He led them to a building that clearly served the more prosperous villagers as a kind of clubhouse. Its large central room featured a charcoal brazier. Richly dressed men sat at tables eating strips of meat broiled over the brazier. As Tracy entered with his guests, the villagers respectfully moved from their tables to clear a path for them. Two elders hurriedly relinquished the brazier table. At the sight of Kirk, one of the attractive girls who were busy setting the table with fresh dishes dropped a cup.

Tracy beckoned her back. ''They were afraid of me,

too, at first," he said. "It's our white skins; our likeness to the Yangs, the white savages."

He might have been a feudal thane graciously permitting his serfs to sit themselves below the salt in his superior company. No acknowledgement was made of his fellow-diners' nods or spoken greetings. His ease with their excessive deference made Kirk more uncomfortable than the deference. He accepted food from one of the girls; and deliberately ignoring Spock, said to Kirk, "Barbecued wild game. Sort of a long-necked rabbit-antelope."

A meat slice was speared and extended to Kirk. Holding it, he watched another girl rush to fill their crude cups with drink.

"You are treated with a considerable honor by these villagers, Captain," Spock said.

Again, he was ignored. Pointedly, Tracy addressed himself to Kirk. "These Kohm villagers asked for help, Jim. If they ever had any spirit, it's been whipped out of them by the savages."

"Are all the Kohm villages under attack?" Kirk said.

Tracy nodded. "This is one of the last. But before the Yangs began decimating them, they appear to have had quite an advanced civilization. There are ruins of large cities out there."

Spock had taken all the snubs he intended to take. Just as pointedly as Tracy, he ignored the *Exeter*'s Captain to speak directly to Kirk. "Though nomad tribes have been known to destroy advanced civilizations, they rarely trouble an unarmed people—spiritless villagers."

Tracy sprang to his feet, furious. "I will not be questioned by a subordinate!"

Unperturbed, Spock merely eyed him curiously. Kirk's voice had become formal. "Captain Tracy," he said, "I think you're forgetting that Mr. Spock is my First Officer. He holds the rank of Commander in the service."

Spock rose to his feet. "I see no purpose in my causing anger to Captain Tracy," he said politely. "May I remove myself, Captain Kirk?"

Kirk took a sip of his drink. Then he nodded. Spock quickly left the table. As he disappeared, Kirk turned a cold face to Tracy. "Let's clear something up right now, Captain.

I have never had a better 'First' than Mr. Spock—or a better personal friend.''

"You're sentimental, Jim. I've yet to meet a Vulcan capable of friendship. Certainly this one is doing his best to sabotage ours.''

Tracy's ruddy face had grown accusing. "And you know what's in his computer mind, too! It's added up a few scanty observations—and clicked to the conclusion I've violated the Prime Directive! He's got it into his machine head I'm interfering in this culture!''

Kirk said to himself, *Take this easy.* To Tracy he said, "Ron, a First Officer's job *is* to be suspicious." He put a smile on his face. "Saves his Captain from appearing to be the villain.''

"I am a fellow starship Captain," Tracy said.

"Fair enough. So you are. Yet I myself saw the local militia recognize our phasers. They also seem to take orders from you." He hesitated. "I'm not making any charges, believe me. I'm merely asking what goes on.''

Tracy's eyes searched Kirk's. "All right. So long as we're asking questions, I'll put one to you. Suppose you were faced with a horde of incredibly vicious savages you knew were massing for a final attack—one that would erase the last trace of a planet's civilization. And suppose there were enough phasers to repel the attack? Can you imagine the power made available to this Kohm culture by just five phasers?''

"Sure," Kirk said. "Like introduction of the atom bomb to the crossbow era.''

Tracy leaned forward intensely. "Jim . . . within forty-eight hours the Yangs would slaughter every adult and child in this village.''

Kirk found the intensity disturbing. He spoke very quietly. "Ron, every time man interferes with the natural evolvement of another world, he ultimately destroys more than he saves.''

"When they attack, Jim, where do *we* go? There's no place left! You and I are finished, too!''

Kirk said, " 'I solemnly pledge I will abide by these regulations even in death.' " He gave the gravity of the words a long moment before he added, "That is the oath we both took.''

Tracy leaned back in his seat, stretching. "So you'll try to stop me."

"I won't 'try,' Ron. I will stop you."

The sole way to enter McCoy's quarters was to sidle in. The village room he'd been assigned was jammed with medical research instruments beamed down to him from the *Enterprise*. Privately, Kirk wondered if the ship's lab had left itself enough equipment to make a simple blood test. Now, as he wriggled over to the electron microscope, McCoy looked up from the slide he'd been studying.

"Our tissue definitely shows a massive infection, Jim. But something down here *is* immunizing us. Otherwise, we'd have been dead ducks hours ago." He removed the slide, frowning at it. "Problem: it could be anything. Some spore, some immunizing pollen, some chemical in the air. Just finding it could take months, even years."

"Bones, we may not have much time to isolate it."

"I've got only one lead. The infection resembles a virus used during Earth's bacteriological war of the 1990s. Hard to believe the human race was once dumb enough to play with such dangerous bugs."

Spock spoke from the door. "A Yang lance, Doctor. It got the Lieutenant under the shoulder." The Vulcan, his uniform begrimed, was supporting the wounded Raintree, pale with loss of the blood that darkened his uniform's shoulder.

"That mat over there," McCoy said, grabbing his medikit. Raintree was groaning with pain as they settled him on the mat. Kirk eyed Spock. "You all right?"

"Just bruised, sir. We were approximately a hundred meters out of the village when five of the savages ambushed us." Kirk glanced quickly at the phaser hanging from his belt. Noting the look, Spock said, "I subdued them with the neck pinch, Captain. Our phasers were not used."

"Good," Kirk said. "Mr. Spock, do you see any hope that these Yangs can be reasoned with? A peace parley, a truce until. . . ."

Raintree struggled to lift his head from the mat. "No, Captain . . . they're too wild, practically insane."

Nodding, Spock said, "Captain Tracy seems to have established several facts. One—the Yangs' total contempt for

death makes for an incredible viciousness. Two—his statement that the Yangs are massing for attack is valid. There are
signs of thousands of them in the foothills beyond." He
paused to remove two objects from under his shirt. Laying
them on the lab bench, he said, "However, in one important
matter, Captain Tracy is less truthful."

"Phaser power units," Kirk said slowly.

"Yes, sir. Captain Tracy's reserve belt packs. Empty.
Left among the remains of several hundred Yang bodies. A
smaller attack on this village occurred a week ago. It was
repelled by Captain Tracy with his phaser. I've found villagers who corroborate this fact."

Kirk, his face hard, replaced the empty phaser pack on
the bench. McCoy looked up from the wound he was swab-
bing. "Jim . . . he'd lost his ship, his crew. Then he finds
himself the sole bulwark between savages and the massacre
of an entire village of a pleasant, peaceful people. . . ."

Spock said, "Regulations are harsh, Doctor—but they
are also quite clear about any violation of the Prime Directive."

"Without a serum we're all trapped here in this village," McCoy said. "Under these circumstances the question
of arresting the man is a purely academic one."

"I agree that formal charges have little meaning now,"
Spock said. "My suggestion is that Captain Kirk confiscate
his weapon."

"Yes," Kirk said. "And file a report." He reached for
his communicator. "Starfleet should be made aware that—"

"It is I who will send the messages, Jim."

Tracy stood in the doorway, his phaser leveled at them.
On his mat Raintree made a move toward his belt. Tracy fired
the phaser at him. Its beam struck him full in the chest, enveloping him.

Kirk lunged. The deadly phaser swung to point directly
at his heart. He halted. Then he just stood, frozen with shock.
The Captain of a starship . . . a phaser . . . and a wounded
member of the service. He didn't turn to look at the charred
mat which had once held Lieutenant Raintree.

Tracy's militia was efficient. Despite the spears they
used to round up the *Enterprise* trio, they first saw to it that

phasers and communicators were removed. As Wu placed them at Tracy's feet, the *Exeter* Captain opened his own communicator.

"*Enterprise*, come in," he said. "This is Captain Tracy of the *Exeter*."

The satisfaction on Tracy's face told Kirk that Uhura had answered him. Sulu, taking his temporary command very seriously, would be standing beside her at her console.

"I'm afraid I've got some bad news for you," Tracy was telling Uhura. "Your Captain and landing party beamed down too late for full immunization. They've been found unconscious. I'm doing everything I can for them."

Kirk waited, hot rage building up in him. Tracy, smiling at him over the communicator, said, "There'd be no point to risking the lives of additional medical staff, Mr. Sulu. This is a fatal disease. They are courageous to volunteer to beam down. However, as I have acquired some immunity, your people may pull through, too. Meanwhile—"

Kirk had torn free. "*Sulu!*" he shouted. "*Don't let—*"

The butt of Wu's sword crashed down on his head. Dark flooded in over him. Spock had pivoted fast. But Wu was just as fast. He'd placed his sword's point on the unconscious Kirk's throat.

Tracy snapped off the communicator. He pointed to Spock and McCoy. "If those two open their mouths, Wu, kill them."

Tracy's communicator beeped. He flicked it open, listening. "Sorry, Mr. Sulu. All members of your landing party are running high fevers. Captain Kirk is delirious. Nobody is in any condition to speak to you. The villagers are helping me to make them as comfortable as we can."

But the strange Captain's words failed to satisfy an agitated Sulu. Tracy's communicator beeped again. He opened it with irritation. But there was no trace of it in the bland voice that said, "Mr. Sulu, let's have an end to this. *I am trying to save the life of your Captain.* What you heard was not the start of an order to you. It was the cry of a man in delirium. Speak to your medical staff. They will tell you that delirious people shout because they are suffering. I am doing my best to reduce your Captain's. I will keep you informed of his state on condition you permit me to attend to it. Tracy out.''

The vague shadow in the doorway gradually assumed the shape of one of Tracy's militiamen. Kirk discovered that he could see again. McCoy's makeshift lab. His arms hurt. They were bound. He sat up. The head at the doorway didn't turn. Then the hot rage surged through him again, galvanic. Head down, he charged the militiaman guard. He knocked him off balance and was preparing to charge again when Tracy pushed the guard aside with a terse "Leave us!"

Kirk sat down on the bench. In his own ears the scorn in his voice bit like acid. "Captain Ronald Tracy, per Starfleet Command regulation six, paragraph four. I merely mention it.''

The smile he got was as false as the man. He'd hit home.

"I know," Tracy said. " 'You must now consider yourself under arrest unless in the presence of your most senior fellow officers, you give satisfactory answers to etcetera, etcetera, etcetera.' " He nodded. "Those are the first words duty requires you to say to me. Consider them said. You're covered. How about moving on to the next subject?''

"Which is 'why?' " Kirk said.

"Good. Direct, succinct." Moving some of McCoy's equipment aside, Tracy sat down on the lab table. "Answer: whatever it is that's immunizing us now has protected the inhabitants of this place against all sickness. And for thousands of generations. Soon your doctor is going to discover what mine did. *No native of this planet has ever experienced any kind of disease.* How long would a man live with all disease erased, Jim?''

"He might stay young a hundred years, live to be two hundred maybe.''

Tracy went to the door, calling. Wu came in. "Tell Captain Kirk your age," Tracy said.

"I have seen forty-two years of the red bird. But my eldest brother—''

Tracy broke in. "Their year of the red bird comes every eleven years. Wu has seen it forty-two times. You can multiply. Wu is four hundred and sixty-two years old. Or more, since the year here is longer. His father is well over a thousand. Interested, Jim?''

"It's not impossible, I suppose," Kirk said.

"I said . . . *are you interested*?''

"Of course I'm interested! I expect McCoy could verify all this easily enough."

"He will if you order it! We must have a doctor researching this!'' He leaned forward with that special intensity characteristic of him. "Are you grasping *all* this immunizing agent here implies? Once it's located, it is a *fountain of youth*! Virtual immortality!''

"For sale by . . . ?''

Kirk waited for Tracy's nod. He got it.

"For sale by those who own the serum," Tracy said. "McCoy will eventually isolate it. Meanwhile, we inform your ship you're still sick. Order it away. When we're ready, we'll bargain for a whole fleet to pick us up if we want it. They'll send it.''

"Yes, I guess they would," Kirk said.

"In the meantime, we've got to stay alive. Let the Yangs destroy what we've got to offer by killing us—and we've committed a crime against all humanity! I'd say that's slightly more important than the Prime Directive, wouldn't you?''

Kirk had gotten one arm free of his bonds. He came to his feet fast; and was yanking the other one loose when he saw Wu stiffen.

"Tra—cee!'' The militiaman shouted.

Cool, easy, self-assured, Tracy rose from the table. Kirk's right arm was held by the thong just an instant too long. Tracy's expert swing cracked against his jaw, sending him stumbling to his knees. He jerked his right arm clear of the noose. Tracy pulled back for a feinted swing; and Kirk, dodging, exposed his jaw to a judo chop that spun him around. He recovered, lashed out with his right fist—and Tracy, moving with the blow, chopped him again, slamming him to the floor.

"Not bad, Jim," he said. "Considering I'm larger, faster, more experienced than you are, it wasn't bad at all." He yanked Kirk to his feet. "In better shape, too, I fancy. Physical fitness has always been one of my—''

Kirk pivoted, lunging for his chin. Tracy ducked. He lifted his hard hand for another chop. Once more he smashed Kirk to the floor.

This time he didn't pull him to his feet. Instead, he strode to the door to call Wu and two militiamen. Pointing to Kirk, he said, "Bring him!"

They took him to the village jail.

There was a rack of swords in its outer room. That was all Kirk had time to register before he was dragged to the inner area. The cells were fitted, not with bars, but with elaborate grills. The first one held the two Yangs who had escaped execution. The powerful male appeared to be anything but grateful. Snarling with rage, he'd thrust an arm through the grillwork, trying to reach the yellow-skinned militiaman who stood guard at the next cell, which confined Spock and McCoy.

Tracy, his own phaser leveled at Kirk, handed the three *Enterprise* weapons to Wu. "Give these to your men. Tell them we leave soon. This time we'll ambush the Yangs with many fireboxes." He pointed to McCoy. "Have the Doctor taken back to his work place. The one with the pointed ears stays."

McCoy made a protesting move; and Kirk said, "Go ahead, Bones, continue your research."

As McCoy left with Wu, Tracy jerked a thumb toward the Yangs' cell. "And you, Jim, take a close look at that."

The male's eyes were a blue blaze of fury. Yet, taking that good look at him, Kirk discerned a certain stoicism underlying the ferocity—a kind of native dignity that suggested the man was a person of consequence in his tribe. As to the young woman, there was a supple grace even in the way she leaned back against the cell wall, her eyes alert under her shock of unkempt blond hair.

"*Animals* which happen to look like us," Tracy said. "You still believe the Prime Directive's for this planet, Jim?"

Kirk said, "We lack the wisdom to interfere in how this planet is evolving."

Tracy wheeled to his men. "Put him in there! If logic won't work, maybe that will!" They hesitated, incredulous. "Put him in there!" Tracy shouted.

Fearfully they opened the cell door. The Yangs rushed at them. Beating them back with sword and spear butts, two militiamen hastily shoved Kirk inside, slamming shut the heavy iron grating. It was locked and the keys replaced in a table drawer. Kirk faced around to see that the Yangs had begun to circle him like wolves stalking fresh meat.

He addressed the male. "If you understand me—"

A foot smashed against his shin. He tripped—and the Yang was on him, hands at his throat. Instead of fighting the choking fingers, he twisted suddenly; and doubling his legs up, lashed out in a hard kick that caught the man in the midriff. But the blow won him only a moment's respite. The Yang used his crash against the wall to roll into a crouch and begin the stalking again.

Tracy, turning to leave, called, "Remember that Prime Directive, Jim!"

The circling went on as though both Yangs drew on inexhaustible springs of energy. The female, seeing an opening, leaped on Kirk's back; and he had to turn to slam her away, pivoting just in time to fight off the male. Then once more the stalking began.

In his own cell, Spock, pressed against the grilled door, was straining to see into Kirk's. "Don't they ever rest, Spock?" Kirk yelled. His uniform shirt was ripped. And he was becoming aware of diminishing strength. There'd been that black-out from Wu's sword-butt crash on the head. Tracy's judo chops hadn't been so salubrious, either. Now here was the strain of a constant vigilance as these tireless Yangs watched for an off-guard moment. Just five seconds rest . . . He spoke to the Yang. "At least tell me *why* you want to kill me!"

Spock called, "Keep trying to reason with them, Captain. It is completely illogical that they—"

"I am very aware that this is illogical, Mr. Spock!"

The Yang jumped him again. The struggle sent the woman flying against the door's iron lattice. Spock reached an arm out to give her his Vulcan neck pinch. The male paused in amazement as she collapsed. He went to her, trying to shake her awake. Disturbed by his failure, he leaned against the door to peer into Spock's cell.

The Vulcan was at its window, pulling at its ornate

grillwork. Watching, the savage saw him heave his full weight against the iron embedded in the ancient mortar. A thin trickle of crumbled dust fell on the sill. Spock called to Kirk. "I think I've loosened my window grill a bit. If the mortar on yours is as old . . ."

"I can't even test it. Not with them on me every moment."

But the Yang had held off. Kirk eyed him. The woman sprawled at his feet was slowly reviving. Once conscious again, would she incite her mate to resume the stalk? "Keep talking, Spock. Don't let me doze off."

"Captain Tracy mentioned there apparently was a considerable civilization here at one time. A war is the most likely explanation of its ruin, Captain. Nuclear destruction or a bacteriological holocaust."

"An interesting theory," Kirk said. "Better keep working on your window, Spock, if we're ever to regain our freedom."

In the very act of renewed attack, the Yang male froze. "Free-dohm?" he said. He was staring at Kirk with mixed curiosity and awe. "Free-dohm," he repeated.

"Spock!"

"I heard, Captain. Ask him if he knows what it means."

"That is a worship word—*Yang* worship!" cried the savage. *"You will not speak it!"*

Kirk said, "It is *our* worship word, too. Perhaps we are brothers."

"You live with the Kohms!"

"Am I not a prisoner of the Kohms now, like yourself?"

He let it rest there. Moving to the cell window, he began to tug at its grillwork. It was immovable. He flung a shoulder against it—and was rewarded with a small sifting of powdered mortar. The Yang looked at his mate. She rose to her feet, lithe as ever, and they both came over to join him. All three pushed their combined weight at the lattice. More mortar fell; and Kirk, turning to the Yang, said, "Why did you not speak until now?"

"You spoke to Kohms. They are for killing only."

The listening Spock called, "Is your window giving, sir?"

"A little . . . we'll get yours next."

Their following heave broke the grill loose at one corner. Now they had leverage. Twisting and bending the iron, they released its top. The old mortar finally surrendered. It was the Yang who wrenched it free. Smiling, Kirk turned his head toward Spock's cell, calling, "Stand by, Mr. Spock. We'll have you out in—"

"Captain!" Spock yelled.

The warning came too late. The heavy grill had caught Kirk on the temple, felling him, unconscious, to the floor.

The Yang shoved his mate through the open window. Spock saw him hoist himself up to the sill, and disappear.

"Captain?"

Spock, crouched at his cell door, tried to reach the unmoving body of Kirk. But it had fallen under the open window at the other side of the cell.

The recovery of consciousness came slower this time. Finally, hearing Kirk move, Spock left his cell window to hurry to its door.

"Captain?"

"Spock? How long?"

"About seven hours, sir."

Seven hours out . . . a rest of sorts. Blood had dried on Kirk's face. Trying to move, he winced at the tide of pain that washed over him. The iron lattice lay beside him. He used its support to get groggily to his feet. Over his head the open window gaped. Stumbling, he put the grill at a slant under the window. Then he climbed it, hauling himself the shortened distance up to the sill. In the alley outside, he located the jail's rear door. It opened; and he hurried to the table drawer where the cells' keys had been placed.

It was Spock who discovered that Tracy had placed a guard in McCoy's quarters. The man stiffened at the scratching noise that came from the door. McCoy, oblivious to everything but his portable computer, didn't so much as look up. When the scratching came again, the guard carefully opened the door. He literally stuck his neck out for Spock's Vulcan pinch. He folded, dropping his sword. Spock had him dragged inside the room before McCoy looked up to register a world beyond his computer.

"Oh . . . Jim," he said. "Good morning."

Spock, eyeing the lab equipment, saw an instrument that might lend itself to conversion into a communications signaler.

"I can cross-circuit this unit, Captain. We can contact the *Enterprise* in a few moments."

"Bones," Kirk said, "what have you found?"

"I'm convinced now that there was once a frightful biological war. The virus still exists. The crew of the *Exeter* was killed by it; we contracted it, too. But over the years nature has built up immunizing agents in the food, water, soil. . . ."

Spock, busy with tools, observed, "The war created an imbalance: nature counterbalanced."

McCoy nodded. "These natural immunizers just need time to work. That's the real tragedy. If the *Exeter* landing party had stayed here just a few hours longer, they never would have died."

Taking in the statement's implications, Kirk said, "Then we can leave any time we want to?"

McCoy nodded again. Kirk's face lightened with his first grin in a long time. Then it disappeared. "Tracy," he said, "is convinced this immunizing agent could become a fountain of youth. Isolate it, make a serum, inject it into others."

"Poppycock!" McCoy snorted.

"Bones, some of them here live to be a thousand years old."

"Possible. Because their ancestors who survived had to have superior resistance. And they developed powerful protective antibodies in their blood during the wars. You want to destroy a whole world, maybe your descendants can develop a longer life—but I hardly think it's worth it."

"Then any serum you develop out of this is useless."

McCoy shrugged. "Who knows? It might finally cure the common cold. But lengthen our lives? I can do more for you if you'd eat right and exercise regularly."

Over at the corner bench where he'd been working on the lab instrument, Spock made some final adjustment; and looked up to say, "Somewhat crude, Captain, but I can signal the ship with this. No voice contact possible, of course."

"That will be quite sufficient, Mr. Spock." Kirk was moving toward the bench when the signaler in Spock's hand glowed red under the brilliant beam of a phaser. It disappeared—and Spock was slammed violently backward, grazed by the fierce energy in the scorching beam.

Tracy, his uniform spattered with blood, was leaning against the doorframe, disheveled, wild-eyed. He lowered the phaser. "No messages," he said. He glanced around the room. "Kirk, the Yang in the cell with you. Did you set him free?"

Kirk ignored him to join McCoy, who was kneeling beside the wounded Spock. "Alive at least," McCoy said briefly.

"The savage, Kirk! Did you send him to warn the tribes?"

Kirk looking up, saw that Tracy was badly shaken. "What happened?" he said. "Where are your men?"

"The Yangs must have been warned. They sacrificed hundreds just to draw out into the open. Then they came . . . and came . . . and came." His voice trembled. *"We drained three of our four phasers and they still came! We killed thousands and they still came!"*

Tracy became suddenly aware that he was shouting. He made a visible effort to control himself, and McCoy, intent on Spock, said, "He'll live. But I'll have to get him to better facilities than these."

"Impossible," Tracy said. "You can't carry the disease back up to your ship."

"He's fully immunized now," McCoy told him. "All of us are!"

"We can beam up any time, Tracy," Kirk said. "Any of us."

"You've isolated the serum?"

"There *is* no serum!" Kirk said. "There are no miracles here—no immortality! All this has been for *nothing*!"

Tracy stared at him, dumbfounded. Then, unbelieving, he looked at McCoy. "Explain to me, Doctor! *Explain!*"

"Leave medicine to medical men, Captain!" McCoy

snapped. "You've found no fountain of youth! They live longer here because it is now natural for them to live longer!"

Color drained from Tracy's face. Even the cuts on it had gone pale. He raised his phaser, motioning Kirk to the door with it. "Outside," he said. "Or I'll burn down both your friends now."

He'd do it, too, Kirk knew. "Do what you can for him, Bones," he said and walked to the door.

The frightened villagers had left the street empty.

Tracy, phaser pointed at Kirk, tossed him a communicator. "Let's see how willing you are to die," he said. "Call your ship!"

Silent, Kirk looked at the communicator. "I need your help, Kirk!" Tracy cried. "They'll attack the village now! My phaser is almost drained; we need more, fresh ones."

So that was it. The *Enterprise* was to get into the weapon-smuggling business to accommodate this madman. At the look on Kirk's face, Tracy shouted, *"You're not just going to stand there and let them kill you, are you? If I put a weapon in your hand, you'll fight, won't you?"*

Reason, sanity. Was Tracy any longer capable of either one? Kirk said, "We can beam back up to the ship. All of us."

"I want five phasers . . . no, make it ten. Three extra power packs each."

"All right," Kirk said. The phaser lifted and aimed at him as Tracy waited. Kirk clicked the communicator open.

"*Enterprise*, this is Captain Kirk."

He could hear the relief in Uhura's voice. "Captain! Are you all right now?"

"Quite all right, Lieutenant. I want ten phasers beamed down, three extra power packs each. Do you have that?"

Uhura didn't answer. "Say again!" Tracy said.

"*Enterprise*, do you read?"

Sulu's voice spoke. "This is Sulu, Captain. We read you—but surely you know that can't be done without verification."

"Not even if we're in danger, Mr. Sulu?"

A good man, Sulu. And smart. "Captain, we have volunteers standing by to beam down. What is your situation?"

Tracy made an impatient gesture.

"It's not an immediate danger, Mr. Sulu. Stand by on the volunteers. We'll let you know. Landing party out."

Kirk snapped off the communicator. Tracy nodded in a begrudged approval. "You have a well trained bridge crew. My compliments." He extended his hand for the communicator. It was the chance Kirk had been waiting for. He grabbed the hand, twisted it; and lashing out with his fist, knocked Tracy off balance, reaching for the phaser. But Tracy eluded the reach and, rolling with the blow, came back with the weapon at the ready. As Kirk dived around a building corner, he fired it. The beam struck a rainbarrel—and the chase began.

The dash around the building corner put Kirk in an alley he recognized. It was the one that passed the jail's cellblock. Racing by a Kohm cart, he made for the jail. Behind him, Tracy leaned against the cart, kneeling to aim at Kirk's back. But his weight was too heavy for the flimsy cart. Its rear wheel collapsed. Kirk ran on. He jumped into cover through the jail's rear door. He was barely inside when a phaser beam blasted a porch support. He heard the porch crash down.

The iron lattice that had felled him—it would still be in his cell. He found it. Not much use against a phaser, but it was all he had. Opposite the jail's front door was the execution block. As he emerged from the door he saw Tracy standing beside it. The phaser came up. Tracy fired it point blank. Nothing happened. Tracy stared at the drained phaser. Then, flinging it aside, he grabbed up the executioner's ax. He charged Kirk, taking a murderous swing at him. Kirk ducked and slammed the iron lattice into his middle. Tracy fell, but kicking out, tripped Kirk; and the two closed, grappling in the dirt.

Tracy had kneed him in the groin when he gave a cry. The point of a spear had pricked his shoulder. Both men looked up. The Yang stood over them. Behind him were ranged other armed white savages.

The brazier had been removed from the central table in the villagers' clubhouse. Now it held a worn parchment document, some ancient-looking books and Tracy's communicator. The whole interior of the room had been altered into what Kirk could only consider to be a primitive court scene. White savages composed the "jury." Among the men Kirk saw the young woman from the jail cell. He, Spock, McCoy and Tracy had been seated to the left of the table.

The male Yang of the jail cell strode to the seat behind the table.

He looked at Kirk. "My name," he said, "is Cloud William." Then he looked away to nod at one of his warriors guarding the door. A procession of Kohm Elders were herded into the room and up to the table. Kirk looked anxiously at the stiff figure of Spock. "I am weak, Captain, but not in difficulty."

McCoy leaned over to Kirk. "He *must* have attention, Jim! And soon."

Spock indicated the Kohms. "Prisoners, Captain. It seems they like killing less than we thought."

Kirk glanced around at the rough courtlike arrangements. "If my ancestors had been forced from their cities into deserts, the hills . . ."

"Yes, Captain," Spock said. "They would have learned to wear animal skins, adopted stoic mannerisms, devised the bow and the lance."

"Living much like Indians . . . and finally even looking like the American Indians." He paused, startled by his own sudden idea. "Spock! Yangs . . . yanks . . . Yankees! Is it possible?"

Spock nodded. "Kohms . . . kohmunists. Almost too close a parallel, Captain. It would mean they fought the war you avoided and here the Asiatics won, took over the Western world."

"And yet if that were true, Spock, all these generations of Yanks fighting to win back their land . . ."

"You're a romantic, Jim," McCoy said.

He sat back in his chair. Yang warriors were pushing their Kohm prisoners into attitudes of respect. The crash of a drumbeat's ceremonial tattoo silenced the room. Proud and tall, Cloud William rose from his seat behind the table.

"That which is ours is ours again! It will never be taken from us again." He pointed to the rear door and a steady drumbeat throbbed. *"For this day we mark with the great Ay Pledgili Holy!"*

Turning to look, Kirk, Spock and McCoy stiffened in unbelieving amazement. The door had opened. A guard—an honor guard—had entered. One carried a staff. From it hung an incredibly old and tattered flag, its red, white and blue faded by time. But its stars and its stripes had outlasted the centuries' ravages. They had triumphed over time.

Kirk, watching the flag proudly planted in its stand at the front of the room, felt his blood chill with awe.

Tracy whispered, "The American flag!"

Kirk turned to Spock. "After so long, I wonder if they really understand what they were fighting for."

"I doubt it, Captain. Some customs remain, but most of them would have become only traditions by now."

"And ritual," McCoy said. "The flag was called a 'holy.' "

Tracy said, "They can be handled, Kirk. Together, it will be easy." He leaned toward the three of them. "I caution you, gentlemen, don't fight me here. I'll win—or at worst, I'll drag you down with—"

He was silenced by a nudge from a spear. Cloud William was speaking. "I, Cloud William, am chief, also the son of chief, Guardian of the holies, Speaker of holy words, leader of warriors. Many have died; but this is the last of the Kohm places. What is ours is ours again."

The words were repeated by the crowd. "What is ours is ours again!"

Cloud William placed his right hand over his heart. "You will say these holy words after me." The Yang guards placed the Kohm prisoners' right hands over their hearts. Cloud William turned to the old flag. "You will all say Ay pledgli ianectu flaggen tupep likfor stahn . . ."

Kirk sprang to his feet. ". . . and to the republic for which it stands. One nation, under God, indivisible, with liberty and justice for all!"

The room exploded in shouts. A guard, moving to Kirk, halted in shock.

Cloud William was in quiet but agitated conversation with an aged savage at his table. The old man, shaking his head, referred to one of the yellowed books on it. Guards were removing the Kohm prisoners from the room. Two warriors, uneasy and uncertain, moved toward Kirk. One motioned him to face the Yang chief.

The chief was rapping the butt of his knife on the table to quiet the room.

"You know many of our high-worship words. How?"

Kirk said, "In my land we have a—a *tribe* like you."

"Where is your tribe?"

Kirk pointed upward. "We come from there. From one of those points of light you see at night."

Uproar broke out again. Kirk tried to go on but his words were drowned by the noise. Cloud William rapped for quiet once more. He turned to nod at the old Yang scholar beside him. The still-keen eyes fixed on Kirk. "Why are you here? Were you cast out?"

The Yang jury waited for his answer. Kirk spoke carefully. "You are confusing the stars with 'heaven' from which—"

"*He was cast out!*" Tracy shouted.

He jumped from his chair to confront the jury. "Don't you recognize the Evil One? Who else would trick you with your own sacred words? Let your God strike me dead if I lie!" He looked upward. "But He won't because I speak for Him!"

The brutal murder of Raintree . . . the betrayal of his service oath . . . now this exploitation of ignorance and superstition. He should have known, Kirk thought. To further his purpose there was nothing that Tracy would not do. But the old Yang scholar had hurriedly opened a thick, black book.

Cloud William was studying Tracy. "Yet you have killed many Yangs," he said.

"To punish them. You would not listen when I tried to speak with you. *You* tried to kill *me*."

Kirk said, "I am a man like yourself. I am not God. I am not the Evil One."

"Would a *man* know your holy words?" cried Tracy. "Could a *man* use them to trick you?" He extended a dramatic finger at Spock. "And see his servant! His face, his ears, his eyes! Do Yang legends describe the Evil One?"

Kirk turned to the tribunal. "Do all *your* faces look

alike? Can you tell from them which of you is good and which is bad?''

The old scholar had pushed the black book before the chief. Cloud William lifted it to kiss it reverently before he opened it. Kirk saw that its worn gold-lettered title was still legible. It read ''Holy Bible.'' A wrinkled hand extended a finger to point to a page.

Many old Bibles contained illustrations. If this one pictured drawings of Lucifer's aides, one of them might bear some resemblance to Spock. One apparently did. Cloud William looked at Spock. Then he looked back at Kirk.

''You command the demon,'' Tracy said to Kirk. ''Everyone has seen it.'' He wheeled to the chief. ''You want more proof? The demon has no heart! Put your ear to him!''

Guards had seized Spock. The chief left the table.

McCoy cried, ''His heart is different! The Vulcan internal organs are—''

''I have seen his sorcery,'' said Cloud William. He fingered the back of his neck. ''When he touched my woman there, she fell into sleep.'' He crossed to Spock and solemnly placed his ear against the Science Officer's chest. Listening, a frown began to gather on his forehead. He straightened up. ''He has no heart.''

The room burst into terrified yells. They subsided as Cloud William raised his right arm. Then he hurried back to his ancient mentor. ''There is a way,'' he was told. Painfully, the aged scholar moved to a large ornate box at the end of the table. Cloud William nodded in obvious relief.

''The greatest of holies,'' he said. ''Chiefs and the sons of chiefs may speak the words . . . but the tongue of the Evil One would surely turn to fire.'' He looked straight at Kirk and Tracy. ''I will begin and you will finish.'' He closed his eyes, chanting, ''Ee'd pebnista nordor formor fektunun . . .''

His lids lifted. He waited.

There was something unplaceable but familiar in the chanted words. As Kirk struggled to identify them, Tracy cried out, ''He fears to speak them for indeed his tongue would burn with fire! Kill his servant unless he speaks, so we may see if the words burn him!''

A Yang knife was poised at Spock's abdomen. The clamor for blood turned the room into bedlam. Cloud William, his face deeply troubled, had given the signal for the knife plunge when Kirk shouted, "No! Wait! There's a better way! Your sacred book, does it not promise good is stronger than evil?"

"Captain . . ." But over Spock's protest rang out the voice of the young Yang woman of the jail cell. "Yes, it is so written! Good will always destroy evil!"

"It is written," said the old scholar.

The guards had bound both Kirk and Tracy. Now a Yang warrior cut their thongs. The room had been cleared of furniture. In its central space Cloud William drove two razor-sharp knives into the floorboards. Kirk tried to rub circulation back into his numbed hands.

"Careful, Jim," McCoy said. "I've found Evil usually triumphs unless Good is very, very careful."

Kirk nodded wordlessly. He walked over to where the two knives thrust upward from the flooring.

"The fight is done when one is dead," Cloud William said. Lifting his arm, he dropped it swiftly, shouting, "Hola!"

Tracy was the first to reach his knife. He shoulder-butted Kirk aside and kicked his knife away. Then he lunged, knife raised. Kirk met him and, seizing his wrist, immobilized the down-thrust. They locked in a wrestle, straining against each other for an opening.

McCoy muttered, "We've got to do something, Spock."

Spock strove with his bound hands. "I am open to suggestions, Doctor."

Kirk broke free. He got a hammerlock on Tracy; but the *Exeter* Captain, wriggling himself out of it, was carried away by the momentum of his own move. Kirk stooped and scooped up his knife. The two began a wary circling of each other.

Spock suddenly became conscious of eyes. They belonged to Cloud William's young woman. He saw a tremor pass over her as their eyes locked. Half-fascinated, half-repelled, she tore her gaze from his. Then she looked at him again. He beckoned her toward him with his head. McCoy saw the gesture. "What are you doing?" he said.

"Making suggestions," Spock said.

Tracy had nicked Kirk. As he withdrew his knife, Kirk drove at him with a swift thrust; but Tracy parried the slash and the young woman, unnoticed, began to make her way through the shouting warriors. Edging along the wall, she reached the table that sill held the old documents, the books and the communicator. She paused, glancing back at the two fighting men. Tracy's knife flashed out, cutting Kirk's sleeve and arm. Blood dripped to the floor. But the young woman had the communicator. Holding it so that it couldn't be seen, she moved toward Spock and McCoy. Spock looked up at her. "Do as my mind instructs you, woman," he said.

"I obey," she said.

Kirk was losing the fight. His shoulder was slashed now and the crowd howled for more blood. Then Tracy finally made his mistake. Caught off guard by a feint from Kirk, he stumbled. Kirk hauled back—and landed a blow that spun Tracy around and down. Kirk was on him, his knife at his throat. He held it there, his left hand reaching for Tracy's weapon. He wrenched it from him and sent it skidding across the floor to Cloud William's feet. A sudden silence fell over the room.

"Kill him," Cloud William said. "It is written Good must destroy Evil."

Kirk lifted the knife from Tracy's throat, rose to his feet and was backing away when he heard a familiar hum in the stillness. He whirled. Sulu and two Security guards had sparkled into shape beside him. Around the room Yang warriors were dropping to their knees. At stiff attention Sulu said, "Sir, we picked up a communicator signal but we couldn't raise anyone. Adding that to—"

"We'll discuss it later, Lieutenant. Put Captain Tracy under arrest. Now, Cloud William . . ."

The Yang chief had crawled to his feet. "You are a great God servant, and we shall be your slaves."

Kirk reached down, lifting him to his feet. "Get up! Stand and face me."

"When you would not say the words of the holy Ee'd Pebnista, I doubted you."

Kirk said, "I did not recognize the words because you say them badly . . . without meaning."

The old Yang scholar had lifted the ornate box high in the air. Kirk approached him and gently removed it. He opened it, took out a ragged fragment of ancient parchment. Aghast, the old man cried, "Only the eyes of a chief may see the Ee'd Pebnista!"

"This was not written for chiefs." Kirk turned. "Hear this, Cloud William. This is *your* world. But perhaps without violating *our* laws, we can teach you what your fathers meant by these words."

He raised the tattered parchment so that all could see it. "Among my people, we carry many such words as this, from many lands, from many worlds. Many are equally good and well respected. But wherever we have gone, there are no words which have ever said this thing of importance in quite this way. Look at these three words written larger than all the others and with a special pride never written before or since . . . in tall words, proudly saying . . ." He paused.

"We the people . . ."

He faced Cloud William. "What you call the Ee'd Pebnista was not for chiefs or kings or warriors or the rich and powerful . . . but for all people. Over the centuries you have slurred the meaning out of the words. They are these. . . ."

Reading from the parchment, he spoke slowly and clearly. "*We . . . the . . . people . . .* of the United States . . . in order to form a more perfect union, to establish justice, insure domestic tranquility, provide for the common defense, promote the general welfare, and secure the blessings of liberty to ourselves and our posterity—do ordain and establish this Constitution."

He reverently restored the parchment to the box. "Those words," he said, "and the words that follow were not meant only for Yangs. They were for Kohms also."

"For Kohms?" repeated Cloud William, shocked.

"They must apply to everyone—or they mean nothing. Do you understand?"

"I do not fully understand, one named Kirk. But the Holy words will be obeyed. I swear it."

Kirk left him to address Sulu. "You and your men will have to stay a few days until your bodies pick up immunization and adjust."

Sulu grinned. "Looks like an interesting place, Captain. You don't suppose there's a Shanghai or Tokyo down here, too?''

"There might be at that," Kirk told him. He clicked open the communicator Spock handed him. "Kirk to *Enterprise*, four to Transport."

"We're locking in on you, Captain," Uhura said.

Kirk, Spock and McCoy, Tracy between them, moved together for upbeam.

As they broke into dazzle, Kirk turned for a last look at the old flag upright in its standard, its stars and its stripes still bright.

ASSIGNMENT: EARTH

Writer: Art Wallace (Story by Gene Roddenberry and
  Art Wallace)
Director: Marc Daniels
Guest stars: Robert Lansing, Terri Garr

Kirk viewed the conversion—however temporary and partial—of the *Enterprise* into a time machine with considerable misgivings. He had to recognize, of course, that an occasional assignment of this kind had become inevitable, the moment the laboratory types had had a chance to investigate the reports of the time-travel he, Spock and McCoy had been subjected to from the City on the edge of Forever, and the time-warp the whole ship had run into when it had hit the black star.

But these two experiences had only made him more acutely aware of the special danger of time-travel: the danger that the tiniest of false moves could change the future—or what was for Kirk the present—and in the process wipe out Kirk, the *Enterprise*, the Federation itself. Hovering in orbit above the Earth of 1969, even in hiding behind deflector screens, was a hair-trigger situation.

For that matter, that was why they were here, for 1969 had been a hair-trigger year. In Kirk's time, nobody really understood how the Earth had survived it. In the terrible scramble with which the year had ended, crucial documents had been lost; still others, it was strongly suspected, had been falsified. And it was not just the historians, but the Federation itself, that wanted to know the answers. They were possibly of military as well as political interest, and in a galaxy that contained the Klingon Empire as well as the Federation, they might be a good deal more than interesting.

Which explained the vast expense of sending a whole

starship back in time to monitor Earth communications. Nevertheless . . .

His musings were interrupted by a faint but unmistakable shuddering of the deck of the bridge beneath his feet. What on Earth . . .

"Alert status," he snapped. "Force shields maximum. Begin sensor scan. Any station with information, report."

Immediately the telltale light for the Transporter Room went on and Kirk flipped the intercom switch.

"Spock here, Captain. We are having transporter trouble; Mr. Scott just called me down to help."

"You shouldn't be using the transporter at all!"

"Nobody was, Captain. It went on by itself and we find we cannot shut it off. We seem accidentally to have intercepted someone else's transporter beam—and one a great deal more powerful than ours."

"Mr. Spock, you know as well as I do that the twentieth century had no such device—" Again he was interrupted by the faint shudder. Spock's voice came back urgently:

"Nevertheless, Captain, someone—or something—is beaming aboard this vessel."

"I'll be right down."

In the Transporter Room, Kirk found the situation as reported. All circuits were locked open; nothing Spock or Scott could do would close them. The familiar shimmering effect was already beginning in the transporter chamber.

"For all its power," Spock said, "that beam is originating at least a thousand light years away."

"Which," Scott added, "is a good deal farther than any transporter beam of our *own* century could reach."

The ship shuddered again, more strongly than before. "Stop fighting it," Kirk said quietly. "Set up our own field for it and let it through. Obviously we'll have serious damage otherwise."

"Aye, sir," Scott said. He worked quickly.

The shimmering grew swiftly in brightness. A haze form appeared in it, and gradually took on solidity. Kirk stared, his jaw dropped.

The figure they had pulled in from incredibly deep space was that of a man impeccably dressed in a twentieth-century business suit. Nor was this all: in his arms he carried a sleek black cat, wearing a necklace collar of glittering white stones.

"Security detail," Kirk said. "On the double."

The stranger seemed as startled as Kirk was. He looked about the Transporter Room in baffled anger, rubbing the huge cat soothingly. The exotic element in no way detracted from his obvious personal force; he was tall, rugged, vital.

"Why have you intercepted me?" he said at once. "Please identify yourselves."

"You're aboard the United Spaceship *Enterprise*. I am Captain James Kirk, commanding."

The black cat made a strange sound, rather like one of the many odd noises a Siamese cat can make, and yet somehow also not catlike at all.

"I hear it, Isis," the stranger said. "A space vessel. But from what planet?"

"Earth."

"Impossible! At the present time Earth has no—" his voice trailed off as he became aware of Spock. Then, "Humans with a Vulcan! No wonder! You're from the future!"

He dropped the cat and reached for the control panel in the transporter chamber. "You must beam me down onto Earth immediately. There's not a moment to . . ."

The doors to the Transporter Room snapped open, admitting the ship's security chief and a guard, phasers drawn. At the sight of the weapons the strange man froze. The cat crouched as if for a spring, but the man said instantly, "Careful, Isis. Please listen to me carefully, all of you. My name is Gary Seven. I am a human being of the Twentieth Century. I have been living on another planet, far more advanced than the Earth is. I was beaming from there when you intercepted me."

"Where is the planet?" Kirk said.

"They wish their existence kept secret. In fact, it will remain unknown even in your time."

"It's impossible to hide a whole planet," Scott said.

"Impossible to you; not to them. Captain Kirk, I am of this time period. You are not. Interfere with me, and with what I must do down there, and you will change history. I am sure you have been thoroughly briefed on the consequence of that."

"I have," Kirk said. "On the other hand, I know nothing about you—even about the truth of anything you've told me."

"We don't have time for that. Every second you delay me is dangerous—this is the most critical year in Earth's history. My planet wants to ensure that Earth survives—an aim which should be of no small interest to you."

Kirk shook his head. "The fact that you know the criticality of the year strongly suggests that you're from the future yourself. It's a risk I can't take until I have more information. I'm afraid I'm going to have to put you in security confinement for the time being."

"You'll regret it."

"Very possibly. Nevertheless, it's what I must do." He gestured to the security chief. The guard bent to pick up the cat, but Gary Seven stepped in his way.

"If you handle Isis," he said, "you will regret *that* even more." He scooped up the cat himself and went out with the security detail.

"I want a special eye kept on that man," Kirk said. "He went along far too docilely. Also, Mr. Spock, ask Dr. McCoy for a fast medical analysis of the prisoner. What I want to know is, is he human? And have the cat checked, too. It may tell us something further about Mr. Seven."

"It seems remarkably intelligent," Spock commented. "As well as strikingly beautiful. All the same, a strange companion to be carrying across a thousand light years on what is supposed to be an urgent mission."

"Exactly. Scotty, could that beam of his have carried him through time as well as space?"

"The theory has always indicated that it's possible," Scott said, "but *we've* never been able to manage it. On the other hand, we've never been able to put that much power into a transporter beam."

"In short, you don't know."

"That's right, sir."

"Very well. See if you can put the machinery back in order. Mr. Spock, please give the necessary orders and then join me on the bridge. We are going to need *lots* of computation."

* * *

The computer said: "Present Earth crises fill an entire tape bank, Captain Kirk. The being Gary Seven could be intervening for *or* against Earth in areas of overpopulation, bush wars, revolutions, critically dangerous bacteriological experiments, various emergent hate movements, rising air and water pollution . . ."

"All right, stop," Kirk said. "What specific events are going on today?"

"Excuse me, Captain," Spock said, "but that question will simply open another floodgate. There were half a hundred critical things going on almost every day during 1969. Library, give us the three most heavily weighted of today's events in the danger file."

"There will be an important assassination today," the computer said promptly in its pleasant feminine voice. "An equally dangerous government coup in Asia Minor; and the launching of an orbital nuclear warhead platform by the United States countering a similar launch by a consortium of other powers."

Kirk whistled. "Orbital nuclear devices were one of the greatest worries of this era, as I recall."

"They were," Spock agreed. "Once the sky was full of orbiting H-bombs, the slightest miscalculation could have brought one of them accidentally down and set off a holocaust."

"Sick bay to bridge," the intercom interrupted.

"Kirk here. What is it, Bones?"

"Jim, there isn't any prisoner in the brig. All I found there were the security chief and one guard, both of them acting as if they'd been hypnotized."

"The Transporter Room!" Kirk shouted. "Quick!"

But they were too late. There was nobody in the Transporter Room but a dazed Chief Engineer, and, a moment later, McCoy.

"I was working with my head inside an open panel," Scott said, his voice still a little blurred, "when I heard someone come in. I turned and saw him with the cat under one arm and a thing like a writing stylus pointed at me."

"A miniaturized stunner, no doubt," McCoy said.

"Well, the next thing I knew, I was willing to do anything he asked me to. In fact I beamed him down to Earth myself. Somewhere in the back of my mind I knew I shouldn't, but I did it anyhow.''

There was a brief silence.

"And so," Spock said at last, "human or alien, contemporary or future, he has gone to do what he came to do—and we still have no idea what it is."

"We are going to find out," Kirk said. "Scotty, where did you beam him to?"

"That I can't say, Captain. He set the coordinates himself, and put the recorder on wipe. I can give you an estimate, within about a thousand square meters."

"If Spock and I beam down, working from the power consumption data alone, inside that thousand square meters, can you triangulate?"

"Aye, I can do that," Scott said. "It still won't be very precise, but it ought at least to bring you within sighting distance of the man—or whatever he is."

"It is also a major risk to history, Captain," Spock said.

"Which is just why I want you and me to be the ones to go; we had had experience with this kind of operation before. We can't find any answers sitting up here. Have ship's stores prepare proper costumes. Scotty, stand by to beam us down."

The spot where they materialized was a street on New York's upper East Side, not far from the canopied entrance of an elegant apartment building. It was a cold winter day, although there was no snow.

"All right, Scotty," Kirk said into his communicator. "Lock in and check."

"Correlated," Scott's voice said. "Readings indicate greater altitude—approximately thirty meters higher."

Kirk looked speculatively up the face of the building. Once they entered a maze like that, they might pass within whispering distance of their quarry, behind some door, and never know it.

Nevertheless, they went into the lobby, found an elevator, and went up. At the prescribed heights, they stepped out into a hallway. Nothing but doors.

"Altitude verified, Captain," Scott's voice said. "Proceed forty-one meters, two-four-seven degrees true."

This maneuver wound them up in front of one of the doors, in no way different from any of the others. Kirk and Spock looked at each other. Then Kirk shrugged and pushed the doorbell button, which responded with a melodious chime.

The door was opened by a pretty blonde girl in her early twenties. Kirk and Spock went in, fast.

"Hey, what do you think you're doing?" the girl demanded. "You can't come breaking in . . ."

"Where's Mr. Seven?" Kirk said sharply.

"I don't know who you're talking about!"

Kirk looked around. It was an ordinary Twentieth-Century living room as far as he could see, though perhaps somewhat on the sumptuous side. There was a closed door at the back. Spock pulled out his tricorder and scanned quickly, then pointed at the closed door. "In there, Captain."

They rushed the door, but it was locked. As they tried to voice in, Kirk heard an unfamiliar, brief whirring sound behind him, and then the girl's voice, all in a rush: "Operator, 811 East 68th Street, Apartment 1212, send the police . . ."

Kirk whirled and snatched the phone out of her hand. "No nonsense, Miss. Spock, burn the door open."

The girl gasped as Spock produced his phaser and burned out the entire knob and lock assembly. They rushed in, forcing the girl to come with them.

Here was another large room, also elegantly furnished. One wall was book-lined from a point about a meter from the floor to an equivalent distance from the ceiling. Under a large window was a heavy, ornate desk.

There was no sign of Gary Seven or anybody else. Kirk noted that this seemed to surprise the girl as much as it did himself.

Spock went to the desk, where there was a scatter of papers.

"I'm warning you," the girl said, "I've already called the police."

"Where is Mr. Seven?" Kirk demanded again.

"Spock, is she Twentieth Century? Or one of Seven's people?"

"Only Doctor McCoy could establish that, I'm afraid, Captain. But I think you will find these papers interesting. They are plans of the United States government's McKinley Rocket Base."

"Aha. So the orbital platform launching *is* the critical event. Now how long do we . . ."

The doorbell rang. The girl, catching them off guard, dashed for the door. Both men raced after her, Kirk reaching her first. As he grabbed her, she bit his hand, and then screamed.

"Open up in there!" a male voice shouted in the hallway outside. "Police!" Then the door shook to a heavy blow.

Spock too seized the girl. Kirk managed to get his communicator back into play. "Kirk to *Enterprise*. Wide scan, Scotty, we'll be moving. Now!"

Another blow on the door, which burst open. Two policemen lunged in, guns drawn. Spock propelled the girl away from the group toward the library door.

At the same instant, the apartment dissolved and all four of the men—Kirk, Spock, the policemen—were standing in the transporter chamber of the *Enterprise*. The policemen looked about, stunned, but Kirk and Spock raced off the platform instantly.

"Scotty, reverse and energize!"

The policemen faded and vanished.

"Fine, fast work, Scotty."

"That poor girl," Spock said, "is going to have a lot to explain."

"I know it, but we've got something much more important to set right first. Let's have a look at those plans. Blazes, the launch is scheduled in forty minutes! Scotty, look at these. Here's a schematic layout of a rocket base. Can you get it on the viewscreen here?"

"Easy, Captain. In fact, there's an old-style weather satellite in orbit below us; if I can bounce off that, I ought to get good closeups." He moved to the screen. In a moment, he had the base. An enormous, crude multistage rocket was already in launch position, being serviced by something Kirk dimly remembered was called a gantry crane.

"If we could spot your man," Scott added, "I could lock on and beam him up."

"The odds are that he is out of sight," Spock said. "Inside the rocket gantry, or at one of the control centers. I suppose he has a transporter hidden somewhere in that library of his. Otherwise I cannot account for his disappearance, seconds after the tricorder said he was there—or at least, *somebody* was there."

"Surely that base has security precautions," Kirk said.

"So did we," Scott pointed out.

"I see your point, Scotty. All right, continue visual scan, and stand by to beam us down again."

"Won't be necessary, sir. There he is."

And there indeed he was, at the top of the gantry. He had a panel off the side of the rocket and was working fever-ishly inside it. Nearby sat the black cat, watching with apparent interest.

"Why does he take a pet with him on a dangerous job like that?" Spock said.

"Immaterial now," Kirk said. "Scotty, yank him out of there!"

It was done within seconds. Gary Seven raged, but there was nothing he could do with four phasers leveled on him.

"Relieve him of that hypo and any other hardware he's carrying," Kirk said in a granite voice, "and then take him to the briefing room. This time, Mr. Seven, we are going to get some answers."

"There's no time for that, you fool! The rocket will be launched in nine minutes—and I hadn't finished working on it!"

"Take him along," Kirk said. "And Mr. Spock, put that cat in a separate cabin. Since it's so important for him to have her along, we'll see how well he stands up without her."

Kirk interviewed Seven alone, but with all intercom circuits open, and standing instructions to intervene at dis-cretion and/or report anything that seemed pertinent.

There was no problem about getting Seven to talk. The words came out of him like water from a pressure hose.

"I am what I say I am, a Twentieth-Century human

being," he said urgently. "I was one of three agents on Earth. We were equipped with an advanced transporter, and a computer, both hidden behind the bookshelves in my library. I was returned to—where I came from—for final instructions. You intercepted me and caused a critical delay. When I escaped I found both my fellow agents had been killed in a simple automobile accident. I had to work fast, and, necessarily, alone. They need the help, Captain. A rival program of orbital nuclear platforms like this destroyed Omicron III a hundred years ago. It will destroy the Earth if it isn't stopped."

"I don't deny that it's a bad program," Kirk said.

"Then why can't you believe my story? Would a truly advanced planet use force to help Earth? Would they come here in their own strange, alien forms? Nonsense! The best of all possible methods would be to take Earthborn humans to their world, train them for generations, send them back when they're needed."

"The rocket has been launched," Scott's voice responded over the intercom.

"There, you see?" Seven said desperately. "And I hadn't finished working on it. If you can beam me into its warhead I can still . . ."

"Not so fast. What were you going to make it do?"

"I armed the warhead, and gave it a flight path which will bring it down over Southeast Asia."

"What! That'll start a world war in nothing flat!"

"Correction, Captain," Scott's voice said. "The rocket has begun to malfunction, and alerts are being broadcast from capitals all over the world. I would say that the war has effectively started."

"So much for your humanitarian pretenses," Kirk said. "Mr. Scott, prepare to intercept that rocket and beam it out into space somewhere . . ."

"No, no, no!" Seven cried. "That would be a highly conspicuous intervention! It would change history! Captain, I beg of you . . ."

"Excuse me, Captain," said Spock's voice from the intercom. "Please come to the next cabin."

"Mr. Spock, that rocket will impact in something like fifteen minutes. Is this crucial?"

"Absolutely so."

After checking the guards outside the briefing room, Kirk went to the cabin where Spock had taken the cat. The cat was still there, curled up in a chair.

"What's this all about, Mr. Spock?"

"Sir, I have found out why he carries this animal with him wherever he goes, even when it is obviously inconvenient. It changes the entire picture."

"In what way? Spit it out, man!"

"We have all been the victims of a drastic illusion—including Seven. The true fact is, Mr. Seven has been under the closest kind of monitoring during every instant of his activities. I suspected this and bent certain efforts to redisciplining my own mind to see the reality. I can now also do this for you. Look."

He pointed to the chair. Seated in it was a staggeringly beautiful woman. She had long black hair, and wore a sleek black dress and a jeweled choker necklace. Her legs were curled under her with feline grace.

"This," Spock said formally, "is Isis. And now . . . ."

The woman was gone; only the cat was there, in a strangely similar position.

"Neither," Spock said, "is likely to be the true form of Mr. Seven's sponsors, but the phenomenon supports the story that he does indeed have sponsors. Whether or not their intentions are malign must be a command decision, and one which I must leave to your human intuition, Captain."

Kirk stared at the illusory cat, which was now washing itself. Then he said, "Mr. Scott!"

"Here, sir."

"Give Mr. Seven back his tools and beam him into the warhead of that rocket—on the double."

The warhead blew at 104 miles. Scott snatched Seven out of it just barely in time.

"You see," Seven told them somewhat later, "it *had* to appear to be a malfunction, which luckily did not do any damage. But it frightened every government on Earth. Already there are signs that nobody will try orbiting such a monster, ever again. So despite your accidental interference from the future, my mission has been completed."

"Correction, Mister Seven," Spock said. "It appears that we did *not* interfere with history. Rather, the *Enterprise* was simply part of what was supposed to happen on this day in 1969."

Seven looked baffled. Kirk added, "We find in our record tapes that, although it was never generally revealed, on this date a malfunctioning suborbital warhead was detonated *exactly* 104 miles above the Earth. And you'll be pleased that our records show it resulted in a new and stronger international agreement against such weapons."

"I am indeed pleased," Seven said. He picked up the cat. "And now I expect to be recalled. It might save time, Captain, if you would allow me the use of your transporter. I mean no reflection on your technology, but I must get back to my own machine for the trip to—where I am going."

"Of course." Kirk rose. "Mr. Scott, take Mr. Seven to our Transporter Room and beam him down."

At the elevator door, Seven paused. "There is one thing that puzzles me. Your accidental interception, and your tracing me, and your interruption of my work—every one of those events was unplanned and should have produced a major disruption. Yet in each case, it turns out that I made exactly the proper next step to advance the business at hand, even though each time I was working blind. Does the course of history exert that much force on even a single individual?"

Kirk eyed the creature in Seven's arms which, whatever it was, was most certainly not a cat.

"Mr. Seven," he said, "I'm afraid that we in our turn can't tell you *everything* we've learned. The credit for this day's work is largely yours—and I strongly advise you to let it rest at that."